The Warlord's body jerked, muscles bunched. He raised his arms as if he would rip the manacles apart. Wounds opened, blood flowed, his chest heaved.

"My lord, stop! It's killing you!" Fideles cried.

"Remarkable, isn't it," said Abdiel, eyeing Sagan in jealous admiration. "After all he's endured, he still has the strength to try to defy me. But, you are right, young brother. It is killing him."

The mind-seizer raised his left hand. Five razor-sharp needles, protruding from the flesh, gleamed in the candle-light.

"And now, Brother Fideles, you will obey your lord's final command."

"Yes," said Brother Fideles, "with God's help, I will obey my lord's command."

"Good, good. And you will carry to the Lady Maigrey a message from me, from Abdiel. Tell her that I have taken Lord Sagan to the galaxy of the Corasians. And when you talk to the Lady Maigrey, you should remind her of something that she may have, perhaps, forgotten. Something that will make this contest all the more entertaining."

"I'm listening," Brother Fideles said, keeping firm control over his voice to prevent it from breaking.

"Remind my lady," said Abdiel, "that if she saves the life of Derek Sagan, she saves the life of the man who is destined to end her own."

STAR OF THE GUARDIANS

Volume Three

KING'S SACRIFICE

BY

MARGARET WEIS

BANTAM BOOKS

NEW YORK · TORONTO · LONDON · SYDNEY · AUCKLAND

KING'S SACRIFICE

Grateful acknowledgement is made for permission to reprint the following: Excerpt from "The Ship of Death", from *The Complete Poems of D.H. Lawrence* by D.H. Lawrence. Copyright © 1964; 1971 by Angelo Ravagli and C.M. Weekley, Executors of the Estate of Frieda Lawrence Ravagli. Used by permission of Viking Penguin, a division of Penguin Books USA, Inc. and Laurence Pollinger Limited. Excerpt from *The King Must Die* by Mary Renault, Copyright © 1958 by Mary Renault. Reprinted by permission of Pantheon Books, a division of Random House, Inc.

A BANTAM BOOK 0 553 40276 5

First Publication in Great Britain

PRINTING HISTORY
Bantam edition published 1992

Bantam Books are published by Transworld Publishers Ltd.,
61-63 Uxbridge Road, Ealing, London W5 5SA,
in Australia by Transworld Publishers (Australia) Pty. Ltd.,
15-23 Helles Avenue, Moorebank, NSW 2170, and in New
Zealand by Transworld Publishers (N.Z.) Ltd., Cnr. Moselle
and Waipareira Avenues, Henderson, Auckland.

Printed and bound in Great Britain by
BPCC Hazells Ltd
Member of BPCC Ltd

*To Janet and Gary Pack
sharing the dream*

Acknowledgments

To Gary Pack, who is now currently in the employ of Xris, and who is responsible for developing much of the cyborg's technology.

To Nicole Harsh, Maigrey's swordmistress, who was concerned about milady's exercise regimen.

To our "special agent" Mike Gibbons, FBI, who has worked with Xris.

To friend, author, and poet, Michael Williams, who didn't know he was also a starship captain.

To my daughter Elizabeth, for being very patient and for keeping her music turned down.

To John Hefter, who is now a prior in the abbey of St. Francis.

To the later Mary Renault, whose wonderful historic novels have provided ideas, pleasure and thought. These include *The Mask of Apollo*, (Bantam Books, 1966) and *The King Must Die* (Bantam Books, 1958).

To Van Gelis, whose music provided inspiration, particularly *Heaven and Hell*, 1975 RCA Limited.

To Steve Youll, for his fantastic covers, Jamie Warren for cover design and both of them for their support.

To Amy Stout, editor and friend, not necessarily in that order.

And to Dave Cole, one of the most caring copy editors ever.

. . . if you will believe with me that the soul is immortal and able to endure all good and ill, we shall keep always to the upward way and in all things pursue justice with the help of wisdom. Then we shall be at peace with Heaven and with ourselves, both during our sojourn here and when, like victors in the Games collecting gifts from their friends, we receive the prize of justice; and so, not here only, but in the journey of a thousand years of which I have told you, we shall fare well.

Plato, *The Republic*

Book One

Dion was, indeed, at this time extremely young in years, but of all the scholars that attended Plato he was the quickest and aptest to learn, and the most prompt and eager to practise the lessons of virtue, as Plato himself reports of him, and his own actions sufficiently testify.

"Dion," *Plutarch's Lives of Illustrious Men*, Volume III

Chapter ·◆═◯═◆· One

"This is a stem
Of that victorious stock; and let us fear
The native mightiness and fate of him."
William Shakespeare,
King Henry V, Act II, Scene 4

"Welcome to *Galaxy in Depth*, the program that discusses the news of today with those who are making it. I am your host, James M. Warden. I am pleased to introduce to you a young man who undoubtedly needs no introduction, a young man who has created an intergalactic sensation. His Royal Highness Dion Starfire."

The robotcam panned left from the rugged, erudite features of GBC's popular news commentator James M. Warden to a young man clad in a military-cut suit of black with short black jacket, high collar, red piping on the cuffs and collar. He wore no medals, epaulets, or insignia except for a small Scimitar pin on the left collar and a brooch that was the face of a lion. Red hair the color of an exploding sun framed the pale, serious face, tumbled shoulder length over the black suit of clothes. Intense eyes of a vibrant cobalt-blue showed well on the vidscreens and the robotcam zoomed in on them frequently, to the intense and swooning delight of millions of this young man's followers.

He sat at ease, poised, confident, unlike many others who had faced an interview with the incisive reporter.

"I am pleased to be here, Mr. Warden," replied the young man in a rich, melodious voice that flowed out of the vidscreens of billions, including that of the President of the Galactic Democratic Republic, Peter Robes. "Thank you for inviting me."

"'Thank you for inviting me,'" mimicked President Peter Robes with a sneer. "I wonder if he knows Sagan did everything in his power to keep his puppet off this stage?"

3

The President paced about an elegantly furnished room in his residence, a residence known publicly as the Common House, because he fashioned himself a "common" man, a man of the people. But when the people were too much for their president, he fled to the Common House, which was located on a tightly secured plot of land as far from civilization as possible and where not one of "the people" could possibly set foot.

"Dion is no puppet," remarked an extremely old man, clad in loose-flowing magenta garments, who sat huddled in a chair, shivering as with a chill. "That is what makes him so dangerous. Mistaking him for one will prove costly, for both you and Sagan. Do sit down, Peter. You are annoying me."

The room was extremely warm; the heat had been turned up expressly to benefit the elderly man. President Peter Robes mopped his forehead with a handkerchief—careful not to disturb the plastiskin smoothness—and shed his suit coat. Tossing it to a waiting servbot, he subsided into a chair next to that of the old man, and glared at the vidscreen.

"Only a short while ago, no one had ever heard of Dion Starfire." James M. Warden swiveled in his chair to face his intergalactic audience. "Then one night a young man walked into the home of the Adonian Snaga Ohme, stood in front of the most powerful people in the galaxy, and announced to them that he was their king.

"Since then, backed by the support of Derek Sagan, one of the wealthiest, most powerful, and most feared men in the galaxy, Dion Starfire has traveled throughout the various star systems, and everywhere he goes, he brings turmoil and unrest."

Warden turned to face his guest. "Your critics charge you with inciting the people to riot and rebellion in an attempt to overthrow the government. How do you answer those charges, Your Majesty?"

"I am not the one who incites the people to rebellion," said Dion quietly. "When I go before them, I *say* very little. Instead, I listen—something no one's done in a long, long time. And the angry voices I hear are the voices of the people, demanding change."

He leaned forward, hands gesturing eloquently, his tone earnest, intense. "The government of Peter Robes is corrupt from the top down. The contagion has spread from the

President throughout the Congress until it now infests every governmental body. Where is the federal agent who cannot be bribed? Where is the Congressman who does not devote all his time and effort to assisting the rich and influential, letting the poor and helpless suffer? The people want change, but they feel powerless to alter a system so rank with disease that it contaminates all who enter it."

"And you are the prince who will ride to their rescue?" asked Warden with a slight smile.

"I am their king," Dion replied gravely, with dignity.

Warden raised an eyebrow. "But, Your Majesty, Peter Robes has been duly elected and reelected President by the democratic process, by these very same people."

Now it was Dion who smiled, charmingly. "I recall one newsman making the comment on election night that Peter Robes had, once again, 'got his money's worth.' I believe that was how you put it, wasn't it, Mr. Warden?"

Warden gave a rueful chuckle. "Very good, Your Majesty." He swiveled back to the audience. "We'll break now for a word from our sponsors."

"The boy *is* good," President Robes stated grudgingly.

"What do you expect?" asked the old man with a shrug. "He's Blood Royal, and he's been well coached."

"You're making a mistake, Abdiel. Not letting me confront the boy publicly."

"And give his claim credence? In the act of refuting it, you acknowledge it. He's baiting you into doing that very thing. No, my dear, far better to keep yourself aloof as you would from any other fad that catches the public fancy."

"But he isn't a fad. You said yourself he was dangerous. We could implicate him in the murder. You were at Ohme's that night. You could come forward and tell—"

"Would that be wise, do you think, my dear?"

Abdiel's interruption was soft. Reaching out with his left hand, he took hold of the President's right hand, turned it to the light. Five swollen, fiery red marks, clearly visible on Robes's palm, corresponded to five sharp small needles protruding from the palm of the old man.

The fingers on Robes's hand twitched, his arm stiffened.

"Would you want it known publicly, my dear, that you and I have formed a—shall we say—liaison?" Abdiel caressed gently Peter Robes's hand. "Would you have it known publicly that the Order of Dark Lightning was not destroyed during the Revolution? That one member still exists? People would start to ask questions. I think you might find them difficult to answer, particularly the one question on everyone's lips—how and why did Snaga Ohme die?"

The President shuddered, swallowed, and swiftly jerked his hand away from that of the old man's. "The public knows how Snaga Ohme died. Sagan murdered him, of course, to obtain the space-rotation bomb. The Grand Jury brought an indictment. The Warlord's a hunted criminal, not to mention a damned rebel."

Abdiel said nothing, shook his head, smiled to himself, and hunched deeper into his robes.

Robes glanced sideways, nervously, at the old man and ran his finger around his collar and loosened his tie. His shirt was soaked with sweat.

"If it comes to that," he said accusingly, "you took a chance yourself that night, Abdiel, going to Ohme's, showing yourself before that crowd. Your arrival might have been recorded."

"Nonsense," Abdiel answered crisply, his gaze fixed on the vidscreen. "No trace of me exists anywhere that I do not want it to exist. Ohme's elaborate security devices carry no record of my presence. Only three people know I was ever there and, like you, they dare not admit it. To all the rest, I was one too many glasses of champagne. Hush, now, Peter, my dear."

The program returned. Warden continued.

"You claim to be the son of the late Crown Prince Augustus and his wife, Princess Semele Starfire. Your parentage has been proven through genetic testing. For those of us who have forgotten our history lessons, would you explain to us, Your Majesty, your relationship to the late king, Amodius Starfire?"

"He was my uncle. He died childless. On his death, his younger brother, my father, would have succeeded to the throne. Since my father, too, is dead, I am next in line."

"Let's be honest, Your Majesty. You are next in line to a throne *that doesn't exist*."

"According to the polls," Dion replied coolly, "there are many who believe it should."

James Warden sat back in his chair. "You are backed by one of the richest, most powerful Warlords in the galaxy. You've said numerous times that you believe you have a mandate from heaven. Why don't you go to war to claim your rightful inheritance?"

"I will not make war upon my own people."

"And yet, Your Majesty, reliable sources report that you have in your possession one of the most destructive weapons ever created, a weapon that some speculate could tear a hole in the fabric of the universe—a space-rotation bomb."

"I am certain you will understand that, for reasons of security, I can neither confirm nor deny such a report."

James Warden shook his head. "You are a king without a crown. You refuse to go to war to gain it. There are those who are saying this is all a publicity stunt."

"One day, I will be king."

Dion spoke with a quiet, firm conviction that impressed even the cynical newsman.

"How, Your Majesty?"

"My people will rise up, like a tidal wave, and sweep away the remains of this corrupt, unsanctioned, and illegal government."

"Peacefully?" Warden's tone was skeptical.

"Peacefully."

"With a warmonger such as Derek Sagan behind you? How can we believe you are sincere, Your Majesty?"

"Derek Sagan is of the Blood Royal, a distant cousin of mine, in fact. He has acknowledged me his liege lord and pledged his allegiance to me."

"Derek Sagan was involved in the overthrow of the monarchy. He was, many believe, responsible for the death of the king, your uncle. For eighteen years, Derek Sagan went about the galaxy systematically rounding up and killing those known as the Guardians. He has been implicated in the murder of the Adonian Snaga Ohme. How can we trust such a man? How can you?"

Warden paused for dramatic effect.

"Do you trust Derek Sagan, Your Majesty?"

The robotcam zeroed in on Dion. His blue eyes deepened in color and intensity, but his facial expression remained unchanged, his voice level and calm.

"Lord Sagan has done many things in his past that I do not condone, though perhaps I have come to understand his reasons for doing them. But I believe Derek Sagan to be innocent of the murder of the king to whom he had pledged his loyalty. He pledged the same oath to me. Yes, Mr. Warden. I trust him."

Warden appeared dubious. "Eyewitness accounts would have us believe otherwise, Your Majesty."

"It is the victor who writes the history, Mr. Warden."

The news commentator turned again to the audience. "Food for thought, ladies and gentlemen. And now, we'll break for local station identification. When we return, we will discuss with His Majesty what is being called the Miracle on Mahab 73."

"He's lying through his teeth." Robes tugged again at his necktie, finally jerked it off.

"What? About trusting Sagan? No, you are wrong there, Peter. Dion trusts Sagan more than he trusts himself. And that, my dear," Abdiel remarked complacently, "is the crack in his armor that will prove his undoing. It is time for you to act. You're slipping in the polls badly, Peter. Three systems, those belonging to DiLuna, Rykilth, and Olefsky, are on the verge of open rebellion—"

Robes jumped to his feet, began to again pace the room.

"What do you expect? The economy's in a shambles. The galaxy's on the verge of civil war. Half the Congress is away trying to prevent their systems from seceding. Six members of my Cabinet are going on trial for corruption, and I'll be damned lucky if I'm not implicated. Every important issue's tied up in committee. I can't get anything accomplished—"

"Stop fooling with them, Peter."

Robes ceased his pacing. He turned to look at Abdiel. "What do you mean?"

"I mean stop fooling with them. You don't need them anymore, Peter, my dear."

"Need who?" Robes was reluctant to understand.

Abdiel shrugged. "The Congress, the Cabinet, the . . . people. They've served you well enough. You've been president eighteen years."

Robes went the color of a dead fish's underbelly. "You're . . . saying I should step down . . . turn over the government to this—this—" He made a feeble gesture at the vidscreen. The interview had resumed.

"Tell us, Your Majesty, about the healing of the child on Mahab 73."

"I have nothing to say concerning that incident except that the press blew it out of proportion."

"But, Your Majesty—"

Abdiel made a motion, and the vidscreen shut itself off.

"On the contrary, Peter. I want you to take charge. This intergalactic emergency offers you the perfect opportunity. Nations seceding. War threatening. The Constitution gives you certain powers and you simply take the rest that you need."

"But the media? They'll chew me up and spit me out—"

Abdiel sighed delicately. "I'm not telling you to rush out and seize control tonight, my dear. It must be carefully thought out, done in stages. When all is over, the public and the media will be groveling at your feet. You can be king yourself, if you like."

"You have a plan?"

"Of course. That's why I came to see you."

Robes smiled, relaxed. "What is it?"

Abdiel gestured to the chair beside him. "Come sit down, Peter. Come sit near me." He spread his hand, the needles embedded in the palm flashed in the light.

Peter Robes's gaze fastened on the needles. He licked dry lips, backed up against a desk, and began rubbing the palm of his own hand against his thigh.

"Just . . . tell me your plan."

"You must rid the galaxy, once and for all, of the Blood Royal. Most especially, you must rid yourself of this boy-king."

"Murder, again." Robes shook his head, swallowed hard. "No. I'd be suspected. You know that. It would ruin me."

Abdiel motioned again. The needles flashed. "Come sit beside me, Peter. Let us talk, be comfortable."

Robes attempted to back up farther, but the solid, massive desk prevented him. His gaze was fixed on the old man.

Robes's lips trembled, his body shook. "No, I won't."

Abdiel's lidless eyes stared into him. The bald head, with its nodes and nodules and flaking patches of decaying skin oscillated and thrust slightly, menacingly forward.

"You are refusing me, Peter?"

"Yes!" Robes gasped.

"Why?"

"You know why." Robes spoke feverishly, like a man in delirium, or a man being tortured, who has reached the limit of his endurance. "In the beginning I was clean. I meant well. My intentions—Abdiel, you knew my intentions! I believed in the people, in democratic rule. I believed in myself!" He paused, struggled for breath. "Now, look at me. Wallowing in the mire you created! Coated in filth, slime, blood.

"You"—Robes pointed a shaking finger—"you, Abdiel. You've dragged me down, deeper and deeper. It started with a lie. Just a little lie. Then a bribe to cover the lie. Another lie to conceal the bribe, and another bribe. You wound your coils around me, pulled me down, dragging me under an inch at a time.

"And then the night of the Revolution. The murder of the king, the slaughter of the Guardians, the destruction of the priests! You, all your doing! I knew nothing!"

"You knew," Abdiel said softly, so very softly.

"No!" Peter Robes cried, clenching his fist. "I swear before God—Listen to me!" He raised an anguished face to heaven. "I'm swearing to a God I don't believe in! Or maybe I do believe in Him! Maybe I feel His eyes on me. Maybe I see in them the same loathing and hatred I see when I look at my own reflection. You've used me, Abdiel. You've used me from the beginning and now"—opening his palm, he stared in horror at the five swollen marks upon it—"now you've sucked my soul dry."

Abdiel said nothing, waited patiently.

Robes wiped his face, cast the old man a bitter, haunted look. "I should kill myself," he said in a low voice.

"You should," Abdiel agreed, "but you won't."

Robes—haggard, gray—stared at the old man. "You're right. I won't. You won't let me."

"Someday, perhaps. But not now. You're of use to me, still."

Spittle frothed on Robes's lips. "I won't do it! I won't go along with you. Not this time!"

"Yes, you will." Abdiel rose to his feet. Gathering the magenta robes around him, he glided over to where Peter Robes stood, hunched in misery. The old man placed a bony arm, its flesh rotting and scabrous, around the President's shoulders.

Robes cringed at the touch, shrank within the old man's grasp. The President was in his forties, in good physical condition. The old man was feeble, sickly, bones likely to snap in two if he coughed. Peter Robes had only to speak a word and his security 'bot would kill the old man instantly. The President had only to speak two words and the room would be filled with bodyguards. His muscles leapt in a sudden, convulsive effort to escape. He raised his head, his mouth opened.

Abdiel placed his hand over the hand of Peter Robes, pressed it gently, caressingly. "There, there, my dear. You're tired. You don't know what you're saying."

Robes gabbled, but no words came from his mouth. He kept his hand clenched tightly shut over the five scars. Abdiel made no move to force it open, but merely continued stroking the flesh with the tips of his long, tapered fingers.

"It will be easy, Peter, my dear. So very easy. No one will suspect a thing. All your worries will be at an end. You will take complete and absolute control. And I will be by your side, to guide you. Come, my dear. Relax. Relax."

Peter shook his head in disbelief. "What can you do against Starfire? He has the space-rotation bomb! He has Sagan and his fleet! He has youth, beauty—"

"I have his bloodsword. And that," Abdiel added, seeing that Robes was still refusing to understand, "gives me much the same influence over him that I wield over you, my dear."

Slowly, Peter Robes lowered his head, his shoulders slumped. His hand went limp, flopped down on his leg; the fingers slowly unclenched, opened, revealing the five swollen marks.

Abdiel gripped Robes's hand tightly, pressed the needles into Peter Robes's flesh.

The President moaned and writhed. Abdiel held on, increased the pressure, drove the needles deeper.

Robes sighed. His pain, through Abdiel's skill in controlling his mind, had changed to pleasure: reward for obedience. He leaned against the old man. Abdiel's arm encompassed the President, drew him near, cradled his head on the bony shoulder.

"And now, my dear, this is what you will do. . . ."

Chapter ◆━ා◯ය━◆ Two

"Most blest believer he!
Who in that land of darkness and blind eyes
Thy long expected healing wings could see . . ."
                              Henry Vaughan, *The Night*

Tusk waited, fidgeting nervously, at the very edge of the studio set. *Galaxy in Depth* was still in progress, though winding down. An alien on the floor was wiggling three of its five antennae in what Tusk supposed was a sign to Warden that he had three minutes to wrap up his interview.

Which meant Tusk had three minutes before he went into action.

A robotcam hurtled straight at him. Tusk dodged, stumbled over a trailing length of cable, and nearly crashed into a nuke lamp. The steadying hand of a centurion reached out, caught hold of Tusk, and helped restore his balance.

"Thanks, Agis," Tusk muttered.

The centurion said nothing; he had, after all, merely done his duty. The iron-disciplined men of Lord Sagan's own personal legion rarely spoke. They acted. Tusk figured that by now he should be used to it, but he wasn't.

The alien glared at him and made a peremptory gesture. A young human female with what appeared to be a satellite dish, revolving radar, and a battery of anti-aircraft guns protruding from a helmet on her head bore down on Tusk.

"What are you doing here? Who let you on the set?"

"No one exactly 'let' us," Tusk began.

A second robotcam trundled past, narrowly missed running over Tusk's foot.

The alien wiggled two antennae.

The young woman glanced up at a dark, glass-encased booth located above the studio. Someone up there was making frantic hand signals. Tusk could hear faint sounds of shouting

12

coming over the various devices in the young woman's headset. She turned to Tusk.

"Mr. Warden won't like this. You'll have to leave. Go out that door and wait in the hall until the red light—"

Tusk grinned, shook his head. "No."

The young woman's face went rigid. James Warden was asking Dion about his stand on education, advising him that he had about thirty seconds in which to give it.

"Please step out that door!" the young woman hissed.

"I'm not stepping anywhere and neither are they." Tusk jerked his thumb back at the centurions, standing at attention as they'd been standing for the last hour.

The young woman glared at him, stomped her foot. "You will be forcibly ejected—"

The centurion's captain shifted his eyes from Dion for the first time since they'd entered the broadcast studio, focused on the young woman. He said nothing, made no move. He merely looked.

The young woman gulped, glanced helplessly back up at the booth. James Warden was thanking Dion and informing the audience of next week's guest. The alien director's purple skin had turned a sickening shade of gray. Every antenna on its head wiggled wildly.

Robotcams swooped down on the two.

"And that's a wrap," stated the alien through its translator.

Warden stood up, said something pleasant to Dion. Dion rose to his feet.

"We'll be heading your direction any minute now," Tusk said into his commlink to the centurions on duty outside the building. "The jet-limo waiting?"

"Yes, sir," came the report.

James Warden and Dion were walking companionably off the set. The news commentator stopped, held out his hand.

"I look forward to following your career, Your Majesty. I don't think we've heard the last of you, by any means. Good luck."

"Thank you, sir." Dion shook hands.

Warden walked off, with only a brief glance at Tusk and the waiting centurions. The young woman hastened after him, apologizing volubly for the disruption.

Dion walked over to Tusk. "How was it?" he asked.

"Good, kid. You did great," Tusk said absently. His mind was on getting Dion out of the building. "You ready to go?"

Dion nodded. He was exhilarated. He hadn't come down yet. He knew he'd done well.

The centurions closed ranks around him. The studio door crashed open, and they were in the hallway. Tusk trotted out in front, comforted by the rhythmic thudding of booted feet behind. "We're on our way," he said into his commlink.

The hall was empty. All nonessential personnel had been cleared from the area.

"Keep it moving," Tusk said unnecessarily.

The centurions would have kept moving through a null-grav steel wall if one had blocked their path. But the distance to the elevators at the end of the black marble hallway seemed to stretch on interminably.

Nola shot out from a side door marked NO ADMITTANCE. AUTHORIZED PERSONNEL ONLY. Tusk scooped her up in his arm as they passed.

"How'd he look?"

"Fantastic. As always."

"What's it like outside?"

Nola shook her head. "A mob. There've been reports of rioting."

They reached an elevator bank. Two centurions stood guard, keeping people away. Doors opened. Agis ordered his men forward. Dion followed, stepping into a ring of armored bodies. Tusk and Nola crowded inside. The doors slid closed, shutting out the noise in the hallway. Damnably cheerful music enveloped them.

"There must be a million people jamming the streets and the route to the spaceport," said Nola in subdued tones.

The elevator whisked downward. The centurions stood stolidly around their king, eyes forward, faces expressionless.

"I know how important it is for His Majesty to be seen." Tusk was clearly unhappy. "I know we need shots of this on the nightly news. But all it takes is one nut with a lasgun—"

"You're doing it again," said Nola.

"What?"

"Talking to yourself."

"No one else'll listen to me."

"I'll be all right, Tusk." Dion smiled at his friend reassuringly from behind the barricade of armor-plated chests and shoulders.

Tusk saw the smile, but he also saw the pallor of Dion's complexion beneath the makeup, saw the sag in the jaw muscles, the droop of the shoulders. Exhilaration was draining from him. He looked tired, on the verge of exhaustion.

Hell, he should be tired! He's been running on sheer momentum for a couple of military-time months, now, Tusk thought bitterly.

Like Warden had said, only a few months ago, Dion Starfire had been a redheaded kid without a last name living on an obscure planet with a poet, pacifist, atheist. Tusk sometimes wondered what that boy might have become, if Lord Sagan hadn't arrived that fateful night? A microchip salesman? Happy at home with the wife and 3.5 kids?

No. Tusk stole another glance at Dion. Not with the fever of the Blood Royal burning in his veins, the lust for power, the desire to guide, direct, control, protect, the need to rule that had been bred in him over countless generations. It would have come out, one way or the other. Fate. Destiny. A "mandate from heaven."

Overnight, over *one* night, Dion had become a "galactic sensation." Romantic, young, handsome, charming, he was the darling of the media. And he was shrouded in mystery, which made him more alluring. The murder of Snaga Ohme, the rumor of a horrific doomsday weapon, the change in Lord Sagan from ruthless exploiter to guiding father figure, the sudden appearance and equally sudden disappearance of Lady Maigrey. The press couldn't quit talking about it all.

The elevator jolted gently to a stop. A pause before the doors opened. Everyone tensed. Dion straightened his shoulders, shook the red hair out of his face, warmed himself at some inner fire. His jaw tightened, smoothing out lines of fatigue. The charming smile curved lips that must be almost numb from constantly smiling; the flame was rekindled in the blue eyes.

Tusk, watching Dion force himself to come back to life, could have sat down and wept.

The elevator doors opened. Dion stepped out, Tusk emerged on one side of the king, Nola at the other. The centurions massed around them. The press surged forward. Nuke lights blinded them, voices shouted at them. The centurions forged their way through the crowd with practiced skill, having practiced this maneuver hundreds of times under Agis's direction. Keep His Majesty moving, keep him safe, but let him be seen.

Tusk—jostled and hassled and elbowed and stepped on— thought with longing of his mercenary days, when he'd done nothing more strenuous than dodge nuclear missiles.

Dion waved and smiled and gave every appearance of having gone deaf as hundreds of questions were hurled at him. Tusk came in for the overflow, replied "no comment" until he was certain his tongue would dry up and fall out of his mouth. He stopped only long enough to extricate Nola from the hands of a reporter who was offering her part ownership in a small resort planet if she'd only give him the "inside story."

The centurions marched through the marble and plastisteel lobby of the GBC building at double-quick time, trampling only a minimal number of reporters on the way, and thrust open steelglass doors that were letting in a flood of brilliant sunlight.

The king and his entourage stepped out onto a marble-columned colonnade. A thunderous roar greeted Dion's appearance. Tusk stopped a moment to adjust his eyes to the bright sun, cast a glance around to make certain the centurions were repositioning themselves. Blinking, he looked down the long flight of wide marble steps they'd have to traverse to reach the jet-limo waiting for them on the bottom.

"Shit," said Tusk, and added a few more epithets for good measure.

Beside him, he felt Dion's body tense.

Thousands of people crowded the steps, held back by a living wall of GBC security agents, local police, the local military, and anyone else this planet had been able to draft into service. Thousands more jammed the street in front of the GBC building, thousands more hung out of windows or stood on rooftops of buildings surrounding them.

Tusk was used to the crowds; they might have been ants for all the notice he took of them. It was the sight of what was on the steps that drove him to use language that would have fried XJ's circuits.

"How the bloody hell could they have let this happen?" Tusk raved. "They were warned, the bastards! We told them over and over—"

"Tusk," interrupted Dion. "Stop it. Robes's people arranged this on purpose. It's obvious. They want to see what I'll do."

"What will you do?" Tusk asked grimly.

"Walk down the steps," Dion answered.

On the steps, directly in the path the king must take to reach the limo, lay or sat or stood Misery. The blind, hearing the cheers, stretched out pleading, groping hands. The deaf, seeing their salvation, cried out in voices that they couldn't hear. The mute cried out in voices no one could hear. The crippled raised themselves up from pallets spread upon the stairs. Dying children, pushed forward by frantic parents, held small bouquets of flowers clutched fast in pitifully thin fists. All the unfortunates left behind by the advancements in medical science stood waiting for something larger, something more wonderful.

Tusk was busy marshaling his forces and his thoughts at the same time. "Here's what we do. We keep moving. We don't stop for anything. Agis, deploy your men on either side of the king. If someone gets in the way, move them. Be as gentle as you can—the damn robotcams are gonna record every second of this—but move them."

Dion gestured. "Let's go."

He descended the stairs. The crowd, held back by the police, heaved and surged and roared. Their noise could not drown out the pleas, the wails, the fervent prayers of the sick and the dying who had been permitted (and encouraged) to move near. The king smiled and waved, but Tusk saw the smile had gone tight, rigid, the blue eyes were dark as deepspace. They moved like a funeral procession down the steps. A descent into hell might have been easier.

The centurions performed their difficult task well. Aware of thousands of electronic eyes that would carry this scene to billions of living eyes, they gently eased the blind out of the way, gently moved aside the beds of the cripples, gently lifted and carried children back to their mother's arms.

Dion was halfway down the steps. Pleas were changing to wails of bitter disappointment. Prayers to curses. His breathing grew short, he licked his lips. Tusk edged his way near him. They were almost at the bottom. The guards around the limo had the doors open. The driver was set, ready to take off.

A young woman broke free of the crowd. She darted around the centurions, lunged straight at Dion, came up against Agis's solid, armor-shielded body. He took firm hold of her, but perhaps moved by pity or the fact that she went limp in his grasp, his grip on her eased. She slid out of his hands like quicksilver and flung herself on the cold stone directly in Dion's path.

"Don't shoot!" he commanded, seeing the centurions' lasguns aimed directly at the woman.

Wise move, thought Tusk, who could see how *that* would play on the vidscreens. *Centurions Incinerate Hapless Teenager*. But he was shaking so he couldn't get his weapon back in its holster.

The girl knelt at Dion's feet and raised her hands in supplication.

Tusk took one look at her, felt his insides twist up, and hastily averted his eyes.

She had a lithe, graceful figure, pretty light brown hair, and a face out of a bad drug trip. Agis hurried forward, caught hold of her by the arm, started to drag her off bodily.

"Stop!" Dion commanded in a voice that was like no voice Tusk had ever heard come from a living man.

The captain, startled, stared at Dion.

"Let her go, Agis," the king commanded.

The captain obeyed reluctantly. A 'droid reporter remote appeared out of nowhere, glass eyes winking. One of the centurions handled the reporter efficiently, sent it clanging and banging down the marble steps. It rolled into the crowd and was immediately dismembered and scavenged for its parts.

The girl paid no attention to the reporter or to anyone else around her. What remained of one eye focused on Dion. What might have been her mouth opened. Tusk fought to keep from gagging. And he'd seen it all . . . or thought he had.

"What happened to you?" Dion asked her gently.

"My planet was at war. The bombs. The chemicals, the fires . . ." She reached her fingers to claw at her ravaged face. "It wasn't my fault! But not even my own mother can stand to look at me! I tried to kill myself, but they brought me back. And now I know why. You will help me. I see it in your eyes. You're not disgusted by me. You are sorry for me. I was beautiful, once, like you are beautiful. Heal me, my liege. Heal me."

What the devil's wrong with us? Tusk demanded of himself

savagely. Have we all been turned to stone? Changed into statues? He looked at Agis, who knew very well that he should have disobeyed Dion's command and taken the young woman away. He looked at Nola, saw tears streaming down her face. He looked at himself, stricken dumb, limbs gone nerveless. Why can't we move? What are we waiting for?

For a miracle.

Dion's skin was so pale it was almost translucent, the flame burning in him was bright and pure and holy. It will devour him, consume him. He lifted his hand, started to lay it on the girl's horribly grotesque face.

"Your Majesty." Agis spoke in a soft undertone, using the military argot of the barracks that the girl wouldn't be likely to understand, "I would be remiss in my duty to Your Majesty if I did not remind him of Lord Sagan's advice—"

"Thank you, Agis," Dion interrupted. "You have done your duty."

But the fingers that had almost touched the girl began to tremble, then curled in on themselves. His hand clenched to a fist, dropped nervelessly to his side.

"I can't."

A bead of sweat trickled down from beneath the red hair, slid down his temple. "I'm sorry," he said without a voice. "I can't. Forgive me."

"No! Please!" The girl screamed, clutched at Dion.

Agis, acting as he should have acted two minutes earlier, firmly hauled her to her feet and hustled her out of sight.

Tusk heaved a sigh that was mostly relief, part something else he didn't like to admit. It was so easy to believe in Dion. Or perhaps it was easy to *want* to believe in him.

This was not the time for metaphysical musings, however. He had to get the king out of here. Tusk's main goal now was the limo and he didn't care how they reached it or what they might look like on the evening news. The fire had died in Dion, the candle's flame snuffed out, leaving him cold and brittle and hard as ice.

Climbing into the waiting limo, the king sat bolt upright in the backseat, looked at nothing, said nothing. He had withdrawn far into himself in what Tusk had come to recognize as a defensive posture, a soldier under attack hunkered flat at the bottom of his foxhole.

"Get us the hell out of here," Tusk ordered the driver.

Chapter ❖ Three

Glorious the comet's train . . .
        Christopher Smart, *A Song to David*

Air locks opened with a soft sigh. The cool, purient air of a vessel in space bit into the nostrils, made sweat-damp skin shiver. The silence of near-empty corridors, which resounded only with the calm and measured tread of a military machine going about its business, eased the pounding ache in Tusk's temples. Dion relaxed, lines of stress eased from his face. His eyes brightened, he almost smiled. The mercenary was about to suggest a nap when the officious Bennett rounded a corner and confronted them.

Tusk saw immediately what was up, attempted a diversion. A glance sent Nola into action.

"Bennett," purred the young woman, sliding her hand over the sergeant-major's arm, "how have you been? How's the general? Did you see Dion on the vid—?"

Safe under this friendly covering fire, Tusk was steering the king down an intersecting corridor. Nola might as well have thrown herself in front of a tank, however. Bennett rumbled right over her.

"Your Majesty, General Dixter's compliments, and could he solicit the honor of your presence and that of Major Tusk in the comm, sir."

Tusk's opening maneuver had failed. The enemy had broken through his front lines and was advancing, leaving Nola standing alone, shaking her curls in the corridor. Tusk hurled himself into the breach.

"Look, Bennett, we had a pretty rough time down there. The kid here's about finished and I'm not much better. Tell Dixter we'll report to him in the morning. . . ."

The creases in the sergeant-major's face went almost as rigid as the knife-edged creases in his neatly pressed uniform.

Bennett could well remember the days when Tusk had been just another mercenary pilot under Dixter's command, Dion a mere civilian passenger. A shift in the tide of the affairs of men had floated Dion to the top, raised Tusk to the status of major under the Warlord's command, and sent General John Dixter drifting into the shoals of uneasy alliance with a former deadly foe and rival. Bennett coped with the changes as he had coped with every other upheaval he'd encountered as aide to General Dixter—the sergeant-major preferred change to regulations and acted accordingly. But he could not forebear, by tone and manner, registering his disapproval of the entire situation and he could not help exulting in his occasional victory.

He sniffed. A corner of a clipped-mustached lip twitched. "Lord Sagan," he said in an undertone. Eyes on the bulkheads, he spoke to no one in particular.

"Damn," Tusk swore beneath his breath, thinking it possible, even at this point, that Dion might not have heard, might yet be persuaded to go to his quarters and rest.

Unfortunately, accustomed as he was to shouting commands on the parade ground, the sergeant-major's voice carried quite well.

Dion had gone white as sunrise on an ice-locked moon.

"Kid—" Tusk began, but the king had turned, was advancing down the corridor, heading toward the communications center aboard ship. Bennett, Captain Agis, and the ever-present centurion guard followed closely behind.

Tusk stood in the corridor, stared grimly after them. The thought came to him that by taking this particular corridor to the left, instead of the right, he would arrive at a lift that would whisk him to the flight deck. There he would find his spaceplane and his irritating, sarcastic, disrespectful, and sorely missed partner, XJ-27.

"Tusk, what is it?" Nola twined her fingers through his, squeezed his hand.

"I'd be a fugitive again," Tusk mused. "But, hell, I've been a fugitive most of my life. I could find work. There's always a war being fought somewhere, 'specially now that the Republic's falling apart. Or maybe turn my hand at smuggling. That pirate we ran into—"

"You can't leave him, Tusk," said Nola softly.

"I can leave anybody I damn well please!" Tusk retorted.

"He's got Sagan, he's got Dixter, he's got a whole fuckin' regiment of armor-plated bootlickers—"

"He hasn't got a friend, Tusk. Only you. You're the only one who cares about him. Not about a king, not about some piece in a huge galactic game, not about a chance for revenge, a chance to restore some long-lost ideal of ages past—but *him*. Dion." Nola moved nearer, slid her arm around Tusk. "You remember Dion, don't you? The seventeen-year-old kid you rescued on Syrac Seven? The kid who threw up the first time he flew your plane? The kid who was scared spitless his first time in combat?" Her voice altered subtly. "The 'kid' who saved our lives on *Defiant*?"

"I know, I know. Lay off, Nola—"

"It's why the Starlady made you his Guardian, Tusk—"

"Yeah, then what does she do? Walks off. Drops outta sight. Leaves us to take the flak—"

"That's not fair. You can't judge her, Tusk. You don't understand."

"Damn right, I don't understand! I don't understand anything except *I'm* the one who's always around. *I'm* the one who watched them stick a crown on that kid's head, then start driving nails into him."

"He put the crown on his own head. It was his choice."

"After they held it up and showed him how bright and fancy it was and let him try it on and told him how great he looked in it and how well it fit and groveled at his feet and messed with his mind. Who knows what ideas that evil old man gave him, sticking needles into him—"

"Don't, Tusk." Nola paled, swallowed. "Don't talk about that time."

"Sorry, sweetheart." Tusk sighed, put his arm around her and hugged her close. "Sorry. I didn't mean to bring up bad memories." He was silent a moment. "I'm scared for him, Nola."

"I know, dear."

"That's why I want to run sometimes. I don't see anything good coming outta this. Like sittin' in a theater, watching a vid, and knowing how it's going to end—"

"You *don't* know how it's going to end."

"I've got a pretty good idea," Tusk said gloomily. "I know the director, and he doesn't believe in happily ever after. Speaking of Sagan, I guess I'd better go see if I can deflect the latest hammer blows. Where'll you be?"

"I'm going to soak in a hot shower and wash my hair. Meet you in the bar?"

"Yeah. Order me a double and have it waiting. I'll need it," Tusk predicted grimly and stalked off, down the corridor, away from the lift and the flight deck and his spaceplane and freedom.

Nola watched after him, sighed. "Oh, Tusk, I wish you understood. Those nails are passing right through Dion. *You're* the only one they're hurting."

··❖·· ➡··

Afraid of being late, Tusk beat it to the comm at a dead run, only to discover on arrival, hot and out of breath, that John Dixter was the sole person—besides the men on duty—present.

Tusk glanced nervously about the room, its hundreds of blinking glass eyes staring outward, reflecting back what they saw, keeping watch on people and events around the galaxy. Operators sat at their posts, monitoring, transmitting, speaking in myriad languages, listening to myriad more. The different images on the various screens shifted rapidly; it made Tusk dizzy to watch, reminded him uncomfortably of the fact that time and events were rocketing forward, out of control, like a spaceplane with a malfunctioning hyperdrive.

"Is it over?" he demanded. Despite his rebellious talk, he couldn't help but feel queasy at the thought of missing one of the Warlord's summons.

"No, no," said Dixter in a soothing tone. He smiled slightly, sympathetic. "Hasn't started yet."

"But Bennett—"

"I sent him after Dion early. Give His Majesty a chance to change his clothes, freshen up . . ."

"Arm himself."

"Yes, that, too," Dixter replied quietly.

Tusk sighed, mopped his forehead with the sleeve of his uniform, completely forgetting to use the standard regulation-issue handkerchief tucked neatly, according to regulations, into his cuff. He saw Dixter's eyebrow raise, saw him glance at the stain on Tusk's sleeve, and it occurred to the former mercenary, belatedly, that he, too, would shortly be in the Warlord's presence.

Tusk groaned and began to try to twitch his uniform coat into place, brush off his trousers. He gave his black boots a quick shine by rubbing them against the backs of his pant legs. This did nothing for the appearance of his uniform, seen from behind, but he wasn't likely to be presenting his posterior to the Warlord.

Not that it wasn't a temptation. Tusk couldn't help grinning at the thought. Looking up, he saw Dixter watching the proceedings with amusement.

Tusk felt his skin grow warm.

"XJ would be proud of you," Dixter said gravely.

"Yeah, well, gotta keep up appearances," Tusk muttered. A shining steel bulkhead reflected his image back to him. He gave himself a quick once over, couldn't help but wonder—at first glance—just who the hell this character was.

The stern, chilling lines of the black uniform, its stiff, high collar and smooth, adhesive-flapped front closing trimmed with red piping and glittering major's insignia, were light-years away from the many-times-washed, army-surplus fatigues Tusk had been accustomed to wearing. Looking at himself, he had a momentary wish that wherever those fatigues were, he was with them.

The jet-black color of the uniform was too near the ebony-black color of his skin; it was difficult to tell—other than by the bloodred lines of the piping—where the uniform left off and Tusk began. Sometimes he had the feeling he was *all* uniform, nothing remained of himself. Even the fit reminded him constantly that he was in the Warlord's service: uncomfortable, rigid, with a tendency to grip him too tightly about the neck. Tusk felt himself continually short of breath, had fallen into the habit of tugging at his collar in an ineffectual attempt to loosen it.

He regarded himself with a small measure of contempt and a large amount of self-pity. Turning away, he saw that Dixter's amusement had broadened into a wide smile.

"You're beautiful," he assured Tusk.

"Oh, stow it . . . sir," Tusk mumbled in return, casting the general a bitter, envious glance.

He didn't know how Dixter managed it. He wore the same type of severely tailored uniform that Tusk wore, yet Dixter always appeared comfortable—his uniform wrinkled and rumpled, the collar undone (the top button missing in action), general's stars half falling off.

Dixter sat at his ease, rump propped on one of the control panels, where he'd been chatting casually with the operator waiting to receive the vid signal from the Warlord's ship, *Phoenix II*. The general might have been back in his old HQ in the desert of Vangelis, except for a few minor changes that no one who hadn't know him a long time would have noticed, someone like Tusk.

Looking at Dixter closely, as the general turned to answer a question from the operator, Tusk saw the older man's hair had gone a little grayer, the lines in the face were a little deeper, the brown eyes in their maze of wrinkles were a little tireder, a lot older. The deep suntanned brown of the skin, obtained after a life of living and fighting on land, would never completely fade, but the tan had gone sallow after months of being confined aboard a spaceship. And there was a faint pallor beneath the tan and the puffiness about the eyes of a man who never feels himself at ease traveling the frigid, black void of space.

Tusk's envy evaporated, replaced by concern and a growing, smoldering anger. For two plastipennies, he'd grab the general and get the hell off this ship and away from the whole fuckin' mess. Tusk was fired up, he could have blasted off himself without benefit of a rocket. He loped across the deck, the words were on his lips, he was—in his mind—already flying out of the hangar when Dixter turned back to face him. One look at the mild brown eyes, and Tusk's energy drained from him.

Dixter wouldn't leave, any more than Tusk—when it came down to it—would leave. Only what held them wasn't precisely the same.

Tusk drew closer, lowered his voice. "Any word from the Lady Maigrey, sir?"

Dixter shook his head. "No." One word, but it held all the pain a man could conceivably hold and go on living.

"Begging the general's pardon, but damn it all to hell!" Tusk's anger found a vent. "One minute she's there and the next she's not, without so much as a 'so long, wasn't it fun, let's do it again sometime.' No, sir! I gotta say this, get this off my chest. If I don't, I—I might hit somebody!"

Noting the fierce expression on the mercenary's face, Dixter closed his mouth on the remonstrance he had been about to utter. He signaled Tusk to contain himself for the moment, rose to his feet, and led the way to the center of the room, which was empty and as quiet as the center of the comm could ever be.

Backed by the low buzzing hum of countless voices and the frequent bleeps of computers, Tusk launched into his grievances. Dixter listened patiently, his eyes fixed on the young soldier who'd become dear as a son to him, with only an occasional straying glance toward the door or to the operator waiting for Sagan's call.

"If the lady were here, she'd put a stop to about three fourths of the stuff that's goin' on. She'd take the kid in hand and help him understand what's happening instead of trying to bully him and telling him 'do this' and 'don't do that' and 'don't ask questions, just do as you're told.' But, no! Right when things start gettin' tough, she runs out."

A dark line, appearing between Dixter's brows, and a glint in the usually mild eyes halted Tusk a moment. But he'd gone too far to quit now, the damage had been done. He had to continue, try to explain himself.

"It wasn't like she was captured or carried off or Lord Sagan did away with her or anything. She left of her own free will! I know, sir. I was there, on base, the morning after the army took over Snaga Ohme's place. I was with Lord Sagan when he returned and they brought him word that the lady'd taken a spaceplane and beat it. I saw him, I saw his face."

Tusk paused, frowning. "He was mad. Hell, *mad* isn't the word." He shook his head. "I'm not sure there is a word for what he was. I'd swear I saw steel walls start to melt and drip all over the floor. And what does he do? Turn out the guard? Send out patrols?"

"Tusk—" Dixter tried to break in.

"Nothin'!" Tusk was past listening. "Not a goddam thing. In one second he goes cold as he was hot and says, 'Very well, my lady, maybe it's better this way,' or words to that effect."

"Tusk, if I—"

"And now, it's been six months. All hell's breaking loose. Two actors battling for the same role. The kid got it and now he's out on center stage, putting on a show for an audience that's come mainly to see this play turn into a tragedy, then they can all have a good cry and go home. And meanwhile, Sagan's working backstage to bring down the curtain on the first act. And when it comes up again, guess who's gonna try to step in and take the lead! And my lady's off somewhere, doing God knows what. And as for how she treated you, sir—"

"Tusk, that's enough." Dixter's voice was whip-sharp, the voice of the old desert-days HQ. It flicked across Tusk, brought him to his senses. He lowered his head, stared at his boots.

"I'm sorry, sir. I know how much you think of her and I didn't mean to get into that. It's none of my business. . . ."

"Damn right, it isn't," Dixter said coldly.

Tusk lifted his head, defiance in his tone. "But I've seen what it's done to you, sir. You can't blame me for being upset."

Dixter glowered at the mercenary in grim and furious silence, but was obviously finding it difficult to be angry with someone whose only fault was that he cared.

Tusk saw the anger seep out, like blood from a wound, saw it replaced by pain and deep sorrow, and felt far worse than before. He knew, then, that much of what he'd said John Dixter must have been thinking; the man wouldn't have been human otherwise. Somehow or other, he'd come to terms with it. Because he loved her.

"Go ahead, sir," Tusk said. "Kick me. Kick me good and hard. Or, if you'll excuse me, I'll just go into a corner and kick myself—"

"That won't be necessary," Dixter said, one corner of his mouth twitching. He paused, grave, indecisive, then sighed, made up his mind. "Son . . ." He clasped a hand on Tusk's shoulder. "I—"

The operator looked in their direction. "Lord Sagan in five minutes, sir."

Dixter did not even glance over. "Inform His Majesty."

"Yes, sir."

"Tusk"—Dixter looked at him earnestly—"I don't have time to explain and I'm not certain I could anyway. I'll say this once, and then the subject will be closed forever between us. I've known Maigrey over twenty years. I've loved her, it seems, longer than that. I loved her when I thought she was dead and lost to me forever.

"I *know* her, Tusk. She didn't just 'leave.' She fled. She ran away. She's trying desperately to escape."

"Escape?" Tusk thought it over. "Yeah, I can understand. That old man, that Abdiel . . . I heard he gave her a rough time. And she outsmarted him, tricked him. He can't be happy about that. Yeah, I guess it makes sense—"

"Tusk!" Dixter sighed in exasperation. "Maigrey's not running from Abdiel. She never ran from an enemy in her life. Yet all her life she's been running, trying to escape the one enemy who has the power to ultimately defeat her."

"Who's that? Sagan?"

"No, son. Herself."

Tusk saw the mingled pain and love on the general's face, saw the pain the love had cost. The mercenary was forced to clear his throat of a sudden husky sensation that clogged his windpipe.

"I think I understand, sir. I ran around in that wire wheel myself not long back." His hand went to an earring in his left earlobe, an earring fashioned in the shape of an eight-pointed star. "Odd, though. It was the lady who helped me climb out."

"It's always easier to help others than ourselves, son."

"Yeah, I guess that's right. Anyway, sir, I'm sorry about what I said. I wasn't thinking—"

"What *did* you say, anyway?" Dixter smiled. Reaching out, he took Tusk's hand and pressed it warmly. "I can't seem to remember. It must not have been all that important."

"Lord Sagan on vidscreen three, sir," reported the operator.

The door to the comm slid open. Dion entered, followed by a fussing Bennett—clothes brush in hand—and the omnipresent Honor Guard.

Dion had changed to the same severe black uniform worn by Tusk and Dixter, worn by all the officers aboard the Warlord's ships. No insignia of rank glittered on the collar or banded his sleeve. A sash of purple satin, attached at his left shoulder, tied at his waist, banding his chest was the mark of his royal stature. That and the brooch, made of gold, with the face of a lion whose mane was the rays of the sun. The lion's eyes were blue sapphires. The brooch had been a gift from the Warlord.

The Honor Guard drew up in a line, snapped to attention.

General Dixter bowed, grave and dignified. "Your Majesty."

Tusk bowed as well, clumsily. He'd practiced and practiced, Nola coaching him, but he could never quite make it come off with ease and grace. The atmosphere in the comm changed, crackled with energy and tension, as if that red hair of Dion's was a generator that sent a jolt of current through everyone present. He fed them. It was exhilarating, exciting to be in his presence.

And they fed off him. Drained him.

Those in the comm who could leave their duties rose and bowed respectfully. Those who couldn't darted glances at him out of the corners of their eyes, hoping for a look, a smile, before turning back to their work.

Dion gave them what they wanted. He smiled, gracious, yet aloof, a perfect blend. How does he know where to draw the line? Tusk wondered, marveling. How does he know what to say and how to act and how to command the respect of these men, men like Agis, men double his age? When had he learned it? How had Tusk missed it?

Or had he missed it? No, he admitted. He was a part of it himself. Had been, all along. Something the general told him a long time back returned to Tusk.

"We've flown too close to the comet," he said to himself. "Now we're trapped, just one more spark in the fiery tail streaking through the heavens, being carried along behind a brilliant, beautiful, flaming ball of ice. He flashed into our lives, and before we could help ourselves, we were lit by his light, warmed by his fire, swept up in the wild ride through the stars. Yet where will the ride end?"

The face of the Warlord appeared on the screen. Immediately, everyone in the room tensed. The buzz and hum of voices hushed, those who could broke off communications or, forced to continue speaking, they did so in tones barely above a whisper. Tusk had the insane impression that even the lights in the room dimmed, the temperature seemed to drop measurably. Thus does the atmosphere change, the crowd fall silent and come alert, when the two combatants enter the arena.

Dion was on his guard, treading warily, knowing the first slip, the first sign of weakness, and he would be lying facedown in the dust, his opponent's boot on his neck. Tusk could see the strain of the contest take its toll, could see Dion's jaw muscles tighten to hold his chin firm, the fingers of one hand twitched spasmodically.

Tusk's fist clenched. Damn it, he *would* hit someone! Right when he got out of here. Too bad Link wasn't aboard. . . .

An elbow prodded Tusk in the ribs.

"You're being watched," Dixter shot out of the corner of his mouth with an oblique glance at various cams stationed throughout the room.

Tusk grunted, scowled, but forced himself to calm down. He was somewhat comforted by the sight of Dixter. The general remained standing at his ease, lounging against a table, arms folded across his chest, his uniform collar undone. (His aide Bennett was futilely endeavoring, by semaphore messages from his eyebrows, to remedy the collar situation.) Dixter's eyes were on Dion, a half smile played on the general's lips.

He's picked the winner. But how can he be sure?

Comets, after all, are held in their orbit by far stronger suns.

Chapter ···❖◐◗❖··· Four

Hell trembled as he strode . . .
>John Milton, *Paradise Lost*

Aboard *Phoenix II*, Warlord Derek Sagan stood alone on the bridge; Admiral Aks having retreated as far from his lord as was physically possible in the cramped surroundings. Sagan was angry, extremely angry, and it was conducive neither to one's health nor well-being to be too near the Warlord when he was in this mood. The admiral would, in fact, have been in another, far-distant part of the ship had not Sagan requested his presence.

The heat of the Warlord's fury seemed to radiate from his ceremonial armor, the golden breastplate fashioned in Roman style, decorated with the phoenix rising from flames. The wretched ensign charged with the task of transmitting his lord's image and anger to another part of the galaxy was sweating as if he were sitting in front of a blast furnace.

"We have established contact, my lord," reported the ensign.

Numerous vidscreens came to life, revealing, from every conceivable angle, a communications center in a spaceship light-years away. One of the shots panned wide, to provide a view of everyone in the room. Others were more selective, focusing in on certain individual faces.

One screen held the image of a young man with flaming red-golden hair, who appeared defensive, defiant. Another portrayed a black man, sullen and angry, and, next to him, an older man, in his early fifties, who seemed slightly amused by the whole proceeding. Sagan's gaze flicked to each of these in turn.

"Your Majesty." Sagan's head inclined slightly in what passed for a bow, the shadowed-eyed gaze focused on Dion. "I trust you are well after the rigors of this day?"

31

The king was outwardly composed. But Aks saw the shoulders stiffen beneath the purple sash, the blue eyes narrow, intent on the eyes of his opponent, searching for the slight shift in focus that would tell where would fall the first blow. The admiral shook his head, caught himself hoping that some minor crisis would arise, call him from the bridge.

"I'm getting too old for these games," he said silently. "They're not fun anymore."

Dion's tone was cool and controlled. "Yes, Lord Sagan, thank you for asking. I am tired, but otherwise well."

"I am pleased to hear it, sire. I have important matters to discuss with Your Majesty, but first I beg your indulgence. I must take disciplinary action against one of your guard. I am sorry Your Majesty is forced to witness such an unpleasant proceeding, but the matter cannot be delayed. Discipline must be maintained. Agis, stand forward."

The captain of the Honor Guard, eyes facing front, stepped to the viewscreen, fist over his heart in salute.

"Captain, repeat to me your orders regarding any person who approaches His Majesty."

The Warlord's gaze was, ostensibly, on his unfortunate captain, but Sagan's eyes—Aks saw—were in fact watching the vidscreen that showed him the face of the king, a face that had gone extremely rigid and pale.

"My lord," answered the captain, standing at attention, "my orders are to prevent said person from coming anywhere near His Majesty."

"And yet, this very day, a person was able not only to come near His Majesty but to detain His Majesty in conversation. Is that true, Captain?"

"Yes, my lord." The cords in the man's neck stood out like iron rods.

"You were derelict in your duty, Captain."

"Yes, my lord."

"What is your excuse, Captain?"

"I have none to give, my lord."

"Captain Agis did his duty. He attempted to prevent the young woman from speaking to me." Dion's clear voice rang out like a silver bell. "I commanded him to let her approach."

Sagan bowed. "It is good of Your Majesty to try to defend this officer. Nevertheless, Agis had his orders."

"Yes, Lord Sagan," returned Dion, "and his orders came from his king."

Aks could have sworn he heard the clash of steel. He saw them toe-to-toe, pushing against each other, neither prepared to give ground. Suddenly, unexpectedly, the Warlord broke free, fell back a pace.

"Captain, you are fortunate that His Majesty, in his gracious magnanimity, has intervened in your behalf. No disciplinary action will be taken against you this time. I advise, Captain, that you do not fail His Majesty again."

"No, my lord. Thank you, my lord."

"Do not thank me, Captain. Thank your king."

No blade of ordinary steel could possibly attain the sharp cutting edge of the Warlord's tone. The blade's point was not held to the guard's throat, however, but to Dion's. Sagan had a high regard for his officer, he knew perfectly well the circumstances under which Agis had acted, for he had watched it all on his own private monitor from cams concealed at various locations, including one in the captain's breastplate and another in the lion pin worn on the king's own breast.

Dion had managed to deflect the first attack. He was not about to let down his guard, however. His adversary had seemed to weaken perhaps, only to draw him into a foolish move.

"Your Majesty, certain matters have arisen that require your immediate attention. With your permission, I will make arrangements with the commander of your vessel to transport you back to *Phoenix*. I respectfully advise that you should leave within the hour."

Dion frowned. "My Lord Sagan, I have appointments, commitments."

"Begging Your Majesty's pardon, but I have taken the liberty of canceling your appointments and commitments. The matter is extremely urgent."

Dion's face flushed, the blue eyes flared. He retained control of himself, however. "I will speak to you in private, my lord."

His image disappeared momentarily from the screen. Aks made an oblique, peremptory gesture with his hand and every man whose duties did not absolutely require him to be on the bridge left in discreet and thankful haste. Dion returned, alone. Flame-red hair, flame-blue eyes, the light of his being was almost blinding, causing Aks to avert his gaze, as if he stared into a sun. But the glow reflected off the Warlord, was unable to penetrate the shadowed darkness.

"*I'm* the one being disciplined. Is that it, my lord?" Dion demanded.

The Warlord did not respond.

"I could have healed that young woman!" Dion persisted, angered at Sagan's silence. "I know it! I felt it inside me, the—the energy. You should have let me! You should have let me!"

Sagan smiled sardonically. "*I* didn't stop you, Your Majesty."

"Yes, you did!" Dion retorted. "Not physically. Mentally. Doubts. You make me doubt myself!"

"Why the devil," Sagan said with biting mockery, "didn't you just tell her to go see a good plastic surgeon?"

Dion stared, blinked.

"No," Sagan continued, anger mounting, "you didn't think of anything that simple, that logical, did you, Your Majesty? You fell into the sentimental trap provided for you. Fortunately, you managed to crawl back out before any harm was done. What would have happened if you had gone ahead and attempted to heal that young woman and you had failed? Failed in full view of several billion watchers throughout the galaxy. Everything lost! Everything we've worked for: gone, disappeared, vanished!"

Crimson stained Dion's cheeks. He started to say something, but Sagan pretended not to notice.

"Why do you think Robes planted that woman there?" the Warlord persisted relentlessly. "Why her and not an assassin? Because an assassin's shot makes you a martyr. The people would be furious. Robes would fall tomorrow, his government toppled in an instant. That girl did far worse than almost kill you. She almost made a fool of you. And Robes deals easily with fools."

The crimson in the king's face faded, leaving behind a deathly pallor. "You are right, my lord," Dion said in a low voice. "I . . . didn't think."

"You escaped this time, barely. You may not be so fortunate again. I suggest you return to *Phoenix* without delay."

Dion's lips tightened. "Very well, my lord."

Sagan bowed. "By your leave, Your Majesty. End transmission," he ordered.

The Warlord turned on his heel, stalked off the bridge, booted footfalls resounding like thunder on the deck. The ensign obeyed his lord's orders with alacrity, slumped in relief over his console when the vidscreens went dark. Aks could sympathize. The admiral himself was starting to relax, now that the storm was receding, when Sagan stopped and looked back.

"Admiral Aks?"

"My lord?"

"Cancel His Majesty's next engagements, whatever they are."

"Yes, my lord." It was hardly an admiral's place to act as a public relations agent, but Aks certainly wasn't going to argue. He would pass the word to where it needed to go.

The Warlord strode on, walking the corridors of his ship in mute fury. The admiral knew his lord's moods and, aware that he was needed, followed after, steering a careful course to keep from being swamped in the tidal wave. Sagan's private elevator carried them to the lord's private quarters. Once inside, with the Honor Guard taking up positions outside the sealed door, the Warlord could unleash his anger in private.

"Damn and blast him! He brought us to the brink of disaster, and then has the gall to defy me, to question *my* actions!"

Sagan removed his helm from his head. Aks had the distinct impression that the Warlord's first impulse was to hurl the helm from him, send it crashing into the bulkhead. The admiral wished fervently his lord would do so, would give way to the hot rage that was a devouring flame. Sagan would never permit himself to lose control, however. He held the ornate metal so tightly that it left behind vivid imprints in the flesh when he finally, with deliberate calm, placed it on its stand.

But Aks knew he stood on fault-lined ground. The pressure of two opposing forces, of Sagan and Dion—two solid rock plates grinding together—had to give, had to be released. The quake, when it came, would be destructive, devastating. It might carry them all to ruin. It would certainly destroy one . . . or the other . . . or both.

The admiral decided to risk causing a small tremor. "My lord, perhaps the Lady Maigrey could be of some assistance—"

The deck might have split beneath his feet. Sagan gave Aks a look that stopped the rest of his sentence, came close to stopping his breath.

"The Lady Maigrey abandoned him," the Warlord said coldly. "You know what happened that night on Laskar."

"Not precisely, my lord." Aks had heard rumors, of course, but the subject of my lady's disappearance always put his lordship in a particularly bad mood and was therefore not often brought up during casual dinner conversation.

Sagan did not answer immediately, but regarded Aks long and thoughtfully. Deciding how much of the truth to tell me, the admiral knew, from long association with his lord.

"That night, Aks, following certain circumstances which I need not go into, my lady was left in sole possession of the space-rotation bomb. She deceived both me and His Majesty into believing she had armed and was prepared to detonate it. Maigrey gave Dion the code needed to disarm it, but refused to tell either of us how much time was left ticking away before it blew up. She wanted to find out if His Majesty would be willing to sacrifice his life to obtain it. Dion was, of course. He is Blood Royal. He was willing to die, and to take us with him, unless I promised to turn the bomb over to him. I did so. He gave me the code and I disarmed a bomb that had, as it turned out, never truly been armed."

Sagan shook his head ruefully.

"But I didn't know that, then. I left the spaceplane, Aks, left Dion, left Maigrey with him. I had work to do. Snaga Ohme was dead and all he owned, all his vast store of weapons and wealth, was up for grabs. I had made arrangements. General Haupt's forces were engaged in securing Ohme's estate—an easy task, but the army was encountering stubborn pockets of resistance from Ohme's men. I needed to be there in person. His Majesty was wounded, on the verge of exhaustion. I expected Maigrey to stay with him, kiss his hurts, make him feel better, tuck him in bed, and keep an eye on the bomb."

Sagan's tone was biting, sardonic. "Instead, Aks, she walked out on him."

Walked out on *you*, my lord, Aks amended silently. But he was immediately so uncomfortable even thinking such a thing—in case Sagan might somehow see inside his head—that the admiral was seized by a sudden fit of coughing, forced to cover his face with his handkerchief.

Fortunately, Sagan was brooding over bitter memory, paying his admiral little attention. "That morning, I came back from Ohme's to discover that my lady had not returned to her quarters. I sent the guard to search for her. She had managed, by faking a message from me, to convince those left behind in command on the base that she was to be given a spaceplane in order to join the fighting at Ohme's. Of course, she never came anywhere near the Adonian's."

"But you could have gone after her, my lord," ventured Aks, recovered and greatly daring. "You knew where she was."

"Yes, I knew where she was," Sagan snapped. "I know where she is. And she can stay there. Maigrey abandoned her duty to her king. She obviously has no interest in him or his welfare. She prefers to hide, lick her wounds. Let her. Let her rot!"

The Warlord poured himself a glass of cool water, drank it. Eyes closed, he breathed deeply, concentrated on his breathing, on cleansing body and mind of the debilitating anger.

At least that's what he thinks he's doing. Aks watched his lord in concern. The flame remains, it will never die, never be tamped down, never snuffed out. His anger was not directed at Maigrey, but at fate. And it was burning him alive.

These past few months had aged Sagan. He was only forty-eight (almost forty-nine, his natal day was approaching, a day Aks dreaded). The Warlord was in life's prime for one of the Blood Royal, whose life span exceeded that of ordinary mortals. But the fire within Sagan was consuming those extra, genetically manufactured years. The gray at the temples had lengthened to streaks through the thick black hair. The lines on the granite face and brow were darker, deeper.

He walked with a slight limp, nothing serious. He had pulled a muscle exercising. But the injury itself was significant. The exercise routines that had once been enjoyable, had once been performed for relaxation, were now done in grim earnest, as if he could outrun time . . . and destiny.

"My lord"—Aks tread delicately—"why not allow young Starfire the chance to test his healing power? We could set up a controlled experiment. Dr. Giesk has suggested how it could be done."

"Bah!" The Warlord's calm had returned, at least on the surface. "'God works in mysterious ways,' not through the mechanical fingers of Giesk's medicbots."

"But if we could prove to His Majesty one way or the other—"

Sagan broke in irritably. "The fact that he needs proof that

he can perform miracles, Admiral, is the surest possible sign
that he can't. And according to the rite, to the ritual of
initiation, God has granted him the powers of the Blood Royal
but not the ability to use them. The ultimate sacrifice.
Although"—the Warlord's voice grew bitter again—"I could be
wrong about what God intends. I've been wrong about His
plans before now."

Aks backed off, detoured around this path in haste. Loyal as
he was to Sagan, the admiral refused to follow his lord into the
deep, dark, and tangled bog of religion.

"Your orders, my lord?"

"Maintain our current position, Admiral. And prepare for
guests. Open up the diplomatic suites."

"Very good, my lord. May I inquire the names?" Aks was
trying to remain nonchalant, but he had the feeling he knew
what was coming.

The Warlord glanced at his admiral, smiled the rare, dark
smile so few ever saw. "You know them, Aks. Olefsky, Rykilth,
Baroness DiLuna . . ."

"It's war, then." Aks rubbed his hands together with pleasure. If anything could blow away the clouds hanging over his
lord, it would be the winds of war.

"We have no choice. President Robes—or whoever's behind
him, advising him—is good." Sagan's brow furrowed. "Very
good. We came near losing without a shot being fired. I dare
not take the chance any longer."

The Warlord's darkness threw a shadow over Aks. The
admiral was ready for aggressive action. In his mind, war was
long overdue. But he scented the gangrenous whiff of fear and
desperation, and that unnerved him. What did his lord mean
by the statement *Robes—or whoever's behind him*?

Derek Sagan was afraid. The sudden realization appalled
Aks, alarmed him beyond the power of speech. He had never
known his lord to fear anything. Sagan had faced down Death
so many times the two must be bored by the sight of each other
by now. What had really happened that night at Snaga
Ohme's? What were these "certain circumstances"?

"Aks?" An impatient snap.

The admiral started guiltily. "My lord?"

"Did you hear what I just said?"

"I—I'm afraid, not, my lord. I was thinking of . . .
arrangements—"

"I realize that thinking does require an extraordinary amount of effort for you, Aks. Perhaps you could pay attention to me now and think later."

"Yes, my lord," replied the admiral gravely.

"I was saying that we should start making preparations for war, although these need not be mentioned to His Majesty. The king will believe himself to be in command, of course."

"Will His Majesty go along with it?"

"He will," Sagan said, his tone ominous, "when I fully explain the circumstances. That is all, Admiral. You have leave to return to your duties."

Aks bowed silently, crossed the room, was near the door, when he paused, turned, and noiselessly crossed the thick heavy carpet that covered the deck in the Warlord's sparsely furnished, Spartan quarters.

Sagan, thinking he was alone, had relaxed his rigid posture. His shoulders slumped in weariness, he ran his hand through sweat-dampened hair.

The admiral was not a brilliant man. He knew this fact about himself, the knowledge had never bothered him. He knew his value to Sagan, knew himself to be an ally who was trusted because he wasn't cunning enough to be feared. Older than Sagan, Aks had known the Warlord over twenty years. They had met after Sagan had left the Academy to begin his career in the now-defunct Royal Air Corps. Aks had long admired his lord, holding him in awe, in mortal dread. Aks had never, until now—the ache of fear and pity in his heart—realized that he loved him.

"Derek," he said, greatly daring, placing his hand upon the Warlord's bare shoulder. "Who is the true enemy? I think I have the right to know."

The muscles beneath Aks's hand tensed, bunched, anger at the liberty, anger at the invasion of the private self that Sagan worked so hard to keep hidden nearly unleashing a storm of outrage upon the admiral. Aks had known the risk, braced himself to face the onslaught. He kept his hand on the battle-scarred flesh, fingers firm, grip steady.

The taut muscles relaxed. Black eyes, dark with the smoke of smoldering fire, looked up, regarded Aks with wry intensity.

"Is it that obvious?"

"To me," Aks reassured gently. "Only to me. I've known you

a long time, Derek." And I deserve better than this, the admiral added, but he added it silently.

Sagan heard the unspoken words, however. For long moments he was quiet, sat unmoving. Finally, he stirred restlessly beneath the admiral's touch.

Aks, taking the hint, removed his hand.

"Abdiel. Does the name mean anything to you also?"

"Good God!"

The Warlord's lips tightened to a dark slash across his face. "I see it does."

"But he's . . . he's dead! You yourself had him assassinated."

"One of my many blunders, Aks, and one for which I am paying dearly. I neglected to drive the stake through his heart, so to speak. And now he has come back to haunt me. He is the one behind Robes, my friend. No, not behind him. He is *inside* him!"

The Warlord lifted his hand, stared at five marks upon the palm, continued in a soft voice, speaking more to himself than to Aks.

"Abdiel, former abbot of the Order of Dark Lightning, was at Snaga Ohme's that night. Abdiel was the one who murdered the Adonian. Abdiel nearly caused Dion to murder me. It was Abdiel who captured the Lady Maigrey. She was strong enough to fight him, and so saved herself and the bomb that he sought to acquire. But she could not overcome him. He escaped her, escaped me, escaped Laskar, and disappeared.

"Now, almost assuredly, he is with Robes again. That wretched girl with the ravaged face who approached Dion—Abdiel's plotting, if not his handiwork. He knows Dion, for he probed his mind. He knows what will affect him, how to manipulate him without ever coming near. What is worse, he has Dion's bloodsword. The fool young man, trusting Abdiel, left it behind the night of Ohme's party."

"But what could Abdiel do—"

"—with the bloodsword? The Blood Royal can communicate with each other through the sword, Admiral. It is even possible for a stronger mind to control a weaker through the sword. Although I don't believe that is the case with Dion, at least not yet. Dion is strong, stronger than he gives himself credit for being sometimes. He defied Abdiel, that night, at

Ohme's. He knows Abdiel now, knows him enough to be wary of him. Still . . ."

"His Majesty is in terrible danger—"

"We are all in danger, Admiral," Sagan snapped, straightening, stiffening. He retreated back inside his stone fortress, the iron gates crashed down. "And you, I believe, have your orders."

Aks, shaken and unnerved, could only nod abruptly. He left in precipitous haste.

One of the Honor Guard, standing outside the golden double doors, decorated with the symbol of the phoenix rising from flames, regarded Aks with silent concern.

The admiral saw his face reflected in the man's shining helm and was shocked. His skin had gone gray beneath its artificial tan. His eyes were red-rimmed, the lids puffed and swollen. A nerve twitched in his cheek.

Abdiel . . . still alive.

The admiral glowered at the centurion, harumphed an unintelligible remark, and stalked into the elevator, ordered it to take him to the bridge. At the last moment he reconsidered.

"Officer's club."

Courage is rarely found at the bottom of a Scotch bottle, but it couldn't hurt to go looking.

··◁■ ■▷··

Tusk was engaged in his own exploration of the bottoms of bottles. He was not in an officer's club; his ship was— ostensibly—not a military vessel. When he first saw the yacht, Tusk had registered a strong protest against trusting Dion's travel through a dangerous galaxy in what appeared to be a space-going spa. On entering and discovering the yacht's many secrets, the mercenary changed his mind.

He should have known, he told himself. The yacht had, after all, once belonged to the late Snaga Ohme. The vessel's sleek, almost sleazy outer appearance belied its true nature. A fake hull, adorned with neon lights that flashed witty epigrams to fellow ships passing in the night, could be rolled up instantaneously, revealing a real hull bristling with lascannons, banks of phasers, hypermissiles—the very latest in death-dealing technology.

Inside the yacht, the lavishly decorated interior altered itself the moment a shot was fired or even contemplated.

Objets d'art retreated back into the bulkheads or sank down into the deck. Classic paintings slid aside to reveal instrument panels and weapons consoles. Plush love seats rose up, swiveled to align themselves with the guns that sprang out of the cedar paneling. The yacht was fast, faster than anything Tusk'd ever flown. Like a rat, it could run if outnumbered, stand and fight if cornered.

Ohme had, in fact, named it *The Rat*. Sagan had ordered the name changed to something better suiting the dignity of the king it now carried. But the crew called the ship by its old name, as a kind of tribute to the late owner. Tusk heard it referred to as *The Rat* so often he couldn't remember half the time what the new name was. He had come to respect it, admire it, though he never could get used to blast doors beautified by the very latest in modern art.

He highly approved of the lounge, that was dimly lit, with large black marble tables and deep white leather sofas. Vidscreens provided vicarious amusement for those who couldn't find it anywhere else. The vidscreen was currently replaying Dion's interview with news commentator James Warden.

They had the lounge practically to themselves, the few crew members who had been present had quietly left, out of respect for the king's need for a few moments privacy. As private as he could ever be, surrounded by aides, bodyguards.

Tusk had his back to the vidscreen, refusing to watch. Dion, seated across from him, glanced up at himself occasionally, but mostly kept his morose gaze fixed on the beer in front of him—beer which he hadn't tasted and which by now must be warm and flat. Nola looked from one to the other and sighed.

"Boy, you two are about as much fun as a TRUC marooned in deepspace. And to think I washed my hair for this. Jeez, I wish Link were here," she added teasingly.

"Me, too," Tusk said, clenching his fist, a gleam in his eyes.

"I wonder what he's plotting," Dion muttered, the first words he'd spoken since they'd left the comm over an hour ago.

Tusk assumed they weren't referring to Link.

"Whatever it is, you'll find out soon enough. Don't worry about it. Look, I'll get you a fresh beer. Drink it and go to bed. . . ."

"I *am* tired," Dion admitted wearily, shoving the glass aside.

He glanced up again at the screen. The interview was approaching the end. He started to say something, when the image abruptly changed.

"We interrupt our deepspace broadcast for this GBC special report."

A premonition swept over Tusk. "Switch that damn thing off!" he shouted at a startled 'droid bartender, who stared at him in mechanical bewilderment.

The controls were located behind the bar. Tusk twisted to his feet, lunged over the polished surface. He broke several glasses and sent a bowl of pretzels flying, but accomplished little else. The voice droned on.

"The body of a human female has been discovered floating in one of the ornamental ponds located on the GBC grounds. She was the victim of an apparent suicide. The body has not been identified, but reliable sources tell us that she is the same person involved in a dramatic confrontation that took place today with Dion Starfire, self-proclaimed king of the galaxy—"

Tusk drew his lasgun, aimed and fired. The vidscreen exploded, raining bits of plastiglass down on the indignant, protesting 'droid. Too late to undo the damage, of course, but shooting the damn screen gave Tusk an infinite amount of satisfaction.

Dion stood frozen, drained of all color, white and cold and stiff. His eyes went vacant, glassy.

"Dion!" Nola cried, frightened.

He didn't respond.

"Tusk, he's not breathing!"

"Kid!" Tusk grabbed Dion's shoulder, shook him hard, fingers pinching the flesh. "Kid, snap out of it. Nola, hand me that beer—" he began, with the intention of throwing it into Dion's face.

But the blue eyes slowly regained their focus, though he did not seem to recognize his surroundings. He drew in a shivering, sucking breath.

"You okay?" Tusk demanded, worried.

"Yes, I'm fine."

Tusk shuddered at the sound. "Come on, kid. I'll take you back to your room—"

"No, I'm fine. I need time to think, that's all."

Dion shook off his friend's hand, walked to the door. The Honor Guard came to attention, saluted.

Tusk followed after him, thinking he should, though he didn't particularly want to. What could he say?

At the door, Dion turned to him. "Tusk, report to the bridge. Tell the ship's captain to take us into the Lanes. I want to reach *Phoenix* immediately."

"Sure, kid," answered Tusk. He exchanged glances with Nola. Her eyes were wide, her freckles stood out like ink blots on her pallid skin. No need to mention that the ship was already in hyperspace.

"Thank you," Dion said in the same flat and lifeless voice.

The centurions were prepared to fall into step behind their king. But Agis, their captain, brought them to a halt. The centurion then did the unthinkable. He broke a rule, spoke without being spoken to.

Coming forward, he said softly and most respectfully, "Your Majesty, I'm sorry."

Dion, who was staring at nothing and seeing, perhaps, the body of the dead girl, her pretty brown hair floating in the water, shifted his gaze to the centurion.

"So am I, Agis," he said quietly. "So am I."

Chapter ❦ Five

She is drowned already, sir, with salt water, though I
seem to drown her remembrance again with more.
William Shakespeare, *Twelfth Night*, Act II, Scene 1

His Majesty, King Dion Starfire, arrived aboard *Phoenix II*
and was met with due ceremony. Ranks of centurions stood to
attention, forming an aisle of gleaming breast-plated human
columns on either side of the path His Majesty tread. Behind
the Honor Guard, those crew members of *Phoenix* not needed
to keep the ship operational, attired in their dress uniforms,
were present to do their king honor.

Lord Sagan, clad in golden armor, golden helm with bloodred feather crest, red cape trimmed in gold with its golden
phoenix stitched on the back, greeted his king with grave and
solemn ceremony and presented him to the other dignitaries.

Dion knew what was expected of him before an audience,
knew it wouldn't be politic to indicate, by either bearing or
manner, that there was a rift between himself and his chief
military commander. He returned his lord's salute with dignity
and aplomb, acknowledged a bow from Admiral Aks, advanced
to meet the dignitaries.

"Lord Rykilth, Your Majesty," said Lord Sagan. "Warlord of
galactic sector twenty-four."

An extremely powerful Warlord, the vapor-breather had
once, during the rule of the old king, been Sagan's mortal
enemy. They were allies now. Rykilth's system had seceded,
he had pledged the new king his support.

Dion spoke the words of formal greeting in the vapor-
breather's language, acknowledged the swirl of yellow fog
in the vapor-breather's bubble helm that was his answer,
remained a moment to exchange meaningless pleasantries.

His mind was not on the polite words, spoken in the
language that sounded rather like a hydraulic leak. His mind

45

was on Sagan. What was he plotting? Why was Rykilth aboard *Phoenix* and not in galactic sector twenty-four, where he belonged?

"Baroness DiLuna, Your Majesty, Warlord of sector sixteen." Sagan, moving along gravely at his king's side, continued the introductions.

Another powerful Warlord, another whose sector had seceded from the Galactic Democratic Republic. Strong, swaggering, DiLuna ran a ship crewed exclusively by women, many of them her daughters. Various Baron DiLunas came and went. Always young, always handsome, they lived to service the baroness. These men were provided one year of sublime pleasure, anything and anyone aboard DiLuna's ship was theirs for the asking. After that year, the barons were "retired." No one ever knew what happened to them, the ceremony of retirement, like the ceremony of marriage, was performed in strictest secrecy, a mystery sacred to the baroness and her women. The following night, however, a new young man warmed DiLuna's bed.

Dion, thinking of all this, understood the woman's sardonic smile and did not take offense at the coldness of her greeting. He may have been king but he was, after all, only a man, an inferior being, who served one useful purpose only. His face grew warm at the thought.

DiLuna's smile broadened, perhaps she read his mind. He saw what he immediately assumed to be glances exchanged between the woman and Lord Sagan—obviously there was *one* man DiLuna respected. Dion's anger swelled and served him well, burning away his embarrassment.

"Bear Olefsky, ruler of the planetary system of Solgart."

"Aye, laddie, well met again!"

No formalities of bowing and scraping for Olefsky. Arms like the limbs of sheltering oaks clasped Dion to a breast rock-solid and big as a mountain. He was nearly stifled by the smells of cowhide and sweat; a trophy of human hair, dangling from the leather armor, tickled his nose; the skull of a small animal (he hoped it was an animal) dug into his cheek.

Dion extricated himself from the embrace, did what he could to recover both his dignity and the breath that had been squeezed out of his body. He felt his anger begin to cool, he could see what was transpiring. These people were the three most powerful in the universe, next to Sagan. He had brought them here to pledge the king their allegiance publicly, for the first time.

Out of the corner of his eye, Dion saw they were under the close scrutiny of vidcams; Sagan's public relations people were hard at work, recording this historic meeting for posterity and the GBC.

Dion's eyes sought those of the Warlord's, but couldn't see them, shadowed by the helm. The two moved away from the line of dignitaries, continued down the aisle of living statues.

"Very impressive, my lord," Dion remarked out of the side of a mouth that was smiling left and right. "But we need to talk. Alone. Now."

"Your wish is my command, sire."

The response was correct, proper, and the sarcasm was like acid falling on Dion's flesh. Neither said another word. The ceremonies were concluded, the troops thanked and dismissed. Admiral Aks and his junior officers acted promptly to herd their guests back to the diplomatic portion of the ship.

The king, accompanied by his apparently attentive lord, headed for the elevator that led to the Warlord's private quarters.

··◁■ ■▷··

"An interesting young man," said DiLuna. She despised men, but was accustomed to sizing them up for breeding purposes, "I'd bed him." A high compliment from the baroness. "What do you think, Rykilth?"

"He's lasted longer in the contest than I'd expected," observed the vapor-breather through his translator.

"The scars of his battles are plain upon him," Olefsky agreed. The huge warrior glanced back at the two figures, one tall and gleaming in gold, the other shorter, red hair burning like flame. "Who will be the ultimate winner?"

"Who do you suppose?" Rykilth asked dryly.

"Bet?" Olefsky raised his gigantic hand.

"What stakes?" DiLuna demanded.

"One hundred golden eagles."

"Terms?"

"That before we leave this ship, the crown will not rest on two heads, but one. The laddie's."

"Ha!" Rykilth gave a snort that sent the fog billowing and nearly blew out his translator. "You might as well hand over your money now, Olefsky. By the time we leave this ship, the 'laddie' will be lucky to retain his head, much less the crown."

"A bet, then?" Olefsky asked coolly, extending his huge hand.

"A bet." Rykilth's small, gloved, three-fingered hand closed over as many of Olefsky's fingers as the vapor-breather could manage.

DiLuna scoffed. "None of the three of us ever defeated Sagan. You're saying this 'boy' will do what we couldn't?"

"I am," the Bear replied imperturbably. "None of us were Blood Royal."

"All thanks to the Goddess for that! It will be a pleasure taking your money, my friend." DiLuna's hand gripped the big man's firmly.

Laughing, the three shifted their conversation to more important topics.

···◁■ ■▷···

The double doors, decorated with the phoenix, closed and sealed. Sagan removed his helm, placed it carefully upon its stand. His hands clasped behind his back, beneath the flowing red cape, he took a turn about the spacious area of his living quarters, glanced out the viewscreen at the other ships in his fleet, looked to see if there were any messages on his computer screen, then turned to face his king.

"What is it you have to say, Your Majesty?" Sagan asked coldly.

Dion's anger was at hand, sharp and shining with the righteousness of his cause.

"The girl died, the one I could have healed! She drowned herself, and it was my fault. Never again. Never again will I listen to you or take your advice. You don't want me to discover my true powers because you're afraid of me. I am king and I will *be* king!"

The Warlord said nothing, did nothing.

"I came to tell you that. I will be in my quarters, should you decide to respond." Dion turned to leave.

"I have a vid I think Your Majesty should see," came Sagan's voice behind him.

Dion stopped, glanced around, eyes narrowed, immediately suspicious.

"I am extremely tired, my lord. It can wait until morning."

The Warlord depressed a button on a console. A vidscreen slid into view. "No, Your Majesty, it cannot. Computer, bring up exhibit number B-221."

A vid appeared on the screen. Blurred at first, it sharpened as the computer adjusted the focus and brought into view the corpse of a teenage girl, her face hideously deformed, laid out upon a steel table. The girl's body was naked, her hair wet, bedraggled. The feet and hands were blue, a numbered tag was wrapped around one toe.

Dion made a strangled sound, shock and fury robbed him of his voice. He continued walking toward the double doors.

"Look at her, Your Majesty!" Sagan's voice grated. "*If* you have the nerve. Her death was, as you say, your fault. Your responsibility, though perhaps not the way you imagine."

Slowly, hands clenching to fists, Dion faced the horrible image on the vidscreen, faced the impassive, shadowed visage of the Warlord.

"You are right, my lord." Dion swallowed, his throat muscles constricting in his neck. "I must accept the burden of this young woman's self-destruction. I have much to learn. I thank your lordship for teaching me."

"You have much to learn, all right!" Sagan snapped.

The cam zoomed in on the body, bringing it closer, closer, studying it from every angle. Dion drew a deep breath, held himself steady.

"Body of Jane Doe," came a voice over the audio, a woman's voice, sounding calm and bored. "Vid taken prior to autopsy for purposes of identification." The coroner gave the planet's date and time, also Standard Military date and time, her own name and official title, adding, "Anyone having information regarding the identity of subject Jane Doe is asked to report to—" name of local police chief.

The cam lingered for a close-up of the hideous face, traveled casually over the upper part of the body, moved down the right arm to focus on the victim's right hand.

"No tattoos. No moles or birthmarks," the coroner continued. "The only wounds found on the body were discovered on palm of the right hand."

White flesh filled the screen—white flesh crisscrossed with the lines used by fortune tellers to trace a human's destiny, white flesh marred by five small puncture marks arranged in a peculiar pattern.

Dion let go his inheld breath. Balls of yellow burst before his eyes, he was suddenly sick and dizzy. Dazed, he lifted his right hand, stared down at his palm. Five scars, five puncture marks, arranged in the same pattern. Draw a line between them, connect the dots, and they'd form a five-pointed star.

Sagan ordered the computer to freeze the frame. It did so, leaving the image of the dead girl's hand on the screen.

"By her report, the coroner had a difficult time determining what these marks were," the Warlord stated, regarding the photo with cool, frowning detachment. "She concluded that they were made by five metal needles, driven into the skin. But for what reason or purpose, she couldn't fathom. She surmised it was some type of drug use, though she couldn't find any trace of drugs in the body. Admittedly, she didn't spend much time investigating. The young woman had obviously died by drowning, obviously finally succeeded in doing what she'd attempted to do several times before. We know differently, however, don't we, my liege? We know it wasn't suicide. It was murder, cold-blooded, calculating murder."

Dion found a chair and sat down before he fell.

"Abdiel." He spoke softly. The name conjured up bitter memory. He stared at his hand, curled the fingers over the palm, hiding the marks.

"Abdiel," Sagan repeated.

"You knew . . . all along."

"I didn't know. I suspected. When I received news of the girl's suicide, I sent Dr. Giesk to examine the body, obtain the coroner's report. He recognized immediately the true cause of death."

"But she drowned! It *was* suicide, the coroner said so." Dion clung to his fragment of hope.

"Yes, death was by drowning. No one actually saw her jump, but, as you heard, no marks were found on the body. There were no indications of a struggle. I have no doubt she took her own life. But did she do so of her own volition?" Sagan shook his head. "You know yourself how Abdiel can manipulate the mind, especially those with whom he has bonded."

Dion shuddered, grasped his right wrist, nursed his hand as if it pained him. "But she wasn't mind-dead. I would have recognized one of his disciples."

"Exactly. Abdiel would know that, of course. The girl was probably a new acquisition, one recently obtained. The effects of bonding with the mind-seizer, such as the lifeless look in the eyes, come only after a period of time."

Dion laughed suddenly, mirthlessly. "What would Abdiel have done if I *had* healed her?"

"He had little cause to fear that. Through your bloodsword, he sees inside you."

The young man flushed, frowned, made no response.

Sagan followed up his advantage. "He sees your doubt, your lack of faith. He can use it all against you. And against me."

Dion opened his mouth to argue, closed it again. The dead hand on the screen seemed raised against him, raised in wrath and vengeful accusation.

"Due to the swift action of the guard in destroying that remote reporter 'droid, the damage that could have been caused by this incident was minimized. If that young woman's plea for healing had been made public, you would have been finished. As it was, we were able to put out the story that she accosted you, attempted to kill you. After which, filled with remorse, she killed herself."

"But that's a lie!"

"Would you prefer us to broadcast the truth, Your Majesty?"

Dion sat silent, thoughtful, unhappy. He looked away from the screen, away from the hand, yet he could still feel its chill touch. "None of this is what I expected," he murmured. "Being a king . . . The lies, the deception. And when I do tell the truth, I'm never permitted to tell all of it. I'm not certain I even know what the truth is, anymore."

Sagan eyed him. "What did you say, Your Majesty?"

Dion regarded him, blue eyes reflecting back golden armor. "Nothing important. Nothing you would understand. What is your counsel, my lord?"

"We escaped destruction this time," Sagan said grimly, "but just barely. We will not be so fortunate again. That is what Abdiel is telling us. That is his warning."

"Warning?" Dion stared at him.

"Of course! Don't tell me that even now, you don't understand. This"—Sagan pointed to the cold, dead hand—"was no blunder on his part. He flaunts his abilities, signs his name to his work."

"But . . . why?"

"Because he knows the debilitating power of fear."

Turning, Sagan again clasped his hands behind his back,

beneath the red cloak trimmed in gold. He walked over to the viewscreen, looked out at the fleet of ships. Destroyers, carriers, torpedo boats, support vessels—a vast armada surrounding the Warlord and his king with an impenetrable ring of steel and fire.

Dion followed his gaze, his thoughts. "Against all this—one frail old man." He shook the mane of red-golden hair. "I'm not afraid of him."

"I am, Your Majesty," Sagan said quietly.

He left the viewscreen, crossed the carpeted deck to the computer. Dion noticed, for the first time, that the Warlord was limping slightly, favoring his right leg.

Sagan caught the boy's glance. "A pulled muscle."

He depressed a key on the computer. The dead hand vanished.

"And what do you suggest we do, my lord?"

Dion asked the question, but he already knew the answer, knew the reason why he'd been requested to return, knew the reason why Rykilth and DiLuna and Olefsky were on board *Phoenix II*.

"We go to war," said Sagan.

Chapter ❦ Six

Commune with your own heart . . . and be still.
                            Prayer Book, *1662*, Psalms 4:4

The Council of War among the allies gathered on *Phoenix* lasted three days, Standard Military Time. The Council's purpose had been to plan the war, but it spent much of its time attempting to convince His Majesty of the need to seize the crown, instead of, as Rykilth put it, "Standing around politely, waiting for it to be handed to you."

They had to convince Dion, because the one weapon the allies wanted, desperately needed, was in the king's possession—the space-rotation bomb. Given to him, albeit under duress, by Lord Sagan.

The king sat in on every meeting, listened attentively to every argument, asked questions to clarify some point, but then said nothing more. What he was thinking, what he was deciding, no one knew. Certainly not Sagan, whose frustration and anger were growing more apparent every SMD that passed.

"I believe you will be owing me some money, Rykilth," rumbled Olefsky, giving the vapor-breather a nudge that nearly deflated his protective spacesuit. "The kinglet has proved stronger than you thought."

The three were in the war room alone together. Sagan had, once again, pressed the king for a decision. Dion had, once again, refused to commit himself. The Warlord had stormed out of the Council meeting in rage. His Majesty himself had left shortly after. Bear Olefsky had ordered lunch.

"I cannot understand why Sagan keeps up this pretence," Rykilth commented through his translator.

The words of his language swirled and writhed like the fog in his helm. Always shifting, sometimes thickening or thinning depending on his body's needs, the mist obscured the vapor-breather's face, making it difficult for most humans to communicate comfortably with him. An eye would suddenly appear, staring at them from the fog, then vanish in the mist and only the toothless mouth could be seen.

The mechanical voice of the translator flattened out all emotion. Those accustomed to dealing with vapor-breathers knew to judge their mental state by the color of the fog. Affected by even the slightest variation in body temperature, the vapor ranged in shade from an almost pure white—a sign of calm—to a dark yellow, stained with brown. Rykilth's vapor was, at the moment, a sort of ochre.

"Lord Sagan should simply tell the boy, 'Your Majesty, we're going to war and if you don't like it you can take a walk out the nearest air lock.'" Rykilth's vapor darkened slightly.

"His Majesty has the bomb and Sagan does not," said Olefsky, winking.

DiLuna glanced significantly around the room. "Careful, my friend. Ears are listening."

The Bear shrugged. A grin split the bearded face. "By my lungs and liver, what's Sagan going to do, shoot me for speaking the truth?"

They were interrupted by orderlies, serving lunch: a huge platter of raw meat and bread for Olefsky, a plate of fruit and rice for DiLuna, and a plastic envelope of congealed red liquid for Rykilth.

"Gracious Mother, accept our thanks for Your bounty," DiLuna prayed to the Goddess.

Rykilth detached a tube from the envelope, attached it to a tube inside his helmet, and sucked up nourishment. The ochre color faded gradually in the enjoyment of his repast. Bear Olefsky forked raw meat into his mouth, wiped away the blood that dribbled down his chin with a hunk of bread.

The orderlies poured wine for the woman, deposited what looked to be a keg of ale at Olefsky's side, asked if anything else was needed, and then disappeared, leaving the three to their meal and their conversation.

Just what is the truth about the space-rotation bomb?" DiLuna questioned.

"That it belongs to Dion Starfire. That he has it hidden away, under lock and key. That he has it in his power to destroy us, to destroy Sagan, to destroy the galaxy, maybe to destroy the universe, if he chooses." Olefsky rolled his eyes, stuffed a wad of bread into his mouth, washed it down with ale.

"And Lord Sagan can't get it back? From a whelp who's still got his mother's milk on his lips?" DiLuna made an impolite gesture.

"Sagan can get the bomb anytime he chooses," Rykilth predicted. The red liquid was nearly gone. It had a slight intoxicating effect; the vapor-breather was in a more relaxed mood, his fog almost pure white. The mists had thinned, two of his eyes were actually almost visible. "What has there ever been that Sagan didn't get if he wanted it?"

"One thing," Bear said with unexpected solemnity. "The one thing he wanted most—the crown. He pledged his word to Dion, you see. Pledged it before the good God."

"Ah, well, that settles it," said DiLuna, nodding. She worshiped a different deity—or perhaps one could say a different aspect of the same deity—but the warrior woman was devout and reverent in her duties to the Goddess Mother. She understood.

Rykilth, who believed in nothing except his own life-giving vapor, made a gurgling sound—a sneer among vapor-breathers. The mist thickened, a faint brown streak wafted up from the region around his neck. "Sagan always has an angle. You can't tell me he doesn't. I trust *we're* not being played for fools—by both of them."

A line marred DiLuna's forehead. She shot a swift, shrewd glance at the other two. "We were each of us Sagan's enemy once. And what do we truly know about this Starfire?"

The vapor-breather's mist turned an ugly shade of naphthol-yellow. Bear Olefsky set down his mug of ale, frowned at it as if it tasted bad.

DiLuna rose to her feet. She was sixty years old, by her planet's reckoning, tall, broad-shouldered. "I'm going to contact my ship. I'm leaving tomorrow. If a decision has not been reached tonight, I'll take matters into my own hands."

She turned, looked directly into what was supposed to be a concealed cam, and shook her long scalp lock of iron-gray hair. Gunmetal earrings jangled. "*I* won't go crawling back to Peter Robes."

"Time for me to switch chemical packs," Rykilth announced. "I believe that I, too, will make arrangements to leave tomorrow. I can only tolerate existence in this oxygen-contaminated atmosphere so long. What about you, Olefsky?"

The Bear glowered into his mug, then looked up, eyes glinting. "Stomach and spleen, I think you are wrong, both of you. And I think that before you leave you two will pay me the money you owe me."

·-◁▮ ▮▷-·

"So much for our trusty allies," said the Warlord dryly. He gestured toward the screen. "Still, I can hardly blame them. That, Your Majesty, is the result of your refusal to act."

Dion stared at the screen, frowned, the full lips petulant. "You're not angry at them?"

"Angry? Over what?"

"This—this disloyalty."

"Loyalty!" Sagan snorted. "The vapor-breather's translator device wouldn't know how to interpret the word. Your royal blood is so much water to him. Talk to him of your divine right to rule and he'll drift off to sleep in a cloud so thick you'll never find him. Talk to him of money and the mists will part. His star systems are impoverished, with only one resource: people. A mixed bag of human and alien life-forms, they have one thing in common—they want what others have and they don't and they're willing to die to get it. And they're willing to back you because they like the odds."

Dion switched the cam to himself, saw his own image on the screen. He was startled by his appearance. His skin was pale, purple smudges shadowed his eyes. He couldn't remember the last time he'd slept the night through.

"Meaning," he said coldly, "that they would back another if the odds were right."

"If the odds were right . . . or if they improved."

Dion heard the implied threat, chose to ignore it.

"As for DiLuna," Sagan continued, "she is loyal only to her Goddess. She despised the Blood Royal once because we worshiped the Creator; she was jealous of the power of the Order of Adamant. Now that the Blood Royal are, in essence, gone from the universe, and the Order of Adamant is no more, DiLuna sees her chance to bring the worship of the Mother to the galaxy. Hers is a holy war."

"How could she expect me to help her in that?"

"DiLuna has a daughter about your age, I believe; a priestess ordained in the worship of the Goddess. Rest assured, young man, that if you manage to overthrow Robes and gain your throne, DiLuna will plot to make this daughter your queen. You might not find it all that bad, however. Her daughters have the reputation for being as skilled as their mother in bed."

Warm blood rushed to Dion's cheeks. He turned stiffly away, but not before he caught a glimpse of the Warlord's sardonic smile. Dion's shame burned; he felt like a schoolboy caught watching a porno vid.

How did Sagan know? Was my unease and discomfort around the baroness that obvious?

Dion was not quite sexually inexperienced, not anymore. Kings throughout the ages have always had their pick of amoretti and the attractive, vibrant, and exciting Starfire was no exception. But Dion's ventures had been less than satisfactory.

The women in whom he took an interest were screened, examined, searched. The evening was directed, managed, staged. The centurions remained standing outside the door the entire time. And although the women had assured the young man in the morning that he'd been wonderful, an angel, he knew himself that he was clumsy, awkward, inadequate. It is difficult to enjoy the softness of silken sheets when you are surrounded by a ring of steel. But at least he'd always supposed that those feelings were private, his to hide and nurse like a wound in the darkness.

Now he saw that even his shame was laid bare. Dion suddenly hated Sagan for knowing, hated him for displaying his knowledge, for using it as a weapon.

"And then, of course, we still have the problem of Abdiel. Or perhaps not a problem for you, Your Majesty. Have you been in contact with him?" the Warlord asked with cool nonchalance.

Dion flared, rounded on him. "Meaning is *he* the one advising me? Is he attempting to use me?"

"Well, is he, Your Majesty?"

"No more than you, my lord," Dion replied. "And with about the same measure of success."

The two eyed each other, blade tips touched, sparked. It was Dion, this time, who lowered his weapon, stepped out of the circle.

"And where does Your Majesty think he is going?"

"I'm tired. I'm going to lie down."

"You still have a great deal of work to do, sire."

"Work! I've done nothing but work these last three days! I don't count sheep when I try to sleep, I count battalions. Supply lines trail me through my dreams. The flash of laser fire wakes me and the sound of bombs . . ." The screams of the dying, the dead eyes staring at me, the blood on my hands, on my uniform.

He bit off the words, shook off the memories. "One problem remains, my lord, that you have not seen fit to address. I've stated publicly, time and again, that I will not make war upon my people. Now, suddenly, you want me to announce cheerfully that I've been lying through my teeth?"

Sagan waved his hand, brushing away gnats. "It is a king's prerogative to change his mind. Say you're giving in, bowing to public pressure. Say the people demand that you free them from a corrupt, defiled presidency. Say you've had a sign from God—"

Dion looked up swiftly at the Warlord, thinking that Sagan might have spoken those last words with some deeper, underlying meaning. He half expected—half hoped—to find the dark eyes staring into his, their shadowed gaze probing his soul.

The Warlord wasn't paying attention to Dion at all. He was glancing over some reports that had just been relayed to him. He had not spoken from penetrating insight, but out of exasperation.

"Two more systems have seceded," he announced with satisfaction. "They haven't yet thrown in with us, but they will, once we make it clear where we stand. Well? Has Your Majesty made his decision?"

The sarcasm flicked like a whip on already bleeding flesh. Dion flinched, remained silent.

"It may not even be necessary to go to war," Sagan pursued. "Fear of the space-rotation bomb will drive many to support your cause."

"I don't want them to come to me out of fear!"

"Then it's quite likely, sire, that they won't come to you at all!"

"It's a terrible responsibility," Dion said softly, "knowing that I hold the lives of billions of people in my care. Knowing that with one word, one command, I can end them. . . ."

"And how you love it!" Sagan spoke each word clearly and distinctly, moved a step nearer with each word until he loomed over the young man, surrounded him with metal and with flame. "How you love the power, the adulation. Like a bright and shining silver globe, falling into your hands from above. Think back to your rite of initiation. Do you remember the silver globe, Your Majesty?" His voice was low, lethal. "Do you remember it falling, remember the spikes, remember your hands impaled upon the spikes?"

Dion remembered. He stared at his hands, saw the spikes tear flesh, sever tendons, shatter bone, felt the pain flash up his arms, explode in his brain. . . .

"Power is like the bright and shining silver globe, Your Majesty. You won it and now you hold it easily. You see yourself reflected in its silver surface, you see youth and beauty and adoring crowds. And then, suddenly, the spikes! Your hands impaled upon the silver, shining globe. Not so easy to hold on to now, is it, sire? Not so easy to look on your reflection and see it smeared with blood! But you must hold on to it and endure the pain."

The Warlord's hand opened, palm empty. "Or drop it."

Illusion. The silver ball, the spikes, the blood, the pain—all illusion. Special effects, created by Sagan and Maigrey to impress him. An All-Seeing, All-Knowing Being controlling the universe, flaunting His Omnipotence by impaling a boy's hands on a silver ball!

Isn't it? Isn't it, Platus? Dion cried silently to his dead mentor. You and I—we reasoned away God before I was six years old. I am alone. I alone am responsible. I alone hold the bright and shining silver ball. That's right, isn't it? Tell me that's right, Platus!

Dion's hands shook. He clenched them to fists, lowered them to his sides. "And if I refuse?" Blue eyes, clear and bright as silver, looked into eyes darkly shadowed behind a golden helm. "If I refuse to go to war?"

Derek Sagan stood silent.

The blue eyes did not waver, did not lower their gaze.

The dark eyes narrowed, grew darker. "I will not let this moment pass me by."

"And what about me, my lord?"

Sagan raised an eyebrow, lips twisted. "Kings, especially foolish kings, have been imprisoned before now . . . or worse. You've been of use to me. You started the ball rolling. It will speed along now under its own momentum."

"I see. You swore your oath of allegiance to me before God, just as you swore it long ago to my uncle. You broke your oath to him. Now you will break it to me."

"If my soul is eternally damned for the first, Your Majesty, it hardly matters what happens to me over the second. I expect you will want to announce your decision this evening, following the banquet that is being given in honor of our guests. Consider well what that decision will be. By your leave, sire."

The Warlord bowed, red cape falling in a tide of crimson over his shoulders. He turned, walked out of the room, left Dion standing, alone.

From somewhere deep inside him, or from somewhere far beyond him, came the voice.

It wasn't Abdiel's. Dion knew the mind-seizer's voice, had heard its seductive whisperings often in the past months. It had been easy to evade him, refuse to respond. He knew the mind-seizer, or thought he did. He assumed he knew the man's game. Offers of power, glory, wealth. Meaningless. Abdiel, after all, could give Dion nothing that he didn't already have.

This new voice offered him nothing. It appalled and terrified him, because it was a voice that he didn't know how to question, a voice he didn't know how to answer. It was still and small, yet he heard it clearly.

Wait, it counseled. Wait.

Chapter ❈⟋❀⟍❈ Seven

> ". . . who knew
> The force of those dire arms. Yet not for those,
> Nor what the potent Victor in his rage
> Can else inflict, do I repent or change . . ."
> John Milton, *Paradise Lost*

Tusk ran his finger around the tight collar of his dress uniform, attempting, for the hundredth time, to ease its iron grip on his throat.

"Stop that!" Nola hissed out of the corner of her mouth. Champagne glass in hand, she smiled on the arriving guests.

"It doesn't matter to you that I'm being slowly strangled!" Tusk retorted.

"Look at Sagan's officers—Captain Williams, for example. *He* isn't squirming around like a man with his head in a kij vine."

"Yeah, well, maybe that's 'cause his uniform fits. This damn thing shrunk." Tusk gave the collar a final vicious, hopeless tug.

"That's impossible." Nola cast Tusk a cool, appraising glance. "If anything, you've gained weight. All this high living."

Tusk opened his mouth to make a smart rejoinder. Nola was not the tall and willowy variety of human female. Her short, compact, muscular figure fought a constant battle against pudginess. But she, as Dion's social secretary, seemed to always find time to exercise. Tusk, as Dion's road manager and unofficial guardian, always seemed to find himself in a bar. Tusk looked down at his protruding gut that had once been hard and flat as sheet metal, and gloomily snapped his mouth shut.

"Champagne?" offered a waiter.

Tusk snarled. A look sent the man and his tray of crystal glasses dashing off hurriedly into the crowd.

61

The banquet chamber, located in the diplomatic section aboard *Phoenix II*, was slowly filling with officers and the Warlord's guests.

Baroness DiLuna arrived, escorted by four of her female guards, all clad in armor. The metal, specially made for them, fit close and tight to their strong, lithe bodies, gleamed like a fish's skin, and left one breast bare, as was the custom among the female warriors. They kept apart, flashing eyes staring boldly and disdainfully at all the men. The only person in whom they seemed to take any interest at all was Nola, who found that interest extremely disconcerting.

Bear Olefsky entered the vast room, seemed to fill it with his hairy, leather-covered body, and rumbling, booming laughter. His two sons, taller and broader than their father by a half meter in all directions, followed after him, grinning sheepishly at the women and accidentally trampling a midshipman.

Rykilth and his party of vapor-breathers wafted into the room. Faint, breath-snatching whiffs of their poisonous atmosphere seeped out of their helms, causing those standing near to cough and gasp. Captain Williams put in a hurried, quiet call to the bridge to increase air circulation in the banquet hall.

Warlord Sagan strolled about, red and gold as flame, speaking to his guests and darting shadowed glances at the door.

His Majesty, the king, had not made an appearance.

Tusk lifted his chin, tried to stretch out his neck. Leaning down, he whispered in Nola's ear, "Let's get married."

"Sure," she said, smiling at Captain Williams, who bowed effortlessly, gracefully, and smiled back.

"I mean let's get married now, tonight," Tusk said urgently. "That'll be our excuse to leave."

Nola turned, stared at him. "You're serious."

"Damn right." Tusk drew near, caught hold of her hand. "There's gonna be war—"

"You don't know that for sure." Nola looked troubled.

"The hell I don't! They've been talkin' nothing else for three days, building the kid up for it, shoving him into it. He'll go along, he's got no choice. And I . . . I just don't want to be around when it happens."

"I never knew you to run from a fight before, Tusk."

The voice belonged to General Dixter, standing slightly behind and to one side of the couple.

Tusk had been so intent on his conversation, he hadn't noticed the older man's approach. He realized how his words must have sounded, frowned, and shook his head. On second thought, he decided he'd have a glass of champagne. He reached out to a passing waiter, snagged one, gulped the bubbling liquid.

"I'm no coward, but there's no percentage in getting involved in a fight that can't be won, sir."

"On the contrary, Dion has a very good chance of winning," Dixter observed.

"Yeah, that's what I mean, sir," the mercenary mumbled, face in his glass. He looked up, met Dixter's shrewd, weary eyes. "If he wins, he loses. I got to admit I don't know much about bein' a king, but it seems to me that it must be hard to keep your seat on a throne that's slippery wet with the blood of a billion or so of your own subjects."

Dixter nodded slowly, understanding. "But he doesn't have many alternatives, Tusk. He's pretty well chained himself to the rock."

"Yeah, well, maybe he has and maybe he hasn't. All I know is I don't have to hang around and watch the eagles swoop down and rip his guts out. C'mon, Nola, what do you say? Williams'll marry us. It's the least he can do after trying to kill us. Dixter can stand up with us and we'll get the kid, too. Make him forget about all this for a while. It'll be like old times. Then we can take XJ and the spaceplane, fly to Zanzi. I should see my mother again before she forgets what I look like—"

"Tusk!" Nola squeezed his hand, stemmed the flood. "I'll marry you anywhere, anytime you say. I'll go anywhere, any place you want, anytime you want. Okay?"

"Okay." Tusk sighed, relaxed, tugged at the earring in his left ear. "Okay. Okay with you, sir?"

"I'd be honored," Dixter said gravely. "You should talk to Dion, though. Don't spring it on him like a land mine. Which, by the way, was what I came over to ask you. Have you seen Dion? He should have been here by now."

"No." Tusk grunted. "Last I saw of him was this afternoon. He looked terrible, like he hadn't slept in days. I told him to go lie down, take a nap. Maybe that's what happened, sir. Maybe he just fell asleep. I could go check—"

"No need. Someone else is looking for him, too," said Nola softly.

Lord Sagan had turned from a conversation with Rykilth to speak a few words to Agis. The centurion left the room. The crowd had grown quiet, except for patches of desultory conversation started by Admiral Aks, conversation that went nowhere and straggled on to an uncomfortable end. DiLuna stood among her women, arms crossed beneath her bare breast, making no attempt to conceal her impatience or suspicions. Olefsky was patting his stomach and looking hungry, an alarming prospect to those who recalled the ravages committed by the big man when he wasn't fed on schedule. The vapor-breather's fog had turned a nasty shade of orange.

The Warlord resumed his discussion with Rykilth smoothly, acting as if nothing were amiss. His voice carried in the silence, the deep baritone calm, level, even. Those who knew him read his anger in the still, unmoving folds of the red cape; in the rigid muscles of war-scarred arms, of the barely shivering red feather crest on the golden helm.

Agis returned. Everyone in the room fell silent, straining to see and hear, waiting with the eager, nervous intensity of an audience who senses that one of the players has abandoned the script and is launching out on his own.

"I don't like this," Tusk muttered. "Something's happened to the kid—"

"Shh!" Nola dug her nails into his flesh.

The centurion, who, it seemed, would have preferred delivering his line off-stage, spoke to his lord in a subdued undertone, made a slight motion with his head toward the door.

The Warlord, an old trooper, apparently realized that such a bit of bad theater would merely increase the audience's excitement, draw out the tension. Better to end it and ring down the curtain swiftly.

"Captain," said Sagan, his deep voice maintaining a pleasant tone, God alone knew through what effort of will, "did you inform His Majesty that we eagerly await his arrival?"

Agis took his cue, delivered his line in a crisp, disciplined monotone.

"His Majesty regrets that extreme exhaustion confines him to his quarters this evening. He trusts his guests will enjoy themselves—"

There might have been more to the message, but the captain, facing his Warlord, suddenly seemed to find it difficult to deliver.

No one moved or spoke or even seemed to breathe. The Warlord continued to stand still, but the folds of the cape began to stir, as if ruffled by a hot wind. One hand, the right one, clenched, unclenched, then slowly became a fist. He walked suddenly and swiftly from the room, his cape flaring crimson behind him like a tidal wave of blood.

"That's torn it," said John Dixter heavily.

"Does this mean we don't get fed?" Bear Olefsky thundered.

··◁■ ■▷··

Following the explosion, Admiral Aks and his officers hastened to do what they could to put out the flames and contain the damage. Dinner was announced, waiters scurried in with food. The officers guided the guests to their tables, tried, as far as possible, to temper anger and distrust with wine and baked chicken.

"Baroness," said the admiral, offering her his arm with nervous gallantry, "if I might have the honor—"

"Thank you, no, " DiLuna replied coolly. "My staff and I will dine in our quarters. Have food sent to us and make certain my shuttle is prepared for takeoff at 0600 hours."

"I'm certain Lord Sagan will be speaking to you before then—"

"I'm certain he'd better," DiLuna returned with a cat-eyed smile. She leaned nearer the disconcerted admiral. "If Sagan has no further use for his king after tonight, tell him to send the young man to me for a year. I like what Dion's made of. He'll breed fine daughters. Oh, and tell Sagan not to damage any of the young man's vital parts."

The baroness gathered her women together and left, leaving the admiral to stare gloomily after them, mop his sweating forehead.

Bear Olefsky, pacified by the smell and sight of food, snagged a passing waiter, took over a tray of plates intended for numerous guests, and settled himself with a contented sigh into one of the specially built chairs designed to accommodate his massive body.

"Ale," he grunted, sweeping the wineglasses to the floor.

The Bear motioned to his sons to seat themselves and they began to consume chicken.

Rykilth, trailed by an apologetic Captain Williams, paused at the table. He held out a three-fingered hand.

"I'll trouble you for my money, Olefsky."

Olefsky grinned, shook his head. His teeth crunched bones. "It is not over yet, my friend. By my balls, it's not over yet!"

General Dixter took advantage of the confusion to draw Tusk and Nola out the door, slipped unnoticed into the corridor.

"What the hell do you think's going on, sir?" Tusk demanded, looking worried and confused.

"I'm not sure, but my guess is that Dion was told to come to the banquet tonight and announce that we were going to war. Not only didn't His Majesty do what he was supposed to do, he made the Warlord look like a fool in front of powerful allies."

"Did you see Sagan's eyes when he walked out?" Nola shuddered.

"There may be murder done before this night is out," Dixter said grimly. He began moving at a brisk pace down the corridor. "Don't run, Tusk! It'll draw attention. Keep calm. Which way's the elevator to Dion's quarters? Down here? I always get turned around in these damn ships!"

"Yes, sir." Tusk slowed, forced himself to move and act with a semblance of normalcy. But the two men took long strides. Nola, with her short legs, had to almost run to keep up.

"We're gonna be too late, you know that, sir," the mercenary predicted ominously.

"I'm not so certain. Sagan was caught completely off-guard. He didn't expect Dion to defy him, obviously wasn't prepared for it. Raise XJ. Tell the computer to have the Scimitar ready for takeoff. The men we left behind on *Rat* are loyal to Dion. They'll support him, back his cause. We could stand off Sagan a long time—"

"XJ!" Tusk was shouting into his commlink on his wrist. "XJ, it's me, Tusk. Make ready for takeoff—"

"Tusk?" came an irascible, mechanical voice. "Tusk who?"

"Tusk who? I'll give you Tusk who! XJ, this is no time for your—"

"I used to know a Tusk," the computer continued. "Lousy pilot. Couldn't fly his way out of his shorts. I took care of the guy, made him the big shot he is today, and what thanks do I get? None. Nothing. Not so much as a—"

"XJ!" Tusk roared, shook the commlink. Men stopped, stared at him curiously.

Dixter took hold of the mercenary's arm, steered him into the elevator. "XJ-27, this is General John Dixter. We have an emergency here. Alert status: red. Do you copy?"

"Yes, sir. General Dixter, sir." XJ was instantly subdued. "Sorry, sir. Didn't know you were present."

"Can you be ready for takeoff in ten minutes?"

"Yes, sir. But it won't do any good, sir."

Dixter and Tusk exchanged glances. Nola sighed, shook her head, slumped back against the side of the elevator.

"What do you mean, XJ?"

"Order just came through, sir. We're grounded. No planes being permitted to take off."

"What's the reason?"

"Dangerous solar winds, sir, caused by an unstable sun in the Ringo system."

Dixter, who was no pilot, cocked an eye at Tusk.

"Bullshit," Tusk answered.

"We're too late," Nola whispered.

"Should I get ready for takeoff anyway, sir?" XJ hinted. "We could blast our way out—"

"No, thank you, XJ. Some other time." Dixter nodded at Tusk, who shut down the transmission.

The elevator came to a stop on Dion's level. The doors slid open. Six armed centurions stood waiting. Tusk reached for his lasgun. Nola cried out, grabbed at his arm.

"No, son," Dixter said calmly, fingers closing over Tusk's gunhand. "That won't help."

"General Dixter, sir," said the centurion respectfully. "Lord Sagan's orders. You and your friends are to come with me."

··◆■ ■▶··

"Have my spaceplane ready. Alert the patrols," Sagan snapped at Agis, who met him outside the banquet hall. "We'll find His Majesty and—"

"We have already found him, my lord. He's in his quarters."

"He is?" The Warlord regarded his captain in surprise, paused to consider this development. Surely Dion knew the fate that awaited him. And yet, after committing an act of such brazen, blatant, ill-judged defiance, he was sitting in his quarters?

"Perhaps he thinks because he is king"—Sagan's lip curled, his voice shook with fury—"he is beyond my reach. He has forgotten who it was made him king. But he will soon remember. Yes, he *will* remember!"

The Warlord started to issue orders, realized he had no idea where he was. He'd walked his ship, blinded by a blood-dimmed mist before his eyes. Glancing around, he found himself standing in front of the private elevator that led to his quarters, could not recall how he'd come to be there.

He felt an ache in his upper arms and wrists, looked down at his hands, saw the fingers curled tightly, painfully. His shoulders were stiff, neck muscles tense. His injured leg throbbed. The flame of his anger died instantly, blown out by the chill, biting wind of self-command.

"Captain."

"My lord."

"General Dixter, Major Tusca, and that woman—What's her name?"

"Rian, my lord?"

"Yes, Rian. Have them all arrested, take their weapons. Dion may consider himself to be above my wrath, but General Dixter will be operating under no such delusion. I'll be surprised if our gallant trio isn't on their way to attempt to rescue their king right now. Have your men keep watch for them near His Majesty's quarters."

"Yes, my lord." Agis relayed the message.

"Bring them all, including the king, to me. And bring me the bomb. I trust it's still in the same hiding place. We've given His Majesty no cause to think we discovered it; I don't suppose he's moved it."

Sagan turned to enter the elevator. The centurions who posted guard stood to either side, the doors slid open.

"What's this?"

The Warlord's sharp eye caught sight of a scrap of paper, lying on the deck near the doors of his own private elevator, almost beneath the boot of one of his guards. The centurion glanced down in astonishment. Agis swooped to remove the trash littering the ship's sterile, immaculate surroundings.

Sagan's hand forestalled his captain's, snatched up the scrap, glanced at it, and crumpled it in his palm.

"I will not tolerate slovenly habits among the crew, Captain. See to it that this does not happen again."

"Yes, my lord."

The Warlord entered the elevator, paused in the doorway. "Did anyone try to use the elevator during my absence, centurion?"

"No one, my lord. No one who would be of interest to your lordship, that is." The centurion's glance shifted to his captain, his mouth twitched in a half grin. "The male nurse was here again—"

"Male nurse." The Warlord was mildly curious. "What male nurse?"

"One of Dr. Giesk's staff, my lord. A young man—around twenty-four years of age."

"Indeed? And this young man has been to see me before now? The matter must be important. Did he say what it was?"

"He has, quite frankly, my lord, been making a nuisance of himself," Agis struck in, somewhat astonished that during this emergency his lord was interested in such a trivial matter. "He's been here nine times during the last three days. I asked what he wanted and he replied that it was a private matter. I told him that your lordship was not in the habit of listening to the grievances of every minor member of his crew. I advised the nurse to go through channels, talk to his superior, fill out the requisite forms."

"Quite proper, Captain. Nonetheless, I think I will see this . . . male nurse. I suppose you could find him?"

"I suppose so, my lord." Agis looked dubious.

"Excellent. Bring him to me now."

"Now, my lord?"

"Are you questioning one of my commands, Captain?"

"No, certainly not, my lord. But—your orders concerning His Majesty . . ."

Sagan's lips tightened to a grim smile. "Confine him to his quarters. Let him wait. Give him time to think long and hard about what he has done . . . and what he faces."

"Yes, my lord. And General Dixter and the other two—?"

"Lock them up with His Majesty."

"Yes, my lord."

"The nurse is to be sent to me immediately."

"Yes, my lord. Very good, my lord."

Agis left swiftly. He'd been having a struggle with his face, trying hard not to appear bemused by his Warlord's sudden shift in commands, and was glad to take his face out of Sagan's sight.

The Warlord entered the elevator. The doors shut. It rose smoothly and swiftly to the upper levels of the ship, to his chamber. Once alone, he opened his palm, carefully smoothed out the paper, and read again the words inscribed in an ancient language.

"*Benedictus, qui venit in nomine Domini.*

"Blessed is he that cometh in the name of the Lord."

Chapter ··❦◯❦·· Eight

A soldier, lying in a hospital bed, dying. A spasm of pain contorts the face. A male nurse moves near, a hypodermic in hand. The Warlord closes his hand over the nurse's arm, stops him, instructs the soldier to continue his report on Dion.

"The eyes . . ." the private whispers, his own widening in awe and horror. "I saw his eyes . . ."

The nurse starts to administer the drug, sees it won't be necessary. The froth on the ashen lips lies undisturbed. The Warlord murmurs something beneath his breath.

"'Requiem aeternam dona eis, Domnie—'"

"'—et lux perpetua luceat eis.'" The nurse's voice slides beneath his.

The Warlord glances at the nurse in astonishment. The two of them are alone. A screen conceals the dying man from his fellows.

"I am one of the Order, my lord," the nurse replies in a soft, low voice. "Many of us are, who serve you in this capacity."

··❦ ❦··

The golden double door slid aside, framed a slender figure dressed in white, flanked by Agis.

"Enter," ordered the Warlord.

He sat in a high-backed chair, busy about some paperwork at his desk. He had removed his helm and the red cape, but he remained clad in his ceremonial armor. He did not glance up from his work.

The male nurse did as commanded, gliding into the room with the noiseless ease of one accustomed to moving silently, lest he disturb the sick, the injured, the dying. He remained

71

standing near the door, arms crossed, hands clasped on his elbows, head bowed, eyes on the ground.

The Warlord noted the posture, out of the corner of his eye; felt a queer, painful constriction of his heart. He calmed himself, scrutinized the young man closely. He was tall and slender, with strong, well-developed muscles in his upper body and arms.

"Thank you, Captain. Continue with your duties."

"Yes, my lord." Agis saluted, left the room.

The golden doors slid shut behind him.

Sagan ceased reading, clasped his hands on the desk before him. "Look at me," he commanded.

The young man lifted his head. The face was masculine, not delicate, yet refined. Its expression was calm in the dread presence of the Warlord. The eyes that met Sagan's were sensitive, intense, penetrating. Eyes that saw clearly both within and without. His sterile white uniform gleamed in the harsh, bright light. He seemed clothed in light.

"I've met you before, haven't I?" Sagan asked.

"Yes, my lord. I worked originally on *Phoenix*. When that ship was destroyed, I was assigned to *Defiant*. I worked in the infirmary on board *Defiant* and I was present the time when you came to interview the dying—"

Sagan cut him short. "How do you come to be on this ship, *Phoenix II*, if you were assigned to *Defiant*?"

"I asked to be transferred, my lord."

"It would seem you are following me."

The nurse flushed, crimson stained his cheeks. "My lord, I know it appears—"

The Warlord waved the young man silent, beckoned him to approach. The nurse, arms folded, as if he were accustomed to hiding them in flowing sleeves, came near. Sagan shoved the scrap of paper toward him, across the desk.

"Did you leave this note for me near my private elevator? Think well before you answer, young man."

The Warlord reached down to his side, removed the blood-sword from its scabbard, and laid it on top of the desk, his hand resting upon the hilt. "You indicated to me on *Defiant* that you have somehow penetrated a secret of mine. It is dangerous to know my secrets. I have long had you under surveillance. You did your job, remained silent, and so I left you alone. But now you have obtruded yourself into my life. The sender of this note is marked for death. Unless you can convince me otherwise, you will not leave this room alive."

The young man smiled faintly. "I was the one who left you the note, my lord," he said without hesitation. The hands that reached out to touch the paper were firm and did not tremble. "I tried many times to see you, but was refused. I was desperate. I didn't know what else to do. The message that I bear is of such importance, such urgency . . ."

"What is your name?" The Warlord's face was grim.

"The name as it reads on my files or my true name, my lord?"

"Whatever name you think it wise to give me."

"You would, of course, know the name on my files. My true name is Brother Fideles, my lord."

The Warlord sat quietly, his expression carefully impassive. Finally, he rose to his feet. He lifted the bloodsword from the desk, inserted the five steel needles that protruded from its hilt into five matching scars on the palm of his hand. The sword flared to life, drawing its energy from Sagan's body. He held the sword in his right hand, pointed with his left.

"You see before you a screen. Step behind it."

The nurse did as he was told, walked calmly behind a screen made of panels of plain black cloth. The Warlord accompanied him, the sword's blade hummed loudly, eagerly.

A low table covered with a black-velvet cloth stood before them.

"Lift the cloth," Sagan commanded.

The young man did as he was bid. On the table, beneath the cloth, were three objects: a small porcelain bowl holding rare and costly oil, a silver dagger with a hilt in the shape of an eight-pointed star, a silver chalice inscribed with eight-pointed stars.

The young man raised his eyes to meet the Warlord's. Sagan nodded, gestured toward the table. The young man lowered his eyes in acquiescence. He knelt down reverently before the table, raised his hands in the air, pronounced the ritual prayer in soft, inaudible tones. Sagan watched the lips move, repeated the prayer himself in his heart.

The prayer ended. The young man struck a match, lit the oil. The bittersweet odor of incense, of sanctity, perfumed the cold, sterile air of the Warlord's quarters. The young man rolled up the sleeve of his shirt, laying bare the flesh of his left arm, an arm marked by scars that had not been made by an enemy, but were self-inflicted. Unhesitatingly, the young man lifted the silver dagger and, murmuring another prayer, placed the sharp point against his skin.

The Warlord bent down, put his hand upon the hand holding the dagger. "Stop. There is no need."

The young man bowed his head, replaced the dagger gently upon the velvet cloth, and rose to his feet. Sagan switched off the bloodsword, returned it to its hilt at his side.

The two remained standing behind the black screen, that partially shut off the harsh glare of the lights in the Warlord's quarters, cast a dark shadow over both. The flame of the oil lamp burned a flickering yellow-blue, which was reflected in the clear eyes of the young man.

Sagan scrutinized him, studied him intently.

"Fideles. Faithful. Brother Faithful. A name of honor."

"I strive to be worthy of it, my lord," the young man said softly, eyes cast down.

"You know the prayers, you are familiar with the ritual. You bear the proof of your faith upon your arm. I would understand this, if you were an old man. But you are young. The Order was destroyed during the Revolution, eighteen years ago, while you were but a child. Who are you, Brother Fideles? And what do you want of me?"

"I am a priest in the Order of Adamant, my lord. The Order sent me to be near you, knowing the time would come when my services would be needed. That time has arrived, my lord"—Brother Fideles lifted his eyes—"but first I see I should explain . . ."

"That would be wise, Brother," the Warlord said dryly.

"I was a child, as you said, when the Revolution came; a child in the Order, my lord. I joined when I was six years old. I have always known my calling, my lord. When I think back on my childhood, I cannot hear my mother's voice or my father's. I remember hearing only God's.

"The priests were reluctant to accept me, because I was not of the Blood Royal. They were going to turn me away, but one came forward, an older priest, grim and stern, dark and silent. He never spoke, but placed his hand upon my head."

The young man paused, as if he thought Sagan had spoken. The Warlord was silent, however, did not move. After waiting a moment Brother Fideles continued.

"From that time on, no word was said against me. I was taken into the monastery and educated and promised that, in time, if I was still of the same mind when I grew old enough to make the decision, I would be taken into the brotherhood. My faith, my determination, never wavered.

"I was almost eight years old the night of the Revolution. The mobs, led by soldiers of the rebel army, stormed the monastery walls. We had received a warning, however. We never knew how or from whence it came—some said God himself warned his faithful."

The priest's eyes were lowered again, he did not look at the Warlord.

"We were ready for them, when they came. We were forbidden to take human life, of course. None of us were warrior-priests. But under the direction of the dark and silent priest, we built cunning traps that captured men alive, rendered them helpless, but did them no harm. We defended the Abbey with fire and water, with rocks, with blasts of air.

"Many of our Order died that night," Brother Fideles continued in low, quiet tones, "but by the Power of the Creator, we defeated our foe. They fled, most of them, in dread and awe. They felt the wrath of God. To this day, no one comes near it. We—those of us who remained—live in peace. I believe you are familiar with the Abbey of which I speak, my lord. The Abbey of St. Francis."

"I know it." Sagan spoke without a voice. "Its walls still stand, then?"

"Yes, my lord."

"I have not been back. I did not think—" The Warlord checked himself, made a gesture to the young man to continue.

"There is little more to tell, my lord. The Order was outlawed, banned, but it was not dead. It went underground. We established a secret network, discovered those who had survived, and kept in contact. Quietly, circumspectly, we continued to do our work for the Lord. Occasionally a priest or nun would be captured, tortured. But each died maintaining he or she was alone in the faith, never revealing the truth. Our numbers have grown, since then. We are not many, for we must be careful who we take in, but there are more of us than you might imagine, my lord."

"None of them, the Blood Royal?"

"No, my lord. They are ordinary, like myself. The work we do is ordinary. We can no longer perform miracles. But it is, I believe, nonetheless blessed in the eyes of God."

"Perhaps it is more blessed, Brother Fideles," said Sagan, but he said it so softly and in a voice laden with such pain that the young man pretended not to have heard, made no response.

"You bear a message," Sagan said abruptly, tightly. "You risked your life to deliver it. Who from? What is it?"

"It is from the head of our Order, my lord. I am to tell you that a certain priest, whom you believed died eighteen years ago, is alive."

"*Deus!* Oh, God!"

It was a prayer, a supplication. The Warlord's flesh chilled, his eyes stared ahead sightlessly, he ceased to breathe.

The male nurse, alarmed, approached the man, laid his hand upon the wrist, felt for a pulse.

"My lord, you are not well—"

"Tell me, damn you! Tell me!" Sagan's voice sounded ghastly, the command burst from his mouth as if torn from the chest. Brother Fideles was frightened to see spots of blood fleck the ashen lips. "Tell me why you came!"

"My lord, this priest lies now upon his deathbed. His last wish is to see you once more, to beg your forgiveness, and to grant his dying blessing to you—his son."

Chapter ❧◦❧ Nine

Moira . . . the finished shape of our fate.
                    Mary Renault, *The King Must Die*

"Why doesn't he come, get it over with!" Tusk demanded, pacing back and forth, ten steps in each direction, with a slight jog halfway to avoid running into a chair.

"The delights of anticipation, Sagan's a master at it," Dixter returned. Lifting his gaze from the book he was pretending to read, he looked intently at Dion.

Why? he wondered silently. *Why have you done this?*

Dion hadn't told them anything, hadn't spoken a word to them since they'd been escorted into the young man's quarters. He stood staring out the viewscreen, stared at the flickering lights of spacecraft, the steady, ever-burning lights of the stars.

"You're right, sir." Tusk stopped in mid-pace, pivoted on his heel, and sat down on the edge of the chair. "By God, I won't give Sagan the satisfaction of thinking he's got me worried."

He threw his arms over the chair's metal back, crossed his legs, and concentrated with grim attention on looking relaxed. Dixter hid a smile, returned to the book.

"I wonder if Sagan would marry us, before he executed us, like the Nazi officer married Humphrey Bogart and Katharine Hepburn in that movie about the boat," said Nola dreamily.

She sat in a chair, her arms stretched out across a desk, her head resting on her hands. They'd been locked in the room for eight hours now.

"Damn it, Nola, stop talking about executions!" Tusk exploded. Bouncing up from his chair, he started to pace again. "Nobody's gonna get executed." He rounded on the general, demanded for the tenth time, "There must be something we can do—"

Dixter looked up from his book. A corner of his mouth

twitched. "The door's locked and sealed. But let's say we did manage to tunnel our way through a meter of solid null-grav steel. That accomplished, the four of us, armed, I suppose, with that pair of scissors lying on the desk, take on ten centurions—"

"I'm sorry you were all involved in this," Dion said suddenly, coolly. "I thank you for your attempt to help, but you needn't have. I know what I'm doing."

There's something different about him, Dixter thought. Something strange. He seems fey, as if he were above this reality or beyond it, as if he were, perhaps, out there with those glittering stars, instead of a prisoner, confined to his own bedroom.

Tusk shook his head, came to stand near Dixter. "Begging the general's pardon, but I think we should try to make a run for it. Some of those men on guard have been with the kid a long time. If push came to shove—"

Dion turned from the viewscreen. "No, Tusk," he said, guessing, by the low tone, what the mercenary was proposing. "I refused to start a civil war in the galaxy. I won't start one aboard this ship."

"You sure you made the right decision?"

"Yes, I'm sure. I know," Dion added, seeing Tusk look skeptical, "because originally I made the wrong one."

"You're not makin' sense, kid. 'Course that wouldn't be the first time," Tusk added, mopping sweat from his neck. He had, by taking the aforementioned pair of las-scissors to his uniform, finally managed to rid himself of the constricting collar.

("You might as well go ahead and cut it off, Tusk," Dixter had recommended wryly. "With what's facing us, I wouldn't be overly concerned about receiving a few demerits for deliberate maltreatment of a uniform.")

"I meant to go to the banquet. I planned to tell them we were going to war."

Tusk stopped his pacing.

Dixter ceased to pretend to read.

"What happened, son?"

Nola lifted her head, shook her curls out of her eyes.

"I told myself that Sagan was right—war was the only alternative. I was going to give him the space-rotation bomb."

"Jeez, kid, I—!" Tusk frowned, clamped his mouth shut.

Dion nodded slowly. "I know what you're thinking. That I'm

a coward and a liar. After everything I said about not making war on my own people. But now I had a way out. I was going to give in to Sagan's threats, let him take over. That way, I could blame him for whatever happens. I wouldn't have to take the responsibility, wouldn't have to blame myself. I could always comfort myself with the fact that I didn't have a choice.

"And so I made my decision. Or I thought I did. But when I went to leave my room for the banquet, when I went to walk out the door, it was like . . ."

Dion paused, considering how best to express himself.

"It was as if a force field had been activated around me. I couldn't walk through that door. Whenever I tried, my insides seemed to shrivel up. I began to sweat. I couldn't breathe."

Nola looked wise, nodded in understanding. Tusk rolled his eyes and glanced at the general. Dixter kept his gaze, intent and penetrating, fixed on Dion.

"What did you do then, son?" The general closed the book, but kept his finger to mark the place. He'd just noticed something on the page that he hadn't been reading, and he wanted to check it, to make certain.

"I told myself I was coming down with something. The flu, maybe. Or stress. I went over to the bed and lay down, thinking I'd rest a little, then go. There was still plenty of time. As I lay there, I admitted to myself that I *did* have a choice. I could refuse to give in to Sagan's threats. I could do what I believed was right. After all, I was the king. I'd taken on the responsibility of caring for the welfare of my people. I couldn't let them down.

"And the moment I made the decision, I felt better, calm and relaxed. And I sent the message," Dion concluded.

"This is all in that correspondence psych course I took," Nola struck in, excited. "You knew subconsciously that what you were doing wasn't right and it was your subconscious that made you sick."

"Subconscious, my ass! More like something he ate for lunch. Well, what the hell do you expect to do now? You won't fight. You just gonna stand there and let him shoot you."

"He won't," said Dion softly. "Any more than I could shoot him that night at Snaga Ohme's."

"Godalmighty . . ."

"You don't have to back me up, you know," Dion pointed out, with a slight smile.

"It's a little late to switch sides, kid," Tusk muttered, threw himself into a chair, and subsided into gloomy silence.

Dion smiled at his friend, walked back over to stare out the viewscreen.

Far out in space, beyond the fleet, a pulsar flashed, twice every second.

Dixter returned to his book, and this time actually saw it. He glanced at the title, an ominous one. *The King Must Die*, by a twentieth-century author, Renault. The book was old. It had fallen open to a page, as Dixter held it in his hands, as if that particular part had been read many times. One paragraph, near the middle, was marked with a dot of red ink.

> . . . When the King was dedicated, he knew his moira. In three years, or seven, or nine, or whenever the custom was, his term would end and the god would call him. And he went consenting, or else he was no king, and power would not fall on him to lead the people. When they came to choose among the Royal Kin, that was his sign: that he chose short life with glory, and to walk with the god, rather than live long, unknown like the stall-fed ox.

Dixter rubbed his stubbled chin, rough with a night's growth of beard. He had heard a sound, barely audible through the steel door, but easily identifiable to those who've been listening for it: the muffled tread of many pairs of booted feet marching in step.

The faint sound became clearer, seemed to boom like thunder through the tension-tight silence of His Majesty's quarters. Tusk's head snapped up. Nola sat straight in her chair, her hand reached out for Tusk's. Dion turned from the window, to stare calmly and dispassionately at the closed, sealed door. But Dixter saw that the young man's fingers, clasped together behind his back, left livid marks on the skin of his hands. The general slowly shut and laid down his book.

Could they truly hear, through the door and the metal bulkheads, the thud of fists striking body armor over the heart, or did they imagine it? Could they truly distinguish one set of booted footfalls from the others?

Tusk, shining black and coiled tense as a cornered panther, rose to his feet. Dion moistened dry lips.

The sealed door slid open, the Warlord entered. He placed his hand on a control panel. The door slid shut behind. He stood alone, no guards accompanied him. He was clad in full battle armor and helm; not his ceremonial armor, but the accoutrements of war. He wore the bloodsword at his side. A long cape fell from the shoulders, attached by golden phoenix pins. The metal face regarded Dion in silence, then Sagan removed his helm, held it in the crook of his left arm.

His long black hair, graying now beyond the temples, was slicked back smooth, tied at the base of the neck with a leather thong. The features of his face were steel-cold, he might have been still wearing the helm.

The young man's unrelenting defiance did not crumble. He stood proud, resolute.

When the Warlord spoke, it was to Dion alone, as if the two of them were alone in the room, perhaps alone in the universe.

"I have come to inform Your Majesty that I am leaving."

Dion had been prepared for anything except this. He stared at the Warlord in astonished silence, wondering if he'd heard correctly.

"Admiral Aks will be in command of the fleet," Sagan continued. "Aks is not particularly bright, but he has sense enough to know his limitations. He is a skilled and experienced commander, you can rely on him. I would suggest to His Majesty that he select General John Dixter to serve as commander in chief of both land and air operations in my absence."

Sagan's eyes flicked sideways, acknowledged the general's presence briefly, coolly. No love lost, but grudging respect.

What the devil does this mean? Dixter wondered.

Apparently, he wasn't the only one trying to figure out what was going on. The Warlord paused, waited for Dion to say something. But Dion obviously didn't know where to begin.

The rock wall of defiance was crumbling. He had realized, as had everyone in the room, that this was no trick. The Warlord was in earnest.

"I have already made the necessary arrangements. It remains only for you, sire, to give the final orders. I have placed Agis, captain of the Honor Guard, in charge of His Majesty's personal safety.

"In capacity as adviser, I suggest that for the time being His Majesty rely on the wisdom, if not necessarily the common sense"—Sagan's mouth twisted slightly—"of Bear Olefsky. He is bullheaded and rough-edged, but his great mound of flesh conceals a shrewd knowledge of men and their thinking. As for DiLuna and Rykilth, use them, get from them what you can, but do not trust either of them. Never betray weakness to them. Once they smell blood, they will tear you to pieces. Never let them forget that you are their king. Farewell, sire."

The Warlord bowed stiffly, turned on his heel, and started for the door.

"Wait!" Dion found his voice. "You can't do this! Where are you going, my lord? When will you be back?"

"I cannot say."

"You're leaving me alone?"

The Warlord spoke in a low and bitter voice. He did not turn around. "Not alone. God is with Your Majesty."

The door slid open. Sagan walked out. The door slid shut behind him.

No one moved or or said a word.

Out in space, the pulsar flashed, once every two seconds; reminded Dixter of the knowing wink of some gigantic eye.

··❖■ ➡··

The following morning, early, the allies were escorted to their ships. Admiral Aks and Captain Williams were both present, ostensibly to see them off, in reality to make certain that they had no time to talk privately among themselves. The Warlord's sudden departure was common knowledge. Where he was going and why was not.

"Keep those three from putting their heads together, monitor every word, and get them off this ship fast," had been Sagan's final instructions.

Surrounded by their own escorts, a guard of honor, sent by His Majesty, and ship's personnel, the three met only briefly in the hangar to say their formal farewells. DiLuna was stern, frowning. Rykilth was "fogged in," as the saying went among vapor-breathers, his face completely shrouded by a thick, swirling mist. Olefsky, however, positively smirked.

"What are they talking about?" Aks asked his captain in a low voice. The admiral appeared to have slept badly. He was endeavoring to overhear what was being said, but the noise inside the hangar and a dull, throbbing ache in his temples was making it difficult.

"Horse racing, sir," said Williams in a whisper. The captain looked grim. He had not slept at all.

"Horse racing?" Aks stared. "Is that all? Are you certain?"

The two sidled a step or two closer.

"And did you hear who won the last race?" the Bear was asking, smoothing his beard.

DiLuna's voice had a sharp edge. "Subspace transmission was garbled. I couldn't be certain I caught the name correctly."

"You did," said Olefsky, "and you each owe me one hundred golden eagles."

Rykilth's mist turned an ugly shade of greenish yellow. "Your horse has yet to cross the finish line."

Aks blinked in astonishment. "How very strange," he murmured. "But, then, perhaps it's one of those mechanical 'droid horses. . . ."

"It matters not!" Olefsky roared. "When one horse drops out of a two-horse race, the contest is ended, as we agreed." The Bear held out a huge hand. "Pay."

DiLuna pulled a purse made of tiny steel rings out from her belt, weighed the jingling purse in her hand, eyed the Bear thoughtfully. With a sudden flashing smile, she tossed the gold to Olefsky.

"A paltry sum, after all, considering the amount of prize money at stake. In fact, I think I may enter a horse of my own."

"I might do the same." Rykilth gave a nasty laugh that came over the translator as a metallic squawk. "I don't think much of that colt of yours, Olefsky. I doubt if he'll last the season. My guess is that he'll come up lame and we'll be forced to put him down."

"He's had good trainers. And he proved himself in his first outing," the Bear said complacently. "Pay up. Cash, not credit."

One of the vapor-breather's eyes was suddenly visible, glowering at Olefsky through the mist. Incoherent gargling sounds came over the translator. Rykilth began to fumble stealthily among the myriad small, zippered pockets and compartments of his flight suit.

"Tightfisted as a vapor-breather," Aks commented in an undertone, shaking his head.

Rykilth removed and deliberately counted out (twice) ten well-worn and obviously well-loved bills, each stamped with ten golden eagles. Slowly, reluctantly, fog roiling in his helm, he handed them over, then turned and stalked angrily to his shuttle.

DiLuna, laughing, bid Olefsky a safe journey, cast Williams and Aks a disdainful glance, and headed for her shuttle. Olefsky stuffed the bills into his fur-topped boot; thrust the purse inside his leather armor. He turned to Aks and Williams, who were trying hard to look as if they hadn't heard a word.

"The fog-sucker may be right. Still, my money on the colt. I like his bloodline." The Bear winked. "Wouldn't you agree, Admiral?"

"I have no idea what you are talking about," Aks returned stiffly.

Olefsky seemed to find this funny. Rounding up his hulking sons, he lumbered off to his shuttlecraft. His booming laughter vied with the roar of the engines warming up for takeoff.

"The galaxy is falling apart around them, and all they can talk about is horse racing!" Aks glared after the three indignantly.

"And yet, sir," said Williams with a tired smile, "it has been called the sport of kings."

Chapter ❧ *Ten*

> . . . then the queen stole away . . . and great penance she took, as ever did sinful lady in this land, and never creature could make her merry. . . .
>
> Sir Thomas Malory, *Le Morte d'Arthur*

The Academy, it was called; named for a garden near Athens where Plato taught. Eighteen years ago, it had been a place where the children of the Blood Royal came to learn how to be rulers.

The Academy was far from Athens, far from Old Earth, light-years from almost any civilized planet in the galaxy. Such isolation had been chosen purposefully. The planet had to be safe from the threat of any type of war, either local or solar in nature. There were no major population centers on the planet, for the same reason, and also to discourage outside interference or distractions that might tempt students away from their studies. Only one small village was located near the Academy, and it had sprung up to serve the Academy's needs.

Those responsible for selecting the location of the school in which the human children of the Blood Royal were to be educated decided that, in addition, the planet on which the Academy was located must be a planet similar in nature to Old Earth. Since so much of human culture emanated from Earth, it was deemed valuable to the students to experience an Earth-like environment. It is difficult to understand the lines of Shakespeare, "In me thou see'st the twilight of such day, As after sunset fadeth in the west . . ." if you come from a planet with three suns, eternal days, and no nights, or perhaps from a planet where the sun is so far distant that it is tantamount to having no sun at all.

The Academy had two separate and distinct campuses—one for girls and one for boys. The courses taught in each were identical in all respects. The educators had decided to separate the sexes due to the fact that females tended to assimilate knowledge faster than males at a young age. When the students were older, in their teen years, they attended school together, mainly for purposes of socialization. These boys and girls, when they became men and women, would be rulers of planets, perhaps entire solar systems. Alliances formed at this age could prevent wars in the future.

Few aliens attended the Academy. There were other schools, located on other planets, where children of the genetically superior of alien races were sent to complete their education. The Academy for humans was the largest, however. It was humans, with their proclivity and ability for rapid breeding, their burning ambition, and their insatiable curiosity, who had become the major force in the galaxy.

There had been children present in the Academy the night of the Revolution. What had happened to these children, whose parents were slaughtered in the royal palace on a distant planet, far away?

President Peter Robes, unwilling to be known as another Herod, issued a statement that the children of the Blood Royal were being taken to a location where their minds could be "re-formed" and they could be "assimilated" into the general population. Vids were broadcast showing the children, clutching their small bundles of clothing, boarding huge transports. The children looked somewhat dazed, having been awakened in the middle of the night, but a few managed to smile and wave on cue. The assimilation process must have worked extremely well, for not one of those children was ever heard of after that night.

The Academy's grounds were extensive, its buildings numerous, designed in a classical motif. Rolling, densely wooded hills, where soft mists settled in the cool mornings, often hid one hall from the other. Trails connected each. Students walked to classes, exercise being considered an important aid to learning. Gardens flourished. Everyone, from the headmaster to the smallest child, worked in the gardens, cultivating not only vegetables for dinner, but a knowledge of and appreciation for plant life. As for its libraries, no vaster collection of knowledge had been known to exist since the great library in Alexandria.

Following the Revolution, Congress voted to turn the Academy into a school for the people. Professors were hired, students flocked to sign up. Merchants moved to the area, planning to establish a city nearby, prepared to meet the needs of students and faculty. President Robes himself cut the ribbon that opened the campus to all and sundry (who could afford the high tuition).

All and sundry soon departed. No one stayed beyond the second semester. Strange rumors circulated. Strange things happened. No plant would grow in the garden. The buildings began to fall apart: windows cracked for no apparent reason, roofs developed leaks in the most unexpected places. Books disappeared from the library the moment anyone wanted to read them. It rained endlessly, terrible thunderstorms, the likes of which no one could remember.

In vain, President Robes pleaded with students and professors to remain. No one did. One professor of advanced mathematics, a noted disbeliever in "psychic phenomenon" did research and announced that, in her opinion, the air was bad for the health. Too much oxygen.

The property was too valuable to give up, however. The Academy was, at various times after that, a low-income housing development, a retirement community, a luxury resort and health spa. All failed dismally. The poor abandoned it and took to the woods, the retired people fled in the night, the luxury resort never opened. Eventually, Congress, tired of pouring money into worthless projects, gave up. The Academy was forgotten, its gardens left to run wild, its buildings empty and abandoned . . . except for those of the dead who were rumored to walk them at night.

And, now, one living person, who walked them by day.

The Warlord's space shuttle set down at what had once been the Academy's spaceport. The port was not large, meant to accommodate only one or two craft at a time. Visitors had not been encouraged; children rarely or never went home for holidays or any other reason. Parents, it was believed, had generally an unsettling effect on their offspring.

His Lordship's Honor Guard marched down the shuttle's ramp and onto a tarmac that had fallen into disrepair. Grass and weeds sprang up through large gaps in the concrete surface. The spaceport's communications tower had been long abandoned. Its foundation was cracking, most of its windows were broken out. Its guidance equipment no longer scanned the skies, no longer paid any attention to the heavens.

One other spaceplane, a long-range Scimitar, was parked at the edge of the landing strip. A canvas cover had been drawn over the plane to protect it from the weather and the planet's wildlife. It had obviously been there many months. Grass grew over its wheels. Autumn's leaves drifted down around it. The Warlord, scrutinizing the plane carefully, thought he detected bird's nests near the region of the cockpit.

Sagan gestured to Agis, who stepped forward with alacrity.

"My lord."

"My respects to the Lady Maigrey. Inform her that I have arrived on planet and that I await the pleasure of her company in"—Sagan paused, considering—"in the headmaster's rose garden."

"Yes, my lord. And where will I find her ladyship?"

The Warlord glanced up at the heavens, judging the planet's time by the sun that hung low in the sky.

"In the gymnasium," he said. "You can see it from here. That domed building there, to your left. When you have delivered your message, return to the shuttle."

"Yes, my lord." Agis was about to detail a portion of his force to go with him, leaving another to stay behind with the Warlord, when Sagan interrupted him.

"Take all the men."

Agis appeared dubious. "My lord—"

"That's an order, Captain."

"Yes, my lord."

Agis could not refrain from casting an uneasy glance at a figure standing directly behind the Warlord. Dark and silent and motionless, the figure might have been Sagan's shadow. The young man was dressed in long brown robes; his arms and hands were invisible in long sleeves, arms folded, hands clasping his elbows. A brown cowl was pulled low over his head, hiding his face from sight. None of the centurions knew who the man was, where he'd come from. He'd simply appeared, mysteriously, on board *Phoenix II*. By coincidence, no doubt, Dr. Giesk had reported at the same time that one of his male nurses had gone AWOL. Agis was able to put two and two together, but the answer made no sense. He therefore kept his mouth shut.

But he didn't like, didn't trust that robed and hooded figure. The man had done something to his lord—aged him, drained him of life, of spirit. Agis was not a fanciful man, and it must have been racial memory that stirred the bottom of humanity's dark caldron and brought to the surface of the mind tales of evil warlocks and black magic, long pins stuck through the hearts of waxen dolls.

"Do you have a question regarding your orders, Captain?" Sagan asked with some impatience.

Yes, Agis had a great many questions, but none that he dared ask. He assembled his men and marched off the broken tarmac, heading for a walkway arched over by the tangled limbs of swaying poplar trees.

The Warlord saw his guard well on their way, then he turned on his heel and started across the tarmac in the opposite direction. He said no word to the robed young man, who hesitated and did not immediately follow, perhaps uncertain whether he was wanted.

Sagan, not hearing the softly slippered shuffle of footsteps behind him, glanced over his shoulder.

"Come along, Brother," he commanded. "My lady will want to meet you."

Brother Fideles bowed his head in response and hastened to catch up, not an easy task. It was occasionally difficult for his own Honor Guard to keep up with their Warlord's long strides. Brother Fideles panted and puffed and fought to keep the skirts of his robes from tripping him as he ran.

Sagan, seeing out of the corner of his eye the young man's difficulty, said nothing, but obligingly slowed his pace. Brother Fideles caught up with him and the two walked side by side. The young brother's arms remained folded and hidden, his head bowed slightly as was proper. Sagan walked with his own head bowed, either lost in thought or burdened by memory. His hands were clasped behind his back, beneath his red, flowing robes.

They left the tarmac, entered and passed through the deserted spaceport building, and out onto its covered walkway. From the porch, the young priest caught a breathtaking glimpse of the Academy, buildings and grounds spread out before him in mist-shrouded valleys and on low, sunlit hills. The Warlord turned to his left, followed a pathway that led down the high rise on which the spaceport was built.

They walked for a long time and covered a vast distance. The beauty of the place overwhelmed the young priest. The afternoon sun gleamed golden against a cloudless azure sky.

The air was cool, touched with the frost that would come with nightfall. Leaves of gold and red streaked with green fluttered downward in the sighing wind, drifted about their feet.

Man had worked with Nature when taking over her lands and making his mark upon them, and it seemed that when man left, Nature returned the favor. Gardens lost none of their charm by becoming wild and overgrown. Trees from the encroaching wilderness did not threaten the buildings, but seemed to offer shelter with their strong, protecting arms. The abandoned halls and libraries, laboratories and classrooms, looked calm and serene, their white marble edifices glistening in the bright sunlight.

But Brother Fideles could well understand why no one could bear to stay long on these lovely grounds, to stroll among the trees, to sit in the echoing halls. Sadness—unbearable, unutterable—was the ghost that walked the Academy grounds, walked it during the bright day, walked it during the moonlit night.

"What a sorrowful, eerie place. I wonder the Lady Maigrey can bear it, all alone," Brother Fideles said, and only when the words were spoken did he realize he'd said his thought aloud, interrupting his lord's meditation.

Sagan stopped, looked long at the surroundings that had changed so much, yet not enough. "Alone, Brother?" he said reflectively. "No, in this place, she would never be alone. Perhaps to her regret."

··◁■ ■▷··

Maigrey heard the door to the gymnasium open, she heard the booted feet tramp across the wooden floor. She did not turn around. Hand on the bar, she continued her exercises, her eyes fixed on the mirror opposite, on the reflection that stared gravely back at her.

"Look into the mirror always." The dance master's voice echoed in her memory. "Come to know your own body. Only then will you understand how it moves and how you can control that movement."

She had performed these exercises every day of her life with only few exceptions since she'd come as a child to the Academy. She had fidgeted and giggled through them when she was little, reveled in them when she was in her teens. She and her squadron, the famous Golden Squadron of the King, had performed them before battle. Many times, she and Sagan had done the exercises alone together.

She had gone through the routine herself, alone, the day before the night of the Revolution.

The days after the Revolution had been one of the few times she did not do the exercises. And then she had been in the hospital, near death, wondering bitterly why she hadn't died.

After her escape, she had continued the exercises on the tropical planet where she'd gone to hide. Seventeen years, every afternoon, just before sundown, she'd performed them, though she couldn't say why. Why keep the body fit? Why keep the mind trained? She did not hold the bloodsword once during those years of exile, did not even look at it. She never expected to hold it again. Still, she exercised.

"You should look only two places in my class, at me and at yourself. You do not look out the window, Maigrey. You do not look at each other. Stavros"—crack went a wooden ruler—"you do not look at the clock."

You do not look at the clock. Not once, in seventeen years. Yet she had been aware of every second that passed, of the change each second brought.

"What is that hand doing at the end of your arm, Maigrey? Has it died, that you allow it to flop around so gracelessly?" Crack went the ruler against her palm.

The dance master carried a wooden ruler, a meter long, that served, at various times, as dancing partner, a baton to tap out the rhythm, and his means of enforcing discipline. He was amazingly quick; he was also their swordmaster. Crack. Maigrey could feel the sting of the wood against her skin.

"The hand is alive now, isn't it? You feel the pain, Maigrey? You feel the life?"

She'd done the exercises on board *Phoenix*, when she'd been a prisoner of the Warlord. She and Dion had done them together; the boy having been taught the routine by Platus. Her brother. The boy's guardian. One of the last of the Guardians.

Do you feel the pain, Maigrey?

The booted measured tread came to a halt almost behind her. A centurion, captain by his insignia, stepped forward, body straight, rigid, fist over his heart in salute.

"Lady Maigrey Morianna, Lord Sagan's respects. He requests the favor of your presence in the headmaster's rose garden."

Do you feel the pain, Maigrey? Do you feel the life?

She kept her gaze steadfastly on the mirror.

"My respects to Lord Sagan and I will attend him presently."

"Yes, my lady."

The captain saluted, wheeled, and marched his men out. Maigrey watched them from the corner of her eye. The centurions did not move with the knife-edged sharpness and precision generally seen in the Warlord's guard of honor. They seemed nervous, ill at ease. They might have been trapped and surrounded by the enemy, instead of wandering about the deserted grounds of an abandoned school, surrounded by the ghosts of dead dreams, dead hopes.

Do you feel the pain?

Their footsteps retreated in the distance. The gymnasium was quiet, except for the voices and the music of memory. Maigrey continued the exercises, worked through them to completion.

--�»■ ■»--

The rose garden of Headmaster Aristos was one of Maigrey's favorite walks. Sagan would know that, of course. Just as she knew he was waiting for her there. Sending the men to her had been a mere formality. Connected as the two of them were by the mind-link, they were close enough to touch, though light-years separated them. She, alone, had known of his coming. He, alone, had known where to find her.

Maigrey returned to her dwelling on the grounds of the Academy—a small house that had once belonged to one of the caretakers. She could have moved into any of the many empty houses, including the beautiful home on the wooded hill that had belonged to the headmaster. But her awe of that frail man, who had seemed ancient to her, and wise beyond anyone she'd ever known, lingered past her childhood. She would not have been comfortable in his house. She would always feel that she must move quietly, hold her breath, keep her hands at her sides, fearful of breaking some rare and priceless object.

She showered, washed, and dried the pale hair, brushed it out until it was smooth as the surface of a placid lake. She dressed in a long gown of dove-gray lamb's wool, draped over her shoulders a mantle of sky-blue lined with eiderdown. The autumn evenings grew chill. She walked alone to the rose garden; the rays of the setting sun slanted golden through the green and orange leaves of the oak trees.

Do you feel the pain?

Chapter ❈ Eleven

> Now conscience wakes despair
> That slumber'd,—wakes the bitter memory
> Of what he was, what is, and what must be . . .
>
> John Milton, *Paradise Lost*

A low stone wall, of irregular shape and design, surrounded the rose garden. A wrought-iron gate, accessed from the headmaster's tree-shaded patio, permitted entry. The garden was large. Stone paths and walkways wound around maple trees and lindens, oaks and pines and spruce. Statuary, copies of famous pieces of antiquity, stood in nooks and niches and crannies. Rosebushes, a thousand varieties, filled the air with their fragrance, filled the soul with their beauty.

Maigrey pushed on the gate, its hinges made no sound. She had taken care, when she first came here, six months ago, to oil them. The silence of the grounds was sacred. It seemed to Maigrey that only Nature's voice, like that of a priest's in a cathedral, had the right to disturb it.

Thinking of priests and cathedrals, she was rather disconcerted to catch a glimpse, as she entered, of a brown-robed and cowled figure, standing in the shadows of an oak tree. Maigrey did not speak, nor make any indication that she had seen the priest. The young man, for his part, remained immobile as one of the statues, keeping his eyes lowered. It was not permitted to those who had taken the vow of chastity to look at women directly.

Maigrey sighed deeply when she shut the gate behind her. She could not see the Warlord, but she knew where he was. It was as if she heard the beating of his heart and could find him by following the sound. She walked the stone paths that had, despite the years, remained in relatively good condition. Maigrey had been surprised, pleasantly surprised, to see that few changes had come to the garden. She had expected to find it dead, bleak and barren. But it teemed with life, though some of the hybrid roses had gone wild and some of the climbers, with their long, thorny runners, had completely overrun certain sections.

The paths had almost vanished, covered with dead leaves, those of this autumn and those of autumns gone by. The hem of her skirt, as she walked, brushed among them, making a soft, whispering sound that was echoed by the gentle breeze and the drifting, falling leaves.

Rounding a corner, she came upon Sagan, seated on a marble bench near a copy of one of Rodin's sculptures, *The Burghers of Calais*. The Warlord had removed his helm, it lay upon the bench at his side. His head was bowed, his arms crossed over his chest. His black hair, streaked with more gray than she remembered, fell loose around his neck and shoulders.

He sat silent, staring at nothing, immovable as the statue of the brave, doomed men standing over him. He had been sitting thus for a long time, Maigrey noticed. Brown and withered leaves had fallen on his shoulders, on the hem of his cloak that trailed on the stone walkway.

Maigrey paused at the bend in the garden path. Whatever had brought her this far—courage, pride—failed her. She could not take another step.

He either heard her or sensed her coming. He lifted his head, saw her standing beneath the oak tree, her hand upon its trunk as a child might have clung to the hand of its mother. He rose to his feet with respectful, soldierly grace.

Maigrey drew a breath, let go of the tree, pushing herself forward slightly with the tips of her fingers, and walked to meet him.

"My lady," he said with a slight inclination of the head.

"My lord."

She held out her hand, wishing that it would not tremble, wishing her chill, numb fingers had some life in them. He took her hand in his, but did not carry it to his lips. He held it fast. His strong, warm fingers closed around hers. He drew her near him.

Can you feel the pain? She had felt it, shared it with him. The battery of emotions assailing him had beaten down his fortress walls, smashed through his defenses, left him, for a brief time, open and vulnerable. Maigrey had wept for him, that first night after he'd heard the news. And though her giving way to tears generally irritated him, this time she'd sensed him grateful, as if through their shared consciousness, he'd found solace in her compassion.

But that was past. He was working to repair the breach, build the walls around him higher, thicker than before. Not a crack remained in the stonework. She could catch no glimmer of light.

"You will go?" she asked, knowing the answer but wishing him, willing him to change his mind.

"Yes, my lady. I will go."

Maigrey removed her hand from his grasp, twisted and twined her fingers together, a habit when she was nervous. She averted her eyes from his steady, intense gaze, stared unseeing at the statue, her brow furrowed, twisting her hands.

A sudden gust of wind swirled dead leaves in a small cyclone down the path. She watched it, her attention caught by the sound and movement. The cyclone ended suddenly, the leaves becoming tangled in the thorns of a bush filled with blood red roses. Maigrey reached out a hand, touched a blossom.

"Have you ever noticed that the roses are most beautiful in autumn? Their colors are more brilliant, vibrant, as if they know what fate awaits them and they are reveling in life."

He said nothing, made no movement. Patiently waiting, he stood near her, still looking at her, she knew, though she was not looking at him. She kept her gaze on the roses.

"My lord," she said softly, "the words I'm going to say we hold captive in the darkest portion of our souls. I'm going to free them, speak them aloud although, God knows," she added, shivering, "I wish I could let them stay there."

Maigrey turned her gray eyes, earnest and intent, full upon him. "One man knows about the crack in your armor. One man knows the weak link in the chain mail that will give way and let the point of the spear drive home. Abdiel was in your mind, my lord. He owns a portion of you, as he owns a portion of . . . a portion of—"

Maigrey's voice broke. She began to shake uncontrollably. Huddling deep within the folds of the sky-blue mantle, she lowered her face, trying to hide her weakness behind the curtain of hair.

Sagan put his arms around her, gathered her close. She stiffened for an instant at his touch, then she relaxed, pressing her head against his breast. Eyes closed, she heard his heartbeat, slow, strong, steady. The warmth of his body, radiating through the armor, drove away the chill from her skin, at least, if not her heart.

"Derek, I used my power."

She spoke hesitantly, uncertain whether her words might not impel him forward, rather than hold him back. The body pressed against hers tensed, muscles went rigid. He ceased to breathe.

Maigrey drew a breath, as if for both of them. "I looked across time and space and . . . and inside the Abbey walls."

His hands closed painfully over her upper arms. He stared at her eagerly, hungrily.

"It's true. Your father is alive. . . ."

Sagan relaxed his grip on her. His eyes closed, he drew a shuddering breath. Maigrey grasped him in turn, digging her strong fingers into his flesh.

"Derek, listen to me. A shadow lies across him, across the Abbey! A shadow my power couldn't penetrate."

"That could be due to many things, my lady." Sagan thrust her away from him. He was suddenly crisp, businesslike, evidently sorry for his former display of emotion. "The priests would not permit you to see within, for one thing. Or," he added, his voice growing cooler, "it could have been the shadow of approaching death. . . ."

"Yes, but whose?" she demanded, fear snapping patience.

He frowned, crossed his arms over his chest. "This wasn't what I came to discuss, my lady—"

"Oh, Derek!" Maigrey caught hold of his arms, felt, beneath her chill fingers, the taut muscles, the smooth skin broken by the scars of his battles and the scars of his devotion to his faith. "You told me, that night at Snaga Ohme's, that we could never fight Abdiel alone. That the only way we could defeat him was to fight him together. Don't you see, my lord? This is the one way he knows he can divide us! I know you must go. At least take me with you!"

He was angry, extremely angry, and she thought for a moment the anger was directed at her. But it wasn't, it was aimed at himself. The flesh beneath her hand trembled. She understood the depth of his fear, understood that he was angry because he had been tempted and he had nearly weakened, nearly let himself be persuaded.

"Derek, please," she urged.

He sighed. Reaching up, he ran his fingers gently over the scar on her face. Her pale hair, tousled by the evening wind, brushed across his hand. He smoothed it back.

"Impossible, my lady. Women are not permitted within the monastery walls—"

"I was once!"

"You would not be again."

"I could wear a disguise. The hooded robes, like those the young priest has on, would hide my face, my body. . . ."

The Warlord almost smiled. "The brethren would know, Maigrey."

Yes, she thought in bitter despair. They would know. But what mattered most was that *he* would know. The warrior-priest would never permit such sacrilege within the walls of his one true sanctuary.

"Besides, my lady," he continued coolly, smoothly, "you have other duties. That is what I came to discuss. You must return to Dion."

Maigrey stared at him. She hadn't been prepared for this, hadn't seen the blow coming. He'd caught her uncovered, off her guard. She went numb, the blood and life drained from her as surely as if he had stabbed her. She turned away from him, walking blindly, tripped, stumbled, and caught hold of the trunk of the oak to save herself from falling.

"I won't go."

"No? Where will you run to this time, my lady?" he asked dryly. "There aren't many hiding places left."

"How can I face him? After what I did? He knows, doesn't he? Knows the truth?"

"Dion knew it before that night, my lady. Abdiel made certain of that."

Maigrey lifted her head, stared out into the garden that was slowly darkening with evening's lengthening shadows.

"Then he knows I failed him. He knows I planned to betray him. *I* was going to keep the space-rotation bomb. *I* was going to be queen!"

"In the end, you didn't."

"But that wasn't *my* fault! Give credit where it's due, my lord. Give it to yourself, to Abdiel. Our blood's all tainted with the same poison."

"Yes," he said somberly, and there was something dark and

ominous and hurting in his tone that made her forget her own grief. She turned, fearfully, to look at him.

"I broke my oath to him, Maigrey," Sagan said. "Or rather, I would have broken it, if Brother Fideles hadn't stopped me with the"—there was the slightest hesitation—"with the message from my father."

"My God!" Maigrey could say nothing more, could only stare at him. She had seen the deepening of the lines of his face, noted the pallor beneath the rich tan, the darkening of the shadows around the eyes, the grim tightness of the lips. But she had accounted them to shock.

Now she knew, now she understood. A wind swept through the garden with the biting cold of winter, scattering the dead leaves. They skittered down the paths like demons dancing for joy at the fall of another soul.

"You're shivering," Sagan said. "We should go inside—" He was drawing the hood of her cloak up over her head.

"No, I want to stay out here. I couldn't breathe . . . inside." She glanced around, shuddered. "I feel sometimes that our lives are like this garden. All the paths surrounded by a stone wall that hems us in and constantly turns our footsteps so that no matter where we walk we must end up in the same place. If God exists at all, Derek, is this what He is? A stone wall?"

Sagan shrugged. "I read somewhere—perhaps in the Kaballah, I can't remember—that the closer man comes to God the less free will he has. The truly devout man knows the mind of God, you see, and to work God's will, man must forfeit his own. The angels," he added grimly, "being the closest to God, are therefore virtual slaves."

Which is why Lucifer rebelled, she thought. *Better to reign in Hell than serve in Heaven*.

"Maigrey," added Sagan quietly. "There is the gate. You are always free to open it and leave."

"You mean run away," she said bitterly.

Run away from my responsibility. From trying to set right what I made wrong. *Those who know the mind of God*. Or if not His mind, at least their own.

Maigrey sighed wearily, bowed her head in resignation. "What must I do?"

"My shuttle will take you back to *Phoenix*. The Honor Guard will be yours to command. Brother Fideles and I will go on in my own private spaceplane."

"Alone? Surely you could take one of the centurions—"

His brows came together in annoyance.

Maigrey saw her words would do no good, saved her breath.

"When you return to *Phoenix*," he continued, "go to my quarters. I have reset the controls to allow you and you alone to enter. Using our code—you know the one—you will have access to all my secret computer files, all my reports, all my wealth. Use the information, use the money. Use whatever you need."

Maigrey shrank back from him, shaking her head, appalled. "No! I don't want—"

"Then turn it over to Dion, if you think that's what's best!" he said impatiently. "I mean," he amended, "to His Majesty."

His hands went to his waist, he unbuckled his sword belt. Folding the straps neatly around the bloodsword, he handed it to her.

"Keep this for me. One does not come armed into the presence of God."

Maigrey took the bloodsword, felt the leather smooth and warm from his body. No need to tell him he might be walking defenseless into the presence of the one enemy in the universe who had the power to destroy him, to destroy them all. He knew.

"I will keep it for you until you return," she said steadily, calmly.

He started to say something, changed his mind. Silently, he reached into the worn and ancient leather script he wore at his side, drew forth a small rosewood box, and held it out to Maigrey.

For a moment she didn't think she had the strength to take it. But her courage would match his. She accepted it, opened it, was surprised to find it empty. She lifted her eyes to him in mute questioning.

In answer, he drew aside the folds of his cloak. The Star of the Guardian hung on a silver chain around his neck. The jewel was dark, unlovely, hideous to look at.

"*My* penance," he said with a rueful, dark smile.

Maigrey felt tears running down her cheek, the moisture cold on her skin. She knew her crying would annoy him, raised her hand to hastily brush the tears away, attempted to hide the motion behind a curtain of pale hair. He saw, however.

"Let's walk," he said. "Warm the blood. Time grows short and I have one more subject to discuss with you."

They walked the garden paths, walked unconsciously in step, each with the other, their footfalls sounding on the stone paths as one. Blue cape and crimson red trailed behind, dragging the dead leaves after them with soft, rustling whispers. They walked shoulder to shoulder, close but not touching. His hands were clasped behind him, beneath his cloak. Hers held the hilt of the bloodsword.

Each knew what the last subject was to be discussed. Neither wanted to bring it up, both planned to avoid it as long as possible. Maigrey hoped fervently he would decide not to mention it at all.

"How have you lived here, my lady?" Sagan asked, striving to speak nonchalantly, his gaze roaming over the low stone wall, going to the abandoned, deserted buildings.

"My needs are simple," she replied. "I live in the caretaker's cottage. Do you remember it? The house is small, with a fireplace for heat and cooking. There's a village near here, now. It was supposed to be a city, when Robes took over the Academy, but it never quite got that far. Now it's a farming community, the inhabitants glad to live isolated lives, away from the world. A young woman comes once a week, with a gift of bread and fruit and meat."

"A gift?" He glanced at her, amused.

Maigrey flushed in embarrassment. "I try to pay her for it, but she refuses. I'm not sure, but I think the people believe I'm a ghost. Either that, or I'm insane. They hope their gifts will keep me from murdering them all in their beds. You should have seen the poor child when they first sent her up here. She was half-dead from fright. She fainted when she saw me. Even now, she puts the food down on the grass, waits until she sees me take it, then runs."

The Warlord made no reply. Maigrey didn't blame him. She was rambling, talking simply to fill the vacuum.

She stole a glance at him, doubted if he'd even heard. The lines in his face had deepened, darkened. He looked gaunt, haggard, weary beyond the ability of sleep to give him ease. She drew near him, placed her hand upon his arm. He closed his own hand over hers, stopped in the middle of the path, standing before a copy of a Pietà, done by some forgotten artist of the past.

"Maigrey, have you ever considered that it might be better if I did *not* come back?"

"No, my lord," she answered calmly, looking up at him.

"You know that you are destined to die by my hand—"

"Destiny, again!" Maigrey interrupted him. "The stone wall, the winding, twisting paths. No, I *won't* believe it! You had a dream. That's all! You were furious with me for failing you that night. You hated me, you wanted revenge. Wishful thinking, that's all it was and—"

"My lady." He finally managed to stop the torrent by placing his fingers gently on her lips. "You are right. I was furious that night, the night we failed each other. And I had the dream soon after. I've dreamed it many times. And at first I reveled in it, I looked forward eagerly to my revenge."

"There, you see?" she said quickly when he stopped to draw a breath. "It's time we were returning. That poor priest of yours you left standing by the gate has probably frozen solid—"

"Maigrey. The dream comes to me still. Now I loathe it. It haunts me. And yet, each time, its images are clearer."

"Which means?" she asked reluctantly, knowing he would never leave until she heard him out.

"That the event is coming closer. Do you still have the silver armor?"

"I won't give it up. It was a gift from Marcus. Now a gift from the dead, doubly precious."

"Or doubly cursed. Heed my words, Maigrey. The time may come when you are forced to make a choice—"

"If so, it will *be* a choice, Derek! And *I* will make the decision. I will determine my own fate. Neither you nor God nor anyone else will determine it for me."

The Warlord regarded her grimly for long moments, then bowed.

"So be it, my lady," he said coldly.

"So be it, my lord."

And that was their farewell.

Twilight gilded the tops of the trees with a golden, red-tinged radiance, driven away by dusk's shadows that crept through the garden, night moving inexorably to overtake and banish day. The two said nothing more. The Warlord retrieved his helm, that he had left upon the bench near the statue of the eternally doomed burghers of Calais. Lord and lady walked in silence to the gate, where Brother Fideles waited patiently.

Two together must walk the paths of darkness before they reach the light. Maigrey recalled the old prophecy, shook her head. Destiny, prophecy. Perhaps it had meant nothing more than that the two of them would walk through a dying rose garden in the dusk. She looked quickly at Sagan, half-afraid he'd heard her unspoken words. He would consider such thoughts blasphemous.

He gave no sign that he had. The fortress of his being stood fast, impenetrable, impervious to assault.

Better to reign in Hell than serve in Heaven.

But I wonder if Lucifer ever thought of repenting, of going back, Maigrey asked herself. And what would God do to him if he did?

Book Two

I will say unto the God of my strength, Why hast thou forgotten me: why go I thus heavily, while the enemy oppresseth me?

My bones are smitten asunder as with a sword: while mine enemies that trouble me cast me in the teeth;

Namely, while they say daily unto me: Where is now thy God?

Prayer Book, 1662, Psalms 42:11

Chapter ◆━◗◯◖━◆ One

. . . the lion does not defend himself against traps, and the fox does not defend himself against wolves. . . .

Niccolo Machiavelli, *The Prince*

"We interrupt this broadcast for a GBC special report. As expected, the former Citizen General Derek Sagan—hero of the Revolution, a hero of the recent battle with the Corasians—has been indicted by a military tribunal for the cold-blooded and brutal murder of the notorious Adonian Snaga Ohme.

"If found guilty, Sagan would, by military law, automatically receive the death penalty. We are standing by, live, for what we are told will be a personal appeal by the President of the Galactic Democratic Republic for Derek Sagan to give himself up.

"No evidence against the citizen general has been made public and will not be, according to the office of the judge advocate general, until the trial. However, private sources reveal that the evidence is extremely damning.

"And now we are going live to the Common House."

An officious voice: "The President of the Galactic Democratic Republic."

The President faced directly into the cam. A shimmer of tears brightened his eyes, his voice broke. "Derek, you and I have known each other a long time. You've always claimed to be a man of honor. Do the honorable thing now, Derek, and turn yourself in. Stand trial. Answer these terrible allegations publicly. You owe it to yourself, Derek, and to your followers.

"And now I have a message for those followers, for the people of the systems who have left the Republic. Citizens, for I still think of you as citizens, you are being led blindly to your own destruction by leaders who care nothing for you or your well-being.

105

"One of those leaders, who had long styled himself Warlord, has been accused of committing a crime whose ferocity shocks the galaxy. Rise up and let your leaders hear your voices. Let your leaders know that you won't put up with their attempts to drag you into a devastating war. For it is you, not they, who will suffer.

"We would add"—the President's voice softened, the facile face molded itself into a look of paternal patience and understanding—"a word to Dion Starfire. We all admire you, young man. We believe that, deep down, you truly believe you are doing the right thing. Derek Sagan proclaims you publicly to be his king, his ruler. Therefore, we trust that in the interests of justice that you claim to uphold, you will encourage him to give himself up. In any case, I am certain you will not want to be embroiled in the scandal and disgrace of harboring a fugitive from the law.

"And finally, I leave you, Derek Sagan, with this warning. You are powerful, but the people are the true power in the galaxy. The people have spoken. You are not above the law. The people will see justice done. If you do not turn yourself in, you will be arrested like any other common felon. I give you forty-eight hours, Standard Military Time."

And how does it feel to be alone, my king? came the insidious voice, the voice through the bloodsword.

Dion knew the voice was Abdiel's, yet it spoke his own words. He knew Abdiel's voice, knew it far better than this other voice, trying to be heard within him. He knew Abdiel's words were lies, deceits, but there was always, disconcertingly, a hint of truth within them. A hint of truth that made him doubt. . . .

Sagan is gone. The Lady Maigrey gone. They discovered they couldn't use you, and so they have left. Plotting some treacherous scheme against you, my king, of that you may be certain!

"Shut it off," Dion ordered.

Tusk did so, lightly touching the controls on the arm of his chair. The vidscreen went blank, but no one in the room moved. They sat in their swivel chairs in the War Council Room, stared in brooding silence at the vast expanse of whiteness or exchanged glances with each other.

"Well, well," said General Dixter.

"This is insane!" Dion shook his head. "Sagan didn't kill

Snaga Ohme! It was—It was . . ." He stopped, unwilling to say the name. He thought he heard, from deep within, silent laughter.

"But no one knows *he* was there," Dixter said grimly. "His image doesn't even show up on the vids. And the only people who know he was the murderer are the Lady Maigrey, you, and Derek Sagan. Give evidence that a mind-seizer, a member of the Order of Dark Lightning, still lives and has done murder and you'd be laughed out of the courtroom."

"We could testify, sir," said Nola. "Tusk and I. Abdiel tried to kill us!"

"And who would corroborate you? That Sparafucile fellow who saved your lives? One of the Warlord's paid assassins? Against this, they have probably obtained evidence that Snaga Ohme attempted to double-cross Sagan over the sale of the space-rotation bomb. Sagan was heard by half the people in the room, the night of the party, making threats against the Adonian's life. And, then, of course, those officers—his peers—who would sit in judgment are all his enemies. All of whom would sleep much better at night with the pleasant sight of Derek Sagan walking into the disrupter in their minds."

"But this phony personal appeal! What is Robes up to?" Dion asked, running his hand through the mane of flaming red-golden hair. The voice had left him and he felt, as always, an unsettling emptiness inside. He hated it, yet he missed it when it was gone.

"Remarkable timing, too. These charges come out right when Sagan disappears. What a coincidence," Tusk added.

"It's no coincidence. Robes *knows* Sagan's not around to answer the charges or turn himself in. The fleet is riddled with spies and no matter how we've tried to keep the Warlord's continued absence quiet, you know the word's leaked out."

General Dixter, hands on his knees, pushed himself to his feet. "I wonder . . ." He paused, frowned as if a sudden thought had occurred to him and he didn't particularly like it. "We know it's not coincidence. But what if it were more than that?"

"More than what, sir?" Tusk stared at him. "What are you saying? I don't understand."

"I don't understand myself, son. Robes is up to something, that's for certain. For openers, it puts Dion in one hell of a spot."

"How? We'll simply issue a statement, saying that the Warlord has disappeared and we have no idea where he is. At least," Dion added wryly, "we'll be telling the truth."

"Yes, but unfortunately, the truth will only get you in worse trouble. Few will believe you. They'll figure—and Robes will be certain to point it out in case they miss it—that you're simply harboring a fugitive."

"The solution is simple. We fight!" said Tusk, slamming his fist on the table. "The Republic's got no right to board this vessel. If they attempt to do so by force, we defend ourselves. That way, we don't start this war. They start it."

"I don't think war is what Robes is after," Dion said thoughtfully. "I'm still extremely popular with a majority of the people and it would mean a lot of bad publicity for the President at a time when he's got to be thinking of holding the Republic together. He could have declared war on the secessionists, but he hasn't. Still, if not war, then what?"

"Your Majesty." Admiral Aks's face appeared on the vid-screen.

"Yes, Admiral?"

"A large fleet has materialized out of hyperspace."

"Whose? Rykilth's? DiLuna's? Olefsky's? All promised when they left to send us support."

"No, Your Majesty. These are ships of the Galactic Democratic Republic, from the fourteenth sector. Their commander is Citizen General Pang, a woman known to be loyal to the President."

Tusk glanced at Dion. "Not war, you said?"

"Are they threatening us in any way, Admiral?" Dion asked, brow furrowed.

"No, Your Majesty. But they've begun weaving the net."

"Weaving the net?" Dion looked questioningly at Dixter, who looked questioningly at Tusk, who looked grim.

"Standard procedure. They're deploying their destroyers to block off all the Lanes, so that we can't make the Jump and disappear on 'em. When they're finished, it'll be 'we've got you surrounded, come out with your hands up.'"

"Or else come out shooting," Dion said.

"That's about it, kid."

"Has Citizen General Pang attempted contact, Admiral?"

"Yes, Your Majesty. She asked permission to come aboard to speak to Lord Sagan."

"What did you tell her?"

"I told her that Lord Sagan wasn't receiving visitors."

"What did she say?"

"She laughed, Your Majesty."

"I see," Dion murmured. "And then, Admiral?"

"Citizen General Pang demands that Lord Sagan surrender himself into her custody. If he does not, she will send an armed force to board the ship and arrest him. If we refuse to permit them to board, it will be considered an act of resistance and they will have no choice but to fire on us. We have forty-eight hours."

"How long before they get this . . . er . . . net in place?"

"Only a few hours, Your Majesty. If we're going to escape, we've got to do it now."

"And play right into Robes's hands," Nola warned. "This would look extremely bad, Dion. The President would claim that Sagan was fleeing arrest, proving his guilt. And now you'd be involved, too. Robes stopped short of trying to implicate you in these crimes, but that would probably be his next step. You'd leave yourself wide open to accusations."

"And neither Rykilth nor DiLuna would take kindly to hearing of their king running away with his tail between his legs. I don't think even Olefsky would stand for that."

"It's heads Robes wins, tails we lose," muttered Tusk.

Dion stood up, began to pace the room. "How could Sagan do this to me? Surely he must have foreseen . . ." He pivoted to face General Dixter. "*That's* what you were thinking, wasn't it, sir? What you said about Robes arranging—"

"Your Majesty," Admiral Aks interrupted, his face excited, inflamed. "Lord Sagan's shuttle has just been reported coming out of hyperspace!"

All looked at each other, doubtful of believing, wondering if this was good news or bad. Dion almost heaved a relieved sigh, caught himself just in time.

"Surely the Republic's fleet must have recognized the shuttle, Admiral. Is his lordship under attack?"

"I don't believe so, sire. If you'll excuse me—" Admiral Aks turned to receive a report. "It appears, Your Majesty, that Lord Sagan was aware of the presence of enemy forces prior to making the Jump. He waited until the last possible moment before coming out of the Lane, which put him well out of range of General Pang's ships. Several short-range Scimitars flew to intercept, but he outmaneuvered them and is now safely within our own perimeter. The shuttle will be landing momentarily."

"Have you spoken to Lord Sagan?"

"Certainly not, Your Majesty." The admiral's tone was faintly rebuking. "We are under the guns of the enemy."

"Yes, of course. I forgot." Dion paused, considering. "I'll meet Lord Sagan in the docking bay. Join us there, Admiral. We can waste no time in deciding what to do."

"Yes, Your Majesty. I quite agree, Your Majesty!"

The admiral's image faded abruptly from the screen.

Dion left the room in haste. Tusk, Nola, and Dixter followed more slowly.

"Jeez! I never thought I'd be glad to see Derek Sagan." Tusk tugged thoughtfully at the small silver star he wore in his left ear.

"We haven't seen him yet, Tusk," said John Dixter. "We haven't seen him yet."

··◁■ ■▷··

Dion waited with ill-concealed impatience for the interminably slow docking bay doors to shut, and air rush in to fill the vacuum. Admiral Aks stood at his side, mopping his brow with a handkerchief. The others present nearly filled the remainder of the small ready room. Dixter's shrewd eyes were narrowed, their gaze fixed on the Warlord's shuttle, as if certain sums in his mind were not adding up.

The red warning light flashed off, the door to the ready room unsealed. Dion slammed his hand on the control, shot through the door before it was more than half-open. Admiral Aks did not lag far behind.

The young man walked swiftly, but proudly, head held high, lips tightly compressed. He was angry, and he told himself he was angry at Sagan. The Warlord had behaved in a cavalier manner, shrugging off responsibility, rushing off recklessly to God knows where. In reality—a reality Dion refused to admit—he was angry at himself for knowing relief at the Warlord's return.

The shuttlecraft's hatch opened. The Honor Guard, led by Agis, descended, formed a double line on the deck, came to attention, fists over their hearts in salute. Dion halted near the head of the line of men, some distance from the shuttle. He held himself stiffly, with dignity.

A figure appeared in the opening in the shuttle's hull. It was clad in armor, but that armor was silver, not gold. It stood tall and straight, but not nearly as tall as the Warlord. A blue cape, not a red one, hung from the figure's gleaming, armor-covered shoulders.

Dion's anger was sucked out of him, like the air out of an air lock when the docking bay doors were opened. Astonishment and perplexity rushed in to fill the vacuum. He recognized the figure . . . or thought he did.

"Lady Maigrey!"

Behind him, he heard Admiral Aks gasp.

She removed her helm, placed it in the crook of her arm in correct military fashion, and walked between the rows of centurions. She faced Dion, her gray eyes fixed on his. Yet, still, he wasn't certain he knew her.

The face was the face he remembered, the pale hair tied in braids and wound around her head to fit neatly beneath the silver helm, the scar slanted down her right cheek, slightly twisting one corner of mouth. Her physical presence was the same, but Dion had the strange feeling he might have been looking at a likeness carved in cold stone. There was no life, no warmth. A chill flowed from her reminiscent of the black void from which she'd come.

She halted before him, bowed low, gracefully, sinking down on one knee, her head bent. The folds of the blue cape fell around her.

"Lady Maigrey," said Dion again. "I—Where—"

Maigrey lifted her head, the expression in the gray eyes stopped the words on the young man's lips. She remained kneeling, glanced downward swiftly. The folds of the cape stirred. Dion shifted his gaze.

In Maigrey's left hand, concealed beneath the cape from all eyes except his, she held a bloodsword. Not her own. Her own was buckled around her waist. Dion recognized the sword, knew to whom it belonged. He caught his breath.

Maigrey rose to her feet. "Your Majesty," she said quietly, hiding the sword from view as she stood up, "we must talk."

·◄■ ■►·

The small group, accompanied by the admiral and Captain Williams, returned to the War Council Room. Dion had, while proceeding through the ship, kept his composure, not allowed his disappointment or his mounting anxiety to show in his face or his attitude while in view of the crew. Once inside the room, however, he gave way to his frustration.

"You know where Sagan is, my lady?"

"Yes, sire."

"But you refuse to tell me?"

Maigrey sighed. This was the fifth time he'd asked.

"I cannot, Your Majesty. It isn't my secret."

"Lady Maigrey isn't one of the enemy, Your Majesty," General Dixter said gently.

Dion felt his skin burn. "I'm sorry, my lady." He turned away, walked over to stare out the viewscreen.

Maigrey inclined her head slightly in acknowledgment. She was pale and cold, untouchable, unapproachable. The jagged scar, pulsing with a faint infusion of blood beneath the skin, seemed, oddly, the only living part of her.

She looked at no one else gathered around the conference table, but kept the gray eyes fixed on Dion or occasionally shifted her gaze to deepspace. At such times, she would lose track of the conversation, blink when anyone spoke to her, and seem to return to them from a long and fruitless—to judge by her wan expression—journey.

Captain Williams rose to his feet, leaned toward her over the table. "But, Lady Maigrey, it seems to me vital that we get in touch with Lord Sagan!"

"I most strongly agree with the captain," interjected Admiral Aks, having recourse to the handkerchief again. "This is an emergency, Lady Maigrey. A situation my lord could not have possibly foreseen when he left. We must know his orders—"

"These are his orders," interrupted Maigrey coldly. "I am in command."

A momentary silence. Dion looked around at her. Tusk cast a startled glance at Dixter, who became exceedingly grave. The silence was broken by Admiral Aks.

"I beg your pardon, Lady Morianna. I do not mean to imply that you are lying, but I would appreciate seeing some token of my lord's authority."

Maigrey wordlessly reached her hand beneath the blue cloak. Drawing out a bloodsword, she laid it upon the table, lowering it gently, not making a sound.

Aks stared at the sword, eyes bulging. "My lord is dead!" he cried in hollow tones, pushing himself away from the table, staggering to his feet.

"No, he is not!" Maigrey returned, her voice sharp, too sharp, her response too quick. She drew a deep breath, let it out before she spoke. "Understand this, all of you. Derek Sagan is gone. He has placed me in command. He has given me access to his quarters, he has given me the code to unlock his computer files, including those that are classified.

"I did not ask for, I do not want this responsibility, Your Majesty." Maigrey shifted her gaze to Dion. "But I had no choice. No choice," she repeated softly, bitterness tinging her voice.

Her gray eyes were dark, no color in them, no color in her voice or anywhere about her. "This may be negative consolation, Your Majesty, but I can tell you this much—even if you knew where my lord was, you could not communicate with him." Her fingers absently worked the leather of the sword belt, caressed it, dug into it.

Admiral Aks subsided slowly back into his seat.

"Now, Your Majesty," Maigrey continued crisply, her hands leaving the sword, fingers clasping together on the table, "I would appreciate an updated report on the situation."

"Tusk, go ahead," Dion ordered.

Turning his back on them, he returned to staring moodily out the viewscreen. The ships of the Galactic Democratic Republic crawled among the stars like small annoying spiders. He heard Tusk's voice in the background, going over what had happened, but the king wasn't listening to him.

Wait . . . counseled the voice inside him. And Dion was at last beginning to understand why.

"And that's the story, your ladyship," Tusk concluded. "General Dixter doesn't think it's any coincidence that Robes chose to pull this stunt the moment Sagan's . . . er . . . back was turned, so to speak."

Dion glanced around, saw the mercenary reclining in his chair, frowning at the toe of his boot.

"I believe that General Dixter is correct," said Maigrey. She was keeping her face averted from the general, though he had several times attempted to catch her eye. "I am certain Robes took advantage of the opportunity. In fact, it may even be worse than that."

So I'm right, Dion thought. He was astonished at his calm.

A terrible calm, he was almost light-headed. He was reminded forcibly of the time he'd killed those men on *Defiant*, or when he'd held Sagan's life in his hands . . .

Silence again. Uncomfortable, ominous, menacing. Maigrey stirred, smoothed back a lock of hair that had straggled out from her braid, then spread her hands flat upon the table. For the first time, she looked around at each of them, gathering them to her.

"You think I understand more about what's going on than the rest of you. But I don't, not really. We know why Robes's has done this: to discredit Dion and the Warlord. We know the President's chosen this particular time to act because his spies informed him that Sagan was not around to defend himself against these charges. Not that my lord would have done so, in any case. What we don't understand—what *I* don't understand—is what Robes is hoping to gain from all this."

"Simple." Tusk shrugged. "He's trying to goad us into war. And I say we give it to him!"

"I agree," said Admiral Aks. "Citizen General Pang has threatened to board this ship in forty-eight hours. Make that forty-four hours now. That would be a disgrace, an affront to Lord Sagan . . . and to His Majesty," the admiral added hastily, as an afterthought. "I would blow this ship up first!"

"And I would be the one to press the button, Admiral," said Maigrey. "But hopefully there are other alternatives."

Dion felt her eyes upon him. Hands clasped behind his back, he had turned again to stare unseeing out the viewscreen.

"There *are* other alternatives, my lady." Aks was holding forth eagerly. "We send for Rykilth and DiLuna. Their fleets join with ours, we surround Pang's forces and we—"

"—start a civil war. Is that what we want?" General Dixter argued. "Listen, Admiral, I've fought in countless civil wars in my time and I've never yet seen a winner. A victor—yes. But a winner—no."

My throne smeared with the blood of my subjects, Dion reflected, watching the tiny, gleaming white dots of the spaceplanes move as close as either side dared, harassing, tempting, luring the opponent to make a mistake. I would rule a kingdom forever divided; steel and fear the glue holding it together.

"Then what do you suggest we do, General Dixter?" Captain Williams demanded acidly.

"Beats the hell out of me," Dixter replied.

"Bah!" Aks exploded. "No wonder you were never more than a money-grubbing mercenary. What amazes me is how you managed to attain the rank of general, even in the Royal Army. But, then, it was always well known that you had influential friends. . . ." He gazed pointedly at Maigrey.

Tusk was on his feet, fist clenched. "You goddam—"

"That will do, Tusk," Dixter said firmly. "Admiral Aks, I don't care what you say about me, but you owe the Lady Maigrey—"

"It seems to me," said Dion, turning abruptly, facing them, his voice cutting cold and sharp through the clamor, "that there is one point you have all overlooked. Admiral, General, Major Tusca . . . if you would all resume your seats."

Another moment's tense silence. Dion's eyes met and held the defiant, anger-filled glares. One by one, he stared them down. Chairs scraped, feet shuffled, places were resumed, not without some muttering and clearing of throats and sidelong glances that promised the hostilities were not ended, merely deferred.

Maigrey had neither moved nor spoken. Dion wondered if she even knew what had been said. She sat staring at the bloodsword and he realized, suddenly, that she was far away from them, far away from him.

She, too, had left him, but he'd known that a long time ago.

"Forty-eight hours," Dion said. "Why forty-eight hours? Lord Sagan's an accused murderer. What other murderer is given so much as forty-eight seconds to turn himself in? Why didn't Robes order Sagan arrested immediately? Why doesn't Pang force this ship to halt and board it this minute?"

Silence again; this time he could see everyone considering, swallowing, digesting the premise. He could tell, by the sudden grimaces, that they were beginning to understand. The taste it left in the mouth was bitter.

"It's Robes who needs the forty-eight hours." Dion answered his own question. "Within that time, he's expecting news. This"—he gestured at the net, closing fast around them—"is a mere diversion, meant to keep us occupied."

"A trap!" Tusk whistled softly, off-key. "He's set a trap for Sagan!"

"You must tell us where my lord is, Lady Maigrey!" Aks was on his feet again, pounding the table. "He must be warned!"

"He knows," Maigrey said quietly. "He knew when he left."

The admiral's mouth moved, but no sound came out.

"We could do nothing to help him anyway." The scar was a leaden streak against Maigrey's livid skin. Her hands closed convulsively over the leather belt of the bloodsword. "He is out of reach, out of touch."

Out of sight, Dion added mentally. Not even you, with the power of the Blood Royal can see him, can you, my lady?

"So what do we do?" Tusk demanded.

"We wait," said Dion.

Chapter ·─◆━⊃◯⊂◆━· Two

Try me, O God, and seek the ground of my heart: prove
me, and examine my thoughts.
Prayer Book, *1662*, Psalms 139:23

The Warlord guided his spaceplane to a landing on a barren,
windswept desert. No planetary government challenged him,
no control tower gave him coordinates, directions, warnings to
avoid other aircraft. There were no other aircraft, there was no
control tower, no government—planetary or otherwise—any
longer. The planet seemed devoid of all life. If it had once had
a name, that name had long since been expunged from the
records.

The spaceplane's systems shut down, with the exception of
life support. The planet's atmosphere was thin; they would
have to wear oxygen masks when they left the plane and began
their trek across the desert.

"We have landed some distance from the Abbey, my lord,"
Fideles stated timidly.

It had taken them the equivalent of a day and a night to
travel the Lanes, reach the isolated, forgotten planet where
the Order had located its headquarters. Despite this length of
time spent together, in the relatively cramped quarters of the
spacecraft, Fideles was still so much in awe of the Warlord that
it took a great deal of courage to venture this remark.

Sagan did not respond. He was absorbed in his work, doing
something with the plane's controls and computer. Fideles,
who knew nothing of the mysterious and complex workings of
a spacecraft, had no idea what.

The Warlord had set the craft down behind a range of
sawtooth rock formations, keeping them between his plane
and the Abbey, whose walls stood black against a lurid red sky.
It occurred to the young priest that the Warlord had landed
here deliberately, was hiding the spaceplane from view.

117

Fideles decided such a precaution was probably an instinctive action, taken by an old soldier, who could not relax his guard.

The Warlord removed his hand from off five gleaming needles embedded in the arm of his pilot's chair. Those needles, linked with his body, worked like the bloodsword, connecting him mentally and physically to his spaceplane. This was, Fideles knew, how Sagan flew and controlled his craft.

But it wasn't the only means available.

The Warlord looked thoughtfully, speculatively at the priest seated in the co-pilot's chair next to his.

"Can you fly a spaceplane, Brother Fideles?"

Fideles's mouth and eyes opened wide at the question. He cast a glance at the dials and switches and flashing lights on the control panel, and shook his head, smiling, thinking that perhaps the Warlord was teasing him.

"No, my lord."

Sagan turned the matter over in his mind one more time, then set to work again, barking sharp commands at the computer, hands moving swiftly and assuredly over the complex instruments. Brother Fideles watched him uneasily, with trepidation, afraid that these complicated maneuvers had something to do with him.

The Warlord turned to him once more. "Brother Fideles, now you can fly this spaceplane."

The young priest shook his head. "It is an engine of war. To operate it would be against my vows. I—"

Sagan raised his hand. "It might be more correct to say that the spaceplane will fly you, Brother. I have set the controls in such a way that all you have to do is give a single verbal command to the computer. It will do the rest."

The Warlord looked intently into the eyes that were gazing back at him in dismay, then continued, speaking in an even, controlled voice, as he might have spoken to a student pilot.

"I have locked the plane's destination onto the last-known coordinates of *Phoenix*. The plane will carry you there, but it will do nothing more for you than that. It will not fight, for example, if anything attacks you. The Lady Maigrey will maintain the ship's position as long as it is possible to do so. If you arrive and the fleet is gone, then, Brother Fideles, you must put your trust in the Creator."

The young man cast a nervous, sidelong glance at the on-board computer, the confusion of incomprehensible mechanical devices, the intimidating flare of ominous-looking lights. He shook his head.

"My lord, I think I understand what you are saying. You plan to remain in the Abbey after your father's death, perhaps take his place. And you make these arrangements in order that I may return to my duties. But that is not necessary, my lord. For if you do not return, then I will not return. I will stay and serve you in whatever capacity you might need me."

Sagan made no reply. He rose from the pilot's chair, moved into the cramped space behind, and began to strip off his armor. Brother Fideles kept his eyes lowered, out of modesty, as was proper. He'd seen naked bodies, of course, but that was during the performance of his duty, treating the sick, the injured, the wounded, the dying. But this instance—alone with another human in the intimate confines of a cramped space—was different. Those who pledge vows of chastity both of mind and of body are taught to avoid temptation.

He acted strictly out of force of habit, doing what he had been taught, not because he felt any uncomfortable stirrings of desire. Fideles wasn't tempted by the beauty and comeliness of the male physique. The dreams that tormented him in the long hours of the night were dreams of women, and the torment was very gentle, for Fideles was truly devout and had never once been led to question his faith.

The young priest heard the clink of battle armor being packed away, neatly, orderly, in bins located on the plane's bulkheads. Sagan's silence continued. Fideles, who couldn't see the man's face, thought perhaps the Warlord was angry.

"My lord, if you are worried that I am a deserter and that by allowing me to stay you are shielding a criminal, you can put your mind at ease. I am not, technically speaking, a member of the ship's crew."

This evoked a response. Sagan paused in his undressing, half turned. "You're not? And how did you manage to sneak aboard my ship, Brother Fideles?"

"With God's help, my lord," the young priest answered serenely.

"Since He is not subject to court-martial and the death penalty, I suggest you tell me your story," Sagan said dryly.

"It is a long one, my lord, and I am not permitted to give details, for I would not want your anger to fall upon any other than myself. Suffice it to say that I met a young man in the medical corps who was newly assigned to serve under your command. He confided in me that he was terrified at the prospect, for it is said, my lord, that those who sign their names on the roll to serve you sign their names on Death's roll, as well."

Fideles heard the rustle of soft cloth sliding over the hard-muscled body. He saw the hem of long black velvet robes, the robes of a warrior-priest, brush the deck. He could not forebear raising his eyes, fascinated. He had never seen the black robes of those who were permitted to do battle for their faith, to engage in physical combat, to injure, maim, kill in the name of the Creator. Once, long ago, such priests and priestesses had defended the Order of Adamant against its enemies. But King Starfire, shocked at the thought of men of God spilling blood, had demanded that the Holy Father, the Lord High Abbot, head of the church, rid the Order of its warriors. The Holy Father had complied—there being some doubt existing with the body of the church itself as to the exact propriety of maintaining this guard. Thus, the night of the Revolution, there had been no one to protect the men and women of the Order from the mobs.

"Well, Brother?"

Fideles blinked. "Forgive me, my lord. I—I'm sorry. I wasn't listening."

He had been wondering how Sagan had managed to become one of the forbidden warrior-priests. Obviously, it must have been done prior to the Revolution. In secret, of course. But why? Unless the Order had foreseen the need. . . .

"How did you get aboard my ship?" the Warlord repeated patiently. Perhaps he guessed the thoughts running through the young priest's mind.

Fideles flushed. "The young man of whom we were speaking came from a wealthy family. He had, I believe, joined the military as an act of rebellion against his parents and come to regret it. He offered me a vast sum of money to take his place. I took the money and—"

"You took it? A member of the Order accepting payment to further a criminal act?"

The young priest appeared much abashed. "I did not view it in that way, my lord. We in the Order take vows of poverty, but the church requires funds to continue its work. God had, in essence, granted this young man's prayers, and I felt it only proper that the young man show his gratitude. I gave all the money to the Order, in the young man's name. I told him I was giving the money to charity, but I don't think he believed me. Such lack of faith in his fellow men will count against his soul, however, not mine," added Fideles gravely.

The Warlord compressed his lips, perhaps to hide a smile. "Continue, Brother. Confess to me the rest of this crime."

Fideles glanced up, startled and somewhat frightened by Sagan's stern tone. The young priest saw the Warlord's thin lips twitch, saw the dark eyes amused, not angry.

Brother Fideles relaxed. "It was easy to slip aboard *Phoenix* in the confusion just prior to launching. The young man's friends knew, of course, that the switch had been made, but I believe he had paid them well to hold their tongues. And so you see, my lord, the person who is now AWOL from your ship was actually a deserter years before. He changed his identity and disappeared long ago."

"You entered my service and, from what Giesk tells me, you have served me and my men well. You are courageous, cool, and levelheaded under fire. During the Corasian attack, Giesk said you remained on board *Phoenix*, treating the wounded, until ordered to take the last evac ship."

"In serving men, I serve the Creator, my lord. My courage comes from Him."

"Does it, indeed?" Sagan murmured, almost to himself. "I hope He has a good supply of it laid up in storage for you, Brother Fideles. I have a presentiment you're going to need it."

The young priest stared at him, incredulous. "What do you mean, my lord?"

The Warlord did not immediately answer; he appeared to be in doubt whether or not to explain or let the statement stand. He wrapped a braided leather belt around his waist. Reaching into a worn scrip—the only object he'd brought with him beside the black robes—he removed the small silver dagger with the star-shaped handle, slid it into its place beneath the belt. The scrip, with its chalice and the silver dish for the oil, remained in the pouch, attached to the belt. Taking hold of the black hood that rested upon his shoulders, Sagan drew it up over his head. Fideles rose to his feet, thinking they were preparing to leave.

The Warlord made up his mind to speak. He put his hand upon the young man's arm, restraining him, holding him.

"Brother Fideles, within those safe and peaceful-looking Abbey walls, we may face greater danger than would be present if we found ourselves surrounded by the entire Corasian nation. In fact," Sagan added grimly, "I would far rather be facing a Corasian battle fleet alone in this small plane than what perhaps lies ahead for us in there."

Fideles considered first that the Warlord was teasing him again, perhaps playing a practical joke. One look at the man's set and rigid jaw, the shadowed eyes, and Fideles realized this was no laughing matter.

"My lord. I don't understand. What harm could possibly come to you on the sacred grounds of our Abbey?"

"Sit down a moment, Brother, and listen."

Fideles returned obediently to the co-pilot's chair. The Warlord remained standing, his tall figure towering over him.

"What do you know of the Order of Dark Lightning?"

Fideles was startled by the question. He didn't know what he knew, for certain. He'd never thought about it. "They were a group of . . . of the Blood Royal, who set themselves up as an antithesis of our Order. They surgically implanted the needles, like those on your chair and on the bloodsword, into their own hands . . ."

"And took the virus and the micromachines that the bloodsword infuses into our bodies into their own bodies, so that they could infuse it into the bodies of others." Sagan spoke implacably, as if he were giving a lecture. "Do you understand?"

"Not completely," answered Fideles hesitantly. "I know about the virus, how it uses the body's energy to operate the sword, how it connects you mentally with either sword or this spaceplane, allowing you to act with the swiftness of a thought. I know its use drains the body of energy, after a time. But I never could understand how or why these people risked taking the virus into their own bodies and nurturing it there. The effect it had upon them must have been dreadful!"

"Yes, it was. Some lost their lives, dying horribly, their bodies refusing to assimilate the virus. Those who survived are forced to consume vast quantities of various types of drugs to maintain a semblance of health. Yet still they endure constant pain. Their skin rots, falls off in patches. The micromachines tend to gather at the location of nerve bundles, forming large nodes at the base of the skull. Their hair falls out. Yet they endure all this gladly.

"By inserting the needles into the flesh of any other human being they are able to speak directly to that person's mind. They can see into the consciousness of another, discover all secrets, even those of the subconscious. They learn, in time, how to manipulate the minds of their victims, how to give sublime pleasure, how to inflict excruciating pain. They gain ascendancy over them, power."

"You speak of them in the present tense, my lord," said Fideles. "They are all dead, aren't they? Their dread Order was destroyed during the Revolution."

"Yes, just as was our own Order, the Order of Adamant," Sagan replied, looking at the young priest.

"May God have mercy! My lord, what are you saying?"

"I'm going to tell you a story, Brother Fideles. Few people know about it, few people left alive, that is. Admiral Aks is one; he was indirectly involved. John Dixter is another; Maigrey told him all her secrets. And Dion. I told him, warned him. Too late, as it turned out. But, still, now he knows. And so must you.

"It happened twenty some years ago, before the Revolution. How it happened doesn't matter, that is a story in and of itself. Suffice it to say that the Lady Maigrey and I fell into a trap laid by one of the most cunning and powerful members of the Dark Order. It is not a memory of which I am proud. Trickery, deception, playing off our own youthful conceit, put us into this man's hands. Abdiel, he called himself. Abdiel . . . one of the angels of God.

"He wanted us for two reasons: He sought to gain control of us and use us for his own purposes, and he was trying to discover the secret of the mind-link that binds my lady and I. We resisted his disciples when they came to take us, but there were only two of us and many of them."

The Warlord looked down at the palm of his right hand, at the five holes in the flesh, fresh and oozing a clear liquid from their contact with the needles on the control pad of the spaceplane. Sagan rubbed the palm, as if it pained him.

"He calls it 'joining,'" he said in a low voice. "It is a physical pleasure for him. Sexual. To the victim, it is rape. Rape of the mind, of the soul."

The Warlord fell silent, rubbed his fingers over the wounds on his hand. His face reflected memories of the bitter struggle, the final defeat.

"Although he invaded us, my lady and I proved too strong for him," said Sagan at last. "We held out against his probing and managed, at last, to escape him. But not before he had gained a portion of each of us. Not before he knew every one of our secret dreams, secret fears, secret desires."

"This man, this Abdiel, lives?" Fideles was bewildered, dazed. "And you're saying that he is . . . that he's . . ." The priest couldn't finish, the idea was unspeakable.

"I don't know for certain," said the Warlord. "But I think it's possible. Abdiel has seen into my mind, my heart. He alone would know of the one summons in this universe that I could not fail to heed."

A horrifying thought struck the young priest. "My lord! Surely you don't think that I . . . that I have betrayed you!"

"No, Brother Fideles." The Warlord smiled, rested his hand upon the young man's shoulder. "I believe that you are what your name claims for you. But," he added more soberly, "Abdiel has made use of the innocent before now."

The priest turned his gaze out the plane's viewscreen toward the Abbey of St. Francis. Its dark windowless walls and towers, sharply defined against the red horizon, had always been to Brother Fideles a fortress against the rest of the universe. Within those walls lay peace, security, brotherly love and concern, knowledge, good works. The very air the priests and monks breathed was of their own making, the thick, specially designed walls contained a self-created, artificial atmosphere.

No voice was ever raised in anger or alarm. No drums beat the call to action that sent a tremor through the limbs. No harsh lights shone on mangled, bleeding bodies. Fideles pictured the cool and soothing shadows through which robed figures passed, going about their business, nodding hooded heads in silent greeting. They would be gathering in the chapel for Vespers now.

"*Alleluja, alleluja, alleluja.*

"*Venite, exultemus Domino . . .*

"Come let us rejoice in the Lord . . ."

His voice blending with the voices of his brothers, chanting the words that carried thought and spirit to God on wings of sublime music, lifted it far above the frailty of the body, the day's temptations, sins, regrets, failures. These voices cleansed the soul, washed it free of impurities, left it pure and fresh to begin anew.

Fideles looked at the dark walls and tried to imagine them stained, defiled, threatening. He couldn't. It wasn't possible. God would not permit it.

"It is written that we must put our trust in the Lord," said the young priest softly.

"I do," responded Sagan, tone grim. "But it is also written that the Lord helps those who help themselves. And thus, though I hope for the best, I prepare for the worst." He pointed toward the computer, the controls on the spaceplane.

"I did not go to the trouble of programming this plane in order to return one male nurse, however sorely needed, to Dr. Giesk. If anything happens to me, Fideles, it will be your duty and your responsibility, as given by God, to inform the Lady Maigrey and His Majesty, the king. If I fall, their lives, especially the life of the king, will be in imminent danger. Do you understand, Brother?"

Fideles was staring at him in shock. "My—my lord! You can't mean it. My vows . . . I can't . . . I couldn't possibly . . ."

"We never know what we can do, Brother, until we are called upon to do it. As for your vows, I do not ask you to break them. You are not being sent into battle. You would be carrying a message, that is all."

Sagan glanced out the viewscreen, measured the distance they must walk with his eye. "Come, Brother. If we leave now, we will arrive just after Vespers."

He positioned the breathable air pack on his back, fit the mask over nose and mouth, and assisted the young priest with his. Exiting the spaceplane, the Warlord showed Fideles how he and he alone could open the hatch once it had shut and sealed behind them.

"Place the palm of the hand flat against this control. Then say something, anything. The words don't matter. It's the sound of your voice that will activate . . '."

Activate . . . Yes, I understand how it operates. But what has it to do with me? Fideles wondered. The Warlord is mistaken. He has been surrounded by death and violence too long. He imagines it everywhere, even in the holy sanctuary of the Creator.

"Can I rely on you, Brother Fideles?" Sagan asked.

The young priest was troubled, uncertain how to answer. "I hope and trust that you can rely on me always, my lord," he said eventually. "But I truly believe that your fears and worries are groundless. God would never permit this evil man to enter our walls."

"And what about the night of the Revolution, Brother?" Sagan's voice, muffled by the mask, seemed to come from a long distance away. "God permitted the mobs to enter the walls, didn't He?"

A shadow of doubt crossed the priest's soul, sliding over him, passing quickly like the shadow of the wing of some bird, flying far over his head.

"Man is not meant to understand God's plans, my lord. We must have faith. I will pray to the Creator for guidance."

Sagan said nothing more, it was necessary to conserve the breath, difficult to talk with the mask on. The two began to make their way through the desert, bearing toward the Abbey.

The walking itself was not difficult, the planet's surface was red rock, covered by a thin layer of reddish dust and yellow sand. But a blasting wind blew against them, driving stinging bits of stone and sand into any area of unprotected skin. Black clouds scudded across the red sky, joining with the gases of a red giant that was its sun in a garish, swirling dance. The two men pulled their hoods low over their faces, bent forward into the wind, and struggled on, robes flapping about their legs and ankles.

They drew near the walls of the Abbey. Fideles looked at them fondly, expecting the sight to gladden his heart. To his shock and dismay, they suddenly seemed no longer a safe haven, a sanctuary. He was reminded of a prison . . . or a mausoleum. He paused, trembling, alarmed, and felt Sagan's strong hand close over his arm.

"Pray your prayers, Brother Fideles," intoned the Warlord. "Pray them swiftly."

Chapter ···✦◦◯◦✦··· Three

> Behold, I shew you a mystery; We shall not all sleep, but
> we shall all be changed . . .
>
> Holy Bible, 1 Corinthians, 15:51

Maigrey sat in the Warlord's quarters, in Sagan's chair, at his
desk, before his computer. The screen glimmered brightly,
the only light in the darkness of the room. The screen was
empty, however, nothing on it. Maigrey stared at it, thought
that this mechanical mind was a good reflection of her
own—blank, empty, waiting for someone to give it life.

She had not intended to use Sagan's quarters. She had
meant to find a room for herself anywhere else on board
Phoenix except Sagan's quarters. But she soon discovered that
his quarters were the one place on the ship where she was
certain of being alone, where no one could gain access to her,
where she could hide.

"My lady," came the voice of Agis, captain of the Honor
Guard.

Maigrey froze, stared fearfully at the door, afraid it might
suddenly open, though she knew there was no possible way it
could. John Dixter. It was John Dixter again. She wouldn't
answer. He'd think she was gone. And, yet, the guard knew
she was here.

"I gave orders not to be disturbed," Maigrey said coldly,
cuttingly.

"His Majesty, the king, to see you, my lady."

Maigrey closed her eyes, sighed. "What are you waiting for,
then?"

The double doors slid silently open. Dion stood in the
aperture. The light from the corridor outside bathed him in
radiance, the red-golden hair shone like a bright flame. He
entered, moving gracefully, his stature reflecting pride but not
arrogance, his walk confident, commanding.

He has changed, thought Maigrey, remembering the night she'd left him. He'd had within him then the propensity to greatness, the charisma, the power of the Blood Royal to gain ascendancy over others. But he'd lacked confidence in himself, lacked wisdom, knowledge. A sword's blade that has been through the fire, cooled, he wanted only the cutting edge. Sagan had sharpened the steel.

Dion could now walk into a room and all eyes were drawn to him, held by him. And this would happen, Maigrey realized, if he wore the purple sash of royalty or the ragged shirt of a beggar. Sagan had given him the outward semblance of a king, but what, Maigrey wondered, looking at the young man intently, had given him the inner?

"Your Majesty." Rising from her chair, she bowed low before him. "You should have sent for me—"

"No," Dion interrupted. "I wanted to talk to you in private, alone. And"—he glanced about the room—"I thought this would be the best place."

No spying eyes or listening ears in the Warlord's chambers. Maigrey nodded in understanding.

"Please sit down," Dion added, seeing that she remained standing. He flushed slightly, embarrassed. "I want to talk to you . . . as a friend. I'm not here as your king," he continued, seeming to feel his words needed clarification. "I want it to be like it used to be between us."

Maigrey saw no need to tell him that this was impossible. He would come to understand, soon enough. She walked over to a couch that appeared, like all the furniture in Sagan's quarters, to be standing at rigid attention, prepared to take into custody anyone who sat upon it. The furniture was not comfortable, nor was it meant to be. Sagan did not encourage visitors and when forced to entertain them, did not encourage them to stay.

Maigrey sat down, smiled at Dion, inviting him with a pat of her hand upon the leather to be seated.

"Thank you, my lady, but I prefer to stand, if you don't mind."

"I don't blame you, Your Majesty," Maigrey said, grimacing, attempting in vain to locate a position on the couch that didn't threaten to cut off the circulation to her legs.

Dion didn't hear her. He had begun pacing back and forth, hands clasped behind his back, his head bowed in thought.

Maigrey had seen Sagan walk thus, countless times. A smothering sensation came over her. She was forced to avert her face, lower her eyes. Her hands curled over the edge of the thin, hard sofa cushion. She took a deep breath.

"I'm sorry for bothering you, my lady." Dion paused in his walking, turned to face her. "You have a lot to do. I'm interrupting your work. I won't take up much of your time."

"My time is completely at Your Majesty's disposal—"

"Don't," Dion said abruptly, the blue eyes bright as flame. "Don't talk to me like that. Talk to me the way you used to, when we were both Sagan's prisoners on board the old *Phoenix*."

"Very well, Dion," Maigrey said gently. "I didn't mean—"

"My lady"—he forced out the words as if he had to say them now or never speak them—"I've seen him!"

"*Seen* him? Seen who?" Maigrey thought for a moment he meant Sagan. She half rose from her chair.

"Platus." He stared at her intently, to see her reaction.

Maigrey sank back down. "What did he say to you?" she asked faintly.

"You believe me?"

"Shouldn't I?"

"It could have been a dream."

"Was it?"

"Don't do this!" Dion snapped. "Don't play these stupid games with me again!"

"What would you have me do, Dion?" Maigrey returned sharply. "Would you have me say: Yes, it was my brother you saw, returned from the grave, or would you have me laugh and say: No, something you ate for dinner disagreed with you? You know the truth in your heart, Your Majesty. You don't need me to either confirm or deny it for you."

Dion frowned, still angry. Then gradually, as he considered her words, his anger cooled. "He didn't say anything to me. He didn't come close to me. He stood in the doorway of my quarters and he looked at me. He just looked at me and he nodded." Dion's voice softened, grew sad. "He reminded me of when we were together back home, and I'd solved an algebra equation. . . ."

He was suddenly irritated.

"Is that some sort of rule with ghosts? That they never talk to you? And I can't believe what I'm saying! And I'm serious!

Look, I'm sorry for bothering you with this. It was probably a dream. I—"

"He could have spoken, if he'd felt he needed to," Maigrey said softly. "He spoke to me."

She stood up, walked around to the back of the couch, ran her hands over the cold metal frame. "It was said that the spirits of the Blood Royal could remain on this plane of existence after the body died, especially if the spirit was closely bound to one of the living. So widely held was this belief, and so many stories were told about people who had seen or been contacted by 'ghosts'—if you will—that our scientists conducted experiments to try to prove or disprove the notion."

"And what did they find?" Dion asked eagerly.

"What I've already told you. That either you believed what you saw or you didn't."

Maigrey smiled at the sight of the king's disappointed expression. "Logically, it makes no sense. Why do some spirits walk and others do not? There was a theory that those who left some important task unfinished would return to complete it. One of these, I remember, was an alien scientist who was working to find a cure for some sort of dreadful plague that was decimating her planet's population. She was reportedly near a breakthrough, but died of the disease herself, before she could complete her work. If anyone had cause to come back, it would be her. Scientists set up instruments and took readings and measurements and waited around her laboratory, but she never appeared. A cure was never found. The plague destroyed the planet's entire population. One entire alien culture ceased to exist and was lost to us forever.

"And yet, we'd hear reports of a mother's spirit returning to find a child's lost toy. A father appearing to his daughter on her wedding day. A dead soldier warning his living comrades of an ambush. Why, for example, has your mother never appeared to you? Her last words, her last thoughts, were of you . . ."

Maigrey sighed. Her gaze fixed on her hand, that moved back and forth over the metal arm of the couch.

"You said you saw Platus." Dion came around to stand beside her. "He spoke to you. What did he say? Unless, of course, it's personal—"

"I can tell you. He came to stop me from taking my own life. It was right after he died, when I knew Sagan had discovered my hiding place and that he was coming to take me captive. I knew that the Warlord would use me to find you and I thought, to protect you, that I must kill myself. My brother's spirit convinced me that I was needed."

Maigrey looked at the young man. "Sagan would tell you that it is the Creator who chooses whether the dead shall return or not. Why didn't you tell him, Dion? Were you afraid he wouldn't believe you?"

"No." Dion paused, grim, thoughtful. "I was afraid he would. I could see him sneer. I could almost hear him say, 'So that's the reason you refuse to go to war. Your pacifist mentor forbids it! You're weak. Just as he was!'"

"And that was why you defied Sagan?"

"No, I'd made the decision already." Dion put his hand to his head, ran his fingers through his hair. "I sent the message, and then I sat down to wait. That time was hardest. I was alone and . . . afraid." He looked at her defiantly, as if expecting her to mock him.

She nodded, understanding. "I don't blame you."

"And then I saw Platus standing there. I saw the expression on his face. It was strange, but I realized why I was afraid. I began to understand my fear."

Maigrey kept silent. Dion was no longer talking to her, but explaining it all at last to himself. "I was afraid, not so much of Sagan, but of failing. Of losing everything. By going to war, I could exert my power, my authority. I could force people to do what I wanted, scare them into following me. Once I thought about it, I knew that wasn't the type of king I wanted to be. It would be better to fail, better to return to a life of being ordinary, even better to die than to do something that I would eventually live to regret. When I realized that, Platus smiled at me and nodded."

"You see," Maigrey said gently, "he had no need to speak to you."

"I guess not. But I didn't really understand that until now. I didn't understand myself." Dion frowned, shook his head. "Platus was an atheist, though. He didn't believe in God."

"He used to, Dion. And I'm not certain he truly did lose his faith. He was like a small child who gets mad at his parents and runs away from home. My brother couldn't understand how God could permit the atrocities committed the night of the

Revolution. Platus got mad and he . . . ran away from home. Perhaps, now, he's come back."

"You know about the healing incident? The child and the . . . the young woman?"

"I read Sagan's report," Maigrey began cautiously, uncomfortably.

"Yes, well, you know about it, then. I know I healed that child, Lady Maigrey! I felt the energy flow through my body into his! And I know I could have helped that girl, even though she was under Abdiel's control.

"Sagan doesn't believe I can. He doesn't believe I have the power. He says I can't because the Creator grants the power and He would never give it to someone who didn't have faith—"

"Unless He gave it to someone to give that person faith," Maigrey amended quietly.

Dion nodded. "I've thought about that, too. And let's suppose that's true. Why that power and no others? I can't do anything the rest of you Blood Royal can do! I can't shut off the electricity with my mind. I can't force open doors with a look. I had the power during the rite. I kept the spiked ball floating in the air. . . ."

"That was because you gave yourself up to the power completely, Dion. You didn't question it or yourself, you didn't try to analyze it—"

"Because I didn't know what the hell it was! I'm sorry, my lady," Dion said, drawing a deep breath. "I didn't mean to shout."

"Dion, what do you want from me?" Maigrey asked wearily. "I would like to be able to tell you that there is a God and that He, She, or It has some grand cosmic plan for us. I would like to believe there was a reason your father was murdered, your mother died in my arms, a reason for Platus's death, a reason my life was spared. I would like to tell you this. I'd like to tell myself—"

"Doesn't Platus's coming to us prove it?"

"It doesn't prove anything. I was about to kill myself. Maybe this was my subconscious way out. You were under stress. The vision could have been a form of hysteria—"

"You don't believe that. And neither do I."

"I don't know what I believe in, anymore. All I know is that faith comes from within and it begins with faith in yourself; the knowledge that you have within you the ability to judge between the dark and the light and to act accordingly."

"Dark and light? Sagan murdered and tortured people and professed all the time to be performing God's will."

"Sagan has heard the still, small voice within. He either refused to listen, rebelled against it outright, or twisted its words to make it say what he wanted to hear. But I don't think he can do that any longer."

Dion waited for her to continue.

Maigrey was silent. After a moment, she sighed, reached out her hand, and lightly touched the fire-opal necklace the young man wore around his neck. "You're not going to get off any easier than the rest of us, Your Majesty. And for you, it may be much, much harder. . . ."

"My lady," the apologetic voice of the captain of the guard.

"I am in conference—"

"I beg your pardon for the interruption, but Mendaharin Tusca is demanding to see you. He says it is urgent."

"Perhaps he's heard something about Sagan," Dion suggested.

Maigrey's pallor increased. "Yes, perhaps he has. Send him in, Agis."

The double doors slid open. Tusk, accompanied by Nola, bounded into the room.

"Great! They told me we'd find you both here! We've been lookin' all over the place for you, kid—"

"Tusca! What's happened?" Maigrey took an eager step forward.

"Happened? Nothing, yet. That's what we wanted to talk about." Tusk stared at her, confused.

Nola grabbed hold of his hand, squeezed it tightly.

He looked down at her and smiled. "Nola and I've decided. We want to get married now. That's okay with you, isn't it, kid? Hell, we're not doing anything else at the moment."

Dion and Maigrey stared at him blankly.

"We decided we don't need anyone to perform the ceremony. I mean, it may not be real legal, but who knows what's legal these days? It's what we say and mean to each other that counts and we want the people we love best to share that with us and . . . well . . . give their blessing to it. So we thought you and General Dixter and the kid here . . ."

Tusk's voice dried up. Nola began to wilt.

"I mean . . . that's all right, isn't it?"

"Tusk," said Nola, edging close to him, "we interrupted something important. I think we'd better go—"

Maigrey recovered herself. "All right? It's wonderful. A wonderful idea. Everyone, every person in this entire ship, needs something to celebrate. A wedding would be perfect."

"Begging your pardon, your ladyship, but we wanted this to be . . . just our friends," Nola said, flushing.

"Of course. But afterward we'll have a party," said Dion enthusiastically. "The biggest party this ship's seen. We'll tell the entire fleet and the reporters. This will show Peter Robes what we think of his threats! Let's see, how long will it take us to get ready . . ."

"You'd better have the ceremony tonight," Maigrey said.

She hadn't meant to sound grim. Nola stared at her with wide eyes, her face grew downcast.

Tusk frowned. "Maybe we shouldn't—"

"We should." Maigrey was deliberately cheerful. "I'll speak to Admiral Aks and Captain Williams and make the arrangements. We can have the ceremony—" She started to say "here" but, glancing around, realized that Sagan's presence in the room was too pervasive, too powerful. Not at all conducive to a wedding.

"I thought maybe the hydroponic vegetable garden," Nola said shyly. "It's not exactly roses and orange blossoms, but it is green and light and airy. . . ."

"I dunno." Tusk shook his head. "I'm not sure I want to get married around a bunch of carrots and brussel sprouts."

Dion laughed. "It'll look great when we fix it up. And perfect background for the vids. No reporters at the ceremony, of course," he added, seeing Tusk frown again, "but afterward will be fine. I wonder how many bottles of champagne are on board? If you'll excuse me, my lady?"

"Yes, certainly, Your Majesty," Maigrey answered, trying not to sound too relieved at his going.

The three left; Tusk looking foolishly happy, Nola surrounded by a golden glow, Dion excited enough to be getting married himself. The double doors shut behind them, shut out their voices, leaving Maigrey alone.

Sagan's quarters were silent, dark, empty of everything except him. Maigrey walked over to the communications terminal and sat down at the console, prepared to astonish, confound, and undoubtedly highly irritate Captain Williams with demands for a wedding reception. She paused, however, and stared at her face in a steel panel opposite. Lifting her hand, her fingers traced, idly, gently, the scar on her cheek.

"And what about me?" she wondered. "Did I run away from home? Or did I come back one day to find the house empty, abandoned . . ."

Chapter ❈❁❈ *Four*

The words of his mouth were softer than butter, having war in his heart; his words were smoother than oil, and yet they be very swords.

Prayer Book, 1662, Psalms 55:22

Sagan and Brother Fideles, their bodies bent against the strong gusts that swept over the planet, struggled toward their goal. Sand blasted their flesh. Clouds of dust swirled up suddenly, half blinding them. The two kept their cowls pulled low over their faces, their hands hidden protectively within the sleeves of their long robes.

At times, they were forced to come to a complete halt; the wind pounding them as if it would blow them over. When they reached the dark, silent, and towering Abbey walls, they were chilled to the bone, breathing heavily from the exertion.

The Abbey of St. Francis was old, one of the first monasteries to be built by the Order. The forbidding location had been chosen purposefully. Here, in these harsh and barren surroundings, young men of eighteen years of age desiring to enter the priesthood were brought to study and meditate and to undergo rigorous testing. Here they learned to abjure all pleasures of the flesh, including those that most humans considered not pleasures but necessities: warmth, comfortable beds, good food, companionship.

The young aspirant slept in his robes on a wooden cot in an unheated cell with only one wool blanket, which he wove himself. His diet, on those days when he was not fasting, consisted of bread, baked in the Abbey, fruit and vegetables, grown in the Abbey, and water. Mornings were given to study, afternoons to physical labor, evenings to further study. He was called upon to cease his labors and come together with his brethren in the chapel to pray three times daily, again before going to bed, and he was roused from his sleep in the deep hours of the night to pray silently in his cell.

Idle talk was forbidden, except for a short relaxation period following the evening meal, lasting exactly fifteen minutes duration. At all other times, speech was permitted only to impart vital information or to respond to the questions of one of the elder brethren. Most communication came to be performed by hand signs.

Once a young man entered these walls, he was as effectively cut off from family and friends as if he—or they—had died. The abbot and the prior were the only two people permitted to have contact with the universe beyond the walls and this contact was almost exclusively confined to other abbeys and to the Order's headquarters, which were, prior to the Revolution, located on Minas Tares. (It is interesting, historically, in view of this restriction, to realize how much power the Order managed to exert on events happening throughout the galaxy.)

Upon completing his training, the young person was either accepted as a novitiate into the Order, in which case he took his vows, or he was rejected, in which case he was sent home. Once rejected, a young man or young woman (for the Order had its nunneries) could never again apply for admittance. Once accepted, a member of the Order, having been initiated into its secrets, could never leave.

To the Order's credit, very few who entered ever desired to quit. Any who had doubts were counseled. Those who were bitterly unhappy, and whom the counseling and the prayers of the community of faithful did not seem to help, simply and quietly disappeared. It was rumored that they were taken to some extraordinarily lovely place, where they were kept safe in pleasant surroundings for the rest of their lives.

A novitiate took vows of poverty, chastity, and obedience. He was not permitted to harm any living thing or to take a life, even in defense of his own. (The warrior-priests were an exception to this rule, being granted the right to kill to defend the Order or the innocent.) After an additional two years study, the novitiate was admitted to the priesthood and deemed ready to be sent out into the world to serve God and man, if that was his choice. He could also choose to remain within the monastery walls, become a monk, one who renounces and withdraws from the world.

Sagan and Brother Fideles stood in the shadow of the Abbey, protected from the wind, whose keening among the sharp-edged rocks was the only sound to reach their ears. The walls towered above them, thick, massive. Unlike other human habitations in hostile environments, no plastisteel dome enclosed the Abbey in a protective bubble. The Abbey's walls and towers were made of the rock of the planet and were solid, airtight. Each stone had been hand-carved to fit precisely with the adjacent stones so that not the tiniest crack or chink existed between them. A special "skin" had then been fused on the exterior, to protect it from the ravages of wind and weather. Inside the Abbey, life-support systems similar to those on board spacecraft produced an oxygen-rich atmosphere. The system was the only mechanical device permitted in the Abbey. Light came from candles, fire for the cooking stoves and to heat the infirmary (the only room in which heat was permitted) came from wood or coal.

"I should never have left," said Sagan softly. He laid his hand upon the solid walls, chill and unyielding.

A large cast-iron bell was mounted on the wall above a small door made of the same heavy iron. A rope hung from the bell. Brother Fideles pulled the rope, rang the bell three times. He paused, as long as a man might count ten heartbeats, then rang the bell three times again. He folded his hands back in his sleeves and waited.

"I was to have been my father's penance," Sagan continued, his gaze on the high, dark, windowless walls, "to give the fruit of his sin back to the Church."

"God willed it otherwise," said Brother Fideles.

Sounds could be heard from within the structure, as of a door opening and closing. A slit window made of one-way steelglass, set in the iron door, slid open. Sagan and the priest took care to stand where they were visible to the unseen scrutiny. The window's shutter slid shut. They heard again the door opening and closing. Then a faint hissing sound, air being pumped out of the room, the pressure inside reduced to match the pressure outside.

"Was it God's doing," Sagan said, shifting his gaze to the door, "or a perversion of His will? I fought against the decision that sent me from the monastery in which I'd been raised. But the king had discovered that a child of the Blood Royal was being reared in ignorance and isolation. He commanded that I be sent to the Academy, and strong as the Order was, it could not go against a royal decree. When I was eighteen, I was given the choice of returning to the Order or remaining in the world. I was ambitious, yearning for power, fame, fortune. I chose the world."

They heard a screech, then a grinding sound. The iron door began to open slowly, operated by hand.

"Yet," said Brother Fideles, "you wear the robes and perform the rites of a warrior-priest, a sect banned at the time by a royal decree."

It took several moments for the heavy door to open. It was used rarely, and the crude mechanism, comprised of chains and wheels, was stiff, occasionally creaking to a stop. The two men waited patiently, each picturing, in his mind, the monk who acted as porter, sweating at turning the large crank on the other side.

"You can imagine, then, that it was a well-kept secret," said Sagan, eyeing the young priest.

Brother Fideles's pale face flushed, he lowered his eyes. "Forgive me, my lord. I didn't mean—"

Sagan waved the apology aside. "The truth can be spoken now, I believe. You should know it anyway," he added in lower, grimmer tones. "It might save your life . . . or the lives of those whom I have given into your keeping."

Brother Fideles's complexion went from burning red to ghastly white. He bit his lip, said nothing. The door shuddered and jolted into movement, but instead of opening, it started to close, stopped, then lurched into action again, this time in the right direction.

"Each child of the Blood Royal must undergo a rite of initiation. The Lady Maigrey and I, being mind-linked, were told that we must take ours together. I was twenty-three at the time, she was sixteen. I was older than was customary, but I had come to my studies late in my childhood, and then we had to wait for Maigrey to attain the proper age before proceeding. We were told that we would undergo the rite here, on the planet of my birth. We assumed it would be in the cathedral.

"When we arrived here, we were met by members of the Order and taken, in secret, under the cover of darkness, to the Abbey. We were admitted inside, the Lady Maigrey being the only woman ever permitted to enter the Abbey's walls. In silence, told nothing, we were led to the altar. My father himself conducted the ritual. He spoke to us—the first time that he had spoken since he'd confessed his sin and taken upon himself the vow of silence. That was the only time that I ever heard his voice. My own father's voice."

The door had opened wide enough to permit entry. The two men stepped within, stood in a small air lock that was a tight fit for the Warlord's broad shoulders. Perhaps it was the cramped surroundings that caused Brother Fideles to rest his hand gently upon Sagan's arm, or perhaps it was the pain, not heard in the man's voice, but crying from within, that caused the young priest to offer silent comfort.

Sagan did not respond to the touch, he seemed lost in memory.

"My father had received a sign from God, he said, that against royal command, against precedent, against tradition, against the rules, I was to be taken into the Order without undergoing the formal training, and made a warrior-priest. My only vow was an oath of fealty to God. My father spoke a prophecy concerning the Lady Maigrey and I, and then my father stepped into the shadows around the altar and was gone. That was the last time I saw him."

The door shut, and sealed itself fast. The sound came of a pump going into action, then a slight hissing—air being forced into the chamber. They waited patiently until it was safe to remove the masks.

"Something is troubling you, Brother?" Sagan asked.

"My lord will forgive me—"

"Yes, yes," the Warlord said, suddenly irritable, perhaps not as calm as he seemed.

"I don't understand, my lord, how you could support a revolution that espoused atheism and the abolition of the Order to which you'd sworn loyalty?"

"You are mistaken, Brother. I had sworn my loyalty to God, not to the Order. I saw a monarchy corrupt and inept. I saw the civilized realms of the galaxy falling into disorder, war, chaos because our king was weak, his laws foolish and ineffectual. The Order itself became corrupted, its members openly broke their vows, began to acquire property and wealth, indulged carnal desires. I believed the Revolution to be God's will."

"Do you still?" asked Brother Fideles softly.

Sagan looked at him intently, eyes dark and shadowed by

the hood. "Yes, Brother. The Order, the universe itself, was cleansed with fire and with blood. It has risen again, pure, holy, sanctified in God's eyes. That is why we have a new king, born in fire and in blood. Do you understand, Brother?"

Fideles could not at first respond, he was overcome by awe and a sudden illuminating flash of insight into—it seemed to him—the mind of God Himself.

"I understand, my lord! For the first time, I truly understand."

"Congratulations, Brother," said Sagan ironically. "It's taken me eighteen years."

The seal on the air lock broke, the inner door opened. The Warlord and Brother Fideles removed their oxygen masks and entered the Abbey of St. Francis.

It was dark inside. The only light came from the stub of a beeswax candle inside a small lantern that stood on the floor, caused their own hooded shadows to loom over them. The monk who served as porter and who had operated the air lock had obviously carried the lantern to light his way, set it down on the floor during the performance of his task. The porter lifted the lantern and held it up, shining its light directly into the faces—and eyes—of the visitors.

"I am Brother Fideles," said the young priest, squinting against the bright glare. "This is Lord Derek Sagan. You've been expecting us."

The monk nodded, at least so it seemed by the slight motion of his hooded head. He kept the light shining in their faces a moment longer, apparently studying them—particularly Sagan—intently. The Warlord stood unmoving and unmoved, his expression impassive. Seeming satisfied, the porter lowered the lantern, bowed in silent greeting, and with a gesture of a white hand that looked ghostly in the candlelight, he invited them to follow him.

All seemed well. The welcome was similar to twenty other welcomes Brother Fideles had received on his return to the Abbey. But the priest felt uneasy. He tried to shake off the sensation, telling himself it was merely the effect of the Warlord's grim tales and dark forebodings.

Fideles glanced at Sagan as they walked silent-footed through the narrow stone corridors. The priest could not see the

Warlord's face; it was hidden in the shadows. But he saw the eyes, the lantern light reflected in them, saw them flick left and right, endeavoring to pierce the thick fabric of the darkness that parted in the light, only to fall more thickly around them when the light passed.

In times previous, when Brother Fideles had returned home—and this Abbey had become his home—the shadows had drawn him into their sweet incense-scented, protective warmth, gently urging him to shut his eyes to the glare of harsh lights in the world outside and, here, find rest. Now, the young priest saw the shadows as ominous, threatening, capable of hiding lurking terrors.

He decided to try to dispel these uncomfortable doubts. Gliding forward, he fell into step beside the porter.

"Brother Chang was gatekeeper when I was here last." Brother Fideles attempted to see the monk's face by the lantern light. The man kept his head lowered, his hood pulled forward, his eyes on the ground. All quite proper, yet Fideles found it disquieting.

"You have been gone a long time, Brother," observed the monk in a voice that was not familiar to Fideles. "Two years, by the Abbey's count, I believe."

That was true enough.

"Forgive me, but I am forced to admit that I do not remember you, Brother. I am ashamed, but I must ask you to refresh my memory and tell me your name."

"No forgiveness is required, Brother. You do not remember me because I was not here when you left. I arrived shortly after your departure. My name is Mikael."

Fideles bowed, a show of respect, but also a movement that provided him with an opportunity to peer upward, attempt to see the monk's face beneath the hood. The endeavor met with failure. Either by chance or by design, Brother Mikael turned his head to look down a shadowed corridor branching off from the one where they walked. He seemed to hesitate, as if trying to make up his mind, then continued walking.

Brother Mikael's moment of indecision had not been long. Fideles would have never noticed it if he had not been so extraordinarily sensitive to the monk's actions. The thought instantly came to Fideles's mind that this monk had, for a split second, become lost or disoriented. The hesitation would have been understandable in someone newly come to the Abbey. At this level and in the subterranean levels below ran an extensive and labyrinthine network of cellars and underground passages. Food was stored below ground in the cool depths. The heart of the life-support system was down here, with its massive array of duct work and pumps and electrical wiring. And in the catacombs were crypts and tombs for the dead. It was extremely easy to lose one's way. But Brother Mikael had been in the Abbey for two years. . . .

"Brother Chang was gatekeeper for a long time," said Fideles, trying hard to sound casual, as if he were making polite conversation to while away the tedium of their journey through to the Abbey proper. "I hope that he was not forced to relinquish his post from ill health?"

"Brother Chang has moved on to other duties," was Brother Mikael's laconic reply.

That was plausible, if not very likely. Brother Chang, a cheerful, jolly man, had been extremely fond of his position as gatekeeper. Although he was devoted to the Order, he missed the outside world and enjoyed even this small opportunity to catch glimpses of it. His beaming face put the new aspirants at their ease and gave a warm welcome to the occasional rare guest of the abbot's. Brother Chang would not have traded such loved duty for the position of abbot itself. Fideles would have liked to inquire further about the friendly Chang, but such curiosity could earn him a rebuke for indulging in idle gossip.

However, he could not be faulted for asking after the health of a brother.

"And what of Brother Nick?" asked Fideles ingenuously. "He was taken extremely ill, just prior to my departure. Something he ate, it was believed, affected him wrongly. I trust that he is quite recovered?"

"You are mistaken, Brother Fideles," said the soft voice of Brother Mikael. "There is no one by that name among us, nor," added the voice, the shadowed face turning toward Fideles, "was there anyone in this Abbey by that name when you left."

Fideles murmured something about dreaming it. Brother Mikael concurred that this must have been the case. Brother Mikael was not inclined to talk on his own and Brother Fideles's thoughts were in such turmoil and confusion that, though he could think of a thousand questions to ask, he could think of none that would not reveal his growing, dark suspicions.

He fell back, therefore, to walk beside the Warlord, tried to intimate, by a glance, that something was amiss.

Sagan refused to meet the priest's eye and, when Fideles would have said something, halted his words by the very slightest motion of his fingers, barely seen in the dim light, slipping out of the sleeves of his robes, then sliding back in again. The Warlord appeared to be rapt in his own thoughts, natural, considering the solemn and sorrowful purpose that brought him within these walls.

Fideles started to sigh, checked even the soft exhale of breath, fearful of its being overheard and taken for a sign of unhappiness and—if it would not have implied a lack of faith to admit to it—fear.

Brother Fideles and Sagan, led by the silent monk, left the lower part of the Abbey, entered the main portion. They walked past classrooms, unoccupied, their tall desks and high-backed chairs visible only for an instant, fine wood gleaming in the lantern's light. They passed through the Abbey's gardens, the only place in the building where sunlight was permitted. The sun had been a fiery red monster viewed from outside. Shining through a skylight in the ceiling far above, it appeared to have been chastised and tamed before being permitted to enter the monastery. Neat, orderly rows of green plants, splashed with the vibrant colors of their fruit, were ready for harvest. Fideles cast a sharp glance at the garden in passing, and bit his lip.

The priests, monks, and novitiates were returning from chapel. They filed out in reverent silence, hands clasped in the sleeves of their robes, heads covered, eyes cast down. Several bowed in greeting to Brother Fideles and the Warlord. No one spoke. The monk led his charges on.

They came to the *dortoir,* the dormitory, the Abbey's living quarters. Numerous small cells branched off from an unlit hallway. Walls and floor and ceiling were of stone, chill and dank. The monk stopped before a wooden door. Reaching into the pocket of his robes, he drew forth an iron key, inserted the key into an iron lock, and opened the door.

"Your room, Lord Sagan," he said. "I have placed Brother Fideles in the room next door."

"I want to see my father," said Sagan, the first words he'd spoken since they entered the Abbey.

"You will be taken to him shortly," returned Brother Mikael in his soft voice. "The abbot thought that after having lived so long among the infidels and evils of the world outside, you might like time to compose and cleanse your soul with prayer."

Sagan's face darkened. He seemed about to thrust the monk aside and go off on his own. Brother Fideles, standing slightly behind the monk, shifted his eyes to the door, made a slight motion with his head.

"A good thought, Brother Mikael," said the Warlord.

The cell was small, the three of them were cramped inside it and Brother Mikael was standing half outside, blocking the door. The bed—a mattress, thin and lumpy, albeit clean, that rested across wooden slats elevated on short legs—took up almost one third of the room's space. A wooden desk, with a chair, filled one corner. An altar, made of stone, stood against the wall opposite the bed.

Sagan sank down upon his knees before the altar, removed the scrip he carried from his belt, opened it, and withdrew the small silver bowl. He filled it with sacred oil from the altar, and lit it. The sweet smell of incense filled the room. The Warlord rested his elbows on the altar, folded his hands, and bowed his head.

Brother Mikael evidently approved of these proceedings. He started to respectfully withdraw.

"If you will come with me, Brother, I will take you to your cell," Mikael whispered, motioning to Fideles.

"Thank you, Brother," said Fideles. "That will not be necessary. Simply give me the key, that I may enter later."

Brother Mikael did not appear to approve of this. He stood in the doorway, the hooded head turning from Lord Sagan to Brother Fideles, as if the unseen eyes were carefully scrutinizing each. The fingers holding on to the iron key clenched.

"I would join my prayers with my lord's," Fideles added humbly. Going to the altar, he knelt down upon his knees next to Sagan.

"*Misere mei, Deus, secundum magnam misericordiam tuam.* Have mercy upon me, O God, according to Thy loving kindness.'"

Fideles's thinner, lighter tenor joined his lord's deep baritone in reciting the prayer. Brother Mikael stood in the doorway. It was an unspeakable offense to disturb a brother in his prayers. While the soul communed with God, only an emergency, a matter of life or death, could be allowed to interfere. Brother Mikael withdrew, closing the door behind him. Fideles heard the key turn in the lock.

The young priest discovered that he couldn't remember the next line to the prayer, a prayer he had recited since his first days in the Order.

"*'Et secundum multitudinem miserationum tuarum, dele iniquitatem meam,'*" said Sagan aloud. "'According unto the multitude of Thy tender mercies blot out my transgressions.' God forgive me," he intoned softly, then leaned close to Fideles, speaking barely above a whisper, his breath warm upon the young priest's cheek. "Since when do they lock doors in a *dortoir*?"

"They don't, my lord," returned Fideles, nervous and unhappy, talking too fast, trembling. "We've never had locks upon our doors. We have no need for them. And did you notice, my lord, that the locks are only on your door and mine? And there are other things, my lord—"

His voice started to rise. Sagan's strong hand closed over Fideles's arm, comforting, warning. The priest regained control of himself, ceased to tremble. The Warlord repeated loudly the prayer's third line.

"'*Amplius lava me ab iniquitate mea, et a peccato meo munda me*. Wash me thoroughly from mine iniquity, and cleanse me from my sin.'"

"God forgive me," Fideles murmured.

The Warlord motioned. Fideles rose to his feet, padded soft-footed to the door, and peered out a small iron grille. He looked long and hard, then, satisfied, he turned and shook his head.

Sagan nodded, gestured for the young man to return to his place at the altar. Fideles continued the prayer, the words returning to him under the Warlord's—or perhaps it was God's—calming influence. Sagan left the altar, moved quietly to the desk, and returned with a sheet of parchment paper, a crude ink pen and a stone jar of foul-smelling ink that brought a rush of memories back to Fideles.

Dipping the pen in the ink, Sagan wrote two words upon the paper.

Tell me.

Fideles, wondering what was going on, opened his mouth. The Warlord shook his head, laid his fingers upon the young priest's lips. Sagan's eyes glanced significantly about the room.

"You think someone might be listening?" Fideles mouthed, miserable, desperately unhappy.

The Warlord nodded. Fideles closed his eyes, asked for strength. When he felt able to continue, he opened his eyes, took the pen in hand firmly, and began to write, even as he prayed.

The garden was filled with weeds. The desks in the class-room were covered with dust.

Sagan shrugged his shoulders, implying such trivial matters could be explained. The two, meanwhile, continued to pray loudly, covering the sound of rustling paper, the scratching of the ink pen.

Fideles wrote swiftly, underlined with a firm, thick stroke.

My lord, there is a Brother Nick.

Satan interrogated the young priest with a look. Brother Fideles started to write, shook his head impatiently. They had come to the conclusion of the *Miserere*.

"Let us each offer silent thanks for our safe arrival, Brother," said the Warlord.

Fideles leaned close, breathed into Sagan's ear, "Brother Nick is a goat."

The Warlord looked considerably astonished, then frowned, reminding the young man with a stern glance that this was no time for levity.

"The brothers raise long-haired goats, my lord, for their milk and the wool. We've done so, since the Revolution, to raise money. And, since that time, the he-goat of the flock has always been called 'Brother Nick.'

"Oh, not officially, my lord," Fideles added hastily. "It was a joke, you see, among the younger brothers. The term 'Nick' used to be, I believe, a slang word for the devil and since the he-goat . . . well . . . I mean, we had to have little goats and that meant . . . You understand, my lord?" Fideles finished, unable to keep from blushing.

Sagan raised an eyebrow, one corner of his lips twitched. Fideles plunged ahead.

"It's a tradition, my lord. Once the abbot himself forgot and made a reference to 'Brother Nick' during a sermon, which caused Brother Chang to laugh aloud in chapel. Realizing what he'd done, the abbot couldn't help but laugh, too, although afterward he assigned a week's penance to himself and to Brother Chang to make up for it.'

Fideles paused for breath. It was a strain to whisper. His chest felt tight, he seemed not to be able to draw enough air into his lungs.

"Don't you understand, my lord?" he said when he could continue. "Even the newest aspirant would know about 'Brother Nick.' And Brother Mikael claimed to have been here two years and has never heard of him."

Fideles gazed at the Warlord anxiously. He found himself hoping Sagan would laugh, shrug it off, as he had shrugged off the other bits of evidence that all was not well within the Abbey walls. The Warlord's face was dark, his expression grim and serious.

"God help us!" Fideles gasped aloud, leaning his elbows on the altar and letting his head sink despairingly into his hands.

"The Lord helps those who help themselves," Sagan reminded him softly. The Warlord placed a firm, steadying hand on the young priest's shoulder. His voice sank again to a whisper. "You showed courage under fire, Brother."

"That was different," the young priest answered bitterly. "Then the danger was real and obvious. But this—vague fears, terrible mysteries, and all in the peace and safety of my home . . ." Tears choked his throat.

"Fear of the unknown is always the most difficult to overcome," said the Warlord. "But you can, Brother. I need you. And so does God."

"Yes, my lord," said Fideles faintly, drawing a deep breath. Swiftly, he brushed his hand across his eyes. "What must I do?"

The Warlord lifted the pen, wrote upon the paper.

When they come to take me to my father, make some excuse to separate yourself from me. Investigate. Find out what is going on.

Sagan looked at the young man intently, to see if he understood, or perhaps to measure his courage. Fideles nodded, lips pressed tightly together, jaw held firm.

The Warlord nodded, apparently satisfied. Lifting the paper, he held it to the flame, laid the burning paper upon the altar and watched the fire consume it to ashes. He stirred the ashes with his fingers, scattered them with a breath. Carefully, he wiped the ink pen clean with the hem of his black robe, replaced pen and ink upon the desk.

··◁■ ■▷··

When the key rattled in the iron lock, Brother Mikael entered the room to find the Warlord and the young priest on their knees, absorbed in prayer. At first, neither seemed to notice the monk's presence.

"Lord Sagan," said Brother Mikael, "your father will see you now."

The Warlord remained kneeling a moment longer. Fideles, glancing at him, was astonished at the man's sudden pallor and ghastly look. Sweat beaded on Sagan's upper lip, his skin was livid beneath its tan, the eyes sunken and darkly shadowed. His breath came quick and fast, his skin burned to the touch. When he started to try to stand, his step faltered. Fideles, rising at the same time, caught and steadied him.

"My lord," said the priest in a low voice, "you are not well. Perhaps I should—"

Sagan said nothing, cast him one sharp, commanding look, and removed his arm from the priest's grasp.

Fideles understood, kept quiet. He took a step forward, after the Warlord. Brother Mikael, who had remained standing aside respectfully to let Sagan out the door, turned his body to block the exit when Fideles approached.

"I had assumed, Brother, that you would want to wait for Lord Sagan's return here, in his cell," said the monk.

"Thank you for your thoughtfulness, Brother," said Fideles, "but I have taken a vow to pray all night, on my knees before the alter of God in the chapel, to ask for salvation for my lord's father's soul."

"May your prayers be answered," said Brother Mikael reverently, bowing his head and standing aside to allow Fideles to pass him. "You remember the way to the chapel, Brother?"

"Yes, certainly," snapped Fideles. Brother Mikael's sudden meek acquiescence was disconcerting. "Thank you, Brother, for your concern," the priest added in gentler tones, "but I lived here for many years. I am not likely to ever forget my way."

Brother Mikael's hooded head nodded. "Then I will offer myself as escort to Lord Sagan."

The two of them left, walking down the hall in the light of Brother Mikael's lantern. Fideles remained alone in the room. He waited until his lord and the monk had passed beyond his sight, then he took the candle from the desk, lit it at the flickering, perfumed flame of the lamp upon the altar.

"'Yea, though I walk through the valley of the shadow of death,'" he said to himself quietly, "'I will fear no evil; for thou art with me.' Be with my lord, as well," he prayed, and walked into the dark and empty hall.

Chapter ···❈❍❈··· Five

In the midst of life we are in death.
Prayer Book, 1662, Burial of the Dead

The monk, Brother Mikael, walked the dark corridors of the Abbey, his lantern held steady to light the way before him. Sagan followed after, his head bowed, his hood pulled low over his face. Neither said a word. The Warlord did not attempt to engage the monk in snare-laden conversation; he did not try to see past the shadows hiding the monk's face.

If this Brother Mikael were truly one of Abdiel's minions, one of the mind-dead, he would be easily recognized by his expressionless face, his empty, vacant stare. Sagan could have, with one swift movement, yanked the hood from off the monk's head, discovered the truth. The Warlord's hands, hidden within his sleeves, were clasped together in prayer. He already knew the truth. He knew he was not following a monk. Derek Sagan was following God.

The narrow hallways they traversed were empty. When they passed open areas, such as the candle-lit, incense-warm chapel, other members of the Order could be seen, moving silently about their business. The hooded heads almost always turned in their direction, unseen eyes watched their slow and solemn progress.

The monk led the way past a herbarium; the Warlord could tell the nature of the room by its smell of moist soil and growing, living things. He caught a glimpse, in the lantern's light, of bunches of dried stalks and leaves hanging in neat rows from the rafters, of flasks carefully and neatly labeled, of a mortar and pestle on a worktable.

We will be near the infirmary, he thought, remembering the layout of the monastery where he had spent the first twelve years of his life. His father would be in the infirmary, where

151

the sick and injured were taken to mend, where the dying were taken to ease their last hours.

A tremor of dread and excitement shook the Warlord's frame, a burning as of a fever swept over his body, his stomach clenched. Pain shot through his hands, clasped together too tightly. Blood pulsed and throbbed in his head, obscuring his vision.

But the monk walked past the infirmary without pausing.

The Warlord went cold, suddenly, as in battle, when the initial adrenal rush wanes and you are left, cold and empty, to simply do a job. He became aware of his surroundings, saw that they were in a cul-de-sac; the hallway ended, there was no passage out. A door, marked with the inscription, *Requiem aeternam*, stood at the end.

Sagan glanced back at the infirmary. A coal fire lit the room, to keep those within comfortably warm. But no one lay in the beds, no invalids sat upright in wheeled chairs, no herbalist fussed over his patients. The monk reached the door. Stretching out his hand, he pushed it open and stood aside humbly, indicating that the Warlord was to enter.

Sagan drew back. He had no need to ask where he was. The inscription, the smell of dank stone, and the flow of chill air that brushed his cheek told him.

"Why have you brought me here?" he asked sternly. "Is my father dead, then? Why didn't you tell me?"

Brother Mikael seemed disinclined to answer. He held the lantern high, lighting the way into the room, indicating, with an almost imperceptible nod, that Sagan was to enter. When it became clear, however, that the Warlord would not stir a step, the monk responded.

"Your father lives."

"Then take me to him!" Sagan demanded.

"I have," Brother Mikael answered softly.

"This is the mortuary!" the Warlord stated, endeavoring to control his rising anger.

"It was his wish," said Brother Mikael.

Sagan stared at the monk, who stood impassive in the doorway, body pressed against it to leave room for the Warlord to go past him. Abruptly, Sagan walked by, entered the chamber.

The mortuary was a large, unheated, windowless room made completely of stone. A grooved channel, cut into the floor, carried away the water used to wash the bodies of the dead, prepare them for the final rest. In the center of the room stood a stone bier, flanked by four wrought-iron candle holders, as tall as the height of a man, supporting thick, round beeswax candles. By the soft candlelight, Sagan saw upon the bier not a corpse, but the body of a living man.

Derek Sagan had, in his time, boarded enemy ships, knowing he was outnumbered ten to one, aware that unless he was quick and cunning, certain death awaited him. He'd done so confidently, boldly, without fear. But he could not now take another step. He was suddenly weak and frightened as a child, lost and alone in the darkness. He looked at the robed figure lying on the bier, its body covered with a thin, worn blanket, and the candle flames grew large in his swimming vision, their fire threatening to engulf him. A faintness seized him, he came near sinking to his knees.

"Deus miserere!" he gasped, and at the sound, the head upon the bier turned, the eyes looked at him.

His father had always seemed old to Sagan, though the priest had been relatively young when he had broken his vows and been forced to reap the bitter fruit of his sin. Derek's earliest memories were of a stern and implacable face, deeply lined with the ravages of shame and guilt and the self-inflicted pain and privation that was the anguished soul's only ease. Before the young child knew this man, called only the Dark Monk, to be his father, Derek sensed a bond between them. It was a terrible bond, never mentioned, never alluded to by anyone, but visible in the burning eyes of the Dark Monk whenever their tormented gaze rested on the child.

When Derek was ten, and it was believed the precocious child could understand, the abbot took the boy into his study one day and, in a few blunt words, explained to Derek his father's sin, his father's chosen penance—a vow of eternal silence—and his father's wish that Derek be raised within the Order's dark, thick, impenetrable walls. A king's command had altered that, but it could not alter the fact that Derek knew, from that moment on, that life had been granted him only at the cost of his father's disgrace and eternal suffering.

During Derek's first twelve years, spent daily in his father's company, the Dark Monk said no word to his child. At the end of those twelve years, when Derek left to enter the world, his father did not come to bid him good-bye.

But now the son had come to bid good-bye to the father.

God heard Sagan's prayer, granted him the strength to move forward. He came to stand beside the bier, near his father. Sickness and old age had smoothed out and softened the stern, grim harshness of the features. Lines of torment that had been carved deeply into the cheeks were now blurred by the wasting away of the flesh. The lips, the stern guardians of the vow, once pressed together so firmly, were flaccid and shriveled. The man's body, formerly strong and muscular and unbent beneath its self-imposed burden of pain, was thin and skeletal and shook beneath the blanket and the too-large brown robes. Derek might not have recognized his father except for the eyes. Their gaze he knew. Their gaze he remembered.

He slowly folded back the cowl from his head.

The eyes of the dying man watched every move, searched the face, absorbed it, and then the head rolled back upon its hard, cold pillow. The eyes closed, not in peace, it seemed, but in bitter despair.

"He is very near the end," came a voice from out of the shadows.

Sagan was not surprised to hear the voice. He realized, when it spoke he'd been expecting it.

The candlelight shone upon a bulbous head, tottering precariously on a neck that was far too slender to support it, and caused the head to seem to spring suddenly from the darkness, like a demon conjured from the shadows. The hairless head was grotesquely disfigured, covered by unsightly patches of decayed skin, several smallish lumps. Two large nodules protruded from the base of the neck.

The man was old, every bit as old as the dying man lying on the bier, and seemed in not much better health, for though wrapped in thick, heavy robes, he shook and shivered. The voice, however, was strong, if thin, and indicative of an indomitable will.

"Abdiel," said Sagan, an acknowledgment rather than an exclamation.

"A pleasure, my lord, to see you again after so many years. I am, however, rather disappointed. You're not surprised to see me. It would almost appear that you were expecting me. I trust Mikael and the others in the cast have not misplaced their roles? Ah, no. I begin to understand. The astute Brother

Fideles could not be fooled. Where is young 'Faithful'? Out investigating, perhaps? You won't tell me? No matter. He will come to me . . . or should I say 'to you,' my lord."

"I'm the one you want. Let the priest go."

"Oh, I intend to, my dear. He'll leave here quite unharmed. I want my message delivered safely. And you've arranged for his departure with your usual efficiency, Sagan; left me nothing to do except to have a little talk with him."

The Warlord did not appear to hear Abdiel, nor care about the ominous implication of the mind-seizer's words. He had, after a first, brief, and almost uninterested glance at the old man, turned his gaze back to his father.

"Now that you have me, remove my father to the infirmary, where he may spend his last hours in peace."

Abdiel appeared faintly insulted. "Really, Derek, I am not such a monster as you suppose. Admittedly I used your father to bait my trap—rather cunning of me, you must admit—but I would never needlessly torment a dying man.

"Believe me, I would myself have been far more comfortable waiting your arrival in a warm room instead of this dank tomb. Mikael told you the truth about this, if very little else.

"We found the Dark Monk here in the mortuary upon our arrival. Apparently, when he discovered his death was imminent, he asked that his living body be brought here and laid upon this bed where customarily only the corpse lies. I deemed it best not to move him, for fear he might not survive the transfer. I knew, you see, that you would not come unless you believed in your heart that he lived. It became critical, therefore, for me to keep him alive. I assure you, Derek, that *his own son* could not have taken better care of him."

Abdiel chuckled at his little joke.

Sagan ignored the mind-seizer. The Warlord knelt beside the dying man's bier, clasped the wasted hand.

"My father, will you die without granting me your final blessing? Do you hate me that much?"

The head turned, the eyes opened. The mouth moved, lips forming words the voice had long ago forgotten, or had perhaps never known, how to speak.

"Hate . . . you? My son. My son . . ."

The eyes closed in wrenching anguish. The hand holding fast to Sagan's tightened, expending the frail body's last energies. Two tears, squeezed from beneath the waxen eyelids, rolled down the gaunt cheeks. The lips moved, stirred perhaps by the last breath. Perhaps forming a last word.

"Forgive . . ."

The hand slowly relaxed its grip. The folds of the blanket across the chest rose and fell no more. Sagan remained kneeling in reverent silence, the thin hand pressed to his breast. Then, rising slowly to his feet, the Warlord kissed his father's hand, placed it on the sunken chest.

"'*Sanctus, Sanctus, Sanctus Dominus, Deus Sabaoth. Pleni sunt caeli et terra gloria tua.* Holy, Holy, Holy, Lord God of Hosts,'" Sagan chanted, moving with solemn mien, bowed head, and slow step around the head of the bier.

Glancing swiftly from beneath reverently lowered eyelids, he saw Abdiel, huddled within the thick robes, shivering, in the shadows, watching with morbid interest. He stood alone. Mikael, guarding the door, could never hope to move fast enough to prevent his master's death at Sagan's hands. The old man's scrawny neck in that bone-crushing grip, a swift twist, a snap. . . .

The Warlord was near the mind-seizer now. Only a few steps separated them. Sagan started to lift the other flaccid hand that lay by the corpse's side, to compose the limbs for their final rest. His voice rose, "'Heaven and earth are full of Thy glory . . .'"

The Warlord turned suddenly, swiftly, made a lunge for Abdiel. He was within arm's length of squeezing the life from the mind-seizer when a glittering object rose up before Sagan's eyes.

His brain reacted instinctively, analyzing the danger, halting his body's forward movement. He jerked backward, lost his balance, fell painfully on one knee. Breathing heavily, he remained crouched on the stone floor at Abdiel's feet, a prey to a terror he hadn't imagined it possible he could know, his eyes staring in disbelief at the object in the mind-seizer's hand.

"I knew nothing else would stop you, Derek." Abdiel smiled unpleasantly. He twisted and twirled the object in his hand, caused its crystal and gold to shine in the light. "Certainly not the threat of death. What would death matter to you, if you could save the life of your precious king? For you know, don't you, my lord, that Dion is my only object. But this . . . the serpent's tooth. . . . You're afraid, aren't you, Derek? I don't need to probe your mind to find out the truth. I see your fear."

The object the mind-seizer held appeared innocuous, some type of elaborate and ceremonial weapon resembling a scythe. Its handle was made of gold and styled to resemble the scaled head and upper body of a striking snake. From the snake's mouth protruded a blade made of gleaming crystal.

The blade gave the weapon its name: serpent's tooth. Shaped like a snake's fang, the clear crystal was actually a hollow vial that had been honed to a needle-sharp point. Such a fragile instrument could not penetrate armor. It seemed too delicate to penetrate flesh. But Derek Sagan, staring at the weapon in the old man's shaking, palsied hand, made no move against him.

The blade didn't need to penetrate. One scratch across the skin, barely breaking the surface, was enough. The poison in the crystal vial entered the body swiftly, and, once within, there was no antidote.

"Every man has his breaking point, even you, Derek Sagan." Abdiel began to withdraw from the room, gliding backward, keeping the serpent's tooth between himself and the Warlord.

The precaution seemed needless. Sagan remained on his knees, head lowered, shoulders hunched. Abdiel never took his gaze from the Warlord. Reaching the door, speaking to Mikael, the mind-seizer still kept watch on his victim.

"Give the signal," Abdiel commanded.

Mikael nodded, shoved open the door. Twenty of the mind-dead stood in the corridor. Robed in brown, disguised as monks, each held a scourge in his hand. One by one, they began to file into the mortuary, ranged themselves around the walls.

"I want him beaten, injured, broken, but not dead. He has information in his head that I need."

Mikael glanced at the huddled figure of the Warlord. "You have defeated him, master. A great victory."

"You think so, my dear? No, Sagan is merely in shock. Soon he will recover his wits, he will start to think, to plot, to plan and figure a way to try to defeat me. Look, Mikael. Look how, even now, he begins to shake off his horror.

"Look at him raise his head, see the gleam in his eyes. If I joined with him now, even under the threat of this"—Abdiel gestured with the serpent's tooth—"his mind would be strong enough to resist me. Pain and suffering and the despair of knowing himself helpless, a prisoner, will soften him up."

"Yes, master."

Mikael made a sign with his hand. The mind-dead began to move forward, wielding the scourges. Small whips, they were made of thirteen strands of leather soaked in brine. Each stroke of the lash inflicted a vicious cut in the flesh; the salt, entering the wound, stung and burned. At the end of each of the thirteen strips dangled a sharpened piece of metal, like a nail, meant to puncture, rip, and tear.

Sagan, seeing them advancing, rose to his feet to meet them, his bare fists—his only weapon—clenched.

"I will be in my room, where it is warm," said Abdiel. "Come and get me when it is over."

Mikael nodded silently.

"What of that young priest?" the mind-seizer added, as an afterthought.

"He has, for the moment, disappeared, master. I have sent teams to search for him. Shall he be killed or apprehended and brought to you?"

"Neither, my dear. Keep an eye on him. No fear. He will come to find his lord. After all, he is not called 'faithful' for nothing."

Abdiel left. The door to the mortuary shut behind him.

The key turned in the lock.

Chapter ·❦· Six

The snares of death compassed me round about: and the pains of hell gat hold upon me.

Prayer Book, 1662, Psalms 116:3

Brother Fideles watched from the hallway until Lord Sagan and the monk had vanished into the shadows.

Fideles's first thought was to follow them, ascertain where they were going. Accordingly, he hastened along behind until he once more caught sight of the tall figure of Sagan, towering over the shorter monk. Fideles slowed his pace, keeping to the shadows, his slippered feet making no more noise than a whisper over the stone floors. He rounded a corner. Three monks emerged unexpectedly from a doorway. Fideles plowed headlong into the group.

"I beg your pardon, Brothers," gasped Fideles, struggling to disentangle himself from a mass of long sleeves, tripping skirts.

The brethren murmured apologies and endeavored to move out of his way, but when he moved to the left, the three brethren moved to the left. When Fideles sought to circumvent them to the right, they had shifted themselves in that direction.

Finally, he bore desperately through the middle of the group, brushed against one of the monks, inadvertently jostled him, knocking the man's hood awry. Light from the priest's candle shone full upon the monk's face. Fideles stared, gasped.

The monk's eyes were the vacant, expressionless eyes of a dead man.

Hearing that shocked intake of breath, the monk swiftly pulled the hood over his head. Fideles endeavored to get a second look at the strange eyes in the shadows of the hood, but the monks had, by this time, hastened on.

Did I see it? he wondered. Or was it a trick of the light? No living man has eyes like that.

Fideles couldn't answer the question to his own satisfaction and was further upset and disappointed to discover that, during the confusion, he had lost sight of his lord and the strange Brother Mikael.

Fideles spent a few moments in fruitless search, then, remembering that he had told Brother Mikael he was going to chapel, thought perhaps he had better do so. If anyone was spying on him, the move would hopefully allay their suspicions. And the young priest felt truly in need of the sanctity and reassurance of God's presence.

He hurried through the monastery, keeping a sharp lookout for his lord, or perhaps that same strange monk. But he saw none of the brethren. An odd circumstance, considering the time of day. He had his lord's command to investigate, but he didn't know where to begin. He considered going to the abbot with his doubts and questions, decided he would do that only after he had contained his soul with prayer. The young priest reached the cathedral, entered it thankfully.

The large nave, built in the style of ancient cathedrals on old Earth, was empty, following the evening service. Fideles made his obeisance to God, slipped among the wooden pews, and knelt to pray. All was quiet around him, the air sweetly scented with the smell of incense and hundreds of flickering votive candles. But Fideles's prayers halted on his lips.

He was ill at ease, trembled with a vague fear. The cathedral was no longer home to him, its sanctity had been defiled, its peace shattered. He lifted his head, glanced around for some token, some sign to confirm his instinctive impression, but everything was in order. Yet, like a child who can sense upon entering a house that his parent is angry, Fideles felt the awful immensity of God's wrath crackle in the air.

He heard a sound, glanced behind him. Three monks, perhaps those who had blocked his way earlier, had entered the back of the cathedral. Fideles knew, suddenly, that he didn't want that monk with the dead eyes to find him. He blew out the candle he held in his hand, dropped it to the floor.

"What can I do?" he begged.

His answer was a flash of light, seen from the corner of his eye. The flash was no more, actually, than the flaring up of a votive candle, before the flame guttered, drowned in the hot wax. But an idea came to Fideles's mind. He glanced about to see if the monks were watching him.

The light was dim, however, and if they noticed him at all, they would see only his vague and shadowy outline. The monks could be in here for some entirely innocent reason, yet Fideles felt threatened. He didn't have much time. He watched them, saw them drawing aside the curtains of the confessionals, peering inside.

Fideles rose to his feet, glided down the central aisle, arrived at the crossing, turned to his left, and entered the transept. He saw, out of the corner of his eye, the monks catch a glimpse of him. They left off their search of the confessionals, started in his direction.

The young priest hastened to the back of the transept, moving toward a large and ornate marble relief, depicting a scene from the Final Judgment. The relief completely covered one portion of wall from ceiling to floor. Passing between banks of votive candles that flanked the carving, Fideles grabbed a candle with one hand. He held the light to the wall, found what he sought, and thrust his index and middle fingers into the hollow eyes of a tongue-lolling demon about to drag a sinful man down into a marble hell.

A door, artfully concealed by the writhing figures of the damned, shot open on oiled hinges. Fideles darted into the darkness beyond, leaned his body against the door, shut it fast, and stood against it, trying to catch his breath, endeavoring to calm his frantically beating heart.

Outside, he heard a scraping and scrabbling sound, hands attempting to find a way within. He could imagine the monks' frustration. It would appear to them, as it appeared to those watching the miracle play every year, as if Fideles had walked through the wall. During the miracle play, the brother chosen to depict the Evil One would emerge from this same trapdoor, to be driven back by the prayers of those portraying the virtues.

"*'Que es, aut unde venis? Tu amplexata es me, et ego foras eduxi te. Sed nunc in reversione tua confundis me—ego autem pugna mea deciam te!'*"

"'Who are you? Where are you coming from? You were in my embrace, I let you out. Yet now you are going back, defying me—but I shall fight you and bring you down!'" the Evil One cried as he chased his prey.

Fideles could imagine those outside the wall, muttering exactly the same threats. Wild laughter surged up in his throat. The young priest, shocked at himself and fearing he was growing hysterical, choked it back. He wasn't out of danger. The monks might accidentally stumble upon the key that opened the hidden door. The fact that they didn't know about the secret of the demon's eyes, known to everyone in the Abbey, proved to Fideles what he had long suspected. They weren't really monks at all.

Holding his votive candle to light his way, the priest descended a spiral staircase carved into the wall. The stairs didn't take him far, leading only to a small room below the nave where the actors in the miracle play dressed for the roles and waited for their cues. But outside the room was a hallway and another door and other stairs that would lead him to the subterranean depths below the Abbey walls.

Fideles ran without any clear idea where he was going, the only thought in his mind to escape those terrifying monks. He descended deeper and deeper. The stairs came to an end. Stepping onto a smooth, dry stone floor, he raised his light. The soft candle's flame reflected off grayish-white marble. The eyes of stone angels stared into his, seeming to offer him the peace of those whose rest they guarded. He was in the mausoleum.

A pain in his side hampered his breathing. Fideles, feeling himself safe, rested the votive candle upon one of the sarcophagi and was about to sit down on the bottom step to rest when he heard a noise.

The burial chamber was actually a long and narrow cave, carved in the rock. Its center aisle was flanked by the marble coffins of dead abbots and priors, whose carven images graced the lids. Farther back stood the humbler wooden coffins of the lower-ranking monks and priests. The noise had come from the back.

Fideles, holding his breath, listened for it above the pounding of his heart.

He heard nothing, could see nobody.

"Rats," he told himself, but at the same time, he picked up the votive candle and walked forward, eyes searching the shadows.

What drove him on, he could never afterward explain, except perhaps the reassuring thought that whatever had made the sound, be it man or animal, was apparently trying to hide from him. One of the threatening monks wouldn't be likely to do that.

Fideles wasn't prepared to find anything, however, and when the candle's light illuminated the pale face, staring up into his from out of the shadows, the young priest very nearly dropped his candle. He started backward, then bent forward, peering into the face intently. He was vastly relieved to see that the man's black and liquid eyes were filled with terror, very much alive. And Fideles thought he recognized them.

"Brother Miguel?" Fideles held the candlelight closer. "Is that you? Have I found someone I know at last?"

The terror in the eyes slowly faded, replaced by astonishment, disbelief.

"Fideles?" he whispered. "Is it truly you? Not one of . . . them? Ah, it *is* you! It *is* you! Thank the Creator!"

The monk crawled forward from his hiding place, clasped Fideles's hand, and fell upon it, weeping. The priest set the candle down, clasped the monk around the shoulders, and held him tightly, nearly weeping with joy and relief himself.

"But, tell me, Brother," Fideles said when it seemed that Miguel had recovered his composure and could speak, "what is going on? What dreadful thing has happened?"

"Tell me first if it is safe? You are here. Does that mean that they are gone?" Miguel was shivering, not so much with cold as a reaction to his fear.

"I don't think so. But I don't know who you mean or what you are talking about. If you mean a monk with very strange eyes . . ."

"Eyes of the dead?" whispered Brother Miguel.

Fideles nodded.

"They are still here, then." The eager, hopeful look disappeared from Miguel's face. He sank back onto the floor, leaned against the coffin.

"At least I will die on holy ground," he said, casting an almost affectionate look at the rows of tombs stretching on into the darkness. "I will die in peace, not like the others . . ." He buried his head in his hands and sobbed like a frightened child.

Fideles gazed at the wretched man, torn between pity and the desperate need to discover what was going on and, if possible, warn his lord.

"Miguel," Fideles said, deliberately making his voice stern, "I am not alone. Someone is with me, someone who may be in terrible danger. Remember that you are in God's hands, Brother. Have you lost your faith? Such behavior is sinful."

"Lost my faith!" Miguel lifted a ghastly, tear-streaked face. "I didn't lose it! It was murdered, butchered, destroyed! All of them. All of them. . . ."

"What?" Fideles knelt down beside the man, took hold of him, forced him to look at him. "What are you saying, Brother? Everyone? . . . They're not . . ." He couldn't speak the word.

"Dead? Yes, everyone. *He* came for me. The bloody knife in his hands, fingers clotted with blood, his arms red . . . to the elbow."

"Who? Who came for you?" Fideles was on his feet. What was the name of the man Sagan had told him about? He couldn't remember. One of the angels of God. . . .

"Prior Gustav!" Miguel could barely speak the name, he shuddered all over at the sound.

Fideles, stunned, sank back down, eyed the young monk warily. He's insane. He's a raving lunatic. "Brother," Fideles said aloud, "you must be mistaken. Prior Gustav is the most gentle man who walks the ground." He reached out, soothed back the black hair from Miguel's fevered face. "You don't know what you are saying . . ."

"You think I'm mad. Madness. That's what drove them to it, you see, Brother. Madness. The madness of the serpent's tooth."

Should I stay here? Fideles pondered, growing increasingly nervous and fearful for his lord's safety. Or should I return and tell my lord what I've discovered? But how can I leave this poor brother of mine here alone in this condition?

"Abdiel," Miguel said.

"What?" Fideles jumped. "What did you say?"

"He calls himself Abdiel. He came to us one night, an old man, frail and bent and sickly. Oh, God!" Miguel groaned. "He pretended to be one of the Order. He had survived the Revolution, he said, had been persecuted and driven from his homeland. He wandered far, searching always for others of the brotherhood, for he knew in his heart we lived. Now, he had found us. He wanted only to end his life among us. We took him in. God help us. We took him in."

These weren't the ravings of a madman. Fideles gazed intently at Miguel. The man was haggard, suffering from the cold and starvation, and frightened half to death. But he wasn't insane.

"Tell me, Brother. I'm listening." Fideles put his hand upon the monk's trembling arm.

"I work in the infirmary now, Brother. That night, the prior came into the herbarium, where I was preparing a poultice for one of the patients. He had a scratch on his arm, asked for some cobweb to stop the bleeding. The scratch wasn't deep and it appeared clean. He wasn't in pain. He laughed about it, in fact. Said that Abdiel had shown him a type of curious weapon he'd picked up on his travels. A serpent's tooth, it was called. Abdiel had, with his palsied hand, accidentally inflicted this scratch on our prior."

Miguel paused, licked dry lips. His voice had grown dry and husky. "Water."

Fideles glanced about.

The monk smiled wanly, pointed to a shadowed corner. "Back there. A trickle leaking from one of the condenser coils. It's all that's kept me alive."

A hollowed-out sliver of marble—part of an angel's wing— served as a cup. Fideles gleaned what water he could from the small stream running down the wall, returned, and gave it to Miguel. The brother drank, continued his story.

"That night Prior Gustav returned to the infirmary and . . . and killed the brother who was on night duty. Then he moved to the patients. The first few, he knifed while they lay sleeping in their beds. One of the other brothers awoke, saw what was happening, and cried out. I was sleeping on a cot in the herbarium. A potion of mine had to be stirred at frequent intervals. The frightful yell woke me. I ran to see what was going on. It was . . . like a terrible dream. I haven't slept since that night for fear I should see it all again!"

Fideles put his arm around his brother, held the shivering body.

"What happened then?" the priest asked. "Forgive me for pressing you, Brother, but I know now that Lord Sagan is in danger and I must warn him. . . ."

"Danger. Sagan?" Miguel looked up. "Yes, a trap. That's what it is. A trap."

"For my lord?" Fideles stared at the man. "Tell me, Brother. Be swift!"

"We managed to . . . restrain Prior Gustav. The look on his face was . . . indescribable, more horrible, even, then the dreadful crimes he'd committed. He knew, you see, what terrible things he was doing! One moment, he would beg us to end his life, end the torture. The next, he was swearing at us, using the foulest language, and trying to break free of his bonds—"

"Brother, please!" Fideles begged. "What does this have to do with my lord?"

"Abdiel came to us that terrible night. He told us, then, who and what he was—a member of the Order of Dark Lightning. He showed us the weapon known as the 'serpent's tooth.' It's nothing more than a crystal scythe, containing a poison—a dreadful poison that does not kill, but perverts the mind, drives the victim to commit the most heinous crimes, to murder, torture, dismember, cannibalize. . . . And what is most terrible—half the mind remains sane. Half the mind knows what frightful deeds the other half is committing, but is powerless to stop it!"

"Abdiel led forth our abbot, showed us the serpent's tooth, and said that if we did not do his bidding, our abbot would be the next to suffer the same living hell as poor mad Prior Gustav. What could we do, Fideles?"

"Pray to God."

"We prayed." Miguel sounded bitter. "You see how our prayers were answered. Why didn't He listen, Brother?" The monk clutched at Fideles. "Why did He destroy us, who lived only to serve Him?"

"I don't know. I only know we must have faith. You did this Abdiel's bidding?"

"His disciples, those he calls mind-dead, entered the Abbey. We clothed them and taught them our routine. God forgive us, we taught them our prayers. All the time, we were certain that God would save us. And then came the night, the dinner . . ." Miguel swallowed. Sweat beaded his face. "I—I didn't eat with the others. I was fasting . . . praying for the souls of those who had died by violence. But the rest, all the rest . . ."

"Poisoned," guessed Fideles.

"They were dead within hours," said the monk in dull

despair. "I tried, but there was nothing I could do for them. And then the mind-dead came for me. Their eyes . . ." He shuddered. "I don't remember how I got down here. I've hidden here since, terrified they would find me. When I saw you, I was certain it was them. I . . . I was almost thankful. Part of me wanted to hide, but another wanted to rush into their arms . . ."

"I have to go, now." Brother Fideles stood up. "It may be too late, but I must try to save my lord."

"Impossible!" cried Miguel, endeavoring to hang on to him, hold him back. "You will die with him."

"If that is all I can do, then I will do that. Hold fast to your faith, Brother. God has not abandoned us, though we do not understand His purpose. He has spared you for a reason, you may be sure. Return to your hiding place and pray to Him, pray for my lord, pray for me."

"I will," said Brother Miguel, his voice sounding stronger. He stretched out his hand. *"Dominicus tecum*. God be with you."

Fideles took the hand. *"Et cum spiritu tuo*. And His spirit with you."

Retrieving the candle, Brother Fideles waited until he saw Brother Miguel safely hidden within the shadows, protected by the dead. Then Fideles left, hurried back up the aisle of cold and silent marble figures. Placing his foot upon the first stair, looking into the darkness above him, Fideles thought of the monk with the dead eyes, of the horrors he had heard about, of the serpent's tooth. His courage almost failed him. He couldn't make himself take that second step.

"God spared Miguel for a reason. Yes, perhaps to warn me. To save my lord's life! And here I stand, cowering in the darkness. God is with me. I am in His hands."

Firmly, swiftly, Brother Fideles began to climb the stairs.

··◁ ▷··

The priest emerged from a cellar door that led him out into the Abbey's large communal kitchen.

He paused in the shadows of the doorway, peered out, "reconnoitered" as the soldiers said. No one was about. The kitchen had not been used in some time, apparently. Perhaps the mind-dead had no need for food. Or maybe they had brought their own.

Fideles pulled his hood low over his head, slid his hands into the sleeves of his robes, and slipped out the door. He hurried through the kitchen, noticed, in passing, that it had not been cleaned after that fatal, last supper. Bowls and pans lay on the floor, a sack of flour was opened, spilled. He thought of the brothers working, feeling the first pangs of the poison. Rats scurried away at his approach. What, he wondered suddenly, had been done with the bodies? Averting his eyes, not wanting to think about it, he hurried through the room.

At the doorway, he stopped again, looked into the hall, expecting to see the monks who were not monks at all but those Miguel called the mind-dead.

The hall was empty.

Maybe they've gone and taken my lord with them! Fideles thought in sudden panic. His fear drove him into the hallway, determined to search the entire Abbey if he had to.

Two robed and hooded figures stepped out suddenly from the shadows, blocked Fideles's path.

The young priest's heart nearly stopped beating.

"We have been expecting you, Brother Fideles," said one.

"Come this way," said another.

Their voices, like the eyes that he could see now, glittering in the darkness of the hoods, were lifeless, expressionless. Once his heart had resumed its normal cycle, Brother Fideles found himself responding to this desperate situation with the calm and steady nerve that sustained him when his ship was under fire.

"I want to see Lord Sagan," he said firmly. "Take me to him."

"That is our command," said one of the mind-dead implacably. "Follow us."

Fideles hadn't expected to be obeyed with such alacrity, wondered uneasily at the sudden cooperation. The monks led him past the infirmary, the herbarium. Fideles pictured the bloody tragedies enacted within, shivered, and said a prayer for the dead. The monks continued walking. Fideles, looking up, saw the door that led to the last room all brothers eventually entered.

"Is my lord . . . dead?" Fideles stopped.

One of the mind-dead turned around. "Come," he said.

Fideles heard, then, the sound of a groan, a cry of terrible agony, coming from behind the mortuary door. He thought he recognized Sagan's voice, and the young priest hurried forward. Pushing aside the mind-dead, no longer thinking of his own danger, Fideles thrust open the door to the mortuary and hastened inside.

"My lord!" he breathed in anguish and in pity.

Sagan lay upon the stone bier, the bier on which the dead rested. A corpse—Fideles recognized it as that of his lord's father—had been removed to make room for the living. It had been dumped unceremoniously in a corner of the stone room, the bodies of several of the mind-dead lay still and motionless near it. The Warlord was bound, hand and foot, with steel manacles, a precaution that seemed unnecessary, considering the terrible severity of the punishment he had endured.

Fideles hurried forward, stared in shocked horror at the tormented body. Sagan was half-naked, his black robes had been torn from his upper body and his legs. He had been beaten so severely that, in places, the flesh had been stripped away, exposing the white bone beneath. Puncture wounds, turning an ugly bluish purple, oozed dark blood. His face had been battered almost past recognition.

Fideles glanced at the bodies on the floor, at the blood that ran in the gutters of the room. The Warlord had not submitted to his torment without a fight.

"My lord!" Fideles repeated in a choked voice, grasping hold of Sagan's right hand. He felt blood, warm and sticky, on his fingers. Turning the hand, palm up, he saw five fresh puncture marks in the flesh.

The priest's voice roused Sagan from his half-conscious stupor. Turning his head with a painful effort, he looked at Fideles. Recognition lighted the dark eyes.

"I, too, must pass through the fire," he whispered through lips that were split and swollen and caked with blood.

"My lord, tell me what to do! How can I help?" Fideles said urgently.

"By carrying out your orders, of course, Brother Fideles," said a voice.

An old man with a disfigured, bulbous head crept out of the shadows of the back of the room. He wore magenta robes, decorated with a streak of jagged, black lightning.

"Abdiel," whispered Brother Fideles.

"Ah, you've heard of me. His lordship told you, no doubt. How convenient. It saves the need of tedious and time-consuming explanation. And you haven't much time, Brother

Fideles. You must return to Lady Maigrey and to His Majesty, the king, immediately! You must warn them, tell them that I, Abdiel, have taken Lord Sagan hostage. Though I think you'll find that your news is not news to them, at all. I'm certain that the Lady Maigrey already knows."

Sagan's eyes narrowed, the swollen lips parted. The fingers of the hand that Fideles held clenched in a spasm of rage and pain.

"I don't understand, my lord," Fideles said, holding fast to Sagan and ignoring Abdiel. "What is it *you* want me to do, my lord? If it is to remain with you, to suffer and die with you here, then I will commend my soul to God and do so."

"Those weren't your orders, however, were they, Brother Fideles?" Abdiel said cunningly. "That wasn't your lord's final command to you. Hasten! The spaceplane is ready to go, to carry you safely to *Phoenix*, where the Lady Maigrey awaits your arrival."

The Warlord's body jerked, muscles bunched. He raised his arms as if he would rip the manacles apart. Wounds opened, blood flowed, his chest heaved.

"My lord, stop! It's killing you!" Fideles cried.

"Remarkable, isn't it," said Abdiel, eyeing Sagan in jealous admiration. "After all he's endured, he still has the strength to try to defy me. But, you are right, young brother. It is killing him."

Abdiel held up a scythe, shaped like the head of a snake. "Before I'd let you die, Derek, I'd use this. I don't want to have to. It would make you extremely difficult to control, but I will, if you force me."

The Warlord's eyes closed, a bloody froth formed on his lips. His head lolled, the body went limp.

Fideles, thinking he had died, placed his hand upon the naked chest, was about to give a thankful prayer to God, when he felt, weak and slow but steady, the beat of the heart.

"He is not dead," said Abdiel. "He has escaped me the only way left to him. His mind has withdrawn deep into its own hiding places. It will be difficult, the task long and tedious, but I have time. I will track him down and find him."

The mind-seizer raised his left hand. Five razor-sharp needles, protruding from the flesh, gleamed in the candle-light.

"And now, Brother Fideles, you will obey your lord's final command."

Fideles remembered the spaceplane, the myriad dials and buttons whose use and function he did not understand. He thought about the long flight through cold and hostile space, helpless, alone, perhaps drifting, lost, marooned. He looked at the wizened old man, who stood leering over the bier at him, and knew that, somehow, he would be doing this evil man's bidding. Yet, Sagan had obviously foreseen something like this happening. He must have had his reasons.

"Yes," said Brother Fideles, "with God's help, I will obey my lord's command."

"Good, good. And you will carry to the Lady Maigrey a message from me, from Abdiel. Tell her that I have taken Lord Sagan to the galaxy of the Corasians. In that mind"—Abdiel pointed at the Warlord's bloodied head—"are the plans and designs for the space-rotation bomb.

"I will gain access to those plans by means of this"—Abdiel made the needles wink and glitter in the light—"and I will pass the knowledge on to the Corasians, who will then construct such a bomb."

Fideles stared at him. "You're mad! You'd give this power to our enemies?"

"No, to myself," Abdiel replied with a wink and a smile. "I will deal with the Corasians when the time comes. In the meanwhile, they will serve me. Tell this to the Lady Maigrey. She will know where to find us."

"A trap," said Fideles. "Another trap. I'll warn her. She won't fall into it."

"She won't fall, she will walk, run! Only she possesses the power to stop me. Only she stands in my way from taking total control of this galaxy . . . and of her king. She must destroy me. I must destroy her. An interesting contest, don't you think?"

Brother Fideles cast one last look at his lord, asking for some sign, some indication if he was doing the right thing or not.

Sagan lay still, unmoving.

Fideles sighed. Lifting the limp hand, he pressed it to his lips. "God be with you, my lord," he whispered. He laid the hand back on the stone bier and turned away abruptly, blinking back the tears that filled his eyes. Bracing himself, he started to walk away from the bier, away from the old man. The thin, cracked voice stopped him.

"And when you talk to the Lady Maigrey, you should remind her of something that she may have, perhaps, forgotten. Something that will make this contest all the more entertaining."

Fideles paused. He could not look around, revulsion and horror had almost overwhelmed him.

"I'm listening," he said, keeping firm control over his voice to prevent it from breaking.

"Remind my lady," said Abdiel, "that if she saves the life of Derek Sagan, she saves the life of the man who is destined to end her own."

Book Three

Build then the ship of death, for you must take
the longest journey, to oblivion.
And die the death, the long and painful death
that lies between the old self and the new.

> D. H. Lawrence, *The Ship of Death*

Chapter ❖──◦◯◦──❖ One

Those whom God hath joined together let no man put asunder.
Prayer Book, 1662, Solemnization of Matrimony

General John Dixter, standing outside the double golden doors, decorated with a phoenix rising from flames, leaned back against one of the bulkheads, folded his arms, and crossed his legs at the ankles.

"Her ladyship is extremely busy, sir," began Agis in apologetic tones, embarrassed at keeping an officer of such high rank standing in a hallway.

"I'm aware of that," said Dixter mildly. "I said I'd wait."

"My lady . . ." The captain had recourse to the commlink.

"Send him in," came the curt reply.

The doors slid open. Dixter stood upright, nodded his thanks to the captain, who saluted the general as he entered the Warlord's quarters. The doors slid shut behind him, the soft sigh of the mechanism masking Dixter's soft sigh as he walked into the room.

Maigrey was seated at a communications center at the far end of Sagan's quarters. Dixter could see an image of Captain Williams, an obviously distraught Captain Williams, on the screen in front of her. Maigrey said nothing to her visitor, but she turned her head to acknowledge his presence and invited him, with a glance and a nod, to be seated.

Dixter, having experienced Sagan's furniture, decided to remain standing. He lounged about the far end of the room, keeping a discreet distance between himself and the communications terminal, and appeared to busy himself by examining a few of the curiosities Sagan had collected to replace those lost in the destruction of *Phoenix*.

The general looked at everything, saw nothing. Now that he was here, now that he was close to her, he was wondering if

175

he'd done the right thing in forcing himself into her presence. He listened to her voice, to one side of the conversation, the volume on the commlink being kept low, and he heard the ragged edge of weariness, the sharpness of fatigue that was not so much of body but of spirit.

"The wedding is scheduled for 1800 hours, Captain. That gives the tailor and his mates six hours. I am certain that in this time—"

Williams interrupted, his tirade inaudible to Dixter, who could, however, guess what was being said.

Maigrey bit her lip, listened patiently, though her fingers drummed restlessly on the console. At length, she cut in.

"Yes, Captain Williams, I am fully aware that Nola Rian is an officer in the Royal Air Corps. I am aware that she has been credited with shooting down twelve Corasian fighters and the disabling of another four. I am aware that she was decorated for her valor in the Corasian battle and I will possibly concede the fact, Captain, that Nola Rian is one of the 'toughest broads' you've ever met. But, damn it, she is also a woman and this is her wedding day and if she wants to be married in a white dress, then *I* say she will be. Besides, it will look well on the GBC nightly news. You know that Lord Sagan would never dream of using those white lace tablecloths anyhow."

Williams was apparently still inclined to argue. Maigrey let him rant on a few moments, then, "It would seem to me, Captain, that sewing a skirt is far easier than sewing trousers. It's just a matter of a few seams. . . . No, I've never done it before myself, but—Tell the tailor I will send down one of my own dresses that he can cut up to use for a pattern. You may also tell him that he will have that wedding dress ready on time or I'll put a seam in his head! Is that understood, Captain?

"Thank you. Now, about the wedding cake." Maigrey brushed back a lock of hair from her face. "A cake designed in the shape of this warship is not particularly romantic. I want something else. I have no idea what. Tell Cook to use his imagination."

Williams made a comment.

"Not quite *that* much imagination, Captain," Maigrey said with a wry smile. "Remember, the reception will be open to the press and available for public broadcast. Every man off-duty is to be in attendance in full dress uniform. And, of course, yourself and Admiral Aks."

Williams made another comment.

Maigrey sighed, placed her hand on the switch. "Believe me, Captain, no one wishes my lord were back more than I do. You have your orders."

She depressed a button. The screen went blank. She sat, staring at the empty screen. "If I ordered them to smash through that blockade out there, I wouldn't hear a murmur. But this?" Her shoulders slumped, her head sank into her hands. "Declaring war would be easier. . . ."

"My lady." Agis's voice came through the commlink. "Admiral Aks requests—"

"Tell the admiral I'm in conference."

"He says it's urgent, my lady. Something about the flowers. . . ."

"I could come back later," Dixter offered.

"No, stay here, John. I—We need to talk. Tell the admiral to do the best he can, Captain. I rely completely on his judgment.

"There." Maigrey rose to her feet, walked around the chair, but she kept her head lowered, her face hidden behind the curtain of pale hair. "God knows what the man will come up with. I'm not sure Aks knows the difference between a rose and a cauliflower. I don't suppose it will matter much, at this point . . ." Her voice trailed off.

An uncomfortable silence fell between the two. Maigrey looked down at her hands, resting on the back of the chair. Dixter carefully replaced whatever object he'd been inspecting back on its stand.

"You've been avoiding me, Maigrey."

"Yes," she answered coolly. "And I would have continued to do so if you hadn't insisted on this meeting that can only be extremely painful to both of us."

"Maigrey, I—"

"Don't, John!" she cried suddenly, raising her hand in a warning gesture. "Don't say it! I won't listen."

"Say what?" Dixter stopped, stared at her, truly puzzled.

"Say that you forgive me. I don't deserve your forgiveness. I don't want it."

"Forgive you?" Dixter said, perplexed. "Forgive you for what? Maigrey, I don't understand—"

"You never did!"

She raised her head, the gray eyes were darker, emptier,

colder than the deepspace he abhorred. "You never did understand, did you, John? You're too damn nice. Too damn honorable. I left you on *Defiant* to die, John Dixter. I left you, I left Dion, knowing that if I had stayed, I could have saved you both! I owed you my loyalty out of friendship. I owed Dion my loyalty out of a sacred trust. I renounced both. As it turned out, Dion saved himself and Sagan saved you."

"But, Maigrey, you had your duty—"

"Duty!" She tossed her hair back from her face, gave a bitter laugh. "Duty. You mean going after that space-rotation bomb? Snatching it out from under Sagan's nose? Do you want to know the real reason I went after it, John? Do you?"

Maigrey took a step toward him. The gray eyes were light now, but the flame that burned within them gave them an ugly cast. She clenched her fist, fingers grasping, clutching. "I wanted it for myself! I wanted the power for myself! My God, I sold my starjewel to get it!"

Her hand closed over the empty place on her breast, the place where the gleaming, glittering starjewel had always rested. John knew where the jewel was. He'd seen it . . . once. Once had been all he could stand. Its clear crystal had darkened. Its aspect was hideous, horrible to look upon. The silver chain, from which it hung, was black with the clotted blood of the Adonian Snaga Ohme. The jewel was now in Dion's possession, it rested in the interior of the space-rotation bomb. The jewel was the bomb's triggering device.

"Sagan was right, John. The scar on my face struck far deeper than flesh. It's in my soul." She drew herself up, tall, majestic. "I think you had better go."

"You've got me right where you want me, don't you, Maigrey?" Dixter asked calmly. "Whatever I say, whatever I do, you despise me. If I say there's no need to talk about forgiveness between us, then you despise me for being a 'nice guy.' And if I say all right, yes, you hurt me but I forgive you, you despise me for being weak. And if I said I despised *you* and I walked out the door, then that would be the best that could happen for you, wouldn't it? All memory erased, the screen blank."

"Yes," she said, staring through shimmering eyes at anything in the room except him, "all memories erased, the screen blank." Her hands curled over the back of the chair.

"And now I'll say what I came to say. I love you, Maigrey.

Although that may be the wrong thing," Dixter added with a rueful smile. "Maybe you've despised me all these years for loving you, knowing that I could never have you."

Maigrey raised her eyes to his, a tear slid down the scarred cheek. "I hope I'm better than that, John," she said softly. "Maybe not much better . . . but a little better than that."

Dixter stepped forward, took her hand. Maigrey held his fast, tightly, too tightly.

"We always joked about never saying good-bye to each other; parting without farewell seemed to mean that we would never part. . . . I said good-bye to you when I left *Defiant*, John. Just as, I imagine"—Maigrey smiled wanly—"you said good-bye to me after I had gone."

Dixter swallowed, but it didn't help. The words wouldn't come past the pain in his chest.

"I know. I understand." Maigrey closed her other hand over his. "I thought we should leave it at that. I thought it would be best that way. But now I'm glad you came."

"And we still haven't said good-bye. Not yet," Dixter added cheerfully, drawing her near. "And the charm is still working. We haven't been parted."

"No," she said softly, coming to stand close to him, as she might huddle beneath a sheltering oak to escape the rain. "We haven't been parted . . ."

"My lady." Agis's voice, sounding slightly harried. "Mendaharin—"

"It's Tusk!" shouted Tusk. "I gotta talk to you!"

"Send him in."

The doors had only barely opened, before Tusk was bounding into the Warlord's quarters.

"The wedding's off! That's it. Finished. Off."

Maigrey shook her head. "Oh, no, it isn't. Not after what I've been through. You're going to get married, Tusca, if I have to hold a lasgun on you!"

"It's just cold feet, son," said Dixter in mollifying tones. "Every bridegroom feels—"

"What the hell does the temperature of my feet have to do with this?" Tusk demanded, beside himself. "My feet are fine! It's XJ!"

"XJ?" Maigrey stared at him blankly. "A computer?"

Tusk groaned. "That damn, interfering—Can you believe it? He managed to plug himself into the ship's central computer. I hope they court-martial him! I hope Sagan rips out his electronic guts. That, that—" Words failed him. Tusk shook his fist in the general direction of his spaceplane.

"Tusca, you're not making any sense. What has XJ done?"

"Done? He's found out about the wedding, that's what he's done! And he's mad 'cause he wasn't invited! And if he isn't invited, he's threatened to freeze all my assets solid, plus send out a message that I'm a deadbeat to every credit computer in the galaxy—and, believe me, he's good buddies with all of 'em—and leave me without a kepler to my name. So you see"—Tusk slammed his hand down on a table—"the wedding's off."

Maigrey looked at Dixter. They tried to stop themselves, but couldn't manage it. Both burst into laughter.

Tusk drew himself up with wounded dignity, cast each of them a hurt, reproachful glance that only increased their hilarity. Maigrey sank down into a chair, her hand pressed against her side, gasping for air. John Dixter leaned against the back of the couch, wiped tears from his eyes.

"Bless you, Tusk," he said quietly. "God bless you."

"Oh, Tusca, I'm sorry," Maigrey said, springing to her feet, halting Tusk as he was about ready to storm out the door. "I know this isn't funny to you. It's just . . . just . . ." She giggled, caught herself, and attempted to speak soberly. "The wedding will go on as planned. I'll take care of everything, XJ included."

"You will?" Tusk looked darkly dubious. "I mean, I know you're Blood Royal and you've got all kinds of powers, my lady, but that computer of mine's possessed! Besides, how're you gonna invite XJ to the wedding anyway? Unless you fly the friggin' spaceplane into the ceremony—"

"Don't you see, Tusca? That's it. Almost. We don't fly your spaceplane to the ceremony. We bring the ceremony to the spaceplane. Nola wouldn't mind getting married on board the plane, would she? Then XJ could be there. I think it's very touching that he wants to share this with you."

"I think he's just trying to make my life a living hell. But, well, now that you mention it, I think Nola might kinda like to be married in the spaceplane. After all, that's sorta how we met and we fought the Corasians together in it and I remember that night she was hurt and I thought she was gonna die and I realized how much I loved her. . . ."

"Yeah." Tusk coughed, voice husky, "I think that might be a real good place to be married, after all. Thanks a lot, my lady, General. I'll go tell Nola."

Tusk hurried away. Maigrey shook her head, sighed, turned to gaze resignedly at the blank commlink screen.

"Wait until Captain Williams hears this. . . ."

It was probably one of the universe's stranger weddings. Held inside a spaceplane on a hangar on board a warship surrounded by an enemy fleet, the wedding opened with an alarm that upgraded alert status. Pilots and crews on standby cheered the wedding procession. The wedding party clambered up the ladder leading over the hull of the long-range Scimitar, dropped down through the hatch and into the plane's cramped living quarters that Tusk had just spent the last hour furiously cleaning.

The bride's dress looked as if it had engaged in a battle with a banquet table and lost, but it had a long train of lace, of which the tailor was extremely proud, and Nola herself was so happy and radiant that, as Captain Williams said somewhat bitterly to Admiral Aks, she could have been dressed as a bosun's mate and no one would have noticed.

There was one frightful moment of panic when the bride's train snagged on a bolt on the exterior of the spaceplane, leaving the bride stuck half in and half out of the hatch. No amount of pulling or tugging would free it and one of the Honor Guard was advancing grimly on it with a knife when the horrified tailor rushed forward to save his creation, freed the bride, and the wedding proceeded. The tailor was universally acclaimed the hero of the day.

Bride, groom, best man, king, and computer came together in the Scimitar, ready to begin the ceremony. But the maid of honor, the Lady Maigrey, was missing.

No one knew where she was or why she wasn't where she was supposed to be.

"Stall," said Dion and left to find her.

General Dixter stalled as long as possible, but he couldn't delay matters forever; the press corps was waiting impatiently, the ice sculpture was melting, and any moment the ship might be called upon to engage the enemy.

"I've just spoken to Agis. He reports that she hasn't left her quarters," Dion said in a low voice to Dixter on his return. "But when he tries to contact her, there's no response."

Dixter looked extremely grave. "This isn't like Maigrey. She knows how important this is to Tusk and Nola."

"Yes, sir. But I believe we're going to have to go ahead with the ceremony."

The general glanced at a fuming Captain Williams, pacing up and down the deck, and Admiral Aks, red-faced and impatient, who glared back at him.

"Hey, what's going on?" Tusk demanded, coming over to them. "Nola says it's hot as hell under that veil and her flowers're starting to wilt. And this damn collar's giving me a rash on my neck. Where's Lady Maigrey?"

"She'll be along in a moment," said Dixter, glancing at Dion.

"We'd better go ahead and get started," Dion added.

"Oh, sure." Tusk appeared downcast for a moment, but nervousness and excitement soon put Maigrey's absence out of his mind.

The wedding party was small, which was good, because the spaceplane barely held them all as it was. The ceremony took place in the Scimitar's living quarters and was very short and very simple.

John Dixter, dress uniform pressed within an inch of its life by the faithful Bennett, but still starting, somehow, to look rumpled and slept in, took his place next to a widely grinning Tusk.

Dion, attired in his dress uniform, with royal purple sash, stood slightly aloof from all of them, serious, solemn in his self-conscious majesty. He had never been part of them, not truly.

Dixter, looking at Dion in the brief pause while everyone waited for XJ's remote unit to bob up from out of the cockpit, suddenly remembered the kid who had come into his office with Tusk, the kid who had demanded to know his own name. He's grown, Dixter realized. Not only in height, though he was taller than Tusk, now, by a good several inches. He's grown in dignity, self-confidence, and assurance.

The severe cut of the uniform became him. He was extraordinarily, remarkably handsome. The luxuriant red hair, full and thick, sprang from the peak on his forehead, fell to shoulder length. The planes of his face were sharp and finely chiseled. He had what Dixter called "the Starfire eyes"—

incandescent blue that, like flame, could burn, scorch, illuminate, warm. His only other heritage from his father's side of the family was the pouting mouth, the full, sensual lips that could stiffen in anger and resolve or tremble in weakness, mumble in indecision.

He has the capability to soar above us all, Dixter thought, light the heavens with a blazing flame, or he can—like his uncle—be defeated by himself, the comet break apart and scatter into nothing but bits of ice and dust, falling into obscurity.

"I wonder what Maigrey thinks of him," Dixter asked himself, looking for the twentieth time at the hatch, his concern and worry growing. "I wonder where she is?"

··◁■ ■▷··

XJ's round remote unit, small metal arms wiggling, lights winking like the eyes of a mischievous monkey, floated and bobbed around the assembled guests until it came to rest between Tusk and Nola.

Standing in the center of the spaceplane's living quarters; Tusk slightly hunched over to keep from striking his head on a long length of tubing, the bride and groom held fast to each other's hands, looked at each other as if no one else existed but the two of them.

XJ gave a preparatory bleep, to make certain he had everyone's attention.

"It's been suggested, by General Dixter, that in lieu of the usual we-gather-here-together crap, that each of us says something that sounds halfway intelligent, which'll be a strain for most of you, particularly Tusk, but do the best you can. I'll begin. First, I'd like to say that I'm truly grateful to her ladyship for suggesting that we hold the wedding on board here. It's the first time Tusk's cleaned the place in the seven years we've been together. And if we're lucky, no one'll notice that pair of shorts hanging over the shower nozzle.

"Next I want to express my gratitude to Nola Rian for agreeing to marry this slob and hopefully end the steady stream of bimbos we've had tromping through here for the last—"

"XJ!" Tusk growled, casting a vicious glance at the remote. Nola giggled.

"And finally, well, er—" XJ stammered. Its lights dimmed,

it seemed to be having difficulty with its programming. "'Scuse me a moment. Technical difficulties." The remote blinked off for a second, came back on, a slight hitch in its audio. "I'm gonna say this once and it's a wedding present and I don't ever expect to have to say it again so listen up. Men-da-ha-rin Tusca . . ." The remote paused, blurted forth rapidly, the words wrenched out of its electronic guts, "you'rethebest-damnpilotIeverflewwithandIdon'tcarewhoknowsitandIwish-youandRianallthebestsothere."

"And," XJ added, optic lights flaring, "if anyone ever says that I said that I'll deny it so none of you better. Now hurry this thing up 'cause it's costing me a fortune to run the air-conditioning."

"XJ, that's really very sweet," said Nola.

"Gosh, XJ." Tusk cleared a lump in his throat. "I don't know what to say. I think . . . yeah . . . I think I could kiss you—"

The remote unit dropped to the floor with a crash, lights out, wiggling arms still. "Keep him away from me!" warned XJ's mechanical voice from its central system, located in the cockpit, "or I swear I'll shut this party down."

"It's all right, XJ," said General Dixter, smiling, "I have Tusk firmly in hand."

"Yeah, well, you just keep an eye on him, that's all. Kiss me . . ." Bleeping indignantly to itself, the computer lapsed into deeply offended silence.

Tusk grinned at Nola and winked. General Dixter stepped forward, placed his hands over both of theirs.

"Tusk, Nola, I only want to say one thing. You've been through a lot of dangers together, you've both faced death together. Now you've got a much harder task, you've got to face life together. Love each other, trust each other, respect each other, befriend each other, and you'll get through it fine. I never had a son or a daughter, but if I did, I would wish for them now just exactly what I'm wishing for each of you. May your lives together be blessed."

Nola put her arms around him, hugged him, and clung to him. "Don't ever say you don't have a daughter, sir," she said softly, "because you do now."

"What she said," Tusk managed to get out, before he lost his voice.

He put one arm around Dixter's rumpled shoulder, the other arm around Nola and the three stood together in silence for so long that XJ, not hearing any action, flickered the lights.

Dion took an unconscious, involuntary step backward, coming up hard against the bulkhead. He stared at the three, standing together, as he had stared at the first alien life-form he'd ever seen. Love, respect, trust, caring. A bond between two people, a bond that says you are the most important person in the universe to me. Dion spoke innumerable alien languages fluently, but he didn't speak this one, the language of love. He didn't speak it, didn't understand it. He was dark and cold and hollow inside. He wanted light, warmth. He wanted filled! He wanted someone to look at him the way Nola looked at Tusk. He wanted someone to reach out to, someone to laugh with him over silly jokes that meant nothing to anyone else. He wanted someone to yell at, fight with, apologize to, make it all up again. He wanted, desperately, someone to love.

"But how could I ever be sure of any woman?" he asked himself bitterly. "I've seen them look at me and they don't see me, they see a crown. They see pomp and ceremony. They see their children on the throne. I understand, now, why my uncle never married. I—"

Five points of searing, burning agony shot into the palm of his right hand. White heat swept through his blood, bile flooded his mouth, fiery dots burst before his eyes. Dion thought for a moment that he might pass out, and he was forced to grab hold of and hang on to the hook from which Tusk suspended the hammocks.

"Abdiel!" The name echoed inside him. The heat that had suffused his body died, leaving him shivering with intense cold. "Abdiel . . ."

The mind-seizer's presence was powerful, terrible laughter running through the young man's veins. Dion glanced wildly around. He wouldn't have been surprised to see the old man drop through the hatch into the spaceplane.

Nothing. No one.

The wedding was proceeding, Tusk and Nola, voices barely audible, were talking only to each other, sharing their vows.

Dion felt suffocated. He had to get out of here. He had to—he knew suddenly—find Maigrey. He didn't understand what was happening, but she would. A supreme effort of will kept him standing silently until the ceremony was over.

"Husband and wife."

Nola ripped the veil from her head, flung her arms around

Tusk. He held her fast, kissed her. She kissed him. XJ set off
the alarm horn and added whistles and bells and other raucous
(and a few rude) noises the computer had on file. Dion
managed to make his way over to them, gasped out congratulations, and left precipitously.

--◁■ ■▷--

"I will see Lady Maigrey!" Dion demanded, bursting out of
Sagan's private elevator.

Agis, standing in front of the golden double doors, moved to
open them. "Yes, Your Majesty."

A cry came from inside Sagan's quarters—a cry of despair
and rage and a bitter protest against fate.

"Excuse me, Your Majesty."

The captain moved into action swiftly, calling his men to him
with a glance. Firmly, yet politely and respectfully, he elbowed Dion out of his way, touched a panel.

The double doors slid open. Weapons drawn, Agis and his
men ran into the room. Dion dashed in after them, thrusting
aside one of the centurions who sought to keep the king safe
until whatever danger threatening them could be determined.

The room was dark. The only light came from the illuminated dials and buttons on the command console, the faint
lambent glow of the computer, and the cold, empty light of the
stars outside the viewscreen.

"My lady!" Agis called out, overturning chairs in his haste
and worry.

"Over here," Dion called, drawn to her by shared pain,
shared grief, shared fear.

A black screen, standing at the far end of the room, hid from
view a small altar. Maigrey, dressed as she had been dressed to
attend the wedding, in royal-blue robes covered by a silver
surplice, lay on the deck before the altar, unconscious.

Dion knelt beside her, lifted her gently in his arms. Her
eyelids fluttered, she looked up at him.

"Maigrey," he said softly, "it's Sagan, isn't it? What's happened? Maigrey, tell us. . . ."

She stared at him without recognition. "I, too, must pass
through the fire," she murmured. Pain contorted her face, and
she lost consciousness.

Chapter ·❦· Two

United thoughts and counsels, equal hope,
And hazard in the glorious enterprise.
John Milton, *Paradise Lost*

Dion came to Maigrey's quarters early in the morning.

"You're to go in, Your Majesty," said the centurion on watch.

Dion glanced questioningly at the guard, who shook his head.

Entering the quiet room, Dion looked at the bed, saw that it hadn't been slept in. He found Maigrey behind the screen, kneeling before the altar, her head resting in her hands. He kept silent, thinking perhaps she'd fallen asleep, and was about to withdraw. Maigrey raised her head, looked at him over her shoulder, through a fine curtain of pale hair.

"No, don't leave. We need to talk. I've . . . sent for the others."

She started to stand, fell back. Dion hurried to her, offered his help. She leaned against him, rose stiffly to her feet. He was alarmed at the chill feeling of her flesh, the terrible pallor of her skin.

"Have you been here all night?" he asked, guiding her to a chair.

Dark circles shadowed her eyes, that were red-rimmed and swollen. Dried blood flecked her lips, the marks of her teeth plain upon them. Her face was drawn and haggard, her hair ragged and uncombed, her blue velvet dress wrinkled and spotted with tears.

"Yes. I waited for . . ." Her voice caught. She shook her head. "No, I don't want to sit down. I need to walk, start the circulation going again. My legs have gone numb. There, thank you. I can manage."

Maigrey pushed Dion's hands away and moved slowly across the deck, rubbing her arms.

"You've heard nothing?" Dion asked.

She didn't turn around, didn't look at him. Her head lowered.

"No."

"He's not . . ." Dion swallowed.

"He's alive." She pressed her hand over her breast. "I know that . . . here. But I can't reach his mind."

"My lady!" Admiral Aks came through the double doors. "Your Majesty, I'm glad you're together. We've been monitoring galactic news wires. You must see what's coming over the vids now."

Aks went to the console, the screen came on, bringing with it a face and a voice.

"The self-styled Warlord Derek Sagan, under indictment for the murder of the Adonian weapons dealer Snaga Ohme, has reportedly eluded capture and fled to the Corasian galaxy. It is rumored that he has with him the space-rotation bomb, the awesome weapon designed by the notorious Snaga Ohme."

"So that's the story," Maigrey murmured.

"That's it," Aks said grimly.

The newsman continued: "It was an argument over this very weapon which presumably led to the Adonian's murder. Now reports have it that Derek Sagan, whose ruthless disregard for life and lust for power are well known, has taken this weapon over to our most feared enemies.

"We switch now to the Common House, where President Peter Robes has called a press conference."

President Robes, wearing a dark and depressing suit, with an expression specially chosen to match, stood on a broad patch of clipped green artificial grass.

"I am shocked at this news," the President was saying, "but not extremely surprised. Derek Sagan, or Lord Sagan as he demands to be called, has always considered himself above the laws that govern the rest of us ordinary people. He assumed he could commit murder with impunity and he was furious when he learned he was to be called to account."

Reporters clamored to be heard. The President nodded at one. The alien spoke through its translator.

"You said, Mr. President, that Sagan's fleet is surrounded by our own warships. How was it that he escaped?"

"Apparently he had received prior warning of our attempt to bring him to justice. We have learned that Sagan had in his pay numerous spies who reported to him every move made by the people's duly elected government officials. He was not on board his ship when the fleet was surrounded. Sources indicate that he flew his shuttlecraft to an obscure planet, there to meet with his cohort, the Lady Maigrey Morianna. His former lover, she is undoubtedly implicated in his flight. Warrants have been issued for her arrest."

"Mr. President! Lord Sagan was a hero in the battle with the Corasians. Why would he defect to the enemy?"

"As always with Sagan, he was a hero when it suited his purpose to be one. We have received several reports, the contents of which we can't discuss at the moment, which indicate that Sagan may have been in collusion with the Corasians all along, that the battle was staged for our benefit to cover up his manufacture of that fiendish weapon, the space-rotation bomb."

"But, Mr. President, Sagan himself circulated reports implying that you had something to do with that attack."

The President was grieved and mildly exasperated. "I state now as I have stated in the past, I see no need to dignify those charges with an answer."

"Mr. President, what do you think Derek Sagan's intent is, taking the bomb to the Corasians?"

"What do you think his intent is, Lizz?" the President asked bluntly. "Derek Sagan is ruthless, ambitious. The free people of the galaxy made it clear that they weren't going to give power to him, and now he's going to take it by force."

"You mean all-out, full-scale war with the Corasians?" The reporter was dramatically solemn.

"I don't want to start a panic, but it has always been my policy to tell the people who elected me to office and who have put their trust in me the truth. We must assume that this is what Derek Sagan plans." The President was calm, but obviously upset. "The Congress has been called into emergency session to determine what action we will take."

"You watching this?" Tusk demanded, entering the room, followed by Nola and General Dixter. "What the hell's going on?"

"I'll explain in a moment," Dion told him.

"And now, before I answer any more questions," President Robes was saying, "I would like to send a personal message to one young man out there."

The President looked directly, intently, and with utmost sincerity into the eyes of the innumerable cams turned on him.

"Dion Starfire, I hope you are listening. You are an honorable young man who has been misguided by bad advice. I truly think that you believe yourself to be acting for the good of the people in this galaxy. I hope that is the case. Derek Sagan has proclaimed publicly, more than once, that he supports your claim to the throne. He has declared, more than once, his loyalty to you as his liege lord. If you do have such influence over him, young man, then you have a chance to save the people of the galaxy.

"Dion Starfire, if you know where Sagan is hiding, if you can talk to him, persuade him, then I hope and trust that you will act at once to alleviate this terrible danger. An ordinary citizen of this galaxy would do no less. A king would do much more."

Dion stared silently at the screen. His glance flicked to Lady Maigrey, who had remained immovable, impassive, except for a pale ghost of a smile when the President mentioned issuing a warrant for her arrest.

"Admiral," an excited voice broke in over the commlink, "Lord Sagan's spaceplane has just materialized out of hyperspace!"

"What?" Aks gasped, looked confused, then hopeful. "Perhaps my lord managed to escape!"

"The plane won't respond to any of our attempts to contact it, sir. It's just sitting out there, dead in space, although our readings indicate that there is someone alive on board. The spaceplanes of the Galactic fleet are moving to intercept—"

"He's injured, then. Lock a tractor beam onto that spaceplane and get it the hell inside here!"

"Lord Sagan isn't aboard that plane," Maigrey said, sighing. "Its passenger is a priest. And the fewer people who know that, the better. Captain"—her gaze turned to Agis—"take your men and meet the priest the moment he sets foot on deck. Bring him here immediately, without any fuss, if you can help it. Make certain he talks to no one on the way."

"Yes, my lady."

"Tusk, go with them." Maigrey's voice softened. "The young man's been through a terrible ordeal. He'll be glad of a friendly face in the midst of all that steel. Do what you can to make his arrival appear normal."

"Yeah, sure," said Tusk, looking dubious. "Priest, huh? What . . . er . . . what's his name?"

"Fideles. Brother Fideles."

"Fiddle," repeated Tusk, leaving on his errand.

"Admiral Aks"—the voice over the commlink again—"the press is demanding access to His Majesty. What shall—"

Dion's eyes met Maigrey's. "I'll be calling a press conference shortly," he said.

She nodded her approval. "Is Lord Sagan's spaceplane aboard?"

"Not yet, my lady. But the tractor beam is locked on and intercept planes have retreated."

"Gave up without a fight?" Aks was disbelieving.

"They know Sagan's not on board," Maigrey said.

The admiral snorted and shook his head. Maigrey ignored him. She had withdrawn from all of them, locked herself away inside herself, surrounded by a wall of ice. Anyone who drew near risked being burned by the cruel cold.

No one spoke, although everyone present had innumerable questions. They had the feeling that their questions would be answered soon; that when the answers did come, they probably weren't going to like them anyway. And so they sat in silence in the Warlord's quarters, waiting for a priest, who had arrived, alone, in the Warlord's private spaceplane.

The golden double doors opened. Tusk entered, shepherding a young man clad in brown robes, his head covered by a hood.

"This is him," said Tusk grimly. "Brother Fiddle. My long-lost cousin come to pay his respects at my wedding. He's the white sheep of the family," he added, jerking a thumb at the young man's white complexion, a marked contrast to Tusk's own ebony-black skin.

"Thank you, Tusk." Maigrey smiled faintly. "Did everything go well?"

"I guess. I called him 'cuz' and hugged him and we slobbered over one another for a while. *Maybe* a few people bought it." Tusk didn't sound at all hopeful.

"It should stop most of the wilder rumors, anyway. That's as much as we can ask. Please, enter and welcome, Brother Fideles."

The young priest had stopped just inside the doorway. He kept his hands in his sleeves, his head down. At Lady

Maigrey's request, he walked into the room, into the light. The brown robes were splotched with dark, ugly stains—dried blood.

Dion rose silently to his feet. Clasping his hands behind him, he walked over to stare out the viewscreen. Admiral Aks's face had gone gray. He sagged in his chair. John Dixter glanced quickly, concernedly at Maigrey. Nola went to stand beside Tusk.

Brother Fideles came to Maigrey, knelt before her on one knee.

"My lady," he said softly, reverently.

Maigrey, composed, pale, gave him her hand. He kissed the tips of her fingers that must have been chill to the touch as the hand of a corpse.

"Rise, Brother, and be seated. I know that you are worn from your long journey and ordeal, but you will have time to rest and refresh yourself later. Now, it is imperative that you tell us what has happened."

"My lady"—Fideles hesitated—"should I speak before all these people? Perhaps you alone—"

"No, all these people are . . . or will be . . . involved. His Majesty is present." She drew his attention to Dion. "The time for secrets is past."

"Yes, my lady."

Fideles rose, bowed to Dion, then sat down in a chair. Nola thoughtfully brought him a glass of water. He accepted it, kept his hood over his head, his eyes cast down, as was proper for a priest when in the presence of women. Those assembled drew chairs nearer his, gathering around him. Dion, however, remained standing at the viewscreen. He could see the young priest's reflection, a ghostly image hovering between the king and the stars beyond.

Fideles told his tale of what had happened to himself and to his lord inside the dark towers of the Abbey of St. Francis. He spoke clearly and concisely in a voice that was steady and firm. He did not stammer or hesitate, had obviously carefully sorted his thoughts, gone over his report in his mind prior to his arrival. He shared his own fears, his doubts. His descriptions were simple, yet poignant and precise, and deeply affected his audience.

Nola and Tusk shivered and drew closer together. Aks, hearing of Sagan's torment, lowered his head, hid his face with his hand. At the mention of Abdiel's name, Dion clutched his left hand over his right, rubbed the scarred palm that ached and burned.

Maigrey remained unmoved, listened to the tale without outward emotion, her gaze fixed steadfastly on the young priest. Dion realized suddenly that she must have, through the mind-link, already known everything that had occurred, had perhaps even shared Sagan's agony.

"When the one who called himself Abdiel told me that I must leave and bring this information back to you, I was confused." Fideles's calm demeanor wavered. "Perhaps I did wrongly, obeying this evil man's command. But it was my lord's command, as well, and it seemed, though my lord couldn't tell me at the end, that this was what he wanted."

"You did well, Brother," reassured Maigrey gravely. "If you had refused, Abdiel would have turned you into one of his 'disciples' and then you would have had no choice."

"How do we know he didn't?" Tusk demanded hoarsely. "Let's get a look at this priest."

"Yes. Remove your hood," Aks commanded.

Fideles did so. His face was pale and thin; his eyes, however, were bright and alert and intelligent. Tusk, peering into the eyes, grunted and stepped back, satisfied. Aks, recognizing the priest as his AWOL nurse, stared at him in astonishment.

"It's not likely Abdiel would send one of the mind-dead, Admiral," Maigrey said. "The mind-seizer had little time to waste. He needed to get his message to us quickly and Sagan had thoughtfully provided him with the means. Abdiel had his prize, he wanted to flee with it. By now, the mind-seizer is undoubtedly halfway on his journey to the Corasian galaxy."

"And Sagan with him," said Dion abruptly.

"Yes," Maigrey said, "Sagan . . . and the knowledge that he carries inside his head . . . with him."

"My lady." Brother Fideles raised his eyes, looked at her unhappily, reluctantly. "My lady, I have one more message to give. A message from Abdiel to you. Perhaps it would be better if I told you alone—"

"No, Brother. As I said, the time for secrets is past. What is your message?"

Brother Fideles repeated, hesitantly, Abdiel's final words.

"'Remind my lady that if she saves the life of Derek Sagan, she saves the life of the man who is destined to end her own.'"

Dion turned around. Dixter rose to his feet, came to stand beside her. Maigrey flushed and bit her lip, appeared to regret exceedingly that she'd ordered the young priest to speak.

"What does that mean, my lady?" Dion demanded.

"Nothing that has any bearing on the subject under discussion. The very *urgent* subject," she remarked coldly. Leaving her chair, escaping Dixter's outstretched hand, she walked rapidly across the room, came to stand in front of the command console. "We must decide what action to take, determine the best course to follow."

"Apparently the time for secrets isn't past," Dion said.

Maigrey lifted her head, gray eyes dark and threatening as a stormy sea. "This is a personal matter, between Lord Sagan and myself. It has nothing to do with anyone else. If, of course, Your Majesty commands me to speak—"

"I do," Dion said calmly.

Maigrey glared at him, the gray eyes flashed lightning. Her face had gone livid with anger, the lips drawn tight and bloodless, the scar an ugly red slash across her skin.

Dion weathered the storm, unbending, unyielding. "What does Abdiel's message mean?"

Maigrey turned away. The fingers of her hands, clenched over the back of a chair, were white with the strain.

"Lord Sagan had a dream. Nothing more than that. He took it as a portent."

"Lord Sagan has great faith in his dreams," stated Admiral Aks, indignant at the slur against his commander. "Perhaps it was coincidence that they often came to pass, as I myself frequently told him, but I must admit that—"

"Oh, shut up, Aks!" Maigrey snapped. "What do you know?"

"I know that my lord discussed this particular dream with me on more than one occasion. He had the dream several times. He said that in it he—"

"Your Majesty!" Maigrey interrupted impatiently. "We must decide what is to be done and we must waste no more time doing it. Didn't you hear me say that Abdiel is halfway to the Corasians by now? The President has challenged you to make good your promises to the people. Refuse to go after Sagan and you are finished."

"But, damn it all, Starlady, it's a trap! Abdiel admitted as much!" Tusk slammed his fist on a table. "You can't send the kid out into it!"

"Of course it's a trap. Don't you see? This is Robes's solution to a most annoying problem. He doesn't dare have Dion killed, make him a martyr. The people would immediately suspect the President, it would end his political career. But if Dion dies in a faraway galaxy, dies during a battle, Robes is home free and clear. He can mourn the young man as a hero, put up a statue to his memory, bring tears to the eyes of everyone when he refers to it in his campaign speeches."

"Then the answer's obvious," stated Tusk. "The kid says he's real sorry to hear about Lord Sagan, he'll do what he can to help, but it ain't his problem. Toss in our cards and fold."

"No," said Maigrey, "Abdiel's made the stakes high, made it worth our while to stay in the game. Nothing less than a golden crown sits in the center of the table. If Dion goes to the Corasian galaxy, and if he survives, and if he comes back victorious, Robes is finished. The people of the galaxy will name Dion their king. They'll carry him to his throne on their shoulders."

"What do we do?" Dion, like everyone else in the room, was mesmerized by her, caught up in her excitement.

"I have a plan, Your Majesty. We'll need to work it out in detail, but basically it is this. You announce that you're going to Corasia. Robes will offer to 'help,' he'll insist that the Galactic fleet convey you to the enemy."

"And when I have crossed over into enemy territory, I fall victim to a convenient enemy bombardment or some such thing." Dion smiled ruefully. "I'm beginning to understand."

"Accept Robes's challenge, but refuse any help. State publicly that the only people you trust are those who support you wholeheartedly—those who have put their trust in you. That sort of thing."

"But the Galactic fleet," Tusk protested. "They've got us webbed in."

"I think we can handle the fleet," Dion replied. "Admiral Aks, call a meeting of top officers. But what about Lord Sagan. And . . . Abdiel."

"The two of them," said Maigrey, "will be my concern."

Dion opened his mouth to argue, command . . . but he saw it would be like trying to break the everlasting cycle of an ocean's tides. This was going to be a bitter argument and one he didn't want to do in public.

"We'll discuss this later. For now, we have plans to make and little time to make them. I propose that we adjourn to the war room." Turning on his heel, he walked out.

"Some honeymoon, huh?" Tusk said, putting his arm around Nola.

"Yeah," she agreed. "Good thing we had ours before the wedding."

General Dixter was the last to leave. Pausing at the door, he looked back at Maigrey. She had turned to the computer, was giving it commands in a smooth, level voice.

John Dixter shook his head, left. The doors shut, sealed behind him.

Maigrey sank, trembling, back into her chair. A rustle of cloth made her jump, look up swiftly in alarm. The young priest stood before her.

"Brother Fideles." She rose haughtily to her feet. "I thought you had left with the others." Her chill tone advised him to immediately make up for his oversight.

The priest remained standing, head bowed, hands hidden in the folds of his sleeves. Suddenly he raised his head, looked her full in the eyes.

"I'm going with you," he said.

She stared, speechless with astonishment.

"God has given me a sign. I'm going with you," Fideles repeated.

Maigrey found her voice. "You don't know what you're asking, Brother. You can't possibly understand the danger, the risks I'll be running. I must enter the Corasian galaxy. Have you ever even *seen* a Corasian, Brother Fideles?"

"No," said the priest steadily, "but I have seen Abdiel. I have seen what he did to . . . my brethren, to my lord. I will go with you. You need help."

"I need help, all right," Maigrey answered, exasperated, uncertain how to cope with such stern, calm resolution. "But the help I need is a fighter, a warrior, someone who isn't forbidden by his vows to kill."

"The help you need is God's help, my lady," said Fideles. "'*Benedictus, qui venit in monine Domini*. Blessed is he that cometh in the name of the Lord.'"

Maigrey's hand went to her breast, to the place where the

starjewel had once hung, to the place where it hung no longer. She thought of it, resting inside the space-rotation bomb, blackened, horrible to look on, cursed.

God has abandoned us, she'd once said to Sagan. Maybe that was wishful thinking.

"I'm against it . . . but I'll consider it," she added grudgingly, forestalling further argument. "Now, I have to leave for the meeting. I think it's best, on second thought, that you remain here, in these quarters, until I return."

Brother Fideles bowed in silent acquiescence.

"I'll have food and water brought to you—"

"Thank you, my lady, but all I need is sleep."

"Then lie down. The bed is through those doors."

"I will sleep on the couch, my lady—"

"I'm not going to be using the bed. I have too much work to do—Oh, very well, sleep where you want."

Fideles nodded. Kneeling beside the couch, he said his prayers, wrapped himself in his robes, and lay down. He was almost immediately asleep.

Maigrey, seating herself back at the computer, watched these proceedings out of the corner of her eye. She had one more command to issue before she left for the meeting. She was running late as it was, but her hands rested limply on the keyboard. What she was about to do would irrevocably set in motion the wheel of fate. There was, now, still time to change her mind. This plan, formed last night, when she could have traced upon her own body every wound Sagan had suffered, was dark, desperate, terrible.

But it was the one plan that might work.

Maigrey placed her fingers on the keyboard. The command she was about to give was far too secret to be spoken aloud, even in a room presumably sealed off to every other ear and eye aboard ship. She typed one word, the only word needed to launch a sequence of coded commands.

SPARAFUCILE.

Chapter ·✦◦◯◦✦· *Three*

Oh build your ship of death, your little ark
and furnish it with food, with little cakes, and wine
for the dark flight down oblivion.

> D. H. Lawrence, *The Ship of Death*

The ship's bells chimed eight times to indicate the changing of the watch at midnight when Maigrey returned, accompanied by Dion. The captain of the Honor Guard was talking quietly with the centurions on duty outside Sagan's quarters. Agis, having a feeling he would be summoned before the night was out, had not gone to bed.

"His Majesty and I are not to be disturbed," Maigrey ordered.

Agis nodded. "Yes, my lady."

The double doors opened, sealed shut behind them.

"Talk quietly," Maigrey said, glancing at the sleeping figure of Brother Fideles, huddled on the couch. "Though I doubt if, at the moment, a bomb blast would wake him."

Each fell silent. The spirit of the Warlord grew strong, was given life and power in this, his room. The spirit wasn't a comfort to Maigrey, but made the empty place inside her darker, colder, as if a chill wind blew through her.

"You're not going to tell me the details of *your* plans, are you, my lady?" Dion broke the silence.

"I can't, Your Majesty."

"Why not? Or"—he was bitter—"perhaps you don't trust me. Because of Abdiel and the bloodsword."

"It's not that, Dion. The reason is—if you knew what I planned, you would never permit me to go through with it.

"What's more," she continued, stopping him as he was about to speak, "when you find out what I have done, you must publicly denounce me, disavow my actions. You must say that

I have gone insane. And you must issue a reward for my capture . . . and my death."

"I can't do that!" he protested.

"You'll have to. I will leave you no choice."

"I have a choice. I can forbid you to go at all."

She smiled wanly. "Don't do it, Your Majesty. It would lead to a confrontation between us. You'd be forced to confine me to quarters or throw me in the brig. That would cause talk. And I'd escape anyway, leaving anger, resentment between us. It will be easier for both of us this way. Don't worry," she added with a sigh, "when word of what I've done, reaches you, you won't have to pretend to be shocked and horrified."

Dion frowned, obviously irresolute, determined to prevent her going. "I don't see what good you can do—by yourself."

"I won't be by myself. I've explained that much." Maigrey reached out her hand to him. "Acting together, we have a chance to defeat Abdiel, but only if I find a way to catch him off-guard. Consider this, Dion. You enter the galaxy with a fleet of warships. The Corasians will sight you, alert Abdiel. No matter how fast you move, he will have time to destroy Sagan, to escape with the plans for the bomb. With luck, I'll be there by then. I'll be able to stop him. I'll return your bloodsword to you. And then you and the fleet will convey me safely back home."

"You make it sound so easy."

"Yes, well, it won't be. It will be exceedingly dangerous. Especially for you."

"Me?" He glanced at her bitterly. "What do I have to do except spend weeks traveling through hyperspace? The only danger I see is that I'm likely to be bored to death!"

"The danger is not physical. Your plan is a good one, Dion. But before you make the final decision to go through with it, I want you to count the cost."

"Cost? I have Sagan's wealth, the captured arsenal at Snaga Ohme's. I can afford it—"

"Money isn't what people want from you, Dion. DiLuna is the matriarch of a vast system of worlds, one of the most powerful forces in the galaxy. Rykilth will never admit it, but that tightfisted vapor-breather has set aside enough to keep himself in fog for generations to come. No, Dion, what they want is you. And that is what Abdiel wants, as well."

He shifted uncomfortably before her serious, gray-eyed gaze.

"I can't say what your allies might ask of you." Maigrey shook her head. "But you can be certain that the cost of their loyalty will run high. It may be higher than you are willing to pay. Higher than, perhaps, you should pay. As for Abdiel, you know what he wants."

"My lady," said Dion, after a moment's thought, "when the silver globe with the sharp spikes dropped into my hands, during the rite of initiation, did either you or Sagan reach out and catch it for me?"

"No . . ." Maigrey faltered, somewhat taken aback.

"No, my lady, you didn't. I caught it. I held my hands beneath it. I felt the spikes slash off my fingers, break my bones, and pierce my flesh. I watched my own blood run down my arms. Don't you understand yet what that meant, my lady?"

"Do you, my liege?" Maigrey asked softly.

"Yes, I think I'm beginning to." He lifted his chin, shook back the red-golden mane of hair that flashed in the room's harsh light. "If I want the shining silver globe, I must pay the price, even if it means letting my body be broken, seeing my own blood spilled. I was prepared to lose my life that night, my lady. I was willing to make the sacrifice and I caught the globe and held on to it."

Is he right? Maigrey wondered, staring at him searchingly. We've been standing before him, shielding him, trying to protect him. But have we, instead, only been standing in his way?

"I will bring the fleet, my lady. And I suppose I have no choice but to let you go."

He brought her hand to his lips, kissed it.

Maigrey clutched suddenly at his fingers, held on to him tightly. "Dion, it could be that you will need to confront Abdiel, take back the sword yourself. Either that"—the gray eyes were dark, fathomless—"or consign the sword to him forever. The decision will be yours. The choice yours."

"What do you mean, 'consign it to him forever'?" He was suspicious, angry.

"After all, Your Majesty, you left it with him that night, didn't you?" Maigrey asked.

Dion faced her, denial on his lips, excuses ready. *It was an oversight. Snaga Ohme said no weapons. I was excited, nervous, my brain seething with plans and plots. I simply forgot. . . .*

He let go her hand, averted his face, ashamed for her to see the truth. It was bad enough knowing it himself.

Maigrey placed her hand on his arm. "When I find out where Abdiel is, I will let you know, Your Majesty. It will be your choice, then, either to come to us surrounded and protected by the fleet . . . or to come by yourself."

"Thank you for that much at least, my lady." Holding himself aloof, Dion walked away from her without looking back, walked out the door alone.

Maigrey stared after him, remembering, wondering . . . regretting. It was when she came to the regretting that she realized she was heading down a dead-end path and stopped herself, returned to the main road.

"Captain Agis, please step inside."

Agis entered. Maigrey paused a moment, looking at the dark, huddled figure of Brother Fideles, asleep on the couch. Should she wake him? Send him away?

Or let him stay?

"Seal the door, Captain," she ordered.

"Yes, my lady."

"You must have been waiting up for me," said Maigrey, smiling at him, yet studying him intently.

"Yes, my lady. I thought, perhaps, I might be needed."

"Do you know what has happened to your lord, Captain?"

The question was unexpected. Agis appeared slightly embarrassed. "My lady, rumors spread rapidly—"

"Lord Sagan has not defected to the enemy."

"I never supposed he did, my lady." The captain of the Honor Guard stood unblinking beneath her scrutiny.

She was satisfied. "What I am going to tell you, Captain, goes no farther than this room. Lord Sagan has been captured by a mind-seizer named Abdiel, one of the Order of Dark Lightning."

"The man Marcus fought?" Agis asked. "The man responsible for my centurion's death?"

"Yes, the same one."

"I know of him, my lady." The captain's voice was steel-edged.

"Abdiel has taken Lord Sagan to the Corasian system and

holds him prisoner there. I am going to attempt to free my lord and destroy this man."

"Yes, my lady." Agis did not seem surprised, did not protest, question, doubt.

Maigrey's smile deepened, twisted the scar upon her cheek. "Captain, I need one man selected from the centurions to accompany me. One man only; our force cannot be large or we would be suspected. He must be willing to travel into the enemy's galaxy. He must be willing to put aside all notions of honor and fight by stealth, by murder, by knives in the back, by throats cut in the darkness."

"Yes, my lady."

"He must obey my orders and the orders of the man who will be my second in command without question, although this person who will be my second may be extremely repugnant to him."

"Yes, my lady."

"He must be reported as AWOL. You will issue an order for his immediate capture and/or termination."

"Yes, my lady."

"He must go, knowing that he will almost assuredly die. He must leave without hope of return. He must, therefore, volunteer to accept this assignment. I will not command anyone, nor will you, Captain, to face such peril unwillingly."

"Yes, my lady."

"Can such a man be found to do this for me, Captain?"

"My lady, this warship could not hold the number of men who might be found to do this for you," said Agis, his grim face relaxing in a smile.

Maigrey was, for a moment, overcome. "Thank you, Captain," she said, when she could speak. "Have the man report to me here, in uniform, at 0600. He will bring with him whatever weapons he considers himself skilled in using."

"Yes, my lady."

"You are dismissed, Captain."

Agis saluted and left. On his way out, he stopped to supervise the changing of the watch. "Have Lieutenant Cato report to me now in my quarters," he said to the centurion leaving duty.

··◀▩ ▩▶··

Agis was working at his computer when the lieutenant entered, saluted, and stood waiting silently for orders.

"Lieutenant," said the captain, shutting the door, "when His Majesty awakes, you will tell him that I have gone AWOL. You will, as ranking officer, take over command. I have already entered the report and the charges against myself. Here is a hard copy."

The lieutenant was too highly disciplined to allow any exclamation of astonishment or questions to pass his lips. Silently, wordlessly, he accepted the document. Glancing at it, he saw the order for capture and/or termination and his lips tightened. He looked up, watched his captain take from his own shoulder the hand-tooled harness that indicated, along with the feather-crested helm, his rank. He handed the harness to Cato, who stood, face impassive, stiffly at attention.

Ceremony complete, both men relaxed.

"Is there anything I can do for you, Agis?"

"No, thank you, Cato. My affairs are in order. Serve His Majesty well."

"Of course." Cato hesitated. "The men will understand—"

"Then I trust they will keep their damn mouths shut," Agis said, grinning. He reached out his hand.

"They will." Cato took his comrade's hand, pressed it warmly. "Good luck, sir. My respects to his lordship."

"Good luck to you . . . Captain."

"Thank you, sir," said Cato softly. Saluting a final time, he left.

The door sealed shut, and Agis began preparing for his journey.

··◁■ ■▷··

"Brother, wake up." Maigrey shook the young man gently by the shoulder.

Fideles blinked, sat up, looked around in confusion. Seeing Maigrey standing by the bed, he flushed, and hastened to scramble off the couch and to his feet.

Maigrey pointed to a pile of clothes, draped over a chair. "You can't go with us dressed in monk's robes. Have you ever worn body armor before?"

Fideles's face flushed with pleasure.

"No, my lady," he answered.

"It fits skintight. It's hard to put on, if you haven't got the knack. If you need help—"

"Thank you, my lady." Fideles's face went crimson, he stared at the floor. "But that won't be necessary. I'm sure I can manage."

"Very well. There's time for a shower, if you want. Dry off thoroughly, then cover your body with talcum powder. The armor will slide on easier. You can change your clothes behind the screen."

The young man's flush deepened.

"Thank you, my lady," he said. Taking the clothes and the body armor, he tucked them under his arm and disappeared into the head.

Maigrey smiled when he couldn't see her, but her smile ended in a sigh. She sighed again when the young priest emerged from behind the screen.

He had apparently succeeded, after a struggle, in putting on the armor, for he walked as stiffly and looked as uncomfortable as a man in a body cast. That didn't worry Maigrey. With wear, the priest would soon get used to the strange, tight, squirmy feel of it. But . . .

"God help us," said Maigrey, eyeing the young man in exasperation.

"I'm sorry, my lady," said Fideles, glancing down at himself.

In an effort to disguise the priest, make him look like an outlaw, Tusk had rummaged out a pair of faded, dark-colored blue jeans, an old, ragged sweatshirt, a leather flight jacket, and a pair of combat boots. Brother Fideles, with his slim body, frank and open face, and long blond hair that fell over his shoulders in gentle waving curls, looked exactly like a priest trying to disguise himself as an outlaw.

"Tie your hair back. That will help some. And for heaven's sake, don't blush and stare at your shoes every time a woman talks to you!"

"I'm sorry, my lady." Fideles's face grew redder than before. "I—I've never been around many women."

"No, I don't suppose you have," said Maigrey, biting her lip, not knowing whether to laugh or cry. "Well, just do the best you can. Maybe, like the body armor, you'll get used to us eventually."

"But are we going to be meeting many women, my lady? I thought—"

"You thought we were going to sail into the Corasian galaxy without a care in the universe, trusting in God to protect us?"

"Well, not exactly—"

"We wouldn't get as far as the outer perimeter. We have to have a reason for being there, Brother. A reason for them not to blast us out of the stars . . . or worse. We have to, therefore, fit in with the humans who travel there."

"*Do* humans travel there?" Fideles asked, eyes glancing up at her in astonishment, immediately lowering again.

"Oh, yes. The Corasians are quite fond of humans, human flesh particularly."

Maigrey said nothing more. Let him think about that one. She turned away, busied herself with packing items in a duffel bag. She had changed her clothes, was dressed all in black, black leather pants, tucked into high black boots; a black, high-collared, long-sleeved tunic, belted around her waist. Occasionally when she moved, there came from beneath the black the flash of shining silver armor. She wore the blood-sword, attached to its scabbard, on her right hip.

"Brother Fideles," Maigrey said suddenly, straightening, facing the priest, "do you know what kind of people go into Corasia? Scum. The stuff that sinks to the bottom of the pot, the dregs of human and alien life. Do you know *why* they go there? Two reasons: One, they have nowhere else to go, which means that they've done things that have put them outside the laws of man and God. Two, they want money so badly that they're willing to do anything to obtain it.

"Those are the kind of people who get into Corasia safely, the kind who do business there. And that's the kind, Brother Fideles, we're going to be . . . only worse."

"I understand," said Fideles, eyes lowered. "God will be with us."

"No, He won't!"

Crossing the deck, Maigrey caught hold of the collar of the young man's shirt, gave it an expert twist, and jerked his head up so that he was forced to stare directly into her face. "Where we are going, God left long ago, if He was ever there at all, which I doubt. You don't believe me, now, but you will, Brother. You will."

If Fideles so much as blanched, twitched, if his eyelids flickered, Maigrey had decided to leave him—sign from God or no sign from God. She would turn him over to the Honor

Guard, have them lock him in the brig, where he could pray to his heart's content. But he met her gaze calmly, listened to her calmly, his face serious, expression firm and resolved.

"I may be a priest, my lady, but that doesn't mean that I am weak or a coward. I'm used to hardship. I've seen pain and suffering. I've proved my mettle in battle, under fire. I proved my mettle to my lord. You can rely on me, my lady. And if I choose to bring God along," he added with a quiet smile, "I'll see to it that He doesn't get in your way."

"Very good, Fideles." Releasing her hold on him, Maigrey smoothed the wrinkles from his shirt. "You even looked at me when you spoke. There may be hope for you yet. Now, just try to stop shaking every time I touch you, and we'll get along fine."

"Yes, my lady." Fideles swallowed. Sweat trickled down his forehead.

Maigrey turned back to resume her packing. "We need another name for you. I don't suppose they called you 'Fideles' below decks?"

"No, my lady. I was known as Daniel."

"Well, Daniel, you're headed for the lions' den. Yes, Captain," she said in answer to a call over the commlink. "Enter."

The double doors slid open, Agis walked inside. The doors slid shut, sealed. Maigrey yanked the ties of the duffel bag closed. She did not look up.

"Is the man I requested here, Captain?"

"He's here, my lady."

Maigrey raised her eyes, saw Agis standing alone before her. He saluted, fist over his heart.

"I hope he will suit, my lady."

"He has suited me in the past," Maigrey said gravely. She noticed that though he wore his armor, he had removed his harness and the crested helm. "Agis meet Daniel. He will also be accompanying us."

The two men looked at each other, examined each other, nodded. If the centurion was surprised or disturbed at this choice of companion, Maigrey was pleased to see that he kept his doubts to himself.

"Now, gentlemen, here is the scenario. I am Lady Maigrey, an outlaw with a price on my head, willing to do anything to escape being brought to justice, on my way to join forces with the notorious Lord Sagan. You, Agis, are a former centurion who has forsaken your sworn duties and come with me, I suppose, because you are desperately in love with me."

"Yes, my lady." Agis grinned.

"And you, Daniel?" Maigrey paused. "What about you?"

"I'm a renegade priest of the Order of Adamant, who broke my vows and fled the brotherhood to escape punishment. Because I've been initiated into their secrets, the Order's punishment would be severe," said Daniel cheerfully. "I'm sure they'd kill me."

"I'm sure they would," Maigrey said dryly. She lifted the duffel bag.

"I'll carry that, my lady." Agis took the bag from her, slung it over his shoulder. "Where to?"

"My lord's spaceplane," said Maigrey, drawing a deep breath. "We're going to make ourselves truly outlaws. We're going to run the blockade."

--◁■ ■▷--

0400. The changing of the watch. An unshaven and bleary-eyed Admiral Aks—an unusual sight on the bridge at this hour—paced back and forth on the captain's walk, a slender bridge that spanned a gigantic viewscreen, opening onto the panorama of stars glittering in the vast deep.

Captain Williams stood rigid, motionless at the far end of the walk. The captain was often on the bridge at the changing of the watch, particularly when the ship was under full alert. But alert status had been downgraded, since it was now common knowledge that Lord Sagan was not to be found on *Phoenix*. His Majesty, the king, had actually opened up friendly negotiations with the Galactic forces.

An ensign, receiving a communication, looked startled, reported, "Captain, a group of heavily armed men have commandeered Lord Sagan's spaceplane! They're threatening to kill anyone who tries to stop them from taking off!"

The Admiral stopped his pacing. He and Williams exchanged glances.

"Attempt to raise it," ordered the captain.

"No response, sir. Their computer says that if they don't receive clearance for takeoff, they'll blow up this ship. Sir"—the ensign looked extremely puzzled—"reports from the han-

gar deck indicate that Lady Morianna and Agis, the captain of
the Honor Guard, are the ones who took the plane."

"Indeed?" Williams raised an eyebrow. "Well, we can't have
them blowing up the ship. Grant them clearance."

"Yes, sir." A momentary pause. "Plane's away, sir."

"Excellent. Now, communicate to her ladyship that unless
she returns to *Phoenix* immediately, she will be fired upon."

"Yes, sir. No response, sir."

"Ah," said Williams. He cleared his throat, stood tapping his
foot on the deck.

"Shall I give the order to fire, sir?"

Williams appeared to consider the matter. "What's the
spaceplane's current location?"

The officer provided it. "The plane's apparently heading for
the Lanes, Captain."

"Undoubtedly." The captain and the admiral both stepped
to the viewscreen, looked out.

"The plane is very near the ships of the Galactic Democratic
Navy," remarked Williams.

"It would be a pity if we were to fire on the stolen
spaceplane and hit one of their cruisers, particularly during
this stage of negotiations," stated Admiral Aks.

"An excellent point, sir. Hold your fire," Williams ordered.

"Yes, sir," said the mystified ensign. "Galactic Navy planes
moving to intercept. Her ladyship is opening fire."

The admiral and the captain and everyone who could sneak
a glance from his duties stared out the viewscreen, at the battle
that, from this distance, appeared to be between one child's
set of toys and another. The play turned deadly. Tracer fire
from the spaceplane disintegrated one of the Galactic planes
opposing it, crippled another. Other planes flew frantically to
join the battle, but by that time Maigrey had locked in a
course. The Lane was clear. She made the Jump, her plane
vanished from sight.

"They've gone into hyperspace, sir."

A ragged cheer echoed through the bridge.

Williams, frowning, turned around. "Belay that nonsense.
Lieutenant, put those men on report."

"Hangar deck reports two men knocked unconscious, sir;
taken to sick bay. Sir," the ensign added, highly astonished,
"one of the men with her ladyship has been identified as that
nurse who went AWOL. . . ."

"This is a disgrace!" Williams snapped. "I want everyone involved put on report. Show in the log that the spaceplane was stolen and that we made every effort, short of risking the lives of those who might be in the line of fire, to recapture it. And now, I must go and explain the situation to General Pang."

Williams smoothed his uniform, straightened his collar, pulled at his cuffs.

"And I," said the admiral gravely, "must report this unfortunate incident to His Majesty."

The two officers left the bridge. The crewmen looked at each other, grinned, and returned to their duties.

The lieutenant, leaving the bridge to file his report, glanced out the viewscreen. "Good luck, my lady," he said beneath his breath.

··◆▬ ▬◆··

General Dixter—a glass of green Laskarian brandy in his hand—stood at his own much smaller viewscreen, waiting. A spaceplane, darting suddenly through space, caught his attention. He focused on it, tensed, watched the attempt to intercept, saw the flash of red fire, the white burst of the explosive hit.

And then the plane was gone from view, as if someone had switched off a light.

John Dixter was left alone in the darkness.

"Good-bye, Maigrey," he said quietly to the stars.

Chapter ❦ Four

The stroke of midnight ceases,
And I lie down alone.
                          A. E. Housman, *Parta Quies*

"You about ready, kid?" Tusk entered Dion's quarters.

"Yes. I'm packed. I just have to change my clothes."

The young man removed the lion-head pin, began to strip off the dress uniform and royal regalia he'd worn for the press conference. Folding them carefully, he thrust them into the rucksack. It wasn't the same sack Platus had given him when he'd bid him farewell that night on Syrac Seven, but it was similar. Perhaps because of Tusk's presence, it reminded Dion of that night.

"What's the official government reaction to the press conference?" he asked abruptly.

"About what you'd expect. Robes said that the notion Sagan'd been abducted by some evil genius was . . . let's see if I can remember it exactly. 'What you'd expect of an eighteen-year-old youth who imagines himself in a fairy tale.' I gotta admit I kinda like that one." Tusk grinned, then sobered. "The bad thing is that they've put out a reward on the Starlady. 'Armed and dangerous.' Which means every bounty-hunting scuzz between here and the Copernicus system will be gunning for her."

"It's what she wanted." And at least I didn't have to do it, Dion added silently. He yanked too hard on one of the straps of the rucksack, tore it off.

"Hey, kid, don't take it out on the equipment," Tusk remonstrated quietly. "You may be living out of that sack a long time. From what I've heard about this godforsaken planet of Olefsky's, he's somewhere back in the twelfth century. He doesn't even have indoor plumbing, the Bear claims it's for wimps. I guess runnin' out in the snow to go to the head in the middle of the night in your altogether with the temperature at thirty below is supposed to make you tough."

Dion couldn't help smiling. He relaxed, felt better. "I know it would make me tough. Either that or make me think twice about drinking beer after dinner. Besides, his theory must work. You've seen Olefsky."

"Flesh mountain? Though I gotta admit most of him's solid. You know what his kid told me? On the day he becomes a 'man,' each of his sons has to kill an ox with one blow of his fist, then carry the carcass home over his shoulders. And women have to go through the same type of ritual. But they probably go easy on girls. I hear he has a daughter," Tusk added ominously.

Dion laughed, zipped himself into a flight suit. "Most likely she gets two hits on the ox, then only has to drag it home."

"Most likely we won't be able to tell her *from* the ox!" Tusk shook his head.

"What are you two talking about? What girl killed an ox? Heavens, Dion, aren't you packed yet? You men. I've been ready for hours." Nola entered the young man's quarters. "XJ sent me to look for you. The computer's about to have a meltdown. Claims he's had life support on for an hour now and you're wasting fuel."

"I'll waste him," Tusk muttered. "The kid's ready to go anyhow. Put your helmet on. No one's supposed to recognize you. The boys out there got their orders?"

"Of course. The centurions will continue to post guard as if I'm still inside my quarters. Food will be brought to my room and one of them will eat it. I'm not making any public appearances due to my deep concern over the current dangerous situation."

"Good." Tusk rubbed his hands. "Well, I guess we're off, like a herd of mad turtles as my dad used to say."

"You're enjoying this," Nola accused him.

"Damn right, sweetheart. No more tight collars and 'droid reporters. No more Captain Williams with his perfect teeth and pressed pants. I'm back to what I do best." He put his arm around her. "Lovin' and fightin'."

Dion grabbed the helmet. "I thought we were going," he said coldly. Seeing the two of them happy together, watching them exchange glances that he knew were bedroom glances, overhearing whispered words that he knew were bedroom words twisted him up inside.

"Where's General Dixter?" he asked more calmly, trying to untie the knot of anger and envy that was tightening his gut. "Already on board?"

Nola's expression was grave. "He's not going with us, Dion."

"Not going? But—"

"Look, kid," Tusk intervened. "You know how the general hates space flight. Cooped up in that little spaceplane that's barely big enough for the three of us, he'd last about a day."

"He's been with us so long, I was counting on him for advice—"

"Dixter says you'll do fine, Dion," interrupted Nola gently. "He has every confidence in you. You've been trained by the best, he says."

"He thinks he should stay aboard *Phoenix*, in case that flippin' Galactic general gets a wild hair up her nose and decides she wants to board the ship."

"Probably a good idea." Dion sighed. One more gone. "I'll go say good-bye—"

"I think the idea was that he'd avoid good-byes, kid. He's had about one too many, if you know what I mean."

Dion nodded, hefted the pack.

"Helmet," said Tusk.

"I haven't forgotten." He fit it over his head. "That look okay?"

Tusk inspected him. Nola tucked wisps of red hair up in the back.

"I'll meet you on the flight deck. We're not supposed to be seen together."

Dion settled the pack on his shoulder, left his quarters. The Honor Guard, pretending he was just another pilot, did not salute him. But one said, in an undertone that was barely picked up by even the helmet's sensitive monitors, "Good luck to Your Majesty."

Dion stopped, glanced around. "Cato, isn't it? You've been promoted?"

"Yes, Your—sir," he said, remembering he was supposed to be speaking to just another pilot.

"Where's Agis? I hope nothing's happened to him."

Cato's face remained impassive. "He went AWOL, sir. He took the news about his lordship very hard. Very hard indeed."

"Ah, I see. You understand your orders, Captain?" he asked in an undertone.

"Perfectly, Your Majesty."

"Then, carry on. Remember, you haven't seen me."

Dion continued on down the corridor alone.

"Here they come," said XJ gloomily. "I want to go on record as saying that I don't approve of this."

"Duly noted," Dion answered.

Now that he was back inside the spaceplane, listening to the computer's complaining, excitement tingled through him, burned away his unhappiness. He was suddenly extremely glad to be going somewhere, extremely glad to be doing something, even if he did face the possibility of being blown to cosmic dust.

A thud hit the side of the spaceplane. The sound of unsteady feet came clomping up the ladder, followed by a pounding on the hatch and a raucous voice, shouting, "Open up in there! you mechanical sonuvabitch!"

XJ's lights flashed in irritation. "Drunk again? I'll fix you, you rummy—"

The computer caused the hatch to drop open with unexpected swiftness. Tusk, leaning on it, slipped and tumbled through headfirst. He landed heavily on the deck on his back, dumping most of the contents of a bottle of champagne over himself on the way down.

XJ chuckled to itself loudly.

Tusk, groaning, got to his feet, shook his fist in the computer's general direction. "You didn't have to do that!"

"I'm a true thespian," returned the computer loftily. "I get into my part."

"Oh, Tusk, honey!" came Nola's voice. "Can you come . . . give me a little help!" She giggled. "I can't seem to make my feet work right. . . ."

"Be right there, schweetheart!" Tusk bawled. Turning his head, his voice suddenly sober, he gave Dion the high sign. "Okay, kid, it's your move. Everybody should be watchin' us, but keep your head down anyway."

Dion nodded.

Tusk, singing loudly, champagne bottle in hand, clambered unsteadily back up the ladder. Dion slipped up another ladder, one that led to the gun turret located above the Scimitar's cockpit. A bubble of steelglass, the gun turret was plainly visible to everyone on the hangar deck. Dion, careful to keep his head down, wedged his body into a tight, cramped shadowed space between the seat and gun, and wondered, as tightly as he was stuck in here, how he was ever going to get out again.

Wriggling about some, trying to keep the circulation from leaving his legs, he peeped up over the rim of the viewscreen to watch the proceedings outside the spaceplane. As Tuck had said, everyone on the hangar deck was watching and laughing at the drunken newlyweds.

Nola, champagne glass in hand, was endeavoring to climb the stairs leading up into the spaceplane. She couldn't seem to find the first rung. Staring at it with the serious, intense concentration of one who sees ten rungs where there should be only one, she lifted her foot, placed it firmly on thin air, and nearly fell over on her nose.

She paused to consider the matter, drank off about half the champagne while thinking about it, and tried again. This time she didn't even come close and staggered across the flight deck. Several helpful flight crew members caught her and aided her back to the spaceplane.

"Hey, you're gettin' pretty friendly with my wife!" Tusk snarled, leaning out over the hatch, waving the champagne bottle. "Just back off! Here, honey. I'll lend you a hand."

The flight crew hoisted Nola, giggling madly, onto their shoulders and gave her a boost up the ladder. Tusk caught hold of her, dragged her on board by the well-rounded seat of her pants. The two disappeared precipitously down through the hatch, accompanied by the sound of breaking glass and wild laughter.

The hatch whirred shut.

Dion heard Tusk climb into the cockpit. A moment later the mercenary's face appeared, peering up at him.

"You okay up there, kid?"

"If you don't expect me to move quickly," Dion retorted. "I'm wedged in here so tight you're going to have to pry me out with a crowbar!"

"You'll move quick enough if they start shooting at us," Tusk predicted. "Okay, Nola, take the co-pilot's seat. Now, XJ, you know what to do."

"Have you ever noticed," stated the computer irritably, "that we never fight our way out of trouble, anymore. We drink our way . . ."

"Just shut up and do what you're supposed to do," Tusk snapped viciously. "This drunk routine was Dixter's idea, by the way."

"Figures," said XJ. "Leave it to the general to know your one strong point."

"Would you two stop it and get us out of here!" Dion demanded. "I've lost all feeling in my feet!"

"Sure thing, boss. Hit the engines, XJ. Kid, tell us what's goin' on from your angle."

The spaceplane's engines started with a roar, the deck on which Dion was sitting began to vibrate, nearly jarring the teeth out of his head. He kept watch out the viewscreen.

"The flight crews are waving their arms and running over here. There go the alarms," he added needlessly. The horn blasts nearly deafened them all. The men on the hangar deck were making frantic hand signals, warning Tusk to shut his engines off. "Too late. The red lights're flashing! There they go!"

As a safety precaution, the hangar bay doors opened automatically within a prescribed time period after a spaceplane's engines were fired. The alarms and flashing lights advised everyone on the deck that the atmosphere and pressure were about to be reduced and it would be advisable to clear the area.

"Scimitar, this is deck control. Just what the devil do you think you're doing?" came a stern voice over the commlink.

"S-sorry," slurred Tusk. "Hit the wrong . . . Nola, get off me. Yeah, sure I like that, sweetheart, but . . . oh, yeah. I really like that!"

Sounds of breathless laughter and kissing.

"The doors are starting to open, Tusk," reported Dion.

He could see Tusk's legs only from the knees down. The mercenary was lying on his back on the console. Nola, leaning over him, was kissing him on the neck. Each had their hands—not on each other—but on the control switches.

"Deck control!" XJ came on. "Would someone get these drunken idiots off my plane?"

"We'd be happy to, computer, as soon as he shuts down his engines!" returned deck control.

"Hangar bay doors open!" Dion reported. "You're clear!"

"Yes, sir," said Tusk. "Shutting down now, sir. I—Oh, shit!"

The spaceplane took off with a blast and a burst of speed that flattened Dion back against the bulkheads and sent Tusk and Nola flying. The Scimitar shot out of the hangar deck and swooped into space.

Dion grabbed hold of the seat of the gunner's chair, which was about level with his nose, and managed to pull himself up. Looking down below, he saw a black hand and arm reach up from the deck, grab hold of the console. Tusk emerged from underneath, grim-faced and red-eyed with fury.

"What's the matter, Tusk?" said XJ, lights flickering innocently. "You didn't want maximum acceleration?"

"You sonuva—"

"No swearing! I got us out of there, didn't I?"

"Yeah. Most of us. If you don't count my guts. *They're* still lyin' on the flight deck. Nola, you all right?"

"Yeah, I'm fine. Just a little shaken." Nola got to her feet. Her eyes were wide. She put her hand to her head. "Wow! That was some ride."

"Kid?" Tusk peered up into the gun turret. "You okay?"

"If you don't count the fact that my spine's on the outside of my skin instead of the inside, I'm dandy. Now what?"

"Get the gun ready. We're not outta this yet. We're comin' up on the blockade. XJ, find us a Lane. And here comes someone to look us over."

"Act one. Scene two," stated the computer. "Places, everyone. . . ."

Dion drew in a deep breath, his fingers closed nervously over the lascannon's handgrips, his thumbs located the firing buttons. A spaceplane zoomed into view. He located it in his sights.

"Got it."

"Good. Don't get an itchy trigger finger, kid. The last thing we want to do is cause a stir. XJ, keep the shields down. We want to look like butter wouldn't melt on our afterburners. Hopefully, we'll just ease on out of here."

The Galactic pilot issued a warning.

Tusk pulled up, hung dead in space, shields down, vulnerable. He had the lights on bright in the cockpit, the pilot would be able to see him clearly. The gun turret's lights were off, however. The enemy pilot wouldn't see anyone up there.

Dion sat in the darkness, hands on the gun, palms sweating, breath coming short and fast.

"Scimitar, where're you off to in such a hurry?" The challenging pilot's voice was female, sounded friendly and extremely bored. "Hell, you shot outta there like you had one of those damn hypermissiles up your ass."

"Aw, my computer's fucked up. It's one of those old XJ-27 models and it's gettin' senile. Doesn't know its disk drive from a hole in the ground anymore."

"I'll get you for that," XJ promised in a low tone.

"Gee, that's too bad," the pilot commiserated. "When you get it replaced, try the M-13. Fast, efficient, no back-talk . . ."

"M-13!" XJ was shocked. "That ramless mass of microchips. Why, I—"

"Shhhush!" Tusk growled. "Yeah, I'll keep that in mind. Thanks for the tip."

"Anytime. I'm always here."

"Blockade duty's no fun," Tusk said sympathetically.

"Damn right. Back and forth. Up and down. Round and round. Fuck it! The only excitement we've had in a week was when the Lady made a run for it. Heard she got away, too."

"Yeah. Good riddance, I say. Damn troublemaker. But now that she and that hard-ass Sagan are gone, maybe the kid'll settle down and get his head screwed on right."

"What kid? You mean the boy who would be king? Do you know him?"

"You might say that. My name's Tusk," said Tusk modestly. "Maybe you've seen me on the vids."

"Tusk! Sure, I've seen you. Seen 'His Majesty,' too. What a cutie! Say, some of the girls and I've been wondering. Is that hair of his for real or is it a transplant?"

Nola's shoulders were shaking with silent laughter. Tusk grinned, glanced up at an appalled Dion, and winked.

"Naw, it's real. Hey, maybe if they call off this blockade crap, I could arrange for you to meet him."

"Could you? That'd be great. They might as well call this off. Everybody we were trying to keep penned up's already got out. Except for the king. And I don't suppose he's planning to go anywhere."

"Shit, no," said Tusk. "He's a nice kid and all that, but he's got no backbone."

"Not anymore!" Dion shifted around in his seat trying to ease the pain of his bruised spine.

"He's locked himself up in his room. Sulking, refuses to come out. That's why I left. Couldn't take the whinin'. Me and the wife here . . . This is Nola. Say 'hello,' Nola."

"Hello," Nola sang out sweetly and waved her hand.

"And you are . . . ?" Tusk asked.

"Epstein, Judi. Lieutenant. Yeah, come to think of it, I saw where you got yourself married. What a pity. You're not a bad-looking guy yourself."

"I think I'm going to short out," muttered XJ.

"Just find us a goddam Lane, will you?" Tusk ordered below his breath.

"I have it already! And I'd just like to add that the M-13 couldn't have come up with it this fast. On the screen . . ."

"Like I was saying," Tusk continued, "me and the wife here thought we'd slip away, grab ourselves some R and R. Things have been kinda tense the last few days. There's a little planet I know of, about two light-years from here—white sand, blue water, green trees . . . orange sky, but then you can't have everything. We thought we'd take a cruise out thataway. Soak up some rays."

"But that's outside the perimeter."

"Sure, yeah, but what the hell difference does it make? You said yourself they're gonna call off this stupid blockade any day now. We just leave an hour or so early, that's all."

"I don't know . . ."

"Lock her in, kid," Tusk said grimly.

"Oh, Tusk!" Nola reached out, grabbed hold of his hand. "We can't shoot her! We know her name!"

"I don't like it any better than you, sweetheart, but if we blow this chance, we'll never get another one. Kid?"

"Don't worry," Dion said coolly. "In my sights."

"What about it, Epstein?" Tusk asked, trying to keep his voice light and cheerful. "No one'll ever miss us. When I get back, maybe His Majesty will be over his snit and I'll get him to throw a party."

"And I'm invited?"

"You betcha," Tusk said. He squeezed Nola's hand.

"All right, then. No one's paying any attention to us. Get going, and if you ever decide you're tired of being married, Tusk, give me a call."

"You can count on it!" Tusk said.

Nola slugged him in the arm. "Don't sound so damn enthusiastic."

The enemy spaceplane veered off. Dion relaxed, slumped over the gun. He was surprised to find himself trembling.

Tusk approached the Lane. "Ready to make the Jump, XJ? You strapped in up there, kid? Here we go . . ."

The first time Dion'd made the Jump, he'd blacked out. He was used to it, now. He no longer lost consciousness. He only ended up feeling nauseous and with a splitting headache.

"We made it," announced Tusk. "Everyone breathe easy."

Dion slid down out of the gun turret, landed on the deck of the cockpit. Three of them were a tight fit. He squeezed past Tusk and Nola, made his way slowly up the ladder to the small sleeping quarters, and crawled into one of the hammocks.

"You okay, kid?" Tusk sounded worried.

"Yes, I'm okay."

"You know, Nola . . . I'm gonna kinda miss that planet with the white sand and the blue trees and the green sky . . ."

"Orange sky," Nola whispered.

Dion heard a rustling sound, as of two flight suits pressing closely together. He lay in his hammock and stared into the shadows above his head and thought about killing someone whose name you knew and whether or not his hair looked fake and why he hadn't stopped Maigrey from going after Sagan and how much it hurt to be alone.

Always alone.

Chapter ·◦··◦◦◦◦·· Five

. . . we cannot make our sun stand still . . .
      Andrew Marvell, *To His Coy Mistress*

"'*Gloria in excelsis Deo.*

"'*Et in terra pax hominibus bonea voluntatis. Laudamus te. Benedicimus te. Adoramus te.*'"

Maigrey sat in the back of the chapel, in the darkness, listening to Derek recite the prayer. The chapel was cold, being unheated, and empty, except for the two of them. Derek avoided the formal Sabbath prayer services, led by a priest of the Order of Adamant and attended by most of the student body and teachers of the Academy. Sagan preferred to pray alone, though the priest—a good, gentle man—often tried to change the boy's mind and draw him into the life of the Church on campus. Sagan politely, coldly refused. Maigrey understood, if no one else did. Derek knew himself to be close to the Creator. It annoyed him to be in company with those who merely mouthed the credo, forgot the responses, and woke up when the service ended.

He prayed, therefore, in solitary aloofness, although he didn't mind Maigrey, on the times she decided to accompany him. She sat in the very back pew, far from where he knelt at the altar. She never spoke, never interrupted. But she listened and it seemed to her as if his prayers carried her nearer a God whom she knew only by reputation, and then only by having heard her father's soldiers take His name in vain.

"'Glory to God in the highest.

"'And on earth peace to men of goodwill. We praise Thee. We bless Thee. We adore Thee.'"

Her presence went unnoticed, it was to him like the presence of the wind that stirred against his cheek, the air that was breathed into his lungs. And his presence was to her . . .

220

"My lady." A hand touched her on the shoulder. "We're near the rendezvous."

Maigrey woke with a start, confused for a moment. She was not in a chapel, but in a spaceplane, yet she still heard the fluid chanting of a long-dead language.

"Thank you, Agis," she said, sitting up.

"Coffee?"

"Yes, please."

Agis brought her a steaming cup of a hot liquid that passed for coffee, but always seemed to taste faintly of hydraulic fluid.

"*Glorificamus te. Gratias agimus tibi propter magnam gloriam tuam.*

"*We glorify Thee. We give thanks to Thee for Thy great glory.*'"

Agis glanced at Brother Fideles—Daniel, Maigrey had to remember to think of him now—and shook his head, shrugging. "I'm surprised you could sleep through that."

Maigrey sipped the coffee. "I was so tired . . . and the prayers were like part of my dream . . . ."

She fell silent, remembering, but the memories hurt, and she shook them off. The present, that's all that mattered. Not the past. Not the future.

"Any sign of a spaceship?" she asked Agis.

"No, my lady. But we're early yet. You have time for a shower and breakfast."

A hot shower sounded wonderful. Breakfast did not, but she had to eat. A throbbing of her temples and a slight dizzy and disoriented feeling were her body's insistent reminder that she had avoided food the last twenty-four hours.

"*Domine Deus, Rex caelestis, Deus Pater omnipotens.*

"*O Lord God, heavenly King, God the Father almighty.*'"

"Pardon me, my lady," Agis said in an undertone, with a glance at the priest, "but he's not going to do that when we're in action, is he?"

Maigrey hid her smile. "No, Agis. He has, if you remember, served on a ship of war. He was commended for his bravery under fire when *Phoenix* was attacked by the Corasians."

Agis raised a skeptical eyebrow, and returned to the cockpit. The spaceplane was operating on automatic pilot, flying to coordinates Maigrey had entered before going to sleep. Which had been, she realized, taking off her clothes, eighteen hours ago.

Maigrey had lived and fought in close quarters with men all her life and had learned the trick of undressing without really undressing. She noticed, however, that Daniel, occupying the same cramped quarters as herself, saw her starting to disrobe and brought his prayers to a speedy conclusion.

Rising to his feet, a faint flush on his cheek, the priest hurried forward, to join Agis in the cockpit. Maigrey smiled, shook her head, wrapped herself in a robe, and locked herself in the tiny shower stall.

The thin trickle of hot water, pouring over her face and hair and body, relaxed her. Closing her eyes, she stretched forth a mental hand, reached out to touch Sagan. Her mind touched nothing. Only his life force remained. She imagined herself locked in a pitch-dark room. She could feel, with her hand, the floor, solid beneath her. But the room itself was empty. She groped about, hoping to touch something, anything. . . .

A stinging pain stabbed her consciousness, as if, in the darkness, she pricked her fingers upon a needle. Maigrey snatched her mind back, shocked, frightened.

Abdiel—attempting to reach her through Sagan.

Which meant that he had Sagan, he'd "joined" with him. Maigrey shuddered, almost gave up in despair. She recovered quickly, realized that Abdiel was stumbling about in the same dark room as herself. Sagan wasn't there. He had withdrawn far, far into his innermost being. She imagined what it would be like, trying to delve into that darkness, trying to bring him back. Resolutely, she pushed the thought out of her mind.

The present—remember, Maigrey? she reminded herself. We're a long way from that point yet.

He was alive. That was what counted. She had never been able to define precisely how she knew he was alive, how she'd known for seventeen years of self-imposed exile, hiding from him, that he was alive. It was hearing footsteps not your own walking beside you. It was feeling the beat of another's heart in tandem with your own. It was hearing clearly a voice speak when everyone around you was silent.

The soap slipped from her fingers. Maigrey swore softly beneath her breath. In the small shower stalls, one had to be practically a contortionist to pick anything up.

What would it be like, she wondered suddenly, retrieving the soap, to lose that life force within hers? What would it be like for her—alive—if he were dead?

The water flowing over her went suddenly cold. Maigrey shut it off abruptly. Soap stung her eyes, she'd neglected to rinse her face. Fortunately her towel was close at hand. She toweled herself off vigorously, rubbing life back into her skin.

The loneliness, for the one left behind, would be unbearable. Separation might not have been difficult to endure during that early time when Sagan'd first found her again on Oha-Lau, during that time before the mind-link had been truly reestablished. But now, they'd grown closer than ever, bound by chains of darkness, chains of adamant. If the chains were broken, the one left behind, the one left living, would have to carry the weight alone.

"My lady!" Agis rapped on the door. "Ship in sight."

"I'll be right there."

The present. The present.

Maigrey wrapped the towel around her hair, hurriedly put on her robe—after a brief struggle with her arm in the wrong sleeve—then hastened forward to the cockpit. The metal deck was ice-cold beneath bare feet, but, as usual, her boots had disappeared. Probably slid under the pull-down bunk.

Standing on one foot, clutching her robe around her, she stared out the viewscreen at the ship that was creeping toward them through the starlit backdrop of space.

Maigrey took a close look at the ship, then glanced at Agis. She saw his jaw muscles stiffen, his expression remain carefully blank. Good, she thought. He recognizes it. This must be the right one. But best to make certain.

She did not attempt to establish verbal contact with the ship, but sent out a general signal, nothing but a meaningless numerical sequence. Collected, translated using the correct key, the numerical sequence would be transformed into music, a line of music from the opera *Rigoletto*.

"*Demonio! E come puoi tanto securo oprar?*"

"You devil! And how do you avoid being caught?" sings the baritone in the opera.

Maigrey, waiting for the reply, hummed the response beneath her breath.

"Coming in now, my lady," reported Agis.

Music and a bass voice sounded from the computer, triggered by the correct code signal.

"*L'uomo di sera aspetto . . . una stoccata, e muor.*"

"I await the man at night . . . one thrust and he's dead."

"That's him," said the centurion, tone grim.

"You disapprove, Agis?" Maigrey asked.

He stared out the viewscreen at the ship, drifting some distance from them.

"No, my lady," he said finally, heavily. "I think you made a wise decision. He is completely and totally devoted to my lord. To *my lord*," the centurion emphasized, glancing back at Maigrey.

She nodded. "I understand. I judged so myself. But he's good. I've seen him at work."

"My lord would have no other," said Agis simply.

"It looks like a peddler." Daniel was staring at the spaceship in confusion.

The ship had come to a halt, waiting for further instructions. A small vessel, it was extremely nondescript in appearance, this particular model having been cranked out by the millions during the space rush toward the end of the second Dark Ages. Cheap and reliable, the saucer-shaped craft had been used to carry a burgeoning population off a desperately sick planet.

The craft's original builders and designers—knowing that once most travelers set forth in these vehicles, they would have a difficult time finding a service station along the route—had made it a selling point that their workmanship would last, and in case it did malfunction, the craft was easily repairable. All parts were interchangeable, detailed repair manuals were included with every purchase, and the "volks-rocket," as it came to be affectionately known, was mainly responsible for the population of other stars.

Due to their high state of reliability, the proliferation of parts, and their sheer numbers, many of the volksrockets were still in existence, surviving mainly by cannibalism. Cheap and fuel efficient, they were used by itinerant traveling salesmen, groupies tagging along after rock stars, drifters, migrant workers.

"A peddler?" repeated Maigrey, studying the vessel that had no weapons, looked shabby and in need of a fresh coat of paint. "Yes, you could say that. A peddler of death."

Daniel looked up at her swiftly, a half smile on his face, thinking she was joking. One glance at her—face pale and serious—and at Agis's grim expression, and the priest's smile slipped.

"I don't understand."

"Soon, Brother Fideles, you will be introduced to one of the most dangerous men in the galaxy. Sparafucile, a professional assassin. He could kill you in less time than it takes to say the word."

Daniel looked grave. "How did you come to meet such a person, my lady?"

"I met him on Laskar. He saved my life. Lord Sagan introduced us. He works for Lord Sagan."

Maigrey and Agis both watched the effect of this information on the young priest's expressive face. The blow was a telling one, striking deep, drawing blood. He realized he was under scrutiny, looked from one to the other, then lowered his eyes beneath the calm, penetrating gazes.

"You mean my lord hires him to kill people. I don't believe it."

Maigrey sighed. "Brother Fideles, look at me. Do you see the scar on my face?"

The young priest lifted unhappy, confused eyes, focused on the terrible disfiguring scar that marred the smooth complexion of the right cheek. He glanced hurriedly away.

"Look at it, Brother," Maigrey commanded. "Look at it closely. The scar represents the flaw—the fatal, tragic flaw—in Sagan, in myself. It led him to betray his king, to commit murder and worse. It led me to break a vow, to betray a sacred trust. We are fallen angels, cast out of heaven. Our redemption—if redemption is possible for us—is Dion. The darkness has overtaken us; it has overtaken Peter Robes. If it overtakes Dion, we are lost."

The young priest sat with head bowed.

"Brother Fideles"—Maigrey's voice was gentle, a whisper to be heard by the heart—"I walk in darkness so thick around me, I can't begin to see my way out. I shouldn't have allowed you to come. And, in fact, I think I'll leave you behind. There's a small planet, not far from here, where you could catch a freighter back to your Abbey. You have duties there."

Brother Fideles didn't answer her. Maigrey kept silent, aware that he was listening to a voice she herself could no longer hear. At last he sighed, raised his head, looked directly at her, at the scar on her face.

"God's will is clear, my lady. I am to stay with you."

Maigrey rocked back on her heels, stared at him, exasperated, not knowing quite what to do. "Listen to me, Brother.

Those of us who walk in darkness must use the ways of darkness. Do you understand what you're letting yourself in for?"

"I understand," said Fideles. His gaze, steady, unwavering, met hers and did not falter.

Maigrey stood up abruptly, turned and walked back to the living quarters.

"He doesn't, of course," she muttered, throwing the wet towel irritably to the deck, kicking it beneath her bunk with her foot. "He has no idea what he's getting into. He's untrained, unfit for this job. He won't carry a weapon, not even to save his own life. He'll end up getting killed . . . if we're lucky. If we're not, he'll end up getting us all killed! Why? Why am I going along with this?"

Because, came the answer, you have no say in this decision. He's gone over your head, to the top. He's acting under Another's orders. You've been outranked.

"All right, then, but if he gets into trouble, You have to get him out!" Maigrey put on her body armor, then her silver armor, pulled the black tunic and pants over it, ran a comb through her wet, straggling hair.

"Agis, I want to talk to Sparafucile."

"Yes, my lady." Agis raised the ship.

A voice, sibilant as a snake's, came over the commlink.

"Starlady! Well met."

The sound of that voice conjured up unwelcome memories. Maigrey shivered involuntarily, steeled herself to the duty at hand. The present. That was all that mattered. The present.

"You received my communication?"

"Sparafucile is here, isn't he?"

"Do you know why I sent for you?"

"I see newsvids. Sagan Lord is truly in Corasia?"

"I have every reason to believe so."

"He not go, like they say, voluntarily?"

"No."

"Then we get him back."

Maigrey smiled at the assassin's confident tone. "Yes. We get him back. I have a plan. But I need men—the kind who'll choose money over scruples—and a small attack ship, a torpedo boat or something similar."

"You have money? Hard money, no credit?"

"Yes."

"Then I know where we can find what you need. I send you course change. You follow me. Your plane is, by the way, hot, Starlady."

"I know. One reason I want to travel together. I presume that thing you're flying is faster and better equipped than it looks."

"She fast, Starlady. More to her than meet the eye."

"I'll bet *that's* true enough," Agis muttered beneath his breath.

Maigrey laid a hand on his shoulder, counseled silence.

Coordinates flashed on the screen. The centurion glanced up questioningly, asking if he should enter them, make the necessary corrections.

"Get up," she said. "I'll take over."

Agis rose to his feet, moved respectfully out of her way, and took his place in the co-pilot's position, which was hastily vacated by Brother Fideles.

Slowly, Maigrey sat down in the pilot's seat, her hand hovering over the needles embedded in the arm of the chair, needles that would link her directly with the spaceplane.

"Where are we headed?" she asked the assassin.

"Hell's Outpost. A place that calls itself the Exile's Cafe. You know it, Starlady?"

"I know it. At least, I knew *of* it. I'm surprised it survived the Revolution."

"Kings come and kings go but business is business forever, Starlady."

"A comforting philosophy, Sparafucile. I'll talk to you on the other side." She cut off communication. "This will suit us, Agis. Exactly what we need. Go ahead and make the course change."

Maigrey rested her hand on the needles, wincing slightly as the virus and micromachines that made her mind one with the spaceplane flowed into her bloodstream.

"Strap yourself in, Brother. We'll be making the Jump. Oh, and now would be an excellent time to say your prayers," she said, glancing back at the priest with a smile.

She meant it as a joke. It must not have come out that way.

"Yes, my lady," said Brother Fideles softly.

Chapter ◆━◗◯◖━◆ Six

> In solitude
> What happiness? Who can enjoy alone,
> Or all enjoying, what contentment find?
>
> John Milton, *Paradise Lost*

"You expect me to land there?"

"That's it, according to the coordinates Olefsky gave us," Tusk answered.

"It's on the side of a mountain!" XJ's audio crackled with shock. "I'll fall off!"

"Scanners indicate a nice wide ledge," Tusk said soothingly.

"Ledge! Ledge!" The computer sputtered. "I want an airfield, a space pad, a long, smooth runway. I want landing lights. I want air traffic control!"

"Well, you're not going to get it. According to the readings there are only two directions on this world—up and down. This ledge looks to be the longest, widest cleared patch of ground around for a few thousand kilometers."

"I refuse to do it. I won't land."

"Fine," said Tusk. "And while you're at it, calculate the amount of fuel we're using orbiting this planet."

XJ was silent, avarice wrestling with self-preservation.

"All right, I'll land. But I want to go on record . . ."

The landing was as tooth-jarring, bone-rattling, and uncomfortable as XJ could possibly make it, including a harrowing dive between two snowcapped peaks, ending in a near collision with the side of the mountain. The plane's roar touched off a small avalanche, snow plummeted down on top of the spaceplane, completely burying it.

"There," said XJ smugly when the plane had come to a shuddering, grinding halt. "I hope you're happy."

"He is, XJ," said Nola, digging her nails into Tusk's arm. "We've never been happier."

228

Dion unstrapped himself, looked ruefully at the bruises on his arms, carefully felt his ribs to see if any were broken. Tusk, wiping blood from his mouth where he'd bitten into his tongue, muttered imprecations and attempted in vain to see out the snow-covered viewscreen.

"Better get out our winter gear. XJ, turn up the heat."

"I will not. If there *is* fuel to be found on this rock, which I doubt, the price these Neanderthals charge is probably outrageous. I'm not wasting any just so you can work up a sweat putting your shorts on. Besides, the sooner you're out of here, the better. I've got repairs to make."

"Repairs!" Tusk swung around. "What repairs? What have you done to my plane—"

"*Your* plane! *Your* plane!" XJ momentarily lost the ability to communicate and simply repeated the two words several times before it could get its system straightened out.

"We'll see when we get outside," said Nola hastily, zipping herself into a fur-lined parka. "C'mon. Let's take a look. It's probably nothing. . . ."

"I dunno," said Tusk, pulling his parka on over his head. "I thought I heard a crunching sound. That left deflector shield— XJ, was it the left deflector shield?"

"I'm not talking," the computer said darkly. "After all, it's *your* plane!"

Tusk headed for the cockpit. "I'll have your microchips for lunch—"

"In case you're interested," XJ continued smugly, "several large and hairy brutes have gathered around *your* plane and are poking at it with sticks."

Thumps and rattles could be heard on the outside of the hull. Tusk, swearing loudly, pulled on his gloves, and hastened up the ladder.

"Open the hatch."

XJ did so, obeying orders with startling alacrity. The hatch whirred open, a shower of snow and ice cascaded down on Tusk's bare head. Nola began to laugh, saw the look on Tusk's face, and buried her giggles in her mittens. Dion bent over, rummaging in his rucksack to hide his smile.

Tusk brushed snow out of his face, stared upward. "Jeez, that looks pretty deep. I don't know how we're gonna—"

A gigantic hand and arm punched down through the snow,

sending another small avalanche into the plane's interior. A
bearded, grinning face thrust through the hatch opening.

"Welcome to Solgart!" boomed Olefsky in a bellow that
shook the plane. "By my ears and eyeballs, it's good to see you
in my homeland. Come up! Come up! Here, I'll give you a
hand."

Reaching down, the Bear caught hold of the hood of Tusk's
parka, lifted the mercenary like a child, and hoisted him up
through the hatch.

"My sons are digging you out," stated Olefsky proudly,
pointing to several large, hulking, fur-covered figures wielding
crude shovels or simply tossing snow into the air using nothing
but their hands and arms.

Half blinded by the white storm the enthusiastic young
Olefskys were creating, Tusk peered through the flying snow,
alarmed at the sound of blows rattling on his plane's hull. "No!
Don't! Thanks, but it's all right! Really!"

The young men looked at him from the depths of long,
shaggy hair, grinned, and waved. Obviously, these two couldn't
understand Standard Military.

"No! Don't do that. . . . Uh, Bear"—Tusk fumbled at his
translator, but his gloved fingers couldn't operate it—"could
you tell them thanks for trying to help but that we can generate
enough heat through the hull to melt the snow and"—he
winced at a particularly loud bang—"I really hate to see them
go to all this trouble—"

"Trouble? It is no trouble!" The Bear laughed, slapped Tusk
on the back, knocking the breath from his body. "You are our
guest. But you are right. These lummoxes would probably do
your vessel harm. Enough! Enough!" Olefsky waved a huge
gloved hand.

The young Olefskys, who looked as if they could have picked
up the spaceplane and shaken the snow off of it if they'd
wanted, backed off, grinning widely. Tusk sat on the hull,
gasped for air that was noticeably thin on top of this mountain,
and wondered if his shoulder blades were still intact. Bear,
reaching down, lifted Nola up through the hatch.

"Thank you, Bear. I can manage. I—"

"I hear you are a wife! I kiss the bride!"

Nola vanished in the embrace of Bear's huge, fur-covered
arms. She emerged flushed and pink-cheeked and laughing.
Glancing over the side of the spaceplane, she saw the ladder

covered with snow and looked somewhat dubiously at the long drop from the top to the ground.

"Ah! The way down is difficult. Do not worry. I will help you."

Gathering Nola up in his arms, Bear called to his sons and, before the woman could utter a cry, tossed her into the waiting arms of his boys. They caught Nola securely, set her gently and respectfully on her feet, each bobbing and ducking a shaggy head in an anxious, friendly manner.

Nola gulped, blinked, and looked up dazedly at Tusk.

"No, thank you!" Tusk said, seeing Bear reaching out his arms for him. "I can manage on my own! Kid!" He leaned over, shouted down the hatch. "You coming?"

"In a minute," Dion returned. "I've got to go over the security measures with XJ."

"Oh, yeah. All the excitement, I forgot. I'm gonna take a look around the plane."

Tusk slithered down the side of the spaceplane, bobbed and ducked in an exchange of greetings with the Olefsky brothers, then clambered around the outside of the plane, endeavoring to determine the extent of the damage.

Inside, Dion and XJ were making certain that the space-rotation bomb was safely stowed away, secure.

"Set up the security the way the Lady Maigrey had it set up," Dion ordered. "You have to hear my voice and mine alone, identify my handprint, and . . . and something of mine—this ring." He lifted the fire-opal ring that he wore around his neck, exhibited it to the computer. "I don't think the bomb'll be in any danger on this planet, but best to be prepared."

"Gotcha. And if anyone starts messing around with it?"

"You've got that new brain gas we installed. Use that. Knock them out and sound the alarm." Dion held up a small device, worn on his wrist. "I'll be here as soon as I can."

"We're not sure the gas works. Say, I've got an idea. Why don't you let me try it out on Tusk?"

Dion smothered a smile. "It works. Sagan developed it. That's the same gas Captain Williams was planning to use on us on *Defiant*."

"But what about—"

"It knocks out most alien life-forms, too. At least according to Dr. Giesk, it does."

"*Most?*" repeated XJ gloomily.

"All those who have the same type of central nervous system or something like that. Quit worrying." Dion put on a parka over his green wool sweater. "Lock up after I'm gone."

"It probably wouldn't have worked on Tusk anyway," XJ muttered. "After all, it is called 'brain' gas."

Dion grinned, climbed up the ladder, made good his escape from the computer, only to find himself half-smothered in the Bear's enthusiastic welcoming hug.

··◁■ ■▷··

A short walk down the steep mountainside from the ledge where XJ was grudgingly parked brought them to another ledge, bathed in sunlight and sheltered by gigantic boulders from the wind and snow. Several enormous beasts were tethered here. At the sight (and undoubtedly the smell) of the Olefskys, the beasts lifted their heads and brayed—a head-splitting squeal that started several minor snowslides. The beasts stood taller than two Olefsky brothers if one had been standing on another's shoulders, and were wider in girth than the Bear himself. Long black hair, which looked rough but was remarkably soft to the touch, covered the beasts' bodies, fell in graceful, shining cascades from head and back to the ground. Their heads were horned, with intelligent eyes. They reminded Dion of gigantic goats.

The Olefskys each mounted one of these creatures—which Bear called grons—pulling themselves up onto the broad backs by grabbing hold of handfuls of the long hair and literally climbing up the side of the patient and apparently thick-skinned animals. Tusk and Nola mounted, each riding in back of a young Olefsky. Bear insisted that Dion travel with him.

"You will explain to me as we ride," said the Bear, "everything that is going on."

The grons picked their way down the steep mountainside with an agility remarkable in such large and seemingly ungainly looking animals. Nola, a muffler wrapped over her nose and mouth, ostensibly to protect her face from the cold but in reality to keep out the smell, held on tightly to the Olefsky in front of her and closed her eyes at the sight of the sheer drops into jagged-edged rock canyons below.

Tusk, jolted and jounced, imagined gloomily what his rump was going to feel like after a few kilometers of this treatment, sighed and wished he'd remembered to bring along the bottle of jump-juice he'd left behind in the spaceplane.

"How far are we going?" he asked his Olefsky.

The young man turned his head, grinned and nodded.

Tusk sighed again, pulled off his gloves, switched on his translator. "How far?"

The young Olefsky leaned at a perilous angle over the gron's neck and pointed. Tusk, holding on for dear life, peered over a ledge that plunged straight down into the tops of a forest of fir trees. A valley with a lake of shining blue water nestled at the bottom of the mountain peaks. A castle, standing at the foot of one of the mountains and looking—from this distance— like a child's toy, was apparently their destination.

"That far, huh?" Tusk groaned, sank back down on the gron's broad but unfortunately lumpy backside, and hunched himself into his parka. "When'll we get there—some time next month?"

The Olefsky thought this particularly hilarious, to judge by his laughter, which sent small rocks bounding down the hillside. Reaching into his coat—it was either his coat or part of his long beard, Tusk couldn't be certain—the younger Olefsky pulled out a bottle and offered it to the mercenary.

"You try?"

Tusk brightened, took hold of the bottle, unscrewed the cap, and sniffed. "What is it?"

The name of the stuff came through the translator roughly as "that which keeps the feet from freezing."

"Hell, I'll try anything once." Tusk took a swig and immediately understood the nomenclature. The burning liquid ran through his body, up into his head, and clear down to his toes.

Cradling the bottle in his arm, Tusk settled down to enjoy the ride.

··◁■ ■▷··

Bear and Dion followed the others at a distance. Though the Bear had asked the young man to tell him his news, Dion could not, at first, reply. He had never been in a land like this before, had never breathed air this pure and cold, sweetly sharp with the spiced smell of pine. The grandeur and harsh, savage beauty of the towering mountains was overwhelming to the senses. He gazed up at the tops of the peaks, towering high above him, white against an azure-blue sky, and suddenly knew what it must be like to stand at the foot of the throne of God.

"Now," said the Bear, settling his bulk comfortably on the gron, "you will tell me the truth about what is going on."

Dion lowered his rapt gaze from the heavens and did so.

Bear listened attentively, did not interrupt, asked no questions. But the broad, cheerful face, turning occasionally to look at Dion over a massive shoulder, lost its grin, became unusually grave and solemn. When Dion concluded, Olefsky heaved a sigh that was like a gust of wind, tugged thoughtfully and painfully on his beard.

"I should have stopped Maigrey. I should have talked her out of going," Dion said.

"Ah, laddie, you would have stood a better chance telling that river to change its course or commanding the sun not to set tonight. You may be a king, and one of the Blood Royal, but you are mortal and there are some forces you cannot control." Bear glanced back over his shoulder, one shrewd eye glinting from the mass of hair and beard.

Dion, remembering the rite of initiation, hearing Maigrey's voice saying to him almost those very same words, said nothing but sat brooding and silent, watching the snow clouds move in to shroud the mountain peaks. A few flakes, sparkling and white in what remained of the sunlight, meandered past him, settled on the Bear's fur coat.

"She would have gone to him no matter what you did or said to her, laddie. You know that, in your heart, so stop pummeling yourself over it."

"Maybe so," Dion said doubtfully. "But why? That's what I don't understand."

"Don't you, laddie?" Bear shifted his girth on the gron's back to regard Dion intently. At length, he shook his head, turned back around to guide the beast. "Well, but you are very young."

The words came drifting back through the snow.

Dion bit his lips, his hands clutched at the gron's hair, fingers dug into the animal's hide. The gron snorted, cast a rolling eyeball backward to see what was amiss.

If the Bear noticed, he made no comment, nor did he look behind him.

"I am sorry for Sagan," he said in a low voice. "A dark and dreadful destiny is his, doomed to kill the only thing he loves."

Dion was shocked. "Loves? Who said anything about love? Not between those two—"

"Said!" Olefsky roared, causing the gron to shy and dance nervously along the path. "Said!"

The Bear brought the animal to a halt, turned around. "By my heart and bowels, laddie, who wakes every morning and takes a deep breath and says to the air, 'Air, I love you.' And yet, without air in our lungs, we would be dead within moments. And who says to the water, 'I love you!' and yet without water, we die. And who says to the fire in the winter, 'I love you!' and yet without warmth, we freeze. What is this talk of 'said'?"

"But how could two people who love each other do such terrible things to each other?"

"Love and hate are twin babes, born of the same mother, but separated at birth. Pride, misunderstanding, jealousy prod hate, urge it to destroy its sibling. But love, if it is armored with respect, will always prove the stronger."

The clouds had covered the sun, a grayness settled over the world. The snow began falling thick and heavy, tumbling straight down out of the sky, not a breath of wind stirring it. The flakes settled on Dion's eyelashes. He blinked rapidly, trying to brush them away. He could taste the icy whiteness on his lips and tongue.

The Bear shook himself, much after the habit of the animal whose name he bore, and shifted back around, facing forward, kicking the gron in the sides to start the animal moving. The others had gone ahead, vanished completely out of sight. The woods, filling up with snow, were suddenly, incredibly silent. Dion wondered if Olefsky was angry, but the Bear's voice, when it spoke again, was filled instead with a sadness as soft as the falling snowflakes.

"Why do you think Sagan spent seventeen years of his life searching for the Guardians? Oh, to find you, of course, laddie. You were important to him. But not nearly so important as finding the other half of himself that had been so long missing. And why did she wait seventeen years in one place for him to find her? Because she could no more run away from the missing half of herself than her body could run off without its heart."

"But he was going to execute her—"

"And did he?" The glinting eye peered at Dion through the snow that was whitening the matted hair.

"Well, no. But only because Maigrey forced him to fight a duel—"

"Forced him, did she? A Warlord, aboard his own ship with a thousand men at his command, and one woman *forces* him to fight her in fair combat?" Olefsky chuckled. "And when that duel took place, laddie, did either actually kill the other?"

"Only because the Corasian attack came—"

"Lucky for them the good God intervened, or they would have had to come up with some other excuse."

"Sagan vowed to kill her," Dion said after a moment. "He asked God to give her life to him."

Bear heaved another sigh that dislodged the snow from his shoulders. "Yes, laddie. And that is why it is said, 'Be careful what you wish for.'"

"But if he does love her, then he couldn't harm her. And if he does do what the dream foretells, then it's because he wills it. Nothing and nobody, not even God, could force Derek Sagan to do something he didn't want to do."

"And yet, he is gone, isn't he? And would he have chosen this time to go? The good God be with him, I say. And with his lady. But I am surprised to hear you talking seriously about dreams and destiny and the good God. You used to scoff at such things."

Dion brushed back his snow-wet hair, smiled ruefully. "I've done some thinking about it. I'm not saying what I believed was wrong. I'm only saying that now I'm not quite certain what's right."

Olefsky cocked the glinting eye over his shoulder again. "Perhaps you aren't as young as I thought."

··◁◼ ◼▷··

The Bear's castle, or Lair, as he dubbed it, half joking and half not, was made entirely of stone and was massive, imposing, medieval, and drafty. Dion had the strange feeling that they had not left the spaceplane and ridden down the side of a mountain. They had left the spaceplane and ridden backward in time.

He'd had a sneaking suspicion, on first entering the castle, that the moat and the drawbridge, the gigantic iron portcullis, the flagstone courtyard with various animals underfoot, were all for show, a pretentious bit of playacting by a man who hadn't quite grown up. But when he saw Bear in the huge stone hall, warming himself before a roaring fire, fondling some sort of enormous dog with one hand, his other hand wringing water from his beard, Dion had to admit that Olefsky lived this way because no other way of life to him would have been living.

And after a few moments, Dion began to understand how the big man felt. Chilled to the bone, his face blue and pinched with cold, snow crusting his eyebrows and eyelashes, the king crowded close to the crackling blaze. Steam rose from his wet clothing. He thought how fascinating it was to watch the flames, what a pleasant smell the wood smoke produced, and how good it felt simply to stand here and revel in the luxury of such a simple pleasure as being warm.

The walls of the high-ceilinged hall were covered with tapestries and shields. Bright-colored flags and bunting hung from a ceiling partially obscured by haze from the fire's smoke. What articles of furniture were present in the hall were plain and functional—consisting of a wooden table that was nearly as long as the hall and numerous heavy, high-backed chairs. The Bear and several of his hulking sons manhandled the chairs to stand before the fire. Olefsky, with his blunt, rough courtesy, invited his guests to be seated.

This simple act was rather difficult for the guests, due to the size and girth of the chairs. The short-statured Nola had to practically climb into hers and nearly disappeared from sight when she tried to rest against the chair's back. Tusk sat rigidly on the very edge of the seat, trying to look as if it didn't bother him that his feet didn't quite touch the floor. Dion, taller than his friend, was somewhat more fortunate. His feet touched the floor but he discovered that he could not rest both arms on the armrests at the same time. He couldn't reach that far across.

They had just settled themselves and Tusk was commenting that he didn't think he was going to have to cut off his frostbitten fingers after all, when a woman entered the room, carrying in her hands a large wooden tray filled with tall flagons. Bear walked forward to meet her, saluted her with a kiss on her cheek.

"The shield-wife," he said, presenting the woman to his guests with as much pride as he would have presented them to the sun, had he been able to catch it. "Sonja, my wife."

The sun might have brought more light and warmth into the room, but the contest between the two would have been close; Sonja's blond hair shone almost as brightly. She was tall, nearly as tall as her husband, and as wide around, with big bones, big hands, big arms, and a smile that was the largest thing about her.

"His Majesty, the king," said the Bear, waving a hand at Dion.

The young man slid out of the chair to his feet and bowed politely. Sonja, laughing, blushed and curtsied, continuing to hold the tray of mugs, never spilling a drop. Bear introduced Tusk and Nola.

"Do not get up," he added, waving at them. "We do not stand on ceremony here."

"Vilcome," said Sonja in a booming voice, pitched only slightly higher than her husband's deep bass.

"That is the only word she knows how to say in Standard Military, I am afraid," said the Bear. "She is a great warrior and there was never such a woman for bringing sons into this world, but she has no gift for languages."

Sonja, seeming to know what her husband was saying about her, laughed again, blushed deeper, and shook her head. She handed round the flagons. Made of metal, filled with a steaming, warming, sweet-tasting drink, each enormous flagon had obviously been designed to be held by an enormous hand. Dion nearly dropped his, and he felt new respect for Sonja's strength. She held five of them, plus the tray, with ease.

"Vilcome," she said again, watching him anxiously as he grasped the flagon firmly with both hands and sipped at his drink.

"It is very good, thank you," he said to her in her own language. "And I am honored to be in your home. May its walls keep trouble always out and happiness always in," he added, dredging up from somewhere in the back of his mind that one was supposed to invoke a blessing on the house when one was the guest of a Solgart.

"You do our house honor, my king," she answered, heartily pleased to hear him speak her tongue. "Its walls were built to shelter you and may they be torn down stone by stone before they allow harm to come to those within."

"I knew I should have brought my translator," muttered Tusk, trying—as most people will when in the presence of those speaking an unfamiliar language—to look as if he had at least some idea of what was being said. "I left it upstairs, in my room. If you'll excuse me . . ."

"No, no!" Bear shook his head, tugged on his beard. "We don't hold with those things. You will have no trouble communicating. I forgot that this one"—he nodded at Dion—"has the head of a computer."

The drink, that Bear called mead, was passed around. Sonja brought out a large jug, set it near the fire to keep it warm, and refilled their flagons the moment the level seemed likely to drop near the mid-point. The drink—wine mixed with honey—slid easily down the throat, warmed the body and the mind, and soon Dion noticed a golden glow light the hall, the table, the chairs, everything and everyone in the room.

Bear's sons gradually drifted into the hall, coming from performing various chores, some bringing in bundles of wood to replenish the fire, others stacking spears and bows in a corner, while still others—the younger ones—brought in baskets of fruit and nuts that they shyly offered to the guests.

The boys—there were fourteen of them—all looked alike, each looked exactly like the Bear. Dion could distinguish the fourteenth son from the first only by the fact that the fourteenth was a baby, who, in the company of the large dog, toddled in to see what all the commotion was about.

"I have a daughter," the Bear said proudly, "that I most particularly wanted you to meet. But since we were not certain when you would arrive, she has gone out on a hunting trip and will not be here for dinner." He looked slightly downcast over this, but cheered up, adding, "She will most likely be back tomorrow, however, and you can meet her then."

Dion said something polite, glanced at Tusk.

The mercenary grinned back at him, mouthed, "Bringing home the ox!"

Sonja rose, excused herself to supervise the preparation of dinner. Dion, knowing that business was never discussed among Solgartians during the all-important anticipatory time before eating, sat in his golden haze and listened to Bear tell stories about their battles, which were fought for honor and pride as much as conquest.

Dion knew, from having studied the Solgarts under Platus's tutelage, that their political system was always in seeming turmoil; wars were common, taking place between families, cities, countries, and sometimes entire planets. But the wars were generally friendly in nature, no one held grudges and the fighting would all cease in a moment if Olefsky—who was their leader and who watched over them as the mother wolf watches over cubs rolling in the dirt—said the word.

"We tried peace once," stated Olefsky, "and we didn't like it. The young people grew restless and bored and got into mischief. A good, clean war is much healthier and does less damage."

"These shield-wives . . ." Tusk was slightly drunk. He waved a vague hand. "I've heard . . . somewhere . . . that you people have some sort of warrior engagement party. Couples proving how well they can fight together." He grinned at Nola, who had climbed out of her chair and was on the floor, playing with the baby.

"It is a custom that dates back to ancient days, when wars were fought honorably with steel and muscle, not in the coward's way we fight today."

Bear heaved a great sigh, his eyes grew moist. He smoothed his long beard with his hand. Dion could see, through the golden haze, sunlight gleaming off bright armor and shining spear tips.

"Couples often fought together. The man, being the stronger, wielded sword and spear. The woman fought at his left side, his heart side"—Bear pressed his hand over his breast—"carrying a huge shield that she used to guard them both. If her man fell, she laid the shield over his body, picked up his weapons, and fought on until death took her, when they would be buried together.

"And if the shield-wife was killed . . ." Bear's face grew stern. "Woe betide the one who felled a shield-wife. Her man would never rest, not even if war ended, until he had avenged her death or died himself.

"Now, war is different." Bear shook his head over the degeneracy of the age. "Some of our own young people wanted to use bombs. We refused to resort to such cowardly weapons. They make killing too easy. One should look an enemy in the eye, know that he is a man like yourself. Thus, we permit only the short-range hand weapons. And we still keep the tradition of the shield-wife, though it is now only a contest. All newly engaged couples must prove their worth on the field of honor, prove that they will protect and defend each other with shield and sword before they can be married."

Nola—the baby in her arms—looked at Tusk, who smiled at her. The golden haze around Dion was suddenly dispersed by a chill wind that tore his dreams into shreds. He rose to his feet, without any clear idea of where he was going or what he was doing. He just wanted out. At that moment, however, Sonja came to invite her guests to dinner.

··◁■ ■▷··

The meal lasted several hours. The Bear refused to be rushed over one of the day's most important events. Afterward, much to Dion's relief, they finally settled down to talk business.

He explained his plan for the fleet. The Bear listened attentively, and though he sighed occasionally and frowned almost constantly, in the end he admitted that the plan was good.

"We must contact DiLuna and Rykilth. You have not done so?"

"No. We figured that the Galactic Navy might be monitoring our transmissions. I had hoped we could contact them from here, but . . ." Dion glanced around at the stone walls, the bright-colored tapestries, the fire burning on the hearth, the dogs lying on the floor. "I guess that's not possible."

Bear, grunting, rose to his feet. "Follow me."

They climbed a spiral staircase, almost too narrow to accommodate Olefsky's massive bulk, that led them to a tower room high atop the castle walls. Bear shoved open the door, stood glowering at the objects inside as if he would be happy to send them all hurtling out the window.

"Jeez!" Tusk breathed, entering. "Would you get a load of this! You could raise President Robes with communications equipment this powerful. Hell, you could probably raise the dead!"

The tower room was covered ceiling to floor with instruments, control panels, and sophisticated communication devices. One of the sons—of course—sat grinning at them from out of the depths of a shaggy beard. It was a strange sight, to see the young man, clad in leather, fur, and homespun cloth, cohabitating with devices that could send his image halfway across a galaxy in the blink of an eye.

"What do you expect?" said the Bear ruefully, in response to their questions. "I am a leader of several star systems. And it is difficult to talk to them like we talked to each other in the old days, using smoke and drums. Tomorrow, we will contact DiLuna and Rykilth. Now, it is the time for sleep."

Dion hadn't felt particularly tired, until the Bear mentioned sleep. Suddenly, weariness overwhelmed him. It took an effort to stay awake long enough to bid his host and hostess a safe night's rest. The Bear and his wife lit the young man to his room. Sonja warmed the sheets by sliding an iron pan filled with hot coals over them. Standing together, arms around each other, they bid him good night.

The room was unheated. Shivering, Dion undressed swiftly, crawled hurriedly into bed. Huddling beneath a heavy goose-down comforter, he was soon warm and slid gently into sleep, where he dreamed of battle and bright armor and shining blades and a tall warrior woman, with golden eyes, who held her shield before him and fought at his side.

Chapter ·◦━⊃◯⊂━◦· Seven

Twice or thrice had I loved thee,
Before I knew thy face or name;
So in a voice, so in a shapeless flame,
Angels affect us oft, and worshipp'd be.
                    John Donne, *Air and Angels*

Dion woke in the morning after the most restful night's sleep he could remember having since the death of his old way of life, the death of Platus. Lying in the warm bed, the comforter pulled up around his neck, he watched his breath turn to frost in the icy-cold room, and avoided, as long as possible, leaving behind the blissful warmth of dreams only half remembered, setting his bare feet on the cold stone floor.

Hunger and a need to relieve himself eventually drove him out of the bed. He dressed in record time and, after losing his way in the castle's corridors, eventually found what Tusk called "the facilities" located in a sheltered courtyard. Joining several of the shaggy sons, who grinned at him and ducked their heads, Dion performed his morning ablutions, washed his face and hands in a bucket of cold water—first breaking the ice—and thought longingly of a hot shower.

After breakfast, they spent the morning endeavoring to make contact with DiLuna and Rykilth. Neither was available to talk, aides of both offered to arrange conferences to take place on the morrow, separately and together.

Dion was relieved. He'd been dreading these meetings. He hated the diplomatic groping, stroking, and fumbling, hated the promises that wouldn't turn out to be promises, hated the lies that might or might not turn out to be truths, hated the truths that would probably end up being lies. He was thankful, at least, to put it all off until tomorrow.

With business over for the day, Tusk and Nola went with the Bear to learn a charming game known as "spear-chucking."

Dion excused himself from joining them, pleading a headache, which was true. All the time he'd been cooped up in the communications room, he'd been aware that the day outside was beautiful—clear blue sky, light breeze, and a warm snow-melting sun. He felt the need to escape into that world and took advantage of the first opportunity to do so.

The afternoon was warm, almost hot. The sun in the cloudless sky beat down on the land below, making it seem as if yesterday's chill had been all in the mind. Water ran in rivulets from beneath the melting snow and ice, rushing down the gentle slope on which the castle was built. Dion followed the water, letting it lead him where it would, content to simply enjoy the warmth of the sun on his aching neck and shoulders, content to admire the beauty of the wild landscape.

The runoff led him to a clear lake, whose blue water mirrored the blue sky with such perfection it made Dion almost giddy to stare into it—gave him the eerie impression that he might, if he fell, tumble up into the sky, instead of down into the water.

No breeze stirred the lake's surface; the wind had died in the heat of the afternoon. Dion sat on a large flat rock and stared across the glasslike lake until the heat of the sun on the rock, baking through his clothes, led him to think longingly of a swim. Gingerly, he put his hand into the water. It was cold, but not icy. He felt grimy, bug-ridden. (He'd observed the dog and a couple of the Olefsky brothers scratching themselves. The unwelcome thought of fleas—which had spread through the galaxy faster than humans—entered his mind.)

Dion looked around. He was alone, all Bear's sons having been eager to exhibit their skill in "spear-chucking." Stripping off his clothes, Dion dove into the sparkling water.

The cold made him catch his breath. He gasped, came up for air, and immediately began swimming toward the opposite side of the lake, knowing that he had to warm the blood, keep moving. He wasn't a bad swimmer, but not particularly good at it, either, having been raised on a planet where the largest body of water he'd ever seen was his bathtub. He'd learned to swim while on board *Phoenix*. His form was clumsy, but it kept him afloat and took him where he wanted to go and that, as his instructor had said, was most important.

Reaching the opposite shore, Dion found a large boulder, worn smooth on top, and guessed it had been used by generations of young Olefskys as a diving platform. Invigorated by the cold water and the exercise, certain he was alone and away from critical eyes, he relaxed and let the child in him come out to play. He clambered up on the rock, dove off, doing cannonballs, shouting, laughing, landing more than once flat on his naked belly. Finally, chilled, exhausted, he climbed onto the boulder to let the hot sun dry and warm him.

He stretched out full length, folded his arms beneath his head, and started to lie down comfortably.

A pair of eyes, fixed boldly on him from across the water on the bank, brought him sitting bolt upright. At first, Dion thought he was being observed by a youth, for the figure had short hair, close-cropped to the head, and was dressed in fur trousers and fur vest. Dion, feeling ebullient, was about to wave to the young man in friendly fashion when he took a closer look at the slender, delicate neck and realized it wasn't a young man. It was a young woman.

"What are you doing?" she asked in a voice as cool and clear as the lake. "Besides ruining my fishing."

Dion moved faster than he'd ever moved in his life. He slid off the rock, tumbled into the water. Clinging to the edge, he put the boulder between himself and the young woman.

"How long have you been here?" he demanded, remembering just in time to speak the woman's own language.

In answer, she reached down into the water and pulled up a stringer of glistening fish—more than twenty.

"That was before you came and starting making all the noise and splashing," she said accusingly.

Dion sputtered. "You've been spying on me this whole time! Why didn't you say something?"

"Spying!" The young woman bristled. "This is my father's lake. I have every right to be here. More than you, I'm certain. And you'd better come out of the water and get dressed. You're starting to turn blue."

"If you've been here that long," said Dion, teeth chattering with cold and embarrassment, "then you know that my clothes are on the opposite bank. I'll—"

"Oh, no, they're not." The young woman exhibited Dion's trousers. "I fetched them for you. I knew you'd be chilled to the bone. You'd better come out now," she repeated, glancing up at the sky, to the sun that was rapidly disappearing behind the mountain peaks. Long shadows were starting to stretch across the lake. "When the sun goes down, the air will turn cold rapidly."

Dion stared at his trousers and the rest of his clothes that he could now see piled neatly behind the young woman. He knew what she said was right. Evening's chill breeze on his wet skin raised the flesh on his arms. As for modesty, he told himself, it was useless now. She'd seen everything there was to see and, he had to admit, she didn't appear to be all that impressed. Yet, he couldn't bring himself to walk out of the water under the gaze of those calm, clear eyes.

"I'll come," he said, starting to splash slowly toward her, the water about waist deep. "But . . . turn around."

"Why? What for?" The young woman was obviously perplexed. Then her brows came together. "You're not planning to steal my fish, are you?"

"I'm not going to steal your fish!" shouted Dion, losing patience, the cold seeping into his bones, his skin burning as if he had a fever. "It's just . . . Damn it, girl, I don't have any clothes on!"

"I can *see* that! You're shivering. You'll catch your death. Be careful. The pebbles there are slippery. Here"—she leaned out over the water, reached out a hand—"let me help you. . . ."

"No!" Dion exclaimed hastily, drawing back. "I can manage on my own, thank you. Look, it's like this. Where I come from, it's not considered"—he searched for but couldn't find an equivalent of the word "proper" in the young woman's language. He was beginning to understand why—"well . . . right . . . for a woman to see a man without his clothes on. Or the other way around," he added, blushing furiously.

The young woman regarded him gravely. "That is true in our realm with betrothed couples or with those who have some reason to be ashamed of their bodies. But we are not betrothed and you have no need to be ashamed of your body. You are well proportioned and muscular. It is a pity no one ever taught you to swim properly."

Dion opened his mouth, closed it again. She wasn't being cute or coy or flirting with him. Her appraisal was spoken with frank, open honesty.

"Look," he said helplessly, "if you'd just turn your back . . ."

The young woman, shrugging, placed his clothes at the edge of the shoreline, then did as she was told, walking over near a stand of fir trees. Her lithe form moved gracefully, yet awkwardly, as if she had only recently acquired a new body and was still getting used to it. Sitting comfortably on the ground, she stared intently straight ahead of her.

Dion climbed out of the water, reached for his underwear.

"You'd better dry off," the young woman advised. "Your clothes will be wet and it is a long walk back to my home. Use my jacket, if you want. The skin beneath the fur is coated with oil. It won't hold the water like yours will."

Dion grabbed hold of a shapeless mass of fur lying near his clothes, toweled off hurriedly, and pulled on his trousers.

"Thank you for the invitation to your home," he said, wringing water out of his long hair and trying unsuccessfully to stop shaking. "And I'd really like to visit you sometime . . ."

He paused, not realizing, until he said the words, how true that statement was. "But," he added with real regret, his gaze lingering on the shining hair, the beautifully formed head, the long and slender neck supporting it, "I'm a guest at the castle—"

"Which is my home," said the young woman, turning around, facing him.

"No, no," said Dion, feeling extremely confused, noticing suddenly that her eyes were golden and her hair, in the slanting sunlight, was glistening silver, "I mean Olefsky's castle. Bear Olefsky. I'm his guest."

"And I'm his daughter," said the young woman. Smiling at him, she stood up, walked over, extended her hand to him. "My name is Maigrey."

"Maigrey!" Dion stared, frozen in place, unable to move for amazement.

"And what's wrong with that?" the young woman flashed, snatching back her hand. She glared at him defiantly. "I am the name-child of a valiant warrior-woman, who is a friend of my father's and who was a guest at the castle the day I was born."

"N-nothing's wrong with it," Dion stammered. "I know the Lady Maigrey and it . . . startled me to hear you say the name—"

"You know her?"

The young woman's eyes opened full and wide, drawing Dion inside.

"Yes," he said, dazzled, his blood pounding hot and fast through his body. "I am Dion. Dion Starfire. Perhaps," he said modestly, "your father has mentioned me—"

"The boy-king," said the young woman. She stretched out her hand again. "My father said you were strange, but that you had some good qualities."

"Thank you, I think," Dion said confusedly, accepting the handshake, which was strong and firm and friendly.

Her fingers were slender and rounded, fingernails cut short as a man's. She was as tall as he was, with well-formed, muscular arms and shoulders, slender waist and hips and long legs. Her skin was tanned, from being outdoors, and made his look white and sickly by contrast. The golden eyes (where had he seen those eyes before?) were large and serious. Her nose was long, too long for classic beauty, her smile wide and ingenuous and . . . friendly.

Friendly! God, friendly! Dion groaned inwardly. He had always laughed at the notion of Eros shooting man with love's arrows, but now Dion understood. He wouldn't have been at all surprised to look down at his chest and see the rascal's shaft sticking out of his heart.

"Have I offended you?" asked the young woman, mistaking his long silence.

"No, no," Dion answered, then shook his head, gazed at her through his wet, tangled mass of red hair. "'Boy-king' doesn't sound very flattering, does it?"

"I'm not certain my father is right," stated the young woman, eyeing Dion with cool appraisal. "You seem a man to me."

Dion wanted to howl and leap about the forest and start a fire by rubbing sticks together and wrestle some great beast and lay it at her feet. But he judged, by looking at her, that she might get the better of him in beast wrestling and she could almost certainly start fires. . . .

He said nothing, couldn't find the words, and that golden-eyed stare of hers was shredding him up inside. Turning, he leaned down, picked up the fur jacket that smelled strongly of fish, and handed it to her. "Here," he said, looking at her tan, bare arms, "you'd better wear this."

The sun had disappeared behind the mountain peaks. Its glow lit the sky; a soft, shimmering purple streaked with bands of red and orange.

"I *have* offended you," said the young woman. "I'm sorry. My mother says I have the charm of a gron." Taking the jacket, she drew near him and wrapped the fur around his shoulders, drawing it close together in the front, smoothing it with her long-fingered hands. "There. You will be warm soon."

Dion caught hold of the hands in his own, held them tightly, drew her nearer to him. His eyes looked into hers, saying those things that can never be spoken aloud, but only heart to heart.

It seemed she understood. Her eyes lowered, long lashes brushed against flushed cheeks. Her head bowed. He could see that the hair, which he had thought was silver, was really a mixture of iridescent white and ash-blond and brown. It was clipped short, probably not to get in her way when hunting. He imagined pressing her head to his chest, running his hand through her hair, ruffling it with his fingers. The burning ache in his throat nearly choked him.

Suddenly, she pulled away from him, ducked around him, behind him. "I have to get the fish."

Dion wasn't sorry to let her go. He felt the need to catch his breath and realign the ground beneath his feet.

She retrieved the fish, flopping about wetly on the stringer. "Hold this a minute," she said, handing it to Dion. Vanishing into the woods, she returned, carrying a leather pack and several long, slender poles tipped with iron points. She slung the pack over her shoulder, hefted the poles, and reached out a hand for the fish.

"No, no," Dion protested. "I'll carry these."

"Are you sure?"

He noticed then that he was holding the wriggling, gasping, slimy creatures at arm's length, his nose wrinkling at the smell.

"I'm sure. I should do something to make amends for ruining your fishing. But don't you think you should take your jacket back?" he added, looking again at her bare arms, the loose-fitting fur vest. She had turned sideways to him and he could see, through the V-necked opening, the swelling round-ness of her small, firm breasts.

"Nonsense!" she said crisply. "You're the one who's cold. I'm not. You've gone all gooseflesh."

Dion could have said that it wasn't the cold that made him shiver, but he thought it best to keep quiet. They left the shoreline, moved into the woods, and struck a path that ran around the lake, a trail worn and trodden by the feet of innumerable Olefskys. The young woman walked like a man—straight-hipped, taking long strides.

Encumbered by the fish, not knowing the path, Dion had trouble keeping up with her. He fell into a hole. She reached out a hand to catch hold of him, steady him, and he noticed, suddenly, that she was walking on his left-hand side, his shield side, and he knew then where he'd seen those golden eyes.

"Are you all right?" she asked him, pausing, alarmed. "You didn't twist your ankle? I should have carried the fish—"

"I'm fine!" he told her, trying to calm the blood pulsing in his temples. He shook off her hand, irrationally angry, wishing she'd stop treating him like a child. "And I'll carry the damn fish!"

The silence grew between them like an ugly bramble bush, prickling with thorns. Each cast furtive, sidelong glances at the other when they thought the other wasn't looking. When their eyes accidentally met, each looked hurriedly and uncomfortably away. They continued walking in silence almost halfway around the lake. The light in the sky had dimmed to a soft, subdued afterglow. Dusk shadowed the woods.

"We won't reach home before darkness falls," said the young woman, stopping to glance around her, "and I didn't bring a lantern. But we'll be able to see the castle lights. They will guide us."

"I think I have found the light to guide me," said Dion softly, moving to stand beside her, thinking regretfully how difficult it was to be romantic when holding a stringer of twenty dead or dying fish.

The young woman at first didn't understand his meaning, was slightly puzzled, as if she thought he might pull a flaming torch out of his pocket. He looked at her intently, however, again letting his eyes speak for his heart.

Her face flushed. She lowered her head, but she kept near him. Together, their silence now warm and companionable, they walked slowly down the path.

"Your name is Dion," she said, almost shyly. "Is that what everyone calls you all the time?"

"Yes," said Dion, shrugging. "Don't they call you M-Maigrey?" It was difficult to say the name in reference to this woman. It didn't fit, carried with it too much pain.

"No. Only on my nameday, and then I think it makes my father and mother sad. I am called by my second name, Kamil. You may call me that, if you like."

"It's a beautiful name, Kamil. And you call me Dion."

"I will . . . Dion. And I think, since you don't know the way, that you should walk closer to me."

"Maybe I should hold your hand," suggested Dion, and thought it suddenly quite charming to be treated like a child. "So that I don't get lost."

They moved nearer, fumbling in the darkness until their hands met and fingers twined together, clasping each other firmly.

Night's shadows wrapped around the tree trunks, obscured the path, forced them to walk slower, take their time. It would have been dangerous to hurry. All too soon, however, the trees gave way to rolling hills and they could see the castle, far above them. Light streamed out the windows, setting the green grass ablaze, welcoming them home.

Chapter ◦◦○◦○◦◦ Eight

> The deep, unutterable woe
> Which none save exiles feel.
> W. E. Aytoun, *The Island of the Scots*

Contrary to the more sensational reports of the vidmags, Hell's Outpost acquired its name from being the last inhabited planet encountered before entering the Lane that led to the Corasian galaxy, not because it was decadent or sin-ridden or any of the other attributes popularly attributed to Lucifer's domicile. Those who had the leisure and time and money to spend on sin traveled to Laskar or any of a thousand other places willing and able to provide it. Those who traveled to Hell's Outpost could not afford the luxury of leisure—their time was generally running out—and they came to find money, not to spend it.

Hell's Outpost was a quiet place, businesslike, reserved, and more secret than the dead. The planet was, in actuality, not a planet at all, but a moon that revolved around a nondescript planet that had no name. The moon's surface was gray, bleak, barren, half of it baking in the light of the sun, the other half frozen and dark. Its one town, located on the sunny side, consisted of innumerable geodesic domes of various sizes, depending on their use, all arranged beneath one gigantic dome with its own artificial atmosphere.

Maigrey located the domed town, then circled the moon while Agis ran checks on the various spacecraft parked on the ground before making preparations to land. No government challenged their approach, no control tower issued coordinates and guided them safely. In landing, as in everything else on Hell's Outpost, you were on your own.

It took some time for the three to outfit themselves in the spacesuits that would be needed to walk from the plane to the dome. Or rather, it took some time for Agis and Maigrey to outfit Daniel in his suit. The priest had worn a spacesuit only a few times prior to this, and that had been during emergency evac drills held at intervals on *Phoenix*. He had always thought he was putting it on wrong, but no one had ever bothered to show him how to put it on right.

"Perhaps Broth . . . I mean Daniel . . . should stay behind," Agis said to Maigrey in a low tone as they worked together to adjust the priest's gravity boots.

"I thought about it," Maigrey whispered back, tugging at the straps. "But he ought to see and hear firsthand what he's getting himself into."

"What if he wants out, my lady? We can't very well leave him here."

"He won't, Agis. Make up your mind to that," said Maigrey. "But I want him walking ahead with his eyes open, knowing what to expect. Like it or not, my friend, he's one of us now."

"What will *he* think?" Agis jerked his head in the general direction of the junker plane parked next to theirs.

Examining the volksrocket through her viewscreen on landing, Maigrey had noted with approval and some amusement the various methods the half-breed had used to camouflage his innocent-looking volksrocket's true deadly capabilities.

"Who knows what he thinks about anything," Maigrey muttered, standing up. "There, Broth—Dan—Oh, the hell with it!" she said to Agis. "Let's introduce him as Brother Daniel. We both keep calling him that. One of us is bound to slip, and considering his cover story, it makes sense anyway."

Agis nodded.

Brother Daniel, unaccustomed to the grav boots, clomped his way clumsily back and forth across the deck, attempting to grow used to the strange sensation of walking when it felt as if his feet were glued to the ground. Maigrey watched him a moment, started to make a helpful suggestion, decided it might simply confuse him, and turned back to the business at hand. She checked—again—the power supply of the bloodsword she wore at her waist, checked to see that she had the rest of the equipment she would need while on the Outpost.

"Lasgun?" Agis offered, holding up one for her inspection.

Maigrey considered. The bloodsword was the best close-range weapon ever developed. It could cut through a steel beam with as much ease as it could slice through a man's flesh. In addition, it gave the Blood Royal the ability to exert a powerful charismatic influence over any mortal, with the exception of the extremely strong-willed or another member of Blood Royal. The bloodsword was not designed, however, to be used in a laser-blasting firefight.

But then, thought Maigrey, neither am I. The Blood Royal were never intended to find themselves in such a menial situation. Maigrey would have never learned to shoot at all, if Sagan hadn't insisted, and then he remarked in disgust that she'd better hope she scared her opponent to death rather than counting on hitting anything.

She shook her head, deciding against the gun. There was the psychological angle to consider. She did not intend to walk into the Exile Cafe armed to the teeth, looking as if she were hiding behind her firepower. Wearing only the bloodsword, she would appear supremely confident of herself, of her ability to deal easily and effectively with any situation.

Maigrey set about her final task of shutting down and securing the spaceplane until their return. Agis, holding the lasgun, turned to the priest.

"Brother Daniel?"

Maigrey, watching out of the corner of her eye, saw the young priest shake his head. "I am armed," he said, pressing the palms of his hands together, a somewhat difficult maneuver due to the insulated gloves he wore to protect him from the moon's frigid cold and lack of atmosphere.

Agis glanced at Maigrey, who shrugged, shook her head, and continued with her task. The centurion came over to assist her.

"Do you really believe, my lady, that he has and can use the power of God?"

"Lord Sagan believed it," said Maigrey shortly.

"But you, my lady?" Agis persisted.

Maigrey's hand went to her breast, to the place where the Star of the Guardians had once hung and now hung no longer. "It's why I permitted him to come, Agis."

"I understand, my lady."

"Do you? Maigrey thought. Then perhaps you could explain it to me.

··◁■ ■▷··

They found Sparafucile, waiting patiently for them outside their spaceplane. Maigrey was thankful to see that the half-breed's helm at least partially obscured his malformed, misshapen features. It wasn't the sight of his disfigurement that would force her to steel herself to look at him again. It was the memories the face would bring back to her. Memories of the time on Laskar he'd saved her life, memories of the mindseizers, memories of Sagan. . . .

"Starlady."

"Sparafucile."

The half-breed was attired in a shabby pressure suit of a type that had been outdated when Maigrey was a little girl. Bulky and heavy, it was encumbered with numerous valves and gauges and a complex system of buckles and straps that clunked and jingled and made enough noise for a circus parade when the half-breed moved. Maigrey smiled grimly, wondering how many and what type weapons the breed had managed to stash inside the suit, wondered what telltale sounds those convenient clunks and jingles masked.

"You remember Agis, captain of my lord's Honor Guard? Former captain," she amended.

Agis and the assassin glanced at each other, said nothing, acknowledged each other with a nod—on the centurion's part—and a sort of shuffling wriggle on Sparafucile's. The two knew each other by sight; Agis having often been required to escort the breed into his lordship's presence.

I warned Agis, Maigrey thought. He knew what to expect. Besides, they don't *have* to like each other. They only have to respect each other.

Which brought her to the priest. And she could tell, by the direction in which the assassin's helm faced, that he'd been curiously eyeing the young man. "This is Brother Daniel. Brother Daniel, Sparafucile." She turned to Brother Daniel. "Sparafucile is a professional assassin."

Daniel, having been prepared for this, made a clumsy bow.

"Brother Daniel"—Maigrey turned to Sparafucile—"is a priest."

"Sagan Lord, a priest."

Maigrey wasn't surprised that the assassin knew the Warlord's most carefully guarded secret. From what little she had seen of the half-breed, and more that she had gleaned from Sagan's files, she knew that Sparafucile was perceptive, intuitive, highly intelligent. Reasons why she had decided to tell him the truth. He would undoubtedly find out anyway and she wanted him—as much as possible—to trust her.

"That is the reason we have brought Brother Daniel with us. He carries no weapon, he will not kill another living being. He goes forth armed with the power of God."

A trifle romantic, but it sounded impressive. And perhaps the assassin was impressed, for he made no protest against Brother Daniel, and when they started walking in the direction of the Cafe, Sparafucile fell into step at the young priest's side.

"You not kill, eh?" the assassin asked.

Brother Daniel, encountering difficulty in using the grav boots, shook his head. He had not learned the trick of rolling forward on the foot or "peeling" the foot off the ground, as the technique was known. Attempting to lift each foot with each step, he looked like a bird performing some bizarre mating ritual.

"Ah, but if I try to kill you, you would try to kill me. Yes?" Sparafucile pursued.

"No, I wouldn't," Brother Daniel replied. He studied the assassin walking beside him, attempting to emulate his rolling gait.

Sparafucile considered this statement, then nodded. "I understand. Your God—He kill for you."

Maigrey, listening to the conversation, wondered how Brother Daniel would slog his way out of this theological morass. She hoped he would realize that this was neither the time nor the place for a sermon and that he would do nothing or say anything to cause the assassin to begin to doubt him—and consequently doubt all the rest of them.

"'We have made a covenant with death,'" quoted Brother Daniel, "'and with hell are we at agreement.'"

Sparafucile made a grunting noise that seemed to indicate he was impressed, though he probably had only a vague understanding of the priest's words. As for Brother Daniel, he spoke of "death" and "hell" glibly enough, but Maigrey knew he didn't understand either, not yet.

Well, she thought grimly, entering the air lock that was the gate into Hell's Outpost, he will. Soon.

The Exile Cafe was the largest structure on Hell's Outpost. A huge dome several kilometers in diameter, it was the central point in town. All roads led to it. All the domed structures built up around it supported it, in one way or another. And all people, human and alien, they met, as they walked toward it, were either heading that direction themselves or leaving.

No one raised a hand (or any other appendage) in greeting; no one said a word to anyone, even if (especially if) the other person was known or recognized. Hell's Outpost had its own special code of etiquette and honor, a code that had been developed over the years of its operation for a reason—to protect the privacy and the lives of those who came to Hell's Outpost to conduct business. The code was broken only at one's extreme peril.

A single door led into Exile Cafe. Another, at the rear, led out. The Cafe proper was designed to accommodate humans, its primary guests, but special rooms had been equipped to handle vapor-breathers and other life-forms if they desired a more familiar and homelike atmosphere.

Weapons were not checked at the entrance, disputes were prohibited—a part of the unwritten code. The Exile Cafe was neutral ground. Mortal enemies, sworn to kill each other on sight, who met in the Cafe were expected, by the code, to buy each other a drink. Weapons were worn for show, for advertising purposes. No weapon had ever been drawn in anger during all the long years that the Exile Cafe had been in business.

Maigrey had never been to the Exile Cafe—or Hell's Outpost—before, but Sagan had and, as was customary with him, he had also amassed an extensive file on it and its operations. She knew how to act, therefore, and what to expect.

She entered the lobby. All rooms in the Exile Cafe were circular with domed ceilings, resembled eggs that have been cut in half. The largest of these "eggs" was the Cafe itself, which occupied the center of the dome. Private meeting rooms, located on the four levels surrounding the Cafe, looked out over it, providing the occupants with a view of all those who entered.

Before one obtained access to the Cafe, one had to pass through the lobby. And before one entered the private meeting rooms, one had to pass through the Cafe.

Maigrey walked a pace ahead of her cohorts, indicating that

she was the leader. She alone would speak for the group. The others ranged in a row behind her—Agis and Sparafucile flanking Brother Daniel; the centurion prepared to muzzle the priest if he seemed likely to make a social misstep. Fortunately, having been raised in the strict discipline of the monastery, Daniel was accustomed to silence and passive obedience.

The lobby was a smallish room, brightly lighted, with walls of plush red velvet. A 'droid made to resemble a human male of the clerk variety stood behind a desk of curved, blond wood. Above the 'droid's head, numerous vidscreens provided constantly shifting pictures of those who were already inside, these photos having been taken when they entered the lobby. Maigrey knew, as she walked up to the desk, that her own image and those of her companions was being transmitted on the thousands of vidscreens throughout the Exile Cafe.

Looking at the vidscreen, Maigrey guessed her group must be occasioning quite a bit of comment inside. Her bloodsword gleamed brightly in the light, showed up well on camera. Those keeping tally inside would see that sword—capable of being used only by the Blood Royal—and would mark their scorecards accordingly.

Agis to Maigrey's left, stood tall, straight-backed, square-shouldered, face impassive, gaze cool, unimpressed, appraising. The scorecards would read: highly trained, highly skilled combat veteran.

Directly behind Maigrey, Brother Daniel. Silent, his face grave and solemn, he had an air of serenity about him that, in this place, was extremely daunting, disconcerting. Those keeping score would put down question marks.

At Maigrey's right and slightly behind her shambled the assassin, looking more like a pile of rags someone had dumped in an alley than a living being. He moved with a shuffling gait, shoulders slumped, malformed head continually oscillating, attempting to focus the misaligned eyes.

The shuffling, the shambling, the lethargic movement—all an act, intended to deceive the careless, the unwary. The scorecards for those who knew him would read: one of the most dangerous men in the galaxy.

An interesting mixture, one that—she hoped—would cause the right people to sit up and take notice.

The door through which they had entered slid shut behind

them. Only single individuals or allied groups were permitted in the lobby at one time.

"Welcome to the Exile Cafe," said the 'droid in a programmed, mechanical voice, devoid of expression. "I will explain the house rules."

The 'droid greeted all those who entered the Cafe in the same manner, no matter how many times they may have been there. Again, part of the code. Once you left the Exile Cafe, it was as if you had never entered.

The rules were simple: Weapons could be worn but not used. No fights, arguments, or brawls were permitted on the premises or within a hundred meters in any direction of the premises. Maigrey listened, indicated that she understood and would abide by the rules, agreed that she would accept the penalty if she did not. The penalty—instant annihilation—had never, as far as anyone could remember, been exacted.

"And now," said the 'droid when the formalities were complete, "how may we serve you?"

"I want a private room," Maigrey replied.

The 'droid assured her that this request could be fulfilled.

"I want the upper room. Six hours," she added.

"One hundred thousand golden eagles," said the 'droid.

Maigrey agreed, ignoring a slight gasping sound that came from behind. Brother Daniel, no doubt.

The 'droid slid forth a credit machine. Maigrey entered Sagan's account number. The 'droid approved.

"Look into this," it ordered, pointing out a scanning device.

Maigrey did so. A tiny ray of intense light shot out, pierced her right eye, momentarily blinding her. The device shut off. She stepped back, blinking, trying to see through the black dot of an afterimage.

"The effect will pass in a few minutes," said the 'droid. A segment of red-velvet wall slid aside, opening into a narrow corridor filled with white-blue light. "That way to the Cafe. Two-drink minimum."

They entered the corridor. A door slid shut behind them. It would not reopen. From this point, everyone moved on into the Cafe. The exit was located on the opposite side of the dome, obtainable only by passing through the Cafe.

The corridor they entered was a tube of steel about six meters long. The only light came from the far end, a round patch of darkness, surrounded by a circle of bright blue neon lights.

"If the drink prices are on a level with the room rates, I doubt if even the Warlord's bank account will cover more than a couple of rounds," Agis murmured, coming up to walk at her side.

"Such a sum would buy the Abbey," said Brother Daniel in disapproving tones. "And we are offered only a single room?"

"And that for only six hours," Maigrey said. "Admittedly, I took the most expensive. The Cafe has others that rent for less, but I'm not only paying for the room, Brother, I'm paying for privacy, secrecy, and prestige. This is no cut-rate job. I intend to hire the best and I want everyone to know I can pay for it."

They reached the entrance to the Cafe proper. It wasn't a door, but was rather like stepping into a black hole. Complete, baffling, disorienting darkness engulfed them. There was, suddenly, no floor beneath their feet, they could feel no walls on either side. Maigrey, recognizing a sensory-deprivation chamber, fought down an involuntary panic reaction. Within moments, light was in her eyes, her feet were on the floor. She had entered the Cafe.

A circular, domed room that extended upward through all four stories, the Cafe presented, at first glance, an eerie contrast of bright lights and deep shadows. A gigantic circular bar, around which several hundred people could have gathered, stood in the center. The bar was made of clear acrylic, lit by white neon tubing that encircled its base three times. The white light shone up through the bar, illuminating the faces of all who sat there.

The remainder of the Cafe's lower level was taken up by innumerable round tables, of various sizes. A globe of light stood in the center of each table. The globes were of differing colors, ranging from white to blue to red to green. As Maigrey and her group entered the globes began to change color, flashing from blue to red, from white to blue, from red to green. Faces could be seen only by the light of the globes and nowhere else. The remainder of the room was shrouded in darkness, lit by the waiters—male and female—in various states of undress, whose painted bodies gave off a phosphorescent glow.

Each table held, in addition to the globe, a vidscreen. On these screens flashed the faces of those who entered, or if so desired, the vids could be used by those seated at the tables to communicate with those upstairs in the private rooms.

Maigrey glanced behind her to make certain her companions were following, worrying that Brother Daniel might have been unable to cope with the sensory deprivation chamber. He emerged apparently unscathed, although appearing considerably bewildered, accompanied by Sparafucile, who had a firm grip on the young priest's arm.

"Fun, eh?" The assassin grinned.

"It was . . . interesting," said Brother Daniel faintly.

Maigrey smiled at him reassuringly, saw his eyes shift to a point behind her, widen, and suddenly lower. His face burned red.

Maigrey turned, was met by a 'droid, this time made to resemble a human female—perfect in every detail as far as they could see, every detail being more or less on display.

"Table for four?" asked the hostess in programmed, seductive tones.

"No, we have a private room. We'll go straight there."

"As you wish. This way, please."

The hostess, her half-naked body glowing a faint green, herself a walking lamp, led the way, at a slow and languid pace, through the tables. Faces, illuminated in the light, floated like disembodied heads in a sea of darkness. Eyes stared at them, followed them.

Maigrey kept herself aloof, allowed her gaze to meet no one's.

The hostess led them to a cylindrical tube that stood at the rear of the Cafe, opposite the entrance. Here was another round black hole that marked the exit. Here, also, was the elevator that led to the upper floors.

"It is an anti-gravator," said the hostess. "Take hold of the brass ring when you arrive at your destination to stop your ascent, then simply step out."

Maigrey nodded. The hostess opened her hand. On the palm was located a small keypad. Maigrey entered the account number and an amount for the tip. The hostess cast Brother Daniel a teasing, provocative glance through lowered, gold-gilded eyelids, and glided away.

Brother Daniel, his gaze riveted to the floor, did not notice.

The gravator had no door. Maigrey stepped inside and

immediately began floating gently upward. The rest followed after her; Sparafucile keeping close to Brother Daniel.

An odd pair, Maigrey thought, looking down on them. Having entered after her, they were slightly beneath her. She could only assume, uneasily, that the assassin was shadowing the priest out of distrust, which would undoubtedly mean trouble sooner or later. It had been a mistake to bring him, a superstitious weakness on her part. Agis certainly thought that was true. God knew what, then, the cold-blooded assassin must be thinking.

"Brother Daniel will simply have to watch out for himself," she muttered, reaching out for the ring on level four and pulling herself to a halt. "Or else You'll have to watch out for him," she added, glancing heavenward. "*I'm* certainly not going to!"

The fourth level, the top of the dome, had only one room. Maigrey eased herself out of the gravator, stood in a narrow corridor, lit by dim, recessed ceiling lights. At the end of the corridor was what appeared to be a blank wall, devoid of decoration except for a single, hieroglyphic-like eye.

Maigrey waited until everyone had joined her before proceeding down the silent, empty corridor. She came to stand before the eye, stared into it. A beam of light shot out, scanned her eyeball, shut off. The wall vanished, replaced by pitch-darkness. She stepped into it. A light flashed on, revealing a small, round room with a domed ceiling. A round table stood in the room's center, surrounded by a round, comfortable sofa. On the table was a vidscreen and a globe of light, identical to the globes they'd seen in the Cafe below.

The four squeezed into a room—a tight fit. When all had crowded inside, the door shut and sealed behind them.

"Cozy," Maigrey said, pressed against the wall. She motioned everyone to stand back. "Don't anyone sit down yet. Agis, check for listening devices."

The centurion drew out a hand-held scanner. He activated it, stared at it, narrow-eyed, listened to its faint humming.

"Clean, my lady," he reported.

Maigrey nodded. "Carry on then."

To Brother Daniel's intense astonishment, Sparafucile pulled out a nuke light, dropped to his hands and knees, and proceeded to crawl under the table. Agis jumped on the sofa, poked and prodded at the ceiling panels, that were firmly fixed in place.

"What are they doing? Looking for dust?" the priest asked with an incredulous laugh.

Maigrey didn't answer. Agis knocked, pushed on each steel wall panel, endeavored to shove his hand between the sofa and the wall. He shook his head, stepped down.

Brother Daniel looked confused. "But, my lady, I thought you said this place was private, secret—"

Hammering and rattling noises, from beneath the table, interrupted the priest, indicated that the assassin might be attempting to tear the furniture apart. Then they heard a grunting sound, the noise ceased.

Maigrey's expression grew grave. The shaggy head and misshapen features of the assassin emerged back into the light. Sparafucile placed on the table what appeared to be a small, round, smooth rock—green stone, streaked with red.

Maigrey felt the strength drain from her body. She sat down, suddenly, on the sofa, stared at the rock.

Brother Daniel started to say something. Agis cast him a warning glance, shook his head. Sparafucile lifted the rock in his hand, closed his palm over it. There came a cracking sound, as of a walnut being crushed. The assassin opened his hand. Green dust mixed with bits of rock fell from his grasp, like sand falling through an hourglass, to form a small mound on the table.

"*Him*, Starlady," said the assassin. "Same device as I find on Laskar. Furniture is bolted to floor. Rock was wedged good and solid back in corner formed by table's base." Sparafucile dusted off his hands.

"Not a bad try," murmured Maigrey. "Considering he didn't have much time—between when we first said we wanted this room and our coming up here. Damn, damn, damn!" She sighed, stared at the rock dust.

"Surely, my lady, you expected this," said Agis gently.

"I did. It was why I looked for it. But that doesn't make it any easier. So much for security. I should demand my money back."

"The mind-dead go where they will. Few can stop them," intoned Sparafucile.

"And no one would believe me anyway." Maigrey shrugged, smiled ruefully. "After all, what was it? A rock. Nothing more."

Brother Daniel caught onto a word. "Mind-dead. My lady, you told me that those monks . . . with the eyes, the terrible eyes . . . were mind-dead. Are you saying that they are here?"

"Yes. And sent by him—the one called Abdiel," the half-breed answered. "Does the priest know of him?"

"Yes," said Brother Daniel in a low voice, his face pale. "I know of him. . . ."

The assassin grunted again, shook himself like a mongrel dog. Maigrey touched gingerly, with the tip of her finger, the mound of rock dust.

"What was that thing?" Agis asked. "Obviously not techno-logical, since it didn't show up on the scanner."

"It isn't. It is what it appears to be—a rock, known as bloodstone. Years ago, the Blood Royal used these stones to communicate, one with the other. The stone acts as a focus for the psychic powers or some such notion. It was a toy, really. Normal communication routes were easier and required less mental discipline. Lovers exchanged bloodstones, that sort of thing. But the mind-seizers came to realize that the stones had a far greater potential.

"The Order of Black Lightning discovered that they, with their enhanced mental energies, could use the stones to spy, to overhear conversations. They could even, so I've been told, use the stones as another eye, to see events transpiring far, far away.

"Through this simple stone, Abdiel could hear me, see me, and, if he chose, perhaps even read my thoughts."

"He knows we're here, then. Will he try to stop us?" Brother Daniel asked, glancing about the room fearfully, as if he expected to see the old man emerge from the walls.

"No. That isn't his purpose, his intent. He knows I'm coming to him. He *wants* me to come. But he doesn't want to be taken by surprise. He would like very much to know *how* I'm coming and *when*. Do you think this room is safe now?" she asked Sparafucile abruptly.

The assassin's misaligned eyes narrowed. "I think no place safe from him, Starlady."

"I agree. And now, gentlemen," she continued briskly, "if you will sit down, we will get on with our business."

Chapter ❖ Nine

How long do you stay fresh in that can?
The Cowardly Lion to the Tin Man,
from *The Wizard of Oz*

Maigrey ordered drinks: a vodka martini, straight up, olive, not a twist, for herself, water for Agis (Sagan's men, like Sagan himself, did not consume alcohol), a pot of hot tea for Brother Daniel, and an impossible-to-pronounce concoction for the half-breed.

"The waiter will bring them," said the hostess. "Anything else I can do for you?"

Maigrey assured her there wasn't, sank back into the sofa cushions, thinking that a martini would be extremely welcome, wishing she could enjoy it. She watched idly the assassin flick through images on the vidscreen, switching from one table to another, from one face to another, with a rapidity that made her dizzy.

At last he grunted—this seemed to be his primary form of communication—and swiveled the computer screen around for her to view.

"This good man, lady-mine," he said, having undoubtedly come up with that appellation from hearing Agis refer to her as "my lady." "He do work for Sagan Lord."

Maigrey saw, by the white light of the globe on his table, a human male of indeterminable age—an old thirty or a young fifty. He was completely bald, his face and scalp were mottled with white splashes—acid burns, Maigrey recognized. Dark, brooding eyes were almost hidden in the shadow of an overhanging forehead. He had a drink on the table in front of him. Two hands rested near the glass. One hand was made of flesh and bone and blood. The other was metal.

"Cyborg," said Sparafucile.

"What percentage?"

"Over seventy. Left side. Hand, leg, foot, face, skull, ear, eye."

"A class job. I wouldn't have guessed the face. Why didn't he get a natural hand to match?"

"That hand of his—special design. Does many special things, lady-mine. And then, it is his way. He does not try to hide what he is."

"No," Maigrey murmured. "He flaunts it, in fact. He looks promising, but he's not for hire. His light's not green. Obviously, he's not in need of work."

"Him never in need." Sparafucile grinned. "People come to Xris. He not go to people. But cyborg always willing to listen."

"Xris, you said his name was."

"Xris."

Maigrey reached out, touched a button, saw the cyborg's gaze shift, focus on the screen before him. Otherwise, he did not move.

"I'd like to buy you a drink," Maigrey said.

The cyborg's hand, the real one, shifted to the glass in front of him.

"Thanks, sister," he said in a voice that had a faint mechanical tinge to it, "but I haven't finished this one yet."

"Too bad. If you change your mind, I'm in the upper room," replied Maigrey with a smile.

The glittering eyes were momentarily hooded. The cyborg lifted his drink, drained it in a gulp, and rose to his feet.

Maigrey removed her portable computer linkup from its case, connected it with the computer aboard her spaceplane.

"Sagan's files. Mercenaries," she commanded.

The computer complied.

"Xris, cyborg."

The computer brought up the file swiftly. Maigrey studied a long list of references, then read the single-sentence remark—Sagan's personal comment—at the end. She smiled, sighed.

A tap on the door, a voice sounded through the commlink. "Waiter."

Agis drew his lasgun. Sparafucile's hand slid inside his rags. Maigrey quit the file, touched a control beneath the table. The door slid aside. A figure, fantastic in dress and appearance, entered, pushing a floating tray bearing glasses, a cup, and a teapot. Maigrey stared.

"Raoul, isn't it?" she said.

The beautiful Adonian bowed gracefully in acknowledgment, flashed her a charming smile. Deftly, he placed the glasses on the table, one in front of each, handing the correct drink to the proper person. When he had finished, he sent the tray to wait for him near the door, and made another low and elaborate bow. Straightening, he flipped his long, straight, shining black hair back over his rainbow-velvet-clad shoulders and favored Maigrey with another charming smile.

"You work here, now, Raoul?" she asked.

"Alas, my most gracious lady," said the Adonian, continuing to smile with the drug-induced euphoria of the Loti, "the untimely and brutal death of my late former employer, Snaga Ohme, forced me to seek other gainful means of support for myself and my friend. You remember my friend?"

"The Little One. Yes, where is he?"

"He remains in our dwelling place. You will understand, my lady, that this den of thieves and murderers, present company excepted," he added, with another fluttering bow, "is no place for the sensitive and delicate nature of an empath."

"Yes, I can imagine," Maigrey replied, doing her best to keep from smiling. "Am I to take it that you are unhappy working here?" It was difficult to tell with the Loti, whose drugged state generally gave the impression that it was impossible for them to be unhappy about anything.

Raoul appeared absolutely blissful as he shook his head sadly. "It is not that, my lady. What is happiness, after all, but the fleeting, transitory butterfly of an emotion that is impossible to catch and hold for long before it flies away."

He allowed a white, delicate hand to emulate the insect of which he spoke. Then, smoothing his hair, he returned from this flight of fancy to what passed for him as reality. "When I saw you enter, my lady, I knew a moment's happiness, the first true happiness I've known in some time. I do not work here strictly for the money. I have many means at my disposal of earning my keep that are not nearly so degrading or that bring me in contact with such low companions. I intend no offense, of course, my lady. I, more than anyone, understand how circumstances have forced you to place yourself in this unsavory locale."

"Truly," said Maigrey gravely, accustomed to talking to Adonians, "we are fellow sufferers of misfortune. Please go on."

"Thank you, my most gracious lady," said the Adonian with a heart-melting smile and another bow. "The Little One and I are here, you see, for a reason. We have a vendetta."

"I'm afraid I don't understand," said Maigrey cautiously, wondering if the Loti knew what the word "vendetta" meant, thinking he may have mistaken it for some type of blow-dryer.

"My late former employer, Snaga Ohme, was a very good employer," said Raoul. The drug-misted eyes were, for a moment, suddenly sharp and clear, fixed on Maigrey with a purpose and conviction that was extremely disconcerting. "A very good employer," repeated Raoul, "and a fellow Adonian. We—the Little One and I—know the name of my late former employer, Snaga Ohme's, murderer."

"It was not Lord Sagan," Maigrey said.

"Oh, no. The Little One and I never supposed that for a moment. We discovered the truth, my lady. That is, the Little One discovered it. We saw the murderer that night. We were close to the one known as Abdiel . . . and to you, my lady, although undoubtedly you did not notice us. You were . . . preoccupied."

Trust the Adonian to phrase it delicately. "I was his prisoner," Maigrey said bluntly.

"Yes, my lady, we knew. That is, the Little One knew. What with the confusion, the report of the bomb about to go off, we were unable to stop the mind-seizer and bring him to justice. Since that unfortunate time, however, we have been keeping track of his whereabouts and . . ." Raoul hesitated.

"—waiting for an opportunity to 'bring him to justice,'" suggested Maigrey.

"Yes," admitted Raoul. "But one never occurred. He came here, but he was well guarded and," the Loti added ingenuously, "he drinks only water that he distills and purifies himself and eats nothing but pills, all of which he makes up in his own laboratory."

"A poisoner's nightmare," said Maigrey sympathetically, remembering the Loti's talent.

"I was considerably disheartened." Raoul looked as downcast as it was possible for a Loti to look.

"Now, Abdiel has jumped galaxies and you have lost him completely."

"The Little One has a particular aversion to Corasians," said Raoul solemnly. "It is difficult to develop a rapport with them.

The two of us would be in extreme peril if we attempted to go after him alone. But the point is moot considering the unhappy circumstance that we do not own a ship capable of making the Jump."

"My lady," Agis said, his eyes on the computer screen, "the person you requested to see is waiting outside."

Maigrey depressed the button, the door slid open.

She had met numerous cyborgs, but not one quite like this. Most people forced by circumstance to become part machine chose to make the machine part appear human. Plastiskin, fleshfoam, and chemblood made artificial limbs not only appear real to the sight and touch, but they would actually bleed if wounded. Internal computer systems, operated by brain impulses, kept the limb moving in harmony with the body's natural parts. Only the most careful observer could generally note the too-perfect function of a cybernetic limb.

But this cyborg, as Maigrey had said, flaunted his machinery, scorned to hide it. A short-sleeved shirt revealed a metal arm, hand, and fingers. LED lights blinked on and off, presumably indicating that all parts were functioning normally. The fingers were jointed, various compartment chambers were visible, containing—Maigrey guessed, considering the cyborg's occupation—weapons. The same undoubtedly held true of the cybernetic leg and foot, visible beneath a pair of altered combat fatigues, whose left pant leg had been cut off at the hip to reveal the mechanical limb.

Maigrey noted as an oddity that the flesh, bone, and muscle half of the cyborg's body was extraordinarily well developed; almost too well developed. Muscles bulged in both legs and arms, contrasting strangely with the smooth-sided mechanized limbs. It was almost as if the human side of the man was competing with the machine.

The cyborg's gaze flicked about the room, making a swift, reflexive, force-of-habit reconnaissance. He did the same with each person seated at the table, summed up Agis with a glance, passed over Sparafucile without the barest hint of recognition, studied Brother Daniel with cool curiosity. His gaze finally settled on Maigrey, who made a slight gesture with her hand, inviting him to be seated. She could hear, in the quiet room, the faint hum and whir of the cyborg's machinery.

"You will excuse me?" she said. "I've run into an old friend."

"Sure, sister. Take your time."

Xris accepted the seat at the end of the round couch, lounged back, studied the ceiling with as much intensity as if he could see through it, which—considering he had an enhanced, artificial eye—perhaps he could. One never knew, with cyborgs.

"The mind-seizer was here on this moon," Maigrey said, returning her attention to Raoul. "You saw him."

"Yes, my lady."

"And"—Maigrey paused—"Lord Sagan was with him?"

"One might say that, my lady."

"What do you mean?"

"The Little One thought Sagan was dead, my lady. But I said that he must be wrong. Why would the mind-seizer bother to transport a corpse?"

"Why, indeed?" Maigrey asked. She lifted the martini glass to her lips. "And what do you want of me, Raoul?"

"Please, my lady," said Raoul with a flip of the hair, a flourish, and a bow, "though I am a Loti, do not take me for a fool. The drugs in which I indulge allow me to see the universe through rose-colored glasses, as the old saying goes. They do not, however, dim or blur my vision. It is not coincidence that you are here, on Hell's Outpost and that the mind-dead are here, as well."

Maigrey set down the martini glass. "You've seen them?"

"Yes, my lady."

"You know, perhaps, who they are? Where they are staying?"

"Yes, my lady."

Maigrey glanced at Sparafucile, who nodded and, uncoiling his body, rose lethargically to his feet.

"How many of them?" the assassin asked.

"Three," answered Raoul.

"In the Cafe?"

"Yes."

"I will have to wait until they leave, Starlady," said Sparafucile.

"I understand. We will meet you back at the spaceplane."

"Perhaps I should accompany him, my lady," offered Agis, starting to rise.

Sparafucile grunted, shook his head. "I work alone. Come, Loti."

"My lady." Raoul, in his earnestness, leaned over the table.

His long hair fell forward, brushed his fingertips. The smell of exotic perfume filled the small room. "This information deserves some reward, don't you agree?"

"Certainly," Maigrey replied. "Your tip will be extremely generous."

"Not money, my lady. Take us with you."

"You and the Little One."

"Of course, my lady. Our help could be of inestimable value."

Maigrey studied him thoughtfully. "Perhaps it could. I will give the matter thought and let you know."

"Thank you, my lady."

"And since you will be busy, would you send someone else up with this gentleman's order?" She glanced at Xris.

"I will be delighted, my lady." The Adonian rose, smoothed back his hair, bowed, and turned gracefully to the cyborg. "What is your pleasure, sir?"

"Nothing gives me pleasure, Loti. Booze makes it a little easier, that's all. And I've reached my limit."

"Very good, sir." Raoul smiled radiantly on all of them, drifted out the door in a cloud of euphoria, leaving behind the fragrance of roses and jasmine.

Sparafucile followed, padding silent as a cat. Brother Daniel sneezed. The cyborg stared at Maigrey.

"Name's Xris. So what's the deal, sister?"

Agis stiffened. "You are in the presence of Lady Maigrey Morianna, sir. You will speak to my lady with respect."

The cyborg slid an inch down in his seat, made himself comfortable, kept his eyes—lids narrowed—on Maigrey. "Yeah, I thought that's who you were. Word's out you're looking for men for a job. I have five. Xris's Commandos. Maybe you've heard of us? We used to be seven, but we lost two."

"How did it happen?"

"We were doing a job on Shilo's Planet I, about eight, nine months ago."

"When the Corasians attacked?"

"Yeah. They were good men. Been with us from the start."

"You could replace them. . . ."

"This"—Xris held his flesh-and-blood hand to the light—"can be replaced, sister. Not men. Not good men."

The cyborg pulled out a plastisteel case, opened the lid, removed an ugly black, braided, particularly strong, and nasty form of tobacco known as a "twist," and stuck it in one corner of his mouth.

"I would appreciate it if you didn't smoke," said Maigrey.

Xris brought the metal hand to the twist's tip. A small flame shot out of the thumb, lit the tobacco. A cloud of noxious gray-green smoke drifted lazily to the ceiling. The cyborg inhaled deeply, let the smoke drizzle out the corner of the tight-lipped mouth.

Agis was on his feet. "My lady asked you not to smoke—"

Maigrey laid a restraining hand on the centurion's arm.

Agis resumed his seat reluctantly, jaw set, face grim. Xris paid him no attention.

"You don't attempt to endear yourself to your potential employers, do you?" Maigrey asked wryly.

"I'm not off to see the wizard, looking for a heart. What's the job, sister?"

"I can't give you details until you accept. I couldn't give them to you here, anyway. We've had a small problem. Someone attempting to . . . eavesdrop." She stirred the rock dust with her finger.

The cyborg would have raised an eyebrow if he'd had any. "Must be damn good to break through the security of this place."

"They are good. We found one listening device, but there may be others."

"So that's where the breed went, huh? He in on this with you?"

"Yes."

Xris removed the twist from his mouth, flicked ashes on the floor beneath the table. "What are the odds of getting back alive?"

"Practically none."

"Suicide mission?"

"That describes it."

"What's it pay?"

"Name your price."

Xris stated a figure.

Maigrey smiled, shook her head. "I could buy twenty men for such a sum."

"You hire us and you'll think you hired twenty."

"Your team is that good?"

Xris took a drag on the twist. Smoke curled up lazily from

the corner of the cyborg's mouth. "We're that good. I lost two men on Shiloh, but I managed to get the rest of my men off alive. We five were the only survivors."

"These are my terms: I'm in command. You report to me. Your men take orders from you."

The ash on the twist glowed brightly, dimmed. "You used to be in the Golden Squadron?"

"Yes."

"Sagan's number two?"

"Yes."

Xris nodded. Taking the twist out of his mouth, he tossed it on the floor, ground it beneath his heel. "These are *my* terms: I draw up the contract. You sign it. We don't do anything that's not in the contract unless we get paid extra. We take cash only. No credit. All of it, in advance."

"Half now. Half on return."

"No dice, sister. From what you say, this is a one-way ticket."

"And from what you say, if you're as good as you say, you've guaranteed me a worry-free round-trip. Half now, half on return."

The cyborg took out another twist, stuck it in his mouth, eyed Maigrey. Then he grinned. "Shoveled myself into my own hole, didn't I?"

Maigrey smiled coolly. Her eyes kept level with his, never shifted.

At length, Xris lifted his metal hand, flexed the fingers. "There's some new parts out on the market. I need to upgrade and I need money to buy them. It'll be worth it to you, sister, I promise. Sixty percent now, forty on return."

"Very well," Maigrey agreed, ignoring Agis's scowl.

Xris's gaze flicked to the linkup. "You've been checking on me, I see."

"Just as you've been checking on me."

"What did you find out?"

"Nothing you don't already know."

The cyborg grunted, stood up. He held out his right hand, his flesh-and-blood hand. "Done?"

Maigrey stood up, clasped her right hand over his. "Done."

Xris turned her hand over, palm up. The five puncture wounds that marked her as Blood Royal shone dark in the room's indirect lighting. He glanced from her palm to the bloodsword.

Maigrey removed her hand from the cyborg's grasp, placed it on the bloodsword's hilt. "You know Sparafucile's plane?"

"That heap? Yeah, I know it."

"Meet me there at 2400. We'll go over the details and I'll have your money."

Xris said nothing, nodded, started to leave. He moved awkwardly, with an uneven gait, as if forcing the human side of his body to move faster and better and smoother than the machine. At the door, he turned, glanced over his shoulder.

"By the way, sister. You'd better put that forty percent you owe us in escrow. We *will* be back to collect."

Maigrey activated the door. The cyborg walked out. She shut the door, sealed it behind him. Thoughtfully, she sat down again.

"What do you think?" she asked.

"A tormented soul," said Brother Daniel, suddenly and unexpectedly.

Maigrey stared at him, startled. "Yes, I believe you're right."

"I don't like him." Agis shook his head, frowning darkly. "But I have little doubt that he's capable. What does my lord say about him?"

Maigrey smiled, switched on the linkup, turned the screen for Agis to read.

At the bottom of the long file, under "Xris, cyborg" was a single comment, wry, grudging.

HE'S ACTUALLY AS GOOD AS HE THINKS HE IS.

Chapter ❖❀❀❖ Ten

Follow, follow, follow . . .

The Wizard of Oz

"Where's Agis?" Brother Daniel asked, emerging from the Café's exit—another sensory deprivation chamber that left the priest feeling slightly dizzy and disoriented.

Maigrey shrugged. "Last I saw him, he was heading for a back room in the company of our fluorescent green hostess."

Brother Daniel gasped, shocked. "He should not have left you—"

"Oh, lighten up," Maigrey said sharply. "We're not all virgins, you know."

Brother Daniel stared at her in disbelief, his skin burning. Hurt and offended, he turned away.

She seemed to regret her words, looked as if she wanted to apologize, then changed her mind. "Come along, Brother," she said abruptly. "It's time we were getting back to the plane."

The three had left the upper room, planning—or so Brother Daniel had assumed—to return to the spaceplane. On the way down in the gravator, Agis had suggested they stop in the bar and have "one for the road." Maigrey had agreed. Brother Daniel had excused himself to use the facilities.

When he had returned, Agis was nowhere to be seen. The priest assumed the centurion had gone about the same business as himself and would meet them at the exit. But the centurion was, it seemed, apparently engaged in more pleasant pursuits. Brother Daniel couldn't understand it. Agis had certainly not seemed the type to indulge in his appetites when they were on such an urgent and dangerous mission. And the priest couldn't understand Maigrey for allowing it. Apparently, he had misjudged both of them.

"This way," said Maigrey. She was cold, cold and colorless as the moon on which they stood.

Brother Daniel didn't argue. The plastisteel domes looked all the same to him. He had no idea where they were.

The two walked rapidly over the planet's gray surface, the rock crunching beneath their boots. Brother Daniel kept nervous watch. They were out late, too late. Although Hell's Outpost never slept, the inhabitants had apparently taken their business and/or pleasure behind closed doors and plastisteel walls. The streets—meandering paths winding around the scattered domes that passed for streets—were almost empty, except for a few dark and furtive figures, who kept closely to the shadows.

Daniel thought he saw one of these figures detach itself from a wall and fall into step behind them. Coincidence, he told himself. Someone heading the same direction we are.

The priest was forced to quicken his pace to catch up with Maigrey, who was walking rapidly, looking neither to her left nor her right, apparently preoccupied by her own thoughts.

"My lady, I think we're going the wrong way," said Brother Daniel.

"Keep moving," Maigrey said softly, beneath her breath.

They were surrounded by several domes, most of them dark and deserted. The priest, glancing behind him out of the corner of his eye, caught a glimpse of a shadow melting into the shadow of a building.

"No, no, this is the right direction. I'm sure of it," Maigrey said suddenly, loudly.

Daniel had no idea what was going on. Fear's hard knot tightened inside him. Maigrey glanced at him, her lips moved.

"Say something," she mouthed. "Keep talking."

He wished desperately he knew what was going on.

"I . . . I don't remember any of these buildings." He swallowed. "And, look. You can see the dome wall from here. That isn't the air lock we came in through. And there are no planes parked out beyond. We've . . . come the wrong way," he repeated helplessly.

Maigrey came to an abrupt stop. Daniel was three steps beyond her before he realized it.

"So we have," she said, and spinning on her heel, she launched off in a different direction. "This is the way. I remember now."

Coming even with her, Brother Daniel looked back over his

shoulder. Their shadow had also changed direction, was moving along after them.

"My lady," he said in a low voice, "I think we're being—"

The sound of a scuffle came from behind them, a choking, agonized scream.

"Damn!" Maigrey swore. Turning, she ran back down the street.

Bewildered, Daniel hurried after.

Agis knelt over the body of a woman, lying on the gray rock. Maigrey came up to him.

"Dead?" she asked.

The centurion rolled the woman's body over. Brother Daniel, looking down, looked hurriedly away. He had seen death, had seen violent death, but never anything quite as horrible as this. The woman's eyes were wide open, stared up at them in sheer terror. Her mouth gaped open, her face was contorted by what must have been unendurable pain.

Agis rose to his feet.

"I'm sorry, my lady. I tried to take her alive, as you commanded, but when I laid my hand on her, she . . . she just screamed and clutched her head and . . . dropped down."

"Was she one of them?" asked Maigrey, regarding the corpse with a cool, dispassionate gaze.

"I believe so, my lady. I couldn't be certain. She was waiting outside the Cafe. She picked up you and Brother Daniel there."

"Yes," said Maigrey. "I hadn't counted on our priest being such an astute observer. He spotted her almost immediately, nearly gave us away."

Daniel stared down at the corpse.

"What killed her, if Agis didn't?"

"Abdiel killed her. Through her mind. God knows what horrible vision he made the poor wretch see, what torment he inflicted on her at the end."

Daniel felt suddenly sick and faint. He swayed where he stood.

"Take it easy, Brother. Sit down. Put your head between your knees," Agis advised, catching hold of the priest before he fell over.

"I'm sorry. I don't know . . . what's the matter with me," Daniel gasped. "I've seen men . . . blown apart . . ."

"It hits you like that sometimes," said Maigrey. "The stress, tension. Take a few deep breaths."

She and Agis turned back to study the body. "There's one way to find out for certain."

Maigrey knelt down, took hold of the dead hand, and turned the palm up to face the light. Daniel leaned his head weakly against his knees, sucked air into his lungs.

"That's it," he heard her say softly, grimly. "She was one of the mind-dead."

"An amateurish job of tailing," Agis remarked.

"Or meant to look that way." Maigrey stood up, glanced around. "She was probably a decoy. Supposed to play games with us, keep us entertained, while her two cohorts went about the real task. Brother Daniel, do you feel up to walking? I doubt if anyone on Hell's Outpost will get upset over a corpse in the street, but I'd rather not have to answer any questions."

"I'm all right," said Daniel, blushing, refusing Agis's proffered assistance. "It's just that I feel . . . such a fool, my lady."

"Sorry we couldn't let you in on our plans. It's not that we didn't trust you, but the walls have ears, as the saying goes. And I'm sorry for what I said to you back there, Brother," she added gently, laying her hand on his arm. "I had to keep her from getting suspicious."

"I'm the one who should apologize, my lady. I should have trusted you. I should have known—"

"Don't praise me too much, Brother Daniel," Maigrey said, harshly cutting him off. "Let's get going."

"One moment more, please, my lady." Brother Daniel leaned over the corpse. Lifting the dead hand, he placed it on the woman's breast, laid her other hand over it. Shutting the staring eyes, he murmured soft words, ending with, "*Exaudi orationem meam; ad te omnis caro veniet*. Hear my prayer, to Thee all flesh must come.'

"She was, after all, one of God's children," he said, rising, pale but composed.

"Once she was," said Maigrey. "But not now. Not when Abdiel was finished with her. She's better off dead. Come on. We've got a long night ahead of us. And I think *this* way," she said with a grave smile for Brother Daniel, "is the right direction."

··◁▪ ▪▷··

Agis kept close watch behind, but they reached the air lock without incident and without unwanted company. Putting on their spacesuits, retrieved from a locker, they walked to the spaceplane in silence. Maigrey and the centurion kept their hands on their weapons, looked sharply into the dark shadows that stood out in clear-cut vivid contrast to the sun's bright light, unfiltered by clouds or atmosphere. But as closely as they watched, none of them saw the half-breed until he appeared right in front of them, as if he had sprung up out of the gray rock.

"You do not need your weapon. It is I, Starlady," said the assassin through the speaker on his helmet.

"Don't do that to me again!" she snapped, irritation concealing relief.

She held the bloodsword; she'd drawn it the split second she'd caught a glimpse of movement in the darkness beneath the belly of the spaceplane. But she was acutely aware of the fact that if the assassin had been her foe, she would more than likely be dead by now. "Next time, whistle or something. I could have sliced you in two!"

"Yes, lady-mine."

Maigrey guessed he was probably laughing at her behind his helmet, but she was too tired to care. And she still had the meeting with the cyborg to get through.

"Well," she said wearily, "did you find the mind-dead? Where did they go?"

"They come here, lady-mine," said the assassin.

Maigrey looked at her spaceplane, nodded. She wasn't surprised. "Where are they now?"

Sparafucile jerked a thumb. Maigrey saw a dark rift in the gray ground some distance from the spaceplane. Walking over, she peered down into a deep ravine. Light reflected off the shattered remains of two helmets, a leg was twisted at an odd and impossible angle. The rest of the bodies were hidden by the darkness.

The assassin came to stand beside her. "They sit in Cafe until certain you safe in private room. Then these two leave. A woman, she stay behind."

"Yes," said Maigrey. "We ran into her."

Sparafucile grunted. "I follow these two. They come here, to spaceplane, try to break in but fail. One stand guard, the other crawl underneath. I take out guard first, then go after the other. He have this in hand."

The assassin pointed with a toe of his boot to a pile of rock dust on the lip of the ravine. Maigrey, glancing at it, saw it was greenish in color, a distinct contrast to the gray rock around it.

"Was that the only one he planted?"

"I think so. I search, find no more."

"Good. But, still, we can't take the chance. We'll meet with Xris on your plane. It isn't likely they would know it, would they? Even if they knew you?"

"No, lady-mine."

Maigrey turned away from the ravine abruptly. *It hits you like that sometimes* or so she'd told Brother Daniel. *God's children. She's better off dead.* They're better off dead, down in that ravine.

We saw you, Raoul had said. *You were preoccupied.* She remembered Abdiel in her mind, remembered the terror, the loneliness, the horror. She remembered the attic, the box of dreadful things. And he was in there, within that box, baiting her, taunting her, hoping she would turn her back, give in, relax. And then the box would slowly open and then his hand would reach out, claim her, and drag her down. . . .

"My lady!" Agis was beside her, concern echoing over the commlink. The assassin, on her left. Brother Daniel hovering before her like some damn angel.

"Go!" Maigrey ordered, waving her hands to dispel them, to shake them loose, to banish them. "Go on ahead . . . to the half-breed's plane. I'll meet you there. Go!" she commanded angrily, seeing them standing, staring at her.

They went. Moving reluctantly, slowly, but they went.

Maigrey waited until they had gone around the back end of the spaceplane, waited until they were out of sight. She would have liked to have slumped down, curled up in a ball, buried her head in her hands. But that was impossible in a pressurized suit, helmet, gloves.

"It's low blood sugar," she told herself, waiting for the dizziness to pass. "I haven't eaten anything all day. Maybe longer than that. I can't remember. And then two drinks on an empty stomach. No wonder the only reason I'm standing is because these damn gravity boots won't let me fall over. I'll be all right in a moment. Oxygen," she said, readjusting the valve on her suit. "I need more oxygen."

She breathed deeply, took firm hold of herself, and started on her way to the assassin's spaceplane.

Chapter ·◈⊃◯⊂◈· Eleven

And all's fish, that comes to my net.
                    Charles Dickens, *Bleak House*

Inside the half-breed's spaceplane, Maigrey removed her helm and breathing apparatus and was immediately sorry she'd done so. The stench was appalling, took her breath. She had to physically restrain herself from putting her hand over her nose and mouth, fought back the inclination to gag.

"This way for'ard, lady-mine," said Sparafucile, offering a hand to assist her.

His assistance was not mere formality or politeness. It was impossible to move more than a step or two into the bowels of the spaceplane (and "bowels" seemed to Maigrey to be an extremely appropriate term) without guidance.

The interior was illuminated by a lambent red glow, shining from various dials and instruments. The dim light gleamed off metal surfaces, showed up most objects as eerie shadows. But Maigrey realized after a close, accidental look at some of the objects that she should be thankful she couldn't see the remainder.

The inside of the volksrocket was like a refuse pit. No, she amended, moving gingerly forward, clutching the half-breed's hand, "refuse" implies unwanted bits of life that the owner has been too careless to discard. Sparafucile wasn't careless or undisciplined. The jumble and clutter that filled the half-breed's plane were parts of his life that he was either unwilling or unable to leave behind.

She groped her way forward. So much for dinner, she thought, her stomach turning at the idea. The others, including the cyborg, were already here, gathered together in one of the volksrocket's few cleared areas. And, at that, it looked as if the half-breed had taken a bulldozer to it. A wall, literally, of

282

junk surrounded them. When anyone moved, bits and pieces of the breed's collection slid off, clattered to the deck.

Maigrey took her place near a pile of human skulls, tread on something that was soft and squishy. She edged it aside with her boot, keeping her eyes level, refusing to look down to see what it was. Or had been.

The half-breed hunkered on the deck, resting on his haunches. The cyborg lounged against one of the bulkheads, the red light reflecting off his metal arm and leg. Agis stood in military posture, at ease, but alert, tense. Brother Daniel perched uncomfortably and unhappily on a metal box. Maigrey glanced at the box's label, stenciled in Standard Military, and wondered if the priest knew he was sitting on a supply of concussion grenades.

"It's late. I, for one, am tired," Maigrey began, her gaze encompassing all those present. "I'll cut the preliminaries, get right to the point, make this as brief and concise as possible. If you have any questions, please ask them as we go along.

"You have all heard, on the GBC, various rumors and reports concerning the mysterious disappearance of the Warlord Derek Sagan. It is important to our cause that we keep these rumors alive, which is why His Majesty—although he knows the truth—has made only vague denials. Here are the facts. Lord Sagan was taken captive by a mind-seizer, a man known as Abdiel, formerly head of the now-defunct Order of Dark Lightning."

Seeing the cyborg frown and about to speak, Maigrey raised a hand, forestalled him. "How my lord was captured, how this Abdiel remains alive after he was reported dead, are not matters we need go into. If you have questions on this, I suggest you refer them to Brother Daniel, who was present when my lord was taken, or to myself at some later time. What I say is true. The mind-seizer lives, and so do those who serve him. We have found three on Hell's Outpost."

"Where are they now?" Xris asked, taking out one of the noxious twists and lighting it. Maigrey was almost grateful to him; the smell of the black tobacco, though rank, was a definite improvement over the other malodors present in the half-breed's spaceplane.

"Dead," answered Maigrey shortly.

The cyborg nodded, said nothing more. Brother Daniel shifted uneasily on his box.

"Abdiel has fled with his captive to the Corasian galaxy. We're going after them."

"You know where they go?" The half-breed's eyelids were almost completely closed, he had appeared to be asleep and Maigrey was slightly startled when he spoke.

"No."

"Then how you find him, lady-mine?"

Maigrey had known this was going to come up, had steeled herself to explain it logically, without emotion. "Lord Sagan and I are what is known as mind-linked, a phenomenon that occurs sometimes in two of the Blood Royal."

"You talk with my lord?"

"No, I can't. He's closed his mind down, retreated before Abdiel's assault on it. But I will be able to find him. Let me put it to you this way. We are like two magnets, whose opposing fields pull them together."

"Abdiel, he know this about you two?"

"Unfortunately, yes. Not only does he know it, but he's counting on it. Lord Sagan and I are the last of the Blood Royal, the last of the Guardians. The mind-seizer has Sagan. He wants me. Only when both of us are out of the way, can Abdiel relax."

"So we're walking into a trap," said Xris.

"Yes, but at least we have the advantage of knowing it's a trap."

Xris blew smoke through his nose. "We're going into Corasia, then, to rescue Sagan—"

"Not primarily," Maigrey corrected.

She'd known this was coming, too. And this wasn't going to be easy. Agis and Brother Daniel both look startled. Sparafucile's misaligned eyes opened a half centimeter, glinted red in the light.

Maigrey took a deep breath, continued: "You have heard about the space-rotation bomb. The plans, the design, the knowledge of how this bomb works and can be produced are all in Lord Sagan's mind. It is Abdiel's intention to force my lord to reveal these plans, have the Corasians build the bomb. I leave you to imagine what Abdiel's plans will be once he has the most destructive weapon in the universe in his possession. To say nothing of the fact that the Corasians will have it in their power to build more.

"Therefore, our primary goal must be to halt this threat to our galaxy."

"In other words," said Agis, "if we cannot rescue my lord, we must destroy him."

"Yes," said Maigrey.

Brother Daniel shuddered. "God have mercy," he whispered.

"How do you know it's not too late?" Xris demanded, taking the twist from his mouth, gesturing with it. "Every man's got a breaking point, even Sagan. I know something about the Order of Dark Lightning, never mind how. But if half of what I've heard about the mind-seizers is true, then this Abdiel could make a man give up his soul, much less every secret Sagan ever knew. And once the Corasians get their robotic claws on that bomb info, it'll be relayed into their central computer system and that'll be all she wrote, sister."

"My lord has the ability to fight Abdiel, but—as you say—every man has his breaking point. In the end, Abdiel will win. Lord Sagan must succumb. But that hasn't happened yet. My lord resists still and can hold out longer. We must move fast, however."

"Into the trap."

"Into the trap. Our goal will be to get in and get out before the jaws shut. In order to succeed, we have to take the mind-seizer completely by surprise. The problem: entering the Corasian galaxy, breaking through their outer defense perimeter without getting ourselves destroyed and without alerting Abdiel to our presence."

Xris pushed himself up from where he'd been leaning against the bulkhead. "Hell, sister. You said this was hopeless, not impossible. Count me out."

"You can't leave," said Maigrey. "You know too much."

"Who's going to stop me?" The cyborg's metal hand flashed in the red light.

"I could," said Maigrey coolly. "But that would mean a fight, which would be a waste of time, energy, and a good man, for I would have to kill you. I have a plan. Why don't you stay and listen to it?"

Xris stared at her incredulously for a moment, then a slow smile crossed the thin lips. He settled back against the bulkheads. "Shoot."

"It's Corasian policy to attack and attempt to capture any

ship coming from this galaxy into theirs—with one exception. One type of ship is permitted to enter. Not only permitted, but welcomed."

Maigrey glanced around, saw dawning comprehension on the face of the cyborg, saw—by Agis's grim expression and dark frown—that the centurion, though he wasn't happy about the plan, understood it. She couldn't tell what Sparafucile was thinking, but the half-breed's eyes had closed again; she presumed he understood and approved. Brother Daniel, of course, had no idea what she was talking about.

"A meat wagon," said Xris, grudging admiration in his voice. "Not bad, sister. Not bad."

"On looking over a list of shipping in the area, I find that the luxury liner, *Galaxy Belle*, will be within jump distance in approximately two Standard Military days. That should give you and your men time enough to get into position?"

She glanced at Xris, who nodded. The twist was almost gone, had burned down to little more than a stump.

"The *Galaxy Belle* is your typical space-going gambling casino, keeping well outside the legal limits to avoid any government hassles, entanglements, and tax collectors. It's one of the smaller pleasure cruise ships of the line, having a crew of twenty humans who serve primarily to run the ship. Most of the work aboard is handled by 'droids. It can carry up to one thousand passengers. Adults only. No children are allowed," Maigrey added in a softer voice. "I checked."

Brother Daniel had risen to his feet. His face was livid, his eyes wide with shock and horror. "You can't mean this, Lady Maigrey! You can't be serious!"

Maigrey ignored him. "We will board the ship, seize control. The passengers and crew will be drugged, enough to keep them comatose, not enough to harm them—the drugs will be the Loti Raoul's responsibility. We fly the ship to Corasia, make it known what valuable cargo we have on board, get passed safely through the outer defenses. Once inside, we head for Abdiel's planet.

"His Majesty plans to raise a fleet of warships and bring them into the Corasian galaxy to assist us. Once we reach Abdiel's location, we will release the *Galaxy Belle*, hopefully with everyone aboard safe and unharmed. If all goes well and the fleet arrives, they can escort the *Belle* back to safety."

"If all goes well!" Brother Daniel cried in a hollow voice. "If all goes well! If it doesn't, you have doomed innocent people to . . . to . . . what did you call it? A meat wagon! God forbid this!"

Maigrey regarded him coldly, gray eyes dark. "Ask God what happens if the Corasians and Abdiel get hold of that bomb, Brother Daniel. Ask Him how many *billions* of innocent people will suffer? I am sorry for what I have to do," she continued resolutely, "but I mean to do it. There is no other way. This is our only chance. The good of the few must be sacrificed for that of the many."

Xris removed the butt end of the twist from his mouth, tossed it to the deck, ground it out with the heel of his artificial leg. "You some kind of a religious nut or something?"

"I am—I was a priest," said Brother Daniel, remembering his cover story. "I was in the Order of Adamant."

"Never heard of it. But if it's any comfort to you, Priest, these gambling cruises are run by the mob, operate outside the law. They cater to people who don't care how they come by their money and less how they spend it. If anything does happen to them, they won't be missed."

Brother Daniel shook his head. "They are God's children."

Agis spoke. "My lady, what about capturing this ship and replacing the civilians with military personnel? At least soldiers would have a fighting chance."

"I considered that," Maigrey said slowly. "But an operation like that would take weeks to bring together. It's too big, word is bound to leak out. The Corasians have spies all through this galaxy—"

"All through the military," Xris commented. The cyborg took another twist from a pocket, put it to his lips, lit it with a flick of his mechanical fingers. "You ever fought Corasians, Priest? Ever been around them?"

"No," Brother Daniel admitted. "But—"

"They're real good at putting two and two together. Better than most. They haven't got eyes, but they see fine without them. Their sonar and radar and internal scanners don't miss much. You can bet they'll board us when we reach Corasia. They'll want to inspect the meat before they invest in it and—"

"Don't call it meat!" Brother Daniel cried, flushing in anger. "These are people we are talking about—"

"You'd better get used to it, Priest," Xris cut in coolly. "If they see anything the least bit suspicious . . . Well, you can figure yourself to be on top of their breakfast menu."

"Why are we wasting time arguing with him," Agis demanded sternly. "You warned him, my lady. You told him not to come."

Brother Daniel stammered, cut himself off, kept quiet long moments. Finally, he spoke. "Again, I've been a fool. Forgive me, my lady. We are in God's hands. He will deliver us." He turned pleading eyes to Maigrey. "Don't leave me behind! You can count on me from now on. I won't fail you, my lady, or my lord."

Maigrey glanced around. Agis looked grim and dubious. Xris, no telling what the cyborg was thinking. Sparafucile didn't appear to have heard a word being said. He crouched on the deck, staring at her through slit eyes that had never once moved.

It was her decision. The most logical—and probably the kindest—thing she could do for the young priest would be to send a laser beam through his head. The situation was going to get darker, grimmer. If he fell apart like that around the Corasians, he could put them all in jeopardy. And how could she trust him now? Might he not decide to take matters out of God's hands and into his own?

Be honest, Maigrey. You can't kill him. You don't have it in you. And you can't leave him behind for the mind-dead to find and interrogate. Which gives you no choice.

Deliberately brusque, businesslike, she turned from him, ordered Sparafucile to call up a diagram of a cruise ship on his vidscreen.

"Now, here's my plan."

···◁▥ ▥▷···

The remainder of the night was spent going over details and finalizing strategy. They discussed tactics, logistics; grappled with cold, harsh reality, and Maigrey finally relaxed, her mind cleared. The hard part was over. She was committed, she couldn't back down or argue herself out of it now. The die was cast. The game afoot. No choice.

She believed she had a good team. Xris made several excellent and intelligent suggestions. Agis was, of course, solid as null-grav steel. The problem of Brother Daniel she'd resolved for herself. As for Raoul and the Little One, no one in his right mind ever trusted a Loti. But this Loti was an Adonian, out to avenge the death of another Adonian. And one of the Adonians' few redeeming characteristics—brought about because they thought so well of themselves—was the fact that they were incredibly loyal to each other. Sparafucile volunteered to keep an eye on Raoul and his diminutive sidekick. Which left her only one lingering doubt—the half-breed himself.

The meeting did not break up until early in the morning.

Agis woke Brother Daniel, who, exhausted, had fallen asleep on a pile of rags. Xris took his money, counted it, nodded, satisfied, and thrust it in a compartment concealed inside his cybernetic leg. Sparafucile escorted them all to the air lock, opened it, then disappeared somewhere into the shadows of his plane.

Xris had a few more questions, dealing with minor details. These settled, he extinguished his twist before putting on his breathing apparatus, and departed. Agis assisted the bleary-eyed, stumbling, half-asleep priest into his spacesuit, then the centurion put on his own.

"Go on," Maigrey told them. "I'll catch up in a minute."

She was so tired she could barely think what she was doing. Standing alone in the air lock, she fumbled at the catch on her helmet. The half-breed was beside her, appearing out of the darkness with a suddenness that startled her. His deft fingers took over the task. Silently, he assisted her. Silently, he opened the air lock.

She was about to thank him. The look in the misshapen eyes froze the words on her lips.

"You not kill my lord," said Sparafucile softly.

So that was it. Maigrey tried to remember what had been said. It was Agis who had spoken. *In other words, if we cannot rescue my lord, we must destroy him.* And she had agreed.

"I trust that will not be necessary," she began, "but circumstances might force—"

The half-breed drew in his breath, let it out in a hiss. "You will die yourself first!"

No good arguing, attempting to explain. He would never understand. Maigrey turned away, stepped into the air lock. It sealed shut. Pressure dropped, stabilized, the lock opened. She stepped out onto the moon's surface. Agis was there, waiting for her. He had sent Brother Daniel on, remained to escort her.

"Problems with the half-breed?"

"I was worried that he might not be loyal enough." Maigrey shook her head. "It never occurred to me that he might be too loyal."

"Do we continue to use him?"

"Yes," she answered, adding wearily what seemed to have become an accursed credo, "we have no choice."

Chapter ···❦··· Twelve

Upon that I kiss your hand, and I call you my queen.
William Shakespeare, *King Henry V*, Act V, Scene 2

Time is, as one noted twentieth-century thinker put it, so that everything doesn't happen at once. The measurement of time, at least by the clock, is exact. The measurement of time by the heart and the head is far different. Time passes, time flies. It creeps or crawls. It moves faster than light. Time, for Maigrey, was running rapidly through her fingers. The hourglass emptying fast. Time, for Dion, was standing still. The stars had ceased to turn. All the suns in the galaxy were shining down on him.

"Isn't she beautiful, Tusk!" Dion demanded.

"Yeah, kid," Tusk agreed, trying unsuccessfully to stifle a yawn. "She's a beauty, all right. Hard to believe. She must take after her mother's side of the family. She sure," he added with heartfelt emphasis, "doesn't take after her father."

"And what do you think of her, Nola?" Dion turned to the young woman, who sat curled up on the bed beside Tusk.

"I like her. There's something very refreshing about her. She's honest, open, unpretentious—"

"Barbaric," Tusk whispered in her ear.

"Be quiet, he'll hear you!" Nola squeezed Tusk's hand.

"No, he won't. Look at him." Tusk yawned again.

Dion didn't hear them. He stood at the window, staring out blissfully at the lake that could be seen in the distance, stars and moon glimmering in its dark water. A golden haze surrounded him with radiance, elevated him above all other mortal beings, filled him with enchanting music that obliterated all sounds except those he wanted, needed to hear.

Tusk and Nola had been ready to retire for the night when Dion appeared at their door. He couldn't sleep, didn't want to end what had been the most marvelous evening of his life. And he couldn't clearly remember any of it. He could only remember her.

"I'm going to ask her to marry me," he said.

Tusk and Nola exchanged alarmed glances, sleepiness startled out of them.

"Uh, isn't this a little sudden, kid. Talk to him!" Tusk urged his wife in an undertone.

"Why me? You're his friend."

"Because women are better at these things."

"Oh, yeah!" She snorted. "I thought the only difference was in X and Y chromosomes. I didn't know we had one labeled 'advice to the love-lorn'!"

"C'mon. It'll be good practice for you—when we have our own kids."

"He's not a kid," Nola retorted. "Or hadn't you noticed?"

"What is it?" Dion turned. "What were you saying? You agree with me, don't you? She's wonderful."

Tusk, making emphatic signs to Nola with his eyebrows and jerks of his head, appeared to have contracted a nervous disorder.

"What's the matter? What's wrong?" Dion asked, the golden haze receding enough to let him see that his friends weren't exactly bounding around the room with joy.

"Nothing, kid," said Tusk, standing up. "Uh, I got to go use the facilities. I'll . . . be back." He dragged out his boots, slid his feet into them, beat it for the door. "You and Nola . . . have a nice little talk while I'm gone."

"I'll get you for this!" Nola shot out of the corner of her mouth.

Tusk grabbed a nuke lamp and fled, slammed shut the door behind him. Out in the hall, he leaned back against the wall, heaved a sigh of relief, wiped sweat from his forehead. "God! What a narrow escape!"

Feeling some remorse that he'd left his wife behind, but not enough to go back, he hastened down the hall, determined to make his stay in the outhouse last as long as it would be humanly possible for him to endure the cold and the smell.

··◁■ ■▷··

"I admit I haven't known Kamil very long," said Dion, leaving his place by the window, coming forward to plead his case, "but look at all the other women I've met in the last few months! I've dated women from all over the galaxy. Every age, every type. None of them come near comparing to her. Do they?"

"No, Dion," Nola answered slowly. "Kamil is different, very different."

"And I never fell in love with any of those others, did I?" Dion demanded. "I'm not like Link, who's in love with somebody on a weekly basis. I knew I hadn't found the right person. I had to keep searching. But when I saw her standing on that rock, when I looked into her eyes, I knew I'd found her, Nola. The only woman I could ever love."

"I know you think so now, Dion," Nola said hesitantly, "but you've been lonely, very lonely. I've seen it, so has Tusk. And what with our getting married, and Lady Maigrey leaving, and all the turmoil and upset . . . well, it's natural that you should be looking for someone to love—"

"And I might latch on to the first person who came along?" Dion asked her quietly. "I thought about that, Nola. I really did, on the walk home tonight. I had to, if I was going to ask her to be my wife. I looked into my heart, and I know the answer. She's the one, Nola, the one I've been waiting to find."

He didn't mention the dream, didn't mention the woman with golden eyes who'd fought at his side, held her shield protectively before him. Despite experiencing the still, small voice within, despite seeing Platus's spirit appear to him, Dion had been unable to come to believe completely in a Creator, in a Will and Force other than his own, guiding his life. But this latest miracle had nearly convinced him. It seemed to him, because of the dream, that his love for Kamil had been foreordained and therefore blessed.

"And I know she's been waiting for me," he added.

"It's something you should think seriously about, Dion," said Nola. "You've been around other women, lots of other women. But Kamil hasn't been with other men. Oh, yes, she's got scads of brothers and probably male friends. But, Dion, despite the fact that she's as old as you are in years, she isn't nearly as old as you are in experience or maturity. She's obviously just barely out of her childhood. In fact, I'll bet she's never before thought about or dreamed of thinking about a man the way she's suddenly starting to think about you."

Dion remembered her sitting on the rock, calmly watching him swim stark naked, with no more passion than if she'd been

looking at one of her brothers, whom she must have seen from
diapers on up. He was forced, reluctantly, to admit that Nola
was right. He himself had witnessed her dawning awareness of
his sexuality, and perhaps her own, as well. He remembered
vividly the warm blush suffusing the smooth, tanned skin,
the eyes that had been bold and laughing, suddenly self-
consciously unable to meet his gaze.

"You believe she does care for me, then?" Dion asked,
skipping over the part of the conversation he didn't want to
hear, landing squarely on the part he did.

His thoughts went to the evening they'd spent together, to
the rowdy, boisterous gathering around the dinner table, to
the girl—almost a woman—who'd talked only to him, who'd
looked only at him. It had seemed to him that they were the
only two people in the room, but now he vaguely recalled her
brothers' nudges and snickers, her father's beard-tugging
ruminations whenever he observed the young couple.

"Oh, Dion," said Nola, smiling at him. "Everyone in the
hall saw how she felt about you, tonight. And that's my point.
She's been raised to be honest, open with her feelings. She
knows nothing about flirting—harmless or otherwise. She
knows nothing about deceit, flattery, playing mind games,
manipulating. Can you have Kamil, Dion, and still be what
you want to be?"

"Can I have Kamil and still be king, that's what you're asking
me, isn't it?"

Nola nodded gravely.

"Of course," he said impatiently. "Why couldn't I?"

"Because you'll put her on display in a glass cage for billions
of people to stare at, poke at. Because they'll stick vidcams in
her face, want to watch her eat, dress, go to the bathroom,
make love, have babies. They'll hate her, love her, become
obsessed with her. . . . You know, Dion! You know what it's
been like. But the difference is that you were born and bred to
it. Fame, adulation—they're mother's milk to you and to all
the Blood Royal, to the Lady Maigrey and Sagan. To Kamil, it
could be poison."

"Oh, come on, Nola! You sound like her big sister and
you've only known her a few—" He stopped, looking rather
foolish.

"Dion," said Nola gently, wisely refusing to press her
advantage on an opponent who'd just inadvertently lowered

his guard, "Kamil's like the jewel the Starlady wore—clear and pure and flawless. I have no doubt, from what I saw tonight, that you could make her love you. But if she gives her heart to you, Dion, she will give herself completely, utterly. Her love will be her life, and she will expect—and deserve—no less from you. And if you ever failed in that . . ." Nola sighed, shook her head.

"I wouldn't fail, Nola. How could I?"

"I don't think you'd have any choice. You aren't some ordinary Joe. Your life isn't your own. Already, you're bound by commitments. You talk of marriage and yet in a few days you're planning to go off to the Corasian galaxy—"

"All right. You've made your point. Just drop it, will you." Moodily, Dion turned away and stared back out the window, stared back out at the moonlight glistening on the lake.

The cost . . . will run high. It may be higher than you are willing to pay. Higher than, perhaps, you should pay.

Maigrey's warning. He'd answered glibly enough, he remembered. But what little he'd had then didn't seem too much to spend. His life. Yes, he'd been willing to give up his life. He knew the dangers he faced in the Corasian galaxy. He'd fought the Corasians, been captured, tortured by them. And that was all he'd supposed she'd meant. A life. Easy to give up a life, especially when it was hollow, empty . . . lonely.

But there'd been the dream. Surely the dream was a portent, a sign. Surely there could be a way to pay the price and withhold just a tiny bit for himself. . . .

Turning abruptly, wanting to be alone to think, Dion nearly fell over Nola, who had come up silently behind him. He tripped, she stumbled, they caught onto each other for balance.

"You're not mad at me, are you, Dion?" she asked wistfully.

Dion was mad at her, mad at fate, mad at himself for having given fate a few healthy pushes along the way. He was tempted to relieve his feelings by shouting, acting like a royal pain, as Tusk sometimes accused him. He mastered himself, however, was startled to feel tears, cold and wet, on his lashes.

Shaking his head, unable to speak, he squeezed Nola's shoulders tightly and then bolted from the room. He didn't even see Tusk, who passed him in the corridor.

··◁■   ■▷··

"For God's sake, sweetheart, what'd you say to the kid?" Tusk demanded, coming inside, shutting the door behind him and locking it, in case Dion might get it into his head to have another midnight chat. "You were supposed to talk to him, not jab a knife into his gut!"

"Oh, Tusk," cried Nola, flying into his arms, burying her head in his chest. "Why do people have to fall in love? Why does it have to hurt so much?"

"What?" Tusk, mystified, stared down at her.

"Leave me alone!" Nola shoved him away.

Flinging herself on the bed—the side of the bed farthest from Tusk's side of the bed—she pulled the sheets and comforters and blanket up over her head, curled into a tight ball, and turned her back on him.

Foreseeing a long and cold night ahead of him, possibly many long and cold nights, Tusk scratched his head ruefully.

"This does it," he muttered. "I definitely got to get back to indoor plumbing."

··◁■   ■▷··

Dion, in his haste, had neglected to take his nuke light with him. The castle's corridors were cold and dark, except for where windows admitted the light of moon and stars, forming patches of ghostly whiteness on the floors and the walls. Dion didn't mind, however. He was glad of the darkness, it suited his mood.

He groped his way through the chill hallways, feeling his tears freeze on his skin.

"Nola's wrong," he told himself. "Kamil isn't some fragile doll. She's strong, a fighter. And she's smart. All she needs is someone to tell her what to wear, how to behave in front of the vidcams, what to say, what not to say."

He tried to picture her in a sleek little number one of his dates had worn—a short, tight skirt; low-cut, tight-sleeved blouse; a cute little hat perched on her forehead. He thought of Kamil's long huntress strides, her free-swinging arms, silver boyish-cropped hair. . . .

"Besides, as queen, she'd set fashion, she wouldn't follow it." He had a sudden mental image of the foremost women in the galaxy wearing leather trousers and deer-hide vests and he almost began to laugh. His laughter changed to a sigh. Clasping his arms in misery, shivering with cold and the ache in his heart, he leaned against the stone wall and shut his eyes.

"Here you are!"

Soft candlelight glimmered beneath his half-closed eyelids. Dion opened his eyes. "Kamil . . ."

She was dressed in a long white gown, the fur-covered skin of some animal thrown around her shoulders for warmth. Her hair glistened spun silver in the light of her candle. Her eyes were dark and liquid and flashing fire. She held, in one strong arm, her youngest brother. His head lolled on her shoulder, secure in the warmth and closeness of his sister's body.

"You went out to take a piss and got lost, didn't you?" she said to Dion gravely. "No wonder. Wandering around without a light. And without a coat. Your room's down this hall. Wait until I put Galen to bed, then I'll show you."

Dion stared at her, had a sudden image of his queen saying to news commentator James M. Warden, "You went out to take a piss . . ." He began to laugh uncontrollably.

"Hush!" Kamil admonished, glancing down at the baby, who started and began to whimper. "I just got him to sleep!"

"Sorry!" Dion stifled his laughter.

She rocked the baby until his whimpering ceased. He sighed, stuck a fat thumb in his mouth, and cuddled against her. "I'll just put Galen in his crib—"

"I—I can find my way," Dion stammered, feeling his knees go weak, thankful he was leaning against the wall. "You don't need to bother—"

"It's no bother," said Kamil, shrugging. "I was up with the baby. He had a bad dream, howling like a wolf had him. I couldn't sleep, so I told Mother I'd get up with him."

She started walking down the hallway, back the way Dion'd come. He hesitated, then turned and followed her. After all, she had the candle and it *was* extremely dark in the castle, now that he thought of it.

He opened the door to the baby's room for her, held the candle while she laid the child in the crib and covered him with a blanket. At her direction, Dion stirred up the dying fire. They discussed adding another log, decided against it. The room was warm enough, she said. After a last peep at the baby, Kamil took the candle from Dion and led him out and into the hallway.

"I couldn't sleep either," Dion said.

Kamil nodded, solemn, serious. "You have important business to do tomorrow. I heard Father and Mother discussing it, before they went to bed. My father says that DiLuna and Rykilth won't be eager to risk their ships and men in the Corasian galaxy. You will have a difficult time convincing them."

"Your father's right," Dion said, "but that wasn't why I couldn't sleep. That wasn't what I was thinking about."

Any other woman Dion had known would have understood the implied compliment, smiled knowingly, or perhaps have teased him until he confessed. Kamil looked at him with her wide, frank, curious eyes.

"Oh? What were you thinking about?"

You can make her love you, Dion.

They reached his room, stood outside the door. She turned to face him, the candle held steady in her hand. This was the time to thank her politely for the light, for showing him the way. This was the time to open the door, walk into that chill and empty room alone, bid her good night, send away the light, shut the door behind him, lock himself in the darkness, and never open the door again.

A strong man would do it. Lord Sagan would do it. Or would he? For seventeen years, he'd searched the galaxy for what? For a lost king? Or for love lost, cast away by the hand that had reached, instead, for the crown. No, that will not happen to me. I won't make the same mistake.

"You," he said, reaching out to her, grasping hold of her gently. "I was thinking of you."

She smiled at him, a smile warmer than the candlelight, whose flame suddenly wavered, trembled in her hand. "I was thinking of you, too," she said.

He drew her close. They were of equal height, their lips met, touched, burned together an instant, parted.

"I want to marry you, Kamil," he said, holding fast to her, his hands stroking, caressing the animal fur that covered her shoulders and was warm from her body's heat. "I want to fight for you in the betrothal ceremony."

"You don't fight *for* me. You fight *with* me. I will be at your side, holding my mother's shield, as she held it for my father."

"Then you will marry me? You'll be my queen?" Dion couldn't believe it, was afraid she'd misunderstood.

"Queen!" Kamil laughed, seemed amused at the thought. "I will be your wife. And, of course, I will marry you. I'd made up my mind to it this night. If you hadn't asked me, I was going to ask you."

The candle flame wavered, a blast of chill air hit it, nearly blew it out. Dion felt the cold breath blow across his rapturous happiness. He didn't understand it, or refused to understand it.

The draft died away, the candle flame burned steadily.

"I will ask your father for permission tomorrow," Dion began.

Kamil bristled at the thought. "I don't need my father's permission to marry!"

"I mean . . ." Dion stammered, "I thought that was customary—"

"We go together to talk with my father and my mother and ask for their blessing. *That* is the custom of my people. We would talk to your father and your mother," she said, more softly, "but my father tells me that they are dead."

Her eyes were warm with sympathy, pity for his loss. It was the first time he could remember that anyone had shown him sympathy, the first time that anyone had cared about him and what he felt. And suddenly, the mystical power that was the birthright—and some might have said the curse—of the Blood Royal lifted the future's opaque curtain for him.

He was given a glimpse ahead, saw the long and convoluted path that would be his life, saw the people crowding alongside that path, for good and for ill, and saw that, of all of them, this one person alone, this one woman, would love and care and think only of him, of Dion. To all others he would be king, to be obeyed, manipulated, wheedled, bribed, worshiped, despised. To her, he would be a man. A man to be loved. She, she alone, would love him. That would be her blessing, and her curse.

The curtain dropped down with a rapidity that left Dion mentally blinking. He could not be certain what he had seen, wondered, after a moment, if he had really seen anything. All he knew, deep inside, was that he could not give this woman up. He needed her.

"It's cold in this hallway," Kamil said suddenly. "You're shivering, your arms are all covered with gooseflesh again. And you have much to do tomorrow. You should sleep, now."

Moving shyly around him, she opened the door to his room, looked inside.

"They didn't lay a fire for you. We never have one at night, except in the baby's room. But I'll build one for you," she said, and started to slip past him.

Dion caught hold of her, held her back. "No, you shouldn't be in my room, not with me, alone."

He was afraid she would argue, perhaps laugh at him. And he wondered how he would make her understand, when he wasn't certain he understood himself. But he didn't have to explain. She paused a moment, then looked back at him, her cheeks faintly flushed.

"You take the light," she said, offering him the candle.

"But you'll need it—"

"No." She shook her head. "I know the way."

He took the candle from her. Leaning forward, he kissed her on the forehead. Their first true kiss had been too special, too sweet, to repeat again quite so soon. He could still taste it, like the honey coating of mead, on his lips. He wanted to keep it through the night, taste it again and again.

"Sleep well," he said to her.

"May your dreams be blessed." She kissed him shyly, on the cheek, then turned and left him, running lightly down the hallway.

Dion watched until the flutter of her white gown and the silver sheen of her cropped hair could no longer be seen. He entered his room, shut the door, forgot to lock it. He lay down in his bed, wrapped himself in the comforter, left the candle burning on the nightstand. Its golden light filled his thoughts, was sometimes flame, sometimes the golden light of her eyes. He fell asleep.

And again he dreamed of the warrior woman, standing at his side during the battle, holding her shield protectively in front of him. But in the dream, when she protected him, she could not protect herself. And he had no shield to hold over her. He was helpless to defend her, was forced to watch her take blow after blow that had been meant for him, until she sank, battered and bleeding, at his feet.

Dion woke with a start, his body bathed in cold sweat.

The candle had guttered out, leaving his room in darkness.

Chapter ❦❦❦ Thirteen

The very pulse of the machine . . .
William Wordsworth,
She Was a Phantom of Delight

The luxury liner, *Galaxy Belle*, appeared as a bright-colored, glittering bauble, set against a backdrop of black, empty space and coldly burning stars. Maigrey watched the ship intently as they drew nearer, waiting with inheld breath for it to alter course, come to a halt, or make any other move that might indicate the *Belle* was suspicious of the small white craft approaching her.

Belle continued sailing through space, however, traveling at a leisurely pace that would disturb neither the expensive wines nor the guests.

"Hailing *Galaxy Belle*. Galactic Federation Agent Gibbons, requesting permission to come aboard. Over." Xris's tone was crisp, official-sounding.

"They're not responding," said Maigrey.

Xris smiled, took a twist from his pocket, examined it, then stuck it in his mouth. "I'll tell you exactly what's going on in there, sister. The captain of that ship has just contacted the big boss, wanting to know why the hell he didn't pay off the government agents in this sector. The boss will come back, inform the captain that he did pay the agents off, same as usual. The captain will want to know who the hell are we, then. The boss will decide that we're probably a hotshot agent, new in the sector, wanting our share. The captain—if he's smart—will tell the boss that maybe this is a trick and they should get the hell out of there, make the Jump, find another sector."

Seeing Maigrey grow uneasy, Xris lit his twist, took a deep drag on it, and smiled at her. "Don't worry, sister. Do you know what it takes to make a Jump in a cruise ship like that? First, you have to get the guests to leave the blackjack tables

301

and slot machines—and you've always got one who has a lucky streak going and refuses to budge—and go to their cabins. That's just the beginning.

"And when you come out of the Jump, three fourths of the high rollers are sicker than dogs and threatening to sue. No, it's much cheaper to invite us on board, show us a good time, fork over a few thousand, and we'll all part the best of friends."

"But—" Maigrey began.

"Agent Gibbons, permission to come aboard granted, sir. Hanger bay nine. Oh, uh, and how do you like your steak, sir?"

Xris glanced at Maigrey. "The way I like my women," he answered. "Lean, hot on the outside, and pink in the middle. Hanger bay nine. Copy. ETA thirty minutes, so don't put that steak on the coals yet. Over and out."

He ended the transmission, laid in the course, then leaned back and blew smoke in the air.

"Very good," said Maigrey, relaxing in the co-pilot's chair. "I'd say you've done this kind of work before."

"Yeah," Xris answered, not looking at her, keeping his gaze fixed on the *Belle*. "Like I told you back on the breed's plane, I used to be a government agent. But that was before—" He raised his cybernetic arm, his lips twisted in a bitter smile.

"How did you get hold of this official spaceplane?"

"Simple. The government sells them at auction. Of course, the agency modifies them first, removes the armaments, gives the planes a new paint job. But it's easy to restore them again . . . if you know what you're doing. I was an agent for ten years. I knew what I was doing."

He sat silently smoking, staring, unseeing, at the garishly lit cruise ship that was growing larger in the vidscreen.

"I was a damn good agent, too," he added. "One of the honest ones. Look what it got me." He flexed the fingers of his metal hand. Lights blinked on his upper arm, a series of small beeps indicated that it was functioning properly. "I'd have been better off dead."

Taking the twist out of his mouth, he tossed it on the deck, ground it out beneath his foot.

"Like I tried to tell her—my wife," he added, glancing at Maigrey, then looking back out the vidscreen.

There were only the two of them aboard the small spaceplane. Federal agents normally traveled in pairs. Anyone else aboard the plane would have looked suspicious, Xris said, in case the cruise ship might actually bother to scan them. Brother Daniel had remained behind with Agis on board Maigrey's plane. Sparafucile carried Raoul and the Little One as his passengers. Neither those two planes nor any of Xris's men could be seen, though all were—Maigrey trusted—on their way, moving into position.

"What happened?" she asked.

It was easy to talk, necessary to take the mind off what faced them. For a few critical moments, the two of them would be by themselves on the cruise ship.

"We raided an illegal munitions factory run by a gang of drug lords on TISar 13. The raid was supposed to be an open and closed job, but the drug lords had been tipped off, probably by someone inside our own agency. They waited until we were in the plant, then blew the son of a bitch sky-high.

"I was lucky, I guess. They were picking up pieces of my partner for three days. But I was alive, more or less. They took me to a hospital, hooked me up to a machine . . . and then turned me into a machine."

"Why didn't you stop them, if that was what you wanted?" Maigrey asked, startled at the cyborg's vehemence.

"I tried to. But I was half out of my head with pain and the drugs. They said I wasn't in my right mind." Again, the bitter smile. "And my wife, she couldn't let me go. She told them to do anything they could to keep me alive. A year I spent in that goddam hospital. A year learning how to walk and talk and see and hear and think all over again. The only thing that kept me going was her. I was doing this all for her. And then they sent me home. I walked in the front door and reached out to touch my wife, reached out with my new, fake hand . . ."

Xris suddenly grabbed hold of Maigrey's arm, the metal fingers closed painfully over her flesh.

"Like that," he said.

She sat unmoving, regarded him calmly. "And what happened?"

"She didn't say a word, but I felt her flinch, shudder." Slowly, he released Maigrey. "And the light in her eyes—love? Hah! Pity. She was sorry for me. I could just imagine what it would be like that night. Her lying in bed, stiff and cold, that pity in her eyes, letting a machine make love to her—"

"You never even gave her a chance, did you?"

"Gave her a chance to what? Hurt me ten times more than

I'd been hurt already? They can't give you drugs to ease that kind of pain, sister. No, I turned around and kicked the door down with this fake leg of mine, and kept on going. I figured she'd divorce me, but she never has. It's been five years now. I guess she heard how much money I was bringing in and decided to try to get hold of it all when my battery pack shuts down for good."

He glanced at Maigrey's arm, saw the marks his metal grip left on her skin. "I don't seem to bother you. Or else you're just really good at keeping it all hidden inside. But then," he added, shifting his gaze pointedly to the scar on her face, "I guess you've been hurt yourself."

"Scar tissue is tougher than ordinary flesh, though not nearly as pretty."

"Hunh. You could cover it up, some makeup, plastiskin—"

"You could do the same. It wouldn't matter, would it?"

"No," he said after a pause, studying her. "I guess it wouldn't."

She looked away from him, stared out into space. "Has it ever occurred to you that your wife hasn't divorced you because she still loves you? Because she took a vow for better, for worse . . ."

"Forget that shit. This wasn't in the contract."

"Perhaps," said Maigrey, "you didn't read the fine print."

Xris snorted derisively. Tilting back in his seat, he took another twist from his pocket, stuck it in his mouth. He glanced at the digital clock on the console. "Ten minutes, thirty-five seconds. You know what to do?"

"It *is* my plan," Maigrey pointed out.

"Okay, sister. Don't get riled. Just remember, when the gas pellets go off, hold your breath for ten seconds."

"I'll try to keep it in mind. I hope those men of yours know what they're supposed to do. *And* when they're supposed to do it. Timing is critical—" She glanced at the viewscreen nervously. "If any of them fly into visual or instrument range too early . . ."

"Relax, sister. Don't worry about my men," said Xris easily. "Worry about your own, especially that monk."

"He's a renegade priest."

Xris removed the twist from his mouth, regarded her, a glint of amusement in his one living eye. "Like hell. The same goes for that supposed deserter, too. You could put him in a dictionary under Loyalty, Duty, and Honor. Still, he looks like a good man. The monk's a different story. Speaking of contracts, working with a gutless wonder like that wasn't in mine. That's going to cost you extra."

"Brother Daniel is no concern of yours. I'll take care of him."

"He's my concern if he snaps." The cyborg clicked his metal fingers together. "He puts everyone else in danger."

"Brother Daniel is stronger than you might imagine. Or than I think he imagines."

"You selling me on him, sister? Or selling yourself? Hey, look, it doesn't matter. First time he screws up, he's gone. That's it. I intend to make it back—if not in one piece, then at least in however many pieces they've put into me. Besides, I didn't manage to spend half that money you paid me and I sure don't plan to let my wife enjoy herself with it."

A hangar bay yawned open. They could see bright lights inside, robot crews standing around waiting to receive them.

"You could divorce *her*, you know," Maigrey pointed out coldly, readying her bloodsword. "Or arrange to will your money to someone else."

"I could," said Xris grimly, the twist balanced precariously again on the corner of his lip, "but knowing she'll get everything when I die is my one incentive for staying alive."

Chapter ···❖·◡◷· Fourteen

. . . upon the sea of death, where still we sail darkly, for
we cannot steer, and have no port.
                    D. H. Lawrence, *The Ship of Death*

Captain Tomi Corbett was in her cabin aboard *Galaxy Belle*,
struggling to get out of her tight-fitting evening gown. She'd
been entertaining at the captain's table when word was
brought to her—in code, of course, not to unduly alarm the
guests—that there was an emergency, she was needed on the
bridge.

"What's up, Church?" she'd asked her second in command.
Discipline was easy and relaxed on board the cruise liner.

"Federal agent. Came out of nowhere. Requesting permission to come aboard."

"I don't like this," Tomi muttered, staring at the small
spaceplane, white paint and GRD insignia gleaming officially
among the stars. "Get hold of the boss."

Tomi Corbett was a shrewd officer and a skilled spacepilot.
She'd been trained in the Galactic Air Corps, left a brilliant
career in the military when it became obvious that they were
going to yank her out of space and promote her up to boredom,
sitting behind some desk, talking at some computer.

In her late thirties, single, attractive, well off, and carefree,
Tomi took a year to consider the job offers that came pouring
in. She accepted the captaincy of the *Galaxy Belle* for one
reason—it paid double the salary of more legit jobs. And Tomi
had, by this time, grown accustomed to the finer things in life.

The job had other advantages. She was, generally speaking,
in sole command of the ship. The boss, *Galaxy Belle*'s owner,
ran the games, looked after the business end. He knew
nothing about space flight or the ship itself, couldn't have told
you the bow from the stern, thought port and starboard were

both after-dinner drinks, and was firmly convinced that a parsec had six legs and wings.

Tomi was, therefore, in charge—up to a point.

"I don't like it," she told the boss bluntly. "We've never had this kind of thing happen with the Feds before."

"There's never been a political situation this screwed up before," the boss replied testily. "These jerks probably figure they'd better get what they can while they can before the government topples and they find themselves out of work."

"It could be pirates . . ."

"When have you ever known pirates to hit a gambling ship?" the boss scoffed. "They know we don't carry cash. Strictly a credit operation."

"What if"—she lowered her voice—"it's a hit. We heard rumors that the syndicate—"

"One blasted spaceplane with two people aboard? Not even Malone's that stupid. The high-stakes poker game's tonight. I don't want my guests disturbed. You deal with it and deal with it quietly, Captain."

"Yes, sir."

When the boss called her captain instead of Tomi, as was usual between them, she knew there was no point in arguing. She didn't like it, but she couldn't give any solid reason for not liking it, beyond the fact that it was out of the ordinary, out of routine. Tomi had learned, from her days with the Galactic Air Corps, that anything out of routine was almost always trouble.

"What do you think?" She looked at her lieutenant.

Jeff Church had been around a long, long time. He was old enough to be Tomi's father, but he didn't resent serving under a woman less than half his age. He didn't resent anything anymore. An intelligent man, he was also a nice man—too nice. He'd seen people with half his brains but twice his chutzpah promoted over him. He'd retired early on an inadequate pension, was forced to find work. He'd accepted this job gratefully; Tomi being the first captain willing to hire a man his age.

Tomi knew she could trust him, knew she could trust his judgment.

"I don't like it either, Tomi. But the boss says do it so I guess we'd better. It might be a good idea to send a security team down to meet them, though."

"Yes, I think you're right."

She gave permission for the agents to come aboard, and arranged everything else, including dinner, a few hundred dollars worth of chips on the house, agreeable companionship.

"And make that security detail look like a welcoming committee. But I want them armed and ready to really 'welcome' these guys, if necessary. Oh, and don't mention this to the boss."

Church nodded, and went off to carry out his orders.

Having done all she could without offending the boss, Tomi hurried to her cabin to change into her uniform. It wouldn't be dignified for the captain to greet government agents, if that's who they were, in a silver, strapless number, no matter how well it set off her dark brown skin. And if they weren't Federation agents, she needed to be ready for action.

Tomi was fumbling at the buttons on the uniform's designer jacket when the call came through to her cabin.

"Captain! This is security. We've got trouble. I . . . I—"

She heard a gasping sound, then a noise as of something heavy—like a body—hitting the deck.

"Security! Security!" Tomi beat her fist on the controls.

No reply.

"Shit!" Tomi hit another control. "Church! We've got trouble on hangar bay nine. What's going on down there? What do the cams show?"

"The cams have gone dead, Tomi," reported her lieutenant. "And the hangar bay door's standing wide open."

"Well, shut it!"

"We can't," he reported. "Someone's jammed the controls."

"Get us out of here!" Tomi commanded. "Send every available man on security to nine—"

"I've already done—"

"Seven spaceplanes on our screens, sir!" squeaked an excited young communications officer in the background. "They're all around us! And . . . And they're firing at us, Lieutenant!"

"Raise shields," was the automatic command that came to Tomi's lips, but she clamped her lips shut without saying it. *Galaxy Belle* had no shields to raise. The ship wasn't even armed. She'd told the boss, time and again, that he should add guns and armaments, but he was afraid it would scare off the paying customers.

"They mean business, Tomi," said Church quietly. "They know what they're doing."

"I'm on my way to the bridge. Get those damn doors shut!"

"Useless, Tomi. We're being boarded."

Nothing to say to that except several words not fit to be spoken over the commlink. Her uniform half-buttoned, her jacket flap hanging open, Tomi grabbed her lasgun belt, buckled it on, left her cabin, and headed at a dead run for the bridge. Guests shrank back against the bulkheads as she flew past, staring at her in drunken amazement, curiosity, or—in some instances when they wouldn't get out of her way fast enough—enraged ire.

She arrived on the bridge, breathless and panting. "Seal that door!" she ordered, pointing at the door through which she'd just run. "At least they won't get on the bridge. Has security reported in?"

"If they've tried, they can't get through!" Church gestured at the control console in disgust. "The commlink's flooded with calls, passengers demanding to know what's going on."

"I wish I knew!" Tomi drew in a seething breath. "Get them off! Now! Clear the lines."

"Should we sound the general alarm?"

Tomi hesitated, shook her head. "No, that would send everyone into a stampede. Have you warned the boss?"

"He's in the poker game. No calls. I've contacted his bodyguards—"

Tomi swore again, tried desperately to think. It had to be a hit. Yet, yet, something just wasn't right. . . .

"Security!" she shouted, fuming.

A banging came from outside the door. "Open up!"

The young ensign gulped, face pale. "What?—" he began.

Tomi motioned furiously for silence.

"We have boarded your ship," came the voice. "It's under our control. Open up or we'll blow it open."

"Good luck," Tomi told them, turning away. "That should keep them busy awhile. Where the hell's—"

"I've got Security," Church reported.

Tomi ran to the console.

The security guard spoke softly, she was probably in hiding. "Seven spaceplanes have landed. They left two men down here, guarding the planes. The rest spread out through the ship. They know what they're doing, all right. They're armed to the teeth. Some sort of gas pellets knocked out the first security team."

"Dead?"

"No, they're coming around. We've got a few wounded, but these guys, whoever they are, seem to be going out of their way not to kill anyone."

"It's not a hit, then," Tomi said to Church. Frustrated, she beat her fist on the console. "What the hell is going on? What do they want? If we knew, maybe we could—"

"Tomi," said the lieutenant, "the door."

Tomi looked, was astounded to see it starting to open. Furious, she rounded on the ensign.

"I told you to seal—"

"I did, Tomi! I swear it!" His voice cracked in panic.

The door was opening, sliding back smoothly, quietly, efficiently. She thought she saw a tiny whiff of blue smoke puff out of the control panel next to the hatch, but that may have been her imagination. She didn't have time to dwell on it. Her lasgun was in her hand, aimed at the entryway.

A bright blue light flared, blinding in intensity. Tomi fired at it, saw it wink out, saw her burst glance off, as if it had struck an invisible shield. A woman clad in black walked in through the half-open door. She held in her hand some sort of weird-looking sword that burned with a bright blue light. Tomi squinted against it, fired again. The blue light vanished. Again her energy burst was reflected, did no damage.

A shield of some sort.

The woman came straight for her. Blue light flared in an arc. Tomi tried to fire again, felt pain sear the flesh of her gunhand. She smelled burning flesh, could see her own skin blister and bubble. And yet the blade had never touched her, it had only come close.

Moving swift as thought, the woman shifted the blade's position. Its blue light glowed near Tomi's breast. She could feel the intense heat radiate from it.

"Drop your weapon," said the woman.

Tomi, despite the pain in her burned hand, gripped the gun tightly. Point-blank range, she couldn't miss if she tried. This woman with her sword or shield or whatever it was couldn't possibly react faster than the speed of laser fire.

Tomi looked the woman in the eyes, to keep her attention from the gun. The blue light of the sword reflected off gray eyes that were cool and dispassionate as a frozen sea. The sword's blue light seemed to envelop Tomi, enclose her in a dazzling halo. She couldn't see anything beyond the light, except the woman standing before her, and the sudden, fearful thought came to Tomi that everything beyond the light had vanished, leaving her isolated, alone, adrift in time and space. Only the woman with the gray eyes was real.

"Drop your weapon," came the voice, speaking from within Tomi, not outside her. "I don't want to have to kill you."

Tomi willed herself to shoot, but her fingers no longer responded to her command. They were under the control of the woman with the blue light and the gray eyes. The lasgun fell to the deck with a clatter.

The blue light vanished, leaving Tomi—so it seemed for an instant—in red-tinged, eye-aching darkness. The woman turned her attention away from her and Tomi felt, suddenly, as if she'd been dropped to the deck with her gun. She was herself again, her will was her own. The bridge, the deck— reality was back.

"All secure, Xris?" the woman asked a cyborg, who had entered behind her.

"All secure, sister."

Tomi glanced around, saw her lieutenant clutching a bleeding arm, a dart sticking out of the flesh. His own side arm lay on the deck. The cyborg, of course. She made a mental note, spotting the sophisticated weapons hand he wore. Her communications officer cowered at his console, his hands held so high in the air it seemed he might, with little effort, grab hold of the ceiling.

The cyborg must have augmented hearing, too. "Someone coming," he reported to the woman, and he moved to stand against the bulkhead, near the open door.

"How many?"

"One."

Tomi strained her ears, couldn't hear anything, but it must be a member of the security team. Probably heard something or seen something to make him wary, suspicious. She could picture him in her mind, treading soft-footed down the corridor, weapon drawn, walking into a trap . . .

Tomi started to shout a warning.

Xris, standing against the wall, looked at her, smiled, shook his head. Laying his real flesh-and-blood finger to his lips, he drew the metal finger across his throat in a slashing motion, then glanced significantly at the open doorway.

"Shout and you won't die. He will," was the unspoken threat.

Tomi kept quiet.

The security man dashed onto the bridge, beam rifle raised, aiming at the woman, who stood watching him with an expression of cool interest. The sword in her hand flared blue. The man paused, startled, eyes blinking.

Xris never moved away from his stance by the wall. He lifted his arm, pointed it at the man. The cyborg's hand flew off the end of his wrist, struck the security man hard on the back of the head. He crumpled onto the deck with a soft groan. The hand fell down beside him with a metallic clang.

"Any more?" asked the woman.

The cyborg listened, seemed satisfied. Walking over, he picked up his hand, reattached it. "No, that's it. Agis's coming . . . and Brother Daniel."

Tomi heard the pause between the names, saw the cyborg's lip curl when he mentioned the second, filed this sign of a possible lapse in team spirit for future reference. Her hand hurt. Trying to ignore the pain, she turned to help her lieutenant.

"Here, sit down," she said, leading him to a seat. "You all right?"

Church's face was ashen, but he managed to smile. Blood welled from beneath his fingers. The metal end of the dart protruded from the flesh. "He needs a medic," Tomi said angrily, turning to the woman. "Let me send for the doctor."

The boss would know what was going on by now. His bodyguards were trained hit men, they'd worked for the syndicate for years. A call to him, pretending to ask for Doc, and . . .

"I don't think so," the woman responded in a pleasant and totally uncaring tone of voice. "I believe that there are enough of us here at present."

"But he's hurt!"

"That's not my concern," said the woman.

A man entered the door, glanced around swiftly, summing up the situation with cool, deliberate calculation. A professional soldier if Tomi ever saw one. Her heart sank. Whoever these people were, whatever they wanted, they were obviously quite capable of taking it.

"Everything's secure, my lady. Xris's men are rounding up

the passengers, escorting them to their rooms. Sparafucile has located the water supply. Raoul is preparing the chemicals now."

"What?" Tomi demanded. "What are you doing to the water supply?"

My lady. He called the woman "my lady." Strange. But then none of this made any sense. What did these people want?

"Casualties, Agis?" My Lady asked, ignoring Tomi's question.

The soldier's eyes flicked to the lieutenant, clutching his bleeding arm. "Only a few, my lady, and most of those are minor. Some of the passengers proved uncooperative, but threats and the butt ends of beam rifles soon settled them. The owner of the ship was more difficult to handle. He and several of his men barricaded themselves in his stateroom. We blew the door, tossed in gas. They'll be unconscious for quite a while, but they'll be all right."

Tomi bit her lips, hoping no one would hear her sigh. Her last hope ended.

"Satisfactory," said My Lady. She pointed at the console. "Cut off all communications. Enter the course change. Xris, see if you can shut that door. Oh, Brother Daniel"—the woman glanced around at a young man who had just entered—"you have three patients who would be grateful for your attention."

The young man, unlike the cyborg and the soldier, appeared uncomfortable, ill at ease, confused, and helpless. He followed the woman's gaze to Tomi and the lieutenant. Tomi saw his eyes widen at the sight of Church's injury.

Brother Daniel, the woman called him. Tomi remembered the sneer in the cyborg's voice. She lowered her eyelids hurriedly, fearful that her exultation would be noticed. She had just found the weak link in the chain.

Church was breathing heavily, his face was soaked with sweat. The young man approached him, his gaze fixed on the lieutenant's wounded arm, his eyes creased with concern. He reached out hands that looked strong, skilled, delicate.

Tomi flung one arm protectively around her lieutenant's shoulders.

"You butcher! Get back! Don't touch him!"

Brother Daniel, riveted by shock, stared at her, wordless.

Tomi was aware, obliquely, of My Lady watching them. The young man quickly regained his composure.

"I assure you, ma'am—"

"Captain!" Tomi snapped.

"I assure you, Captain," the young man said, flushing, not looking at her while he talked, "that I am a trained nurse. That wound needs attention—" His lowered gaze caught sight of her own injury. "And so does that burn on your hand," he said, at last lifting his eyes to meet hers.

Swiftly, he lowered them again.

"Don't worry about me. You're right about Lieutenant Church. He needs treatment, but I'm not letting any of you butchers touch him. The infirmary's right down the corridor—"

"You're not leaving the bridge, either of you," said My Lady with utter finality. "And no one else enters. Brother Daniel treats the lieutenant here and now or he bleeds to death."

Church was obviously on the verge of passing out. Tomi, with a show of reluctance, grudgingly moved to one side. "You'll be all right," she said to Church, who managed a weak smile.

Brother Daniel hurried forward. Tomi backed off, managed, as she was doing so, to brush up against the young man. She was startled to feel his body go rigid at her touch. He shrank away from her, his face flushed a burning crimson. He moved swiftly, hurriedly, past her to his patient.

"You should lie down."

Brother Daniel put his arm around Church, guided him to a low, cushioned bench that ran along one far wall, provided for the comfort of the guests when they made their tour of the luxury liner after first coming on board.

Tomi looked around the bridge—what had been, until moments ago, *her* bridge. The man, Agis, was altering the course. Nursing her burned hand, Tomi leaned over to see what figures he punched in.

She stared in disbelief. "No, wait! You've made a mistake."

"Have you made a mistake, Agis?" My Lady asked.

"No, my lady. These are the correct coordinates."

Tomi rounded on the woman. "But that will take us into the Corasian galaxy!"

"Yes, it will, Captain."

"Who are you?" Tomi, for the first time, felt fear slither inside her. "What do you want?"

"My name is Maigrey Morianna. Perhaps you've heard of me?"

"Yes, I've heard of you," answered Tomi grimly. "You're one of the Blood Royal. One of the last. There's a bounty on you—dead or alive."

She glanced at the strange weapon the woman wielded, remembered the terrible feeling of being forced to obey this woman's will. At least that much was explained. Other pieces were starting to fall into place.

"One of the other last surviving members of the Blood Royal—what's his name, Sagan—fled to Corasia to escape being executed for murder. And you're off to join your lover. That's why you want this ship, isn't it?"

The soldier stirred in his chair, looked around at Tomi with a frown.

"Complete your work, Agis."

"Yes, my lady."

Maigrey shrugged, started to turn away.

"And you also need us to bribe your way into the galaxy safely!" Tomi cried. Fear and anger were making her lose control. "You're going to sell us to the Corasians! You bitch!"

Tomi lunged, intent on killing the woman, not thinking, not caring what happened to herself. Somewhere, in the back of her mind, was the panicked thought that dying like this would be far preferable to the fate that awaited her in the Corasian galaxy.

An arm of steel blocked her way, a steel fist on her jaw knocked her flat. Tomi staggered back into a chair, fell, landed heavily on the deck. The blow made her dizzy, she almost lost consciousness. Fighting the pain and mists threatening to engulf her, she forced herself to a sitting position, clinging to the overturned chair for support.

Xris stood over her, apparently waiting to see if there was any fight left in her. There was, but Tomi decided this was neither the time nor the place. She shook her head weakly, wiped away blood with the back of her hand, and spit out a dislodged tooth.

The cyborg, satisfied, turned to Maigrey. "You fried those door controls good, sister. It's jammed. It won't shut."

"Can you fix it?"

"Sure. Take a couple of hours—"

"Then do so."

"What about the captain here?"

"I'll keep an eye on her. When Sparafucile's finished his work, he can escort her and her lieutenant to their quarters. Good work, Xris," Maigrey added with a smile. "You and your men."

"All in the contract, sister."

Removing his weapons hand, the cyborg cracked open a plate in the cybernetic leg, snapped the weapons hand back into its place, removed another hand whose fingers were far smaller, with intricate jointing, designed for working with delicate precision and skill. He snapped that hand on his wrist, returned to the hatch.

Maigrey offered to help Tomi stand.

The captain refused, sullenly, pulled herself up by hanging onto the chair. She saw out of the corner of her eye, the young man, Brother Daniel, watching. His face had gone white, he looked shocked and upset.

Good. Very good.

"Are you all right, Captain?" Maigrey asked.

"Yeah, your meat isn't damaged!" Tomi said bitterly, rubbing an aching jaw. "What's with the water supply? You drugging it?"

Maigrey nodded. "We can't have the passengers and crew causing us trouble. You'll be in a state of hibernation—we want the meat delivered fresh, of course; the Corasians won't buy frozen goods."

"I'll stop you," Tomi said softly, her black eyes fixed on the woman's gray ones. "If it's the last thing I do, I'll stop you."

"Oh, I don't think so," said Maigrey. Lifting a canteen from its place on a belt at her waist, she tilted it to her lips, took a long drink, lowered it, wiped her mouth with the back of her hand. "Sooner or later, Captain, you're bound to get thirsty."

Chapter ·◆⊃○⊂◆· Fifteen

And I had done a hellish thing . . .
Samuel Taylor Coleridge,
The Rime of the Ancient Mariner

Maigrey sat on the bridge of the *Galaxy Belle*, staring out into the black gulf beyond, the Void that separated their galaxy from the galaxy of their enemy. No stars. Nothing, except the occasional atom, drifting through the vastness.

Inside, she was like that Void. Black, empty, nothing. She was transporting a thousand innocent people to what would undoubtedly be horrible death—for she admitted to herself, the odds of this plan working were very slim—taking them to be placed, literally, in a Corasian meat locker, and she felt nothing.

"My lady." Brother Daniel's voice, softly respectful.

Maigrey was vaguely aware of the priest standing before her, a tray of food in his hand. She shook her head.

"My lady," he said, gently chiding, "you must eat."

"Eat." Maigrey shivered. "Have you ever seen Corasians eat, Brother Daniel? I have. Corasians—themselves energy—feed off energy, feed off humans, aliens, trees, any living energy-rich being."

Daniel, face pale, sat down beside her, laid his hand on her arm. "My lady, don't do this to yourself—"

Maigrey turned, looked at him, the gray eyes seeming to reflect the Void. "Or maybe it will be worse than that." Her gaze left him, shifted back to the black gulf. "The Corasians need slaves to work for them in their factories, building ships and planes capable of carrying them across the Void and into our galaxy. And as you work, you know in your heart that you are developing the tools that will soon enslave others. But not to work is punished most horribly."

"You're only tired, my lady. You haven't slept—"

"He's dying, Daniel."

The young priest caught his breath. The hand on her arm involuntarily tightened its grip. "Who, my lady?" he asked in a low voice, though he knew the answer well enough.

"I can't put it into words or define it or even make logical sense of it. A man can sit on the shore of an ocean for hours on end, watching the tide go out, but it recedes so slowly and imperceptibly that he is rarely conscious of the fact. Only when he looks down at the wet sand at his feet and realizes that, hours before, water stood in deep pools or lapped gently on the shore, is he aware of the change. I look into myself, Brother, and see nothing but a long stretch of empty sand."

"The mind-seizer—" Brother Daniel began.

"No, I sense Abdiel's fury, his helplessness and frustration. Knowing Sagan as he does, he had not foreseen this possibility. He assumed that Derek was the same driven, ambitious man that he was in his youth. Abdiel couldn't know of the changes that have come to my lord since that time. Sagan is giving up," she added simply. "He is using death to flee his enemy."

"My lord would never do such a thing," Brother Daniel said. "To take one's own life is to commit a terrible sin."

Maigrey smiled sadly. "If it was Abdiel alone my lord fought, you are right. He could hold out, withstand whatever torture the mind-seizer inflicted on him. But Sagan's true battle is against himself. The only way he can win that battle is to lose, and he prefers to simply withdraw peacefully from the field of contest.

"And what will I do, Brother Daniel?" Maigrey's voice was laden with pain. "I must confront him, halt his retreat, drive him back to the battlefield, force him to fight—a fight he can't possibly win, a fight that will leave him irreparably damaged, inflict wounds that will never heal. I will do this to him and then I will leave him, leave him to struggle on alone."

She stared out again into the eternal darkness. Her eyes burned. No tears would come to bring comfort.

"One is never alone with God—"

"Do you believe in Sagan's dream, then, Brother Daniel? Do you believe such is our fate and that we cannot alter it? If so, what makes the Creator better than a puppet master, and we poor mortals nothing but His toys?"

"I've heard you say, my lady: 'I have no choice.' But that isn't precisely true, is it? You've been given choices. Right or wrong, you've chosen to follow one path over another. And now consider this, my lady. If God chooses to shine His light on a path that would ordinarily be dark, couldn't it be that He is trying to show the way?"

Or trying to prevent it, Maigrey was about to reply when they were interrupted by Agis and Xris returning from an inspection of the engine room.

"All is well, my lady," Agis reported. "This ship is quite capable of making the Jump to the other galaxy. Fuel supply is more than adequate to take us there—"

"And return?" Maigrey asked, coming back briskly to the problems at hand.

"It will be close, but I trust His Majesty's armada will carry its own fuel supply. When this ship joins the fleet, it can refuel at that time."

Maigrey's ironic smile twisted the scar on her face. "Of course it can. What about engineering? Can you and your men take over?"

"No problem," Xris answered. "The engines are in good shape. Better than usual for these tubs. This captain runs a tight ship."

Maigrey nodded. "Satisfactory. Did you warn your men not to drink the water?"

"Yes, my lady. We provided them with their own supply." Agis crossed over, took a seat beside her. "Shall I prepare for the Jump, my lady?"

"Yes, and send the signal to His Majesty. I've input the code and the destination. All you have to do is transmit. When you've finished that, pass the word for Sparafucile and Raoul."

"Yes, my lady."

Agis set about his task. Xris, having acquired the parts he needed from the electrical room, returned to his work, attempting to fix the door. Maigrey shifted in her chair, stared back out into empty space.

··◁■ ■▷··

Brother Daniel folded his hands, sought to pray. But the simple gesture of clasping his hands together reminded him that he had his own problems, though they were of the flesh, not the spirit. He'd come to discuss them with her but he found he couldn't. His problems seemed petty, now. He wasn't at all certain that she would understand him.

And he was ashamed. He could speak glibly enough of God when it came to dealing with the problems of another, but with his own . . . His attempt at prayer wasn't a success. His thoughts refused to ascend to heaven, but lurked in a warm darkness, far lower.

Daniel's first care had been for the most seriously wounded patient aboard the ship, the lieutenant. He and Agis carried the man to the sick bay, where the shipboard doctor, with curt efficiency, removed the dart from the arm.

Brother Daniel made certain, during the surgery, that the doctor ingested no water. When the operation was finished, however, and the patient resting comfortably, Daniel watched in silence as the doctor poured himself a glass of water from the tap, drank it down. Within moments, the doctor was, himself, lying on one of his own berths, drifting off into a deep, deep sleep.

The priest went over the medical supplies, took what he needed to treat the captain's burned hand, and left, repeating to himself that drugging everyone was much better than holding their victims captive, in a state of perpetual, mind-numbing terror; better than the threats, the beatings, the attempts at escape, the killings that must certainly take place in a protracted hostage situation.

Returning to the bridge, he found Lady Maigrey and Agis deep in discussion over the best route into Corasia. Xris was conversing with his men, checking on their status through a commlink device that was, apparently, built directly into the cyborg's skull. Daniel glanced around. The captain was gone.

"Excuse me, my lady, but where is the . . . the captain?" For some reason, Daniel couldn't talk about the woman without feeling his skin burn, his insides knot up.

Maigrey turned from her work, glanced at him.

Daniel felt immediately guilty, although of what he wasn't quite certain. He held up ointment and bandages. "For her hand," he said, lamely.

It seemed the lady saw right through him, but she only said, "Sparafucile escorted the captain to her quarters. It's located for'ard, on the engine deck. I can't spare anyone to take you, at the moment . . ."

"I . . . I can find it," stammered Brother Daniel, anxious to escape the lady's amused, albeit somewhat concerned, scrutiny. The thought, too, of the female captain in the hands of the half-breed assassin appalled the priest. He hurried off, and thanks to the cruise ship having numerous maps with "You Are Here" arrows posted on the bulkheads, for the convenience of the passengers, he descended from the bridge, which was on something called Boat deck, found Engineering deck with relative ease.

Wandering the corridor, searching for the captain's cabin, Daniel almost ran into Sparafucile, emerging from a room. The priest heard—through the partially opened door—the sound of a woman moaning in pain.

"What did you do to her?" Daniel demanded, confronting the half-breed.

The misaligned eyes in the cruel and brutish face squinted, narrowed in silent laughter. The mouth, barely visible behind the mass of ragged hair hanging over the face, curled in a leer.

"Woman try to have some fun with Sparafucile," said the assassin. "She think maybe Sparafucile is not smart. Or maybe that he is not dedicated to his job. Woman knows better now. I do not think she will try to have fun with Sparafucile again."

The voice was soft, with a slight hissing sound. Daniel felt his insides shrivel, cold pervade his bowels. He was overcome by revulsion, but—seeing those cunning eyes closely observant of him—he tried to keep his feelings concealed. He took a step forward.

The half-breed blocked the priest's way through the door.

"Let me pass," Daniel said, starting to grow angry.

"What you want with woman?" The half-breed grinned, as if he could guess the answer.

"The Lady Maigrey sent me," Brother Daniel replied. "I have medicine, bandages." He took another step forward until he was almost touching the half-breed. "Let me past."

"Lady send you." Sparafucile considered the matter. He stepped aside slowly, with the grace of a slithering snake. "I stay with you."

"No," said Brother Daniel. "Thank you, but that won't be necessary. Besides, her ladyship wants you to report to her on the bridge."

That was a lie, but the priest trusted God would forgive a lie in a good cause.

The assassin moved away from the door.

"Be careful," the half-breed warned. "The woman is tricksy.

Maybe she try to have some fun with you, too. If you need help, you call Sparafucile."

One of the eyes, the higher of the two on the grotesquely deformed face, closed in a wink. The assassin moved down the corridor, silently, swiftly.

Daniel glanced into the room, saw the woman lying on the bed. When he looked back, the assassin had disappeared, as if he had melted into the bulkheads. Daniel shivered, entered the room, and shut the door behind him.

The woman groaned. Daniel forgot his anger and revulsion and any other intrusive feelings in his pity and compassion for someone hurting. Hurrying to her bedside, he examined her swiftly, could find no trace of blood or any visible wound. Her almond-shaped black eyes were shadowed with pain, but alert, watching him. Her groans had ceased, stifled when she saw him come near her. She was breathing heavily, but deeply. Her dark brown skin glistened with sweat. Her hair, shaved on the sides above the ears, but luxuriant above, was so black as to be almost blue. It sprang from a central peak at her forehead, stood up, glistening, like an ebony crown on her well-shaped head.

Lying on the bed, weakened by pain, her body nevertheless taut and coiled, tense for action, she reminded Daniel of a wild animal, caught in a trap, yet prepared to fight for its life. Her uniform jacket had been unbuttoned when they'd first encountered her on the bridge. The flap now hung open, as if tearing hands had ripped it, partially revealing the large bare, firm breasts beneath.

Daniel stared, caught himself staring, and turned away abruptly.

Hardly knowing what he was doing, moving blindly, acting out of well-trained instinct, he set the medicine and bandages down on a nightstand and hastened into the bathroom. He drew a glass of water from the tap, returned to the woman.

She lay in a more relaxed position, though the eyes fixed on him remained dark with suspicion.

Trying to imagine her as just another of his male patients aboard *Phoenix*, Brother Daniel came to her bedside, leaned down to support her to a sitting position, and held the water to her lips.

"Drink this," he said.

The violent thrust of her strong hand knocked the glass out of Daniel's fingers. It fell to the floor, shattered.

"Get away from me!" Tomi said through clenched teeth. "Get out! Go back to your murdering bitch and tell her I didn't fall for it!"

Brother Daniel stared at the broken glass at his feet, at the water seeping into the carpet that covered the ship's metal deck.

"I'm sorry. I didn't mean—Please, believe me. I had no intention. I . . . saw only that you were in pain. I thought to give you ease . . ."

He couldn't look at her. Bending down, he began to pick up the shards of glass. "I'll remove this . . . you might cut yourself. And then, I will leave. . . ."

The woman said nothing more to him. Brother Daniel concentrated on his work, but he was acutely aware of the woman lying on the bed, of her black eyes watching him, of her breathing growing easier, of the smell of some type of exotic perfume that came from her. His hand trembled, he almost cut himself. He deposited the larger pieces of glass in a trash compactor. Returning to the bathroom, he soaked a towel in water, came back and used it to wipe up the smaller pieces. Uncertain, then, what to do with the glass-encrusted towel, he finally stuffed it, too, in the trash compactor. He never once looked at the woman but he knew, the entire time, that she never once took her eyes from him.

When he was finished, he came to stand beside the bed, his hands folded before him, his eyes staring at the lemon yellow sheet covering the mattress.

"I will leave the ointment for your burn. Apply it liberally, then cover it with the bandage. That will stop the pain and keep the wound sterile. You can wash your hand, but always reapply the ointment afterward. You can only live for a few days without water." He started to turn to go.

The woman's long-fingered, brown-skinned hand reached out, caught hold of his.

"I can manage the ointment," she said, in grudging tones, "but not the bandage. I never . . . had the knack. You'd better do it."

Brother Daniel shut his eyes, asked for strength. The touch of her hand sent tongues of flame flickering over his body. He reached into his memory, brought forth a picture of the false monks with the dead eyes; of Brother Miguel, crouched among the tombs; of Lord Sagan, bleeding, perhaps dying. Resolution returned. He opened his eyes, set about calmly dressing the wound.

The woman was staring at him, forehead creased in puzzlement.

"I heard them call you 'brother.' You related to one of them, the bitch maybe?"

"I am . . . or rather was . . . a priest," said Daniel. "In the Order of Adamant."

"Priest!" the woman scoffed, stared at him, then shook her head in disgust. She lay back on the pillow. "You expect me to believe that?"

"It doesn't matter whether you do or not," replied Daniel softly, steadily, spreading ointment on her fingers that were incredibly long, with tapered ends and colorfully polished nails. "I'm sorry," he said after a moment. "Am I hurting you, Captain?"

"Tomi," she said. "Call me Tomi." Her hand had clenched suddenly over his, a spasm of pain crossed her face. She swallowed, gulped in a breath, relaxed. "No, not you. That freak of nature—"

"What did Sparafucile do to you?" Brother Daniel asked in renewed concern, deftly wrapping the bandage over the blistered skin. He glanced over her body again. "I see no trace of an injury—"

"No, he's good, that one," admitted Tomi, forcing a grim smile. "I judged him by his looks, figured he was dim-witted. I thought I could jump him, take his gun. I never saw anyone move so fast." Ruefully, she rubbed her right arm. "I'll bet I'm not the first to make that mistake with him. He's a high-class, cold-blooded killer. The bitch must have money to be able to afford talent like—"

"Please, don't call her that," said Brother Daniel, his gaze on the yellow sheet. "She's a great lady. You don't understand—"

"No, *you* don't understand!" Tomi propped herself up on one elbow, reached out, grabbed hold of his arm. Long nails drove into his flesh. "Look at me, damn you! Priest! What do you do, Brother? Bless the bodies after this crew murders 'em? Is that what you're going to do for us, when the Corasians have finished with us? Only there won't be much left behind to bless . . . And what do you expect to do with your share of the blood-money, Priest? Got a few favorite charities to support—"

Her hand was strong, trembled in her earnestness. He was conscious of her body's warmth, the musky smell of her perfume or perhaps her own skin, the beautiful clarity of her eyes, the startling whiteness of her sharp teeth against her dusky complexion, the pain of her nails in his flesh. And the pain of her words. She made him see how different he was from the rest, made him consider the vast gulf that lay between him and them, even between him and the Lady Maigrey. A gulf wider than the one that separated galaxies . . .

She was drawing closer to him, the almond eyes half-closed, the wide, full lips that were moist and tinged with coral were coming near his lips. She pulled him down toward her. The jacket flap opened, her breasts were bare. He could imagine the softness, the full swelling beneath his fingers.

The tongues of flame that swept over his body seemed to emanate from his loins. The aching pain was both sweet and appalling, forbidden to him by his vows, inviting because it was forbidden. He made no move to encourage her, but he made no move to stop her, either. He shut his eyes, smelling her fragrance, her touch fueling the fire.

Her hand slid inside his shirt, contacted bare skin, and he shivered at her touch that was cool . . . cool and searching.

Brother Daniel stood up suddenly, wrenched himself away from the woman, away from the feeling fingers. "I carry no weapons," he said coldly.

The almond eyes stared into his. She seemed abashed for a brief moment, then her eyes flashed defiance. "You can't blame me for trying!" Throwing herself back on the bed, she took hold of the flap of her uniform jacket, drew it up, covered herself. "Get out."

Brother Daniel, trembling with shame, wrapped himself in what shreds of dignity he had remaining to him and walked away. He opened the door, started to leave.

"Tell the bitch I'll die of thirst," Tomi hissed behind him. "Maybe you can say a prayer over me, Brother!"

Daniel paused, but did not turn around, did not answer. Walking out the door, he shut it, sealed it without truly knowing what he was doing. He started down the corridor, had to stop. Waves of nausea swept over him. He slumped weakly against the bulkhead, fought to keep from being sick.

"God forgive me!" he cried, shuddering. "God forgive me!"

··◁■　■▷··

"Brother Daniel . . ." It was Lady Maigrey, her voice penetrating through the dark and roiling clouds that encompassed him.

Daniel looked up, lifted his head, realized that she had been speaking to him a long time. His face flushed a burning red. "Y-yes, my lady?"

"Brother Daniel, are you all right?"

No, he was all wrong. Her tone was gentle, filled with understanding. He was on the verge of confessing, of pouring out his blackened soul to her. The words burned on his lips. He lifted beseeching eyes and saw Agis, standing behind her, the man's face grim and stern. He saw the half-breed, leering, knowing; saw Xris, cool, amused; the Loti, Raoul, smiling at him blissfully. They knew. They all knew.

Daniel swallowed, pressed his lips together. "Don't worry about me. I'm fine."

Maigrey had seen his gaze shift to the men standing around her. "Agis, have you had a reply from our signal to Dion?"

"No, my lady."

"We should have heard by now. Send it again."

"Yes, my lady." Agis, hearing a faint note of rebuke in her voice, went quickly back to his duties.

"I've got the door fixed," said Xris, seeing her gaze shift to him.

"Inspect the ship. Check on the status of the passengers."

"Sure thing, sister." Xris cast a look at the priest, shook his head, and walked off.

Sparafucile, taking the hint, shambled to a distant part of the bridge.

Maigrey turned back to Daniel.

"I think you came earlier to tell me something. I'm sorry." She smiled ruefully. "I didn't give you a chance. What was it?"

They were alone. What he said to her, he knew would remain locked in her heart. And he had the distinct impression, from the look in her eyes, that she knew already.

But should he shift this burden onto her? Would she even

understand? She was having her own battle with God. Daniel sighed, determined to fight on alone.

"It's the captain, my lady," he said, his voice steady, in control. "She refuses to drink the drugged water. She claims that she will die of thirst before she gives in."

If Maigrey had been expecting something else and was disappointed not to hear it from him, she kept her disappointment hidden, contented herself with one long, scrutinizing look.

And if the priest lowered his eyes before that penetrating gaze, it was nothing unusual for him.

"Yes, I can believe she'd do it, too," Maigrey said. "A woman of strong character, she's not used to being thwarted. When she goes after something, my guess is she gets it."

Was that a warning to him? Brother Daniel kept silent.

"Raoul," Maigrey called, gestured to the Adonian, who was gazing out the vidscreen with his accustomed drug-glazed rapture.

The Loti came at her command, long hair wafting around him, all lace and ruffles and glittering jewels. In Raoul's wake moved an odd personage that Daniel had not previously seen. The person was short in height. Its race, sex, and species were indeterminable, for it was clad in what appeared to be an overlarge raincoat, its head topped by a fedora. Daniel was aware only of two bright eyes that fixed him with a disconcerting stare.

"How may the Little One and I have the privilege of serving my lady?" Raoul asked with a bow and a flourish.

"I need this drug of yours made into an injection to be given to the captain of this vessel, and anyone else who may take it into their heads not to drink the water. Can you do that?"

"With the greatest of ease, my lady. In fact, I took the liberty of anticipating my lady's wishes along these lines. The injections are prepared." Raoul fluttered his hand gracefully over a kit he had brought with him. "Shall I undertake the task?"

Maigrey considered a moment. "No, Raoul. This captain is an extremely active, strong-minded individual. I think the half-breed had better deal with her."

Brother Daniel rose to his feet, hands clasped before him. "I will give the captain the injection."

Maigrey was obviously surprised, hesitated. "Are you certain, Brother?" She gazed at him searchingly.

This time, Brother Daniel's eyes met hers. "Yes, my lady."

"Very well. Raoul, give Brother Daniel what he needs."

The Loti did as commanded. The priest accepted the kit, listened attentively to the instructions for the correct dosage, left the bridge, his outward demeanor calm.

··◁▦ ▦▷··

Maigrey watched him go. Turning, with a sigh, she found everyone on the bridge staring at her.

Raoul, head cocked, appeared to be listening to the silent voice of his diminutive companion. "The Little One says, my lady, that the priest is confused. He has thoughts of traitorous intent that are being fed by a lust for this woman, the captain."

"I don't think one needs to be an empath to figure that out," said Maigrey dryly. She put her hands to her aching temples.

Dear God! Couldn't You have chosen another time, another place? Don't I have problems enough? And what do I do about it? Brother Daniel has to wrestle with the devil himself. No one can fight this battle for him. And yet this mission is far too important to risk it on a priest's fall . . . or his triumph.

"Sparafucile, go after him. Don't interfere, just keep an eye on him. And," she added, after a pause, "don't let him know he's being watched."

The half-breed nodded, slid out the door.

"I don't like doing that," she said, coming over to Agis. "I don't like spying on him."

"You have no choice, my lady," said the centurion.

Maigrey sighed, shook her head. "Any word from His Majesty?"

"No, my lady."

Chapter ❖ Sixteen

O hard, when love and duty clash!
Alfred, Lord Tennyson, *The Princess*

Dion was fuzzy-headed after a night that had alternated between golden dreams of love and dark and terrible nightmares. And today, of all days, he needed to be alert and in full possession of his faculties, for today he had to bargain with DiLuna and Rykilth for men, ships, and money to launch the battle that would, God willing, win Dion his crown.

His waking and sleeping dreams had been so mixed up during the night, he wasn't sure what was reality and what had been manufactured in his subconscious. One thing only he knew, knew it because of the warmth enveloping him on the inside, if not the out, for his room was bitterly cold. Kamil loved him and had promised to become his wife.

But he had to rouse himself, get rid of what felt like the goose-down comforter inside his head. He recalled yesterday's awakening, recalled seeing Bear and his hulking sons indulging in what passed for a shower bath. They stood naked in an enclosed courtyard beneath a barrel of water, perched precariously on a roof. At the signal, servants upended the barrel, sending a cascade of water, mingled with chunks of ice, down over them. Dion, watching yesterday in mingled awe and amusement, had shuddered at the thought.

Today, grimly, gritting his teeth together to keep them from chattering, he stood in the courtyard, the cold wind cutting through his flesh to the very bone and gasped in shock as the deluge of icy water thundered down on him. Shaking his head, blinking and puffing and doing a little dance to warm himself, he groped blindly for a towel, was nearly knocked over by one tossed at him.

"Thanks!" Dion managed, huddling thankfully in the soft woolen fabric, drying his face.

"I've heard of guys taking cold showers after a date, but don't you think this is carrying things a little too far?"

Tusk, enveloped in his fur-lined parka, was staring at him in horror.

Dion laughed. The cold water had felt good, invigorating. It dispelled the clouds in his head, banished the nightmares. He was young, he was king, Kamil loved him. That was all that mattered. He rubbed the rough towel briskly over his skin, watched it glow red with the exertion. His body dry, he ran the towel over his mane of red hair, emerged with it flaring out in all directions, like the rays of the sun.

Grinning, he snapped the towel at Tusk. "C'mon. You should try it."

Tusk, shivering in his heavy coat, clasped his arms around himself, shook his head. "I'm a married man, kid. I can't afford to freeze my balls off. Though, considering the night I spent, I don't suppose it would much matter if they got frozen off here or up there." He nodded gloomily in the general direction of the bedroom.

"You and Nola had a fight?"

"I s'pose so," said Tusk, shaking his head in perplexity. "I'm not sure. If we did, I wasn't there."

"Don't worry," Dion counseled, feeling suddenly old and wise, knowledgeable and experienced in the ways of love. "Whatever it was, she'll get over it. Women do, you know." Throwing the towel back at Tusk, Dion began to get dressed.

Tusk eyed him suspiciously. "What happened to you, kid? Last night you looked like someone'd just shot you."

Dion hadn't been going to tell anyone, but now he found he couldn't keep his love a secret. It seemed that it must be written in the sky above, flaring across it in rainbow colors by day, flashing across it in sparkling starlight by night. Dion paused in the act of putting on his shirt, apparently oblivious to the chill wind stinging his bare flesh.

"Tusk," he said, coming close to his friend, speaking in an excited undertone, though no one was around to hear them, except the servants, and they were refilling the barrel with water, "I asked Kamil to marry me last night."

He stood back, waited eagerly for Tusk's reaction.

"You did, huh, kid." Tusk eyed him speculatively. "What'd she say?".

"Yes!" Dion could have sung the word, thought it should be sung. Speaking it seemed so inadequate. "She said yes!"

"Yeah, I coulda probably guessed that," Tusk replied.

It occurred to Dion that his friend wasn't responding in quite the proper spirit. "Tusk! Come off it. Don't look at me like I decided to jump off the battlements! Remember how you and Nola felt, the first time you met?"

"Yeah, we hated each other's guts."

"Oh, yes, that's right," said Dion, momentarily deflated. "But after that—"

"Kid, Nola told me this morning what she said to you. Didn't you hear any of it?"

Dion was silent, finished dressing, tugging the heavy shirt over his head. Sitting down on an upended barrel, he pulled on his socks and his boots. "I did, Tusk," he said, more soberly. "I thought about it, I really did."

"How long? Two seconds?"

"It was just that—When I saw Kamil I—We met in the hall last night, purely by accident—"

"And your hormones got the better of you."

"It's not like that!" Dion flashed angrily. "It's—Oh, forget it! Just forget it! I shouldn't have said anything. Don't tell anyone else, will you?" He glared at his friend. "Promise?"

"No, kid, I won't tell anyone else," Tusk said with a sigh. He laid a hand on Dion's arm. "I'm real happy for you, kid. Honest. I hope everything works out. You've been through a lot. You deserve it. You really do."

"Thanks, Tusk," said Dion, putting his hand over his friend's, squeezing it. "I—I'm sorry for what I said. I'm glad you know. I haven't told you—I guess I hoped you'd knew— but through this all—everything I mean, not just this—you've been the one person—well, Nola, too—that I've felt like I could count on. Lady Maigrey, Sagan, even General Dixter— they all want something from me. You never did. You were just there . . . for me. And I guess what I'm trying to say is that I appreciate it—"

"All right, kid, all right," broke in Tusk, wiping his nose, clearing his throat. "Next thing I know you'll be askin' *me* to marry you!"

"No, I won't! Ever!" Dion laughed, then sobered. "You can tell Nola. And tell her thanks for her advice, but, by then, it was already too late."

"I think she knew that, kid," Tusk said, remembering the tears in the night. "I think she knew it all along."

··◁■ ■▷··

Breakfast was a noisy, boisterous meal. Unlike evening's supper, which was a time for relaxation and family gathering, breakfast was haphazard, grab it when you came, sit if you had time and stand if you didn't. Sonja and her women hastened to and from the kitchen, where kettles of water were being heated for laundry. Bear and his sons and several cousins, who had arrived early that morning, discussed their plans for the day, all talking—or rather shouting—at the top of their lungs. There was to be a hunting party, and spears and knives clattered on the table, excited dogs nipped at their heels, snapped at each other, and tried their best to urge their masters up and away.

Kamil was going on the hunt and Dion longed to go himself, though he rather doubted his ability to help net and spear a wild boar. But he had his duty to perform, arrangements to make with DiLuna and Rykilth.

"We'll be going on our own hunting party soon," the Bear reminded him, with a wink. He was also forgoing the hunt, remaining behind to offer counsel and advice.

Dion and Kamil said little to each other during breakfast, fearing that if they said anything, too much would follow. They contented themselves with exchanging glances and smiles, each fondly believing the secret locked safely within, neither realizing that it shone from them like sunlight breaking through the clouds.

Sonja and her husband did their own share of glance exchanging. Sonja shook her head, shrugged, smiled, and seemed to say, "What did you expect?" The Bear, alternating between frowns and grins, tugged so frequently at his beard it seemed likely he would pull it out by the roots.

Amid a clatter of spears, barking, roared laughter, and the inadvertent overturning of several chairs and a cousin, the hunting party left the castle. Dion was aware, for the first time in his life, of the sense of family, of home, of love and joy and pain and sorrow shared, not borne alone. He held the toddler—wailing dismally over being left behind—and watched Kamil leave. Dion thought ahead to evening, when she would be back and they would sit together at the table, bodies near but not touching or perhaps hands clasped beneath the cloth, where no one could see.

He knew happiness in that moment, not bliss or rapture or joy but happiness, plain and simple. He was content. He wanted nothing except for this moment to last forever.

Die now!

The words came to him in Sagan's voice, startled the young man, cast a shadow over his heart. In ancient Greece, this call had been the response to great good fortune.

Die now! For you can never be as happy as you are at this moment and it would be better to die with this feeling in your heart than know the bitterness of its loss.

Tusk was at his elbow. "We got a message, kid, from the Lady Maigrey. She has the ship, they're ready to make the Jump. She wants to know if everything's okay on this end, when you expect to rendezvous . . ." Tusk paused, added with significant emphasis, "*if* you expect to rendezvous."

Dion set the toddler on his feet, bid him run to his mother, and followed after the Bear up the winding stairs to the tower room. And there came, in the whistling of the wind through the cracks and crannies of the castle walls, the urging voice of fate.

"Die now."

··◁■ ■▷··

Entering the room with the high-tech equipment, Dion was forced to pause a moment to reacclimate his thinking, wrench himself back to a former life that suddenly seemed sterile and cold and achingly lonely. He told himself it would be different, now that he had Kamil. Everything would change for the better. But he found himself staring at the vidscreen with a feeling of dread.

"Baroness DiLuna, standing by, Your Majesty," said one of Bear's sons through his translator.

Bear, Tusk, and Nola were waiting, watching him. Dion sat down, clasped his hands in front of him.

"Very well. Put her through. Baroness," he said with a cool smile for the image on the screen. "It is a pleasure to talk to you once more."

"What pleasure either of us derives from this conversation remains to be seen . . . Your Majesty," DiLuna said with a slight inclination of her helmed head and derisive laughter in her eyes.

Dion, lost in his dream of happiness, was wearing blue jeans, a homespun tunic loaned to him by Sonja, who had told him, with a knowing smile, that Kamil had woven the cloth. Dion instantly realized his mistake. He should have been wearing his dress uniform, the purple sash, and other symbols of royalty. He had committed a serious tactical error, lost ground before the battle even began.

Sagan would never have made such a blunder, Dion told himself bitterly, or let me make it. What was I thinking about?

He knew, all too well, what he had been thinking about. Nothing for it, but to make the best of it. He relaxed, appeared supremely confident that what he wanted, he would obtain. This meeting was, after all, a mere formality.

"You received my report on the status of affairs, Baroness. You know where we stand, the danger we are in. I've told you about Abdiel, the head of the former Order of Dark Lightning. I've told you about the scheme he has for turning the space-rotation bomb plans over to the enemy. I trust you have gone over my proposal on how to deal with him, Baroness. I know I can count on your aid in this time of crisis. When may I expect your ships to join the fleet?"

"When I'm damn good and ready to send them," DiLuna responded.

Dion replied with a frown. "Are you telling me, Baroness, that you are refusing to come to my aid? Are you saying that the promises you made meant nothing to you? Or is it, perhaps, that your promise means one thing when all is safe and secure and quite another when there is danger? Is this the honor of the people of Ceres?"

The baroness was an experienced warrior, not to be tricked into losing her temper, making wild swings that would leave her open to an opponent's skilled verbal thrust.

"My promise, Your Majesty, was to support you in a battle against the corrupt government of this galaxy. In such a war, we would stand to gain a lot—restoration of star systems taken from us unjustly, a reopening of trade routes now closed to us, increased power in the galaxy. My people and I are willing to risk our lives and money for that. But this war you are proposing! You offer us nothing except the opportunity to die so that *you* might wear a crown on your head."

"I thought I made myself clear, Baroness," said Dion, controlling his growing anger. "The threat to our galaxy is very real. You know the power wielded long ago by those of the Order of Dark Lightning. The opposition of the Blood Royal alone kept them at bay and, eventually, that failed. Is there any doubt in your mind, after reading my report, that it is Abdiel who has long ruled this galaxy? That Peter Robes is nothing but a husk sucked dry by the mind-seizer, a puppet who dances at Abdiel's bidding?

"All Abdiel needs is the space-rotation bomb and he will blackmail the remainder of the galaxy into submission. And, unless we stop him, he will obtain it. Or, as seems more likely, the Corasians will wait for him to acquire the plans and then they will build it themselves. We have the chance to stop this now, to crush it!"

Dion clenched his fist. "We have a chance to prove Peter Robes is a pawn of the mind-seizer. Yes, that will mean putting the crown on my head, Baroness, but you will have everything you want and everything will come to you in peace, without turning the people of the galaxy against each other in a bloody and bitter civil war."

DiLuna gazed at him, cold-eyed, speculative, then, suddenly, she smiled.

Dion, not liking that feline smile, tensed.

"Lord Sagan has taught you well, Your Majesty," DiLuna conceded. "I am impressed. Your plan is a good one. I have no objections to fighting the Corasians, and then have the grateful citizens of this galaxy shower on me what otherwise I must take by force. I have no objection to placing the crown on your head. You have the makings of a strong king. But you must admit that what you ask goes far beyond what I ever promised. I know I can win a war against the puny armies of the Galactic Democratic Republic. I'm not certain about defeating the Corasians in their home territory. This battle you propose will cost a great deal more in money and lives than war here at home.

The baroness raised a hand, forestalled Dion's interrupting her.

"I didn't say I would not be willing to pay that price. But you're asking more from me than originally bargained. I want something more from you."

"Name it, Baroness," said Dion.

"First, sire, I want the worship of the Goddess restored throughout the galaxy."

Dion waved a deprecating hand. "When I am king, all will be free to worship as they choose. The Order of Adamant, banned by the current government, will be restored, as will—"

"You misunderstand me, Your Majesty," broke in DiLuna. "I want the worship of the Goddess given official status and sanction, placed exactly on the same level with the Order of Adamant—something that the Blood Royal would never previously allow," she added with a curl of her lip.

"Very well, Baroness," said Dion graciously, thinking that agreement to this could do little harm. He was getting off cheap. "Restoration of this ancient religion will be one of my first proclamations."

"Thank you for that, Your Majesty, and that will be an answer to our prayers, but I fear it will not be enough. The people of the galaxy need to see that you yourself take the worship of the Goddess seriously, that you respect it and honor it. Then they will come to it themselves."

"I assure you, Baroness," said Dion, "that I will make it clear—"

"Indeed you will, Your Majesty. Your wife, your queen, will be the Head Priestess."

Dion was confounded, couldn't speak for a moment, tried to grasp what the woman was implying. He had the sudden image in his mind of Kamil standing before an altar, performing solemn rites, and he nearly laughed aloud.

"As you know, Baroness, to my regret, I have no queen—"

"But you will, Your Majesty. You will agree to marry one of my daughters."

Die now! sighed the wind, only it was the mournful echo of a chance forever lost.

"I must think about this," said Dion. His teeth were clenched tightly, a stabbing pain shot through the nerves of his jaw.

Tusk was in the background, reminded him urgently, "Kid! The Lady Maigrey's waiting. You don't have much time."

I can't say what your allies might ask of you. Maigrey was saying to him once more. *But you can be certain that the cost of their loyalty will run high. It may be higher than you are willing to pay. Higher than, perhaps, you should pay.*

"An hour, Baroness," said Dion. "I need an hour to consider this."

"In an hour, then, Your Majesty," said DiLuna, smiling, as one who has won and who knows it. The vidscreen went blank.

The room was silent. Even the faint mechanical hum and whir of the high-tech equipment seemed to hush. Dion stared at the empty screen, still seeing the image of the woman burned into it, as it was burned into his mind. He was vaguely aware of Tusk starting to say something, of Nola putting a restraining hand on his arm, of Bear Olefsky considering him gravely. Dion knew, in that moment, that Olefsky knew—if not in his head, then at least in the father's loving heart—all that had transpired between Dion and his daughter.

"By my lungs and liver, I fear the woman has you where it hurts, laddie," said the Bear, heaving a sigh that came from his toes. "We need her, there's no doubt. And she knows it."

"With our forces and Rykilth's—" Dion began, trying to draw breath, feeling as if he were suffocating.

"It won't be enough, laddie," Bear said. "And I've more than a presentiment that Rykilth has been drawn into this with her. I'll bet my beard that he won't commit his forces unless DiLuna commits hers."

I could give it up, Dion said silently. Give it up and be ordinary. Live my life here, in this castle, with her. Let the rest of the galaxy go to hell. What do they care about me anyway? Nothing. They huddle behind me, shove me forward to fight for them, defend them, give up my life, my happiness, for them. And in return they will revile me, mock me, plot against me.

Here, I could be happy, father children, grow old, die peacefully in my sleep. It might be a long time before the Corasians acquired the bomb. Let another generation worry about it. Another king . . .

The palm of his right hand started to itch, to burn. He slowly unclenched his fist, looked at the skin of the palm, at the lines fate had drawn on it, at the five scars he himself had chosen to accept. He thought back to the rite of initiation or passage or whatever it had been. He saw the spikes of the silver ball cut into his flesh; he felt, again, the terrible agonizing pain; saw, again, the blood flow from the wounds . . .

So it had been real. Not illusion. He knew, because the pain he felt now was the same.

He could give it up. The choice was his.

Or could he? He saw Maigrey standing in the Audience Hall on board *Phoenix*, saw her glimmer in his mind, pale and cold as the moon.

It's too late for that now, Dion. Don't blame yourself. I think it was too late from the moment you were born.

"Kid"—it was Tusk, reluctant, shoving something in the king's unfeeling, unresponsive hand—"messages, kid. One from Rykilth. The Bear was right. The vapor-breather's in this with DiLuna. He won't go unless she does. And another message from the Lady Maigrey. It's urgent, kid. She needs to know what your plans are."

"Look, Dion." Tusk squatted down on his haunches, put his arm around his friend's shoulder. "You have to go along with this. Agree to the marriage. What can it hurt? Hell, a lot can happen between now and then. We'll work on it, find some way to back out. In the meantime, we keep it quiet. No one'll know except us. You don't have to tell Kamil."

Already, Dion thought, I'm hiding things from her, keeping secrets. Already, it's begun . . .

Die now . . .

Too late.

Chapter ·•➤○◀•· Seventeen

Und wenn du lange in einen Abgrund blickst, blickt der Abgrund auch in dich hinein.

And if you gaze for long into an abyss, the abyss gazes also into you.

Friedrich Nietzsche, *Jenseits von Gut and Böse*

"I'm sorry, Dion," said Maigrey. "Truly sorry."

"My lady?" Agis glanced at her. "Did you say something?"

She was far away, her eyes gazing off into a distant world, into a castle, a tower room. Agis's voice brought her back. When she returned, she sighed, removed her hand from the hilt of the bloodsword.

"You were with His Majesty?" pursued Agis.

"Yes. There are disadvantages to this means of communication, Agis." Maigrey looked somberly at the five red marks on her palm. "Unlike commlinks, it transmits pain."

"Is there a problem?"

"We will hear from him. He knows what he must do, what is born in him to do. But for a while he can pretend he doesn't have to. He can pretend to be . . . ordinary."

Agis said nothing more, accepted her word without question, though he must be wondering what they would do if Dion didn't agree to join them. Maigrey wished she could be as confident of him as she'd forced herself to sound. He was only eighteen. The burdens of kingship already sat heavily on him. But he was old enough and wise enough to look ahead with clear eyes, and see that, Atlas-like, he would bear them all his life. How could she blame him if he chose to cast the heavy crown aside and walk bareheaded into happy obscurity?

And what would she do if he did?

Maigrey leaned back in her chair, closed her eyes, and thought longingly of a hot shower and bed, sleep, oblivion. She suddenly, fiercely envied those poor wretches who were

339

now burrowed deep in their drug-enduced hibernation, all bodily functions slowed to an absolute minimum, mental faculties shut down. They didn't even dream. . . .

"My lady," said Agis, voice low and warning, "trouble."

Maigrey jerked awake, cursed herself for having dozed off. Sparafucile stood in the doorway.

"What is it?" she demanded. "What's wrong?"

"You come," said the assassin.

Maigrey rose quickly, followed him out into the corridor, where she found Raoul and the Little One, waiting. "Brother Daniel?" she asked, and was startled to feel bitter disappointment. It was then she realized that she'd been using the priest as a kind of good-luck mascot, God's sign that He was with her. If she lost Brother Daniel, if he betrayed her . . .

"The priest okay," said Sparafucile, grinning at her. "Him not fail my lord."

Maigrey noted, as a point of interest, that the assassin said "my lord." Not "Him not fail you, my lady."

"The tricksy woman say nothing to him. He say nothing to tricksy woman. I know. I listen."

"How—"

"I think maybe something like this happen when captain want to have fun with me. I put bug in room when I there. Now I hear everything, even her breathing." The half-breed leered.

Maigrey swallowed her revulsion. "Go on," she said coldly.

"Priest, he give her injection—"

"Then what's the problem?" she demanded irritably.

"Captain not go under."

"What?" She stared at him.

"Tricksy woman not respond to drug. Oh, she not walk very well and she take long naps and her tongue is very thick, but she not sleep."

Maigrey shifted her gaze to Raoul and the Little One. The empath seemed to shrivel up beneath his fedora.

"How is this possible? Are we going to have more passengers like this? I thought you said you knew what you were doing—"

"My lady," broke in Raoul, hands spreading gracefully in a pretty pleading gesture, "truly, I can understand your anger but it is not justified. False pride is unhealthy, you feed yourself lies. It is, however, right and good to feel proud of what one does well and thus I may say with pride that I am an expert in my field, as oftentimes my former employer, the late Snaga Ohme, had reason to comment. Indeed, my former employer, the late Snaga Ohme—"

"Get on with it!" Maigrey snapped, too tired to put up with the Loti's meanderings.

The Little One, eyes fixed on Maigrey, edged nearer his partner. Reaching out a tiny hand from the pocket of his raincoat, the empath grabbed hold of the Loti's velvet coattail and tugged. Raoul glanced down at him; they shared their silent communication.

"I understand. My lady," he said, turning back to her, speaking more clearly and precisely than she had ever before heard him, "the other passengers are completely somnambulent. A periodic injection, administered every so often, will maintain them. I have no idea why the ship's captain has not reacted to the drug in a similar manner."

The half-breed grunted. Raoul glanced at him, eyelids lowered in acquiescence. "My friend here has expressed an opinion that the priest may have given the woman only part of the injection. That would account for the unaccountable. Being a trained nurse, he would, of course, know how to decrease the dosage without being discovered—"

"Of course," said Maigrey coldly.

The Little One blenched. Raoul paused, smoothed his hair and perhaps his thoughts at the same time. "There is also the possibility, although it is a remote one and I have never known it to previously occur, but—I repeat—it is possible that the woman herself is of such a strong will that she has the ability to put mind over matter, so to speak."

It took Maigrey a moment to disentangle the meaning from the words, but eventually she understood. "What can you do if that's the case? Increase the dosage?"

"That would not be wise, unless you wanted her to sleep for a long, *long* time. Which could be arranged," Raoul added, as an afterthought, adjusting a froth of lace that fell over his delicate-boned wrists.

"I take care of her," said the assassin. "Faster, better than any drug."

"I beg to differ, my friend," said Raoul politely, bowing. "I have, at the moment, on my person, a poison which can cause—"

Angrily, Maigrey shoved the Loti out of her way, stalked off down the corridor. She heard, behind her, after a moment's pause, the tap-tap of Raoul's high heels on the deck, the rustle of the hem of the Little One's raincoat trailing along the floor. She did not hear Sparafucile, but she knew he was following. He would not allow anything to interfere with the rescue of his lord.

Reaching the captain's quarters, Maigrey activated the controls, opened the door. She found the captain—what was her name? Corbett?—leaning drunkenly over her bed, supporting herself on the nightstand. Brother Daniel was near her, speaking to her in low earnest tones. At the whooshing sound of the door's opening, he looked up, sprang back away from the woman. A crimson flush stained his cheeks.

"What is going on, here, Brother Daniel?" demanded Maigrey.

"I don't know, my lady. I gave her the injection, as you commanded. She has, as you can see, only gone partially under."

"You're certain you gave her all the drug?"

"Yes, my lady," he answered, his eyes level with hers.

Maigrey believed him, sighed inwardly, in relief and was immediately irritated at herself for having done so.

The captain, it seemed, had just realized that someone else was in the room. She lifted her head, gazed at Maigrey with drug-glazed eyes.

"Hullo, bitch," she said, and though her speech was slurred and thick, Maigrey could hear the fury, the hatred in the woman's voice, see it glint through the drugged mists that clouded the eyes.

So that's what was keeping her going.

The captain swayed, nearly fell. She caught herself, held fast to the nightstand with hands that shook with the effort. Her breathing came fast and shallow, sweat glistened on the brown skin.

"I've been trying to make her lie down. I'm afraid she'll hurt herself, my lady," said Brother Daniel.

"If she does, she does," said Maigrey. "Come with me, Brother." Turning on her heel, she walked out the door.

Brother Daniel, with a sigh, folded his hands together and started to follow.

The captain shouted after them, "Aren't you afraid your

meat'll get damaged, bitch?" and then pitched forward onto her face on the bed.

Daniel, when he joined her in the corridor, was extremely pale. Maigrey shut the door.

The trio was waiting for them outside. Raoul looked aggrieved, wounded, unusual emotions for a Loti, but then he was obviously taking this failure as a personal affront to his skills. The Little One had his gaze fixed on Daniel, as did—perhaps—Sparafucile. One never knew for certain exactly what the misaligned eyes were looking at.

"According to Brother Daniel," Maigrey began, "he gave the woman the correct dosage of the drug—"

"And he is telling the truth," interrupted Raoul with a smile and bow for Brother Daniel. "According to the Little One."

"Thank you," said Maigrey. "When I want the Little One's opinion, I'll ask for it. The question is, what do we do now? And your other 'solution' is not an option. When we reach Corasia—safely we all hope—and have no further need of this ship, we will turn it back over to its captain, who will then join up with His Majesty's armada and fly it and the passengers safely back to our galaxy. Therefore, we need the captain alive and well.

"You saw her." Maigrey gestured at the closed door. "I admit she doesn't look dangerous in that condition, but anyone with that much guts and determination could do about anything. Well?"

Raoul's eyelashes fluttered. "My lady, I cannot possibly give her any additional injections of the drug until it begins to wear off, which will be, if she continues to struggle against it, in about seventy-two hours."

"A sedative along with it?"

"That is, of course, a possibility, but it might prove extremely toxic, my lady. If it is imperative that we keep this woman alive, I would not advise risking it."

Maigrey heard Brother Daniel, standing beside her, exhale softly, saw his taut face relax, some color return to his cheeks. It never occurred to him, of course, that this increased her problems, doubled their danger, imperiled the success of the mission.

You won't be so pleased, Brother, when you hear what I'm about to propose, she promised him silently, bitterly. Let's see what happens when the devil takes *you* to the top of the mountain!

"Very well, then," said Maigrey. "She'll have to be restrained, for her own protection. And someone will have to stay with her, perform the duties of nurse and guard. Fortunately, we have with us someone who can handle both."

Brother Daniel realized what she was asking—stay with the woman, guard her day and night. The color in his face deepened, then fled altogether. He stared at Maigrey wildly, his lips trembled.

"My lady—"

"Brother Daniel, you are the only one I can spare for this duty. I need Xris and his men to run the ship, maintain security. Agis and Sparafucile and I will man the bridge, share the watch, spell each other as pilot and co-pilot.

"Raoul and what's-its-name here will be able to give you a break, now and then. But Raoul has to monitor the other passengers and he will be required to manufacture and administer additional injections of the drug in order to keep them from coming out of the hibernation prematurely.

"If you refuse, Brother Daniel," Maigrey continued relentlessly, "I will have to give the woman a sedative and risk the consequences. She is far too dangerous to leave unattended."

Brother Daniel had regained his composure. "I will do what is required of me, my lady."

"Satisfactory," she said, softening her severe tone. "I have every confidence in you, Brother."

"Thank you, my lady," he said quietly, but his eyes were cast down, the hands—clasped together—were clenched tightly.

Maigrey was, it seemed, the only one who had confidence in him. He certainly didn't have it in himself. Or in God.

That makes two of us, she told him silently. She knew she should feel something, remorse that she had been vengefully pleased to inflict this suffering on him, sympathy for him, even human curiosity to see whether or not he broke his vows. But she didn't. She felt nothing except irritation that this stupid problem should have been foisted upon her.

She felt nothing for Dion either. Be careful what you wish for. . . . His wish had come true, he'd made it come true. It wasn't exactly what he'd wanted, what he dreamed it would be. The shining silver ball had spikes.

They were all standing there, staring at her expectantly.

Maigrey realized she'd wandered off again on some inner excursion. She wrenched herself back, prodded her weary mind to continue plodding along.

"Sparafucile, rig up some type of restraints for the woman. Make them comfortable, but make them effective."

"I already think such a thing might be wanted, lady-mine," said the half-breed and reached a hand into the bundle of rags that passed for clothing. He removed a metal box, opened it, displayed its contents.

"Sometimes I paid not to kill a person but to keep a person very much alive. I am paid to have pleasant conversation with a person. But sometimes a person does not want to have pleasant conversation with Sparafucile."

"Paralyzers," said Maigrey. "Satisfactory."

"They won't hurt her, will they?" asked the priest, staring at the four objects lined up in a neat row in the metal case.

"Not at all. Here." Maigrey reached in, lifted out what appeared to be a thick metal bracelet. "Hold out your hand."

Brother Daniel did as he was told, eyeing the mechanical device dubiously. He flinched when Maigrey locked the contraption around his left wrist, stared at it curiously when it was in place. It was lightweight, fit loosely, slid easily up and down his slender arm. He might truly have been wearing nothing more than a bracelet. Maigrey, smiling slightly, reached out and activated a switch.

The bracelet began to hum faintly, a row of lights flickered. Daniel stared at the contraption, eyes wide, mouth gaping wide.

"I . . . I can't move my fingers!" he said, voice squeezed in panic. "I can't feel my hand!"

Maigrey deactivated the device. The hum faded, the lights went dark. Daniel flexed his hand, curled the fingers in on the palm, uncurled them. He examined them in perplexity, looked up. "What?"

"It's all in your mind," explained Maigrey. "The paralyzers simply block the nerve impulses from the brain to the hand and, when you put them on the ankles, the feet. They don't disrupt the blood flow, don't injure the body in any way. But it's quite an effective restraint. Sparafucile, put them on the woman—"

"No," said Brother Daniel firmly, taking the box, casting a

grim glance at the half-breed. "Show me how to operate them. I will put them on her."

Sparafucile chuckled low in his throat, a sound that was much like an animal growling and chortling over a fresh kill.

Maigrey hesitated, then decided wearily that it didn't matter. The half-breed had his listening device. He would be able to warn her if . . . But who would spy on the half-breed?

Maigrey was suddenly sick and tired of the whole lot of them, sick and tired of herself. "I'll be on the bridge," she said. "Report to me there."

··◁■ ■▷··

Brother Daniel paid close attention to the half-breed's tutelage, though it took an effort of will on the young priest's part to stand that close to the assassin, who seemed to Daniel to smell of blood and death.

"I understand," said the priest, voice level, even. "This activates it. This shuts it off."

"These two fit over ankles, these over wrists. You can increase size, if you want. But I think that will not be necessary. The lady have very long legs, very fine ankles. A man could put his hand around them—"

"I am certain that they will fit properly," interrupted Brother Daniel. Grasping the box awkwardly under one arm, he walked to the door, activated it.

Tomi lay on the bed. She did not stir. He hoped she was asleep. That would make his heinous task easier. He took a step into the room, realized that the assassin was silently following right behind him.

Daniel turned, blocked the door with his body.

"What do you want?"

He tried to remain calm. If once the half-breed caught the scent of fear, he'd go for the throat, rip him to shreds.

"I watch, check to see that you put them on right." The assassin took a step nearer.

"I'll put them on right."

Daniel did not move. A swift glance showed him Raoul and the Little One, standing across the corridor. They would be of no help, however. One was watching with amused curiosity. God knew what the other was doing or thinking beneath that hat, behind the turned-up collar of the raincoat.

Sparafucile came a step nearer. The deformed face was horrible, close up. He was grinning, which had the effect of nearly shutting the lowest of the two eyes. Daniel couldn't help but involuntarily turn his own face away. The assassin's foul breath was hot upon his cheek.

"You ask what I want. I tell you, priest. I want only to have a little fun. The Starlady, she not care. I not hurt woman. Maybe woman enjoy it, eh? Maybe you enjoy it, priest? We not that much different, you and I. We both want same thing, eh?"

Brother Daniel looked back at him in horror, looked into the misaligned eyes of the half-breed, and shuddered. He saw the lust, the desire, and it was like looking into a mirror, held up by his soul. He saw, in those eyes, what he feared the half-breed must be seeing in his. They were alike. Too much alike.

"Get away from this door," said Brother Daniel.

The half-breed's eyes squinted, narrowed. The leer changed to an ugly snarl that showed rows of white, sharp-edged teeth. "How you stop me, priest? You have no weapon." He shoved Daniel with his body that was hard-muscled, strong, and powerful.

The priest staggered, caught himself, stood firm, held his ground. "Get away from the door."

Sparafucile's body tensed. Daniel braced himself, for the knife, the hands, whatever . . . He started to pray. The words stuck in his throat. Unworthy.

The assassin's hands moved with lightning-swift speed, but not to attack. He clapped Daniel soundly on both shoulders, eyed the priest with approval.

"You brave. You stand up to Sparafucile. This God you serve, the God of my lord, He gives you such courage?"

"Yes," said Brother Daniel faintly, not at all certain he understood what was going on, not at all certain danger had passed.

The half-breed nodded once, abruptly, shaking a quantity of dirty hair over his face. "Lady-mine choose wisely when she bring you. I wonder, at first. Now I know, eh? We be good friends, now, you and Sparafucile." The half-breed held out his hand, grinned. "Like brothers."

Like brothers, Daniel thought in silent misery. Once I would have scorned to touch that hand. Once I would have refused to dirty myself. But now, I no longer have that right." He clasped the assassin's hand in his, pressed it tightly.

"And maybe you tell me something of this God of my lord's."

Daniel replied with a nod. He had lost the power of speech. Sparafucile grinned, flashed a swift look past the priest to the woman, lying on the bed. Turning with a shrug, he ambled away, his shuffling step and hunched shoulders a deceit, a sham.

Raoul, across the corridor, sparkled and bowed. "Most impressive," he said with a toss of his head, as if he'd just come from watching a particularly entertaining bit of theater.

He and the Little One, whose eyes beneath the fedora glinted wickedly, minced daintily along down the corridor after the assassin.

Brother Daniel shut the door, sealed it, started to move, found he couldn't. He leaned weakly against the wall, shivering, sweat chilling on his body.

"You're not like . . . those others," came a slurred, soft voice behind him. "Why are you doing this?"

Daniel jerked around. "I thought you were asleep," he said, eyes on the bedspread. "I'm sorry you heard."

Step firm, he crossed over to the nightstand, put down the metal box, opened it.

"You . . . stood up to him. No weapon. You knew what he meant to do to me. . . ."

"It was only some sort of test," said Daniel, removing one of the bracelets from the box. His gaze focused on the woman's arm, brown-skinned, smooth. "He didn't mean it."

"Like hell," said Tomi.

She yawned, drowsy. Her eyes were liquid, black as the night, warm as the dreams that sometimes tormented his nights. She propped herself up on one elbow, watched him position the bracelet on her arm with only faint interest, as if the arm didn't really belong to her, but to someone else in the next bed.

"I've never met . . . man like you." She ran her fingers over the hand that was clasping the paralyzer around her wrist. "Gentle hands. A touch . . . like a woman's. No weapon, he said. No weapon. And you stood there. That killer. Never seen . . . so brave." Her eyes shut. Her head lolled back on the pillow.

The drug proved too powerful. She had fallen asleep.

Daniel paused before activating the paralyzer, studied her intently. Perhaps it wouldn't be needed. Perhaps, after all, she would sink into the hibernation. He drew nearer, hand outstretched, thinking to check her pulse.

The black eyelashes fluttered on her cheeks, eyes opened. "Free me," she whispered. Her arm slid around his, drew him in to her softness, her warmth. "You and I . . . together . . . take control . . ."

Daniel stood up, breaking the hold that had, after all, been flimsy, flaccid. Tomi smiled at him, sweetly, sleepily.

He clamped the paralyzer firmly on her wrist, activated it, and reached for another bracelet.

◆━ ━◆

"My lady," said Agis when Maigrey returned to the bridge. "I have received a signal from His Majesty. All is arranged. The fleets belonging to Baroness DiLuna and the vapor-breather Rykilth are on their way. If everything goes as planned, His Majesty will meet us at the rendezvous point on schedule."

Poor Dion. He'd caught the silver ball, spikes and all.

"Very good." Maigrey rubbed her burning eyes. "Course plotted?"

"Yes, my lady. Xris reports from engineering that they're ready down there. Do I make the Jump?"

Maigrey looked out into the Void, the darkness that was cold and empty.

"Make the Jump," she said.

Chapter ··❦··❦·· Eighteen

Now I, to comfort him, bid him a' should not think of
God . . .
   William Shakespeare, *King Henry V*, Act II, Scene 3

The king's shuttlecraft was returning to *Phoenix*.

The shuttle took its time; wending its way among the ships
of the line, assembled for inspection, assembled to do him
honor. Bursts of lascannon fire exploded from each ship as the
shuttle passed, the traditional salutes unheard but visible,
tiny, sparkling stars flashing yellow-red amid the blackness.

Dion, in formal dress uniform with purple sash, stood at
attention, watched with solemn gravity from the bow of the
shuttlecraft. The Honor Guard in splendid panoply formed
ranks behind him. This image was being transmitted to every
ship in the fleet and to countless billions watching the galaxy
over. All eyes were on him, the boy-king, the romantic hero of
human legend throughout the centuries, going forth to do
battle against evil. He had been compared to Achilles before
the walls of Troy, to David facing Goliath, to Alexander
conquering the world, to John F. Kennedy and the Cuban
missile crisis. President Robes had sent the king a message,
lauding his courage.

Dion, standing in lonely grandeur on the deck of the
shuttle, thought of all the countless numbers watching, entranced as humanity is always entranced and seduced by
parade, pomp and circumstance. He was reminded of something Sagan had said to him, quoting Bertold Brecht.

"Unglücklich das Land, das keine Helden hat! . . . Unhappy the land that has no heroes."

And the reply.

"Nein, unglücklich das Land, das Helden nötig hat. No,
unhappy the land that needs heroes."

This was a land, a universe, that desperately needed a hero, a savior—someone to fight their battles, bear their burdens; someone to die for them, make them feel alive.

Dion was the elect, the chosen—either by God or by circumstance. Or himself.

I have to be who and what I am.

Flying that stolen Scimitar, flying to *Phoenix* to find a name, to find destiny. He recalled, with a kind of regretful sorrow, as for innocence lost, how awed he'd been at the sight of the magnificent warship, shining brightly as a sun, of its attendant planets. And how insignificant he'd felt, a speck of dust in comparison.

He remembered, too, how lonely he'd been, as lonely as he was now. How much everything had changed . . . and how little.

The shuttlecraft landed on *Phoenix*, His Majesty descended, to be received by a glittering assemblage: Admiral Aks, looking worried and gray and harried around the edges; Captain Williams, smooth and personable and determined to cover himself with glory; Baroness DiLuna, daunting, haughty, self-satisfied; Rykilth, pleased with himself, to judge by the color of the vaporous fog surrounding him; Bear Olefsky, huge, stalwart, towering as a mountain; General John Dixter, stolid, reassuring, slightly rumpled.

Dion tread the red carpet that spread beneath his feet like a river of blood and received their formal bows with calm dignity, mindful of the watching eyes.

Soon, when all was ended and the vidcams were shut down, the 'droid reporters escorted from the ship, the people would shut off their vids and go about their ordinary lives.

Dion would descend into hell.

And if he came back, they would cheer him and love him and crown him their king. And if he failed, they would forget him and wait for someone else.

Had he ever had a choice? Was what Maigrey said true? Was he standing here now by an act of divine intervention? Or had he made the decisions that brought him to this point? Was he acting of his own free will? Or was he being fooled into thinking he was by some snickering omnipotent being?

He remembered Platus, who wanted the child to be ordinary, but who had named that child after Plato's hope of a good and wise ruler.

He remembered Sagan, killing Platus. He heard again the Warlord's voice, *Perhaps I came to rescue you*.

And Abdiel's voice, *You can use the power of the Blood Royal. You have only to reach out your hand, my king, and take it*.

He remembered golden eyes, a shield held in front of him. He hadn't spoken of what he intended. He hadn't had the courage. Oh, he'd told her about DiLuna, about his promise to marry another. That much, Kamil had a right to know. There would be no lies between them. But not this. Not his decision to do . . . what must be done. Tusk was right, something might happen. Fate . . . God . . . chance . . . might intervene.

Might save him from himself? Is that what he wanted?

"Your Majesty." Admiral Aks came forward. "We have received a signal from the Lady Maigrey. She is making the Jump across the Void."

"We will follow," said Dion, rubbing the palm of his right hand, as if it pained him.

Book Four

Where all life dies, death lives. . . .

John Milton, *Paradise Lost*

Chapter ❖◗◯◖❖ One

Day after day, day after day
We stuck, nor breath nor motion:
As idle as a painted ship
Upon a painted ocean.

> Samuel Taylor Coleridge,
> *The Rime of the Ancient Mariner*

Night watch.

No different from the day watch, except by the clock. Powered by strange winds of pulled-apart quarks, racing past the light of stars left far behind, the *Belle* sailed across the Void at speeds only the aweless minds of computers could calculate.

And yet, to those aboard, it seemed they stood motionless, becalmed.

❖◗ ◖❖

Agis came onto the bridge, stood behind the pilot's chair, looked over the half-breed's shoulder at the instrument readings.

"All goes well?"

"She go very well," said Sparafucile, stretching in lazy satisfaction.

The half-breed uncoiled himself from his seat, unwinding body parts as if he had no bones. Just how he sat for hours unmoving, Agis had never been able to determine. Eyes almost completely shut beneath his thatch of tangled hair, Sparafucile either hunched over or curled up or slouched down, or perhaps a grotesque combination of all three. Settling himself in, he never shifted position for the duration of his watch, which was four hours. A casual observer might have supposed the half-breed had fallen asleep. That casual observer, trying to sneak past Sparafucile, would have been dead wrong.

Agis remained standing, after the assassin had removed himself. The centurion disliked sitting down just after the half-breed had vacated the chair. He left behind an unpleasant warmth, to say nothing of the lingering, objectionable odor. Agis always spent the first half hour of his watch standing.

Sparafucile grinned at him, as if he knew exactly what the centurion was thinking, and left the bridge, heading out to do God knows what.

Agis gave the chair a disgusted glance and, pouring himself a cup of hot coffee, leaned against the console and concentrated on monitoring the instruments.

Watch was extremely boring, vitally necessary, which was why the Lady Maigrey had scheduled the three of them—herself, Agis, and the half-breed—four hours on, eight hours off.

Agis kept his eyes on the instruments, fixing one part of his mind on its monitoring duties, setting his inner mental alarm to go off when required. That done, he sipped his coffee and allowed the other portion of his mind not currently engaged to travel through time and space in the opposite direction, travel back to where it always traveled at times like this: back aboard *Phoenix*.

The centurion could not remember a time in his life when he had not been a soldier. He assumed there had been one. He assumed he'd had a childhood, parents, a home, perhaps a dog. No conscious memories of such a past existed for him, however. It wasn't that such memories were unhappy ones, deliberately shoved aside. They were simply unimportant. He couldn't have told, without looking up his record, his real name.

Life began for Agis when he entered the military. He'd been an exemplary pilot, whose skill and daring won him the attention of the Warlord. The proudest moment in Agis's life was his acceptance into the ranks of the Honor Guard. Agis's second proudest moment was when he'd attained the rank of captain of that elite corps.

He was with them now, in spirit, if not in body.

"Cato is a good commander," he said to the flashing numbers on the screen. "He will serve the young king well. And he'll be able to adapt to being captain of the Guard for a king, as opposed to that of a Warlord. I'm not certain I could have. He'll be going through hell now, though."

Agis pictured in his mind the myriad duties required of a captain whose king is not only going to war, but was going to war in the company of dubious allies against an extremely hostile neighbor in that neighbor's own territory, outnumbered zillions to one.

But if all went well, if they beat the odds, if they pulled this off, Cato could find himself captain of the Palace Guard, a force whose existence had been wiped out the night of the Revolution. Honor, glory, wealth, even a chance for retirement, a pension—a thing never expected in the Warlord's Honor Guard. One rarely grew old in Sagan's service.

I won't, Agis thought with a smile.

The coffee had grown cold, he set the cup down.

Agis had no regrets. On the contrary, he would have had it no other way.

"No matter what happens, even if we win, even if we defeat our enemy, I have the foreboding that I will be the last of the Guard to serve my lord. And so it's better this way. Cato will make a good captain of the Palace Guard. Yes, it's better this way."

Calmly, at peace, Agis took his seat in the now-cool leather of the chair and devoted his full and complete attention to his duty.

··◁■ ■▷··

Night watch. Another night.

Xris made his way to the engine room, prepared to take over the watch from one of his men. Like Agis, Xris was mainly responsible for watching numbers, monitoring equipment. But the numbers he watched indicated the functioning of the engines and the computers that ran the engines, and unlike Agis, Xris and his men were required to spend considerable amounts of time constantly adjusting, altering, repairing the complex systems.

The cyborg read the log from the last watch, checked his instruments, ordered his men to go get some sleep. Harry complied. Britt emerged from somewhere back in the depths of the engine just as his replacement, Bernard, came through the door. Two men were required in engineering, working eight-hour shifts.

"Never thought," said Britt grimly, removing the badge that measured the amount of radioactivity his body had absorbed and tossing it down on the desk, "that you'd turn me into an engineer, Xris. Being bored to death is a hell of a way to go."

The cyborg smiled, shook his head. Leaning back in his chair, he pulled one of the black twists of tobacco from a pack stashed in a pocket, lit it. "Things'll liven up soon enough."

"Yeah? Well, I tell you, I'm going to be so happy to get to Corasia that I'm liable to throw my arms around one of the buggers and give it a big hug. Maybe kiss the ground it rolls on. Can I bum one of those from you?"

Xris blew smoke. "I thought you quit."

"Yeah, I did. Thanks."

"Speaking of hugging the Corasians, that's about what we're going to be expected to do when they come on board."

"Yeah, so Lee said. How do we know that they just won't decide to add us to the items already on their menu?"

"We don't. But the lady plans to convince them that we're wanting to establish a regular supply route. 'Fresh meat delivered right to your door.'"

"You think it'll work."

"It's got possibilities. The black market trade in human flesh and technology has picked up over the years. Back when I was with the agency, rumor had it that people in very high places were involved. The Corasians aren't stupid, even if they do all think with one brain. They're bound to figure that they can gain more by cooperating with us than making us a midday snack."

The augmented hearing of the cyborg caught the sound of the mincing, high-heeled gait of the Adonian, the shuffling whisper of his raincoated companion.

"Company coming," he warned Britt.

"Who?"

"The pretty boy."

"Cripes!" Britt looked alarmed. "I'm out of here. That guy gives me the creeps."

"Did I hear someone mention a midday snack?" asked Raoul, entering the engineering room. "I made sandwiches." He held in his bejeweled hands a box containing food and steaming cups of coffee.

Britt gave the sandwiches a horrified glance, shook his head. "No, thanks. The boys and me, we've been cooking our own meals." He edged his way out the door, disappeared in haste.

Raoul gazed after him. The Little One rustled in his

raincoat, shook what presumably was its head beneath the large hat.

"The Little One remarks that this man of yours seems to hold an antipathy toward us."

Xris nodded, puffed on the twist. "Got a thing against being poisoned. He's funny that way." Reaching for a sandwich, he removed the twist from his mouth, took a bite, chewed it stolidly.

"But not you?" Raoul asked, placing the box upon the console, removing hard-boiled eggs, fancifully cut slices of pickle, knives and forks, and silk napkins monogrammed with the liner's name.

"Me," said Xris, eyeing the sandwich, "I figure poison would be the lucky way to go. Don't you, Adonian?"

Raoul smiled in polite agreement, flipped his long hair back over his shoulders with a graceful gesture of his hands, then returned to fussing with the pickles. Xris finished one sandwich, picked up another, paused to frown at a flickering indicator light.

The cyborg tapped at the light with the fingernail of his good hand. The light began to burn steadily. He leaned back in his chair, chewed on the sandwich, gazed at the Loti.

Raoul was looking particularly charming today, wearing a long-sleeved silk blouse tucked into skintight black toreador pants with lace stockings and six-inch heels.

"I hear you and your friend there are planning to go in with us when we reach—what is that name her ladyship calls our destination—the Stygian caverns."

"Yes." Raoul was repacking the box that contained additional sandwiches, redistributing the coffee cups to balance them better. "Your information is correct."

"You going in there high heels and all?"

"I believe," said Raoul pleasantly, "that for the battle I will change into flats."

Xris grunted, took the twist from his mouth. "Can you shoot?"

"Oh, dear, no," said the Loti, the shock sending a mild ripple through his euphoria. "At least I could," he added, after some consideration, "but there's simply no telling what I'd hit."

Xris put the twist back between his lips. "Going to be kind of difficult, poisoning Corasians, isn't it?"

"I don't really care much about the Corasians," said Raoul, lifting the box, preparing to depart. "I trust those who can shoot them will shoot them. It is Abdiel and his mind-dead disciples against whom the Little One and I"—he nodded at his diminutive companion—"have sworn to take revenge."

"And how are you going to manage that in the middle of a firefight? Run up in between laser bursts and ask them if they'd like a bite to eat?" Xris snubbed out the butt end of the twist on the china saucer of the coffee cup.

"How amusing." Raoul laughed delicately. "But not to worry. We have our little ways." He paused, cast a limpid glance at the sandwich from beneath blue- and green-drenched eyelids. "Enjoy," he said, and he and his companion tripped off down the corridor.

Xris looked at the sandwich, shook his head, shrugged, and finished eating it. Lighting another twist, he stuck it in his mouth, went back to his work.

··◁■ ■▷··

Night watch. Again.

Brother Daniel rose from his kneeling posture, grimacing slightly at the tingling sensation of blood returning to numb legs. Carefully he folded the leather scourge, whose numerous strips felt incongruously soft in his hands, soft and wet with blood. He tucked it away, thrusting it in a nondescript bag that contained a silver chalice, a small dagger, his prayer book.

"What the hell are you doing?" Tomi's voice was lucid, only slightly groggy.

Brother Daniel, startled, very nearly dropped the bag. Had he miscalculated? Surely, she should not be coming out of the drug so soon. How many hours, days had passed? Not that many . . . ? He looked at the clock, but was confused. He couldn't remember when he'd last given his patient the injection—an unpardonable sin for a nurse.

He glanced at the record sheet, kept on the nightstand, at the record made in his neat, precise handwriting, since he lacked a personal computer that he would have had aboard *Phoenix*. Yes, he'd miscalculated, made a mistake.

Silently, inwardly, he rebuked, reproached himself. Never before had anything like this occurred. He had been the model, the one all looked to for support in times of crisis. He was one of the few who had remained calm during the enemy bombardment of *Phoenix*, one of the few who had remembered to keep records at all during that terrible time.

Now he was falling apart, crumbling, failing his patient, failing himself, failing God.

Or was God failing him? Why weren't his prayers, his desperate prayers, being answered?

Biting his lips against the pain, Brother Daniel drew on gingerly a shirt over the fresh and bleeding wounds that striped his back. The shirt was too big, fit loosely over the slender frame, fit more loosely than it had when this voyage of the damned began.

Daniel heard the sheets rustle. Looking in the mirror, opposite him, he saw Tomi struggle to prop herself up on her elbows. "I've seen a lot of weird things in my time," she stated. "I've seen guys who paid women to whip them, and women who paid guys to whip them, and just about every combination beyond that, but I never saw anyone whip himself. You get some sort of sick thrill out of that?"

Daniel did not respond. Carefully, he buttoned the shirt. Then, carefully, he prepared the next injection. Turning around, keeping his eyes on the bed sheet that he would change when the patient was, once again, comatose, he stepped forward.

"Don't, please!" Tomi pleaded. Her tone was no longer tough, but soft, vulnerable, frightened. "Not for a little while, at least. An hour. Give me an hour. Just to . . . talk. I promise I won't say anything you don't want to hear. We'll talk about . . . each other. About you. I want to understand you."

Daniel hesitated. The hand holding the air injector trembled. He kept his eyes fixed on the rumpled sheet, but he could see her arm, bare, round, shapely, muscles well defined, skin dark and smooth against the lemon-yellow fabric.

"You don't know how horrible it is," she continued, her tone pitched low. The hand, numbed by the paralyzer around the wrist, twitched involuntarily. "I keep thinking, when you give me that drug, that I'll go to sleep and never wake up. Or that if I do wake up, it'll be in some Corasian slave—No! I'm sorry. I won't talk about it! I promise. Tell me, tell me why you did . . . that . . . to yourself. I want to understand you, truly."

Daniel shifted his line of vision, moving up the arm to the

face. Her black eyes, still clouded somewhat by the drug, held nothing in them that he did not already hear in her words—fear, desperation, and interest, an interest in him.

Surely, an hour wouldn't hurt. He laid the injector down on the nightstand and drew up his chair, this chair where he had spent so many long and tortured night watches.

Tomi's arm moved. If the hand had been capable, it would have reached out to him. He saw her trying, saw the effort of will that the paralyzers disrupted at the wrist. His heart twisted within him, the pain of his self-inflicted wounds could never obviate the pain of his longing.

"You wouldn't understand," he told her, sitting down, being careful not to rest his injured back against the cushions.

"Maybe I would. I had a fight with my boyfriend, once. I went home and I slammed my fist into a wall. Split my knuckles wide open and punched a hole in the plasterboard. But it made me feel better. Though I wished at the time it had been his head instead of the wall I broke." She sank back on the pillow. "Oh, God! I wish I could think straight! I know what I want to say. I know this sounds crazy, but is that why you're hurting yourself? To make yourself feel better?"

"Yes," lied Brother Daniel.

"It's me, isn't it? You want me. And you won't take advantage of me. That's sweet." Tomi closed her eyes, smiled dreamily. "I never met a man so sweet. And gentle. I bet you're a real gentle lover. And sensitive. Your touch." Tomi sighed, stretched, arms, legs, her body moving beneath the sheets. "You'd know where to touch a woman so that she—"

Tomi opened her eyes suddenly. Her voice was husky, muted. "You can have me. We can be lovers. You know that. So what's the matter? You've never been with a woman before? But you know about love, don't you? You've dreamed about it at night. You've dreamed about me!" she guessed, the strange ties that sometimes bind captor and captive providing her sudden insight.

Daniel stood up. He didn't know he was standing until he was on his feet, and then he knew only because he nearly fell. Turning, he gripped the top of the bureau, bent over it, shaking.

"The real thing is better. Better than anything you've imagined! Of course, you'd have to take off these damn paralyzers—"

Daniel raised his head, saw her face reflected in the mirror, saw—for a split second—the coldness, the calculation in the black eyes. It was gone in an instant, when she saw he was watching. But, too late . . . too late.

Whirling, he lurched over to the nightstand, grabbed the injector, pressed it against the woman's arm.

Tomi said nothing, stared up at him. He watched her grimly, waited for the drug to take effect. Her eyes began to lose their focus, the lids grew heavy.

"All right," she murmured. "So I tried. You can't . . . blame me."

The eyes closed, flared open. They were clouded, soft. She looked up at him, sighed. "Such a gentle . . . lover."

She slept.

Brother Daniel hurled the injector from him. Sinking to his knees, he covered his face with his hands and sobbed aloud.

··❈▪ ▪❈▪··

Night watch, another.

Maigrey was awake. They were near the end of their journey. She sat in her cabin, located on C deck, next to an anti-grav lift that led directly to the bridge on the deck above. Two slumbering passengers, a rotund human male and robust human female in probably their mid-sixties, had been removed from the cabin to make room for Maigrey. Sparafucile and Agis had carried them, not without difficulty, to other quarters.

"Lots of meat on those bones," Sparafucile had stated on his return, his ugly face split in a grin. "They will not lose much during hibernation. We take Corasians to see them first, yes?"

Maigrey had ignored him at the time; the half-breed had a warped sense of humor. But she found herself remembering that remark every time she entered the room, every time she saw the man's clothes, hanging in the closet, the woman's jewels, arranged neatly in a case upon the vanity, photos of what Maigrey supposed must be grandchildren on the nightstand. If something went wrong . . .

Nothing was going to go wrong. Maigrey put the thought firmly out of her mind, concentrated on completing her calculations on the fuel consumption. Everything had gone smoothly so far, almost too smoothly. They were almost three quarters of the way across the Void. Tomorrow or the next day they would have to leave hyperspace, prepare to enter the Corasian outer defense perimeter. Maigrey almost wished something would go wrong between now and then. Nothing major, mind you, but just enough to propitiate the gods, who—so it was rumored—never liked to see man grow too content.

She switched on the small desktop computer.

"Blackjack?" it said brightly.

"No, bring up—"

"Craps? Bridge? Solitaire?"

"No. Bring up the latest fuel consumption reports."

The computer, aggrieved, did as it was told.

A knock on the door interrupted her.

"Enter," said Maigrey, her voice activating the controls. "Put it down there," she ordered, not looking up, thinking it was Raoul with dinner.

"My lady."

It wasn't Raoul. Maigrey glanced around, saw Brother Daniel standing in the doorway.

"I need to talk to you, my lady." His hands were folded, his eyes dutifully cast down. But when he spoke, he raised his eyes level with hers and she saw, in the eyes, the shadow of pain.

Maigrey sighed, supposing that, after all, she should feel thankful. Her prayer had been answered. Something was undoubtedly wrong.

"What about your prisoner? You didn't leave her alone?"

"Raoul has agreed to stay with her for the time being," said Brother Daniel. "She is sleeping now, anyway."

"Very well. I'll be with you in a minute. I have to finish this first. Shut the door and sit down."

Brother Daniel did as he was told.

Maigrey endeavored to complete her complex mathematical figuring, but she was acutely aware of the young priest's presence, though he spoke no word, made no sound.

"That's enough for today," she informed the computer, finally. The numbers swam before her eyes.

"Perhaps you'd care to wager on whether or not we have enough fuel to make it back safely to this galaxy?" the computer asked cheerily. "Double or nothing?"

Maigrey shut it off, turned around to face the priest.

"There'll be enough," she assured him. "Provided we don't take any detours."

He looked relieved, nodded. A nerve twitched in his face, at the corner of one eye. His hands trembled on his lap, his complexion, normally pale, was gray. He was thin, had visibly lost weight.

"Brother Daniel, how long has it been since you slept?" Maigrey asked severely. "Or eaten anything? Good God, if you collapse—"

"I won't," he said with a wan smile. "We're trained to fast. I've been doing it deliberately—fasting, praying." He flushed slightly, his cheeks gaining a semblance of color. "And other things." He pressed his lips together, swallowed.

Maigrey, taking his meaning, glanced at the back of his shirt, reflected in the vanity mirror behind him. Faint traces of blood could be seen, staining the fabric, evidence of the scourge, self-flagellation. She said nothing, waited for him to continue.

He saw she understood. "It hasn't helped."

He drew a deep breath, suddenly left his chair, sank down upon his knees before her. "My lady, may I make my confession to you?"

Maigrey stared at him, startled. "Brother Daniel, I—I hardly think that would be . . . right. I'm not a priest, as is Lord Sagan. I've never taken holy orders. I can't offer you absolution—"

"I am aware of this," said Brother Daniel, and his voice had grown firmer, stronger. His gaze fixed on her and it was steady, unwavering. "But you are close to God, my lady. I feel it. I know. The half-breed, Sparafucile, tells me that we will be entering the Corasian galaxy soon, perhaps as soon as tomorrow. We will be in mortal peril from that moment on, won't we, my lady?"

"Yes," said Maigrey.

"I could not die at peace with this burden on my soul. Hear my confession, my lady. Part of it concerns you. Part of it requires human forgiveness. As for God, I must put my faith in Him, that He will be understanding."

"Very well," said Maigrey, growing suddenly cold, fearful.

Was this all a plot, hatched by the priest and his prisoner? Brother Daniel had never approved this plan. Maybe this was his way out. Was that captain, even now, perhaps, stealing

onto the bridge? Sparafucile had been spying on them, but the
assassin couldn't watch them all the time. Perhaps he'd missed
this.

It was on the tip of Maigrey's tongue to make some excuse,
warn Agis. . . .

You fool, she told herself. You're panicking. She forced
herself to think logically. She herself had seen Captain Corbett
yesterday. The woman was still drugged, still only half-
conscious about half the time. Raoul had said that even when
they quit giving the woman the drug, it would take days for the
effects to wear off. Agis was quite capable of dealing with
Captain Corbett, if she managed to make it that far. And
Sparafucile was undoubtedly close at hand, as he always was,
whether anyone wanted him or not.

"My lady," said the young priest, "I have fallen in love."

He fell silent, head bowed.

Not "I am in love" but "I have fallen in love." Fallen. Yes,
that's how he would think of it.

"Is that all?" Maigrey asked, exasperated, speaking before
she thought.

He looked up, stricken, his agony evident in the body's rigid
lines, taut muscles, straining tendons, the stripes of blood
across the slender shoulder blades.

"I'm sorry, Brother Daniel," she said, sighing, "but I
imagined— I am the one who needs to ask forgiveness."

"No, you don't, my lady." His voice was almost fierce. "I
know what you imagined. And you wouldn't be far wrong.
That, too, is part of my sin. I considered betraying you,
betraying my lord. I planned, plotted. I thought, time and
again, of how it might be done. She and I talked. She has lucid
moments, rational, especially when the drug begins to wear
off. It grew harder and harder for me to continue giving her the
injections. I—" He choked, was forced to quit speaking,
lowered his head again.

"Brother Fideles," Maigrey said gently, knowing this would
hurt, but thinking it might eventually help, "did it ever occur
to you that she's been using you? That she doesn't really care
for you?"

"I know," said the young priest quietly. "I'm not such a fool
as that. I knew the first day what she was after." He flushed,
continued in low tones, "And how she would try to get it. But
there have been times, especially lately, when I thought

that perhaps . . . that is . . . that she might be coming to care . . ."

"The woman is a good captain," said Maigrey. This should be cut off swiftly, cleanly, the wound cauterized with flame before it festered. "She cares about one thing and that's her ship, her command, her responsibility to her crew, her passengers. She discovered a weakness in her enemy and took advantage of it, using the only weapon at her disposal. It is unfortunate you got hurt, Brother Fideles, but war is hell."

He glanced up, to see if she were mocking him, laughing at him. But she was earnest, serious. He went extremely pale.

"Yes," he said steadily, "you are right. I mean nothing to her."

"Have you broken your vows of chastity?" Maigrey asked. If he was going to confess, he should dig down to the bottom of his soul.

"Many times. In my mind only. But there is no difference in the eyes of the Creator," he added swiftly.

"I give Him a little more credit than that," Maigrey said dryly. "After all, He was the One who developed the concept. It seems to me, Brother, that your besetting sin is the sin of pride, and I believe it is for that you need to beg God's forgiveness."

"Pride?" Brother Daniel stared at her in confusion.

"You're one of us now, my friend," said Maigrey, gently smiling. "You're no longer perfect, no longer living up among the angels. You have indeed 'fallen,' fallen to our level. You are human."

Brother Daniel frowned, not quite understanding, wondering again if she was teasing him. He looked into her eyes, saw sympathy, pity, but also admonition, rebuke.

"I've been that insufferable?" he asked ruefully.

"On occasion."

"Yes, I suppose I have," he admitted after a moment's thought, ashamed. He rose to his feet. "Thank you, my lady. I will return to my duties."

"I can take you away from her, now, Brother, if you would like," Maigrey offered. "Raoul could—"

"No, my lady. It is my responsibility. Besides, Tomi—I mean, Captain Corbett—is now fairly certain that I will not succumb to her seductions. I don't believe she'll try anything further."

No, Maigrey had the feeling the woman knew when she'd been beaten. The young priest was pale but composed, saddened but tranquil. The captain must see, in that face, that she had lost. But did she see, too, what wounds she had inflicted? Did she know what terrible torment the young man had suffered, alone, in the dark? What fevered, aching dreams of desire he had sought to drive out of his mind by torturing his own flesh?

Maigrey ushered Brother Daniel out the door, watched him wend his way down the corridor.

War was hell. Before returning to her work, Maigrey promised herself a woman-to-woman talk with Captain Tomi Corbett.

·◁■ ■▷·

The night watches came to an end, finally.

Maigrey stood on the bridge, hands clasping the back of the pilot's chair. She watched, over Agis's shoulder, the numbers flash past until her eyes burned with the strain.

"And . . . mark, my lady," he reported.

"Prepare to bring us out of hyperspace."

"Yes, my lady." He and the half-breed did as commanded.

Maigrey activated the commlink that would carry her words throughout the slumbering ship.

"We're coming out of the Jump," she reported. "We are now in the Corasian galaxy."

A red light flashed, winking ominously. Maigrey saw it, saw Agis's glance at her, making certain she had noticed.

"In fact," she added grimly, "we've just tripped one of their alarms. I should say we can expect company almost anytime now. You know what you're supposed to do. Remain calm, and everything will be fine. Secure the ship for reentry."

Sitting down, she strapped herself in and tried to recall, idly, how much it was you were supposed to pay the ferryman that took you across the river Styx.

Chapter ⚬ Two

About, about, in reel and rout
The death-fires danced at night . . .
> Samuel Taylor Coleridge,
> *The Rime of the Ancient Mariner*

One moment the Corasians were not there and the next moment there were swarms of their small planes flying from the mother ship, surrounding the *Galaxy Belle*, weaving their tractor beam web around the luxury liner. Fortunately, it was not the Corasian way to shoot first and ask questions later, even against a ship that had violated their territory. Corasians value human technology too much to risk damaging a prize. Far better to haul it off, dismantle it, study it, learn from it, then scavenge the parts.

And, in addition, the collective mind—that was really quite intelligent, if not particularly creative—was curious. Why was this ship, a pleasure craft, here? It could not possibly have strayed off-course. The *Belle* must be in their galaxy for a reason and the Corasians were interested in knowing what that reason was.

"Pass the word for Xris," ordered Maigrey.

Agis complied, relayed the message to engineering.

A thin mechanical voice, translated from electronic impulses broadcast by the Corasian mother ship, sounded through the stillness on the bridge, "Alien vessel, you have deliberately flown through our defensive barriers. This is a hostile act. You are our prisoner. Prepare to be boarded. Repeat. Prepare to be boarded."

"Transmit this message," ordered Maigrey. "*Galaxy Belle* to Corasian people. We have no hostile intent. This ship is not armed. We have a business proposition."

"State your business proposition."

369

"My lady," said Agis in an undertone, "the tractor beam net is closing around us."

"Yes, thank you," murmured Maigrey. "This is our proposition. We have nine hundred and seventy-five prime specimens of human flesh aboard this vessel. All adults, in good health, suitable for work or the slaughterhouse. We're seeking a buyer."

"We do not make deals with aliens who have violated the terms of the treaty between our galaxies and who have entered our territory illegally. Your ship and its cargo are considered contraband and are hereby confiscated. Prepare to be boarded."

The door slid open. The cyborg entered.

Maigrey glanced questioningly at him. Xris nodded, pointed at a button on the console on the arm of her chair. "Push that, sister, and they'll think a star went nova. Only it won't be a star. It'll be us."

"Satisfactory," Maigrey said to Xris. "*Galaxy Belle* to the Corasian people. This ship is wired to explode. Make any attempt to board, without our permission, and you will lose the vessel and its cargo. Your scanners will verify."

The Corasians did not respond.

"We are being scanned, lady-mine," reported Sparafucile.

Maigrey said nothing, sat back to wait, her hand resting near the button.

The thin mechanical voice returned. "We ask permission to come aboard and inspect your cargo."

"Permission granted," said Maigrey with a tight smile, rising to her feet, moving briskly across the deck. "Agis, you have the helm. Xris, Sparafucile, come with me." Pausing in the open door, she turned. "Agis, if I give the command, you know what you must do?"

"Yes, my lady," he said calmly. His gaze shifted to the button, looked up at her.

Maigrey, satisfied, went out, the cyborg and the half-breed accompanying her. Sparafucile did not walk with them, but shuffled a few paces behind; either acting as rear guard, or keeping an eye on her, Maigrey could never be certain which.

She glanced curiously at Xris, who was arming his weapons hand. Cracking open the metal fingers, he removed the gas pellets and darts appropriate for use in fighting humans. From the compartment in his cybernetic leg, he took out ten objects made of metal, shaped like small torpedoes.

"My own speciality. A Corasian killer. I designed them myself, after the battle on Shilo. They act like heat-seeking missiles," he explained, inserting the projectiles swiftly and deftly into the fingers of his weapons hand. "They're attracted to the abnormally high temperature of the Corasian, explode on impact."

"That would shatter the robot body," said Maigrey, eyeing the weapons curiously, "but not the Corasian itself. In fact, it would probably thrive on the energy of the explosion."

"I thought of that. Each is armed with a small anti-matter charge. Minute, but hopefully enough to disrupt the Corasian energy field and turn them to jelly."

"Hopefully?" Maigrey raised her eyebrows.

Xris smiled, clicked shut the fingers of his hand. Lights flashed up and down the artificial arm, accompanied by a series of beeps. The cyborg listened attentively to the tone, watched the lights—that ranged from green to yellow—and appeared satisfied. He relaxed, removed a twist from his uniform pocket, stuck the length of black tobacco in his mouth.

"I haven't exactly had a chance to test them yet, sister."

"You'll undoubtedly have the opportunity before this is ended, but not here, not now. The last thing we want at this point is a fight."

She was aware of the half-breed's shambling footsteps behind her. He had crept up to examine, over Xris's shoulder, the new weaponry, then had resumed his place again. It was interesting, Maigrey noted, that his footfalls could be heard when he wanted them to be heard; that he could move as silently as the night if he didn't.

"Apparently they don't want a fight either. Not much chance we'll have to use that button now," said Xris, lighting the twist with a flick of his hand. "They're hooked."

"There never was much doubt. They didn't dare risk losing a catch like this. They've got us and they know it. What harm in stringing us along?"

"I wonder, though," said Xris, glancing at her out of the corner of his eye, his good eye, the twist's smoke curling from his lips, "if you'd have done it."

"What do you think?" Maigrey retorted coldly.

Xris took the twist from his mouth, examined it. "I think you're disappointed you didn't have to."

Behind her, Maigrey heard a gurgling sound—Sparafucile's

version of a chuckle. Maigrey ignored the assassin, ignored the cyborg, ignored the jab of conscience that reminded her of her thoughts an instant back there on the bridge. The fleeting, wistful realization that all her troubles could end in a flash. A very bright flash.

·‥◄■ ■►‥·

The Corasian delegation arrived aboard a shuttlecraft sent from the mother ship. She and Xris and Sparafucile stood waiting for the docking bay doors to boom shut, the breathable atmosphere and pressure inside the docking bay to return to normal conditions. She was nervous, tense, ill at ease. She'd never spoken to a Corasian before, previous contact having been limited to killing them before they had a chance to kill her. She knew something of how their minds worked; it had been a dictum of Sagan's—know your enemy. She knew, for example, that those boarding her ship would be soldiers, nothing less . . . nothing more.

The Corasian collective mind, or "hive" as humans tended to think of it, divided its "people" into various categories: soldiers, sailors, tinkers, spies, as one of her sociology instructors had put it. Each Corasian operated within boundaries proscribed by the collective mind, not dreaming—for they had no dreams—of doing anything else. This made for a highly efficient and orderly society that did not, however, deal well with new and unforeseen situations.

"Stay calm," she repeated to herself. "Stay calm." But her fingers clenched tightly over the hilt of the bloodsword.

Xris jerked the twist from his mouth with a sudden movement that startled Maigrey and sent a ripple of tense, involuntary reaction through the half-breed, caused his gunhand to twitch.

"Don't do that!" Maigrey snapped, beneath her breath, though there was absolutely no possibility of anyone hearing them.

The shuttlecraft had touched down, was making itself secure. The docking bay doors shivered and began to shut.

Xris tossed the twist to the deck, ground it beneath his heel.

"You ever seen how those things kill people, sister?"

"Yes," said Maigrey, "and I don't think this is the time to discuss—" but Xris wasn't listening.

"I saw them kill Chico. And I couldn't do anything but stand there and watch. Our weapons were useless. Hell, how long had it been since anyone in the galaxy had seen one of these things?

"We kept firing at the damn things, but it didn't stop them. Finally, we ran out of juice. The lasguns were almost drained. Our one hope was to reach our spaceplanes, turn the lascannons on 'em. We almost made it. Then Chico was hit. He went down. I was going back for him. You know what happened?"

Xris looked at her. Maigrey shook her head, silently.

"My battery went dead. Half my body locked up solid. I couldn't move. Hell, it was all I could do to stand. The arm, the leg, like carrying lead weights. The Corasians were right behind Chico. When he saw me seize up, saw the lights go out, he knew what'd happened. He grinned at me, raised himself up on one arm, and said, 'Next time, before we go out, get a recharge!' And then they had him."

Maigrey let him talk. The shuttle's hatch opened, the fiery red bodies, encased in their robot shells, started to trundle down the ramp.

"They broke out of those damn shells of theirs, and it was like molten lava, flowing over the ground, only fast. Real fast. They started at his feet. I could smell the leather of his boots burn and then the flesh . . . He began to scream. They'd been fast, getting to him, but now they took their time . . ."

Xris took a twist from his pocket, started to put it in his mouth, looked at it, stuffed it back in his shirt again.

"I shot him. It was all I could do for him. It drained the gun, and I threw it at them. Worthless piece of junk. About like me. By that time, Harry and Britt had come back for me, dragged me on board the plane, plugged me in." His voice was bitter. "Recharged me."

Maigrey frowned, glanced at him in concern. "Are you going to be all right?"

"Meaning am I going to do anything stupid?" Xris shook his head, smiled a half smile, tight-lipped, grim. "I'll stay cool. I just wanted to say, sister, in case I don't get the chance, thanks for bringing me along."

Maigrey didn't find this particularly reassuring but it was too late to do anything now. Xris wasn't the type to go on some wild, vengeance-driven rampage. But Maigrey, watching the Corasians come aboard, seeing the ameboid, fiery red bodies encased in their steelglass robot shells roll toward her, was forced to fight down her own feelings of revulsion, horror, fear; forced to battle the sudden, instinctive, panicked urge to strike out at them before they could destroy her. And she judged by the rigid, carefully impassive expression on Xris's face that he ws fighting the same inner battle.

She glanced at Sparafucile, saw him staring at the Corasians, the malformed face thoughtful.

"These things have made my lord captive?" asked Sparafucile, voice low. The fiery red bodies gleamed brightly in the reptilelike eyes.

"Along with Abdiel, yes," answered Maigrey, surprised at the question, wondering uneasily what lay beneath it.

But the half-breed only nodded silently, impassively.

Whatever it was, she couldn't worry about it now. She walked forward to greet the enemy.

··◁■ ■▷··

The Corasians trundled through the ship, inspecting the "cargo," paying at least as much attention to the technology aboard as to the living flesh and blood. The luxury liner offered little in the way of technological breakthroughs and Maigrey gathered—from their silence—that the soldiers were not impressed.

The human cargo passed inspection. Sparafucile opened the doors to all the cabins, permitting the Corasians to peer inside. Since they had no eyes, Maigrey wasn't certain what they saw, but presumably they were able to sense the life-forms slumbering peacefully, without any notion of the danger lurking near. What would it be like for these poor wretches, if they woke to find themselves in the Corasian version of a meat locker?

Maigrey pushed the thought from her mind. She had her own worries. The Corasians were quite capable of offering to pay her off, transfer the human cargo to their own ship, and order her out of the galaxy. And that was supposing that they kept their part of the bargain. They were also quite capable of taking her and her people prisoner. Agis could be trusted to put a swift end to their captivity, however.

Maigrey had counted on Corasians wanting the ship, for spare parts, if nothing else. She was trying desperately to think up some tempting lie to tell them about the nuclear reactors, anything to get them to permit her to take the liner farther into the galaxy's interior, when the Corasians and their hosts entered the gambling casino.

"What is this machine?" one of the Corasians demanded in its squeaky, simulated voice.

Preoccupied, Maigrey barely glanced at it. "A roulette wheel."

"What is its function?"

Maigrey, whose knowledge of games began with chess and ended with bridge, looked at Xris. The cyborg coolly explained the nature of the game, the operation of the computer-controlled wheel, and gave the soldiers a demonstration.

The concept of gambling had, apparently, never occurred to the collective mind. Xris spent the next hour explaining the workings of every machine in the casino to the fascinated Corasians. Maigrey breathed easier, began to think they might pull this off, after all.

"Do we have a deal?" she asked, the tour of inspection complete.

They were on the engineering deck, heading for the docking bay and the Corasian shuttlecraft. "We'll transport the cargo and the liner into the interior for you—"

"That won't be necessary," said the soldier, its voice flat, mechanical. "You will turn the ship and the cargo over to us now. You have your spaceplanes. You will leave in those. We will escort you safely to the perimeter."

Maigrey and Xris exchanged glances over the robotic heads of the Corasians. This was precisely what they didn't want.

"Very well," said Maigrey slowly, considering. "You will give us our money now."

The Corasians, it seemed, had to contact the collective brain, for they were all silent long moments, the lights on their robot casings flickering and fading as they withdrew their thoughts from their bodies' functions. The lights winked back brightly.

"That is not possible," replied the soldier. "We have nothing of what you term 'money' on board our mother ship. The sum you require will be credited to your account in whichever currency of your galaxy you find preferable."

It would be interesting, Maigrey thought, to know just how they come by that money.

"And what happens if payment isn't made? We fly back and sue you?"

"We do not understand—"

"That's damn obvious!" Maigrey folded her arms across her chest. "Look, we're out a lot of cash for this operation. We want payment and we want it before we go. If you can't give us cash, then give us permission to take our cargo into the interior, find someone who can."

The Corasian again consulted the collective mind. Maigrey held her breath.

"What is that?" the soldier said suddenly, robotic head swiveling. "Life-form readings."

"What's that got to do—"

The soldier's head pivoted toward the captain's berth. "There are other life-forms aboard this ship which you have not shown us."

"It's only the ship's captain and her guard. We had to take her prisoner, of course. She's drugged. Now what about our money? Do we have a deal or—?"

"We would like to see these life-forms."

Maigrey eyed the Corasians, tried to determine if this was a trick, stalling for time. Or were they merely exerting their authority? There was really no good reason why the Corasians shouldn't see the captain and Brother Daniel. Just as there was no good reason why they should. Maigrey didn't like it.

"Xris, the door," she ordered.

The cyborg did as commanded, opening the door—with his good hand, Maigrey noted. Small beeps and tiny bright flashes indicated he was giving his weapons hand a system check.

Maigrey entered, cast a swift warning glance at Brother Daniel. The priest rose to his feet, took an involuntary step nearer the bed. Captain Corbett was groggily alert, fear and outrage successfully combating the effects of the drug.

"Hullo, bitch," Tomi slurred. "What's the occasion?"

Maigrey took her place at the foot of the bed, turned to face the Corasian that rolled rapidly into the room. She heard the captain suck in a shocked, frightened breath, heard Brother Daniel murmur something reassuring.

I wish someone would say something reassuring to me, Maigrey thought bitterly and irrationally. She was tense, nervous. The soldier was up to something and she had no idea what.

Sparafucile glided silently in after Maigrey, stood near the bathroom opposite the bed. Xris took his place by the door, lounging against it, but actually blocking, with his body, the seven other Corasian soldiers who remained standing in the corridor. The green and yellow lights on his weapons arm had all shifted color to red.

The Corasian soldier trundled near the foot of the bed.

"We will have this one," it said.

The lights in the robot head winked off, the robotic arms froze, fixed and locked in position. The soldier's steelglass case cracked wide open, down the front. The flaming red ameboid body oozed out and slid to the floor. Moving slowly and deliberately, it crawled across the room toward the bed.

Tomi dragged herself backward, scrabbling with her elbows and pushing with her legs. "Take these things off me, Daniel!" she gasped. "Don't let me die like this! Help me, Daniel! Please, help me."

The priest was staring in shock at the Corasian, moving relentlessly forward. The body was like a horrible blob of fire that pulsed and breathed with intelligent, terrible life.

"Daniel! Take these off—"

The priest turned toward her.

Maigrey made a swift gesture. Sparafucile left his post, glided round the bed to the far side. He clapped one hand over Tomi's mouth, held a knife to her throat with the other.

The captain ceased to struggle. Her body froze, terror-filled eyes on the Corasian that was drawing closer with every breath.

Brother Daniel's motion was arrested by the warning in the half-breed's eyes. "Back away from bed!" the half-breed mouthed.

Tomi moaned in her throat, the black eyes shifted for an instant from the Corasian to the priest. She moaned again, her gaze pleading, desperate.

Sparafucile clasped his hand tighter, the flashing blade rested on the dark brown skin of the woman's neck.

"Back away!" he snarled silently. "Trust lady!"

Brother Daniel, pale and trembling, looked from Tomi to Maigrey. Head bowed, he did as he was told, shrank back against the wall.

The Corasian was within half a meter's distance from the bottom of the bed. Maigrey took a step forward, stood in front of it, placed herself between the soldier and the helpless woman.

"No free samples," Maigrey said. "We want our money."

The fiery mass edged nearer the toes of Maigrey's boots.

She had little fear for herself. She had the bloodsword, the needles were already jabbed in the palm of her hand. Xris's weapons arm was lined up, fingers aiming directly at the other Corasians in the corridor. His men—waiting in the wings, alert for his signal—could be counted on to take care of any that escaped the cyborg's missiles. But being forced to kill these Corasians would seriously hamper, if not outright destroy, her plans.

"Back off," she said. "Or the deal's ended."

The Corasian's body quivered, heaved, then suddenly reversed direction, flowed back across the deck. Reaching its robot case, it oozed its way inside.

"Now," she continued coolly, "about the money—"

The robot head came to life, the case snapped shut with a click. "We do not understand this concept of money. You risk life for it, for a thing that can be of no value to you after death. You sell us secrets of technology in return for it—secrets that must eventually mean your galaxy's doom. You even sell each other for it."

"It's what's made us what we are today. Well?"

"Your terms will be met. We will provide you with coordinates and an escort to your destination."

"Good." Maigrey limited herself to that one syllable, afraid the relief would sound in her voice if she said more. An escort would be a nuisance, but one that could be managed.

The soldier pivoted on its wheels, headed for the door. It rolled past Xris, whose weapons arm slowly lowered to his side. The Corasian rejoined its fellows in the corridor.

"We will now return to our mother ship," it said.

Maigrey glanced back at Sparafucile. The assassin removed his hand from Tomi's mouth, the knife from her throat. Flicking the blade shut, sliding it into some dark recess in his rags, the half-breed grinned and glided over to join Maigrey, who was heading for the door.

Tomi gasped, shuddered, gulped in air. "Wait!" she managed to call out.

Maigrey paused, looked back, stopped. "Go on ahead," she ordered Xris and Sparafucile. "I'll catch up to you in a moment. Well"—hand on the bloodsword, she turned toward the captain—"what is it?"

"You saved my life," Tomi said, her tone sullen, disbelieving. "At the risk of your own? Why? Why didn't you just let that thing have me?"

Maigrey studied the woman, gaze calm, cool. "I could have. I thought about it. And if it's any comfort to you, Captain, saving you wasn't a noble gesture on my part. I acted out of necessity. They were testing me, wanted to see if I was serious. I am, Captain. I assure you. I am."

"I'm glad to know it, bitch." Tomi's head fell back onto the pillow. Her eyes closed, the reaction to her ordeal setting in. "I was afraid I was going to have to . . . reevaluate my opinion . . . of you."

Maigrey smiled, the smile that twisted the scar on her face. "Brother Daniel, a word with you."

The priest crossed the room, came to stand near her.

"No more injections," Maigrey told him, talking in an undertone. "We'll be at our destination in about two days time. Raoul says it will take that long for the effects of the drug to wear off completely. She's got to be alert, by then, capable of resuming command."

"Yes, my lady."

"Keep the paralyzers on her, though. God knows what she'd try if she were loose."

"Yes, my lady. What if she wants to know the reason why? What do I tell her?"

"I don't know," Maigrey snapped. She was suddenly tired, felt drained, empty. She wanted to be alone, shut herself up in her room. "Let her think she's gotten to you, maybe."

"Yes, my lady. And . . . thank you, my lady. What you did—" His voice, earnest, trembling, broke.

"What I did I did for the reasons I said I did, Brother Daniel," Maigrey told him wearily. "Don't go sentimental on me. Now, return to your post."

The priest did as he was told. But his glance, as he left her, was filled with awe and admiration.

Maigrey was strongly tempted to hit him.

She stalked out the door, slammed her hand against the controls, shutting it behind her. If only he knew how close she'd come to letting the Corasian have the woman. If only any of them knew how seriously she'd considered it. . . .

Maigrey walked past her room with a brief longing glance. Returning to the bridge, she informed Agis of their status,

received Xris's report on the status of the Corasians, who had
left the ship without further incident.

Outside the viewscreen, the stars of the strange and alien
galaxy glittered brightly. The Corasian mother ship began to
withdraw, the small Corasian spaceplanes ended their web
building, returned home, with the exception of those detailed
to stay behind, act as escort.

Maigrey stared at it, saw none of it. She saw only the abyss.

Chapter ⊷⊶ Three

An oath, an oath, I have an oath in heaven:
Shall I lay perjury upon my soul?
William Shakespeare,
The Merchant of Venice, Act IV, Scene 1

"Coming up on the Lane, my lady. Or at least that's what I assume it is. The readings are identical—"

"The Corasians stole our technology, so it's probably a Lane. The coordinates are in the computer." Maigrey took her place behind Agis, looked out through the bridge's viewscreen. "I've plotted the course as nearly as I can, all things considered. What are our escorts doing?"

"Flanking us. Six to port, six starboard."

"They don't seem much interested," commented Xris. He had left engineering, come to watch the attempt at the Jump.

"They're not," said Maigrey. "If they were, they'd have six hundred out there, with a net around us. But, then, why should they be suspicious? Escaping from them, making a run for it is the last thing they expect us to do. We're in it for the money, remember? They figure we'll meekly follow where they lead. They're going to be shocked as hell when we blast off in the opposite direction."

"There may be six hundred of them waiting for us on the other side."

"I doubt if they can figure out where we're going. This move of ours is bound to baffle the collective mind. It's so completely illogical. And by that time, His Majesty's fleet will have arrived. That should keep them occupied."

"Coming up on the Jump, my lady." Agis sounded the alarm that would send everyone conscious aboard ship scrambling.

Maigrey sat down, strapped herself in, waited, watched the Corasian escorts floating leisurely alongside. They'd be floating leisurely alongside nothing in a moment.

"I've determined our destination," she said. "I've found what appears to be either several large asteroids trapped in an orbit around a small sun or else the remains of a planet. This is where we'll find Abdiel. The system's near the edge of the Void, which makes sense from his viewpoint. In case anything went wrong, the mind-seizer could always slip back to friendly territory. It's uncharted, far from any major Corasian population centers, so that he won't be disturbed in his work. And these fragments are the only objects of any size anywhere near the coordinates that could successfully support life."

"How did you come to know these coordinates of yours, sister?" Xris asked, blowing smoke.

"How could I *not* know them?" Maigrey muttered, not for him to hear.

"That mind-link thing?"

The stars disappeared, the Corasian escort vanished. Maigrey stared into endless nothing.

"Yes," she said aloud. "That mind-link thing."

"Jump completed, my lady," said Agis.

"Thank you. How long until we arrive?"

"Less than twenty-four hours, my lady."

"Very good." Maigrey unstrapped herself, rose to her feet. "I'll send Sparafucile to relieve you. You'd better get some rest, Agis. Xris, are those engineers regaining consciousness?"

"Yeah. They're not feeling real well. Looks like they're suffering from the galaxy's worst hangover. But they'll be able to take over when the time comes."

"Good. I'm going below, to have a little talk with our ship's captain."

Maigrey left. Xris watched after her, then sat down, took the twist from his mouth, examined it.

"You married?" he asked Agis.

The centurion shook his head. "My lord does not permit married men to serve in his Honor Guard. Divided loyalties, he says, make a divided man."

"You sign a contract?

Agis glanced at him, smiled wryly. "A contract is a man's name on paper. It may bind him legally, though that's not certain. Witness the number of lawyers flourishing in the galaxy. We swear an oath."

"Oaths can be broken, same as contracts."

"Yes," replied Agis quietly, "but, if so, the oath breaker

cannot pass the responsibility to another. The matter is between him and God."

Xris leaned back, propped his flesh-and-blood leg on the console. "I'll stick to lawyers."

--◁■ ■▷--

Maigrey entered the captain's quarters without knocking and interrupted what appeared to be an extremely interesting conversation, on Tomi's part, at least. The captain was leaning near Brother Daniel, talking to him in argumentative tones. She snapped her mouth shut when Maigrey came in, cast a swift glance at the priest, and sank back into her pillow. Closing her eyes, she seemed to have fallen into her drugged stupor.

Brother Daniel was flushed scarlet. Seated in his chair, hands folded together, he had not been looking at the woman, consequently missed that conspiratorial glance.

Maigrey guessed what Tomi must be thinking. "Brother Daniel, report to Xris on the bridge. I want you to take a look at the engineers, make certain they are recovering from the effects of the drug."

She was watching Tomi closely, saw her black eyes flick open in involuntary astonishment. The eyes shut quickly again, however.

Brother Daniel stood up. "Yes, my lady."

"And then go to your quarters, lie down, get some sleep. Your duty here is ended," Maigrey added, seeing him start to protest. "The captain will soon be returning to the bridge. You have done an excellent job, Brother Daniel. You are to be commended."

Raising his gaze from the floor, the priest looked once at the woman lying on the bed. Her eyes had opened again. Confused, she was staring at him, her expression pleading. Was she begging him to stay? Hoping, perhaps, that he'd turn on his leader?

Brother Daniel regarded Tomi steadily, calmly. Turning then to Maigrey, he said, "Thank you, my lady," and left the room without another word, without a backward glance. The door slid shut behind him.

Tomi glared at her.

"All right, bitch, you got rid of him. What for? So you can

kill me, not have to worry about him?" Her voice was slurred, her eyes open, but unfocused.

Maigrey came near the bed, stood over it. "You can drop the act, Captain. It isn't necessary. I ordered Brother Daniel to stop giving you the drug. What did you think? That you'd managed finally to seduce him?"

Tomi blinked, her eyes narrowed. "If this is some sort of trick—"

Maigrey leaned down, shut off the paralyzer on the woman's hands. "No trick."

Tomi, continuing to watch her warily, sat upright.

"Your hands and feet will feel numb for a while," Maigrey continued. "It takes the brain time to readjust. You won't do much walking around for an hour or two yet. After that, I presume you'd like to shower, change into your uniform. Then, if you'll come to the bridge, I'll show you our location when we come out of the Jump, give you a report on fuel consumption. You should have enough left to make it back safely across the Void.

"As for us, we'll be disembarking shortly. You'll have to run the ship by yourself for a while. Your lieutenant's injury wasn't serious. He's making progress, but he's not in a fit state to resume his duties yet. As for the passengers, if I were you, I'd leave them in hibernation until you return to our galaxy. Raoul has prepared enough of the drug to keep them under. That will, of course, be your decision. Any questions?"

Tomi was staring at her, incredulous, suspicious. Her limp hands dangled between her knees. "Where are the Corasians?"

"Gone. We shook them when we made the Jump. I presume we'll run into them again before long. It is their galaxy, after all. But, by then, hopefully you will have joined up with His Majesty's fleet."

"His Majesty." Tomi was still fuzzy. "His Majesty who?"

"I'm sorry, Captain. I really don't have time to explain it all to you. I trust that someday you will come to understand."

"You're not turning us over to the Corasians?"

"No, Captain."

"You're giving me back command of my ship—an unarmed cruise liner—in the middle of an enemy galaxy—"

"On the fringes, Captain. It's not as bad as you suppose."

"And I'm supposed to team up with some king? What's he king of? A penal colony?"

"You can do anything you please, Captain. It's your ship again, or it will be in about six hours. I'm offering you what I consider to be your best chance of survival."

"Yeah, well, don't do me any more favors, bitch."

Tomi removed the paralyzers from her ankles. Balancing herself on the nightstand, she tried to stand. Her feet wouldn't support her. She tottered, started to fall, and sat back down on the bed. Swearing softly, she reached down, rubbed her feet and ankles, attempted to bring some semblance of life back to them. Putting her hand on the nightstand, she struggled to stand, swayed unsteadily a moment, then managed to hobble from the nightstand to the bureau, grabbing hold of it just before she fell.

Looking up, her face glistening with sweat, Tomi saw Maigrey, watching her. "You enjoying this, are you, bitch?"

"I was waiting to see if you needed help," Maigrey answered calmly.

"I don't. Not from you. And not from that weak, gimpy-handed virgin you brought—"

Maigrey reached out, caught hold of Tomi's arm. The captain tried to twist free, but Maigrey's grip was strong.

"Listen to me, Captain. And this is just between us, woman to woman. That 'gimpy virgin' as you term him was strong enough in his beliefs and what he perceives as his duty, both to his God and to a man who is his friend and lord, that he was able to overcome not only his desire for you, but his love.

"Yes, he loves you, Captain. Loves you despite the fact that he knows you were only trying to use him. Or maybe he loves you because of that. He understood that your one thought was to try to save the lives entrusted to you. You may not believe me, but we never intended to turn you over to the Corasians. If Daniel had thought that you were in any real and imminent danger, he would have aided you in a minute, as he was about to do when the Corasian threatened you."

"You're damn right. I don't believe you."

"It doesn't matter. I want you only to understand and believe one thing. Brother Daniel is truly a priest. He has been one since he was a child. His life is dedicated to his God. He has taken vows of obedience, poverty . . . and chastity. If it is any consolation to you, Captain, in revenge for what you've suffered, you managed to hurt him deeply in return.

"I don't blame you for what you did, Captain. Neither does Brother Daniel. Remember this, though. You'll recover from what happened to you. The drug will wear off. The memories of the terror will soon fade. You'll be a hero, a celebrity, when you return to the galaxy. I'm no seer, Captain Corbett, but I predict that this adventure will be the making of you. That you will glean from it fame, wealth, status.

"But not him. Not Brother Daniel. He will be forced to bear, for the rest of his life, the scars of the wounds you inflicted on him. Dreams of you will torment his nights. Memories of you will interrupt his prayers—and all the while he'll know that you were just using him, that you despise him. He will ask his God for help and, for him, that help will be forthcoming. But think about suffering like that, Captain, before you ever again call Brother Daniel 'weak.'"

Maigrey let loose her grip on the woman, turned and walked out the door.

Tomi stood, clutching the bureau to keep from falling. On it she saw, where he had left it, the soft leather scrip that belonged to the priest. Fingers feeling stiff and clumsy, she fumbled at it, opened it.

The scourge lay there, neatly coiled together, the thongs stained dark with the young man's own blood.

"Just using him." Tomi's eyes filled with tears. "A lot you know . . . bitch."

Chapter ❖❖❖ Four

Stood on the brink of Hell and looked awhile,
Pondering his voyage . . .

John Milton, *Paradise Lost*

The woman and her male cohorts were on the bridge when Tomi entered. Maigrey stood staring at one of the monitors on which the captain could see portrayed a star map, featuring a smallish star, orbited by what appeared to be an asteroid belt. The soldier was at the helm, the cyborg manning the ship's long-range scanner. The half-breed lounged against a console, legs crossed, arms hidden inside his rags. The priest, Brother Daniel, leaned over the woman's chair, talking with her quietly, apparently discussing the image on the vid before them.

Tomi glanced out the viewscreen. They had come out of the Jump. A star, presumably the one portrayed on the map, could be seen, burning hotly in the distance. She couldn't see the asteroids or, more likely, fragments from a broken-up planet. The *Belle* was on the far side of the star, keeping the star between the planet's remains and the ship. No Corasians in sight.

Maigrey had glanced around on hearing the door open, greeted Tomi with a cool nod, then turned back to her viewing of the map on the screen. The men looked up from their work, as well, gazes flicking over Tomi with varying degrees of interest—the soldier, uninterested, remote; the cyborg, cynical and amused; the half-breed, dark, shadowed, lethal. In his hand, she noticed suddenly, glinted a knife.

Tomi ignored him, ignored the others, looked only at the young priest, the only one who had not looked at her. Brother Daniel, standing with his back to her, must have guessed, from the reaction of the others, who it was who had entered. But he did not turn around.

"Captain is armed," reported the half-breed, eyeing the lasgun Tomi wore defiantly at her side. "You want me to take weapon?"

"Only if she starts making a nuisance of herself," Maigrey answered.

Tomi felt distinctly her own helplessness—armed though she was—against these people. Her skin burned, her fingers curled over the gun, tucked into its holster on her hip. But the vague and desperate plan she'd formed, while in the shower, to seize back control of her ship, take these people prisoner, bring them to justice, crumbled and dissolved. She'd worn the gun mostly out of bravado anyway, and the lurking suspicion that this was still, somehow, all a trick, that she would be seized and taken prisoner again. And she'd use the gun on herself first before she let that happen.

No one made a move toward her, however. No one—except the half-breed—paid any attention to her at all.

Her head ached, the after-effects of the drug. Her legs were wobbly, she was more than half-afraid she might pass out. But she'd be damned if she gave them the satisfaction. Besides, she had to admit she was now extremely curious to know what was going on.

"I wish we could scan it," Xris said, talking through the twist in his mouth. "I don't like going in there blind."

"Not a chance. They might detect us. And we won't be going in blind," said Maigrey. "Here. I've drawn a diagram for you."

"How the hell do you know what it looks like, sister? You been there?"

"No, but I've seen it. Just one of my little talents," she said with a smile that twisted the scar on her face.

"My lady, we've received a signal from His Majesty. The fleet has safely crossed the Void. They're now coming out of hyperspace."

"Right on time."

"According to the code, they're taking up position on the edge of the Void, my lady, awaiting our coordinates."

"Send them to Dion. Private code. No one else."

"Yes, my lady." A pause. "Coordinates received. Transmission ended."

"Are we picking up any sign of the fleet on our instruments?"

Feeling awkward and self-conscious, her head throbbing,

Tomi walked defiantly over to join them. She was aware, the entire time, of the half-breed's suspicious, watchful gaze.

"No, my lady," answered Agis. "Not this far away."

"Then I doubt if Abdiel will."

"What would he do if he did, my lady?" Brother Daniel asked.

Tomi found her gaze straying to the priest's hands, clasped before him. She remembered their touch, strong, yet gentle. . . .

"The Corasians could dump their computer files, make it impossible for us to tell if they've got the complete plans for the space-rotation bomb or not. Or, if they have the plans but haven't transmitted them yet, they might be driven to do so."

"But they'll know we're there when our planes touch down."

"By then, hopefully"—Maigrey glanced at the cyborg—"they'll be too busy."

"And what about my lord?" asked Brother Daniel softly. "Once the mind-seizer knows we're there, isn't it possible that he will . . . will—"

"Kill Sagan?" Maigrey finished bluntly. "No. You see, Brother Daniel, Abdiel always prefers using live bait. If Sagan was dead, I wouldn't come. How long will it take *Phoenix* to make the Jump from the Void to these coordinates?"

Agis referred the matter to the computer. "Four hours," was the answer.

"What's *Phoenix* going to do? Burial detail?" asked Xris.

"If His Majesty doesn't hear from me, or if I tell him we've failed, the warship will attack and destroy the planet."

Xris blew smoke. "Nice to know that if we're captured, we won't suffer long."

"I thought you'd appreciate it. Now, as I was saying before we got off the subject, this is a blueprint of where we're going. The structure appears to be several years old. These rooms you see here are filled with various types of machinery. I'm not certain, but I would guess that it was used as a sort of service station for the planes on the outer perimeter."

"It looks like a goddam ant farm," said Xris, studying the detailed schematic that appeared on the screen.

"Typical Corasian design—everything built below the planet's surface, no need to cope with temperature fluctuations and atmospheric disturbances aboveground. Easy to generate a breathable atmosphere for the slave labor . . . or for the mind-seizer and his disciples."

"We get in . . . where? Through these cavelike things?"

"Yes. You and your men follow this route to the mainframe computer, located here. You will break into the files, determine how far along they are on actually building a space-rotation bomb. Find out, too, how much information on the bomb has been sent into the Interior."

"How many Corasians do you figure we'll run into?"

"An outpost like this would normally have several hundred. But I'm not certain. It appears that they've ceased functioning as a refueling stop. Probably concentrating all their efforts on manufacturing this bomb."

"Several hundred, huh. And while we're breaking into computers, what will you be doing, sister?"

"What I have to. It's no concern of yours."

"Except if you decide His Majesty should blow us all to hell."

She smiled without warmth, pale and cold as moonlight. "We're going into hell. Death's the way out. And now, if there are no further questions . . ."

Agis turned to Tomi. "Captain, you have the helm. The fleet will be here in approximately four hours. I'm picking up no sign of Corasian activity. You should be safe enough until help arrives, provided you do nothing to alert the enemy to your presence."

Tomi grunted, sneered. "If you're waiting for my grateful thanks, don't bother!" Her gaze shifted, fixed on the priest. "And you're going to go down there with her, with them? Onto a planet that's crawling with Corasians?"

"Yes," Brother Daniel answered steadily.

"Don't be a fool! Don't go. It's suicide. She's crazy. This woman—she's Blood Royal. They were all crazy. Stay here . . . on the ship. Stay . . ."

Tomi's voice faltered. She felt Maigrey's eyes on her, continued defiantly: "Stay on board here, with me." Her voice softened. "I want you to. No tricks now. I mean it."

Brother Daniel shook his head.

"All right! Go with them!" Tomi told him. "It won't do any good. They'll still despise you. Just like I do!"

Brother Daniel flinched, the scorn in her voice flicking across him like the lash.

"I'm sorry," he said, looking up at her. "I did what I believed was best. I don't expect you to understand. But I hope someday that you can forgive me."

A sob welled up in Tomi's throat. Angrily, she turned away, stared out at the fiery sun.

"You, bitch," she said abruptly. "Get rid of them. I want to talk to you a minute. Alone."

"The rest of you go on. I'll meet you at the docking bay. I'll be all right," Maigrey added to Agis and Sparafucile, who appeared reluctant to leave her by herself with the captain. "That's an order."

The men filed out. The door shut behind them. Maigrey turned to Tomi. "What is it, Captain? Be brief."

"The Corasians have the space-rotation bomb? Is that on the level? That's why you've done . . . all this?"

"I could tell you that was the reason. But I don't know why you should believe me."

"I don't know why either." Tomi's hands gripped the back of the pilot's seat, her fingers digging into the leather. "And I don't know why I should give a damn what you think about me, but I wanted to tell you that you were wrong. What you said to me . . . back in my room . . . about the priest."

Tomi sighed, put her hand to her head that felt like it was splitting apart.

"I don't despise him. I don't know why I said that. I really do care about him. I didn't, at the beginning. I meant to try to seduce him, to use him to escape. And part of me still meant it. But part of me didn't. Maybe you could tell him that, if you think it would help."

Maigrey regarded the woman silently, her face impassive. "Good-bye, Captain Corbett. Good luck."

"I'm not the one who'll need it." Tomi cast her a grim glance. "You haven't got a prayer and you know it."

"On the contrary," Maigrey replied gravely. "That's the one thing we do have."

Chapter ❦ Five

*And he went consenting, or he was no king, and power
would not fall on him to lead the people.*

Mary Renault, *The King Must Die*

Dion was in Lord Sagan's quarters on board *Phoenix*,
quarters that were now his. Except they weren't his, not really.
Too much reminded him of Sagan, too much of Maigrey. He
heard their voices . . .

Reprimanding, forbidding, ridiculing . . .

And Tusk's and Dixter's and Nola's . . .

Arguing, pleading, advising . . .

DiLuna's, Rykilth's . . .

Flattering, deceiving, lying . . .

And Abdiel. His voice had returned, his whisperings louder
now that Dion was drawing nearer.

Promising, tempting . . .

The cacophony was deafening, confusing.

Opposed to the tumult was silence, terrifying, appalling, the
silence of being alone. Yet, in that silence, he might hear that
still, small voice that had spoken to him before. He might, if he
listened closely, hear his own voice.

And he thought he knew what it was trying to say.

But he would never know until he could listen to the
silence.

"Your Majesty." Another voice.

"Yes, Admiral." Dion switched on the commlink, saw the
admiral's lined and care-worn face on the viewscreen.

"Has Your Majesty received the coordinates from the Lady
Maigrey?"

"Yes, Admiral. I have."

"Time is of the essence, Your Majesty. . . ."

"I'm aware of that, Admiral. I'll be bringing them to the
bridge myself."

He shut down the transmission, stood staring unseeing at the screen.

His choice. His decision.

Dion turned, headed for the doors, the double doors, embellished with a golden phoenix, rising from flames. The centurion standing guard outside came to attention.

"Cato," said Dion, confronting his captain. "You were appointed to the Guard by Lord Sagan. You were loyal to him."

"I would have given my life for him, Your Majesty, and deemed it an honor."

"Would you do the same for me, Captain?" Dion asked.

The centurion's gaze shifted, met Dion's. "Yes, Your Majesty."

"Very good, Captain. Turn out your men, and come with me."

··◁■ ■▷··

General John Dixter stood on the bridge of *Phoenix*, waiting stoically for the Jump. He knew it would make him sick, it always did. The long trip across the Void had been sheer hell. Dr. Giesk had tried this remedy and that, none of which had worked. Giesk had finally given up. It was the doctor's considered medical opinion that this sickness was all in Dixter's head and that if he would put his mind to it, he'd get over it.

Dixter had told Giesk just exactly what the doctor could do with his considered medical opinion and where he could go after he finished doing it. Having dealt with the doctor previously under far from pleasant circumstances, Dixter received considerable satisfaction from this conversation, recalled his words with pleasure as he had staggered back to his cabin and collapsed on his bunk. John Dixter was undoubtedly the only person in the fleet who had actually breathed a heartfelt sigh of relief when they entered the Corasian galaxy.

But they had come out of the Jump, only to make it again. The general should really be in his quarters, now, but there were last-minute details to cover concerning troop landing and deployment, should such be necessary. At least that's what he told himself. Actually he was on the bridge for one reason and one reason alone.

He had the distinct feeling that His Majesty was plotting

something. The allies knew Maigrey'd sent the coordinates of their destination to the king and the king alone. The allies all assumed that he'd share.

Everyone except John Dixter.

"Excuse me, sir."

The general jerked his mind back, tried to remember what it was they'd been discussing. "I'm sorry, Tusk. What were you saying?"

"If the main objective is to get Lady Maigrey and her team off-planet and back to *Phoenix*, then shouldn't we send the marines in, first units lay down covering fire and—"

Tusk stopped talking. Dixter looked around. Admiral Aks had just returned from the commlink.

"His Majesty is bringing the coordinates in person," the admiral informed Captain Williams.

"About time! What took him so long?"

The two had drawn away from the other personnel on the bridge, walked over to stare out the large viewscreen at the assembled ships of the fleet, massed in battle formation, prepared for the inevitable enemy attack once their presence in the alien galaxy became known.

Dixter and Tusk, sitting at a command console, concealed behind a bank of instruments, could hear clearly the conversation between the two officers.

"What the devil has he been doing all this time, sir?" Williams repeated.

"Who knows? Trying to make up his mind what to do, I suppose."

"I'll be glad when Lord Sagan is back to put an end to this nonsense," said Captain Williams.

"You're not the only one." Aks heaved a sigh.

"I suppose, when my lord returns, there can be no question over who is really the ruler of the galaxy?"

The two exchanged significant glances.

"No question whatsoever. There would have been none before this, if Lord Sagan had not been forced to deal with Abdiel."

"I must say, sir, that His Majesty managed the disposition of the fleet quite brilliantly."

"The young man has paid attention to what my lord has taught him. But I fear—"

The rhythmic, measured tramp of booted feet interrupted

them. The entire complement of Honor Guard, dressed in battle armor, accompanied their king onto the bridge.

Adjusting his expression and his uniform, the admiral moved forward, Captain Williams following, to greet their king.

His Majesty smiled pleasantly.

Dixter and Tusk exchanged glances, both of them knew that smile.

"Admiral, all going well?"

"As well as can be expected, Your Majesty." Aks fidgeted nervously.

Williams, handsome face rigid, stood stiffly at attention. "Your Majesty, we have wasted enough time! We are at full alert status, behind enemy lines with an enemy force on the way. Give me the coordinates . . ."

"I am well aware of the situation, Captain," Dion interrupted. "I came to tell you that there has been a change in plans. I will not be giving you the coordinates. I am taking a spaceplane, flying to the Corasian planet alone."

Everyone began talking at once.

"Quite impossible, Your Majesty! Lord Sagan would never permit—"

"Errant nonsense! You have no idea what you're saying. Captain of the Guard, escort His Majesty back to his quarters—"

"Captain of the Guard," intervened Dion, "place Captain Williams and Admiral Aks and anyone else who opens his mouth under arrest."

The centurions brought their weapons to bear on their targets. Aks, face blotchy, red, mottled with patches of white, stared at the beam rifle pointed at him in astonishment. His mouth worked, but no sound came out. Williams was spluttering with outrage.

"Captain Cato, deploy your men." Dion gestured. He glanced around at the crew on the bridge. "You people are relieved of your duties. Stand back, do what you're told, and no one will get hurt."

The Honor Guard moved into position, weapons drawn. Bridge personnel stared at them in astonishment, then, glancing at their officers and finding no help, they raised their hands, stood up, and moved away from their instrument panels. The centurions lined them up against a wall, forced them to sit down on the deck, hands on their heads.

"You, too, Tusk, I'm afraid," said Dion. "I'm going to take your Scimitar and I'll have enough trouble with XJ as it is. I don't want you interfering—"

Tusk stood stock still, his hands at his side, ignoring the beam rifle a centurion held on him. "Damn right I'm gonna interfere. I'm gonna interfere good. I'm coming with you."

"Tusk . . ." Dion looked annoyed, tried to be patient. "You don't understand—"

"And Nola, too. You'll need a gunner."

Dion shook his head. "I'm sorry, Tusk, but I can't let you."

Tusk shoved the beam rifle out of his way, began to walk toward Dion. "I said I was coming."

"Tusk, they'll shoot—"

"Go ahead." Tusk kept walking.

The centurion leveled his weapon on the mercenary.

"Hold your fire," Dion commanded, exasperated. "Tusk, you don't understand! You don't know what I have to do."

"I've got a pretty good guess."

"Maigrey and Sagan tried to protect me from this, Tusk, but they can't. I've got to make the sacrifice."

"I know, kid."

"It may be that this was all I was ever meant to do. All the mistakes, all the evils of the Blood Royal have culminated in me. If I'm the last, the end, then everyone can start over being ordinary. Tusk, I'm taking the bomb with me! And I'll detonate it, if I have to."

"I figured that, too. Don't forget, kid, I'm Blood Royal. Half of me, at least. I guess I got a responsibility myself. I think maybe that's why my old man dumped this on me." He fingered the star he wore in his left earlobe. "He hoped I'd stop and face myself, instead of running from myself all my life. Well, I just quit runnin', kid."

Dion hesitated a moment.

Tusk grinned. "It's up to you, kid. Either take me or shoot me."

"I ought to shoot you. But, all right. Go find Nola and get the plane ready. I'll be there in a minute."

"General Dixter, I'm placing you in command while I'm gone. I'm sorry"—Dion smiled wryly—"but I'm afraid you're getting the rotten end of the deal. You'll have to explain to Rykilth and DiLuna that there's been a change in plans, and unless I miss my guess, they're not going to take this very well.

Wait for my signal. You'll either fly *Phoenix* in to bring us out or be prepared to make the Jump back across the Void. And if that's what's required, you'll have to move fast."

"I understand, sire."

"I'll give you what time I can. I've made calculations, based on Sagan's analysis of the space-rotation bomb. According to my findings, the Void should dissipate the expanding force of the explosion. The destruction should be limited to this galaxy."

"You're insane!" Captain Williams started forward, found a centurion's beam rifle against his chest.

"I trust I can count on you, sir?" Dion asked quietly, ignoring the interruption and the captain.

John Dixter looked at the flaming red-golden mane of hair, the calm blue eyes, and he thought back to that hot day on Vangelis when he'd first seen the face, first experienced that riveting shock of looking into those blue eyes and seeing simultaneously a future and a past.

"You can count on me, sire."

"And if you'd do one more thing for me. I've left messages in my computer files for . . . certain people. If I don't come back, would you see that they are delivered?"

"Certainly, son," said John Dixter.

"Thank you, sir," Dion turned to leave.

I tried to deny him, Dixter said to himself. I kept my mouth shut, hoped he would go away. But I think, all along, I'd been waiting for him. I'd been waiting seventeen years for the story to end. And is this it? Was he meant only to die for us?

Dion left the bridge.

"Don't just stand there, General!" shouted Captain Williams. "The boy's obviously gone mad! You have influence over him. Go after him! Talk some sense into him!"

"I don't think that's possible, Captain. His Majesty wouldn't hear. He isn't listening . . . to us."

··◄■ ■►··

"If you ask me—"

"No one did," growled Tusk.

"If you ask me," repeated XJ loudly, preparing for takeoff, "there are easier ways to avoid getting married."

Chapter ·◦◦◦ Six

As one great furnace flamed, yet from those flames
No light, but rather darkness visible,
Served only to discover sights of woe . . .

John Milton, *Paradise Lost*

The spaceplanes streaked out of the darkness, leaving behind a trail of fire that must remind the Creator of the day when He hurled his rebel angels from heaven. An apt analogy, Maigrey thought, especially considering where it was the fallen angels landed. Her plane touched on the planet's barren surface.

The broken planet was thickly covered with some sort of carbon-based vegetation, probably planted by the Corasians since it was unlikely anything would have sprung up on its own following the cataclysmic destruction of the planet itself. The vegetation, with its numerous twisted limbs and stunted, gnarled trunks, had a treelike look to it.

"Atmosphere thin, but breathable," Agis reported, studying the instrument readings. "Apparently that plant life exudes oxygen."

"Developed for the convenience of their slave labor, no doubt. Another reason why Abdiel would have picked this place."

Maigrey recalled descriptions of the mind-seizer's dwelling on Laskar, recalled her own experience with him, although that had been twenty years ago, when he was both younger and stronger. Even then, Abdiel had been forced to pamper his fragile, frail body like a hothouse violet. He could not last long living in harsh or hostile conditions.

"Will we find any of them here, my lady, do you think?" Agis was asking.

"Any what? Human slaves?" Maigrey looked out at numerous charred tree stumps—a crude food supply for the Corasians, when they couldn't come by anything they liked better. "I doubt it," she said shortly.

She began shutting down her plane's systems. Agis, stoic and reliable, was strapping on his weapons—lasgun, beam rifle, grenades. Brother Daniel, a faint flush on his cheeks, was keeping himself out of the centurion's way. Maigrey had heard, though she had pretended not to, Agis trying earlier to convince Brother Daniel to carry a weapon.

The priest had calmly, adamantly refused. The power of God was with him, he said, and nothing Agis could argue in return would shake Brother Daniel's conviction. Maigrey did not attempt to intervene. She knew how much his faith had cost the young man. She could only trust the Creator would give him some sort of return on his investment.

Maigrey looked out her viewscreen, saw Xris and his men making a dash across the short stretch of open ground between the planes and the tunnel entrances that resembled mounds of dirt thrown up by some burrowing animal. The cyborg and his crew deployed commando style around the mounds, but met no resistance, not a glimmer of the red glow that presaged an encounter with the Corasians.

Following after him, two strange figures traipsed slowly and unconcernedly over the wide-open patch of ground, heading for the tunnel entrance. Raoul, dressed in what the Loti perhaps dimly assumed was camouflage, was wearing a Corasian-red jumpsuit, complete with matching red gloves and flat-heeled pumps. Shuffling along at his side was the Little One, a walking raincoat, topped by the battered fedora.

Xris waved his arm at her, indicating all clear.

"Time to go," she said.

Leaving the pilot's chair, she went to one of the storage compartments, knelt down, and removed an object wrapped in black velvet. The velvet slid unheeded to the deck. Rising, she walked to Agis, held the bloodsword out to him.

"This is my lord's. You will carry it for him, give it to him when we reach him."

"Yes, my lady." Agis took reverent hold of the weapon, and carefully inserted the sword into the weapon's belt around his waist. "Thank you, my lady."

Maigrey buckled on her bloodsword, strapped it on over the black tunic that was her own camouflage in the dark tunnels of the Corasians. Where the folds of the fabric failed to cover it, however, shining silver armor glinted bright in the plane's light. Agis wore his centurion body armor. Brother Daniel had returned to his brown monk's robes; all the arguing in the galaxy had not been able to convince the priest to wear protective clothing.

Maigrey opened the hatch.

Agis jumped out first, beam rifle held ready, met Sparafucile standing watch at the bottom of the ladder. Brother Daniel followed, moving with more ease in the long robes than he had in the less confining layman's clothing. Maigrey stepped out of the hatch, looked over the barren landscape, whose black twisting mass of vegetation contrasted sharply with patches of barren ground.

It was dark, presumably night, though perhaps no day ever came to this fragment of a planet, far from a weak, distant sun. Looking up, she could see clearly the cold, bright stars of a strange galaxy.

Beneath these stars, my lady, you will die.

Was it Sagan's voice warning her? Her nearness already acting to draw him back from the shadowed places that he walked? Or Abdiel's. Taunting, hoping to burn her spirit as laser fire burns the flesh. She saw, in one brief, illuminating flash, as if lightning had split the darkness, an image of silver armor, and a small silver knife, and silver stars. And then the image was gone.

She was, she realized suddenly, being given a choice. Turn back.

And break her vow—her several vows—again?

Turn back! Beneath these stars, you will die.

"Come ahead, lady-mine." The assassin held out his hand to her.

God, if He was around, certainly had a warped sense of humor.

Turn back. . . .

Maigrey gave her hand to Sparafucile. He assisted her to descend to the ground. She inserted the needles of the bloodsword into her palm.

··◆ ➡··

They ran the distance from the planes to the underground entrance, arrived out of breath and light-headed due to the thinness of the atmosphere. The cyborg lounged against the mound of slag and rock, the faint glow of the twist lighting the darkness. He was alone, waiting for them.

"My men went inside to have a look around," he said in answer to Maigrey's questioning glance. "No sign of a welcoming committee. My feelings are hurt. Maybe we weren't expected, after all."

Maigrey activated the bloodsword. Its blue-white plasma blaze illuminated the cavern a short distance ahead, lit a passageway that delved straight and smooth into the rock.

"Never could see much purpose in those things," Xris remarked, eyeing the bloodsword.

"It has its advantages. Like the fact that I'm now connected to Abdiel's mind," said Maigrey quietly. "He knows I'm here. He knows—or thinks he does—what I'm after."

"Quite an advantage," said Xris dryly.

"It is. I'll keep him focused on me and those with me. He won't know about you, or what you're doing."

Guardian. The last of the Guardians come to do battle. You did not heed my warning. Turn back, Lady Maigrey, or here you will be defeated.

Maigrey heard him, did not choose to answer. As in fighting with the bloodsword, she kept her mental shield activated, refusing to lower it to lash out at her opponent. She could never hope to win a contest with the mind-seizer. She could merely hope to hold her own, keep him occupied, maintain her discipline and self-control.

She was now engaged in what would amount to a running battle with him. She could feel him probing, jabbing, seeking to find a way to penetrate her mind's armor; hitting, hacking, slashing, trying to discover the weak point in her defense, force it to give way before his brutal onslaught.

And he was more fortunate than she was. He could afford to devote his entire attention to her. She, on the other hand, had to divide her forces, send forth a portion to find Sagan, reserve a portion to defend herself and her comrades against a real physical enemy. All designed to weaken her, enable him to seize her mind, her soul.

Wary, alert, she moved into the passage. Xris walked at her side. The bloodsword lit their way, but she was using it for more than light. She was using it to focus Abdiel's mind, forcing him to concentrate on her.

A clatter of footsteps distracted her. A man she recognized as belonging to Xris's team appeared out of the darkness.

"About three meters down, this passage splits in two. One heads to the right, slopes at a pretty good angle. The other goes left, runs straight as far as I could see. And we got company coming. A red glow, down the right-hand side."

"That's the way I need to go," said Maigrey.

Xris had switched on a small vidscreen located on the cybernetic arm, studied a diagram of the Corasian outpost. "According to this, we take the left. The central computer room's three levels down, a straight shot. I hope this vision of yours is accurate, sister."

Britt led them to the branching portion of the passage, where they met up with the rest of Xris's men, their weapons drawn and aimed down the right-hand side of the tunnel. Maigrey could see the red glow shining ominously brighter. She glanced around, saw the cyborg still standing in the passage.

"What are you waiting for?" Maigrey snapped. "We'll take care of them. Hurry up, before they see you."

Xris appeared undecided. "You sure you don't need me, sister?"

"I need you," said Maigrey grimly. "I need you to do what I paid you to do. *That's* in the contract," she added with a half smile.

Xris shrugged. "You heard the boss, men. Move out." His force—including Raoul and the Little One—started down the dark left-hand tunnel.

The cyborg drew a twist from his pocket.

"Are you crazy?" Maigrey whispered angrily. "In these passages, they'd smell the smoke from that thing a kilometer away!"

Xris smiled. "Don't worry, sister. When I work, I don't smoke." He put the twist in his mouth, clamped down on it with his teeth. "I chew."

He looked down the passage. The red glow was growing steadily brighter.

"Take care of yourselves," he advised, and took out after his squad.

Maigrey sighed, shook her head.

"Don't worry over man-machine," stated Sparafucile, shrugging, grinning. "His odds . . . better than ours, I think."

"You're right there," Maigrey admitted.

She peered down the tunnel, but couldn't see him or his men for the darkness.

"Let's go."

--◄■ ■►--

Xris adjusted his artificial eye to the night vision lens that made full use of even the faintest light to enhance his visual range. In this instance, the light was coming from somewhere up ahead of him and it, too, was faintly tinged with red.

"Corasian," he muttered, but listening, he couldn't hear the telltale squeak of gears, the faint whir of their motors, the crunch of their wheels over the gritty rock floor of the tunnel.

He did hear the sound of explosions and the high-pitched whine of a beam rifle, but that came from some distance away, behind him, and far to his right.

"Good luck, sister," he said softly.

He continued on, passed several openings that were apparently additional passageways converging into this one. He remembered what he'd said about an ant farm. He attempted to scan them as he passed, but discovered that his scanning device was being jammed, either deliberately or by some sort of weird energy flux. The side tunnels appeared dark and empty, however.

Removing the butt end of the soggy twist from his mouth, Xris tossed it aside, drew out another, and started after his men. Two shadows—one large and one small—blocked his path.

The cyborg raised his weapons hand, started to fire, caught himself just in time. He had recognized the fedora.

"What the hell are you two doing back here?" he demanded in a harsh whisper. "My men are up ahead. Why aren't you with them?"

"I am most extremely sorry, friend Xris." Raoul breathed into his ear. "But the Little One is not as locomotory as your friends and they seemed disinclined to wait for us. In consequence, we fell behind. Then, you see, we have not thought to bring a source of light—"

"Shit," said Xris.

He heard a strange sound, a combination of a growl and chuckle. Looking down, he saw the eyes of the Little One glisten from behind the engulfing collar of the raincoat.

"Please continue on," Raoul said pleasantly. "According to

the Little One, your men are waiting for you up ahead. They do not want to proceed farther without orders. We will have no trouble finding our way now. And we will serve as—how do you military types put it?—the guardians of your rear end."

Xris had the feeling he was more likely to end up with his rear end in a sling by leaving these two behind him, but time was pressing and he didn't relish the thought of tagging along with the Loti and the ambulatory raincoat.

Shrugging his human shoulder, gnawing on the end of the twist, he continued on down the passage. He could hear, behind him, the mincing steps of Raoul—wearing flats—and the hem of a raincoat brushing against the floor.

Xris found his men waiting for him at a bend in the passageway. Beyond that, light shone brightly enough that his eye readjusted to normal vision. He could hear a faint thrumming and beating, some type of heavy machinery, possibly a generator. Above that, the sound of robot bodies, but they were relatively far away.

"Where's the poisoner?" asked Britt uneasily.

"Right behind me," Xris said. "What's up?"

"The passage ends, opens into a large cavelike room filled with water. An underground lake, maybe. The path runs over it, like a bridge."

"Is that where the light's coming from? What's the source?"

"You won't believe this," Lee predicted. "Take a look. The goddam lake's on fire. See for yourself."

Xris edged his way forward, peered into the cavern room. Lee had a slight tendency to exaggerate, but in this instance he hadn't been far wrong. Yellow flame rippled over the surface of the black water, casting an eerie light that flickered, wavered, and danced on the glistening walls of the cave. The flame moved and shifted with the drafts that whistled through the cavern walls. Xris watched, expecting to see the fire die out, but the flame continued burning. Sniffing, he detected an oily smell, like gasoline.

"It's just what it looks like," reported Lee, holding an analyzer, used to test air samples, water, and anything they came across that might prove hazardous. "H_2O with some type of oil floating on the surface. Don't know what the oil is, I'd have to test it further, but it's probably exuded naturally by the rock."

Bernard ran his fingers over the wall. "Nothing in here."

"No," said Lee, consulting his equipment. "This section of the tunnel walls appears to be coated with some type of flame retardant. Safety measure, no doubt. But they couldn't use it in there. It'd put out the lights."

"Toxic?" Xris asked, looking hard at the wavering flames skittering and dancing over the water.

"Not to breathe. In fact, this stuff, when it catches fire, seems to improve the air quality. I'm reading higher oxygen content down here than on the surface. Pretty ingenious, whoever figured it out. Cheap source of light and heat. But," Lee added, "I wouldn't suggest you take a bath in it."

Xris glanced out at the flame-covered lake, the bridge spanning it. "I hadn't planned on it."

"Oh, and, boss . . . I don't think firing lasguns would be such a hot idea in there, either. Or rather, it might be a real hot idea."

"One blast inside that cavern," added Bernard, "and we're likely to find ourselves in the galaxy's biggest toaster oven."

Xris looked at the flames swirling over the surface of the water, the tunnel walls, covered with glistening oil. He holstered his lasgun. "From now on we stick to dart guns, bolt pistols. Britt, looks like you get to use your crossbow. Stash the beam rifles. No sense dragging them around. We'll pick them up on our way back."

Britt lowered his beam rifle to the floor of the cavern, then cast a nervous glance back down the passage. "I thought you said that poisoner was coming along behind. Shouldn't he be here by now?"

The passageway was empty, no sign of Raoul or the Little One. Xris tried his scanner once more, gave it up. Nothing but static.

"I don't trust that Loti. Do what you can to hide the weapons, shove 'em under a rock or something. I'm going back."

The cyborg headed down the passage, moving away from the light. He listened intently, but couldn't hear a sound. The mincing footfalls had ceased, the dragging of the raincoat quieted. He cursed himself for leaving them behind, cursed the woman for bringing them along. Maybe they were in league with this Abdiel character—

His night-vision eye caught sight of motion—Raoul, hiding in a niche in the cavern wall, beckoning to him.

Distrustfully, weapons hand activated, Xris advanced.

"What?" he began.

The Loti shook his head emphatically, placed a gloved finger near his lips. He motioned Xris closer. The cyborg stepped into the niche, was disconcerted to feel the Loti's slender body press up against his, the gloss-covered lips brush against his ear.

"The Little One says that there are two mind-dead moving this way," Raoul whispered, his words little more than a breath. "That direction."

He motioned down the converging tunnel Xris had passed earlier.

The cyborg looked down it, listened. He heard faintly the sound of footsteps.

"They must not know we are here. Make no sound. If they detect anything suspicious, they will report it instantly to their master."

The poisoner's breath was moist on Xris's face, the faint scent of perfume cloying in his nostrils. The passages were deathly silent. The sounds of battle had ceased; the lady had either won or lost. He could hear the footsteps drawing nearer.

His men, at the opposite end, were going about their business quietly, stealthily. That was habitual, routine. And they could easily deal with two of these humans, but from what he had learned about the mind-dead, all it would take was one glimpse of his men and the alarm would be sounded.

The footsteps were nearer, he could hear their voices.

"The woman has entered."

"We are not to stop her?"

"No. Our master is dealing with her. We are to wait here for the young king, who is—"

A series of beeps broke the silence, lights flashed. Xris looked down at his cybernetic arm. The systems were running through their normal checking sequence, advising him that all was in proper working order.

"Shut it off!" Raoul hissed urgently.

Xris glared at him.

"You must!" the Loti insisted.

Xris knew he must. The mind-dead, discussing their orders, hadn't heard anything yet, but it would only be a matter of time. They were near the tunnel entrance. The stabbing beams of their nuke lamps sliced through the darkness, probed here and there.

Cursing bitterly beneath his breath, the cyborg reached over, switched off the arm, felt it fall heavily, uselessly to his side. It was dead weight now, dragging him down, reminding him that he was, in reality, nothing but a cripple. A helpless, useless cripple . . .

"We will patrol this area first," said one of the mind-dead, stepping into the passageway. He turned in the direction of Xris's men. "Then we will take up our position near the outside entrance."

"What do we do when the young king arrives? Apprehend him?" The other mind-dead, the one asking the questions, was a woman.

The two proceeded at a slow pace down the tunnel, moving away from Xris, heading toward his men.

"We are to take him to Abdiel—"

Xris started to activate his arm. So what if they heard him. So what if they alerted their master. So what if everyone in this whole goddam place knew he and his squad were here. He hadn't expected to get out of this without a fight anyway. . . .

Raoul was shaking a gloved finger in front of his nose.

Xris was about to shove the poisoner out of his way when the Little One suddenly darted out of the niche. He clapped a small tube to his mouth, aimed it in the direction of the mind-dead, and blew. Shifting his aim, he blew again.

One of the mind-dead slapped his hand against the back of his neck, as if killing a stinging insect. The female turned to look at him. Her hand came up to her cheek. The male slumped to the ground. A split second later the female toppled down beside him. Their bodies lay still, inert on the cavern floor.

"Now, friend cyborg," said Raoul softly, "you may turn yourself back on. They are dead in body as well as in mind."

Xris activated his arm. He was breathing heavily, sweating, a prey to the panicked reaction he always experienced when his mechanized half—the half he loathed, the half that kept him alive because he was too much a coward to die—shut down.

He moved through the tunnel, stopped to look intently at

the bodies lying at his feet. Putting his toe beneath one of the mind-dead, he flipped her over. She was dead, all right.

"What killed them?"

Raoul knelt down, pointed to a small black object on the woman's cheek—a tiny metal dart.

"Allow me," Raoul advised.

He plucked it out, held it gingerly between gloved fingers, handed it to the Little One. The empath held open one of the many pockets of the voluminous raincoat. Raoul dropped in the dart, retrieved the other, held it up for Xris to examine.

"Do not touch. The poison kills instantly, as you saw. It is quite a painless way to die. The victim feels only a slight stinging sensation, then . . . nothing."

Xris looked over at the Little One. His small hands—and presumably the blowgun—had both vanished back inside the raincoat. The cyborg thought of all the times he'd turned his back on what he had assumed was the harmless empath.

"He got any more of those?"

"Yes, certainly," said Raoul. "It is his favorite weapon. He is so sensitive, you know. It was difficult for him to kill anything without being terribly disturbed by his victim's suffering. This is much easier on him."

"I'm glad we didn't upset his sensibilities," Xris said dryly. He chewed on the end of his twist, glanced up and down the passageway. "Any more of these mind-dead around?"

Raoul looked at the Little One. The fedora replied in the negative.

"No, it is safe to proceed, although we should make haste. Your men have sighted Corasians, entering the Room of Fire."

"That tears it." Xris took the twist from his mouth. "They're going to know we're here, now."

"A pity," agreed Raoul, shrugging. "But it cannot be helped. And this did not go to waste. Abdiel, at least, does not know we are here. And these mind-dead will not be around to apprehend the young king."

Britt appeared at the end of the tunnel, waving his hand.

"Boss!" he called in a low, urgent voice. "We got company!"

"I'm coming," Xris looked at the Loti, still kneeling beside the bodies. "What about you two?"

"In a minute, friend cyborg. We have something we must do first." Raoul raised his eyes to meet those of the Little One.

Xris clamped his teeth over the twist, shook his head, turned, and started down the tunnel.

"Not yet, Abdiel does not know you and I are here. But he will." The voice was Raoul's. Only a murmur, but it came clearly to the cyborg's ear.

"Now what?" Xris muttered, paused, looked back.

The Little One removed a small case from the pocket of his coat, handed it solemnly to Raoul. The Loti opened it with equal solemnity, took something out, slid it into the hand of the corpse.

Xris adjusted his cybernetic eye, brought the object in the corpse's hand into sharp focus.

A gold-embossed business card carried the message:
COMPLIMENTS OF SNAGA OHME.

Chapter ❦ Seven

> . . . of whom to ask
> Which way the nearest coast of darkness lies . . .
>
> John Milton, *Paradise Lost*

Maigrey, Agis, and the half-breed crouched on opposite sides of the dark tunnel, weapons ready, waiting. Brother Daniel was some distance behind them, posted near the intersection of the two passageways. He had orders to run back quickly if he saw anything. Up ahead, the red light at the tunnel's entrance was bright, glowing, but no sign of Corasians.

"What the hell are they doing?" Maigrey snapped irritably. "Why don't they attack?" She had shut off the bloodsword, shut off its telltale light. Unfortunately she couldn't shut off the voice that came with it.

They are waiting for you, my lady. You must go that way, you know. You must go that way in order to reach Sagan.

"Maybe they're waiting for us," suggested Agis, an unknowing echo. "Hoping to draw us out into the open."

"I go have look," volunteered Sparafucile, and before Maigrey could stop him, the assassin was gliding silent as death down the passage.

She watched him, his body a shapeless dark mass silhouetted against the red light, until he merged with the shadows and vanished.

A short time later he reappeared again, almost directly in front of her, startling her.

"Not fire-bots. Dead-ones"—(the half-breed's term for mind-dead)—"only. Many dead-ones, carrying red lamps. We meant to think they are fire-bots."

"Why?" demanded Agis, suspicious. "That doesn't make sense."

"A mind game," said Maigrey. "Anything to keep us off-balance."

Yes, my lady. Mind games. You are so good at them, too. But you find them wearing, don't you? It saps the ability to concentrate on more important matters. Dion is coming, Maigrey? Did you know?

"Lady, we go now. We not stay here! Dangerous!"

Sparafucile's hand on her arm, shaking her.

He's been talking and talking. I heard his voice, Maigrey realized. I wonder what it was he's been saying? I suppose it must have been important. . . .

"Dead-ones block passage. But wall like arm. We hide behind arm, shoot." The assassin gestured, as if firing over a barricade. "Weird place," he added. "Water burn."

"Burning water," Maigrey repeated absently.

Certainly Dion is coming, Mind-seizer. That's the plan. He's coming to destroy you.

Destroy me? Or join me? Not that it matters to you, my lady. Dion comes to me alone. And you won't be around to help him.

"You'll find he doesn't need my help, Mind-seizer," Maigrey said aloud. Alone! Surely, not alone! He was wiser than that now, wasn't he? She could see Dion clearly, see him in the cockpit of the Scimitar, see . . .

Maigrey sighed in relief. He wasn't alone. But he was deceiving Abdiel into thinking he was. And she was the one who might shatter the illusion. Abruptly, she wrenched her mind away from Dion, before the mind-seizer could touch him through her, discover the truth.

"My lady." It was Agis, quiet, respectful. Brother Daniel stood beside him; both regarding her with concern. "Are you all right?"

My God, what a stupid question! No, she wasn't all right. She was threatening empty air, shouting answers to questions no one had asked. She looked at Agis, saw Abdiel's face. And she didn't dare banish the mind-seizer's image. She had to keep him before her, keep that keen mental gaze fixed on her, not on Dion.

Half of me's not here, she wanted to tell Agis. Half of me's fighting a battle you can't see or understand. And, if I lose, there's no way you can save me!

She wanted to say all this . . . But how could she, to Abdiel's mocking visage?

"Move out," was what she finally said, aloud.

They continued down the tunnel, no longer worried about keeping silent. Sparafucile made less noise than the darkness, but Agis's boots thudded on the rock floor. The heavy beam rifle he carried rattled, whined as it powered up. Maigrey's armor jingled like myriad small, silver bells. Brother Daniel's robes swished and flapped.

Stealth wasn't important now. Abdiel knew they were there, knew they were coming. Haste was important. Maigrey had to reach Sagan. When she found him, she would be whole again.

The half-breed's "arm" in the wall turned out to be a natural rock formation—a groin, that stretched out into the passageway, forming a crude barricade. Beyond, Maigrey could see the red nuke lamps clearly now, against a backdrop of yellow light that wavered like flames.

Water burn. She recalled the half-breed's words, wished she'd asked him then what he meant. It was too late now. Shadowy figures were visible, moving back and forth across the light.

Something whizzed past her, making an odd sound that she didn't at first identify.

"Bolts," said Agis. "They're shooting bolts at us."

Odd, Maigrey thought. Why not lasguns? Beam rifles? Far deadlier, far less need for accuracy.

"Hold your fire!" she commanded, though there was really no need. Agis and Sparafucile were expert enough to realize that the mind-dead could only shoot blindly into the darkness. Returning fire from this distance would do little damage to the enemy, give away their position.

More bolts shot past, striking the walls, the ceiling, clattering on the rock floor.

Maigrey had switched the bloodsword from offensive to defensive, dimming its bright light, using it to shield herself and Brother Daniel, who had been instructed to keep close behind her. But, she realized, she need not waste the energy.

Either these mind-dead were terrible shots or they were purposefully firing so as not to hit anything.

Ah, but you mustn't die, my dear. That wouldn't suit my plans at all.

You better kill me, Abdiel. Now, when you have the chance.

Maigrey crouched behind the barricade. Bolts slammed into it, whistled above it. Brother Daniel huddled beside her.

Sparafucile put his hand on the priest's shoulder, shoved him roughly to the floor.

"Priest, lie down!" the assassin ordered.

Brother Daniel meekly obeyed. Maigrey took a grenade from her belt, intending to lob it over the barricade. The half-breed stopped her.

"No good. Fall in water. Make only big splash."

Water again. "I've got to see what it's like in there," Maigrey said irritably. "Agis, cover me. Make them keep their heads down while I take a look."

The centurion lifted the beam rifle, positioned it on the top of the rock barricade, and fired.

The result was completely, totally unexpected.

A roaring sound, an explosion. Clouds of flame, that roiled out of the cavern, burst over the barricade.

Agis dropped the beam rifle, ducked behind the barricade, pulled Maigrey down with him. She had the vague impression of Sparafucile hurling himself to the floor.

Maigrey covered her face, her eyes, wished desperately she could cover her ears. Screams—the screams of humans being burned alive—rose horribly above the crackling and hissing of the fire. From somewhere near her, Brother Daniel, voice breaking, prayed for the souls of the dying.

In an instant it was over.

The screams were silenced. The flames died to the flickering, wavering yellow light they'd seen earlier.

"My lady!" Agis, face black with soot, leaned over her.

She coughed, pushed him aside. Sitting up, she glanced around dazedly. "What . . . happened?" she managed to gasp.

Sparafucile peered cautiously over the barricade. The half-breed's deformed face was awed. "Look, lady-mine!"

Yellow flames flickered on the surface of a small lake, located at the far end of a domed cavern room. Scattered around the floor in front of the water lay the charred remains of the mind-dead, perhaps as many as twenty. The bodies were burned beyond recognition. It was obvious, from the distorted postures, that each had died in agony.

"Dear God, have mercy!" Brother Daniel whispered.

"I fired and . . . the room exploded," said Agis, shaken out of his accustomed stoic calm. He looked down perplexedly at the beam rifle. "I never saw one do that before."

"Oil," said Maigrey, sniffing. Running her fingers along the surface of the rock barricade, she held them to the faint glow of the light. "It's on the surface of the water, maybe on the walls themselves. That's why they were using bolt weapons."

"But they knew," Agis protested. "They had to know we'd use laser fire—"

"They didn't know," Maigrey said softly, sliding back down behind the barricade. "But *he* knew. *He* sent them to die like that."

"It not make sense," remarked Sparafucile, rubbing a grizzled chin. "There were many of them, they could have killed one, maybe two of us."

"He doesn't want us to die," Maigrey said flatly. "At least not yet. Not now." She tried to tell herself it didn't matter how these poor, wretched, trapped souls of his died. She would have been forced to kill the mind-dead anyway. God's children. Abdiel had done them a favor.

It does matter, doesn't it, my dear? You hear their screams echo in your head. Your spirit sinks. Your energy seeps away. And you are right about one thing, Lady Maigrey. I don't want you to die. And don't you wonder why? You should, my dear. You really should.

Maigrey rose to her feet. She couldn't believe, suddenly, how tired she was.

"We'd better keep going. No, Brother Daniel," she added. "There's no time for that. Besides, their souls are resting in far more peace now than the wretches ever knew when they were alive."

Agis picked up his beam rifle.

"I think you not use that anymore, eh?" said Sparafucile, grinning.

"I think you're right," agreed Agis ruefully and slung the rifle over his shoulder.

"Ancient weapons best, anyway. Never fail you. Never need charging. Only sharpened."

The half-breed flicked his wrist. A gleaming knife slid out into his palm, the blade appearing in his hand like a sixth finger. He flipped the knife in the air, expertly caught it, thrust it back into his belt, from which protruded the hilts of several more "ancient weapons."

"These won't do us much good against Corasians," observed the centurion.

"They're better than nothing," Maigrey said wearily. "It doesn't—" She stopped, bit her lip.

It doesn't matter what weapons you carry, isn't that what you were about to tell them, my dear? How true. I want you alive, not them. You'll watch them die, one by one, with the knowledge that you brought them to their deaths! And the loss of each will drain you that much more.

"Let's go," Maigrey said, and moved around the barricade into the cavern lit by the fiery water, the cavern that smelled of oil and burned flesh.

She picked her way among the bodies, refusing to look at them, refusing to hear the echo of their screams. She wished she could refuse to play Abdiel's game, because he was good. He was getting to her. Why wasn't he going to kill her? Surely, he must know that if she reached Sagan, the two of them would destroy him. Yet Abdiel didn't even appear to feel threatened! What did he have that he knew she feared more than death? . . .

She crossed the cavern room, the others coming behind her, reached the entrance to another passageway, sloping downward. Beyond it she could see a cavern chamber, larger than the one in which they stood. Nuke lamps hung from the ceiling. The room was filled with machines of some sort, working busily, to judge by the noise and vibration beneath their feet. Beyond that room she'd find Sagan. . . .

Yes, go. Wake Sagan. Bring him back to life. He will not thank you, my dear. The life you both face is a terrible one.

Notice I said "life" you face, Lady Maigrey. Not death. I have no intention of killing you, though you must kill me.

And that may not be so easy. But by all means, keep trying, my dear. Only the dead are without hope.

The dead, and those who wish they were dead.

"The serpent's tooth," said Maigrey.

She stopped in the entrance, unable to move, staring into the darkness. At last, she understood.

The others looked at her, looked uneasily at each other. She began to shake, leaned against the oil-slick wall. Agis started to go to her aid, but Brother Daniel stopped him.

"No, this is her battle. We cannot help her. We cannot defend her."

The serpent's tooth. Now you understand. The two of you—Sagan, yourself—infected by the poison.

What will happen to the two of you? You will return to your galaxy. You will travel from planet to planet, and from each begins to come rumors of the atrocities you will commit. Torture, rape, mass murder, cannibalism—your crimes will grow ever more heinous. And who can stop you? The power of the Blood Royal is yours to command! You are superhuman— devils, demons.

The people curse your names, curse the Guardians, curse the Blood Royal.

But, as much as you horrify others, even more do you horrify yourselves. Half of you, sane, watches the other half turn into a homicidal maniac. You long to die; the instinct of survival is strong, however. When at last they do manage to trap you, they will drag you to your execution, struggling and shrieking like the cowards you are.

And the people of the galaxy, friends, relatives of those you butchered, will watch you die and rejoice in the final downfall of the last of the Guardians.

Maigrey drew a deep, shivering breath, pushed herself away from the wall. "We haven't fallen yet!" she said to the empty darkness. "Derek and I! Together, we will fulfill our destiny and destroy you!"

There is that possibility. It is the risk I run and well worth it for such a reward. But for you there is no risk, Lady Maigrey. There is only a terrible choice. For if you rescue the Warlord and if, by some chance, you two destroy me, Derek Sagan will fulfill his destiny and destroy you!

··◄■ ■►··

Xris and his squad ambushed the Corasians in a largish tunnel, located on the opposite side of the room with the fiery lake. Cover was practically nonexistent, but Xris didn't dare use his missiles around the oil-slick water. The commandos squeezed into niches, crannies, hid themselves behind places where the rock jutted out, and waited.

If this doesn't work, Xris thought, arming his weapons hand with his specially-designed missiles, we can kiss ourselves good-bye. He counted, by the sound, ten soldiers. And he only had ten missiles.

The Corasians trundled into the passageway. The moment the lead alien gave a sign that it had, with its sophisticated sensing device, detected the danger, Xris lifted his weapons hand, fired. The missile rocketed directly into the robot "head".

The Corasian exploded. Its casing blew apart, electronic arcs crackled and surged around it. But the alien inside wasn't dead. The fiery red ameboid body slid to the floor. His men began to fire bolts at it. They might have thrown rocks.

The other Corasians were firing now. Laser beams streaked through the darkness. A blast caught Britt in the leg, knocked him off his feet. The red blob, pulsing with horrible life, slithered toward him.

Cursing bitterly beneath his breath, Xris prepared to fire again.

This means we come up short. This means we're finished. This means . . .

A laser beam streaked past him, shattered the rock wall behind him. Xris didn't even duck. Was it imagination? A trick of the eyes, half-blinded by the energy bursts? Or was the Corasian dying.

"Xris! You killed it!" Lee shouted. "Hit 'em again! Hit 'em again!"

··◆= =◆··

The cyborg kicked aside shattered pieces of steelglass casing, prodded the slowly darkening blob that had once been inside it with the toe of his boot.

"That's the last one," said Lee, coming up behind him. "At least we know now those missiles of yours work."

"Yeah," Xris muttered, spitting tobacco, "everyone in the whole goddam place knows they work."

"You got any idea where we are? How far we need to go?"

Xris activated the small screen on his cybernetic arm, consulted the diagram. "Not far, according to this. But it's going to seem a lot farther if every Corasian in the place stands between it and us."

Turning, he walked back to the cavern room entrance. Britt sat propped up against a wall. The flickering firelight glistened on sweat that covered his face. His eyes were closed. Raoul was packing up a medi-kit.

"How's that leg?" Xris asked, kneeling beside him.

Britt opened his eyes, tried to smile. He swallowed, grit his teeth. "Fine. I'm just . . . taking a little rest. But I'll be ready to move out when you give the word. Boy, those missiles of yours are really something."

"Too bad I didn't bring more."

"Say, could I bum a twist?"

"You're quitting. Remember?"

Britt grinned weakly. "Yeah, this'll be my last one."

Xris handed over a twist, lit it for him. "Guess the lady won't mind if we smoke now."

He stood up in response to a look from Raoul, who drew him off to one side.

"The Little One says the man is lying. He is *not* fine," Raoul stated, shaking his head.

"I know he's lying! He knows he's lying! If that's all you've got to tell me, we don't have time—"

"If you please, I've frozen the injured portion of the leg," continued the Loti, "and stopped the bleeding, but that is only temporary. He should not be moved—"

"We're not leaving him behind. You know what those things would do to him. They'd eat him alive! *After* they made him talk."

Raoul lowered his voice. "I am aware of that. And I have with me a certain drug—"

Xris grabbed hold of the Loti by the collar of the red jumpsuit, twisted, half choking him. "Don't even think it!" he said softly, lethally.

Releasing his grip, he shoved the Loti away. "We'll work out something."

"I was about to say, before you got emotional"—Raoul, mildly offended, smoothed his wrinkled clothes—"that I have a drug that will kill any sensation of pain. Your friend would be under the illusion that the leg *was* fine. Of course, what harm he will do to himself while walking on it is—"

"—a damn sight better than the harm that will come if we left him. Go ahead. Give him the drug. And, thanks," Xris added grudgingly. "I'm sorry if I was rough on you. But I thought—"

"I have that, as well," replied Raoul, smiling serenely, removing a vial from the belt he wore around his waist, "but I did not think you would take kindly to the suggestion. The painkiller takes effect quickly. He will be ready to travel in only a few minutes."

"Good." Xris stepped over and around hunks of broken

steelglass. The cyborg moved cautiously, the floor was slippery with oil and dead Corasians. "See anything?"

Harry was covering their exit. He shook his head.

"No, but that wailing noise is slicing right through my skull! What the devil do you figure it is?"

"An alarm of some sort. We're about ready to move out. We head down this passage, then into another one of these caverns. Off that, there should be another passage leading to the computer room."

"How's Britt?"

"That shot tore hell out of his leg. He's in shock, lost a lot of blood. But the Loti's giving him something. He'll be feeling no pain, at least."

"Goes till he drops over dead, huh, boss?"

"You got a better suggestion?" Xris asked grimly.

Harry glanced down at the dead Corasians, shook his head. "No, boss. Sorry."

Britt hobbled up to meet them. "This guy's a genius." He threw his arm around Raoul, squeezed him tight. "The leg feels great! I feel great! In fact, I've never felt this good in my whole life!"

The Loti flushed delicately, shook his head in modest deprecation.

"Who knows," Britt continued with ghastly cheerfulness, "I might have 'em amputate the damn leg, give me one like yours, Xris."

"You should be so lucky," said the cyborg, smiling.

Britt laughed, limped ahead, on down the tunnel.

"You and Bernard stay with him," Xris ordered Harry, who nodded.

The cyborg glanced down at the rock floor, at the bloody footprints his friend left behind.

Taking a twist from his pocket, Xris stuck it between his teeth.

"Yeah, you should be so lucky."

Chapter ✦ Eight

> . . . I fled and cried out *Death!*
> Hell trembled at the hideous name, and sighed
> From all her caves, and back resounded *Death!*
> John Milton, *Paradise Lost*

The tunnel was dark, silent, dimly lit by the flickering light coming from the cavern ahead. Maigrey and her small force moved forward cautiously, Agis in front, the half-breed guarding the rear. When they reached the entrance to the machine room, the mind-dead opened fire.

Laser bursts exploded around them. Apparently, as Agis said grimly, this area of the caverns was "safe" for laser fire, probably due to the presence of the machines. Nuke lamps hung from various portions of the machinery's anatomy, lit the room. The lamps swung and rocked with the machinery's pounding vibrations, their light stabbed erratically here and there, caused the shadows to expand and contract, made the lifeless metal come alive.

The four took refuge behind one of the strange machines that looked as if it had been designed by a drug-crazed Loti on a bad trip, and attempted to get a fix on the enemy's position. It became quickly obvious that they were outnumbered, outgunned, and pinned down. They fought until the beam rifles were drained of energy, the lasguns' firepower depleted. They flung the useless weapons to the floor, drew dart pistols and bolt guns, and fought on.

Time and again, the mind-dead could have taken them. Time and again, it seemed that their position must be overrun. But the enemy held back.

And then, abruptly, all firing ceased.

"What does it mean?" whispered Brother Daniel. Creeping up to Agis, he handed the centurion what spent bolts and darts he'd been able to glean from those fired at them. "I'm sorry.

This is all the ammunition I could find. But perhaps they've gone?"

"Not likely," said Agis grimly. He'd taken a bolt in the right arm, was white-faced with the pain, but had transferred his gun to his left hand and continued fighting. "Regrouping for the final assault."

Sparafucile perched above them on a ledge formed by a part of the machine. His rags hung around him. His eyes, peering intently into the darkness, gleamed with blood lust. He held long knives in both hands and reminded Maigrey of some hulking, sharp-taloned bird of ill omen, eager to swoop down and deal death.

"I think there be nothing out there," said the half-breed. He sounded disappointed.

"Impossible," Agis snapped, fighting against the pain of his wound. "They're trying to trick us, make us let down our guard."

"No," said Maigrey, "Sparafucile's right. They're gone. They were ordered to go."

She stood up, looked past the machines to the opposite side of the room, to a cavern in which it seemed she had lived herself for these last weeks.

"It's safe. We can go on." But she didn't move, except to lower her bloodsword, close her eyes.

She was exhausted. And it wasn't physical fatigue. A little rest, time to catch her breath, ease cramped muscles, and her body would be able to proceed. It was her spirit that longed to crawl quietly into darkness and find refuge there, as had Sagan's. She was frightened, frightened for her men, for Dion, frightened for Sagan, for herself.

Fear was Abdiel's weapon. She knew it. She continued to try to fight, but it was a losing battle. She was alone, the silver armor that protected her flesh could not save her spirit from the continued jabs that portrayed to her the lives of those bitten by the serpent's tooth, the soul forced to watch in appalled horror from behind prison walls erected by the mind.

"My lady! Are you hurt?" Brother Daniel asked, hovering.

Maigrey shook her head, smiled bitterly. "That would be difficult. Not a shot came near me. See to Agis's wound."

Sagan. She needed Sagan. She couldn't bear being alone like this.

Agis leaned up against a portion of the machine, was trying unsuccessfully to tie a crude bandage around his arm.

"Let me do that," offered Daniel. "Move over here, into the light."

"It's nothing," said the centurion, jerking away from the priest's touch.

"That's an order, Agis," said Maigrey.

She looked around. Sparafucile had leapt from his perch, disappeared into the darkness on some errand of his own. Maigrey, sighing, turned back to the centurion.

"How bad is it?"

"Not as bad as it might have been," said Brother Daniel.

The priest probed the wound with gentle expert hands. Agis stood quiet beneath Daniel's touch, jaw clenched, lips pressed tightly together. "A small explosive charge on the tip drove the dart through his armor, but the armor still kept it from penetrating too deeply and entering the bone."

"Can you take it out?" Agis asked. Sweat glistened on his face.

"Yes. But it's one of the barbed kind."

"I know. You have to push it on through. Go ahead. If you're strong enough." Agis looked into Brother Daniel's pale face.

"I'm strong enough," the priest said quietly. "I have some painkiller in my kit, but I don't suppose you'd take it."

Agis shook his head, braced himself.

Maigrey knelt beside him. "Hold on to me," she said.

At first, she thought he would refuse, but then his hand clasped around her forearm. She took hold of his arm and held tightly.

"Lord Sagan is in the next room," she said to divert his mind from what must come.

"I won't take you by surprise," said Brother Daniel. "It's best to be prepared. When I count three. One . . ."

"The chamber is large and filled with the burning water. Four bridges span it, meeting in the center."

"Two . . ."

Maigrey felt Agis's grip on her arm tighten. He kept his eyes open, focused on her. "Yes, my lady," he said steadily. "Go on."

"There are four entrances into the room, located at ninety-degree angles from each other. You and Sparafucile will guard those while Brother Daniel and I—"

"Three."

Brother Daniel gave a sudden shove. Agis caught his breath, stifled a groan. His eyes shut, his fingers clenched painfully over Maigrey's arm. She held him fast. He drew a deep, quivering breath, relaxed his grip.

Brother Daniel held up the blood-covered bolt for Agis to see, then sprayed the wound with the combination bandage and disinfectant he carried with him in his medkit.

"This will numb your arm. I can't help that," he said, seeing Agis's frown. "It's either that or you'll bleed to death."

Maigrey offered him her canteen. "Only water. I wish it were stronger."

Agis took it, smiled at her. "Thank you, my lady."

"Don't thank me. Thank Brother Daniel."

"All thanks should be offered to God," said the priest. Packing up his kit, he stood up, reached out his hand to Agis.

The centurion hesitated, then slowly raised his hand to the priest's. Brother Daniel eased Agis to a standing position, steadied him when he swayed on his feet.

"I'll be fine. Where's the half-breed?"

"Here," said Sparafucile, materializing out of the darkness as if he were made of it and had only decided at the last moment to take shape and form. "I bring weapons. The dead provide." He gestured. "It safe to go on. I look. Dead-ones gone."

Of course, it's safe to proceed. I have cleared the way. I would have enjoyed amusing myself with you longer, but Dion's spaceplane is arriving, and I must put my forces to better use. The young man has brought the bomb with him. Extremely thoughtful, to save me the trouble of going after it. Yes, my dear, I'm to have that, too.

I should warn Dion, Maigrey thought, and it took an effort to think, just as it seemed to take an effort to breathe. No, she decided wearily. He knows the danger already.

Sparafucile plucked at her sleeve. "We wait here long enough, maybe more mind-dead come to let us kill them. Except maybe this time they find their aim and kill us."

"He's right, my lady," said Agis. "We should leave this place."

"It's the silver armor," she told him. "It's so heavy. I could walk easier if it weren't for the armor."

They were all staring at her, puzzled, concerned.

Maigrey shook her head. "Never mind." She sighed, and moved on.

··⇐ ⇒··

"Xris!" called Lee urgently.

The cyborg halted, turned.

Britt had collapsed. He lay on the floor of the dark tunnel, Lee's arm cradling his head.

"Sorry, Xris. Damn stuff that poisoner gave me's makin' me drowsy. I'll take a little nap—" His eyes closed.

"Sure," said Xris, kneeling beside him. "You rest. We'll pick you up on the way . . ."

"He can't hear you, Xris." Lee laid the flaccid body down on the rock floor. "He's gone."

Xris removed the half-smoked twist from the corpse's ashen lips, tossed it with a sudden, angry jerk to one side of the passage. Then he stood up. "Move out."

"We just gonna leave him?" Harry demanded.

"He's not going to care one way or the other now. Go on. Move out."

The others left. Xris stood a moment longer, staring down at the body. "You'd have made a rotten cyborg anyway."

They continued down the tunnel, moving warily, weapons drawn. No red glow appeared, however. The corridor was dark, silent. Rounding a corner, they came to a section where several passageways converged.

Xris motioned to his companions to fall back. Cautiously, keeping his body flat against the wall, he looked down one of the passages. About ten meters distant, at the end of the long corridor, was a dimly lit room, filled with banks of winking, blinking light. He adjusted his vision, enhanced the image, brought it nearer. He could see the computers themselves now, in sharp focus.

"That's their main frame system?" he muttered. "Hell, I haven't seen anything like that outside of a museum."

"Sure seems quiet," said Lee uneasily.

"Sure does. I don't like it." Xris flattened himself against the wall.

Actually, it wasn't quiet. Strange machines were clanking and clattering and pounding, added to that were whining and whirring sounds he could hear coming from the antique computers and the teeth-jarring wail of a siren. But Xris knew what Lee meant. It was too damn quiet.

The cyborg risked another look at the room that housed the Corasians' central computer system. It was large and would have ordinarily been dark, since Corasians needed no lights by which to work. But nuke lamps had been added, probably for the convenience of the mind-dead, whose human eyes required light to see.

Two of the mind-dead stood outside the door of the room. Guards, most likely. By their rigid, unmoving stances, they could have been either asleep or truly dead, but he had the distinct and unpleasant feeling that they were very much awake and alive.

He pulled back. "Two zombies guarding the entrance. No sign of Corasians, though. I wonder where those bastards have got to all of a sudden."

"They are preparing to attack the young king and steal the space-rotation bomb," stated Raoul.

Xris glared at him. "Oh, yeah? How the hell do you know that?"

"I do not know. The Little One knows."

"He reads Corasian minds, too?" Xris eyed the raincoated figure suspiciously.

"He reads the collective mind. It is not pleasant for him and he does not enjoy it. Corasians think of little else except devouring."

"So where are they now?" Xris asked, putting a twist in his mouth.

"They have an army, massed on the surface. When the spaceplane belonging to the young king sets down, they will launch an attack. Mind-dead fight among them. What are we to do?"

"What we were paid to do. Check out these files." Xris took the twist out, pointed it toward the empath. "He know of any more zombies around?"

"No. Only the two at the end of the corridor, who are currently unaware of our presence."

"They're going to be aware of us pretty soon, unless your friend has a real good set of lungs."

"His lungs are in excellent condition for someone his age, but I am not sure—"

"I was referring to his talent with that blowgun," Xris said shortly.

"Ah, you were being facetious." Raoul gave a polite smile. "Might I see for myself?" He slid around the cyborg, glanced down the tunnel, and came back, shaking his head. "The distance is far too great."

"Damn! I'd like to get in there without them or anyone else knowing about it." Xris stuck the twist back in his mouth, chewed on it irritably. "Just what the hell are you doing?"

"I will deal with the mind-dead." Raoul was pulling back his long hair, tying it behind his head in a knot. "Please, allow me," he added, giving Xris a charming smile. "It's my turn."

"How—"

"Wait, please."

The Loti closed his eyes, concentrated a moment, then opened them. The pupils were fixed, unmoving. The eyes held no expression, the face was smooth, impassive.

"Do you think I can pass?" he asked in the dull, lifeless tone of the mind-dead.

"You're crazy," said Xris. "All right, you look like one of them, but these guys must all know each other by sight. They'll shoot you before you can get close enough—"

Raoul shook his head, began to carefully draw his gloves off his hands. "The mind-dead have one flaw. Each is connected to only one being and that is Abdiel. They do not care about anyone else, including each other. Consequently, they do not know each other. Don't touch, please."

Raoul drew his hands aside.

"You're going to need this." Xris was holding out a dart pistol. "Unless you're afraid you'll break a nail."

"My nails are quite strong. It is the cuticles with which I have a—Ah, facetious again." Raoul smiled, bowed. "Thank you, but I have no use for your weapon."

Flexing his hands, he turned and, before Xris could stop him, strolled languidly and gracefully out into the passageway. As he walked, the Loti's body posture altered. He set his shoulders, stiffened his back and neck. He stared straight ahead, proceeded down the corridor with the fixed and unalterable purpose of one of the mind-dead, whose mental faculties have been directed toward a single goal.

"Spooky character, that poisoner," said Lee.

Xris glanced meaningfully at the empath, whose eyes glittered brightly beneath the brim of the overlarge hat. He wondered suddenly what Raoul meant by "someone his age."

"Hell, the little guy knows I'm thinking it," Lee asserted defensively. "I might as well say it."

Xris had to admit Lee had a point. The cyborg turned back to see what was happening in the tunnel.

Raoul walked with even, measured steps toward the computer room. The two guards couldn't see him, due to the darkness, but they must surely hear him. If so, they gave no sign of noticing.

Xris refocused his eye, kept the Loti in sight.

Raoul stepped into a pool of harsh light. The mind-dead moved, at last. Xris swore softly.

"What's going on?" demanded Harry in a loud whisper. "Well, damn it, I can't see anything!"

"They've pulled guns on him," reported the cyborg.

"Should we go?" Lee held his weapon ready.

"No, give him a chance. They haven't shot him yet."

"What are you doing here?" The mind-dead raised their weapons. "This zone is restricted."

"Abdiel sent me," Raoul answered. He stood between the two mind-dead, his hands open, palms out, to indicate he was unarmed. "I have a message for you."

"What is your message?"

The mind-dead lowered their weapons; the name of Abdiel removing any suspicions they might have had.

"The Lady Maigrey is coming. There she is!"

Raoul moved, as if to point. The mind-dead started to turn to look. The Loti glided forward. One hand grasped hold of the gunhand of the mind-dead on his right, his other hand closed over the wrist of the mind-dead on his left.

Shock, pain contorted the faces of the mind-dead. Their knees buckled. Raoul let loose his grip, and both mind-dead slid to the floor.

The Little One sprang out from his hiding place, began running down the hall, tripping on the hem of the raincoat. The small empath could run fast for someone his age.

"Move out!" Xris ordered.

Reaching the computer room, his men took up positions in the passageway. The cyborg inspected the bodies. The light shone on faces grotesquely contorted, mouths parted in the screams of pain neither had been alive long enough to utter.

The Little One stood over them, making chortling animal noise in his throat. Raoul gazed down complacently at the corpses.

"Compliments of my former employer, Snaga Ohme," he said languidly.

Removing the pair of gloves from his belt, he drew them back onto his hands. "Poison." He wiggled his fingers. "That's why I warned you not to touch," he added, glancing at Xris. "Plastiskin over the palms protects me from the poison's effects. And it's remarkably versatile. I've even had it made into my favorite shade of lip gloss."

"Lip gloss." Xris took the twist from his mouth, looked at it, looked at the Loti, started to put the twist back and changed his mind. He thrust what was left in his pocket. "They didn't have time to send a message back to that master of theirs, did they?"

"The pain they experience is brief, but quite debilitating. It would prevent them from thinking about anything except possibly their own impending demise."

"Yeah, well, I guess you know what you're doing. I'm going into the computer room, do a little work. If your friend 'hears' anything, let me know."

"Certainly." Raoul fluttered, glittered. The Little One was removing the gold card case from his pocket.

Xris didn't wait to see what came next.

It took him a while to readjust his thinking to using the old-style computers, and he learned, fumbling with Corasian technology, that although they copied accurately from humans, they occasionally had no idea of what it was they were copying or how it worked.

He jabbed away at the keys. One good thing about the collective mind, each Corasian trusted every other Corasian. No need for passwords, locking codes, any of that nonsense.

"This is just plain weird," he said to himself.

He was conscious of time passing, conscious of the desperate need to hurry, conscious of danger around them. But all that seemed remote, hard to believe. The room was quiet, except for the whirring of the computers. He might as well be in a museum. A glance out the door showed Raoul, letting his hair down.

Xris searched the files. But he caught himself wondering about how her ladyship was doing, wondered if she was still alive. He wondered about Agis, about the priest. Probably not. Probably dead, like Britt.

"And likely all the rest of us soon enough. A goddam army on the surface. There you are!" he said at last.

He'd found the file. Pulling it up, he glanced through it,

skipped over the complex technical language, paused when he discovered numerous three-dimensional schematics. Xris had no idea what a space-rotation bomb looked like, but he had the feeling these weren't it.

"It appears to me, sister, that they've got the pieces to the bomb, they just don't know what to do with them. But we'll let the experts decide."

Switching on his own internal computer, Xris hooked himself to the Corasian machines and downloaded all the files he could find that appeared to have anything to do with bombs, humans, or the Milky Way galaxy in general.

All the while, he kept one eye on the door, expecting any moment to see his men spring to attention.

He was about to shut down and leave when a thought occurred to him. The Corasians had all or most of the basic parts, but were obviously, from the number of models, having difficulty figuring out how they went together. It wouldn't help to erase the files. The lady herself had figured that once in the central computer system these files would go all over the Corasian galaxy.

"But what if we added a few more parts?"

He created a new file and transmitted. A three-dimensional drawing of his own cybernetic limb appeared on the screen. Beneath it he added, in Standard Military, "Arming device."

This complete, he covered his electronic footsteps, left the computer humming and whirring to itself in ignorant intelligence.

"Any sign of the enemy? Good. Then let's get the hell out of here. Our job's finished. I got the dope stored inside me. If anything happens to me, make certain that my files get back to whoever's in charge. All right, move out. That means the two of you, unless you're thinking of staying."

"The Little One says that the Starlady is in much trouble."

"Yeah? Well that's her concern, not mine. We're going to be in a hell of a lot of trouble ourselves, if there's an army between us and our spaceplanes."

"The Little One says you could be of assistance to her."

Xris took a twist from his pocket, inserted it between his lips. His men stood, looking at him in silence.

"It's not in the contract," he said finally, and, turning, began to retrace his steps, back up the tunnel toward the planet's surface.

Chapter ···❦❧❦··· Nine

What I have done is yours; what I have to do is yours;
being part in all I have, devoted yours.

> William Shakespeare, dedication

Maigrey entered the chamber in which Abdiel held Sagan
captive, her heart and soul hushed. Four passages opened into
the room, one at each of the cardinal points. Four bridges led
from each entrance, met in the center to form the shape of a
cross over a vast pool of flaming black water beneath the high
point of the domed ceiling.

In the center of the chamber stood a bier, made of stones
piled up, one on another. Derek Sagan lay on the bier, his eyes
closed, arms at his sides. He was dressed in his red cape and
golden armor, his ceremonial armor, which he wore on
illustrious occasions. The armor was a copy of the real armor,
currently aboard *Phoenix*. The mind-dead did good work.

It was like Abdiel to have added that touch, Maigrey
thought bitterly. Making a mockery of Sagan's victories in this,
his ultimate defeat.

The flames lit the chamber; firelight gleamed on the golden
armor, shone on the face, composed, peaceful, cold and still as
the rock that pillowed the head. The hands that lay at his sides
did not move, the breastplate did not move.

On the threshold, Maigrey stopped, physically unable to go
farther. She reached out a trembling hand to catch hold of the
wall, found Agis's strong arm there to support her.

"We are too late," Agis said. "My lord is dead."

Sparafucile gave a fierce, harsh cry, like that of a wounded
animal.

"No!" Maigrey drew a deep breath, trying to recover from
her first, terrifying shock. "We are meant to think he is."

The soul had not left the body, but had shut itself up inside.

Windows were sealed, entrances closed and locked. No light gleamed from within. It was up to Maigrey to find the door.

Sparafucile shot her a dark, suspicious glance. Gliding forward, soft-footed, the half-breed hurried onto the bridge.

Agis started after him, but Maigrey stopped him, her hand clasping his arm.

"Let him go," she said.

The centurion looked at her, his face grim, doubtful whether or not to obey.

Maigrey understood. Agis's loyalty, like that of the half-breed's, was first and always to his lord. She had only borrowed it awhile.

"He can do no harm," she said.

Sparafucile came to stand beside the bier, the still, unmoving body. The assassin stared down at it, eyes searching the cold face with its harsh, uncompromising lines of strong purpose and resolve. Reaching out a hand that shivered with the temerity of doing that which he would have never dared do while Sagan was alive, the half-breed touched gently the Warlord's arm.

"She is right!" he hissed. "Tricksy woman is right. Flesh is warm. You live. You fool them, eh? Sagan Lord! You fool them all, including Sparafucile. That is very clever. I laugh, Sagan Lord."

The half-breed gave a laugh that was more like a sob. Drawing near, he plucked timidly at the red cape.

"You wake up now, Sagan Lord. Sparafucile is here. Sparafucile make report, eh? Same as always?" The half-breed's voice cracked. He shouted hoarsely. "Sagan Lord!"

"May God have mercy," whispered Brother Daniel.

Maigrey began to understand. This wasn't loyalty, but—in the half-breed's own dark and twisted way—love.

"Agis, stay here and guard the doorway. Brother Daniel, come with me."

Maigrey walked across the bridge. The assassin, hearing her footfalls, whirled to glare at her, keeping his body between her and his lord. His hand darted into the rags.

"I can help him, Sparafucile," said Maigrey, continuing to approach, keeping her gaze fixed on his. "I need you to guard the other entrance." She pointed south, Agis stood at the western passage.

The half-breed eyed her warily, glanced back at Sagan, who had not moved.

"I can help him," she repeated. "I'm the only one. You know that, Sparafucile. I am Blood Royal."

Slowly, the assassin stepped aside.

"Tricksy woman." He snarled the words, jealousy burned in the black eyes like the flame on the surface of the oily water. "You bring back my lord. I guard door. I keep good watch. But"—he raised a crooked finger, whose long dirty nail was like the point of a dagger—"I keep one eye on you!"

Slouching into his rags, he crossed the bridge and came to stand beside the open doorway. Maigrey had the disquieting impression that he meant literally what he said. One of the misaligned eyes was focused on the passageway outside, the other stared directly at her.

She turned away. She couldn't worry about the half-breed now, couldn't worry about mind-dead or Corasians. She had to concentrate on finding Sagan and it was likely, she knew, to be the most difficult task she had ever undertaken. Perhaps impossible.

His face was stern, forbidding. Standing beside him, she lifted his hand in hers. The flesh was warm, she felt the faint stirring of his blood. She pressed his hand against her cheek, the cheek marred by the lashing scar, her skin wet with her tears. Closing her eyes, holding fast to his hand, she entered his mind.

··◁■ ■▷··

All was completely and utterly dark, a hollow, empty darkness that was forever and eternal, vast and unending, like the Void between the galaxies. But that Void eventually had an end. She could travel this darkness on and on and never see the light of a single star. Death, oblivion, her own death. No God, no Creator, no afterlife, no mercy, pity, compassion, no solace. Nothing. It was fearful, more frightening than anything in life she'd ever faced. Her first impulse was to run, flee, escape.

"No. I don't believe this. It is a lie."

A light appeared in the darkness. Sighing in relief, Maigrey hurried forward and found herself on board *Phoenix*. And there was Sagan, standing on the bridge.

She was startled to see him here, amazed to find him so

easily, with such little difficulty. She drew closer. He turned to face her. She stopped, shocked, horrified.

He was hideously changed. His features, no longer noble, proud, were twisted and deformed by every evil passion. The red cape he wore had altered to a gruesome color, as if it had been steeped in blood. The golden armor had changed to dross.

She read his history in his eyes. He had become a despot, a tyrant, cruel, murderous, a Caligula, a Hitler. His own men feared him, loathed him, despised him. His name was cursed throughout the galaxy.

He saw her and he laughed horribly, and drew the blood-sword and came toward her.

He will fulfill his destiny and destroy you.

She drew her sword in despair. It was better, better that he die, that she die. They both longed for death. . . .

Something struck her from behind, jolted her, knocked the sword from her hand. Her concentration wavered. The blow had been real, it had come from the world outside the one in which she stood. Danger, dire, imminent, threatened. She hesitated, confused, knowing she should go back, yet afraid to leave, afraid she might never find her way here again.

Shouts, distant shouting. She had to go back. She knelt down, reached out, groping for the bloodsword.

A robed and hooded monk blocked her way.

"Two must walk the paths of darkness, Daughter, to reach the light."

Maigrey remembered the voice, remembered it husky, rusted, as if long unused. She looked up, from where she crouched at the monk's feet, to see his face. It was hidden in the darkness cast by the cowl that covered the head, but she knew who he was, knew why he had come.

Behind her, a struggle, life and death.

"Father, wait for me!" she cried. "I will come back."

He said nothing, but shook his head. And she heard, in her heart, *To turn back now would do no good. You yourself made the choice that will determine the outcome. Let go of that world, and enter his.*

Reluctantly, Maigrey stood up, left the bloodsword lying on the floor, and followed the monk.

A storm wind rose, blasting, stinging, harsh. It tore at the clothes she wore, the black tunic, and ripped it off. Beneath it, like the moon appearing from behind rent and driven clouds, her armor shone, cold, argent, bright.

The monk turned his back on the wind, which whipped his robes around him. Maigrey lifted her head to see where they were bound.

Towering above her, stern and forbidding, were the walls of an abbey. She recognized it, though she had been there only once before, long ago, and she ran forward, eager to gain entry.

But the doors were shut and bolted against her. She beat on them and shouted, to make them hear her. Her cries were blown away in the wind. Despairing, she turned to the priest. Silently, he raised his hand.

The doors shivered, parted. She stood aside, humbly, thankfully, allowed him to precede her. As he passed, his head bowed, the light shining from her silver armor illuminated his face.

The lines of pride, of stern resolve, recalled to her his son. But the father's face was softened by suffering, self-inflicted punishment, the stripes of the scourge that had laid bare the soul. He looked up at her, and she saw tears glisten on the gaunt cheeks.

He did not say a word as he walked past her. Darkness closed over him, and his face was once more hidden from her sight.

Maigrey, silently, followed him inside the Abbey walls.

··◄■ ■►··

"Brother Daniel, come with me," Lady Maigrey had told him and the priest had obeyed, although just why he was there or what good he could do was not readily apparent.

He had expected her to give him some command, but she said nothing more. She drew near the still figure of Lord Sagan, and the young priest guessed that she had forgotten his existence.

Brother Daniel stood near, prepared to offer silent comfort and sympathy, if he could do nothing more. Looking into her face, he saw her love for this man, her regret for a past lost forever, the knowledge that no future for them existed unless it was one far, far beyond this dark realm.

He saw the tears, sacred as holy water, slide down her face and fall on the hand she held.

Brother Daniel averted his head. This moment was not his to share. When he looked again, he realized that she had left him. Though she stood there, she was gone.

He knew, then, that he was in the presence of God.

He was awed, humbled. He'd felt the Presence before: when in the cathedral, lifting his voice with his brothers in praise, or sometimes in the darkness of the quiet night, kneeling at his own little altar, his voice alone breaking the holy silence. But he'd never felt God this near him before.

He didn't know what to do. The experience was exhilarating, but terrifying. He thought he must pray, he should pray. It was expected. Words vanished from his mind when he summoned them. He was left stammering, trembling, tongue-tied, torn between fright and joy, as he had been when, as a small child, he'd come to the altar to take his first vows.

Daniel had no idea what was happening. Lady Maigrey's face was empty, devoid of expression. She made no sound. Drawing the bloodsword, she activated it, held it above Sagan's body. She said no word, her face was calm, almost serene.

Brother Daniel watched in awe. What was happening was God's will. The priest dared not interfere, although it came to him that she was about to slay Sagan, slay herself, and that would mean death for them all.

It was God's will.

What made him turn his head, Brother Daniel never knew. It couldn't have been a sound, for no one had ever known the assassin to make a sound before he struck. Agis cried out a warning, but that came a split second later. It would have been too late, if Brother Daniel hadn't turned already and seen what was coming.

Sparafucile snaked past him, knife raised, firelight flashing from the blade.

"You not kill my lord!" Sparafucile's arm lifted to stab Maigrey.

Daniel hurled himself bodily at the assassin. The priest's hands grappled for the knife. The attack, coming from a direction he had obviously not expected, caught Sparafucile by surprise. He lost his balance beneath the onslaught. Both of them fell, crashed into Maigrey. The shock of the blow jolted the bloodsword from her hand, knocked it to the floor. She bent to pick it up, to come to the aid of the struggling priest.

And then she dropped the sword, turned her back upon both savior and attacker.

··◁■ ■▷··

From his vantage point, guarding one of the two doorways, Agis saw the assassin break from his post, saw the knife flash.

The centurion's cry had been for Maigrey, hoping to alert her to her danger. He sprang forward, but the distance he had to cover was great. Weakened from his wound, he knew with certain despair that he would never reach her side in time.

Agis ran across the bridge, then stopped, brought up short by the amazing sight of Brother Daniel, unarmed, hands grasping for the knife, flinging himself bodily on the assassin.

The two fell into Maigrey, knocked the bloodsword from her hand. She lunged for the sword; Agis expected her to turn and fight. But she paused, the sword fell from her grasp. She was far away, Agis realized, perhaps locked in her own desperate struggle.

The two combatants reeled back, flailing. Sparafucile shrieked terrible curses, strove to shake the priest loose. Daniel clung to the assassin with grim determination. The two crashed to the floor behind the bier, out of Agis's view.

Recovering from his astonishment, the centurion raced around the bier, found the two locked in a deadly embrace, rolling on the floor. Brother Daniel, wrestling with the crazed half-breed, seemed to be struggling to calm him, as he might have tried to calm a patient gone berserk.

Daniel had the assassin pinned, for an instant, but Sparafucile was strong and lithe as a panther and slipped easily from the young priest's grasp.

Agis stood over them, frustrated, his dart gun drawn, ready to shoot, but forced to hold his fire, afraid—in the dim, shadow-dodging light—of hitting Daniel.

Sparafucile leapt on the priest, straddled him; strong legs held his victim fast. Fire flashed on the blade of the assassin's knife. Agis had a clear shot at last, but in that split second the assassin struck.

A pain-filled scream shattered the silence. Both bodies froze, motionless, immobile. Agis lowered his weapon, grabbed hold of Sparafucile, who crouched over the young priest. Agis flung the assassin back, prepared to kill him. But he looked into the half-breed's face and saw, in the startled eyes, the shadows of approaching death.

Startled, the centurion released his grasp. Sparafucile sank to the floor, hands clutching at his middle. The hilt of the assassin's own knife protruded from the rags that were slowly darkening with blood. The half-breed's lips parted, his pain-shadowed gaze focused on the priest.

Brother Daniel, shaken, sat up, stared around.

"Are you all right?" Agis asked him.

"Yes, praise God. What . . . what happened?" Daniel looked dazedly over at the assassin.

Sparafucile grinned horribly. "You kill me, I think, Priest, eh?"

Daniel saw the knife's hilt, the blood.

"No!" He crawled over to the dying man, caught hold of the bloody hand. "No, I swear before God, I never—"

"Be careful!" Agis tensed, fearing Sparafucile might try to take his killer with him.

But a spasm of pain twisted the grotesque features of the half-breed, his breath gurgled in his throat.

"God!" Sparafucile seemed to grasp feebly at what was, perhaps, the only word he had heard. "Your God . . . He kill me!"

The half-breed's head lolled to one side, blood ran from the open mouth. Lank hair fell forward, covering the misaligned eyes that stared blankly into the darkness.

Brother Daniel sat back on his heels. His face was ashen, his breathing harsh and shallow.

"I never touched the knife! I swear it! Before God, I swear it. You saw, didn't you?" He looked up at Agis.

"Yes, I saw," the centurion lied. Reaching down, he put an awkward hand on the young man's shoulder. "The half-breed's knee slipped. He fell, stabbed himself."

Daniel's gaze shifted back to the corpse. "No," he said. "That was not the way it happened."

"However it happened, you saved my lady's life," said Agis gruffly.

Brother Daniel seemed to recall where he was, what was transpiring around him. Turning his head, he saw Maigrey holding Sagan's hand, her head bent over his, her pale hair falling forward, hiding them both behind a silken curtain.

Brother Daniel sighed softly. "Who knows?"

He closed the staring, misaligned eyes, and began to repeat the prayer for the dead.

·-◁▮ ▮▷-·

Inside the Abbey walls, the darkness was not threatening or fearful, but warm, comforting, offering solace after a day's hard labor, ease for pain. Maigrey walked the halls, following behind the monk. She saw none of the other brethren; it being forbidden them to set eyes upon a woman. She was aware of their presence, however. Shadowy figures moved in the corner of her vision, vanished when she turned her head to look at them directly.

And, far away, in the distance, she heard the voices lifted in supplication.

"'*Kyrie eleison*. . . .

"'Lord, have mercy. . . .'"

The darkness, the warmth, the music, were a reproach to Maigrey, whose armor pierced the soft shadows with a harsh, warlike, metallic light. She sensed the priests' resentment, their disapproval.

"I'm doing my duty," she told them, and her voice was jarring, discordant, echoed through the halls whose stones knew only the sound of prayer and soft, muted discussions of the necessary, the mundane.

Ashamed, she glanced sideways at the tall priest, to see if he was angry at her, but the hood was pulled low over his head, she could not see his face. He said nothing, continued on. Bowing her head, she followed.

They descended a flight of stairs, came to the *dortoir*, the living quarters, turned into a hallway that was dark, narrow. Maigrey could touch the walls on either side of her by barely extending her arms. She had only to reach up to brush her fingers against the ceiling. The tall monk was forced to stoop as he moved along.

It was difficult to see. The monk carried a thin white taper, but its fragile flame wavered and glimmered in the gentle draft created by their movement. What light it did shed was eclipsed by the priest's body, engulfed in the shroudlike folds of his robes. He knew where he was going, could have undoubtedly walked it blind. Maigrey tripped and stumbled, for though the stone was worn smooth by countless feet, the floor was not level, dipped and rose unexpectedly. Her armor clashed and clattered.

They passed countless wooden doors, all of them shut. No light gleamed from beneath, no sound came from the still and silent rooms. They had almost reached the end of the hallway, when the priest halted.

Maigrey had no need to ask which door. She knew. She looked at the priest, seeking a sign, reassurance, approval. He stood quietly, his face hidden, offering no comfort, no urging. The choice was hers.

Sighing softly, Maigrey pushed gently on the wooden door. It swung open.

A man, clad in robes, knelt before an altar. He kept his back to her, though he must have heard her enter, for her armor made a silvery ringing sound. She knew him, however, by the long black hair that fell over his shoulders, knew him by the pain in her heart.

Standing straight and tall, silver armor illuminating the room more brightly than moonlight, she spoke to him.

"Lord Derek Sagan, I call you to fulfill your oath. I call you to the service of your king."

He remained kneeling long moments, then, finally, he rose and turned to face her. His face was grim and forbidding and dark and in his eyes was the bitter reproach she'd felt the moment she'd entered his sanctuary. She sensed him about to refuse and she was frightened, wondering what she would say to persuade him, having nothing to offer him in exchange for this peace but despair, terror, death. . . .

His gaze shifted.

"Father," he said, and the fire of his reproach glimmered and died, even as the flame of the candle the monk carried wavered and guttered out.

The only light in the darkness shone from Maigrey's silver armor.

Sagan looked back to her, sighed deeply.

"You should not have come," he said.

··◁▭ ▭▷··

Agis and Brother Daniel stood beside the bier, watching. Agis felt increasingly uneasy, nervous. He kept his hand on his dartgun, glanced continually around.

"The enemy's near," he muttered. "I can feel them . . ."

"Not without," said Brother Daniel. The priest had his eyes on the still, unmoving figure on the bier. "But within."

Agis stared at him questioningly, not understanding.

"My lord is dying," the priest responded. "My lady fights to hold him to this life, but her heart is not in the battle. How could it be? Fear for herself, fear for him—"

"She must save him!"

"Yes," said Daniel sadly. "She must. She knows it, and I think she will. But her choice is bitter. *Kyrie eleison*. Lord have mercy. Lord have mercy on them both."

Agis had once visited a world of oceans and tides and he was reminded suddenly of standing upon the shore and watching a wave crash upon the beach. He saw again the water rush away from him, and take—so it seemed—the world with it. Sand, pebbles, shells, seaweed, were sucked away from beneath his feet and he remembered experiencing the strange sensation that he was next, that the wave would catch hold of him and draw him out to vanish beneath the green water.

But then another wave came, returned the water, returned the shells and sand and seaweed, sent them back to him, brought life flooding over his feet that stood in the sand. And so it would continue, always.

"It is over," said Brother Daniel softly.

Maigrey laid her head on Sagan's chest.

The centurion knew, then, that his lord was dead. He unbuckled the bloodsword from his waist, made ready to lay it on the bier, as his lord would have wanted. He took a step forward, stopped.

Sagan drew a deep breath, let it out in a sigh. He put his arm around Maigrey, held her close, pressed her to him.

"You should not have come," he said.

Chapter ❀❁❀ Ten

Hail, holy light, offspring of Heaven . . .
                              John Milton, *Paradise Lost*

"Lady Maigrey's spaceplane," reported Tusk, his Scimitar making a low pass over the broken planet's barren surface. "And I recognize the junker. It belongs to that assassin, Spara-something-or-other."

"He saved our lives," Nola reminded him.

Tusk grunted. "Only because he had more use for us alive than dead. I don't know who those other planes belong to, probably those commandos the lady hired."

"This must be the place," said Dion. "Make one more orbit. Scanners reading anything, XJ?"

"All the weird energy levels bouncing around here, and you want me to find a few measly humans!" the computer scoffed. "Ask me next time to look for a lit match in a forest fire."

"Scimitar." A voice came over the commlink. "Scimitar, this is *Galaxy Belle*. Can you read me?"

"Verified," reported XJ. "Transmission's coming from the liner."

"Yes, we can read you," Tusk said. "We've been tryin' to raise you—"

"I had to check you out, first. This is the captain. Corbett, Tomi. And I want to talk to whoever's in charge."

"Captain Corbett," Dion began. "I am—"

"Shut up! I don't care who you are. I was told a goddam fleet was coming to pick us up. I suppose you're it?"

"No, Captain. There has been a change in plans. I am Dion Starfire, in command of the fleet. It's currently stationed on the Corasian perimeter."

"That does me a hell of a lot of good!"

"I will transmit their coordinates to you. I suggest, Captain," Dion continued, "that you make the Jump as soon as possible.

I'm carrying with me the space-rotation bomb and I may be forced to detonate it. In that eventuality, the fleet will be warned in advance to make the Jump into the Void. You should be with them. XJ, transmit the coordinates."

Silence on the other end, then the captain's voice came back, strangely altered.

"I don't understand. You mean . . . something's happened to them down there?"

"Have you received the coordinates?" Dion asked, ignoring the question.

"Yeah, I got them." Silence again, then, "I don't suppose there'd be any way I could help?"

"Thank you, Captain, but you have a responsibility to your passengers—"

"Those rich bastards. This is probably the only good they've ever done for anyone else in their lives, and wouldn't you know, they had to be unconscious to do it."

The captain's voice sounded odd, thick and slurred. Tusk looked at Dion, rolled his eyes, raised an eyebrow. "Jump-juice."

"Captain," Dion repeated, "have you received the coordinates?"

"Yeah, I got them. And I heard that. I'm not on the juice. It's that damn drug your friends gave me. It's wearing off, though. Don't worry. I'll make the Jump. I'm programming for it now. That goddam fleet better be there—"

"They will be," Dion promised.

"Look, one thing before I go. Have you . . . Have you heard any word from . . . anybody that went down there. If they're okay, I mean? One in particular . . ."

Dion waited for the captain to finish, but the voice trailed off.

"No," he said finally. "I'm sorry. I haven't."

"That's all right." After a pause. "It wouldn't have worked out anyway."

The transmission abruptly ended.

"How strange." Dion frowned. "I hope she can operate the ship safely—"

"I would like to remind everyone that it is actually her computer who is running the ship," stated XJ in lofty tones, "and the computer who will be in charge of the Jump. Any human involvement is strictly superfluous—the only reason Tusk has managed to live this long."

XJ waited smugly for Tusk to attempt a verbal riposte.

Tusk said nothing. He stared at the controls, silent, thoughtful. Nola reached out, took his hand, twined his fingers through hers.

"Hey, Tusk, it was a joke," said the computer.

Tusk didn't answer.

"Look, Tusk, I'm sorr—"

"Jeez!" The mercenary leapt to his feet. "Don't do that!"

"Do what?" XJ's lights blinked in astonishment.

"Apologize to me! Shit! Now I know my time has come! Damn computer, apologizin'."

"I did nothing of the sort!"

"You were about to. I heard you start to say 'I'm sorry'—"

"I'm sorry, all right!" XJ shouted, turning up its audio, nearly deafening everyone within earshot. "Sorry I ever set my optics on you, you sorry excuse for a spacepilot."

"That's better," said Tusk, looking relieved, sitting back down."

"XJ, land the plane," Dion ordered.

"One more orbit, kid. I don't like the looks of that landing site. And I'm picking up lots of strange energy readings."

"The landing site's flat rock, XJ. And you said yourself that the energy levels made it impossible to read anything."

"Look, kid, listen to the voice of reason, the voice of intelligence, which, considering the present company you're keeping, means that you listen to my voice. Call General Dixter. Send for the fleet. Send for the marines. Send ten thousand or so soldiers down that rat hole. Let them take care of this mind-seizer."

"It wouldn't work, XJ. Abdiel could make himself appear as ten thousand different things to ten thousand different people, if he wanted. He'd escape, slip away, or maybe even make the ten thousand turn on each other. No. Sooner or later, I have to face him. Lady Maigrey knew it. Dixter knew it. Tusk knows it. That's why he's here with me."

"He's here with you because he's a big boob. As I told him when he got us into this in the first place. A sack of gold coins. That's what we got for taking you on, kid. And the money wasn't much, either, what with the bottom dropping out of the gold market. When I think of what it's cost us since then—"

"Land the goddam plane!" Tusk roared.

Bleeping irritably to itself, the computer started the landing cycle.

··◁▬ ▬▷··

They didn't say anything to each other as the plane touched down. They went about their tasks in silence. When those tasks were finished, they found things to do that didn't need to be done. There was too much to say and no one quite knew how to begin saying it, except to themselves.

Nola went up into the bubble, again, to test the gun that didn't need testing now any more than it had needed testing ten minutes previous. Instead she sat there, alone, staring out at the stars.

"I want kids, Tusk," she said, talking to her reflection in the bubble. "I want a whole bunch of them, rug-rats, running around, driving us crazy, keeping us up all night. Though God knows what they'll look like, poor things. What with my freckles and your nose. And they can play vidgames with Grandpa XJ. We'll be a family. A family . . ."

Tusk punched buttons on the console, running systems checks that did nothing except irritate the computer.

"Soon as we leave here," he promised himself, "I'll take Nola to meet my mother. They'll like each other. Nola complains all the time she never has any other women to talk to. They could talk about . . . women things. And what're those? You know, sitting in gun turrets, blowing people to pieces; lying, wounded, on a pile of bloody flak jackets; landing far behind enemy lines; detonating bombs."

Tusk sighed, rubbed his eyes. "You know, women things."

Dion removed Maigrey's starjewel from an inner pocket, intending to place it into the space-rotation bomb. He started to do it quickly, keeping his gaze averted from the unlovely object. But he paused, forced himself to look at it, look at it deliberately, long and hard.

"I remember the first time I saw her, the first time I saw the starjewel. It gleamed with a radiance that seemed to come from its own bright heart, or maybe hers. But now the heart is dead. The jewel's turned black. Not the shining black of jet or obsidian, not the warm black of ebony, not the cold empty black of outer space or the shades of black that make up the night. It is the black of decay, rot, gangrene.

"'The taint in our blood,' as Maigrey used to say. But if the bomb were detonated, the starjewel would, for one brief second, shine more brilliantly than any sun.

"And so would all the fallen angels."

Dion placed the starjewel in the bomb, typed in the code sentence that would detonate it, the line from a poet's dark vision of a second coming. He typed it all except for the last letter of the last word.

The center cannot hol_ .

The three went on with their work. And it occurred to each of the three, as each continued to do what didn't need to be done, that when they did finally speak to each other, it would be to say good-bye.

Chapter ··◦◖◗◦·· Eleven

> . . . so matched they stood;
> For never but once more was either like
> To meet so great a foe . . .
>
> John Milton, *Paradise Lost*

Sagan sat up too swiftly. A wave of dizziness assailed him. He closed his eyes, put his hand to his head.

"I could give you a stimulation shot, my lord," said a concerned voice.

The Warlord opened his eyes, glanced down from the bier on which he sat, saw the young priest, standing respectfully nearby, a medkit in his hands.

"Brother Fideles?" Sagan wondered, at first, if he'd left the monastery.

"Praise be to God for your safety, my lord."

"I wouldn't be too quick to praise Him, Brother," said the Warlord bitterly. "And no, I don't need a stimulation shot. I haven't atrophied, if that's what you're afraid of.

"This"—he gestured at the bier—"was all a set-piece designed entirely for my lady's benefit. The mind-seizer was forced to keep my body alive, despite the fact that I wasn't in it. I've been fed, exercised. You remember how it was, when he captured us the last time, my lady? Like rats, in a laboratory."

She nodded, shivered, and looked involuntarily around, though what she sought couldn't be seen with the body's eyes, only those of the mind. "Abdiel's coming. We don't have much time. I brought your sword. "

The centurion stepped forward. Kneeling, he lifted the bloodsword in outstretched hands and offered it to Sagan.

"What? You here, too, Captain?"

"Yes, my lord. Your weapon, my lord."

The Warlord did not immediately take the sword, but turned, looked intently at Maigrey.

"Did you think I would forget?" she asked.

"Not forget," he said, after a moment's hesitation, "but perhaps think it best not to bring it to me."

Maigrey smiled, shook her head. "I'm not afraid of you, my lord. Or of my destiny. You see, I wear the silver armor."

The vision of her death came to him again, clear, more real than anything around him. Blood streaming down silver armor. Only it wasn't the bloodsword he held. It was the dagger, the small dagger, its hilt designed in the shape of an eight-pointed star, used by priests to make their offering of their own life's blood to the Creator. Sagan breathed deeply, closed his eyes in thankfulness. His dagger was not here. It was far away, left behind in the monastery when Abdiel had taken him captive.

The dream was a lie. It couldn't come true. Or maybe not a lie, for that would be to deny his faith. Perhaps one of them, he or Maigrey, or perhaps someone else—Dion maybe—had done something, offered some other sacrifice, that had altered the course of the future.

Flexing his muscles, stretching, he reached out briskly to take the sword from Agis.

"Wishful thinking, Sagan," came a dry, cracked voice.

The Warlord caught up his sword, turned. Maigrey drew her sword, activated it, came to stand beside him. Once again together, lord and lady prepared to walk the paths of darkness.

Abdiel's frail and wizened form emerged from the shadows of a doorway to the north, crept along the bridge and into the light. The flames burning on the dark water shimmered on the heavy magenta robes, decorated with a slash of dark lightning.

"How touching," he continued, "to witness a reunion of lovers long parted. I've been moved almost to nausea. And you would have me believe you are united? Lovers who betrayed their love? Guardians who betrayed their king? Dion doesn't trust you. You don't trust each other. You don't even trust yourselves."

He paused, the lidless eyes flitted from Maigrey to Sagan, stealthily trying the door handles, rattling the locks, peering through cracks, seeking an opening. The lidless eyes glinted in the firelight. The wizened body drew back, huddled into its robes.

Sagan shook his head. "Long ago, that strategy worked for you, Abdiel. Long ago, you found the entry into each of us you sought. Pride, fear, jealousy, distrust. My lady and I defeated you, only—in the end—to defeat ourselves. But you will not find your way in now. We stand against you. Two together."

"Two who will feel the bite of the serpent's tooth." Abdiel's hand slid into his robes.

Agis, concealed behind the bier, took advantage of the mind-seizer's preoccupation with Maigrey and Sagan to draw his dartgun. He was an expert shot. The old man was an easy target, standing alone, illuminated by the firelight. Agis took aim.

"Ah, would you, centurion?" The lidless eyes glowed red. "And which of us would you shoot?"

The voice came from his right. Agis saw movement out of the corner of his eye, a flash of magenta. He glanced that direction. The mind-seizer stood in the doorway to the east. Startled, Agis looked back to the north. Abdiel stood there.

"You should never turn your back on me, centurion."

This time, the voice was from behind.

Agis refused to fall for the old trick, though the hair on the back of his neck rose and prickled, instinct warning him to turn.

The shot came from behind, struck him in the back. The laser beam blasted through his armor, burned flesh, melted bone. Agis pitched forward, landed face-down upon the span of rock.

In the doorway behind him stood one of the mind-dead, a beam rifle in his hand.

Brother Daniel flashed a defiant look at the mind-dead, whose rifle was turned on him, and ran to the centurion's side.

"Hold your fire, Mikael," Abdiel ordered. "This should prove amusing."

The mind-dead did as commanded.

"You had no reason to shoot him!" Maigrey said angrily. "Your illusions fooled him! He couldn't have harmed you!"

"On the contrary, my dear." Abdiel smiled unpleasantly. "I had a very good reason."

"Agis!" Daniel said softly, kneeling to examine the extent of the man's injuries. "Lie still. Don't move."

The centurion lifted his head, looked at Daniel.

"Is the old man watching?"

Daniel looked up furtively. "No . . ."

"Take my gun!" Agis pushed the weapon along the floor toward the priest. "Quickly!"

Daniel hesitated. He could scoop it up swiftly, hide it in his robes.

"Take it!" Agis urged. "Save . . . my lord!"

The priest reached out, saw his hand closing over the gun's hilt. His own fingers were red-stained, gummed with blood: Agis's blood, the assassin's.

Daniel dropped the gun, shrank away from it. "No . . . I cannot . . ."

"Coward!" The centurion snarled, grabbed hold of the gun. "Get out of my way."

Daniel tried to stop him. "No, you'll kill yourself—"

Agis gave the priest a violent shove, struggled to push himself up. The exertion was too much. Moaning, he slumped over, shuddered, went limp. The gun clattered to the stone floor.

Hunched in misery, Daniel buried his hands in the folds of his robes.

"A show of power," Abdiel commented. "Ostentatious, perhaps, but necessary. You might, perhaps, save yourselves. But you can't save those you brought with you. Anymore than you will be able to save Dion. And you needn't bother to look for your assassin, Lady Maigrey. He's dead, too. You'll find his corpse there, on the floor behind you. The priest killed him."

"As God is my witness," Daniel cried in misery, "if I killed him, I didn't mean to. He went mad, attacked my lady. I tried to stop him." He lifted his hands, stared at them in horror. "The next thing I knew . . . he was dead."

Maigrey remembered the blow, striking her from behind. It had knocked the sword from her grasp. She remembered, vaguely, the glint of a knife. The words of the monk came back to her, *You yourself made the choice that will determine the outcome*.

"How he died doesn't matter, Brother Daniel," Maigrey said quietly. "You did what you had to do."

"You broke your vows, didn't you, Brother?" Abdiel smiled, his mouth seemed to have no lips, as his eyes had no lids. "God has turned his face away from you, false, lying Priest! Turned away in wrath! You will die and your soul will be eternally damned!"

Daniel tried to clasp his bloody hands together as if to pray, but couldn't bring himself to do so. Frantically, he wiped them on the hem of his robes.

"Don't listen to him, Brother," Sagan warned. "He's trying to destroy you as surely as he destroyed Agis. Keep your faith in God."

"I?" The mind-seizer looked amazed. "I've done nothing. He's destroyed himself—as do all who have the misfortune to come around you two."

Abdiel cocked his head, listening. "Ah, and speaking of God, His Anointed has landed. No, no, my lord. Make no move." This to Sagan, who had started to take a step forward, bloodsword shining. "It would be impolite to conclude this meeting before His Majesty has had a chance to visit with old friends. Mikael, go and offer your services as escort to the king. My lord and my lady and I will endeavor to amuse ourselves while we await his arrival.

"Lady Maigrey, if you so much as flicker an eyelid, Mikael has orders to return not with his Royal Highness, but with his royal corpse.

"Once His Majesty comes, he and I will be so rude as to ignore you both and enjoy a talk together—just the two of us. You will not disturb us or attempt to interfere. For remember, my lord and my lady, that I have in my hand the serpent's tooth. It's bite is sharp, and the king's flesh is tender."

Chapter ··◄─⊃○⊂─► Twelve

The sacrifice of God is a troubled spirit: a broken and contrite heart . . .

> *Prayer Book, 1662*, Psalms 51:15

"Test the commlink," said Tusk.

"Testing," said Dion. "Can you hear me?"

"Loud and clear, kid. Loud and clear."

Dion nodded. Tusk handed him a weapons belt.

The young man shook his head. "Abdiel won't let anything happen to me."

"Maybe not, but how much control does even he have over the Corasians?"

Dion took the belt, strapped it around his waist.

"Anti-matter grenades. Lasgun," said Tusk, pointing. "The grenades are for humans and Corasians. The lasgun's just for humans. Got that?"

"Yes." Dion barely glanced at them.

Tusk eyed him, chewed his lip. "I dunno, kid. I got to admit maybe XJ is right. I don't like the thought of you going in there alone."

"Alone," repeated Dion softly to himself, smiling as if over some private joke.

"Look, maybe I should—"

"No, Tusk, you shouldn't. You can't." Dion raised his head, looked at his friend earnestly. "You have to do this for me, Tusk. You're the only one who understands, the only one I trust." He put his hands over Tusk's. "You will do this for me? If I say so?"

"Yeah, sure, kid," Tusk mumbled, looking down at the white-skinned hands that stood out in sharp contrast against his black-skinned ones.

"The space-rotation bomb is armed. All you have to do is punch in the symbol 'd.' Then leave. You'll have six hours—

time to get back, warn the fleet, and make the Jump into the Void. You *will leave*, Tusk. You won't try to find me or rescue me. Because if I tell you to blow up the bomb, it will be too late to save me. You know that, don't you?"

The mercenary didn't answer.

"Tusk?"

"Yeah, sure. I'll leave."

"I want it this way. It has to be this way to save my people. Now—"

"Damn it, kid, enough already!"

"No, I just have to say one more thing. I've been thinking, and XJ was right when he said what you did for me cost you more than I can ever repay—"

"I didn't mean it!" XJ called out suddenly. For the past few minutes, odd, blubbering sounds had been emanating from the computer.

Tusk was vehemently shaking his head. "Kid, listen—"

"No, you listen. You've been a true friend, Tusk. You've stood by me no matter how stupid I was or how obnoxious I acted. And now you've risked your life for me. More than that, you've risked your happiness, you and Nola both."

A muffled sob came from the gun turret.

"I wish I could tell you that I'd make it up to you, but I can't, ever. I only want you to know that I appreciate it, that your friendship has meant . . . that my last thoughts will be . . ."

"I can't take this!" XJ wailed.

The lights went out.

Tusk, for once, was grateful. He drew Dion into a swift, fierce embrace and was reminded suddenly of watching Platus embrace the young man, of seeing the knowledge of approaching death on the Guardian's face. Tusk knew that if the lights came on, he'd see that same expression on his own face.

Laughing nervously, awkwardly, he wiped his nose, started to tell XJ to turn the lights back on, thought better of it.

Dion fumbled in the darkness, searching for the ladder that led up and out. Life support had shut down as well as the lights. The plane was quiet, the silence broken only by an occasional mechanical-sounding hiccup.

Putting his foot on the first rung, Dion paused. "Good-bye, Nola. Good-bye, XJ."

An incoherent sob from the gun turret and a spasmodic flicker of the lights—on and then off—were the only answers.

"Good-bye, Tusk."

"Good-bye, kid," said Tusk, from the darkness.

··◖ ▶··

Dion pulled himself up and out of the hatch. He stopped, studied the planet's surface. The night-sky, with its lambent starlight, was far brighter than the darkness of the plane he'd just left. He saw nothing, heard nothing. But there was no cover between himself and the mound-covered openings that led below the surface. Drawing his lasgun, he climbed down the side of the spaceplane, hit the ground running.

Undoubtedly Maigrey had come this way, he supposed, glancing at her spaceplane, gleaming white, as he ran past.

He could have reached out to her, could have discovered where she was, what she was doing. He could have reached out to Sagan, as well, if the Warlord was still alive. But Dion knew that to open himself to them was to open himself to Abdiel and he wasn't ready for that yet.

He kept his thoughts and mind focused on his decision, on the fate that lay ahead of him. The sacrifice must go willingly, or it would all be in vain.

And he never noticed, in the distance, hiding in the darkness, among the stumps of charred trees, the army of mind-dead, waiting. He never noticed, when he entered the passages that led blow, the lurid red glow starting to light the sky behind him.

··◖ ▶··

Dion groped his way along the passage slowly, cautiously. The darkness was intense. He should have brought along Tusk's night-vision goggles. Dion was considering switching on a small nuke beam he carried in his weapons belt, debating on whether the risks he would incur using the light would outweigh stumbling around in the dark, when the voice spoke.

"Dion Starfire. We have been expecting you. This way, please."

Nervous, tense, Dion swung around, gun in hand. It took a moment for him to make sense of the words, barely heard over the sudden pounding of his heart.

He switched on the nuke beam, aimed it about eye level,

hoping to blind whoever it was talking until he had a good look at them.

The light illuminated the figure of human male, standing composedly near a rock wall. The beam caught him full in the eyes, but whether or not his vision was impaired by it was impossible to judge. His eyes squinted involuntarily, but no expression of pain, irritation, or annoyance crossed the impassive face. The eyes, once they had adjusted to the light, reflected it back, flat as mirrors, with no light of their own.

"Mind-dead," said Dion to himself, keeping the lasgun fixed on the man. Aloud he asked, "Who are you?"

"My name is Mikael," said the man, detaching himself from the wall.

Dion was momentarily confused. He'd met Mikael before, the time he'd first met Abdiel on Laskar, and this wasn't the same man. That Mikael had died, struck down by the centurion Marcus. Dion dimly remembered someone—Sagan, Maigrey, someone—telling him that Abdiel called each of his most favored servants by that name, promoting a new Mikael to the position whenever the previous Mikael passed on.

"I want to see your master," Dion said.

Mikael bowed. "My orders are to take you to him, Your Majesty. Please, follow me. You will not need your light."

The man switched on a nuke lamp of his own. Dion, ignoring him, kept his own light turned on, played it over every centimeter of ground, wall, and ceiling.

The passageway appeared empty, except for themselves.

"Go on, then," ordered Dion. "You first."

This Mikael was a taller, broader, more muscular Mikael than the last one, but the expression on the two faces was so similar that they might have been created in the same womb. Which, to a certain extent, they had been, Dion thought, eyeing with repugnance the man moving ahead of him.

His senses heightened, tense, and alert, Dion was suddenly aware of Maigrey's presence in the passage. She wasn't here now, but she had been here, been this way, recently, too. It was as if he could smell a lingering fragrance, see a faint glimmer of silver light shining phosphorescently on the dark rock. He longed to reach out to her, but to touch her would be to touch Abdiel. All of them were so close, they could not help but mentally bump into each other.

Better, Dion decided, to remain alone.

They continued walking. He saw, some distance ahead, what he thought was firelight, its reflection flickering yellow, flaring brightly one moment, waning another. He was curious to see the source, but Mikael, at the last second, turned aside, entered a smaller, narrower passage that branched off to the right.

Dion stopped. He had lost Maigrey's trail. She had taken a different path.

"Is this the right way?" he demanded.

"It is for you, Your Majesty," answered Mikael, as if he knew what Dion was thinking.

They traveled downward, the tunnel floor sloping at a steep angle, spiraling round itself. Other passages slanted off. Dion saw their dark entryways, sometimes thought he heard the sound of machines thumping, pulsing. Once, rounding a turn, he saw the red glow that meant Corasians. Terrible memories of his captivity aboard the Corasian mother ship came back to him. His hand closed over a grenade on his belt.

"Have no fear, Dion Starfire," advised Mikael in his lifeless voice. "They will do you no harm."

The disciple continued walking, moving straight toward the Corasians.

Not wanting to appear weak or fearful, Dion did the same, although he kept his fingers wrapped tightly around the grenade. The Corasians came into view, trundling down the same corridor, passing so close that Dion felt the intense heat radiating from their steelglass bodies, could see the inner workings of the robot mechanisms that propelled them.

He stood prepared to fight, but the Corasians wheeled past, giving no sign that they were aware of him or his companion, beyond a slight hissing sound, like steam escaping from an overheated kettle. Dion relaxed his grip on the grenade, continued after Mikael.

The tunnel grew narrower. Dion gradually became aware of a light shining from somewhere below them, reflecting off the walls, growing steadily brighter. He became aware, at the same time, and in almost the same way, of Abdiel's presence, reflecting off Dion's mind, growing steadily stronger.

The passage ceased its downward slant, leveled out sharply, suddenly, causing Dion, accustomed to the slope, to miss his footing and nearly fall. He caught himself on the wall, steadied himself.

Mikael turned to him. "Why do you stop? My master awaits you."

"I'll go when I choose," Dion said harshly.

The passage opened into a large, round cavelike room with a low, domed ceiling. It was hot, reminded Dion of Abdiel's saunalike "house" on Laskar. The young man moved forward, came to stand in the doorway, and he saw the source of the heat. At first he thought the room was on fire. Flames burned in every part of it, yet there was no smoke and the air, if anything, was easier to breathe than in the tunnel.

"Come in, my king," said a well-remembered voice that sent an electric shock through Dion's nerves. "Come in where it is warm and we can talk together comfortably. Old friends of yours are here, awaiting your arrival with considerable impatience."

"Stay on the bridge," warned Mikael, "and you will avoid the fire."

Dion saw Sagan, saw Maigrey, and for a confused moment he was back on *Phoenix*, entering another domed chamber, meeting them both for the first time.

The sun and the moon. He was in the presence of both and he felt their pull on him, felt his blood surge like the tide, his body move in response. It would be very easy to take his place in orbit around these two. . . .

But he hadn't. Nor would he. He'd become his own sun.

Maigrey was looking at him expressively, her eyes gray and cold as ashes.

And he was once again back on *Phoenix* but now he had entered the Warlord's chamber. He was there for the rite, the test. He'd looked into her eyes, seen there a reflection of his own fear.

"I'm going to die," he'd told her then.

And when he'd spoken the fear aloud, he'd been filled with sudden peace, imbued with a terrible calm. A calm such as he felt now.

Dion walked unhesitatingly into the chamber filled with fire.

A span made of rock lifted him up and over flames burning on the surface of a vast pool of black water beneath him.

He studied the cavern, taking note of his surroundings as he'd been taught. Four passageways opened into the room, four bridges led from each entrance, formed the shape of a cross over the flaming water. In the center stood what might have been a tomb. Lady Maigrey and Lord Sagan were on one side of the tomb, Abdiel on the other. Resting on top of the tomb was Dion's bloodsword.

"A long journey, my king," said Abdiel solicitously. "Long and dangerous. And yet you've taken this risk to come to talk to me. I am flattered."

Dion hesitated. Only a moment, a split-second. He didn't mean to, he tried to cover it, but he knew by the sudden narrowing of Sagan's eyes, by the lowering of Lady Maigrey's, that his hesitation had been observed, understood.

Dion set his jaw. "I didn't come to talk to you or to them." His gaze flicked to Maigrey, Sagan. "I came," he continued resolutely, "to get my sword."

He drew near the tomb. No one moved, no one seemed even to breathe.

"And if you try to stop me," he said, speaking to everyone in the firelit room, "I've brought the space-rotation bomb with me. On my orders, Tusk will detonate it. *This time,*" he added with emphasis and a meaningful glance at Maigrey, "the bomb is armed. This time it's not a test—"

"'This time,'" Abdiel mimicked him, "the space-rotation bomb is mine. Tusk," he added conversationally, "is dead."

Dion had approached the tomb, his hand outstretched for the sword. At the mind-seizer's words, he halted, his hand wavered.

"I don't believe you."

"Yes, you do. I can't lie to you. You would know it. Just as you can't lie to me." Abdiel smiled, the lidless eyes bored into Dion. "Try to contact your friend. Go ahead."

Dion swallowed, but the dryness in his throat increased. He had no need to use the commlink. He knew, by the sudden, searing pain in his chest, that the mind-seizer was right. Something had happened to Tusk. Something terrible . . .

And so I've failed, Dion realized. My sacrifice is now meaningless. The true sacrifice was my people, my friends.

Dion lunged forward, grabbed for the sword.

Abdiel was watching, waiting. His left hand snaked out, closed over Dion's left shoulder, sharp needles jabbing deep into the young man's flesh. Dion cried out, more in anger and frustration than in pain.

"Don't move, my lord, my lady," Abdiel warned. "You know

what will happen if I inject the virus into him at this point on his body, this point near the heart. The virus and micro-machines, entering the body outside their usual, proscribed paths, will flare in his blood like liquid fire."

Both froze, motion arrested. The bloodswords they held burned. They were both within striking distance of Abdiel, though he stood on the other side of the bier.

He read their thoughts, nodded. "Yes, a danger. But not for long. Throw your swords into the water."

Sagan sucked in a breath, his face went livid with fury.

"If you don't," Abdiel continued, "I'll kill your king. And you took an oath to protect—"

"I'll die!" Dion cried, voice hollow. "It's what I came to do. You understand, don't you, Maigrey! I came to make the sacrifice. Kill him! Then go to Tusk. Set off the bomb!"

Abdiel jabbed the needles in deeper. Dion gasped, sank to his knees before the tomb. Blood trickled down his arm.

"Kill him!" he gasped.

"You are strong, my king," said Abdiel in admiration. "Not like that fool, your uncle. With my help, you will make an excellent ruler. Much as you would have, Sagan, if you had accepted my offer. Or you, Lady Maigrey. Throw your swords into the water, Guardians."

Sagan, dark, grim, shook his head. "I'd throw myself in first, Mind-seizer!"

"Then do so, by all means," said Abdiel.

The Warlord took a furious step toward the bier, his sword raised.

Abdiel drove the needles deeper into Dion's flesh.

"Go ahead, my lord!" Dion shouted, flinching. He clutched desperately at the mind-seizer's hand, tried to tear it from him. "I command you! Kill him!"

"Don't!" Maigrey caught hold of the Warlord's arm. "We have . . . no choice," she said softly, bitterly.

Turning, she threw the bloodsword away from her, sent it spiraling over the rock span. It fell into the flames, struck the black water with a splash of fire, and sank into the darkness.

Sagan glared at Abdiel in rage, impotent, frustrated. Then, with a bitter curse, he hurled his bloodsword far from him. It smashed into a wall, exploded in a ball of blue-white fire, brighter, for a moment, than a star. And then it was gone.

Abdiel removed the needles from Dion's flesh. The king

slumped over the bier, shivering, his hand grasping his bleeding shoulder.

"Mikael," the mind-seizer ordered, "watch over my lord and lady. You, Priest, come join them. I'm certain they would appreciate your prayers."

Brother Daniel, eyes lowered, hands hidden in the folds of his sleeves, rose to his feet and came to stand beside Lord Sagan. The mind-seizer aimed the beam rifle directly at them.

"And now, His Majesty and I will have our little talk. For you did come to talk to me, didn't you, my king?" Abdiel continued.

"I won't talk with you," said Dion, his eyes on the needles imbedded in Abdiel's palm. "Not like that. Not again. I'd die first."

"No, you would die last. The lady"—Abdiel glanced at Maigrey—"will die first. And then the priest, then the Warlord. You speak very glibly of sacrifice, my king. Will you sacrifice these, as you have already sacrificed your friend Tusk? And for what? Are you afraid to talk with me? Afraid to hear the truth?"

"Perhaps I am," Dion answered softly. "Perhaps that's why I came, after all. Far easier to die." He shook his head, then raised his eyes, looked directly at the mind-seizer. "But, no, I won't sacrifice them or anyone else. We will talk, if that's what you want."

Abdiel smiled at him. Reaching out, he took hold of Dion's hand, caressed it, then pressed the needles into the five scars on Dion's palm.

His muscles jerked. The virus flowed into his body, warming, burning, like dark lightning. Dion sighed and relaxed.

The mind-seizer put his arm around the young man, drew him near.

Chapter ···❈··· Thirteen

"The time has come," the Walrus said,
   "To talk of many things:
Of shoes—and ships—and sealing-wax—
   Of cabbages—and kings . . ."
      Lewis Carroll, *Through the Looking Glass*

The virus and micromachines flowed from Abdiel's body into Dion's. Their minds joined together and Dion was once again in the mind-seizer's dwelling he had first entered on Laskar.

Dion gazed around, wondering at the change, but not terribly astonished by it. The house was enormous, filled with rooms and in each room were valuable treasures, waiting to be explored, discovered. Treasures of ancient wisdom and vast knowledge stood next to treasures of cunning tricks, deceits, machinations.

I could roam among them freely, pick, choose. . . .

Abdiel sat on a sofa in the sweltering hot room. He held the long-stemmed pipe of a hookah in his shriveled hand. A puff of smoke wafted occasionally in the air, coming from his lips. The hookah made a gurgling sound.

"Please be seated, my king," Abdiel said.

Dion accepted the invitation, made himself comfortable. On the table, in front of the mind-seizer, were a handful of pills—Abdiel's dinner—Dion's bloodsword, and another weapon, a sort of scythe, he supposed, though it was unlike any he'd ever seen before. Made of crystal, it looked fragile and insubstantial, harmless, liable to shatter if one grasped it too tightly—almost like Abdiel himself.

"How nice to see you again, my king," continued Abdiel, as if they had just recently bumped into each other. "You are looking well. The royal bowings and scrapings suit you. You were born to it.

"Forgive the heat." Abdiel waved his hand vaguely. Dion could not see them but he had the impression of leaping flames, burning not too distantly beneath them. "You remember my infirmity. I live here, sleep here, eat here. A virtual prisoner. No other room in this blasted warren is warm enough. But then, we all make sacrifices . . ."

The lidless eyes gazed fixedly into Dion's, probed and prodded their way into his mind.

"Open up to me, my king. Don't fight me. We have much to discuss and little time. That ill-advised marriage you've agreed to, for example. Disastrous." The mind-seizer shook his head, sucked on the pipe. "Mark my words," he said, the stem clenched between his rotting teeth, "DiLuna means to rule, through her daughter, of course. She means to bring back the worship of the Goddess. Those women have ways, you know, of enticing men to do their bidding, of enslaving them.

"Or perhaps you don't know," added the old man, eyeing Dion shrewdly. "You haven't slept with the girl yet. But the contract hasn't been made that cannot be broken, my king. Acting on my advice, with my help, you should be able—"

"Your help!" Dion almost laughed. "Why should I invite your help? The last time you offered it, you betrayed me, tried to kill me."

"Yes," said Abdiel, nodding complacently.

"You have the effrontery to admit it?" Dion marveled.

"Of course," said the mind-seizer dryly. "I could hardly do otherwise. I was afraid of you, my king! Fear? Is that such a grievous fault in a minister? The great Machiavelli himself advised that 'it is better to be feared than loved.'

"With fear comes admiration, respect. You have humbled me, my king. Set me in my place. Allow me to serve you, then, as only I can. You have seen what doors I can unlock to your mind. And that was only a few, so very few. This is, after all, why you came to me, isn't it?"

"And what must I give you in return?"

"Give!" Abdiel chuckled, but he seemed irritated, put out. "What is all this talk of giving, of sacrifice? You are king, Dion Starfire! Kings take what they want. If you want that daughter of Olefsky's, take her. If you want Sagan's wealth and power, take it! If you don't want DiLuna, use her and cast her aside. I can show you how."

"And what is the difference between you and DiLuna?

Between you and Sagan? You want to use me, just as they do. You tried, once, and you failed, Abdiel. Remember?"

"I admit it freely, my king. I made a mistake. I underestimated you. I thought you were like those of the Blood Royal who produced you: your uncle—poor weak king. Your father, that giggling sycophant. Peter Robes, Derek Sagan, Platus Morianna, and his sister, Maigrey. Weak, all of them weak. And flawed. How could I suppose that you would be otherwise?

"But I discovered my mistake. You are far stronger than any of them, Dion. Far stronger than even you know. You have no need to fear me. I could never gain ascendancy over you, just as they've never been able to. I'm not flattering you. I'm speaking the truth, and you know it, my king. You are just beginning to understand, to feel your power. I can enhance that power, teach you the ways to use it to best advantage, as I taught Peter Robes."

"And in the end, you abandon him for me?" Dion looked at the bloodsword, lying on the table, near the crystal scythe.

Abdiel sniffed, took the pipe from his lips, coiled the tube around the hookah's base.

"Peter Robes! Weak like all the rest. Weak and shallow. I poured into him what I could. I had more to give—much more—but he lacked the capacity to hold it.

"You, Dion!" Abdiel sighed, closed his eyes in a kind of ecstasy. "I could empty my being into yours. Together, we would create a young and vital king, yet one who possesses the subtle knowledge and wisdom of my years."

Dion trembled, not with fear, but with desire. He knew, as Abdiel had said, that the mind-seizer was telling him the truth. This time, Abdiel had no intention of killing his king. This time, the mind-seizer meant what he said. He would deliver as promised.

The sacrifice? Myself. But then, I came prepared to make that sacrifice anyway.

"And what would become of me when you are gone?" Dion asked. "For you are mortal. Not all the biochemistry in the galaxy can keep you alive much longer."

"Sadly true, my king. But I foresee that a bond such as we will forge between ourselves will not be broken, even by death. You are still resisting me, my king. Open yourself to me completely. You will understand then what I mean. We have much to talk over."

Talk. Always that voice inside me. I'd hear it and no other. Never my own.

His voice, a voice he only recently learned to hear, one he had yet to learn to trust, to rely on. He had no doubt it would advise him wrongly, sometimes. It would make mistakes. It was young, inexperienced, flawed.

Dion smiled sadly. Perhaps this was one of those times. If so, it would likely be the final time. But when he died, the last voice he heard would be his own, not the voice of any others.

"Thank you, Abdiel," said Dion clearly. He stood tall and straight. "I know what you want to give me and I reject it. After all, I came only to get my sword."

He withdrew his hand from the mind-seizer's.

Abdiel did not try to stop him.

The lidless eyes stared at him. "Is that your final decision, my king?"

The vision of the dwelling lingered before Dion's eyes. He was filled with a deep sense of regret, suddenly, a sense of loss. All those rooms, all the knowledge held within, so much to have gained.

"It is," said Dion.

The vision began to fade.

"A poor one."

Abdiel lifted his hand, started to slide it into his robes. Patches of decaying skin flaked off, fell on the table, near the fragile-looking crystal scythe.

Dion was once more back in the chamber of burning water. His bloodsword lay before him on the tomb. The crystal scythe was nowhere in sight. Deeming the scythe unimportant, having more urgent matters on his mind, Dion forgot about it, forgot to wonder what it was or why it had been there.

He saw, out of the corner of his eyes, Mikael turn in his direction, aim the beam rifle at him. The disciple moved slowly, time moved slowly. It seemed to Dion he had all the time in the universe, time to notice small things, like the five glistening spots of blood in the palm of the hand that reached for the sword. Time to search within himself and know that what he was doing was right and that he wasn't afraid.

The last fight of the last of the Guardians, the last fight of the last king. We will fall, but we will be victorious. And the people will come to hear of our sacrifice and it will touch them and out of the ashes will rise a new order . . . like a phoenix. . . .

Dion's hand closed over the hilt of the bloodsword.

Abdiel's hand, hidden within the magenta robes, closed over the hilt of the serpent's tooth.

Chapter ·◆━○━◆· Fourteen

"Take the Long Way Home."

Super Tramp

Tusk groped his way through the dark spaceplane, making a mental note to duck to avoid hitting his head on the same metal beam on which he always hit his head and promptly rammed his knee painfully into the corner of a storage compartment. He swore briefly, bitterly. For once, XJ said nothing in reproach. The lights and life-support systems switched back on.

"You all right?" Nola called down anxiously.

"Yeah, I'm okay. You see anything of the kid?"

"He just walked into the cave or whatever it is."

"Nobody tried to stop him?"

"No, there's no one around."

"I don't like it. It's too damn quiet. You're positive you don't see anything? Maybe I should come up there, have a look myself."

"Sure, Tusk. If that's what you think's best." Her voice was too soft, too understanding.

Tusk knew he was behaving irrationally, knew Nola was dependable. Hell, he could depend on her more than he could on himself.

"I'll . . . be up in a minute," he muttered.

Sliding down the ladder into the cockpit, he subsided into the pilot's chair, moodily rubbed his bruised knee.

"So what was that little emotional outburst you treated us to," he remarked to the computer. "Jeez, you'd think you actually felt something for the kid."

"Emotional outburst!" XJ's lights flared indignantly. "Feelings! How dare you accuse me of such a thing! That was an electrical malfunction, occasioned by—"

"Yeah, yeah." Tusk eyed the space-rotation bomb gloomily. "Just how unstable is this thing?"

"You have insulted me for the last time!" XJ seethed, ignoring the question. "I've put up with a great deal from you, Mendaharin Tusca. Your juicing and your swearing and your refusal to pick up wet towels off the deck when you know how that irritates me, to say nothing of dragging me to an alien galaxy, putting our investment in extreme peril, with no hope of recouping our expenses. I—I—"

XJ was forced to pause, wait for its overloaded systems to cool down. "This is the end of our relationship! I've spoken with Captain Link. He's looking for a new partner. I believe—"

"Sure, yeah, fine."

Tusk wasn't listening. He fidgeted, stood up, sat down again. Something was wrong. Every nerve in his body was jumping and twitching. He felt like a guy who'd been on the juice for a week straight and was trying to come off.

"What are your scanners picking up?"

"Nothing," stated XJ. "I turned them off. The energy levels were beginning to—"

"Turned them off!"

"Tusk!" Nola shouted warningly.

He leapt to his feet, started for the ladder leading up to the gun turret.

The deck slid sideways, out from under him. Tusk grabbed onto the back of the pilot's chair. The plane jolted and rocked, settled back down.

"What the—"

"Tusk! There's a whole army out here!"

"Shit!" Tusk swore. "I knew it. XJ, take us up! Now, XJ!"

He swung himself back into the pilot's seat, began flipping switches. The lights flickered, but nothing happened. The plane remained sitting stolidly on the ground. Another shot rocketed into it.

"Tusk!" Nola shrieked.

"XJ!" Tusk said through clenched teeth. "This is no time to screw around! Get us the hell outta here!"

"Sorry," said the computer.

"What do you mean 'sorry'?"

"We can't take off!" XJ's audio crackled. "The anti-grav. That first shot—"

"Hit it? That's not possible. The shielding—" Tusk could hear, up above him, Nola open fire.

"It didn't hit it!" the computer shouted above the noise. "It's jammed, stuck! You remember? We had this same problem on Alpha Phi Delta Twenty-seven—"

"Fuck it!" Tusk slammed his fist into the console, then kicked it. He had some wild, irrational idea of jarring the anti-grav—located on the plane's underbelly—loose.

"Tusk!" Nola called.

He jumped out of the chair, climbed the ladder, stuck his head up into the bubble. "What's out there?"

"About seventy or so humans and God knows how many Corasians! It's the humans who're attacking. They've got some sort of lascannon. That's what hit us the first time."

The mind-dead, armed with lasguns and beam rifles, were swarming out of the ravaged forest, advancing steadily on his plane and his alone, paying no attention to the other space-planes—the lady's and those belonging to her commandos—parked nearby.

"They're after the bomb," guessed Tusk. "And us stuck down here, sitting ducks."

Nola fired, drove the mind-dead back. Only for a moment. Tusk made up his mind.

"I'm going out there. Maybe I can knock the drive loose. That's what I did the last time this happened."

"What?" Nola let go of the gun, made a grab for him, missed. "Tusk!" She tumbled down the ladder. "That's insane! You'll get yourself killed!"

"What're our odds if I don't, sweetheart? You keep me covered. With our firepower, they won't get close."

Grabbing a beam rifle and as many grenades as he could carry, Tusk kissed her swiftly on the cheek and was gone before she could hang on to him.

Another shot hit the spaceplane, right above where she was standing. Nola ducked, shielding her head. Bits of plastisteel and twisted metal rained down on top of her. When it cleared, she looked up into the bubble. It was no longer there.

"That . . . that was the gun, Tusk!" she cried.

"Glad you weren't with it, baby," Tusk said, starting up the ladder.

"But . . . but . . ." She began to protest, looked at Tusk's face. Gulping, she swallowed her words and the fear surging up inside her. "I'm going with you. Give me the rifle."

Tusk shook his head. He had reached the Scimitar's hatch. "Open up, XJ! It wouldn't work, Nola. Someone's got to stay inside, fly the plane if I get that mother knocked loose." Pausing, his hand on the hatch controls, he looked at her intently. "You understand, Nola? You've got to take this plane outta here, fast."

"You'll fly it, Tusk. When you get back on board."

"There may not be time for that, sweetheart."

She stared at him, shaking her head. "No."

"You got to. It's that simple. Look, I'll try to make it back, but if I don't, we can't let them get hold of the bomb. When I give the word, take off. You hear that, XJ?"

The computer's lights dimmed. "Yes, Tusk," it said.

Tusk climbed the ladder, pushed open the hatch, and was gone.

··◁▮ ▮▷··

Xris and his commandos had reached the planet's surface; their return trip uneventful.

"Boring as hell," Lee described it.

Several meters from the exit, however, the cyborg brought his squad to a halt.

"What's that?" Harry asked, listening. "Sounds like an explosion."

"Lascannon fire," said Xris. Taking the twist out of his mouth, he looked at it grimly, stuck it back in his pocket. "I thought this was too easy. Looks like they plan on throwing us a going-away party. C'mon."

The sound of lascannon fire nearly drowned out every other noise, but in between rounds, they heard blasts of answering fire.

"That's a Scimitar's gun. I'd recognize that weird whine they make anywhere," Bernard said, puzzled. "What's a Scimitar doin' out there?"

"It is as I said," stated Raoul, "the young king has arrived. He and his friends are under attack." He paused, listened to the Little One. "I beg your pardon. The Little One says that the young king is not there. His friends alone are being attacked by mind-dead."

"Yeah, well pardon me if I don't trust the Little One. I'll go see for myself."

Xris ran to the entrance into the mounds. Craning his head, he risked a look. After a moment he motioned. The others hurried up to join him.

"That's what's coming down, all right. There's a small army out there." Xris took the twist from his pocket, stuck it in his mouth, and lit it. "They've left our planes alone, though, at least. For the time being."

"What's that Scimitar doin' still on the ground? Why don't the guy take off?" Harry demanded.

"The Little One says that there is something wrong with the plane."

Bernard squinted to see. "Yeah, that must be it. Look, the pilot's coming out. Gonna try to fix it, I'll bet."

Safe in the tunnel's sheltering darkness, they watched the Scimitar's hatch pop open. A human male pulled himself out. Sliding down the ladder, he stopped at the bottom, fired off several rounds from the beam rifle he carried.

The mind-dead, surging across the open stretch of land between forest and the Scimitar, paused, hit the ground or ran for cover.

"Bastards're using our planes to hide behind," commented Harry. "I don't much like that. Good way to get our planes shot up."

The pilot ceased his fire, dashed around to the front of the spaceplane, crouched down beneath the underbelly. They could see him under the plane, peering at something.

"That's it," Xris commented, watching. "When it doesn't work, give it a good, swift kick."

"Anti-grav's stuck," said Lee. "Happens all the time to those old Scimitars. I heard they fixed it in the new ones."

The mind-dead dashed forward, beam rifle aimed directly at the pilot. Laser bursts flared around him, sparks showered down over him. The pilot hugged the ground, covering his head with his arms.

"They got him."

"No. No, they didn't. He's back up again. Looks like he's got help."

Another person appeared at the Scimitar's hatch. Beam rifle bursts forced the mind-dead to take cover. The pilot was kicking frantically at the jammed unit, began to beat on it with the butt end of the beam rifle.

The mind-dead fell back momentarily, but it was only to regroup, make a change in plans, shift their aim.

Harry, Lee, and Bernard exchanged glances.

"He's never gonna make it."

"We could help. Hell, they're not paying any attention to us."

They looked at Xris, who was staring grimly out the tunnel exit.

"The other person, the one covering him. It's a woman," said Lee.

"Girlfriend, maybe," Bernard commented.

"Or his wife," said Xris quietly, unexpectedly. He put the twist in his mouth, activated his weapons arm. "Give me five, then take off, get to the planes. They're our ticket off this blasted rock. Understand? You two"—he looked at Raoul and his companion—"stay here until the area's cleared, then run like hell."

Raoul nodded complacently. "Yes, I think it would be wise for us to stay here." He glanced down at his companion, who was whimpering into the fedora. "The Little One finds this all highly disturbing."

"What're you gonna do, boss?" Lee asked.

"Kick that damn Scimitar off the ground, if I have to. Ready? All right. I'm moving out. Don't shoot until it looks like they've spotted me."

"Boss," said Bernard, grinning. "This ain't in the contract."

"Yeah, it is," said Xris, taking the twist from his mouth and tossing it away. "Like the lady says, you've got to read the fine print."

Head down, Xris ran full tilt across the ground toward the Scimitar. The cybernetic part of his body operated smoothly, efficiently, the human half moved awkwardly, but kept up easily, sometimes seeming even determined to outrun the machine half.

The mind-dead caught a glimpse of him. A few turned their heads.

Xris's commandos shot out of the tunnel, yelling, drawing the enemy's attention. Blasting a hole in the line of mind-dead, they caught most of them completely by surprise, cut them down before they had a chance to see what was killing them from this unexpected direction.

But the attack failed to divert the zombies from their single-minded purpose, given to them by their master. They continued to advance on the Scimitar. The only thing that caused them to stop was death.

Lee peered through the blasts of laser fire, smoke, and sparks, saw Xris dive for cover beneath the belly of the spaceplane. Then the mind-dead closed in around the Scimitar and he lost sight of the cyborg and the pilot.

"Come on!" Bernard grabbed him. "Get to the planes! It's our only chance. Look what's coming!"

Lee looked, thought for a moment the woods had caught fire. But it wasn't. It was the Corasians.

···◅▮ ▮▻···

Xris ducked beneath the Scimitar's sheltering wing. Two rockets, launched from his weapons hand, exploded in the midst of the mind-dead, decimating their ranks, creating a momentary lull in their fire. The cyborg raced around to the plane's belly, crawled under. He found the pilot—a black human male—lying facedown on the ground. A pool of blood spread beneath him.

Shaking his head grimly, figuring the guy was dead, Xris turned his attention to the anti-grav unit, wondered what the hell it was he was looking at. He knew nothing about Scimitars.

". . . stuck," came a weak voice.

Xris glanced down. The pilot had rolled over onto his side. His hands were clasped over his chest, blood welled out from between the fingers. His face was twisted in pain, the black skin glistened.

"Kick it . . . there," he said, lifting a shaking finger, pointing.

Xris nodded, no sense in wasting words. Turning back, he aimed, slammed the cybernetic foot into the jammed part. It didn't budge, didn't even wiggle. Laser fire burst around him. Two grenades, tossed by the woman up above in the hatch, drove the zombies back.

Xris kicked the device again. No dice. Turning away, he reached down, took hold of the wounded pilot.

"What are you doing?" the man gasped. "You got to . . . keep trying!"

"It's stuck good and tight, brother. If this leg of mine won't knock it loose, nothing will. And we've got a better chance inside than out here."

"You maybe," said the pilot, trying to smile. "Not me. Go on. Leave me. Go . . . take care of Nola."

"What's your name?"

"Tusk."

"You a doctor, Tusk?" Xris grunted.

Tusk started to protest. The cyborg wrapped the remnants of the pilot's flight suit around him, hauled him up. Tusk groaned in agony, and passed out.

"Just as well," Xris said to himself. "This is going to be a rough trip."

He balanced the pilot's limp body over his left shoulder, clasped the strong cybernetic arm firmly around his legs, then dashed out from beneath the plane. Running around to reach the ladder, he began to climb. The woman, seeing him coming, crawled out onto the spaceplane's hull, flopped down on her stomach, poured a continuous stream of laser fire into the mind-dead below.

The cyborg didn't have time to be gentle. The body across his shoulder bounced, flaccid arms dangling down behind. Xris's clothes were wet with blood.

"If you're lucky, you'll be dead by the time we get inside," Xris told the unconscious man grimly.

A shot slammed into the cyborg's leg, nearly knocked him from the ladder. He held on, continued to climb. They'd hit his artificial leg. Fortunately, they hadn't hit the battery pack.

Xris made it to the hatch. The woman ceased firing, slung the beam rifle over her shoulder, reached to help. Her face went white when she saw the injured man, but she stayed calm, composed.

"Get below," Xris instructed. "I'll hand him down to you."

The woman nodded, did as he told her. Capable, gentle hands caught hold of the wounded man, lowered him to the deck.

"Toss me the rifle," Xris ordered.

The woman did so. The cyborg fired several bursts, stayed in the hatchway long enough to make certain his men reached their planes safely. He saw the Corasians, but their advance had been halted by, ironically, the mind-dead. The Corasians had stopped to feed off the bodies of their allies.

Satisfied, Xris slid down, shut and sealed the hatch.

"Who is it? What's going on?" came a voice from the front of the plane.

Xris stared into the cockpit, saw nothing, heard no sounds of any living being. "Who the hell's that?"

"Plane's computer," said the woman in an undertone. "It's all right, XJ," she called out. "Just . . . Tusk, coming back. He brought help."

"Tusk! What's that worthless excuse for a pilot doing inside here? He didn't get that anti-grav knocked loose yet! Send him up. I want a word with him."

"He . . . he can't come right now, XJ," said the woman. "Give him time to catch his breath."

"I'll let him catch his breath all right," snapped the computer viciously. "Five minutes, Tusk!"

"The mind-dead will probably storm the plane," Nola told Xris, not looking up at him, doing what she could to make the wounded man comfortable. "We have a space-rotation bomb on board and they want it."

"Yeah, so I heard," Xris said. "I don't think they'll get very far. You hear that racket out there? Those're my men, getting set to take off. Once they're airborne, they'll drop a few bombs themselves, make it tough for anything to survive long out there."

The woman looked up at him, smiled briefly, then turned back to the injured man, who had regained consciousness. She placed a pillow beneath his head and attempted, gently, to move the hands clutched over his chest and stomach.

"Don't, Nola," said Tusk softly. "It's bad. Real bad. Just . . . leave it . . . alone."

"Oh, Tusk!" she whispered and buried her face in his shoulder.

He attempted a smile, tried to say something. His voice choked, his face twisted in agony. He bit his lip to keep from crying out.

Nola heard, felt his pain, held him closer, as if she could hold him together.

Xris saw, near him, a storage compartment marked with a red cross. He rummaged in it, found what he wanted. Even then, he waited a moment longer to go back.

Nola was sitting up. "We need painkiller," she said briskly, "and blankets."

Xris held up a syringe. "I'll take care of him," he offered. "You go get the blanket."

The woman's eyes gleamed with unshed tears. Hurrying away, she opened a closet, pulled out a blanket. Xris gave Tusk the injection, saw Nola's shoulders slump, her head sink. She hid her face in the blanket. His augmented hearing picked up the sound of the sobs she was trying to muffle in the thick cloth.

Xris took a twist from his pocket, shoved it between his lips. The cyborg had also heard the sounds of footsteps outside the spaceplane, a faint thud now and then on the hull. Probably setting explosive charges planning to blow their way in.

The spaceplane shook. The inside of the Scimitar was lit by a bright flare of light. The banging on the hull ceased abruptly.

"What's going on out there? Tusk! I said five minutes," came a mechanical voice. A remote unit, small arms wiggling in frustration, popped out from the cockpit. "Where is that good-for-nothing? Ah, ha!" XJ pounced on the pilot. "Lying around, eh? Been in the jump-juice again, eh?"

The lines of pain had eased from Tusk's face. He opened one eye, peered fuzzily at the remote unit, and managed a grin. "XJ . . . go to hell," he whispered.

The remote's lights flared in fury. It hovered over the mercenary. "How dare you? I'll shut off every system in this plane! You won't have water for a week! I'll—What . . . what's wrong with him?" The computer's tone altered. "Look! His fluid's leaking out! Well, don't just stand around! Somebody do something! Repair him. You there, Tin Man!" XJ whirled furiously on Xris. "Make yourself useful! Boil some water. That's it! Boil water. Roll bandages. Unroll bandages—"

"That won't be necessary, XJ," Nola said, returning with the blanket. "Everything's under control."

She was, at least. She had dried her tears, cleaned all trace of them from her face. Gently, she covered Tusk, drawing the blanket up over his shoulders, studiously avoiding looking at the large crimson stain that immediately began spreading over the cloth.

"I guess this is the end, sweetheart," Tusk said quietly, looking at her, filling his mind with her light to drive back the dark shadows. "It's been kind of a strange life, but like the song says, we took the long way home. I guess I'm gonna get there before you do, but—"

"Nonsense, Tusk, don't talk like this." Nola quickly wiped away two tears that had crept past her guard. "We're going to get you to a hospital and you're going to be fine. Aren't you?" She ran her hand over Tusk's tight-curled hair, adjusted the pillow beneath his head.

"Nola, the fleet's four hours away and that's banking on everything going good." He coughed. He shifted his gaze to the cyborg. "You tell her."

Xris understood. "I'm sorry, sister, but I have to be honest. He won't last that long. Nothing short of a miracle can save him. The pain will get worse, much worse, until even the drug won't block it." The cyborg held the syringe to the light. "The best thing we could do for him would be to . . ."

Nola wasn't listening. "Miracle!" she repeated softly to herself. She was staring in the direction of the mounds. Swiftly, she bent down, kissed Tusk, fussed over his blanket. "Don't give him any more of that stuff."

"Nola!" Tusk groaned.

"Well, maybe just enough to keep him quiet," she added severely.

Getting to her feet, Nola walked over, took hold of the beam rifle, and, before Xris fully realized her intention, started to climb the ladder leading to the hatch. "You stay here, guard the bomb," she told him.

"Not so fast, sister!" The cyborg grabbed her wrist. "Just where do you think you're going?"

"Inside there." Nola gestured toward the mounds with a shake of her curly hair. "I have to find someone."

Xris stared at her. "Listen, sister! Those aren't grapefruit my boys are dropping outside there!"

The spaceplane rocked, shivered. Laser fire burst around them. Nola turned her head, looked reluctantly out the viewscreen. Spaceplanes dived, bright beams slanted along the ground, killing anything they hit. The forest was burning. Some of the Corasians, feeding off the fire's energy, were growing stronger, but anti-matter bombs were now falling among them. Blackened dying blobs littered the area in front of the mounds.

"And if you did manage to make it to the tunnels alive, you're going to face more of those things, not to mention those human zombies. You haven't got a chance, sister!" Xris's strong cybernetic hand tightened its grip.

"Neither has he," said Nola, looking at him steadfastly. Tears glimmered in her eyelashes. "And do you think that if anything happened to him, I'd want to go on?"

Xris regarded her thoughtfully. Slowly, the cyborg released his hand.

"All right. I'll contact my men, tell them to give you covering fire if they can, at least watch out for you if they can't. Once you make it inside, there's a Loti who might be able to help you find whoever it is you're looking for and keep you from falling in with the wrong crowd. His name's Raoul. He's got a buddy, an empath."

He was rewarded with a smile that rearranged the freckles on the woman's pale face, lit her green eyes.

"Stay with Tusk, XJ," Nola called to the remote. "Don't let him die. Remember, he owes you money."

"Die!" The remote's lights flickered. It sank to the deck. Then, with a struggle, XJ roused itself. "Owes me money. That's right. If this isn't just like you, Tusk. You'd do anything to try to screw me out of money. You d-die"—XJ's audio fluttered, but it managed to hang on—"and I'll sue your black ass! And now, I . . . I have to go . . . figure out how much . . . you owe me!"

Wobbling unsteadily, the remote fled back to the cockpit. "Excuse me," it said. "System failure."

The lights went out.

Tusk shouted. "Nola! For God's sake—"

"Good-bye, Tusk. Don't go anywhere without me."

Nola's footsteps clattered on the ladder, the hatch whirred open, shut again.

"Why'd you let her go?" Tusk demanded.

The cyborg lit the twist in his mouth, blew smoke.

"I had a wife . . . once," he said.

Chapter ❖ *Fifteen*

One equal temper of heroic hearts,
Made weak by time and fate, but strong in will
To strive, to seek, to find, and not to yield.
Alfred, Lord Tennyson, *Ulysses*

The fire burning on the water seemed to burn in Sagan's brain. He could literally neither see nor hear clearly for the rage that consumed him. The flames of his fury roared in his ears, the smoke clouded his vision, the heat sucked the air from his lungs. He had to struggle to breathe, to draw a breath. Pain shot through his chest, sweat chilled his body. He alternately shivered and burned with the fever of his anger.

He had experienced fury like this only one other time in his life: the night Maigrey had betrayed him. It had been in a red rage like this one that he'd struck her down. And now, again, she had been the one to stop him, thwart him. . . .

Sagan struggled with himself, but the flames licked his soul, seared his mind. The pain in his chest increased, blood boiled in his head. It seemed something must burst and it occurred to him, suddenly, that unless he could regain control, he would die, consumed by the fire.

"You counseled me to keep my faith, my lord," came a voice, soft, gentle, soothing as balm. "I do not understand His ways, but I rest my trust in Him."

A hand touched Sagan's. He felt an object press hard against his palm, a dagger, its metal warm from being carried near the body, its blade small but extremely sharp, its hilt—an eight-pointed star.

"'*Benedictus, qui venit in nomine Domini.* Blessed is he that cometh in the name of the Lord,'" whispered Brother Fideles.

❖❖

Maigrey watched Brother Daniel move nearer Sagan, heard the priest's gentle voice, and was afraid, for a moment, from the dark fury on Sagan's face that he might strike the young man.

"'*Benedictus, qui venit in nomine Domini.* Blessed is he that comes in the name of the Lord,'" Brother Daniel said softly.

The expression on the Warlord's face did not alter, the rage smoldered inside, but the fire no longer blazed wild, out of control. He was rational once more, thinking. Either Brother Daniel's prayers were extremely powerful, or he had offered something besides prayer.

Maigrey did not dare risk the mind-link. Abdiel was preoccupied with Dion, his mental probes darting, jabbing into the young man, but part of him would be alert to their thoughts, their plans.

She was aware of Sagan staring at her strangely, intently, as if he had some dark and dreadful choice to make and was asking her for help.

She smiled at him, reminding him silently that no matter how deep the darkness around them, they were together once more. Nothing, no one had ever defeated them, when they acted together.

Abruptly Sagan averted his gaze. He sighed, long, shuddering. His mind touched hers, but it came to her from a far distance. He had withdrawn, retreated behind the walls of his soul.

Be ready.

He had a plan, but gave no hint of it. Of course, he dared not. Abdiel would be listening.

Tense, Maigrey measured distances with her eyes, tried to anticipate what Sagan had in mind. Mikael, the mind-dead who stood guard over them, was nearest the Warlord and would, therefore, be Sagan's responsibility.

She was nearest Abdiel and Dion, though the bier separated them. But there was no telling what the mind-seizer would do, when Dion refused him.

If Dion refused him.

He would. He was Semele's son, after all. She had seen from the moment he entered that he was his own person now; he had chosen to be the hero of his own life. After this, he would no longer need them, his Guardians. And that was right, the way it should be. And when he made his choice, his decision, he would reach for his sword. As he was doing, now. His right hand, separating itself from Abdiel's deadly touch. The left, reaching out . . .

"I know what you want to give me and I reject it. After all, I came only to get my sword." Dion spoke aloud.

Maigrey, looking at Sagan but not looking, saw the muscles in his arms and shoulders tighten, saw him flick his gaze swiftly at her, nod obliquely at the mind-dead guard.

"Is that your final decision, my king?" Abdiel was asking.

Mikael, hearing the voice, turned his dead eyes toward Abdiel, the one who gave him life. Maigrey answered the Warlord, lowering her eyelids slightly, imperceptibly to show she understood. Sagan opened the fingers of his left hand, the hand near Brother Daniel. Maigrey saw a flash of silver in his palm, then the fingers closed over it.

She understood. He had the priest's dagger.

"It is," said Dion.

"A poor one." Abdiel's hand slid inside the folds of the magenta robes.

Mikael raised the beam rifle, but uncertain who to shoot, he looked to Abdiel for orders. The mind-seizer's thoughts were not on his disciple, however.

The crystal scythe glittered in the firelight.

"Dion, get back!" Maigrey cried.

Dion saw the flash of the blade. Twisting sideways, he hurled his body across the bier, making, in the same motion, a wild, desperate grab for his sword.

Abdiel's blow sliced harmlessly through the air. He raised the blade again, brought it slashing down on the rock bier.

Dion rolled, fell off the tomb, and landed heavily on the floor. He scrambled to his feet, fumbling at the sword, trying to fit the needles into a hand that shook with excitement and tension.

"Kill the Guardians!" Abdiel ordered his disciple. "I will deal with the king!"

Mikael spun around, facing Maigrey, beam rifle aimed, ready to fire.

The Warlord sprang, stabbed swiftly, skillfully, driving the small blade of the priest's dagger into the mind-dead's neck, severing the spinal cord.

Mikael dropped without a cry.

"You're finished, mind-seizer!" Sagan shouted. "Give up!"

Abdiel, swinging the scythe, advanced on Dion.

The young man looked up at the fragile crystal scythe. It

seemed he couldn't believe he was being seriously attacked with such a weapon.

"Don't let the blade touch you!" Maigrey cried, climbing over the bier, trying desperately to reach him.

Startled, obeying, if not understanding, Dion dodged, just as Abdiel swung the scythe. The serpent's tooth whistled past the young man's chest.

Dion managed to drive the needles of the bloodsword into his hand. He raised the weapon against the mind-seizer.

The bloodsword wouldn't activate.

Dion stared at it in dismay, shook it.

Abdiel struck again. Dion blocked the scythe's blow with the bloodsword's hilt.

"What's wrong with it?" he shouted.

"He's drained the power!" Maigrey caught her breath in terror, but the hand-guard on the bloodsword protected the young man's flesh from the tooth's dreadful bite.

Dion turned the blow, fell back before the old man's frantic attack.

Maigrey made a lunge for the mind-seizer, hoping to grasp the wrist of his knife hand, break it. Abdiel was aware of her, aware of her intent. Whirling, he slashed out at her with the crystal blade.

"Keep your distance," he warned.

Maigrey halted.

"Mind-seizer!" The Warlord sprang on top of the bier. The small dagger in his hand, he jumped to the ground behind Abdiel. "You can't fight all three of us!"

Abdiel turned, scythe shaking slightly in the palsied hand. Slowly, talking the while, he began to retreat down the narrow span of rock, heading for the entrance to the northern passage that lay behind him.

"I don't intend to fight you, Derek. I have no need. My forces by this time have acquired the space-rotation bomb, compliments of His Majesty. I have a working bomb. I don't need the plans to build another. I shall simply walk out of here, leave you to the Corasians. That is *not*, unfortunately, how I intended to destroy you, but I will try to bear up under the disappointment.

"I suppose I shall have to go back to that fool, Peter Robes." Abdiel grimaced, transferred the lidless gaze to Dion. "One final offer, my king. One last chance to become a true ruler of men? Ah, don't try it, Derek!" The mind-seizer whirled, faced Sagan, held up the serpent's tooth. "Unless you'd prefer this 'life' to death in a Corasian meat locker?"

The Warlord's fingers clenched and unclenched around the hilt of the small ceremonial dagger. He said nothing to her, but Maigrey understood his plan, as they'd always understood each other. He was going to risk it all on one desperate lunge.

Maigrey glanced swiftly around, gauged the situation. Dion stood about three paces from her, to her right. Abdiel was directly in front of her, on the bridge, Sagan six paces to her left. She was closest to Dion. It would be her duty to guard the king.

She looked back at Derek, saw him prepared, mentally, physically, to strike. She put out of her mind what might happen to him, to them both, and braced herself to run.

"We can't just let him go!" Dion shouted, frustrated. He was still gripping the useless bloodsword. "He has the bomb—"

"No . . . no, he doesn't, kid. . . ."

Dion lowered the bloodsword, pressed his hand over the commlink at the base of his skull, behind his left ear. "Tusk?"

The voice was weak, barely audible.

"I heard, kid. And I've got the bomb. Safe. Tell that bastard . . . to go to . . . to go to . . ."

"Tusk!" Dion cried, but there was no answer.

The young man raised his eyes, fixed his gaze on Abdiel. "The space-rotation bomb is safe. Your forces have been defeated."

"You expect me to believe you?" asked Abdiel coolly.

"I can't lie to you. You told me that yourself. Contact your disciples, mind-seizer." Dion stood tall, blue eyes shining cold and brilliant, reflecting the flame, fire on ice. "Does anyone respond? Anyone at all?"

"They won't," added Maigrey, silver armor shining. "I will share the vision with you, if you want, mind-seizer. The cyborg and his men have wiped out your mind-dead. The Corasians are under attack and will soon be destroyed."

"You're finished, mind-seizer." The Warlord straightened. "Throw *your* blade into the water."

Abdiel's face did not alter expression, the lidless eyes left Dion, slid to Sagan, and from Sagan to Maigrey.

"*I'm* finished?" the mind-seizer hissed, and laughed. "Who are really the losers here? An old man who brought down a royal house? An old man who has ruled a galaxy for eighteen years? An old man who made three of the most powerful people in the universe bow to his will?

"Or the three of you. This is the end of the Blood Royal, and you know it. You are fighting a battle that, though you win, you must inevitably lose. For this 'king' will be the last. . . ."

Abdiel whirled, aimed the crystal scythe at Dion, and threw.

Maigrey sensed the mind-seizer's thoughts shift to Dion, saw Abdiel's eyes follow the thought, his hand follow the eyes. Sagan was racing to stop the mind-seizer, but the Warlord would be too late. Maigrey sprang forward, shoved Dion as far from danger as she could, shielded him with her body.

The crystal scythe flashed in the air, a small, fiery comet. It struck shining silver armor. The scythe shattered. Shards of glass glittered in the blazing light, a myriad tiny, fiery suns fell, gleaming, to the rock floor, flickered, and went out.

Dion was knocked to the floor by Maigrey's blow. He started to get to his feet.

"Don't touch any of the crystal," she warned. "Even the smallest slivers are still deadly."

Gingerly, keeping his bare hands off the bits of broken glass, he stood up, hurried over to her.

"Are you all right, my lady?" he asked anxiously.

"Yes, sire." Maigrey smiled, quickly moved her left hand to cover her right. "And you, Your Majesty?"

"I'm fine." Dion looked over to Abdiel.

Sagan had one arm locked around the mind-seizer's chest, his other hand grasped the needle-glistening palm, kept it pinned firmly to the old man's side. Abdiel hung limply in the Warlord's grasp. The lidless eyes glinted malevolently.

Dion stepped forward. "You are our prisoner, mind-seizer. You will be taken back to our galaxy and put on trial for your crimes—"

Sagan tightened his grip. "He must die, Your Majesty. As long as he lives, you are not safe from him."

Brother Daniel, standing behind the bier, forgotten, came hurrying forward. "You can't mean to murder him, my lord."

"It wouldn't be murder. An execution. Long overdue."

Dion frowned. "No, he can do nothing to me now. I know him for what he is. He's old and feeble and helpless. It would be dishonorable to kill him. I won't have his murder on my conscience."

The old man laughed. "You think Derek will obey you? He's

long wanted my death. You won't stop him. And night after night, you will dream of this place, of this time, my king. And when you dream, Dion, you will dream of *me*. . . ." He chuckled again, dryly, a hoarse croak. "Go ahead. Kill me, Lord Derek Sagan. I've done far worse to you!"

The lidless eyes looked to Maigrey, and they shone with a strange and terrible exultation.

Maigrey stood quietly, calmly, her left hand covering her right. The grey eyes were mirrors, without expression, letting no one inside. Sagan saw, on her fingers, a thin, glistening trail of blood.

The old man disdained to struggle. He seemed almost to nestle in the Warlord's arms. "Kill me, Derek!" he breathed. "Kill me now! Kill me while the boy watches. Kill me, as you killed his Guardian. . . . Kill me as you *will* kill the one, the only person you ever loved. . . ."

"Sagan, no!" Dion shouted. "I command you!"

"My lord, stop! For the sake of your own soul!" Brother Daniel endeavored to fling his arms around Sagan.

The Warlord didn't hear, couldn't hear for the roaring of the raging anger within him. He hurled Daniel from him, knocked Dion away. Sagan's strong hands took firm hold of the old man's frail neck, twisted, jerked.

Bones cracked and crunched. Abdiel screamed horribly. His head flopped like the head of a broken doll, the feeble body went limp. But the lidless eyes stared at Sagan, seemed to be laughing at him. The dead lips were parted in a smile. The Warlord flung the corpse to the ground, kicked the body, kicked it to the edge of the bridge.

Brother Daniel ran to stop the desecration. "My lord, no more!" he pleaded.

Sagan kicked the corpse off the bridge. It fell into the fiery water with a splash, floated on the surface amid the flames. The magenta robes began to smoke, smolder. Abdiel's face looked up at them, smiling.

Daniel saw the madness in the Warlord's eyes. The priest turned to Maigrey, hoping she might help. "My lady!" he began, but his words died on his lips.

She had moved swiftly to wipe away the blood, wipe it on the silver armor. But not swiftly enough.

"*Deus!*" Brother Daniel whispered.

Maigrey saw he knew the truth.

"Say nothing to him." She spoke without a voice, glanced meaningfully at Dion.

Sick at heart, horror-stricken, Brother Daniel turned away. Abdiel's body, floating in the water, had caught fire and was blazing brightly. The smell of burned flesh drifted up with the smoke. The prayer for the salvation of the soul of the dead was bitter on the priest's lips. He placed his hand on the Warlord's arm.

"My lord, I know, I understand," Daniel said softly. "She needs you now. His Majesty needs you. Don't abandon them."

The Warlord drew a long, shuddering breath. The fire died in his eyes, died in his heart.

"Dion!" A woman's clear voice echoed through the chamber. "Dion! Where are you? Are you in there?"

"Nola?" Dion turned toward the eastern tunnel entrance. "Nola! I'm here!"

Sagan took advantage of the distraction to grab hold of Brother Daniel's arm, draw him near.

"You know?" Sagan repeated. "You understand what will happen to her?"

"Yes, my lord."

"Then you know you've got to get the king out of here. Take him up to the surface. Stay with him."

"God help me!" the priest whispered. "What do I say?"

"Anything! Make some excuse! Just—"

A woman ran inside the chamber. Ignoring everyone else, she hurried to Dion, grasped hold of him. "It's Tusk, Dion. He's hurt. Bad, really bad. He's—" She paused, unable to keep from crying. Shaking the tears from her eyes, she continued steadily, "he's dying. He needs you."

"Tusk . . . dying." Dion stared at her.

"You must go to him, Dion," Maigrey said. She swayed where she stood, but her voice was firm. "He's your friend. He needs you now. You owe him a great deal."

The Warlord put his arm around her. Maigrey leaned against him, grateful for the support.

"I owe him more than I can ever possibly repay," Dion said quietly.

"Dion, come, please!" Nola clasped hold of him.

"Of course, I'll come. Don't cry, Nola. He's going to be fine. It's probably just a flesh wound. You know what a fuss he makes."

"I'm a nurse, Your Majesty," said Brother Daniel, thanking God his prayer had been answered. One of them, at least. "Perhaps I could be of assistance. If . . . if my lord doesn't need me—?"

"Go with His Majesty, Brother. I will do what needs to be done here."

The priest heard the bitter grief in the man's tone, saw it in the face, dark, ravaged. Maigrey's skin was deathly white, the livid scar had all but disappeared. And though the Warlord supported her, it seemed that she was the one giving him strength, not needing it. She smiled at the priest.

Brother Daniel came to her, placed his hand on her wrist. "God is with you," he said in a low voice.

"It makes no difference," she said steadily. "The choice was mine."

The Warlord's faced darkened. "Is He with us, Brother? Where?"

The priest started to reply, to give the proper response, the response he'd known and trusted in all his life. But his hand on Maigrey's arm could feel, already, the fever of the poison burn in her flesh. Abruptly, he turned away.

"I'll be sending for *Phoenix*, my lord," Dion was saying. Sheathing his bloodsword, he strapped the weapon around his waist. "The warship will destroy this planet and its machines for good. We'll get Tusk to the sick bay. I'll be on his Scimitar, if I'm needed."

Dion glanced at Maigrey, frowned. "You should come back with us, my lady. That cut on your hand doesn't look serious, but it should be attended to."

Maigrey's lips parted to answer. Her voice failed her. Sagan clasped her tightly, lent her his strength.

She drew a deep breath. "Go to Tusk, Dion. He made this sacrifice for you. Only you can help him now, if you choose to do so."

Dion didn't know how to respond. He had the feeling that something was dreadfully, terribly wrong, but it was as if a thick curtain of darkness had been dropped before his eyes. He struggled to part it. Stronger hands and minds than his kept it intact.

Nola fidgeted nervously beside him, tugged at his sleeve.

"God go with Your Majesty," said Maigrey.

Dion stared at her, stared at Sagan, trying to penetrate the shadows.

The curtain remained lowered.

Turning on his heel, back stiff, head held high, the king walked out, left his Guardians behind.

Chapter ··◆◐◯◑◆·· Sixteen

E quindi uscimmo a riveder le stelle.
Thence we came forth to see the stars again.
    Dante, *Divina Commedia. Inferno.*

Maigrey and Sagan stood alone in the chamber of burning water, alone, except for the dead.

"Dion's angry," said Maigrey, looking after the king, her last image of him blurred by her tears. "He doesn't understand."

"He will, soon enough," replied Sagan.

Maigrey felt her reason slipping from her. The pain was intense, sapping her strength, wearing her down. It had taken all the courage and effort of her will to remain standing, to hide the truth from Dion. Darkness came over her. On the horizon of her mind, she could see armies of twisted, demented creatures rising up to do battle. They did not come to kill her, she knew, but to arm her with terrible weapons, and carry her, triumphant, to be their leader in murderous insanity.

"My lady . . ." Sagan's voice, gentle, called her.

He caught her when she fell, held her in his arms, and for a moment the armies were driven back, daunted by the bright gleam of his golden armor. Clashing their weapons, they howled and gibbered in impatience. But they kept their distance. For the time being. They were patient. They knew victory must ultimately be theirs.

"You'll . . . stay with Dion?" Maigrey asked.

"He doesn't need me now, my lady. He will do better on his own. Abdiel was right. Though we won the battle, we must lose the war. We are the end. He is the last. After him, the crown returns to ordinary mortals."

"Men created by God, not by men. The victory is His." Maigrey closed her eyes, rested her head against his chest. The breastplate that covered his flesh was warm from the heat

486

of his body. She could feel the beating of his heart, strong and steady; she heard each indrawn breath.

Closely as he held her, he could not hold her close enough. She felt herself begin to slip from his grasp. A cloud rose to cover the sun, dimming the golden armor. The armies raised a terrible cheer, began to surge forward. Frightened, shuddering, she hid from the ghastly sight, hid her face in his shoulder.

"Derek, stop them! Don't let them take me!" she cried, clinging to him.

"I'm here, my lady," he answered, and his strength comforted her. "Trust me, Maigrey. I won't fail you."

Once more, the armies retreated, fell back. But they came a little closer, every time.

Maigrey looked around, shivering. "Not down here," she whispered. "They have us trapped down here. We must go to the surface, go to where we can see the stars."

·◆ ➡·

He carried her through the dark tunnels, not knowing where he was going, not caring. From the slope of the rock floor and the increasing biting coolness of the flowing air, he guessed that he was moving upward.

At times, she was with him. And at other times, she was not. He sensed her leave him and followed after her, and through the mind-link, he succeeded. He stood on a blasted plain, an empty battlefield beneath a glaring sun. She fought, alone, against legions of apparitions sprung from the appalling depths of human depravity. Apparitions whose intent was not to slay her but to make her their queen.

He was powerless to defend her, for he had no weapon, nothing but a small ceremonial dagger with a hilt in the shape of an eight-pointed star.

He saw her once as she would appear on the other side. A woman savage, brutal, silver armor changed to steel, her beauty made hideous by her cruelty.

He called to her fiercely, loudly, and she managed to free herself from the grasping, clutching hands and return to him, but she was weak, wrung by pain and by her own fear, for she had seen herself, knew what she would become, knew she was powerless to stop it.

The glaring sun beat down on them with blinding white-hot

fury. Her body burned with fever. She begged for water to quench a thirst that would never be satisfied, writhed in an anguish that would never be soothed. No sleep, no rest, no ease; no difference between sleeping and waking except that she lived by day the nightmares she dreamed by night.

He held her close, pressed her to him, and for a brief time he shaded her from the burning sun, his voice silenced the braying of the iron trumpets, the beating of the heartless drums, the laughter of her tormentors. In that fleeting moment of stillness and peace they said to each other what they had never said in the turmoil of their lives.

And then the armies dashed forward, the trumpets shrieked, the drums boomed, steel clashed. Skeletal hands, wiry tendrils, misshapen coils snaked out, wrapped around her. She fought, struggled against them. Raising herself up, she put both hands on his face and looked at him long, earnestly, keeping him between her and the sight of the horror.

And he knew it must be now.

"My lady!" he cried and snatched her away from the terror and saw the sun go out.

···◁■ ■▷···

Sagan came to himself in cold and in darkness. He was on the planet's surface, kneeling on the chill, rock-strewn ground. He cradled Maigrey in his arms. His right hand was wet with blood that made glistening trails down the silver armor. In his right hand, he held the dagger; its sharp blade glimmered in the starlight.

"My lady!" he whispered and, looking down at her, saw she was at peace, her pain ended, lying quiet on the empty battlefield.

"I'm sorry, my lord," she said softly, with a sigh that took the last breath from her body. "Mine is the easy part."

"My lady!" he cried.

But her gaze had shifted from him. She looked up into the night sky and smiled.

And he saw, reflected in her eyes, the bright and shining stars.

Chapter ❧◦◦◦❧ Seventeen

The darkness is no darkness with thee . . .
Prayer Book, 1662, Psalms 139:5

The planet's surface was quiet when Dion emerged from the mounds. A man, armed with a beam rifle, stood alert in the entryway. He had apparently heard their approach long before they saw him, for he had his rifle aimed and ready. Dion came to a halt, wished he'd thought to ask Nola for her lasgun. The man ignored him, however.

"You Nola?" he asked, lowering the rifle.

"Yes."

"I'm Lee. Xris sent me. It's all clear. Brother Daniel, glad to see you're still in one piece." He sounded considerably astonished. "Guess that God of yours pulled you through, huh?"

"I was spared, though I'm not certain why," said Brother Daniel quietly. "Others were not as fortunate."

Lee's expression grew somber. "Yeah. I hear you're needed in that Scimitar. Go on ahead. I'm pullin' guard duty. Don't worry about that," he added, indicating several explosions that lit the night sky. "Harry and Bernard are mopping up."

"We will remain here," stated a Loti, whom Dion vaguely recognized as someone he'd seen before, though he couldn't remember where. "The Little One is extremely tired following his exertions."

"Thank you for your help," said Dion.

"We were pleased to have been of service to Your Majesty." The Loti fluttered, bowed gracefully, handed Dion a gold-embossed card.

COMPLIMENTS OF SNAGA OHME.

Dion thrust it in his pocket.

Nola didn't hear the Loti, she had already hurried on ahead.

Dion had the feeling she would have gone even if the area had been crawling with Corasians.

He went after her, saw Lee's glance flick over him curiously. "King, huh?" he thought he heard the man say as he passed him. Lee sounded impressed.

Dion himself wasn't feeling particularly impressed. His victory was yet still unreal to him, the golden gleam dimmed by a shadow of impending loss, sorrow, bitter regret.

He couldn't understand it, but the farther he walked from that chamber of burning water, the heavier his heart grew, the more difficult it became to move through the darkness. At one point, he halted, with the idea of turning back, but the priest, hand on his arm, reminded Dion gently that his obligation lay to his friend, who had been wounded in the king's cause.

They came within sight of the Scimitar. Nola flung down the heavy beam rifle, broke into a run. Dion was hard-pressed to keep up with her. The ground was uneven, covered with rocks and littered with the bodies and pieces of bodies of the mind-dead. He heard Brother Daniel, hastening along at his side, mutter whispered words of prayer that sounded, to Dion, as if they were flung at the Creator in defiance, rather than offered in the spirit of a contrite heart.

Dion reached the Scimitar, began to climb up the side toward the hatch. Memories assailed him suddenly, and for a moment he couldn't have told if he was on this tortured fragment of an unnamed planet or back on Syrac Seven.

It had been night, then, too. He remembered scrambling up the side of the Scimitar in the darkness, remembered Tusk swearing at him one moment, offering rough sympathy the next, pushing and prodding him along. If it had been up to Dion, the boy would have sat down on the empty sidewalk and waited, uncaring, for whatever might have come.

Dion lowered himself through the hatch, slid down the ladder, remembered the first time he'd come down that ladder. He'd come down slowly, terrified he'd slip, fall, look like a fool.

Landing lightly on the deck, he saw a tall, muscular man hunkered over Tusk. Not man, Dion corrected, looking at him again, but half man, half machine. The cyborg, a long, thin piece of tobacco in his mouth, spent no more than a minute regarding Dion, as if his mechanical eye, with its augmented vision, could see through the young man's flesh, analyze every part of him, snap his image, and carry it forever.

"How is he, Xris?" Nola asked, her heart on her lips.

"Alive." The cyborg stood up, shifted the twist in his mouth from one side to the other.

Nola knelt down on the deck. Tusk lay beneath a blanket, his black skin shining with sweat, body shivering with fever and pain. The blanket covering him was soaked with blood. Blood lay in a pool on the deck, was slippery beneath their feet.

Dion's throat constricted.

Brother Daniel came up behind him.

"Are you all right, Your Majesty?"

"I didn't . . . expect it to be this bad," Dion said, the burning ache of fear and grief nearly choking him.

"You must be strong, for his sake."

Nola caressed Tusk's forehead, ran her hand through the tight-curled hair.

Tusk looked up at her. "Let me go, sweetheart!" His breath came in gasps. "Let me go!"

"Tusk, I've brought Dion," she said, forcing a smile.

"The kid?" Tusk looked pleased. "He's okay—" He coughed, gagged. Blood trickled out the side of his mouth.

Brother Daniel was at his side, skilled, gentle hands doing what they could to make the wounded man more comfortable. He wiped away the blood, mopped the sweat-covered face with a soft cloth, offered by the cyborg.

Nola's face grew paler, she kept smiling, kept soothing him. But when she turned to Dion, her eyes were anguished, pleading.

Dion started to kneel down beside Tusk when the lights on board the spaceplane suddenly flared, nearly blinding him. In the next instant, the plane's interior was plunged into darkness.

"Get those lights back on!" ordered Brother Daniel sharply.

An odd blurping sound came from the front of the plane. Dion noticed then a wild fluctuation in the air temperature. A chill blast blew down the back of his neck, hot air baked his feet.

"XJ?" Dion called, afraid to move, afraid to fall over Tusk. "XJ, damn it, turn on the lights!"

"Swearing! Don't swear. You know . . . how I . . . how I . . . Underwear . . . on the deck. In the fridge. Can't move . . . 'out tripping over . . . shorts. And towels. Wet towels . . . wet towels."

The lights flickered, came on dimly.

"I didn't mean it!" XJ hiccuped. "I didn't mean it about Link! He's not half the pilot Tusk is! No one could fly this baby like Tusk! And I don't care about the money he owes me. What's one hundred and seventy-three kilnors and forty-nine . . . forty-nine . . ."

Dion crouched down beside Tusk. The mercenary looked up at him, managed a weak grin. "Jeez, it's almost been worth it," he breathed, "just to hear old XJ . . . carryin' on."

He closed his eyes, drew a ragged breath that clicked in his throat.

"How bad is it?" Dion asked the priest in a low tone.

Brother Daniel lifted the blanket, glanced beneath it. His face grim, he replaced the blanket, looked at Dion, and motioned him to stand. They walked over to where the medkit rested on top of a storage chest.

"I'm sorry, Your Majesty. If he'd been in a hospital, he might have had a chance. But now . . ." The priest shook his head. Lifting the syringe, he began to fill it with the remainder of the painkiller. "This will make him sleep. If you have anything to say to him, say it now. He won't wake up."

Dion sighed, lowered his head. "Let me tell him good-bye—"

"No!"

The men turned, saw Nola standing behind them. Her face was white, but firm and resolute. The green eyes were fixed on Dion. "You can help him!"

Dion licked his lips. "Nola, I'm not a doctor—"

"You can heal him! You did it before! And that was a stranger! Tusk risked his life for you, Dion. You can't let him die."

"Nola, I don't know . . . That other . . . may have been a . . . a coincidence. Sagan himself said . . ."

"Lady Maigrey said you could help your friend." Brother Daniel reminded him.

Was that what Maigrey had meant? Dion wondered dazedly. Had she been giving him her sanction? Her blessing? Her reassurance? And what about Sagan. After all the arguments. Everything he'd said. The bitter sarcasm. . . . Had he meant any of that? Or had the arguments been an attempt to force me to mean it?

Nola's face became a blur. Brother Daniel's was too sharp, too vivid. Xris's mechanical eye stared into him, like another eye, a calm, unblinking eye. Dion was frightened, more frightened than he had been facing certain death. He was frightened of himself, of failing. For if he did fail, it meant he would fail, always.

God go with Your Majesty, came a voice. Maigrey's voice, or maybe the priest's.

And Dion knew he wouldn't fail. He would be granted the power, but not without cost. And, at last, he understood what that cost would be. He had come prepared to sacrifice his life. He would do so, only not in the way he had imagined.

He would give it up, little by little, piece by piece, everyone wanting, taking a tiny part of him, eating his food to sustain themselves, drinking his water to quench their thirst, warming themselves at his fire.

This is what the rite had tried to teach him. This is what it meant to be king.

"I can't do it alone!" he said and didn't realize he'd spoken aloud until Brother Daniel answered him.

"You won't be alone, Your Majesty. I am here for you and"— the priest hesitated a moment, then said firmly—"and so is He."

"I want to believe you, but I can't see Him and I don't know where to look."

"Within, Your Majesty." Brother Daniel placed his hand on his heart. "You look within."

Dion closed his eyes. In his mind, he went back to Syrac Seven, went back to the house in the middle of the prairie, back to the garden and his music, back to the open window, the breeze ruffling his hair, the pages of his book.

Dion went back to Platus, who had loved him for himself.

Dion went back.

And he took Tusk with him.

Chapter ❖❖❖ Eighteen

. . . to lose thee were to lose myself.
John Milton, *Paradise Lost*

Phoenix had arrived at the Corasian outpost. The warship maintained a stationary position between planet and sun. Its short-range Scimitars patrolled deepspace, keeping watch for the Corasian strike force that was reportedly on the way.

The cruise liner, *Galaxy Belle*, had joined it. Its captain had, for some reason, refused to leave the vicinity, though she had been given the coordinates necessary to make the Jump. A contingent of men was sent over to assist the captain. Scimitars surrounded the liner protectively, in case of attack.

Phoenix would remain in the vicinity only long enough to remove those on the planet, then destroy the outpost. A demolition squad, armed with proton bombs, had been sent below.

Xris and his commandos were taken aboard *Phoenix*, along with Raoul and the Little One. Men and officers eyed the Loti and his small friend with suspicion, particularly when it became known that the two had been discovered moving among the bodies of the mind-dead on the surface, leaving business cards on the corpses. Word spread that the formidable cyborg and his commando squad had taken the pair under their protection, however. Xris had made the two a part of his team. Once again, they were six.

Admiral Aks was again in command, having received a very handsome apology from His Majesty. Captain Williams proved somewhat more difficult to placate, but his wounded dignity and injured pride were eventually assuaged, a major's bars for his collar assisting in the process.

The young king, looking worn and tired, arrived on board to a hero's welcome, which he graciously acknowledged, then immediately disappeared into the sick bay in company with his critically wounded friend. Rumors, spawned by the medical staff, soon began to circulate concerning this friend. Men listened, shook their heads in disbelief.

"I've seen nothing like it in all my years," Dr. Giesk said to General Dixter, who stood outside Tusk's room, waiting for Dion. "Evidence of massive internal injuries, to say nothing of the loss of blood. He shouldn't be alive. Should not be alive." The doctor appeared to take Tusk's living as a personal affront.

"They're talking miracle." Giesk sniffed. "There's a rational explanation. Somewhere. I'm running tests. I'll soon come across it. Tusca's half-Blood Royal, you know. That may account for it."

Dion emerged from Tusk's room. The young king was pale, drawn with weariness and anxiety. But a radiance shone about him, coming from deep within, that illuminated the eyes, like the sun rising into a cloudless blue sky.

"You wanted to see me, General?"

Dixter shook his head to counsel silence for the moment, waited until Dr. Giesk had hustled back, eager to get his hands on his patient. "Poor Tusk," said Dixter sympathetically.

"Brother Daniel is with him," said Dion. "He'll keep the doctor from harassing Tusk too much."

"How is he?"

"Fine. He's going to be fine." Dion smiled to himself, a smile that was both elated and sad. Glancing around the corridor in which they stood, he saw men regarding him in awe. "How is everything going, sir?"

"That's what I came to tell you, Your Majesty. The demolition squad reports that the bombs are set and primed. They're on their way back. The Corasian strike force is drawing near. It's an armada, two of those of mother ships, plus God knows how many fighters. We've got to clear out of here and soon."

"Everything's ready. When the demolition squad returns, give the order. Why not? What's the matter."

"Dion," said Dixter quietly, drawing the young man aside, into a nearby doorway, "Lord Sagan hasn't returned. There's been no word from him. Have you seen him or Lady Maigrey?"

"No. I thought she might be in sick bay. She had a cut on her hand. But Dr. Giesk hasn't seen her and—General Dixter, sir. Are you all right?"

The general had gone gray. "What do you mean—a cut?" He could barely speak. "The crystal scythe shattered on her armor. You didn't tell me she'd been hurt."

Dion stared at him, perplexed. "She said she cut herself on a rock." He stopped. The shadow that had laid across his heart deepened, darkened. "I'm going back down there."

"We'll have to hurry," said Dixter grimly. "We don't have much time."

·-◁■ ■▷-·

Dion arrived on planet just as the shuttle carrying the demolition squad was leaving. He was flying Tusk's long-range Scimitar, its anti-grav unit having been hastily repaired. If the Corasian armada was sighted, Aks had orders to make the Jump. Dion and Dixter would follow, find their own way back across the Void. The space-rotation bomb was still aboard. Dion had not had time to disarm it.

XJ, having been assured innumerable times that Tusk was safe, finally believed Dion was telling him the truth. The computer spent the entire trip complaining bitterly about the blood on the deck.

"There's Maigrey's plane," Dion reported, pointing out the viewscreen. The sun's feeble rays were beginning to drive back the darkness on the planet's surface, illuminating the white spaceplane on the ground below. "But my instruments don't show anyone nearby. Wait. There. I've got a life-form reading. Some distance away. On the other side of those trees. I'm going to put the plane down here."

John Dixter said nothing. He had not said anything since they'd left *Phoenix*.

Dion landed the spaceplane, shut it down, prepared to leave the cockpit.

"Is that Maigrey's starjewel?" Dixter asked suddenly. He was staring gravely, fixedly, at the space-rotation bomb.

"Yes," Dion answered, startled.

"I think you should bring it with you."

"But that would mean disarming the bomb."

"You weren't planning to use it, were you, son?"

"No," Dion said after a moment's thought. "I'm not planning to use it. Ever."

"And it would be safer not to leave it—"

Carefully, Dion removed the starjewel, stood a moment,

staring at it, as if willing it to give him a sign. It lay in his hand, dark, unlovely. He closed his hand over it, and prepared to exit the spaceplane.

···◁■ ■▷···

They found Derek Sagan standing at the head of three rock cairns on which lay three bodies. His hands were clasped before him; his red cape, ruffled by the morning breeze, fluttered on the wind. His golden armor gleamed, reflecting the burning red sliver of a new and fiery sun, rising up over the tops of the ruined trees.

Dion clasped the starjewel tightly in his hand, the sharp points dug into his flesh, leaving eight tiny bruise marks that he would find the next day. He could not see the figures on the cairns clearly, but he could see, on the one in the center, silver armor, shining in the sunlight.

Starjewel in his left hand, Dion drew the bloodsword with his right. The sword had, during the intervening hours, been recharged. It burst into life, its blue-white blade flared. The flame, the fluttering red cape, the golden armor, the terrible, burning ache in his throat and heart, all combined to remind him vividly of the night Platus had died, this sword in his hand. Dion ran forward with a shout, a challenge.

Derek Sagan did not move.

Strong arms clasped around Dion. A voice, deep and heavy with grief, but sharp and stern from years of command, sounded above the roar of blood pounding in his head.

"Dion, stop!" Dixter wrestled him backward. "You don't know what you're doing!"

"Maigrey's dead! Can't you see that?" Dion cried. "And look at him! Her blood on his hands! Just as Abdiel said—"

"Dion! The crystal scythe! That was the serpent's tooth! That cut on her hand . . ."

The shadow lifted from Dion's heart, the curtain parted. Light flooded in, he saw and understood. The bloodsword's fire faded, went out. His arm was weak, numb. He slid the sword back into its sheath before he dropped it.

"Oh, God!" he whispered in agony. "She knew. They both knew and they kept it from me. They . . . they sent me away. But if I had stayed . . . I could have helped her . . ."

"And Tusk would have died." John Dixter put his arm

around the young man's shoulders. "I'm not sure there would have been anything you could have done for her, son."

The general looked at Sagan, tears glistened on the weathered cheeks.

"Her destiny . . . and his . . . are fulfilled."

··◁■ ■▷··

Three cairns, made of rocks piled one on top of the other, stood together, in a row. The one in the center rose higher than the other two. On it lay the body of Lady Maigrey Morianna, King's Guardian. She was clad in the silver armor that had been washed free of blood. Her hands were clasped upon her chest. The bloodsword's empty sheath had been removed from around her waist and rested at her feet, to denote her victory over her enemy. The pale, fine hair had been loosened from its braids, arranged over her shoulders.

Dion leaned down to fasten the starjewel around her neck, felt the hair brush against his hand. It seemed warm, alive; the flesh his hand touched was chill. He looked into her face, saw it white, cold, fair. He knew her, and he didn't. He realized, after a moment, that she looked unfamiliar to him because the scar was gone. The deathly pallor overspreading her complexion had absorbed the scar, made it one with the marble flesh.

Dion adjusted the Star of the Guardians to lie on her breast. Drawing his hand back, he paused, waiting, hoping to see its darkness fade, as had the scar. He waited to see it catch the sun's bright rays.

The sun touched it, the starjewel altered in appearance. It did not burst into blazing fire, however, did not regain the shining brilliance he remembered. Or if it did, he saw its fire as he saw the fire of the stars, far removed from him, their warmth diminished by distance, by time. The starjewel, like her armor, gleamed with a pale, cold light.

On Maigrey's right lay Agis, centurion, captain of the Guard. On her left, Sparafucile, half-breed, assassin. Disparate companions for her long journey. And yet, thought Dion, somehow right and fitting.

John Dixter looked down at the still, calm face. He reached out his hand, softly stroked the pale, fine hair.

"No more good-byes for us," he said to her softly. "Ever."

The sun climbed steadily higher.

Dion cleared his throat, turned to Sagan. "My lord, a

Corasian strike force is on the way. We've set proton bombs in the tunnels. We're going to destroy the outpost before we leave."

Derek Sagan said nothing, did not move from where he stood at the head of her cairn. His face was impassive, registered no expression, neither grief nor anger, sadness nor regret. Nothing.

"We have to go, my lord," Dion prompted gently.

Sagan made no response.

Dion glanced helplessly at Dixter, who only shook his head. Suddenly, the Warlord turned the dark eyes, looked into Dion's. Lifting his hand to his neck, he seemed about to remove his own starjewel.

"No," said Dion, confused for a moment, then understanding Sagan's intent. "I don't need the jewel. I don't intend to arm the bomb . . . ever again. I will keep it, but only to make certain that it doesn't fall into the hands of another. I will"—he paused, amended—"I hope to rule without fear."

Sagan's bloodstained hand fell, nerveless, to his side.

John Dixter reached out, clasped the bloodstained hand, whispered something to the Warlord, something between only the two of them. The empty expression on Sagan's face did not alter. His hand tightened around Dixter's for a brief instant, then released its hold. He withdrew more deeply into himself. The stones of the cairn seemed more alive than he did.

"Your Majesty," said John Dixter, "it's time for us to leave."

Dion laid his hand over Maigrey's still fingers. "Go with God, my lady," he said. He looked into Sagan's dark, empty eyes. "My lord."

Turning, the king left the dead, walked into the dawn.

··◁■ ■▷··

Phoenix was ready to depart. The demolition squad was safely on board. The short-range Scimitars had been called back. One task remained.

Captain Williams approached the admiral. "Should I give the order to explode the proton bombs, sir?"

Aks, troubled, glanced at Dion. The king had just arrived on the bridge. He stood staring out the viewscreen at the planet, that appeared nothing more than a nondescript mote of dust at this distance.

"Your Majesty, we haven't received any word from Lord Sagan. It's possible that he's still—"

"Are you picking up any life-form readings from that planet, Admiral?" Dion asked quietly.

"No, Your Majesty, but—"

"Do your scanners indicate that the spaceplane is still on the planet?"

"No, Your Majesty. It took off a short time ago, but if Lord Sagan were flying it he would have contacted—"

"Proceed with the destruction of the planet."

"But, Your Majesty!"

"Proceed, Admiral."

Jaw working, face blotchy, Admiral Aks did as he was commanded. "Detonate the proton bombs."

Dion turned back to the viewscreen. General Dixter came to stand by his side.

A flash of light, white-hot, blinding in its intensity, flared in the viewscreen. The planet became a fireball, burned, for an instant, brightly as a star.

Then darkness.

Chapter ❦ Nineteen

God save the king.

The man and woman walked the long and echoing hallways of the Glitter Palace, trailing in the wake of a velvet-coated footman, who, after a journey of what seemed like several kilometers, turned them over to a velvet-coated chamberlain, who cast an extremely shocked and highly disapproving look at the man's flak jacket and battle fatigues and was on the verge of refusing them admittance.

"We're expected," growled the man, fishing around in the pockets of his flak jacket. Finally, after much fumbling (the chamberlain's face becoming increasingly frozen), the man produced a card with His Majesty's seal—a golden, lion-faced sun.

"Mendaharin Tusca and Nola Rian," said the man, pointing to the names engraved on the invitation. "That's us."

"I see," said the chamberlain, glancing askance at a ketchup stain and a ring left by the bottom of a bottle on the invitation that appeared to have served time as a coaster.

"They have security clearance," reported the footman.

The chamberlain indicated, by his expression, to consider this a vast mistake. He said only, "This way, if you please," turned and headed for the massive, double doors, made of steel, emblazoned with the king's seal.

Two members of the Honor Guard (now Palace Guard), wearing the same Romanesque armor as always, blocked the door, beam rifles across their chests. At the chamberlain's approach, they relaxed their watchful stance, stepped aside.

Tusk recognized both men, having served with them aboard *Phoenix*. He started to greet them. Both merely glanced at him, however, and that scrutiny, he realized, was to make certain that he posed no threat. They didn't remember him.

The chamberlain threw open the double doors with a

501

flourish. Feeling considerably uncomfortable, wishing that he hadn't come, Tusk entered what he presumed were the king's private quarters.

The Glitter Palace had stood abandoned and empty for nineteen years, was now currently undergoing extensive restoration. The royal antechamber—an enormous room, once extraordinarily elegant and beautiful—had been among the most heavily damaged during the Revolution. The room was being returned to its former glory, but repairs would take some time.

Although most traces of the workmen had been cleared away in honor of today's ceremony, drop cloths covered the paintings hanging on the walls. The crystal chandeliers, swathed in cotton, looked mummified. Multicolored bunting had been hung in an attempt to hide the scaffolding.

Tusk looked around, curious. "My father must have stood here, where I'm standing."

He could almost see his father, dressed in the blue ceremonial robes of a Guardian, robes that had been too short on the tall, muscular Danha Tusca, striding about this room, arguing in his booming voice, laughing his booming laugh.

There had been a time when that ghost would have intimidated Tusk, made him angry, guilty. But now Tusk could look on the ghost with only a melancholy sadness and he could, at last, bid it farewell and wish it rest.

"They've had six months to work on the place," said Nola, trying not to seem awed. "You'd think they'd be further along by now."

Six months since the fleet had returned in triumph from the Corasian galaxy, escaping unscathed after a now-epic battle. Six months since President Peter Robes had been discovered in his private office, dead, having melted his skull with the self-inflicted blast of a lasgun, his suicide recorded—horribly—for posterity on the security cams.

The vid pictured him rambling, almost incoherent, screaming that "his mind was dead, the voice gone." And then he'd shot himself. The news media interviewed every -ologist, -analyst, -iatrist, and talk-show hostess in the galaxy and, while all had opinions, no one could say precisely what Robes had meant by this bizarre statement. All concluded that the President had received advanced warning from his extensive and secret spy network that Dion Starfire had discovered extremely damaging information linking Robes with the Corasians. The knowledge of his impending disgrace and certain impeachment led to the unbalanced mental state that led to his suicide.

The constitution made provision for the takeover of the government, but it took some time to discover who the vice president actually was and then, when they found his name, no one could recall having seen him in several years. Meanwhile, allegations surfaced concerning the corrupt activities of the Cabinet members. Several prominent Congressmen were revealed to have been in Robes's pay. The government collapsed, the galaxy was in chaos. The last act of the Galactic Democratic Republic was to make a humble appeal to Dion Starfire, rightful heir, to accept the crown and restore order.

Dion Starfire accepted. This day marked his coronation and his wedding.

"Do I look all right?" Nola asked, trying to catch a quick glimpse of her reflection in a shining steelglass wall.

"Hell, yes. Would you quit worrying? It's the kid, remember?"

"No, it isn't," said Nola gravely. Reaching out, she took hold of Tusk's hand. "Not anymore."

Tusk, who knew what she meant, said nothing, looked uncomfortable.

"His Majesty will see you now."

Another set of double doors, guarded by yet another pair of centurions, opened. Tusk and Nola, hand in hand, entered.

This room, the private office of the king, was—in contrast to the stark, bleak antechamber—warm and inviting with just enough elegance to remind the visitor that he was in the presence of royalty.

Tusk had a fleeting, confused impression of dark, polished wood, shelves of books, sumptuous leather furniture, greens and browns, rich carpet, soft lighting.

Behind a massive desk, ornately carved, sat a man. He was engaged in perusing numerous documents that had, by their stiff and unrelenting whiteness, an official look about them.

Tusk and Nola entered the room, stood feeling rather lost. The secretary who had ushered them inside urged them forward with a graceful and silent gesture. Venturing around the desk, the secretary bent down, said something to the man in a low voice. The man nodded.

"Leave us," he said.

The secretary, bowing, removed himself, exiting by a side door.

The man raised his head, saw Tusk and Nola, and smiled.

Tusk had known him at first by the red-golden hair that fell in thick and luxuriant waves over the shoulders of the formal dress, military-cut uniform. He knew him now by the intense blue eyes that were always somehow startling when Tusk looked into them after a long absence. Memory faded the color, he supposed. Perhaps it was simply difficult to believe that eyes could be that clear, that vibrant, that . . . blue.

But if it hadn't been for the eyes and hair, Tusk had the feeling he wouldn't have known him. This wasn't, as Nola had said, "the kid."

Dion rose to his feet, came around the desk, his hand outstretched in greeting. His face was thinner than Tusk remembered, graver, more serious, solemn. He seemed older and, Tusk thought confusedly, taller. When he spoke, his voice sounded deeper, different.

"Nola, Tusk," Dion said, taking each of them by the hand. "I'm so glad you could come. I hope you've changed your mind and will stay for the ceremony tonight?"

"No, uh, thanks, ki—" The word stuck in Tusk's throat. Feeling his face burn, he amended it. "Your Majesty. We've got to be clearing out of here. You see it's . . . well . . ."

"Tusk's mother's birthday is tomorrow," Nola broke in nervously, "and Tusk's missed so many of her birthdays that we thought it would be nice if he could be there. . . ."

Both of them stammered, tongue-tied, realizing their excuse was lame, not knowing how to make it sound better.

Tusk was suddenly conscious of his hand—sweaty, clammy, still clasped in Dion's hand that was warm and dry and strong. The mercenary broke the grip, started to thrust his hand in his pocket, decided that this wouldn't be polite, dropped his hand to his side.

"I understand," said Dion, and something in his voice told Tusk that he truly did understand.

"Probably more than I do," Tusk muttered to himself.

He was finding it difficult to look directly into those bright blue eyes, as if he were staring into the sun. He shifted his gaze around the room.

"Nice place you've got here, Your Majesty." The formality was coming easier.

"Yes," said Dion with a smile. "I seem to spend too much time in it, however. I miss flying. I don't suppose I'll be doing much of that now. I'm keeping my Scimitar pin, though," he added, fingering the small silver pin that looked shabby and out of place on the elegant, gold-trimmed collar.

Tusk remembered when and how Dion had come by that pin, was forced to blink his eyes rapidly to keep the room from dissolving in a blur.

Nola gave Tusk a prod in the ribs, jerked her head toward Dion. "What we came for?" she prompted.

"Uh, yeah." Tusk cleared his throat. "Uh, I never got around to thanking you for . . . uh . . . saving my—"

The side door opened a crack, the secretary glided in, ostensibly to lay another document on His Majesty's desk. But a glance from beneath lowered eyelids was obviously a reminder that His Majesty had other people to see this day.

Dion received the reminder with a cool look, turned back to Tusk, stopped him before he could go on.

"I'm the one who owes you, Tusk. You don't owe me anything."

They stood looking at each other, the silence awkward. The secretary gave a polite cough.

"Look, uh, we got to be going," said Tusk.

Dion accompanied them to the door. He seemed to want, at the last moment, to detain them. To hang on. "What are your plans, now? I'll never forgive you for turning down that commission in the Royal Navy."

"Yeah, thanks, but well, Nola and me, we figure it's time to settle down. Maybe raise a few kids. We're going to Vangelis. Nola has her old job back, drivin' a TRUC for Marek. He won that war of his, you know. And me. Well, XJ and I are takin' over a taxi route, shuttlin' passengers between planets, that sort of thing. Link's comin' in as a partner."

"Link?" Dion was startled, dubious.

"Yeah. He's a blowhard and an A-number-one jerk, but he's not a bad sort, underneath. I know how far I can trust him and how far I can't and I'd rather have someone like that than someone I don't know at all. And he and XJ get along."

"How is XJ?"

They'd reached the door to the office.

"He's speaking to me again," Tusk said, shaking his head. "Which is more than he'd been doing. He's convinced I faked that whole bit, getting wounded and everything, just to weasel out of paying him off. You wouldn't believe the hell he's put me through since then," he added gloomily.

Dion laughed.

The secretary slid around them, between them, opened the door. The Honor Guard snapped to attention. The chamberlain loomed, waiting to whisk them away.

Tusk fumbled in the pocket of his flak jacket.

"I know you got a whole army to protect you now, so I don't suppose you'll be needin' me. But if you ever do . . ."

He brought out a small object, almost invisible to sight, handed it to Dion, placing it on the palm of the right hand, the palm scarred with the five marks of the bloodsword.

"Just send this. I'll know what it means."

Dion had no need to look to see what it was. He recognized, by feel, the small earring shaped in the form of an eight-pointed star that Tusk had worn as long as he'd known him.

"Thank you," said Dion, closing his hand over it.

Tusk looked up into the blue eyes and the sun's fire warmed him. He smiled. No more needed to be said.

Nola, at his side, was weeping softly.

"Good-bye, Tusk," said Dion. "The best of everything to you both."

The double doors shut.

"Good-bye, kid," Tusk answered softly.

··◁■ ■▷··

"His Majesty will see you now, Sir John."

"That's you, milord," said Bennett in an undertone, trying futilely to twitch several of the more obvious wrinkles out of Dixter's uniform.

"Who? Oh, um, yes." John Dixter brushed away his aide's solicitous hands. "And I've told you not to call me that," he added in an aside, walking toward the double doors.

Bennett kept up with him until the last possible moment, making swift grabs at invisible bits of lint.

"It's your proper title now, milord." The aide caught hold of a dangling silk braid and looped it back up over one shoulder.

"It's not official yet."

"It will be by tomorrow, milord," Bennett said stiffly, "and we should get into the habit."

"First Lord of the Admiralty," the secretary announced. "Sir John Dixter."

The Honor Guard came to attention, saluted smartly. Dixter returned their salute, entered the king's presence. The doors shut behind him.

Bennett looked after him with fond exasperation, began pacing the antechamber in regulation step, whistling a military march.

"That title's not official yet," Dixter protested.

"It might as well be," Dion answered, rising from his desk. "You're only two sword taps on the shoulders away from it."

"Not the bloodsword, I hope," Dixter said, grimacing at the thought of the forthcoming formalities.

"No. A sword that was my father's. Someone discovered it in a museum somewhere."

"Was that Tusk I passed in the corridor?" Dixter asked after a moment. "Dressed in battle fatigues?"

"Yes. That was Tusk."

"He didn't see me and he looked as if he were in a hurry so I didn't stop him. He's not staying for the ceremony."

"No," Dion answered briefly.

"I'm sorry," said Dixter.

"Don't be." Dion looked up, smiled. "Everything's all right. He and Nola will have twelve kids with curly hair and freckles. Link'll lose half of what they make in ante-up and XJ'll stash away the other half and between them Tusk will never see a penny. But he'll be happy. He'll be completely happy."

"Yes, he will," Dixter agreed. He looked at Dion, wished he could add something, but the only words that came to mind were "I'm sorry" again and that wouldn't do at all.

"Has my fiancée arrived?" Dion asked coolly, as if one thought had led to another.

"Yes, Your Majesty," Dixter replied gravely. "Her shuttle landed just a few moments ago. The Palace Guard is escorting the young woman . . . and her mother . . . to the palace."

Dixter hadn't meant to insert the pause, but he didn't like the Baroness DiLuna and knew that the feeling was mutual. He did his best to keep his animosity concealed from the king, however, who had enough problems.

"Thank you," said Dion. "I'm glad they arrived safely."

Dixter couldn't wholeheartedly concur with this statement, thought he would probably say something he shouldn't, decided to leave.

"If there's nothing else I can do for Your Majesty, it's getting late and Bennett has to shoehorn me into that confounded getup I'm supposed to wear tonight—"

"You need to be going. I understand. Thank you for handling my fiancée's passage for me. And thank you for accepting the appointment as First Lord of the Admiralty. I realize you didn't particularly want the job and that you took it as a favor to me. But you're the only one I can trust. Our navy is the galaxy's lifeblood."

"I am glad to be able to serve you, Your Majesty," Dixter said quietly. "Thank you for giving me the chance."

"I understand you want to make Williams your flagship commander. I must say I'm a bit surprised. I didn't know you two got along that well."

"He's a good officer, Your Majesty. I should know. He damn near got me killed. He's young, ambitious, and what with Aks retiring, he was looking for an opportunity to move on. And I can use his advice. We've discussed our differences frankly and we respect each other. In time, I may even get to like the man."

"Very well. I'll make the appointment."

The secretary opened the door. The Honor Guard came to attention. Bennett, seeing the king, bowed from the waist with such stiffness and precision it seemed likely he might snap cleanly in two.

"Bennett," said Dion, attempting to maintain a straight face, "it's good to see you again."

"Yes, Your Majesty. Thank you, Your Majesty." Bennett stood ramrod-straight, his chin disappeared into his collar. "May I offer my congratulations on the occasion of your wedding, Your Majesty."

"Thank you, Bennett," Dion replied.

"Thank *you*, Your Majesty," Bennett said, clicking his heels together smartly.

"We're leaving now, Bennett." Dixter noticed that Dion had another visitor waiting.

"Very good, milord," said Bennett.

"Don't call me that—" John Dixter began, sighed.

He supposed he might as well start getting used to it.

··<= =>··

"Your Majesty, Bear Olefsky."

"My friend," Dion said, smiling warmly at the big man.

Pressing the huge hand that completely engulfed his, he attempted valiantly to ignore the fact that the Bear, on entering the room, overturned three chairs and upset an end table.

Bear eyed him anxiously. "Laddie. What's the matter? Don't they feed you in this palace?"

"Not like they do at your house, Bear."

Dion tried to speak lightly, but the memories that came back were too intense, too sweetly painful. His voice sank near the end of the polite phrase. He turned slightly to avert his face from the light.

Any polished courtier would have immediately noted his king's discomfiture and obligingly removed himself, or at the least affected to become suddenly and intensely interested in the books on the shelf. Olefsky, bluff, crude, rugged as the mountains he loved, bent down, hands on his knees, and peered directly into the shadowed face.

"Eh, laddie? What's this? If you miss the shield-wife's cooking so much it brings tears to your eyes I can arrange to ship you some of our leftovers. Though after my sons have finished, I think you might well starve."

Dion smiled, but made no answer.

"Aye, and speaking of my sons," the Bear continued jovially, "I've brought them with me. And Sonja, as well. I wanted to bring her to pay her respects to you beforehand but she says it will take all her time between now and the ceremony to dress herself. I swear, I do not understand it," the Bear added solemnly, tugging at his beard as was his habit when perplexed. "I've seen that woman jump from her bed, arm herself with shield and spear, and be ready to fight all before I barely got my pants on.

"And yet, for a simple thing like watching a man get a crown put on his head, she must spend hours cinching up this and flattening that and painting this and for what? So that by the end of it all, I do not recognize her and there is no soft part of her left to grab."

The Bear heaved a sigh that whistled through the office like a gale.

His long-winded conversation had given Dion a chance to compose himself. "Did all your family come with you?"

"Aye," said the Bear, watching Dion closely. "Even the little one, who will, in all probability, scream his head off during the ceremony and disgrace us all. They are all here . . . except my daughter."

Dion closed his eyes, bitter disappointment in his heart, relief flooding through his mind.

A strong hand clasped hold of his shoulder, almost instantly numbing it. "Ah, laddie," said the Bear in a tone so kind that it came near unmanning his king, "I am not blind. And even if I was blind, by my ears and eyeballs, I think I could have seen what has been going on."

Dion was silent, unable to respond in words, though he rested his hand gratefully over the top portion of the Bear's gigantic arm.

"I promised your daughter I would marry her. And now I can't keep my promise. You know that?" he asked in a low voice when he could talk.

The big man nodded his head sadly. "Aye, laddie. I know everything. She told me. Kamil can no more keep a secret than an eagle can keep from spreading its wings and flying with the wind. She told her mother and me that very night, in fact."

"You knew?" Dion raised his head, stared at him. "You knew, then, that day, the day I had to pledge myself to DiLuna. You must despise me."

"Despise you?" the Bear rumbled, his voice bouncing around the room, rattling various fragile objects on the mantelpiece. "No, laddie, I don't despise you. In fact, I said to myself, 'The Lady Maigrey was right. Derek Sagan was right. Now, we have, at last, a true king.'"

"Thank you, Bear," said Dion softly. "That means a great deal to me. More than you know."

"Ach, say no more." The Bear rumpled his beard. "The shield-wife and I thought it would be easier on both of you this night if Kamil did not come. I have decided to send her to the Academy, now you have reopened it. My sons are good boys, but their heads are filled with mutton. My daughter, though, my daughter is smart. She needs to be educated, needs to see that there is a universe above and beyond our mountains."

"Yes, that's a good idea," Dion said briskly.

Shaking free of the Bear's grasp, he righted a chair, then

walked over to stand behind his desk, lifted one of the documents, and pretended to read it. "She'll meet other young people her age. Meet someone else . . ." He stared, hard, frowning, at the document.

The Bear pulled on his beard until it seemed likely he'd pull it out. "Do you still love her, laddie?"

Dion glanced up. He was calm now, composed. "I'm marrying another woman this night, my friend."

"Do you still love Kamil?" the Bear repeated softly.

Dion started to say no, even though it was a lie. Lies were part of being a king.

The big man's gaze reached inside, lay hold of the truth.

Dion replaced the document on the desk, stood staring down at it, unseeing.

"Do you remember, Bear, that day when we were riding to your palace, riding through the snow. We were talking about Sagan and Lady Maigrey. You said—Do you remember?"

"'By my heart and bowels, laddie, who wakes every morning and takes a deep breath and says to the air, "Air, I love you." And yet, without air in our lungs, we would be dead within moments. And who says to the water, "I love you!" and yet without water, we die. And who says to the fire in the winter, "I love you!" and yet without warmth, we die.' That is what you said, my friend.

"And that"—Dion drew a deep breath, lifted the blue eyes—"and that is how I love Kamil."

The Bear heaved another typhoon sigh, dabbed his eyes with the ends of his beard. "I feared as much. My heart grieves for you, laddie. Yet you are doing what is right. What is honorable. You are doing what is best for the people, as well. This strong alliance you forge with DiLuna will be the means of pulling the fragments of the galaxy back together. But you know that, better than the old Bear, who is a fighter, not a smooth-tongued diplomat."

A silver bell rang. "Your Majesty." The secretary's face appeared on a vidscreen. "I am sorry to interrupt but you asked to be notified when His Holiness arrived—"

"Yes, yes!" Bear waved a hand at him. "I know. I must be going."

The secretary vanished. Olefsky made his way to the door, upsetting the remainder of the furniture he'd missed on the way in. He paused, turned.

"I don't know whether I am right in saying what I am going to say, laddie. This tongue of mine does much damage, sometimes. The shield-wife tells me often that I should open my mouth only to shovel meat into it and the rest of the time I should leave it closed. But it seems to me it never hurts a man to know the truth.

"The way you love Kamil, laddie, is the way Kamil loves you. I don't think she will be finding anyone else."

····⊶ ⇥····

"Your Majesty, His Holiness, the Lord High Abbot of the Order of Adamant."

The abbot, resplendent in red and gold and white ceremonial robes, entered the king's chamber. He was a young man, extremely young to be the head of the galaxy's newly reestablished religious order, some said. But there was an air of serenity about him, a calm, firm conviction in his face and in the way he carried himself that soon convinced those who doubted him that he had complete faith not only in himself but in the One who guided him.

The abbot glanced around at the destruction in the room, smiled. "Olefsky's been here, I see."

Dion righted an upended end table. "Yes. From now on, I must remember to hold audience with him on a cleared airstrip. Thank you for coming. I know how busy you are, with the restoration of your abbey and the restructuring of your church, but it seemed only fitting that you should be the one to place the crown on my head and anoint me king."

"It is I who am honored, Your Majesty."

"I hope you don't mind if I call you Brother Daniel. Abbot Fideles just doesn't sound familiar to me, yet."

"I must admit," said Daniel, face flushing, "that it doesn't to me either. Prior John said something to me the other day, referring to me by that name and title, and I walked clean past the man, thinking he was talking to someone else!"

The two laughed, though Dion's laughter ended in a sigh.

The priest gazed at him thoughtfully, placed his hands over Dion's. "Are you at peace, Your Majesty? With yourself and with God?"

"Yes," Dion answered steadily. "I am. With myself, at least. God may take more time. But I'm working at it."

"I am pleased to hear it, Your Majesty," said the priest, reassured.

"Is all in readiness for the ceremony?" Dion asked.

"Yes, sire. The cathedral is filled to capacity. Crowds line the streets. They tell me"—Brother Daniel looked somewhat abashed—"that I will have to wear makeup, because of the vids."

"Yes, I'm afraid so," Dion said, hiding his smile.

The priest sighed. "I don't know what the brethren will make of it. I've allowed vidscreens in the Abbey, you know. I thought it only fitting that they view this historic occasion which marks not only your ascending to the throne but the restoration of the Church. I can only imagine what Prior John will have to say about this. He will be most displeased. Still, I suppose we all must make some sacrifice.

"And now I had better be going. I left the choir boys with Brother Miguel and I wouldn't doubt but that they have him tied to a pew by now."

"Brother, just a moment," said Dion as the priest was about to leave. "Have you heard any word from Lord Sagan?"

Brother Daniel paused, stood with his back to the king, thinking, perhaps, how to answer. Then, turning, he said gently, "He is with God, Your Majesty."

"He's . . . dead?" Dion faltered.

"I have said all that I can say, Your Majesty."

Dion, thinking he understood, nodded.

··◁■ ■▷··

They were gone. All of them. The secretary had been sent on a manufactured errand. Dion was alone.

Soon they would come with the royal robes, recovered from a museum. Soon they would come with the diadem and scepter, removed from the dwelling place of the late Snaga Ohme and returned, with the crown jewels, to the palace. Soon they would come with the crown, a blood red ruby placed in the center, placed in the hole left by the laser that had pierced it the night of the Revolution.

Dion reached beneath the collar of his royal uniform, took out the eight-pointed star earring Tusk had given to him. Clasping it fast in his hand, he looked around the room.

They were all here: his uncle, strong in his faith if nothing else; his mother, beautiful, laughing; his father, proud of his son; Platus, gentle, loving; Maigrey, her silver armor shining in the moonlight. They were with him. After all, he wasn't alone.

"Make me worthy," he said to them.

A tap came at the door. The ghosts departed. But, like Tusk, they would come back if he needed them.

"Enter."

The captain of the Palace Guard stood in the doorway.

"Is it time, Cato?" asked Dion.

"It is time, Your Majesty."

The Palace Guard, armor polished and gleaming, formed two lines, one on either side of the doorway.

Dion tucked the small earring in his pocket. Drawing a deep breath, he walked out, took the first step to his throne.

The Palace Guard came to attention, saluted, fists over their hearts.

"God save His Majesty!" the men shouted in one voice.

And Dion echoed them in his heart.

God save the king.

Afterword

The brethren of the Abbey of St. Francis gathered together in the courtyard, crowding around an enormous vidscreen that several brothers with mechanical and electrical skills had spent most of the two previous days installing. The brethren, habitual silence broken, chatted and talked among themselves, excited not only over the prospect of witnessing the coronation and wedding ceremony of a new king, but also (and perhaps more) over the unusual circumstance of the outside modern world invading their peaceful monastic life.

Prior John, in charge now that Abbot Fideles was away, fussed over the machine, about which he knew absolutely nothing, got in the way of the electrical-minded brothers (who prayed for patience beneath their breaths), and nearly ruined everything by pushing the wrong button at the wrong time, resulting in an alarming explosion and a shower of sparks.

Finally, however, the generator started with a roar and a strong smell of gasoline. The vidscreen came to life. The coronation ceremony began. The choir sang, lifting their voices in praise. Their abbot took his place before the altar in the cathedral. He called on God to anoint and bless His Majesty. The youthful king, dressed in royal robes, with scepter and diadem, came walking down the aisle. He was pale, solemn, touched by a radiance that made the bright, glaring lights shining down on him dim in comparison.

Their attention given to the vidscreen, their prayers going to the Creator, few of the priests noticed the hooded and robed brother coming late to join them, near the ceremony's end. Those who did notice paid him scant attention, not even a smile of greeting or brotherly nod, for they knew that neither would be returned.

The man was a lay brother, one who had taken the habit and vows of a priest of the Order of Adamant, but, either through his own choosing or by the judgment of his superiors, would never be ordained.

The lay brothers performed most of the heavy, manual labor
about the Abbey and it was obvious from the condition of this
man's robes, which were covered with dirt at the knees, the
sleeves splattered with mud, that it was his duties—perhaps in
the garden—that had kept him from seeing the beginning of
the coronation.

It was not surprising to the brethren to find this man at his
labors upon this day, which had been declared a holiday in the
Abbey. He was always working at some task or other, generally
the most menial or those that required exhausting, backbreak-
ing toil. If a brother was taken sick in the night, this man's
strong arms lifted him. If a windstorm damaged the roof, this
man made the perilous climb to repair it.

He was the tallest among them, but thin and gaunt, his body
wasted from fasting. Still, for a man in his middle years, his
strength was remarkable. He rarely spoke to anyone and few
spoke to him; he was not well liked. A darkness shrouded him,
literally and physically, for he never removed the cowl that
covered his head, never showed his face to the light. Those
who—by chance or by the curiosity that is the besetting sin of
even the most devout—had seen his face wished always
afterward they hadn't. The shadow of the hood that covered it
was bright light compared to the shadow in the eyes.

He kept himself apart from the community. He did not even
join his brethren in their prayers, but prayed alone, in his cell,
refusing to enter the cathedral, as if he deemed himself
unworthy of being there.

No one knew his real name or anything about his past. That
was not unusual. When one entered God's service, one
severed all ties with the world outside. He had taken for his
monastic name *Pænitens*—the Penitent One. But because of
his refusal to enter into the presence of God, he became
known unofficially among them as The Unforgiven.

Abbot Fideles alone was the only person who ever noticed
the man or went out of his way to speak to him; the man having
been taken into the monastery by the abbot's recommendation
and under his auspices. The abbot's greetings were never
returned, but the man would, at least, bow his head in
acknowledgment.

Brother Pænitens stood unmoving, presumably watching
the ceremony, though no one could see his eyes. The young
king was kneeling, humbly, reverently before Abbot Fideles.

Holding aloft the crown, the priest was calling upon the Creator to expurgate the blood that had stained it, forgive the sins of those who had defiled it, accept the sacrifices of those who had fought to restore it to its shining glory.

The brothers forgot their excitement. The Presence filled the monastery, was all around them. They fell to their knees, bowed their heads, whispered words of fervent prayer for the young king, for his subjects.

A few of them cast resentful glances at the lay brother, standing on the fringes of the crowd, for he cast a pall over their joy and they wished he would leave.

Abbot Fideles placed the crown upon the young king's head. The king rose, faced his people. Bells pealed in the royal city, bells would ring out at this moment all over the galaxy. The cathedral's own bells began to chime. The brethren smiled and nodded and spoke quietly of their pleasure, except for one young novitiate, who was so carried away that he actually burst out with a loud cheer. The offender was immediately collared by Prior John, told to repeat his prayers twenty times over until he could behave in a more seemly manner.

The vidscreen was immediately shut off. The brothers, singing, began to file away toward the cathedral, where a *Te Deum* would be chanted.

"Te Deum laudamus; Te Dominum confitemur.

"We praise thee, God; we own thee Lord."

The lay brother, forgotten in the general happiness and joy, did not join them, but walked the opposite direction, toward his own solitary cell. But one of the young novitiates (the same who had so disgraced himself) boldly peered beneath the man's hood, sought to penetrate the shadow.

This brother whispered, next day, among his fellows, that he had seen upon the man's lips a sad, dark smile.

Requiem

Someone once asked a famous author (I forget who) how long he had been working on a particular book.

"All my life" was his answer.

I feel that, in many ways, I've been working on this series of books all my life.

One of my earliest childhood memories was of a television program popular in the fifties—Tom Corbet and his Space Cadets. The cadets became good friends of mine. They lived in the bathtub (we had a small house) and were faithful companions.

The romance and excitement of adventure in outer space caught hold of me at that early age and increased, as I grew up. The bathtub was too small to hold all the real life astronauts and fictional space-voyagers who filled my dreams. I looked for them in books, for I am an avid reader, but I failed to find anything in science fiction literature at that time that took my fantasies and brought them to life.

I was complaining about this lack to my agent, Ray Puechner. He said (probably to shut me up): "Why don't you write the kind of book you want to read?"

And, I did.

That was over ten years ago. I completed the first two manuscripts in about two years' time. I must admit, they were terrible. A friend of mine, who has a copy of the original, is hanging on to it, threatening to blackmail me if he ever gets hard up. The books made the rounds of publishers and were deservedly rejected (although I did receive several letters of encouragement. One, especially, from Susan Allison, meant a great deal to me.)

The books were raw, too emotional. But then so was I. And the books served a purpose. They carried me through some hard times. One good thing about being a writer, you can always leave this world and find solace in another.

The next year, I met Tracy Hickman and he introduced me to Raistlin and Simkin and Mathew and a host of other wonderful characters. I enjoyed writing those books, I learned a lot about my craft. But I never forgot Maigrey and Dion and Sagan. I kept thinking about them, dreaming of them, making mental refinements to their story.

Pulling the manuscripts out, one day, I reread them, blushed to see how dreadful they were, and began to rewrite. Friends offered help and suggestions, became part of the book. Raoul and the Little One came into being. Tracy suggested the "evil democracy." Gary Pack gleefully developed weapons of mass destruction. Jim Ward told me Cary Grant was not Darth Vader. (Believe me, it made sense at the time.)

And all the while, Ray had faith in Star and in me. He'd tell me, when I was discouraged, that one day I would be able to share my dreams of the romance of space travel with other people, share them with you. Then, in the mid-eighties, Ray was diagnosed with cancer. About that time, I offered the Star of the Guardians to Bantam. I wanted to have the series published for Ray's sake, almost as much as my own.

Ray was too ill to handle the negotiations, but he was pleased when I sold the series, said he'd known I'd make it all along. Sadly, he didn't live to see the first book published, but the last promise I made to him was to dedicate Star to his memory.

This is for you, Ray. For friendship—the shining star that lights death's darkness.

About the Author

Born in Independence, Missouri, MARGARET WEIS graduated from the University of Missouri and worked as a book editor before teaming up with Tracy Hickman to develop the *Dragonlance* novels. Margaret lives in a renovated barn in Wisconsin with her teenage daughter, Elizabeth Baldwin, and two dogs and one cat, where she is working on a new *Star of the Guardians* novel. She enjoys reading (especially Charles Dickens), opera, and aqua-aerobics.